I0831819

# The Novels of George Gissing, Volume Two

By

George Gissing

Cover Photograph: Keith Ellwood

ISBN: 978-1-78139-554-7

# Contents

## THE ODD WOMEN

## EVE'S RANSOM

## THE PAYING GUEST



## WILL WARBURTON

# THE ODD WOMEN

# CHAPTER I - THE FOLD AND THE SHEPHERD

'So to-morrow, Alice,' said Dr. Madden, as he walked with his eldest daughter on the coast-downs by Clevedon, 'I shall take steps for insuring my life for a thousand pounds.'

It was the outcome of a long and intimate conversation. Alice Madden, aged nineteen, a plain, shy, gentle-mannered girl, short of stature, and in movement something less than graceful, wore a pleased look as she glanced at her father's face and then turned her eyes across the blue channel to the Welsh hills. She was flattered by the confidence reposed in her, for Dr. Madden, reticent by nature, had never been known to speak in the domestic circle about his pecuniary affairs. He seemed to be the kind of man who would inspire his children with affection: grave but benign, amiably diffident, with a hint of lurking mirthfulness about his eyes and lips. And to-day he was in the best of humours; professional prospects, as he had just explained to Alice, were more encouraging than hitherto; for twenty years he had practised medicine at Clevedon, but with such trifling emolument that the needs of his large family left him scarce a margin over expenditure; now, at the age of forty-nine—it was 1872—he looked forward with a larger hope. Might he not reasonably count on ten or fifteen more years of activity? Clevedon was growing in repute as a seaside resort; new houses were rising; assuredly his practice would continue to extend.

'I don't think girls ought to be troubled about this kind of thing,' he added apologetically. 'Let men grapple with the world; for, as the old hymn says, "'tis their nature to." I should grieve indeed if I thought my girls would ever have to distress themselves about money matters. But I find I have got into the habit, Alice, of talking to you very much as I should talk with your dear mother if she were with us.'

Mrs. Madden, having given birth to six daughters, had fulfilled her function in this wonderful world; for two years she had been resting in the old churchyard that looks upon the Severn sea. Father and daughter sighed as they recalled her memory. A sweet, calm, unpretending woman; admirable in the domesticities; in speech and thought distinguished by a native refinement, which in the most fastidious eyes would have established her claim to the title of lady. She had known but little repose, and secret anxieties told upon her countenance long before the final collapse of health.

'And yet,' pursued the doctor—doctor only by courtesy—when he had stooped to pluck and examine a flower, 'I made a point of never discussing these matters with her. As no doubt you guess, life has been rather an uphill journey with us. But the home must be guarded against sordid cares to the last possible moment; nothing upsets me more than the sight of those poor homes where wife and children are obliged to talk from morning to night of how the sorry earnings shall be laid out. No, no; women, old or young, should never have to think about money.

The magnificent summer sunshine, and the western breeze that tasted of ocean, heightened his natural cheeriness. Dr. Madden fell into a familiar strain of prescience.

'There will come a day, Alice, when neither man nor woman is troubled with such sordid care. Not yet awhile; no, no; but the day will come. Human beings are not destined to struggle for ever like beasts of prey. Give them time; let civilization grow. You know what our poet says: "There the common sense of most shall hold a fretful realm in awe—"'

He quoted the couplet with a subdued fervour which characterized the man and explained his worldly lot. Elkanah Madden should never have entered the medical profession; mere humanitarianism had prompted the choice in his dreamy youth; he became an empiric, nothing more. 'Our poet,' said the doctor; Clevedon was chiefly interesting to him for its literary associations. Tennyson he worshipped; he never passed Coleridge's cottage without bowing in spirit. From the contact of coarse actualities his nature shrank.

When he and Alice returned from their walk it was the hour of family tea. A guest was present this afternoon; the eight persons who sat down to table were as many as the little parlour could comfortably contain. Of the sisters, next in age to Alice came Virginia, a pretty but delicate girl of seventeen. Gertrude, Martha, and Isabel, ranging from fourteen to ten, had no physical charm but that of youthfulness; Isabel surpassed her eldest sister in downright plainness of feature. The youngest, Monica, was a bonny little maiden only just five years old, dark and bright-eyed.

## CHAPTER I - THE FOLD AND THE SHEPHERD

The parents had omitted no care in shepherding their fold. Partly at home, and partly in local schools, the young ladies had received instruction suitable to their breeding, and the elder ones were disposed to better this education by private study. The atmosphere of the house was intellectual; books, especially the poets, lay in every room. But it never occurred to Dr. Madden that his daughters would do well to study with a professional object. In hours of melancholy he had of course dreaded the risks of life, and resolved, always with postponement, to make some practical provision for his family; in educating them as well as circumstances allowed, he conceived that he was doing the next best thing to saving money, for, if a fatality befell, teaching would always be their resource. The thought, however, of his girls having to work for money was so utterly repulsive to him that he could never seriously dwell upon it. A vague piety supported his courage. Providence would not deal harshly with him and his dear ones. He enjoyed excellent health; his practice decidedly improved. The one duty clearly before him was to set an example of righteous life, and to develop the girls' minds—in every proper direction. For, as to training them for any path save those trodden by English ladies of the familiar type, he could not have dreamt of any such thing. Dr. Madden's hopes for the race were inseparable from a maintenance of morals and conventions such as the average man assumes in his estimate of women.

The guest at table was a young girl named Rhoda Nunn. Tall, thin, eager-looking, but with promise of bodily vigour, she was singled at a glance as no member of the Madden family. Her immaturity (but fifteen, she looked two years older) appeared in nervous restlessness, and in her manner of speaking, childish at times in the hustling of inconsequent thoughts, yet striving to imitate the talk of her seniors. She had a good head, in both senses of the phrase; might or might not develop a certain beauty, but would assuredly put forth the fruits of intellect. Her mother, an invalid, was spending the summer months at Clevedon, with Dr. Madden for medical adviser, and in this way the girl became friendly with the Madden household. Its younger members she treated rather condescendingly; childish things she had long ago put away, and her sole pleasure was in intellectual talk. With a frankness peculiar to her, indicative of pride, Miss Nunn let it be known that she would have to earn her living, probably as a school teacher; study for examinations occupied most of her day, and her hours of leisure were frequently spent either at the Maddens or with a family named Smithson—people, these latter, for whom she had a profound and somewhat mysterious admiration. Mr. Smithson, a widower with a consumptive daughter, was a harsh-featured, rough-voiced man of about five-and-thirty, secretly much disliked by Dr. Madden because of his aggressive radicalism; if women's observation could be trusted, Rhoda Nunn had simply fallen in love with him, had made him, perhaps unconsciously, the object of her earliest passion. Alice and Virginia commented on the fact in their private colloquy with a shamefaced amusement; they feared that it spoke ill for the young lady's breeding. None the less they thought Rhoda a remarkable person, and listened to her utterances respectfully.

'And what is your latest paradox, Miss Nunn?' inquired the doctor, with grave facetiousness, when he had looked round the young faces at his board.

'Really, I forget, doctor. Oh, but I wanted to ask you, Do you think women ought to sit in Parliament?'

'Why, no,' was the response, as if after due consideration. 'If they are there at all they ought to stand.'

'Oh, I can't get you to talk seriously,' rejoined Rhoda, with an air of vexation, whilst the others were good-naturedly laughing. 'Mr. Smithson thinks there ought to be female members of Parliament.

'Does he? Have the girls told you that there's a nightingale in Mr. Williams's orchard?'

It was always thus. Dr. Madden did not care to discuss even playfully the radical notions which Rhoda got from her objectionable friend. His daughters would not have ventured to express an opinion on such topics when he was present; apart with Miss Nunn, they betrayed a timid interest in whatever proposition she advanced, but no gleam of originality distinguished their arguments.

After tea the little company fell into groups—some out of doors beneath the apple-trees, others near the piano at which Virginia was playing Mendelssohn. Monica ran about among them with her five-year-old prattle, ever watched by her father, who lounged in a canvas chair against the sunny ivied wall, pipe in mouth. Dr. Madden was thinking how happy they made him, these kind, gentle girls; how his love for them seemed to ripen with every summer; what a delightful old age his would be, when some were married and had children of their own, and the others tended him—they whom he had tended. Virginia would probably be sought in marriage; she had good looks, a graceful demeanour, a bright understanding. Gertrude also, perhaps. And little Monica—ah, little Monica! she would be the beauty of the family. When Monica had grown up it would be time for him to retire from practice; by then he would doubtless have saved money.

He must find more society for them; they had always been too much alone, whence their shyness among strangers. If their mother had but lived!

'Rhoda wishes you to read us something, father,' said his eldest girl, who had approached whilst he was lost in dream.

He often read aloud to them from the poets; Coleridge and Tennyson by preference. Little persuasion was needed. Alice brought the volume, and he selected 'The Lotus-Eaters.' The girls grouped themselves about him, delighted to listen. Many an hour of summer evening had they thus spent, none more peaceful than the present. The reader's cadenced voice blended with the song of a thrush.

'"Let us alone. Time driveth onward fast, And in a little while our lips are dumb. Let us alone. What is it that will last? All thing' are taken from us—"'

There came an interruption, hurried, peremptory. A farmer over at Kingston Seymour had been seized with alarming illness; the doctor must come at once.

'Very sorry, girls. Tell James to put the horse in, sharp as he can.

In ten minutes Dr. Madden was driving at full speed, alone in his dog-cart, towards the scene of duty.

About seven o'clock Rhoda Nunn took leave, remarking with her usual directness, that before going home she would walk along the sea-front in the hope of a meeting with Mr. Smithson and his daughter. Mrs. Nunn was not well enough to leave the house to-day; but, said Rhoda, the invalid preferred being left alone at such times.

'Are you sure she prefers it?' Alice ventured to ask. The girl gave her a look of surprise.

'Why should mother say what she doesn't mean?'

It was uttered with an ingenuousness which threw some light on Rhoda's character.

By nine o'clock the younger trio of sisters had gone to bed; Alice, Virginia, and Gertrude sat in the parlour, occupied with books, from time to time exchanging a quiet remark. A tap at the door scarcely drew their attention, for they supposed it was the maid-servant coming to lay supper. But when the door opened there was a mysterious silence; Alice looked up and saw the expected face, wearing, however, so strange an expression that she rose with sudden fear.

'Can I speak to you, please, miss?'

The dialogue out in the passage was brief. A messenger had just arrived with the tidings that Dr. Madden, driving back from Kingston

Seymour, had been thrown from his vehicle and lay insensible at a roadside cottage.

For some time the doctor had been intending to buy a new horse; his faithful old roadster was very weak in the knees. As in other matters, so in this, postponement became fatality; the horse stumbled and fell, and its driver was flung head forward into the road. Some hours later they brought him to his home, and for a day or two there were hopes that he might rally. But the sufferer's respite only permitted him to dictate and sign a brief will; this duty performed, Dr. Madden closed his lips for ever.

# CHAPTER II - ADRIFT

Just before Christmas of 1887, a lady past her twenties, and with a look of discouraged weariness on her thin face, knocked at a house-door in a little street by Lavender Hill. A card in the window gave notice that a bedroom was here to let. When the door opened, and a clean, grave, elderly woman presented herself, the visitor, regarding her anxiously, made known that she was in search of a lodging.

'It may be for a few weeks only, or it may be for a longer period,' she said in a low, tired voice, with an accent of good breeding. 'I have a difficulty in finding precisely what I want. One room would be sufficient, and I ask for very little attendance.'

She had but one room to let, replied the other. It might be inspected.

They went upstairs. The room was at the back of the house, small, but neatly furnished. Its appearance seemed to gratify the visitor, for she smiled timidly.

'What rent should you ask?'

'That would depend, mum, on what attendance was required.'

'Yes—of course. I think—will you permit me to sit down? I am really very tired. Thank you. I require very little attendance indeed. My ways are very simple. I should make the bed myself, and—and, do the other little things that are necessary from day to day. Perhaps I might ask you to sweep the room out—once a week or so.'

The landlady grew meditative. Possibly she had had experience of lodgers who were anxious to give as little trouble as possible. She glanced furtively at the stranger.

'And what,' was her question at length, 'would you be thinking of paying?'

'Perhaps I had better explain my position. For several years I have been companion to a lady in Hampshire. Her death has thrown me on my own resources—I hope only for a short time. I have come to London because a younger sister of mine is employed here in a house of business; she recommended me to seek for lodgings in this part; I might as well be near her whilst I am endeavouring to find another post; perhaps I may be fortunate enough to find one in London. Quietness and economy are necessary to me. A house like yours would suit me very well—very well indeed. Could we not agree upon terms within my—within my power?'

Again the landlady pondered.

'Would you be willing to pay five and sixpence?'

'Yes, I would pay five and sixpence—if you are quite sure that you could let me live in my own way with satisfaction to yourself. I—in fact, I am a vegetarian, and as the meals I take are so very simple, I feel that I might just as well prepare them myself. Would you object to my doing so in this room? A kettle and a saucepan are really all—absolutely all—that I should need to use. As I shall be much at home, it will be of course necessary for me to have a fire.'

In the course of half an hour an agreement had been devised which seemed fairly satisfactory to both parties.

'I'm not one of the graspin' ones,' remarked the landlady. 'I think I may say that of myself. If I make five or six shillings a week out of my spare room, I don't grumble. But the party as takes it must do their duty on *their* side. You haven't told me your name yet, mum.'

'Miss Madden. My luggage is at the railway station; it shall be brought here this evening. And, as I am quite unknown to you, I shall be glad to pay my rent in advance.'

'Well, I don't ask for that; but it's just as you like.'

'Then I will pay you five and sixpence at once. Be so kind as to let me have a receipt.'

So Miss Madden established herself at Lavender Hill, and dwelt there alone for three months.

She received letters frequently, but only one person called upon her. This was her sister Monica, now serving at a draper's in Walworth Road. The young lady came every Sunday, and in bad weather spent the whole day up in the little bedroom. Lodger and landlady were on remarkably good terms; the one paid her dues with exactness, and the other did many a little kindness not bargained for in the original contract.

Time went on to the spring of '88. Then, one afternoon, Miss Madden descended to the kitchen and tapped in her usual timid way at the door.

'Are you at leisure, Mrs. Conisbee? Could I have a little conversation with you?'

## CHAPTER II - ADRIFT

The landlady was alone, and with no more engrossing occupation than the ironing of some linen she had recently washed.

'I have mentioned my elder sister now and then. I am sorry to say she is leaving her post with the family at Hereford. The children are going to school, so that her services are no longer needed.'

'Indeed, mum?'

'Yes. For a shorter or longer time she will be in need of a home. Now it has occurred to me, Mrs. Conisbee, that—that I would ask you whether you would have any objection to her sharing my room with me? Of course there must be an extra payment. The room is small for two persons, but then the arrangement would only be temporary. My sister is a good and experienced teacher, and I am sure she will have no difficulty in obtaining another engagement.'

Mrs. Conisbee reflected, but without a shade of discontent. By this time she knew that her lodger was thoroughly to be trusted.

'Well, it's if *you* can manage, mum,' she replied. 'I don't see as I could have any fault to find, if you thought you could both live in that little room. And as for the rent, *I* should be quite satisfied if we said seven shillings instead of five and six.'

'Thank you, Mrs. Conisbee; thank you very much indeed. I will write to my sister at once; the news will be a great relief to her. We shall have quite an enjoyable little holiday together.'

A week later the eldest of the three Miss Maddens arrived. As it was quite impossible to find space for her boxes in the bedroom, Mrs. Conisbee allowed them to be deposited in the room occupied by her daughter, which was on the same floor. In a day or two the sisters had begun a life of orderly tenor. When weather permitted they were out either in the morning or afternoon. Alice Madden was in London for the first time; she desired to see the sights, but suffered the restrictions of poverty and ill-health. After nightfall, neither she nor Virginia ever left home.

There was not much personal likeness between them.

The elder (now five-and-thirty) tended to corpulence, the result of sedentary life; she had round shoulders and very short legs. Her face would not have been disagreeable but for its spoilt complexion; the homely features, if health had but rounded and coloured them, would have expressed pleasantly enough the gentleness and sincerity of her character. Her cheeks were loose, puffy, and permanently of the hue which is produced by cold; her forehead generally had a few pimples; her shapeless chin lost itself in two or three fleshy fissures. Scarcely less shy than in girlhood, she walked with a quick, ungainly movement as if seeking to escape from some one, her head bent forward.

Virginia (about thirty-three) had also an unhealthy look, but the poverty, or vitiation, of her blood manifested itself in less unsightly forms. One saw that she had been comely, and from certain points of view her countenance still had a grace, a sweetness, all the more noticeable because of its threatened extinction. For she was rapidly ageing; her lax lips grew laxer, with emphasis of a characteristic one would rather not have perceived there; her eyes sank into deeper hollows; wrinkles extended their network; the flesh of her neck wore away. Her tall meagre body did not seem strong enough to hold itself upright.

Alice had brown hair, but very little of it. Virginia's was inclined to be ruddy; it surmounted her small head in coils and plaits not without beauty. The voice of the elder sister had contracted an unpleasant hoarseness, but she spoke with good enunciation; a slight stiffness and pedantry of phrase came, no doubt, of her scholastic habits. Virginia was much more natural in manner and fluent in speech, even as she moved far more gracefully.

It was now sixteen years since the death of Dr. Madden of Clevedon. The story of his daughters' lives in the interval may be told with brevity suitable to so unexciting a narrative.

When the doctor's affairs were set in order, it was found that the patrimony of his six girls amounted, as nearly as possible, to eight hundred pounds.

Eight hundred pounds is, to be sure, a sum of money; but how, in these circumstances, was it to be applied?

There came over from Cheltenham a bachelor uncle, aged about sixty. This gentleman lived on an annuity of seventy pounds, which would terminate when *he* did. It might be reckoned to him for righteousness that he spent the railway fare between Cheltenham and Clevedon to attend his brother's funeral, and to speak a kind word to his nieces. Influence he had none; initiative, very little. There was no reckoning upon him for aid of any kind.

From Richmond in Yorkshire, in reply to a letter from Alice, wrote an old, old aunt of the late Mrs. Madden, who had occasionally sent the girls presents. Her communication was barely legible; it seemed to contain fortifying texts of Scripture, but nothing in the way of worldly counsel. This old lady had no possessions to bequeath. And, as far as the girls knew, she was their mother's only surviving relative.

## CHAPTER II - ADRIFT

The executor of the will was a Clevedon tradesman, a kind and capable friend of the family for many years, a man of parts and attainments superior to his station. In council with certain other well-disposed persons, who regarded the Maddens' circumstances with friendly anxiety, Mr. Hungerford (testamentary instruction allowing him much freedom of action) decided that the three elder girls must forthwith become self-supporting, and that the three younger should live together in the care of a lady of small means, who offered to house and keep them for the bare outlay necessitated. A prudent investment of the eight hundred pounds might, by this arrangement, feed, clothe, and in some sort educate Martha, Isabel, and Monica. To see thus far ahead sufficed for the present; fresh circumstances could be dealt with as they arose.

Alice obtained a situation as nursery-governess at sixteen pounds a year. Virginia was fortunate enough to be accepted as companion by a gentlewoman at Weston-super-Mare; her payment, twelve pounds. Gertrude, fourteen years old, also went to Weston, where she was offered employment in a fancy-goods shop—her payment nothing at all, but lodging, board, and dress assured to her.

Ten years went by, and saw many changes.

Gertrude and Martha were dead; the former of consumption, the other drowned by the overturning of a pleasure-boat. Mr. Hungerford also was dead, and a new guardian administered the fund which was still a common property of the four surviving daughters. Alice plied her domestic teaching; Virginia remained a 'companion.' Isabel, now aged twenty, taught in a Board School at Bridgewater, and Monica, just fifteen, was on the point of being apprenticed to a draper at Weston, where Virginia abode. To serve behind a counter would not have been Monica's choice if any more liberal employment had seemed within her reach. She had no aptitude whatever for giving instruction; indeed, had no aptitude for anything but being a pretty, cheerful, engaging girl, much dependent on the love and gentleness of those about her. In speech and bearing Monica greatly resembled her mother; that is to say, she had native elegance. Certainly it might be deemed a pity that such a girl could not be introduced to one of the higher walks of life; but the time had come when she must 'do something', and the people to whose guidance she looked had but narrow experience of life. Alice and Virginia sighed over the contrast with bygone hopes, but their own careers made it seem probable that Monica would be better off 'in business' than in a more strictly genteel position. And there was every likelihood that, at such a place as Weston, with her sister for occasional chaperon, she would ere long find herself relieved of the necessity of working for a livelihood.

To the others, no wooer had yet presented himself. Alice, if she had ever dreamt of marriage, must by now have resigned herself to spinsterhood. Virginia could scarce hope that her faded prettiness, her health damaged by attendance upon an exacting invalid and in profitless study when she ought to have been sleeping, would attract any man in search of a wife. Poor Isabel was so extremely plain. Monica, if her promise were fulfilled, would be by far the best looking, as well as the sprightliest, of the family. She must marry; of course she must marry! Her sisters gladdened in the thought.

Isabel was soon worked into illness. Brain trouble came on, resulting in melancholia. A charitable institution ultimately received her, and there, at two-and-twenty, the poor hard-featured girl drowned herself in a bath.

Their numbers had thus been reduced by half. Up to now, the income of their eight hundred pounds had served, impartially, the ends now of this, now of that one, doing a little good to all, saving them from many an hour of bitterness which must else have been added to their lot. By a new arrangement, the capital was at length made over to Alice and Virginia jointly, the youngest sister having a claim upon them to the extent of an annual nine pounds. A trifle, but it would buy her clothing—and then Monica was sure to marry. Thank Heaven, she was sure to marry!

Without notable event, matrimonial or other, time went on to this present year of 1888.

Late in June, Monica would complete her twenty-first year; the elders, full of affection for the sister, who so notably surpassed them in beauty of person, talked much about her as the time approached, devising how to procure her a little pleasure on her birthday. Virginia thought a suitable present would be a copy of 'the Christian Year'.

'She has really no time for continuous reading. A verse of Keble—just one verse at bedtime and in the morning might be strength to the poor girl.'

Alice assented.

'We must join to buy it, dear,' she added, with anxious look. 'It wouldn't be justifiable to spend more than two or three shillings.'

'I fear not.'

They were preparing their midday meal, the substantial repast of the day. In a little saucepan on an oil cooking-stove was some plain rice, bubbling as Alice stirred it. Virginia fetched from downstairs

(Mrs. Conisbee had assigned to them a shelf in her larder) bread, butter, cheese, a pot of preserve, and arranged the table (three feet by one and a half) at which they were accustomed to eat. The rice being ready, it was turned out in two proportions; made savoury with a little butter, pepper, and salt, it invited them to sit down.

As they had been out in the morning, the afternoon would be spent in domestic occupations. The low cane-chair Virginia had appropriated to her sister, because of the latter's headaches and backaches, and other disorders; she herself sat on an ordinary chair of the bedside species, to which by this time she had become used. Their sewing, when they did any, was strictly indispensable; if nothing demanded the needle, both preferred a book. Alice, who had never been a student in the proper sense of the word, read for the twentieth time a few volumes in her possession—poetry, popular history, and half a dozen novels such as the average mother of children would have approved in the governess's hands. With Virginia the case was somewhat different. Up to about her twenty-fourth year she had pursued one subject with a zeal limited only by her opportunities; study absolutely disinterested, seeing that she had never supposed it would increase her value as a 'companion', or enable her to take any better position. Her one intellectual desire was to know as much as possible about ecclesiastical history. Not in a spirit of fanaticism; she was devout, but in moderation, and never spoke bitterly on religious topics. The growth of the Christian Church, old sects and schisms, the Councils, affairs of Papal policy—these things had a very genuine interest for her; circumstances favouring, she might have become an erudite woman; But the conditions were so far from favourable that all she succeeded in doing was to undermine her health. Upon a sudden breakdown there followed mental lassitude, from which she never recovered. It being subsequently her duty to read novels aloud for the lady whom she 'companioned,' new novels at the rate of a volume a day, she lost all power of giving her mind to anything but the feebler fiction. Nowadays she procured such works from a lending library, on a subscription of a shilling a month. Ashamed at first to indulge this taste before Alice, she tried more solid literature, but this either sent her to sleep or induced headache. The feeble novels reappeared, and as Alice made no adverse comment, they soon came and went with the old regularity.

This afternoon the sisters were disposed for conversation. The same grave thought preoccupied both of them, and they soon made it their subject.

'Surely,' Alice began by murmuring, half absently, 'I shall soon hear of something.'

'I am dreadfully uneasy on my own account,' her sister replied.

'You think the person at Southend won't write again?'

'I'm afraid not. And she seemed so *very* unsatisfactory. Positively illiterate—oh, I couldn't bear that.' Virginia gave a shudder as she spoke.

'I almost wish,' said Alice, 'that I had accepted the place at Plymouth.'

'Oh, my dear! Five children and not a penny of salary. It was a shameless proposal.'

'It was, indeed,' sighed the poor governess. 'But there is so little choice for people like myself. Certificates, and even degrees, are asked for on every hand. With nothing but references to past employers, what can one expect? I know it will end in my taking a place without salary.'

'People seem to have still less need of *me*,' lamented the companion. 'I wish now that I had gone to Norwich as lady-help.'

'Dear, your health would *never* have supported it.'

'I don't know. Possibly the more active life might do me good. It *might*, you know, Alice.'

The other admitted this possibility with a deep sigh.

'Let us review our position,' she then exclaimed.

It was a phrase frequently on her lips, and always made her more cheerful. Virginia also seemed to welcome it as an encouragement.

'Mine,' said the companion, 'is almost as serious as it could be. I have only one pound left, with the exception of the dividend.'

'I have rather more than four pounds still. Now, let us think,' Alice paused. 'Supposing we neither of us obtain employment before the end of this year. We have to live, in that case, more than six months—you on seven pounds, and I on ten.'

'It's impossible,' said Virginia.

'Let us see. Put it in another form. We have both to live together on seventeen pounds. That is—' she made a computation on a piece of paper—'that is two pounds, sixteen shillings and eightpence a month—let us suppose this month at an end. That represents fourteen shillings and twopence a week. Yes, we can do it!'

She laid down her pencil with an air of triumph. Her dull eyes brightened as though she had discovered a new source of income.

## CHAPTER II - ADRIFT

'We cannot, dear,' urged Virginia in a subdued voice. 'Seven shillings rent; that leaves only seven and twopence a week for everything—everything.'

'We *could* do it, dear,' persisted the other. 'If it came to the very worst, our food need not cost more than sixpence a day—three and sixpence a week. I do really believe, Virgie, we could support life on less—say, on fourpence. Yes, we could dear!'

They looked fixedly at each other, like people about to stake everything on their courage.

'Is such a life worthy of the name?' asked Virginia in tones of awe.

'We shan't be driven to that. Oh, we certainly shall not. But it helps one to know that, strictly speaking, we are *independent* for another six months.'

That word gave Virginia an obvious thrill.

'Independent! Oh, Alice, what a blessed thing is independence! Do you know, my dear, I am afraid I have not exerted myself as I might have done to find a new place. These comfortable lodgings, and the pleasure of seeing Monica once a week, have tempted me into idleness. It isn't really my wish to be idle; I know the harm it does me; but oh! if one could work in a home of one's own!'

Alice had a startled, apprehensive look, as if her sister were touching on a subject hardly proper for discussion, or at least dangerous.

'I'm afraid it's no use thinking of that, dear,' she answered awkwardly.

'No use; no use whatever. I am wrong to indulge in such thoughts.'

'Whatever happens, my dear,' said Alice presently, with all the impressiveness of tone she could command, 'we must never entrench upon our capital—never—never!'

'Oh, never! If we grow old and useless—'

'If no one will give us even board and lodging for our services—'

'If we haven't a friend to look to,' Alice threw in, as though they were answering each other in a doleful litany, 'then indeed we shall be glad that nothing tempted us to entrench on our capital! It would just keep us'—her voice sank—'from the workhouse.'

After this each took up a volume, and until teatime they read quietly.

From six to nine in the evening they again talked and read alternately. Their conversation was now retrospective; each revived memories of what she had endured in one or the other house of bondage. Never had it been their lot to serve 'really nice' people—this phrase of theirs was anything but meaningless. They had lived with more or less well-to-do families in the lower middle class—people who could not have inherited refinement, and had not acquired any, neither proletarians nor gentlefolk, consumed with a disease of vulgar pretentiousness, inflated with the miasma of democracy. It would have been but a natural result of such a life if the sisters had commented upon it in a spirit somewhat akin to that of their employers; but they spoke without rancour, without scandalmongering. They knew themselves superior to the women who had grudgingly paid them, and often smiled at recollections which would have moved the servile mind to venomous abuse.

At nine o'clock they took a cup of cocoa and a biscuit, and half an hour later they went to bed. Lamp oil was costly; and indeed they felt glad to say as early as possible that another day had gone by.

Their hour of rising was eight. Mrs. Conisbee provided hot water for their breakfast. On descending to fetch it, Virginia found that the postman had left a letter for her. The writing on the envelope seemed to be a stranger's. She ran upstairs again in excitement.

'Who can this be from, Alice?'

The elder sister had one of her headaches this morning; she was clay colour, and tottered in moving about. The close atmosphere of the bedroom would alone have accounted for such a malady. But an unexpected letter made her for the moment oblivious of suffering.

'Posted in London,' she said, examining the envelope eagerly.

'Some one you have been in correspondence with?'

'It's months since I wrote to any one in London.'

For full five minutes they debated the mystery, afraid of dashing their hopes by breaking the envelope. At length Virginia summoned courage. Standing at a distance from the other, she took out the sheet of paper with tremulous hand, and glanced fearfully at the signature.

'What *do* you think? It's Miss Nunn!'

'Miss Nunn! Never! How could she have got the address?'

Again the difficulty was discussed whilst its ready solution lay neglected.

'Do read it!' said Alice at length, her throbbing head, made worse by the agitation, obliging her to sink down into the chair.

The letter ran thus:—

> 'DEAR Miss MADDEN,—This morning I chanced to meet with Mrs. Darby, who was passing through London on her way home from the seaside. We had only five minutes' talk (it was at a railway station), but she mentioned that you were at present in London, and gave me

your address. After all these years, how glad I should be to see you! The struggle of life has made me selfish; I have neglected my old friends. And yet I am bound to add that some of *them* have neglected *me*. Would you rather that I came to your lodgings or you to mine? Which you like. I hear that your elder sister is with you, and that Monica is also in London somewhere. Do let us all see each other once more. Write as soon as you can. My kindest regards to all of you.—Sincerely yours,

RHODA NUNN.'

'How like her,' exclaimed Virginia, when she had read this aloud, 'to remember that perhaps we may not care to receive visitors! She was always so thoughtful. And it is true that I *ought* to have written to her.'

'We shall go to her, of course?'

'Oh yes, as she gives us the choice. How delightful! I wonder what she is doing? She writes cheerfully; I am sure she must be in a good position. What is the address? Queen's Road, Chelsea. Oh, I'm so glad it's not very far. We can walk there and back easily.'

For several years they had lost sight of Rhoda Nunn. She left Clevedon shortly after the Maddens were scattered, and they heard she had become a teacher. About the date of Monica's apprenticeship at Weston, Miss Nunn had a chance meeting with Virginia and the younger girl; she was still teaching, but spoke of her work with extreme discontent, and hinted at vague projects. Whether she succeeded in releasing herself the Maddens never heard.

It was a morning of doubtful fairness. Before going to bed last night they had decided to walk out together this morning and purchase the present for Monica's birthday, which was next Sunday. But Alice felt too unwell to leave the house. Virginia should write a reply to Miss Nunn's letter, and then go to the bookseller's alone.

She set forth at half-past nine. With extreme care she had preserved an out-of-doors dress into the third summer; it did not look shabby. Her mantle was in its second year only; the original fawn colour had gone to an indeterminate grey. Her hat of brown straw was a possession for ever; it underwent new trimming, at an outlay of a few pence, when that became unavoidable. Yet Virginia could not have been judged anything but a lady. She wore her garments as only a lady can (the position and movement of the arms has much to do with this), and had the step never to be acquired by a person of vulgar instincts.

A very long walk was before her. She wished to get as far as the Strand bookshops, not only for the sake of choice, but because this region pleased her and gave her a sense of holiday. Past Battersea Park, over Chelsea Bridge, then the weary stretch to Victoria Station, and the upward labour to Charing Cross. Five miles, at least, measured by pavement. But Virginia walked quickly; at half-past eleven she was within sight of her goal.

A presentable copy of Keble's work cost less than she had imagined. This rejoiced her. But after leaving the shop she had a singular expression on her face—something more than weariness, something less than anxiety, something other than calculation. In front of Charing Cross Station she stopped, looking vaguely about her. Perhaps she had it in her mind to return home by omnibus, and was dreading the expense. Yet of a sudden she turned and went up the approach to the railway.

At the entrance again she stopped. Her features were now working in the strangest way, as though a difficulty of breathing had assailed her. In her eyes was an eager yet frightened look; her lips stood apart.

Another quick movement, and she entered the station. She went straight to the door of the refreshment room, and looked in through the glass. Two or three people were standing inside. She drew back, a tremor passing through her.

A lady came out. Then again Virginia approached the door. Two men only were within, talking together. With a hurried, nervous movement, she pushed the door open and went up to a part of the counter as far as possible from the two customers. Bending forward, she said to the barmaid in a voice just above a whisper,—

'Kindly give me a little brandy.'

Beads of perspiration were on her face, which had turned to a ghastly pallor. The barmaid, concluding that she was ill, served her promptly and with a sympathetic look.

Virginia added to the spirit twice its quantity of water, standing, as she did so, half turned from the bar. Then she sipped hurriedly two or three times, and at length took a draught. Colour flowed to her cheeks; her eyes lost their frightened glare. Another draught finished the stimulant. She hastily wiped her lips, and walked away with firm step.

In the meantime a threatening cloud had passed from the sun; warm rays fell upon the street and its clamorous life. Virginia felt tired in body, but a delightful animation, rarest of boons, gave her new strength. She walked into Trafalgar Square and viewed it like a person who stands there for the first time, smiling, interested. A quarter of an hour passed whilst she merely enjoyed the air, the sunshine, and the scene about her. Such a quarter of an hour—so calm, contented, unconsciously hopeful—as she had not known since Alice's coming to London.

She reached the house by half-past one, bringing in a paper bag something which was to serve for dinner. Alice had a wretched appearance; her head ached worse than ever.

'Virgie,' she moaned, 'we never took account of illness, you know.'

'Oh, we must keep that off,' replied the other, sitting down with a look of exhaustion. She smiled, but no longer as in the sunlight of Trafalgar Square.

'Yes, I must struggle against it. We will have dinner as soon as possible. I feel faint.'

If both of them had avowed their faintness as often as they felt it, the complaint would have been perpetual. But they generally made a point of deceiving each other, and tried to delude themselves; professing that no diet could be better for their particular needs than this which poverty imposed.

'Ah! it's a good sign to be hungry,' exclaimed Virginia. 'You'll be better this afternoon, dear.'

Alice turned over 'The Christian Year,' and endeavoured to console herself out of it, whilst her sister prepared the meal.

## CHAPTER III - AN INDEPENDENT WOMAN

Virginia's reply to Miss Nunn's letter brought another note next morning—Saturday. It was to request a call from the sisters that same afternoon.

Alice, unfortunately, would not be able to leave home. Her disorder had become a feverish cold—caught, doubtless, between open window and door whilst the bedroom was being aired for breakfast. She lay in bed, and her sister administered remedies of the chemist's advising.

But she insisted on Virginia leaving her in the afternoon. Miss Nunn might have something of importance to tell or to suggest. Mrs. Conisbee, sympathetic in her crude way, would see that the invalid wanted for nothing.

So, after a dinner of mashed potatoes and milk ('The Irish peasantry live almost entirely on that,' croaked Alice, 'and they are physically a fine race'), the younger sister started on her walk to Chelsea. Her destination was a plain, low roomy old house in Queen's Road, over against the hospital gardens. On asking for Miss Nunn, she was led to a back room on the ground floor, and there waited for a few moments. Several large bookcases, a well-equipped writing-table, and kindred objects, indicated that the occupant of the house was studious; the numerous bunches of cut flowers, which agreeably scented the air, seemed to prove the student was a woman.

Miss Nunn entered. Younger only by a year or two than Virginia, she was yet far from presenting any sorrowful image of a person on the way to old-maidenhood. She had a clear though pale skin, a vigorous frame, a brisk movement—all the signs of fairly good health. Whether or not she could be called a comely woman might have furnished matter for male discussion; the prevailing voice of her own sex would have denied her charm of feature. At first view the countenance seemed masculine, its expression somewhat aggressive—eyes shrewdly observant and lips consciously impregnable. But the connoisseur delayed his verdict. It was a face that invited, that compelled, study. Self-confidence, intellectual keenness, a bright humour, frank courage, were traits legible enough; and when the lips parted to show their warmth, their fullness, when the eyelids drooped a little in meditation, one became aware of a suggestiveness directed not solely to the intellect, of something like an unfamiliar sexual type, remote indeed from the voluptuous, but hinting a possibility of subtle feminine forces that might be released by circumstance. She wore a black serge gown, with white collar and cuffs; her thick hair rippled low upon each side of the forehead, and behind was gathered into loose vertical coils; in shadow the hue seemed black, but when illumined it was seen to be the darkest, warmest brown.

Offering a strong, shapely hand, she looked at her visitor with a smile which betrayed some mixture of pain in the hearty welcome.

'And how long have you been in London?'

It was the tone of a busy, practical person. Her voice had not much softness of timbre, and perhaps on that account she kept it carefully subdued.

'So long as that? How I wish I had known you were so near! I have been in London myself about two years. And your sisters?'

Virginia explained Alice's absence, adding,—

'As for poor Monica, she has only Sunday free—except one evening a month. She is at business till half-past nine, and on Saturday till half-past eleven or twelve.'

'Oh, dear, dear, dear!' exclaimed the other rapidly, making a motion with her hand as if to brush away something disagreeable. 'That will never do. You must put a stop to that.'

'I am sure we ought to.'

Virginia's thin, timid voice and weak manner were thrown into painful contrast by Miss Nunn's personality.

'Yes, yes; we will talk about it presently. Poor little Monica! But do tell me about yourself and Miss Madden. It is so long since I heard about you.'

'Indeed I ought to have written. I remember that at the end of our correspondence I remained in your debt. But it was a troublesome and depressing time with me. I had nothing but groans and moans to send.'

'You didn't stay long, I trust, with that trying Mrs. Carr?'

'Three years!' sighed Virginia.

'Oh, your patience!'

'I wished to leave again and again. But at the end she always begged me not to desert her—that was how she put it. After all, I never had the heart to go.'

'Very kind of you, but—those questions are so difficult to decide. Self-sacrifice may be quite wrong, I'm afraid.'

'Do you think so?' asked Virginia anxiously.

'Yes, I am sure it is often wrong—all the more so because people proclaim it a virtue without any reference to circumstances. Then how did you get away at last?'

'The poor woman died. Then I had a place scarcely less disagreeable. Now I have none at all; but I really must find one very soon.'

She laughed at this allusion to her poverty, and made nervous motions.

'Let me tell you what my own course has been,' said Miss Nunn, after a short reflection. 'When my mother died, I determined to have done with teaching—you know that. I disliked it too much, and partly, of course, because I was incapable. Half my teaching was a sham—a pretence of knowing what I neither knew nor cared to know. I had gone into it like most girls, as a dreary matter of course.'

'Like poor Alice, I'm afraid.'

'Oh, it's a distressing subject. When my mother left me that little sum of money I took a bold step. I went to Bristol to learn everything I could that would help me out of school life. Shorthand, book-keeping, commercial correspondence—I had lessons in them all, and worked desperately for a year. It did me good; at the end of the year I was vastly improved in health, and felt myself worth something in the world. I got a place as cashier in a large shop. That soon tired me, and by dint of advertising I found a place in an office at Bath. It was a move towards London, and I couldn't rest till I had come the whole way. My first engagement here was as shorthand writer to the secretary of a company. But he soon wanted some one who could use a typewriter. That was a suggestion. I went to learn typewriting, and the lady who taught me asked me in the end to stay with her as an assistant. This is her house, and here I live with her.'

'How energetic you have been!'

'How fortunate, perhaps. I must tell you about this lady—Miss Barfoot. She has private means—not large, but sufficient to allow of her combining benevolence with business. She makes it her object to train young girls for work in offices, teaching them the things that I learnt in Bristol, and typewriting as well. Some pay for their lessons, and some get them for nothing. Our workrooms are in Great Portland Street, over a picture-cleaner's shop. One or two girls have evening lessons, but our pupils for the most part are able to come in the day. Miss Barfoot hasn't much interest in the lower classes; she wishes to be of use to the daughters of educated people. And she is of use. She is doing admirable work.'

'Oh, I am sure she must be! What a wonderful person!'

'It occurs to me that she might help Monica.'

'Oh, do you think she would?' exclaimed Virginia, with eager attention. 'How grateful we should be!'

'Where is Monica employed?'

'At a draper's in Walworth Road. She is worked to death. Every week I see a difference in her, poor child. We hoped to persuade her to go back to the shop at Weston; but if this you speak of were possible—how *much* better! We have never reconciled ourselves to her being in that position—never.'

'I see no harm in the position itself,' replied Miss Nunn in her rather blunt tone, 'but I see a great deal in those outrageous hours. She won't easily do better in London, without special qualifications; and probably she is reluctant to go back to the country.'

'Yes, she is; very reluctant.'

'I understand it,' said the other, with a nod. 'Will you ask her to come and see me?'

A servant entered with tea. Miss Nunn caught the expression in her visitor's eyes, and said cheerfully—

'I had no midday meal to-day, and really I feel the omission. Mary, please do put tea in the dining-room, and bring up some meat—Miss Barfoot,' she added, in explanation to Virginia, is out of town, and I am a shockingly irregular person about meals. I am sure you will sit down with me?'

Virginia sported with the subject. Months of miserable eating and drinking in her stuffy bedroom made an invitation such as this a veritable delight to her. Seated in the dining-room, she at first refused the offer of meat, alleging her vegetarianism; but Miss Nunn, convinced that the poor woman was starving, succeeded in persuading her. A slice of good beef had much the same effect upon Virginia as her more dangerous indulgence at Charing Cross Station. She brightened wonderfully.

'Now let us go back to the library,' said Miss Nunn, when their meal was over. 'We shall soon see each other again, I hope, but we might as well talk of serious things whilst we have the opportunity. Will you allow me to be very frank with you?'

The other looked startled.

'What could you possibly say that would offend me?'

'In the old days you told me all about your circumstances. Are they still the same?'

'Precisely the same. Most happily, we have never needed to entrench upon our capital. Whatever happens, we must avoid that—whatever happens!'

'I quite understand you. But wouldn't it be possible to make a better use of that money? It is eight hundred pounds, I think? Have you never thought of employing it in some practical enterprise?'

Virginia at first shrank in alarm, then trembled deliciously at her friend's bold views.

'Would it be possible? Really? You think—'

'I can only suggest, of course. One mustn't argue about others from one's own habit of thought. Heaven forbid'—this sounded rather profane to the listener—'that I should urge you to do anything you would think rash. But how much better if you could somehow secure independence.'

'Ah, if we could! The very thing we were saying the other day! But how? I have no idea how.'

Miss Nunn seemed to hesitate.

'I don't advise. You mustn't give any weight to what I say, except in so far as your own judgment approves it. But couldn't one open a preparatory school, for instance? At Weston, suppose, where already you know a good many people. Or even at Clevedon.'

Virginia drew in her breath, and it was easy for Miss Nunn to perceive that the proposal went altogether beyond her friend's scope. Impossible, perhaps, to inspire these worn and discouraged women with a particle of her own enterprise. Perchance they altogether lacked ability to manage a school for even the youngest children. She did not press the subject; it might come up on another occasion. Virginia begged for time to think it over; then, remembering her invalid sister, felt that she must not prolong the visit.

'Do take some of these flowers,' said Miss Nunn, collecting a rich nosegay from the vases. 'Let them be my message to your sister. And I should be so glad to see Monica. Sunday is a good time; I am always at home in the afternoon.'

With a fluttering heart Virginia made what haste she could homewards. The interview had filled her with a turmoil of strange new thoughts, which she was impatient to pour forth for Alice's wondering comment. It was the first time in her life that she had spoken with a woman daring enough to think and act for herself.

# CHAPTER IV - MONICA'S MAJORITY

In the drapery establishment where Monica Madden worked and lived it was not (as is sometimes the case) positively forbidden to the resident employees to remain at home on Sunday; but they were strongly recommended to make the utmost possible use of that weekly vacation. Herein, no doubt, appeared a laudable regard for their health. Young people, especially young women, who are laboriously engaged in a shop for thirteen hours and a half every weekday, and on Saturday for an average of sixteen, may be supposed to need a Sabbath of open air. Messrs. Scotcher and Co. acted like conscientious men in driving them forth immediately after breakfast, and enjoining upon them not to return until bedtime. By way of well-meaning constraint, it was directed that only the very scantiest meals (plain bread and cheese, in fact) should be supplied to those who did not take advantage of the holiday.

Messrs. Scotcher and Co. were large-minded men. Not only did they insist that the Sunday ought to be used for bodily recreation, but they had no objection whatever to their young friends taking a stroll after closing-time each evening. Nay, so generous and confiding were they, that to each young person they allowed a latchkey. The air of Walworth Road is pure and invigorating about midnight; why should the reposeful ramble be hurried by consideration for weary domestics?

Monica always felt too tired to walk after ten o'clock; moreover, the usual conversation in the dormitory which she shared with five other young women was so little to her taste that she wished to be asleep when the talkers came up to bed. But on Sunday she gladly followed the counsel of her employers. If the weather were bad, the little room at Lavender Hill offered her a retreat; when the sun shone, she liked to spend a part of the day in free wandering about London, which even yet had not quite disillusioned her.

And to-day it shone brightly. This was her birthday, the completion of her one-and-twentieth year. Alice and Virginia of course expected her early in the morning, and of course they were all to dine together—at the table measuring three feet by one and a half; but the afternoon and evening she must have to herself. The afternoon, because a few hours of her sisters' talk invariably depressed her; and the evening, because she had an appointment to keep. As she left the big ugly 'establishment' her heart beat cheerfully, and a smile fluttered about her lips. She did not feel very well, but that was a matter of course; the ride in an omnibus would perhaps make her head clearer.

Monica's face was of a recognized type of prettiness; a pure oval; from the smooth forehead to the dimpled little chin all its lines were soft and graceful. Her lack of colour, by heightening the effect of black eyebrows and darkly lustrous eyes, gave her at present a more spiritual cast than her character justified; but a thoughtful firmness was native to her lips, and no possibility of smirk or simper lurked in the attractive features. The slim figure was well fitted in a costume of pale blue, cheap but becoming; a modest little hat rested on her black hair; her gloves and her sunshade completed the dainty picture.

An omnibus would be met in Kennington Park Road. On her way thither, in a quiet cross-street, she was overtaken by a young man who had left the house of business a moment after her, and had followed at a short distance timidly. A young man of unhealthy countenance, with a red pimple on the side of his nose, but not otherwise ill-looking. He was clad with propriety—stove-pipe hat, diagonal frockcoat, grey trousers, and he walked with a springy gait.

'Miss Madden—'

He had ventured, with perturbation in his face, to overtake, Monica. She stopped.

'What is it, Mr. Bullivant?'

Her tone was far from encouraging, but the young man smiled upon her with timorous tenderness.

'What a beautiful morning! Are you going far?'

He had the Cockney accent, but not in an offensive degree; his manners were not flagrantly of the shop.

'Yes; some distance.' Monica walked slowly on.

'Will you allow me to walk a little way with you?' he pleaded, bending towards her.

'I shall take the omnibus at the end of this street.'

They went forward together. Monica no longer smiled, but neither did she look angry. Her expression was one of trouble.

'Where shall *you* spend the day, Mr. Bullivant?' she asked at length, with an effort to seem unconcerned.

'I really don't know.'

'I should think it would be very nice up the river.' And she added diffidently, 'Miss Eade is going to Richmond.'

'Is she?' he replied vaguely.

'At least she wished to go—if she could find a companion.'

'I hope she will enjoy herself,' said Mr. Bullivant, with careful civility.

'But of course she won't enjoy it very much if she has to go alone. As you have no particular engagement, Mr. Bullivant, wouldn't it be kind to—?'

The suggestion was incomplete, but intelligible.

'I couldn't ask Miss Eade to let me accompany her,' said the young man gravely.

'Oh, I think you could. She would like it.'

Monica looked rather frightened at her boldness, and quickly added—

'Now I must say good-bye. There comes the bus.'

Bullivant turned desperately in that direction. He saw there was as yet no inside passenger.

'Do allow me to go a short way with you?' burst from his lips. 'I positively don't know how I shall spend the morning.'

Monica had signalled to the driver, and was hurrying forward. Bullivant followed, reckless of consequences. In a minute both were seated within.

'You will forgive me?' pleaded the young fellow, remarking a look of serious irritation on his companion's face. 'I must be with you a few minutes longer.'

'I think when I have begged you not to—'

'I know how bad my behaviour must seem. But, Miss Madden, may I not be on terms of friendship with you?'

'Of course you may—but you are not content with that.'

'Yes—indeed—I *will* be content—'

'It's foolish to say so. Haven't you broken the understanding three or four times?'

The bus stopped for a passenger, a man, who mounted to the top.

'I am so sorry,' murmured Bullivant, as the starting horses jolted them together. 'I try not to worry you. Think of my position. You have told me that there is no one else who—whose rights I ought to respect. Feeling as I do, it isn't in human nature to give up hope!'

'Then will you let me ask you a rude question?'

'Ask me *any* question, Miss Madden.'

'How would it be possible for you to support a wife?'

She flushed and smiled. Bullivant, dreadfully discomposed, did not move his eyes from her.

'It wouldn't be possible for some time,' he answered in a thick voice. 'I have nothing but my wretched salary. But every one hopes.'

'What reasonable hope have you?' Monica urged, forcing herself to be cruel, because it seemed the only way of putting an end to this situation.

'Oh, there are so many opportunities in our business. I could point to half a dozen successful men who were at the counter a few years ago. I may become a walker, and get at least three pounds a week. If I were lucky enough to be taken on as a buyer, I might make—why, some make many hundreds a year—many hundreds.'

'And you would ask me to wait on and on for one of these wonderful chances?'

'If I could move your feelings, Miss Madden,' he began, with a certain dolorous dignity; but there his voice broke. He saw too plainly that the girl had neither faith in him nor liking for him.

'Mr. Bullivant, I think you ought to wait until you really have prospects. If you were encouraged by some person, it would be a different thing. And indeed you haven't to look far. But where there has never been the slightest encouragement, you are really wrong to act in this way. A long engagement, where everything remains doubtful for years, is so wretched that—oh, if I were a man, I would *never* try to persuade a girl into that! I think it wrong and cruel.'

The stroke was effectual. Bullivant averted his face, naturally woebegone, and sat for some minutes without speaking. The bus again drew up; four or five people were about to ascend.

'I will say good-morning, Miss Madden,' he whispered hurriedly.

She gave her hand, glanced at him with embarrassment, and so let him depart.

Ten minutes restored the mood in which she had set out. Once more she smiled to herself. Indeed, her head was better for the fresh air and the movement. If only the sisters would allow her to get away soon after dinner!

It was Virginia who opened the door to her, and embraced and kissed her with wonted fondness.

'You are nice and early! Poor Alice has been in bed since the day before yesterday; a dreadful cold and one of her very worst headaches. But I think she is a little better this morning.'

Alice—a sad spectacle—was propped up on pillows.

'Don't kiss me, darling,' she said, in a voice barely audible. 'You mustn't risk getting a sore throat. How well you look!'

'I'm afraid she doesn't look *well,*' corrected Virginia; 'but perhaps she has a little more colour than of late. Monica, dear, as Alice can hardly use her voice, I will speak for both of us, and wish you many, many happy returns of the day. And we ask you to accept this little book from us. It may be a comfort to you from time to time.'

'You are good, kind dears!' replied Monica, kissing the one on the lips and the other on her thinly-tressed head. 'It's no use saying you oughtn't to have spent money on me; you *will* always do it. What a nice "Christian Year"! I'll do my best to read some of it now and then.'

With a half-guilty air, Virginia then brought from some corner of the room a very small but delicate currant cake. Monica must eat a mouthful of this; she always had such a wretched breakfast, and the journey from Walworth Road was enough to give an appetite.

'But you are ruining yourselves, foolish people!'

The others exchanged a look, and smiled with such a strange air that Monica could not but notice it.

'I know!' she cried. 'There's good news. You have found something, and better than usual Virgie.'

'Perhaps so. Who knows? Eat your slice of cake like a good child, and then I shall have something to tell you.'

Obviously the two were excited. Virginia moved about with the recovered step of girlhood, held herself upright, and could not steady her hands.

'You would never guess whom I have seen,' she began, when Monica was quite ready to listen. 'We had a letter the other morning which did puzzle us so—I mean the writing before we opened it. And it was from—Miss Nunn!'

This name did not greatly stir Monica.

'You had quite lost sight of her, hadn't you?' she remarked.

'Quite. I didn't suppose we should ever hear of her again. But nothing more fortunate could have happened. My dear, she is wonderful!'

At considerable length Virginia detailed all she had learnt of Miss Nunn's career, and described her present position.

'She will be the most valuable friend to us. Oh, her strength, her resolution! The way in which she discovers the right thing to do! You are to call upon her as soon as possible. This very after noon you had better go. She will relieve you from all your troubles darling. Her friend, Miss Barfoot, will teach you typewriting, and put you in the way of earning an easy and pleasant livelihood. She will, indeed!'

'But how long does it take?' asked the astonished girl.

'Oh, quite a short time, I should think. We didn't speak of details; they were postponed. You will hear everything yourself. And she suggested all sorts of ways,' pursued Virginia, with quite unintentional exaggeration, 'in which we could make better use of our invested money. She is *full* of practical expedients. The most wonderful person! She is quite like a *man* in energy and resources. I never imagined that one of our sex could resolve and plan and act as she does!'

Monica inquired anxiously what the projects for improving their income might be.

'Nothing is decided yet,' was the reply, given with a confident smile. 'Let us first of all put *you* in comfort and security; that is the immediate need.'

The listener was interested, but did not show any eagerness for the change proposed. Presently she stood at the window and lost herself in thought. Alice gave signs of an inclination to doze; she had had a sleepless night, in spite of soporifics. Though no sun entered the room, it was very hot, and the presence of a third person made the air oppressive.

'Don't you think we might go out for half an hour?' Monica whispered, when Virginia had pointed to the invalid's closed eves. 'I'm sure it's very unhealthy for us all to be in this little place.'

I don't like to leave her,' the other whispered back. 'But I certainly think it would be better for you to have fresh air. Wouldn't you like to go to church, dear? The bells haven't stopped yet.'

The elder sisters were not quite regular in their church-going. When weather or lassitude kept them at home on Sunday morning they read the service aloud. Monica found the duty of listening rather grievous. During the months that she was alone in London she had fallen into neglect of public worship; not from any conscious emancipation, but because her companions at the house of business never dreamt of entering a church, and their example by degrees affected her with carelessness. At present she was glad of the pretext for escaping until dinner-time.

She went forth with the intention of deceiving her sisters, of walking to Clapham Common, and on her return inventing some sermon at a church the others never visited. But before she had gone many yards conscience overcame her. Was she not getting to be a very lax-minded girl? And it was shameful to impose upon the two after their loving-kindness to her. As usual, her little prayer-book was in her pocket. She walked quickly to the familiar church, and reached it just as the doors were being closed.

Of all the congregation she probably was the one who went through the service most mechanically. Not a word reached her understanding. Sitting, standing, or on her knees, she wore the same preoccupied look, with ever and again a slight smile or a movement of the lips, as if she were recalling some conversation of special interest.

Last Sunday she had had an adventure, the first of any real moment that had befallen her in London. She had arranged to go with Miss Eade on a steamboat up the river. They were to meet at the Battersea Park landing-stage at half-past two. But Miss Eade did not keep her appointment, and Monica, unwilling to lose the trip, started alone.

She disembarked at Richmond and strayed about for an hour or two, then had a cup of tea and a bun. As it was still far too early to return, she went down to the riverside and seated herself on one of the benches. Many boats were going by, a majority of them containing only two persons—a young man who pulled, and a girl who held the strings of the tiller. Some of these couples Monica disregarded; but occasionally there passed a skiff from which she could not take her eyes. To lie back like that on the cushions and converse with a companion who had nothing of the *shop* about him!

It seemed hard that she must be alone. Poor Mr. Bullivant would gladly have taken her on the river; but Mr. Bullivant—

She thought of her sisters. Their loneliness was for life, poor things. Already they were old; and they would grow older, sadder, perpetually struggling to supplement that dividend from the precious capital—and merely that they might keep alive. Oh!—her heart ached at the misery of such a prospect. How much better if the poor girls had never been born.

Her own future was more hopeful than theirs had ever been. She knew herself good-looking. Men had followed her in the street and tried to make her acquaintance. Some of the girls with whom she lived regarded her enviously, spitefully. But had she really the least chance of marrying a man whom she could respect—not to say love?

One-and-twenty a week hence. At Weston she had kept tolerable health, but certainly her constitution was not strong, and the slavery of Walworth Road threatened her with premature decay. Her sisters counselled wisely. Coming to London was a mistake. She would have had better chances at Weston, notwithstanding the extreme discretion with which she was obliged to conduct herself.

While she mused thus, a profound discouragement settling on her sweet face, some one took a seat by her—on the same bench, that is to say. Glancing aside, she saw that it was an oldish man, with grizzled whiskers and rather a stern visage. Monica sighed.

Was it possible that he had heard her? He looked this way, and with curiosity. Ashamed of herself, she kept her eyes averted for a long time. Presently, following the movement of a boat, her face turned unconsciously towards the silent companion; again he was looking at her, and he spoke. The gravity of his appearance and manner, the good-natured commonplace that fell from his lips, could not alarm her; a dialogue began, and went on for about half an hour.

How old might he be? After all, he was probably not fifty—perchance not much more than forty. His utterance fell short of perfect refinement, but seemed that of an educated man. And certainly his clothes were such as a gentleman wears. He had thin, hairy hands, unmarked by any effect of labour; the nails could not have been better cared for. Was it a bad sign that he carried neither gloves nor walking-stick?

His talk aimed at nothing but sober friendliness; it was perfectly inoffensive—indeed, respectful. Now and then—not too often—he fixed his eyes upon her for an instant. After the introductory phrases, he mentioned that he had had a long drive, alone; his horse was baiting in preparation for the journey back to London. He often took such drives in the summer, though generally on a weekday; the magnificent sky had tempted him out this morning. He lived at Herne Hill.

At length he ventured a question. Monica affected no reluctance to tell him that she was in a house of business, that she had relatives in London, that only by chance she found herself alone to-day.

'I should be sorry if I never saw you again.'

These words he uttered with embarrassment, his eyes on the ground. Monica could only keep silence. Half an hour ago she would not have thought it possible for any remark of this man's seriously to occupy her mind, yet now she waited for the next sentence in discomposure which was quite free from resentment.

'We meet in this casual way, and talk, and then say good-bye. Why mayn't I tell you that you interest me very much, and that I am afraid to trust only to chance for another meeting? If you were a man'—he smiled—'I should give you my card, and ask you to my house. The card I may at all events offer.'

Whilst speaking, he drew out a little case, and laid a visiting-card on the bench within Monica's reach. Murmuring her 'thank you,' she took the bit of pasteboard, but did not look at it.

'You are on my side of the river,' he continued, still with scrupulous modesty of tone. 'May I not hope to see you some day, when you are walking? All days and times are the same to me; but I am afraid it is only on Sunday that you are at leisure?'

'Yes, only on a Sunday.'

It took a long time, and many circumlocutions, but in the end an appointment was made. Monica would see her acquaintance next Sunday evening on the river front of Battersea Park; if it rained, then the Sunday after. She was ashamed and confused. Other girls were constantly doing this kind of thing—other girls in business; but it seemed to put her on the level of a servant. And why had she consented? The man could never be anything to her; he was too old, too hard-featured, too grave. Well, on that very account there would be no harm in meeting him. In truth, she had not felt the courage to refuse; in a manner he had overawed her.

And perhaps she would not keep the engagement. Nothing compelled her. She had not told him her name, nor the house where she was employed. There was a week to think it over.

All days and times were the same to him—he said. And he drove about the country for his pleasure. A man of means. His name, according to the card, was Edmund Widdowson.

He was upright in his walk, and strongly built. She noticed this as he moved away from her. Fearful lest he should turn round, her eyes glanced at his figure from moment to moment. But he did not once look back.

'And now to God the Father.' The bustle throughout the church wakened her from reverie so complete that she knew not a syllable of the sermon. After all she must deceive her sisters by inventing a text, and perhaps a comment.

By an arrangement with Mrs. Conisbee, dinner was down in the parlour to-day. A luxurious meal, moreover; for in her excitement Virginia had resolved to make a feast of Monica's birthday. There was a tiny piece of salmon, a dainty cutlet, and a cold blackcurrant tart. Virginia, at home a constant vegetarian, took no share of the fish and meat—which was only enough for one person. Alice, alone upstairs, made a dinner of gruel.

Monica was to be at Queen's Road, Chelsea, by three o'clock. The sisters hoped she would return to Lavender Hill with her news, but that was left uncertain—by Monica herself purposely. As an amusement, she had decided to keep her promise to Mr. Edmund Widdowson. She was curious to see him again, and receive a new impression of his personality. If he behaved as inoffensively as at Richmond, acquaintance with him might be continued for the variety it brought into her life. If anything unpleasant happened, she had only to walk away. The slight, very slight, tremor of anticipation was reasonably to be prized by a shop-girl at Messrs. Scotcher's.

Drawing near to Queen's Road—the wrapped-up Keble in her hand—she began to wonder whether Miss Nunn would have any serious proposal to offer. Virginia's report and ecstatic forecasts were, she knew, not completely trustworthy; though more than ten years her sister's junior, Monica saw the world with eyes much less disposed to magnify and colour ordinary facts.

Miss Barfoot was still from home. Rhoda Nunn received the visitor in a pleasant, old-fashioned drawing-room, where there was nothing costly, nothing luxurious; yet to Monica it appeared richly furnished. A sense of strangeness amid such surroundings had more to do with her constrained silence for the first few minutes than the difficulty with which she recognized in this lady before her the Miss Nunn whom she had known years ago.

'I should never have known you,' said Rhoda, equally surprised. 'For one thing, you look like a fever patient just recovering. What can be expected? Your sister gave me a shocking account of how you live.'

'The work is very hard.'

'Preposterous. Why do you stay at such a place, Monica?'

'I am getting experience.'

'To be used in the next world?'

They laughed.

'Miss Madden is better to-day, I hope?'

'Alice? Not much, I'm sorry to say.'

'Will you tell me something more about the "experience" you are getting? For instance, what time is given you for meals?'

Rhoda Nunn was not the person to manufacture light gossip when a matter of the gravest interest waited for discussion. With a face that expressed thoughtful sympathy, she encouraged the girl to speak and confide in her.

'There's twenty minutes for each meal,' Monica explained; 'but at dinner and tea one is very likely to be called into the shop before finishing. If you are long away you find the table cleared.'

'Charming arrangement! No sitting down behind the counter, I suppose?'

'Oh, of course not. We suffer a great deal from that. Some of us get diseases. A girl has just gone to the hospital with varicose veins, and two or three others have the same thing in a less troublesome form. Sometimes, on Saturday night, I lose all feeling in my feet; I have to stamp on the floor to be sure it's still under me.'

'Ah, that Saturday night!'

'Yes, it's bad enough now; but at Christmas! There was a week or more of Saturday night—going on to one o'clock in the morning. A girl by me was twice carried out fainting, one night after another. They gave her brandy, and she came back again.'

'They compelled her to?'

'Well, no, it was her own wish. Her "book of takings" wasn't very good, poor thing, and if it didn't come up to a certain figure at the end of the week she would lose her place. She lost it after all. They told her she was too weak. After Christmas she was lucky enough to get a place as a lady's-maid at twenty-five pounds a year—at Scotcher's she had fifteen. But we heard that she burst a blood-vessel, and now she's in the hospital at Brompton.'

'Delightful story! Haven't you an early-closing day?'

'They had before I went there; but only for about three months. Then the agreement broke down.'

'Like the assistants. A pity the establishment doesn't follow suit.'

'But you wouldn't say so, Miss Nunn, if you knew how terribly hard it is for many girls to find a place, even now.'

'I know it perfectly well. And I wish it were harder. I wish girls fell down and died of hunger in the streets, instead of creeping to their garrets and the hospitals. I should like to see their dead bodies collected together in some open place for the crowd to stare at.'

Monica gazed at her with wide eyes.

'You mean, I suppose, that people would try to reform things.'

'Who knows? Perhaps they might only congratulate each other that a few of the superfluous females had been struck off. Do they give you any summer holiday?'

'A week, with salary continued.'

'Really? With salary continued? That takes one's breath away.--Are many of the girls ladies?'

'None, at Scotcher's. They nearly all come from the country. Several are daughters of small farmers and those are dreadfully ignorant. One of them asked me the other day in what country Africa was.'

'You don't find them very pleasant company?'

'One or two are nice quiet girls.'

Rhoda drew a deep sigh, and moved with impatience.

'Well, don't you think you've had about enough of it—experience and all?'

'I might go into a country business: it would be easier.'

'But you don't care for the thought?'

'I wish now they had brought me up to something different. Alice and Virginia were afraid of having me trained for a school; you remember that one of our sisters who went through it died of overwork. And I'm not clever, Miss Nunn. I never did much at school.'

Rhoda regarded her, smiling gently.

'You have no inclination to study now?'

'I'm afraid not,' replied the other, looking away. 'Certainly I should like to be better educated, but I don't think I could study seriously, to earn my living by it. The time for that has gone by.'

'Perhaps so. But there are things you might manage. No doubt your sister told you how I get my living. There's a good deal of employment for women who learn to use a typewriter. Did you ever have piano lessons?'

'No.'

'No more did I, and I was sorry for it when I went to typewriting. The fingers have to be light and supple and quick. Come with me, and I'll show you one of the machines.'

They went to a room downstairs—a bare little room by the library. Here were two Remingtons, and Rhoda patiently explained their use.

'One must practise until one can do fifty words a minute at least. I know one or two people who have reached almost twice that speed. It takes a good six months' work to learn for any profitable use. Miss Barfoot takes pupils.'

Monica, at first very attentive, was growing absent. Her eyes wandered about the room. The other observed her closely, and, it seemed, doubtfully.

'Do you feel any impulse to try for it?'

'I should have to live for six months without earning anything.'

'That is by no means impossible for you, I think?'

'Not really impossible,' Monica replied with hesitation.

Something like dissatisfaction passed over Miss Nunn's face, though she did not allow Monica to see it. Her lips moved in a way that perhaps signified disdain for such timidity. Tolerance was not one of the virtues expressed in her physiognomy.

'Let us go back to the drawing-room and have some tea.'

Monica could not become quite at ease. This energetic woman had little attraction for her. She saw the characteristics which made Virginia enthusiastic, but feared rather than admired them. To put herself in Miss Nunn's hands might possibly result in a worse form of bondage than she suffered at the shop; she would never be able to please such a person, and failure, she imagined, would result in more or less contemptuous dismissal.

Then of a sudden, as it she had divined these thoughts, Rhoda assumed an air of gaiety of frank kindness.

'So it is your birthday? I no longer keep count of mine, and couldn't tell you without a calculation what I am exactly. It doesn't matter, you see. Thirty-one or fifty-one is much the same for a woman who has made up her mind to live alone and work steadily for a definite object. But you are still a young girl, Monica. My best wishes!'

Monica emboldened herself to ask what the object was for which her friend worked.

'How shall I put it?' replied the other, smiling. 'To make women hard-hearted.'

'Hard-hearted? I think I understand.'

'Do you?'

'You mean that you like to see them live unmarried.'

Rhoda laughed merrily.

'You say that almost with resentment.'

'No—indeed—I didn't intend it.'

Monica reddened a little.

'Nothing more natural if you have done. At your age, I should have resented it.'

'But—' the girl hesitated—'don't you approve of any one marrying?'

'Oh, I'm not so severe! But do you know that there are half a million more women than men in this happy country of ours?'

'Half a million!'

Her naive alarm again excited Rhoda to laughter.

'Something like that, they say. So many *odd* women—no making a pair with them. The pessimists call them useless, lost, futile lives. I, naturally—being one of them myself—take another view. I look upon them as a great reserve. When one woman vanishes in matrimony, the reserve offers a substitute for the world's work. True, they are not all trained yet—far from it. I want to help in that—to train the reserve.'

'But married woman are not idle,' protested Monica earnestly.

'Not all of them. Some cook and rock cradles.'

Again Miss Nunn's mood changed. She laughed the subject away, and abruptly began to talk of old days down in Somerset, of rambles about Cheddar Cliffs, or at Glastonbury, or on the Quantocks. Monica, however, could not listen, and with difficulty commanded her face to a pleasant smile.

'Will you come and see Miss Barfoot?' Rhoda asked, when it had become clear to her that the girl would gladly get away. 'I am only her subordinate, but I know she will wish to be of all the use to you she can.'

Monica expressed her thanks, and promised to act as soon as possible on any invitation that was sent her. She took leave just as the servant announced another caller.

## CHAPTER V - THE CASUAL ACQUAINTANCE

At that corner of Battersea Park which is near Albert Bridge there has lain for more than twenty years a curious collection of architectural fragments, chiefly dismembered columns, spread in order upon the ground, and looking like portions of a razed temple. It is the colonnade of old Burlington House, conveyed hither from Piccadilly who knows why, and likely to rest here, the sporting ground for adventurous infants, until its origin is lost in the abyss of time.

It was at this spot that Monica had agreed to meet with her casual acquaintance, Edmund Widdowson, and there, from a distance, she saw his lank, upright, well-dressed figure moving backwards and forwards upon the grass. Even at the last moment Monica doubted whether to approach. Emotional interest in him she had none, and the knowledge of life she had gained in London assured her that in thus encouraging a perfect stranger she was doing a very hazardous thing. But the evening must somehow be spent, and if she went off in another direction it would only be to wander about with an adventurous mind; for her conversation with Miss Nunn had had precisely the opposite effect of that which Rhoda doubtless intended; she felt something of the recklessness which formerly excited her wonder when she remarked it in the other shop-girls. She could no longer be without a male companion, and as she had given her promise to this man—

He had seen her, and was coming forward. Today he carried a walking-stick, and wore gloves; otherwise his appearance was the same as at Richmond. At the distance of a few yards he raised his hat, not very gracefully. Monica did not offer her hand, nor did Widdowson seem to expect it. But he gave proof of an intense pleasure in the meeting; his sallow cheeks grew warm, and in the many wrinkles about his eyes played a singular smile, good-natured but anxious, apprehensive.

'I am so glad you were able to come,' he said in a low voice, bending towards her.

'It has been even finer than last Sunday,' was Monica's rather vague reply, as she glanced at some people who were passing.

'Yes, a wonderful day. But I only left home an hour ago. Shall we walk this way?'

They went along the path by the river. Widdowson exhibited none of the artifices of gallantry practised by men who are in the habit of picking up an acquaintance with shop-girls. His smile did not return; an extreme sobriety characterized his manner and speech; for the most part he kept his eyes on the ground, and when silent he had the look of one who inwardly debates a grave question.

'Have you been into the country?' was one of his first inquiries.

'No. I spent the morning with my sisters, and in the afternoon I had to see a lady in Chelsea.'

'Your sisters are older than yourself?'

'Yes, some years older.'

'Is it long since you went to live apart from them?'

'We have never had a home of our own since I was quite a child.'

And, after a moment's hesitation, she went on to give a brief account of her history. Widdowson listened with the closest attention, his lips twitching now and then, his eyes half closed. But for cheek-bones that were too prominent and nostrils rather too large, he was not ill-featured. No particular force of character declared itself in his countenance, and his mode of speech did not suggest a very active brain. Speculating again about his age, Monica concluded that he must be two or three and forty, in spite of the fact that his grizzled beard argued for a higher figure. He had brown hair untouched by any sign of advanced life, his teeth were white and regular, and something—she could not make clear to her mind exactly what—convinced her that he had a right to judge himself comparatively young.

'I supposed you were not a Londoner,' he said, when she came to a pause.

'How?'

'Your speech. Not,' he added quickly, 'that you have any provincial accent. And even if you had been a Londoner you would not have shown it in that way.'

He seemed to be reproving himself for a blunder, and after a short silence asked in a tone of kindness,—

'Do you prefer the town?'

'In some ways—not in all.'

'I am glad you have relatives here, and friends. So many young ladies come up from the country who are quite alone.'

'Yes, many.'

Their progress to familiarity could hardly have been slower. Now and then they spoke with a formal coldness which threatened absolute silence. Monica's brain was so actively at work that she lost consciousness of the people who were moving about them, and at times her companion was scarcely more to her than a voice.

They had walked along the whole front of the park, and were near Chelsea Bridge. Widdowson gazed at the pleasure-boats lying below on the strand, and said diffidently,—

'Would you care to go on the river?'

The proposal was so unexpected that Monica looked up with a startled air. She had not thought of the man as likely to offer any kind of amusement.

'It would be pleasant, I think,' he added. 'The tide is still running up. We might go very quietly for a mile or two, and be back as soon as you like.'

'Yes, I should like it.'

He brightened up, and moved with a livelier step. In a few minutes they had chosen their boat, had pushed off, and were gliding to the middle of the broad water. Widdowson managed the sculls without awkwardness, but by no means like a man well trained in this form of exercise. On sitting down, he had taken off his hat, stowed it away, and put on a little travelling-cap, which he drew from his pocket. Monica thought this became him. After all, he was not a companion to be ashamed of. She looked with pleasure at his white hairy hands with their firm grip; then at his boots—very good boots indeed. He had gold links in his white shirt-cuffs, and a gold watch-guard chosen with a gentleman's taste.

'I am at your service,' he said, with an approach to gaiety. 'Direct me. Shall we go quickly—some distance, or only just a little quicker than the tide would float us?'

'Which you like. To row much would make you too hot.'

'You would like to go some distance—I see.'

'No, no. Do exactly what you like. Of course we must be back in an hour or two.'

He drew out his watch.

'It's now ten minutes past six, and there is daylight till nine or after. When do you wish to be home?'

'Not much later than nine,' Monica answered, with the insincerity of prudence.

'Then we will just go quietly along. I wish we could have started early in the afternoon. But that may be for another day, I hope.'

On her lap Monica had the little brown-paper parcel which contained her present. She saw that Widdowson glanced at it from time to time, but she could not bring herself to explain what it was.

'I was very much afraid that I should not see you to-day,' he said, as they glided softly by Chelsea Embankment.

'But I promised to come if it was fine.'

'Yes. I feared something might prevent you. You are very kind to give me your company.' He was looking at the tips of her little boots. 'I can't say how I thank you.'

Much embarrassed, Monica could only gaze at one of the sculls, as it rose and fell, the water dripping from it in bright beads.

'Last year,' he pursued, 'I went on the river two or three times, but alone. This year I haven't been in a boat till to-day.'

'You prefer driving?'

'Oh, it's only chance. I do drive a good deal, however. I wish it were possible to take you through the splendid country I saw a day or two ago—down in Surrey. Perhaps some day you will let me. I live rather a lonely life, as you see. I have a housekeeper; no relative lives with me. My only relative in London is a sister-in-law, and we very seldom meet.'

'But don't you employ yourself in any way?'

'I'm very idle. But that's partly because I have worked very hard and hopelessly all my life—till a year and a half ago. I began to earn my own living when I was fourteen, and now I am forty-four—to-day.'

'This is your birthday?' said Monica, with an odd look the other could not understand.

'Yes—I only remembered it a few hours ago. Strange that such a treat should have been provided for me. Yes, I am very idle. A year and a half ago my only brother died. He had been very successful in life, and he left me what I regard as a fortune, though it was only a small part of what he had.'

The listener's heart throbbed. Without intending it, she pulled the tiller so that the boat began to turn towards land.

'The left hand a little,' said Widdowson, smiling correctly. 'That's right. Many days I don't leave home. I am fond of reading, and now I make up for all the time lost in years gone by. Do you care for books?'

'I never read very much, and I feel very ignorant.'

'But that is only for want of opportunity, I'm sure.'

## CHAPTER V - THE CASUAL ACQUAINTANCE

He glanced at the brown-paper parcel. Acting on an impulse which perturbed her, Monica began to slip off the loosely-tied string, and to unfold the paper.

'I thought it was a book!' exclaimed Widdowson merrily, when she had revealed a part of her present.

'When you told me your name,' said Monica, 'I ought perhaps to have told you mine. It's written here. My sisters gave me this to-day.'

She offered the little volume. He took it as though it were something fragile, and—the sculls fixed under his elbows—turned to the fly-leaf.

'What? It is *your* birthday?'

'Yes. I am twenty-one.'

'Will you let me shake hands with you?' His pressure of her fingers was the lightest possible. 'Now that's rather a strange thing—isn't it? Oh, I remember this book very well, though I haven't seen it or heard of it for twenty years. My mother used to read it on Sundays. And it is really your birthday? I am more than twice your age, Miss Madden.'

The last remark was uttered anxiously, mournfully. Then, as if to reassure himself by exerting physical strength, he drove the boat along with half a dozen vigorous strokes. Monica was rustling over the pages, but without seeing them.

'I don't think,' said her companion presently, 'you are very well contented with your life in that house of business.'

'No, I am not.'

'I have heard a good deal of the hardships of such a life. Will you tell me something about yours?'

Readily she gave him a sketch of her existence from Sunday to Sunday, but without indignation, and as if the subject had no great interest for her.

'You must be very strong,' was Widdowson's comment.

'The lady I went to see this afternoon told me I looked ill.'

'Of course I can see the effects of overwork. My wonder is that you endure it at all. Is that lady an old acquaintance?'

Monica answered with all necessary detail, and went on to mention the proposal that had been made to her. The hearer reflected, and put further questions. Unwilling to speak of the little capital she possessed, Monica told him that her sisters might perhaps help her to live whilst she was learning a new occupation. But Widdowson had become abstracted; he ceased pulling, crossed his arms on the oars, and watched other boats that were near. Two deep wrinkles, rippling in their course, had formed across his forehead, and his eyes widened in a gaze of complete abstraction at the farther shore.

'Yes,' fell from him at length, as though in continuation of something he had been saying, 'I began to earn my bread when I was fourteen. My father was an auctioneer at Brighton. A few years after his marriage he had a bad illness, which left him completely deaf. His partnership with another man was dissolved, and as things went worse and worse with him, my mother started a lodging-house, which somehow supported us for a long time. She was a sensible, good, and brave woman. I'm afraid my father had a good many faults that made her life hard. He was of a violent temper, and of course the deafness didn't improve it. Well, one day a cab knocked him down in the King's Road, and from that injury, though not until a year after, he died. There were only two children; I was the elder. My mother couldn't keep me at school very long, so, at fourteen, I was sent into the office of the man who had been my father's partner, to serve him and learn the business. I did serve him for years, and for next to no payment, but he taught me nothing more than he could help. He was one of those heartless, utterly selfish men that one meets too often in the business world. I ought never to have been sent there, for my father had always an ill opinion of him; but he pretended a friendly interest in me—just, I am convinced, to make the use of me that he did.'

He was silent, and began rowing again.

'What happened them?' asked Monica.

'I mustn't make out that I was a faultless boy,' he continued, with the smile that graved wrinkles about his eyes; 'quite the opposite. I had a good deal of my father's temper; I often behaved very badly to my mother; what I needed was some stern but conscientious man to look after me and make me work. In my spare time I lay about on the shore, or got into mischief with other boys. It needed my mother's death to make a more sensible fellow of me, and by that time it was too late. I mean I was too old to be trained into profitable business habits. Up to nineteen I had been little more than an errand and office boy, and all through the after years I never got a much better position.'

'I can't understand that,' remarked Monica thoughtfully.

'Why not?'

'You seem to—to be the kind of man that would make your way.'

'Do I?' The description pleased him; he laughed cheerfully. 'But I never found what my way was to be. I have always hated office work, and business of every kind; yet I could never see an opening in any other direction. I have been all my life a clerk—like so many thousands of other men. Nowadays, if I happen to be in the City when all the clerks are coming away from business, I feel an inexpressible pity for them. I feel I should like to find two or three of the hardest driven, and just divide my superfluous income between. A clerk's life—a life of the office without any hope of rising—that is a hideous fate!'

'But your brother got on well. Why didn't he help you?'

'We couldn't agree. We always quarrelled.'

'Are you really so ill-tempered?'

It was asked in Monica's most naive tone, with a serious air of investigation which at first confused Widdowson, then made him laugh.

'Since I was a lad,' he replied, 'I have never quarrelled with any one except my brother. I think it's only very unreasonable people that irritate me. Some men have told me that I was far too easy-going, too good-natured. Certainly I *desire* to be good-natured. But I don't easily make friends; as a rule I can't talk to strangers. I keep so much to myself that those who know me only a little think me surly and unsociable.'

'So your brother always refused to help you?'

'It wasn't easy for him to help me. He got into a stockbroker's, and went on step by step until he had saved a little money; then he speculated in all sorts of ways. He couldn't employ me himself—and if he could have done so, we should never have got on together. It was impossible for him to recommend me to any one except as a clerk. He was a born money-maker. I'll give you an example of how he grew rich. In consequence of some mortgage business he came into possession of a field at Clapham. As late as 1875 this field brought him only a rent of forty pounds; it was freehold property, and he refused many offers of purchase. Well, in 1885, the year before he died, the ground-rents from that field—now covered with houses—were seven hundred and ninety pounds a year. That's how men get on who have capital and know how to use it. If *I* had had capital, it would never have yielded me more than three or four per cent. I was doomed to work for other people who were growing rich. It doesn't matter much now, except that so many years of life have been lost.'

'Had your brother any children?'

'No children. All the same, it astonished me when I heard his will; I had expected nothing. In one day—in one hour—I passed from slavery to freedom, from poverty to more than comfort. We never *hated* each other; I don't want you to think that.'

'But—didn't it bring you friends as well as comfort?'

'Oh,' he laughed, 'I am not so rich as to have people pressing for my acquaintance. I have only about six hundred a year.'

Monica drew in her breath silently, then gazed at the distance.

'No, I haven't made any new friends. The one or two men I care for are not much better off than I used to be, and I always feel ashamed to ask them to come and see me. Perhaps they think I shun them because of their position, and I don't know how to justify myself. Life has always been full of worrying problems for me. I can't take things in the simple way that comes natural to other men.'

'Don't you think we ought to be turning back, Mr. Widdowson?'

'Yes, we will. I am sorry the time goes so quickly.'

When a few minutes had passed in silence, he asked,—

'Do you feel that I am no longer quite a stranger to you, Miss Madden?'

'Yes—you have told me so much.'

'It's very kind of you to listen so patiently. I wish I had more interesting things to tell, but you see what a dull life mine has been.' He paused, and let the boat waver on the stream for a moment. 'When I dared to speak to you last Sunday I had only the faintest hope that you would grant me your acquaintance. You can't, I am sure, repent of having done me that kindness—?'

'One never knows. I doubted whether I ought to talk with a stranger—'

'Rightly—quite rightly. It was my perseverance—you saw, I hope, that I could never dream of giving you offence. The rule is necessary, but you see there may be exceptional cases.' He was giving a lazy stroke now and then, which, as the tide was still, just moved the boat onwards. 'I saw something in your face that *compelled* me to speak to you. And now we may really be friends, I hope?'

'Yes—I can think of you as a friend, Mr. Widdowson.'

A large boat was passing with four or five young men and girls who sang in good time and tune. Only a song of the music-hall or of the nigger minstrels, but it sounded pleasantly with the plash of the oars. A fine sunset had begun to glow upon the river; its warmth gave a tone to Monica's thin cheeks.

'And you will let me see you again before long? Let me drive you to Hampton Court next Sunday—or any other place you would choose.'

'Very likely I shall be invited to my friend's in Chelsea.'

'Do you seriously think of leaving the shop?'

'I don't know—I must have time to think about it—'

'Yes—yes. But if I write a line to you, say on Friday, would you let me know whether you can come?'

'Please to let me refuse for next Sunday. The one after, perhaps—'

He bent his head, looked desperately grave, and drove the boat on Monica was disturbed, but held to her resolution, which Widdowson silently accepted. The rest of the way they exchanged only brief sentences, about the beauty of the sky, the scenes on river or bank, and other impersonal matters. After landing, they walked in silence towards Chelsea Bridge.

'Now I must go quickly home,' said Monica.

'But how?'

'By train—from York Road to Walworth Road.'

Widdowson cast a curious glance at her. One would have imagined that he found something to disapprove in this ready knowledge of London transit.

'I will go with you to the station, then.'

Without a word spoken, they walked the short distance to York Road. Monica took her ticket, and offered a hand for good-bye.

'I may write to you,' said Widdowson, his face set in an expression of anxiety, 'and make an appointment, if possible, for the Sunday after next?'

'I shall be glad to come—if I can.'

'It will be a very long time to me.'

With a faint smile, Monica hurried away to the platform. In the train she looked like one whose mind is occupied with grave trouble. Fatigue had suddenly overcome her; she leaned back and closed her eyes.

At a street corner very near to Messrs. Scotcher's establishment she was intercepted by a tall, showily-dressed, rather coarse-featured girl, who seemed to have been loitering about. It was Miss Eade.

'I want to speak to you, Miss Madden. Where did you go with Mr. Bullivant this morning?'

The voice could not have been more distinctive of a London shop-girl; its tone signified irritation.

'With Mr. Bullivant? I went nowhere with him.'

'But I *saw* you both get into the bus in Kennington Park Road.'

'Did you?' Monica returned coldly. 'I can't help it if Mr. Bullivant happened to be going the same way.'

'Oh, very well! I thought you was to be trusted. It's nothing to me—'

'You behave very foolishly, Miss Eade,' exclaimed the other, whose nerves at this moment would not allow her to use patience with the jealous girl. 'I can only tell you that I have never thought again of Mr. Bullivant since he left the bus somewhere in Clapham Road. I'm tired of talking about such things.'

'Now, see here, don't be cross. Come and walk a bit and tell me—'

'I'm too tired. And there's nothing whatever to tell you.'

'Oh, well, if you're going to be narsty?'

Monica walked on, but the girl caught her up.

'Don't be so sharp with me, Miss Madden. I don't say as you wanted him to go in the bus with you. But you might tell me what he had to say.'

'Nothing at all; except that he wished to know where I was going, which was no business of his. I did what I could for you. I told him that if he asked you to go up the river with him I felt sure you wouldn't refuse.'

'Oh, you did!' Miss Eade threw up her head. 'I don't think it was a very delicate thing to say.'

'You are very unreasonable. I myself don't think it was very delicate, but haven't you worried me to say something of the kind?'

'No, that I'm sure I haven't! Worrited you, indeed!'

'Then please never to speak to me on the subject again. I'm tired of it.'

'And what did *he* say, when you'd said that?'

'I can't remember.'

'Oh, you *are* narsty to-day! Really you are! If it had been the other way about, I'd never have treated *you* like this, that I wouldn't.'

'Good-night!'

They were close to the door by which Messrs. Scotcher's resident employees entered at night. Monica had taken out her latchkey. But Miss Eade could not endure the thought of being left in torturing ignorance.

'*Do* tell me!' she whispered. 'I'll do anything for you I can. Don't be unkind, Miss Madden!'

Monica turned back again.

'If I were you, I wouldn't be so silly. I can't do more than assure you and promise you that I shall never listen to Mr. Bullivant.'

'But what did he say about *me*, dear?'

'Nothing.'

Miss Eade kept a mortified silence.

'You had much better not think of him at all. I would have more pride. I wish I could make you see him as I do.'

'And you did really speak about me? Oh, I do wish you'd find some one to go out with. Then perhaps—'

Monica stood still, hesitated, and at length said,—

'Well—I *have* found some one.'

'You have?' The girl all but danced with joy. 'You really have?'

'Yes—so now don't trouble me any more.'

This time she was allowed to turn back and enter the house.

No one else had yet come in. Monica ate a mouthful of bread and cheese, which was in readiness on the long table down in the basement, and at once went to bed. But no welcome drowsiness fell upon her. At half-past eleven, when two of the other five girls who slept in the room made their appearance, she was still changing uneasily from side to side. They lit the gas (it was not turned off till midnight, after which hour the late arrivals had to use a candle of their own procuring), and began a lively conversation on the events of the day. Afraid of being obliged to talk, Monica feigned sleep.

At twelve, just as the gas went out, another pair came to repose. They had been quarrelling, and were very gloomy. After a long and acrimonious discussion in the dark as to which of them should find a candle—it ended in one of the girls who was in bed impatiently supplying a light—they began sullenly to throw off their garments.

'Is Miss Madden awake?' said one of them, looking in Monica's direction.

There was no reply.

'She's picked up some feller to-day,' continued the speaker, lowering her voice, and glancing round at her companions with a grin. 'Or else she's had him all along—I shouldn't wonder.'

Heads were put forward eagerly, and inquiries whispered.

'He's oldish, I should say. I caught sight of them just as they was going off in a boat from Battersea Park, but I couldn't see his face very well. He looked rather like Mr. Thomas.'

Mr. Thomas was a member of the drapery firm, a man of fifty, ugly and austere. At this description the listeners giggled and uttered exclamations.

'Was he a swell?' asked one.

'Shouldn't wonder if he was. You can trust Miss M. to keep her eyes open. She's one of the sly and quiet 'uns.'

'Oh, is she?' murmured another enviously. 'She's just one of those as gets made a fool of—that's *my* opinion.'

The point was argued for some minutes. It led to talk about Miss Eade, who was treated with frank contempt because of her ill-disguised pursuit of a mere counter-man. These other damsels had, at present, more exalted views, for they were all younger than Miss Eade.

Just before one o'clock, when silence had reigned for a quarter of an hour, there entered with much bustle the last occupant of the bed-room. She was a young woman with a morally unenviable reputation, though some of her colleagues certainly envied her. Money came to her with remarkable readiness whenever she had need of it. As usual, she began to talk very loud, at first with innocent vulgarity; exciting a little laughter, she became anecdotic and very scandalous. It took her a long time to disrobe, and when the candle was out, she still had her richest story to relate—of point so Rabelaisian that one or two voices made themselves heard in serious protest. The gifted anecdotist replied with a long laugh, then cried, 'Good-night, young ladies!' and sank peacefully to slumber.

As for Monica, she saw the white dawn peep at the window, and closed her tear-stained eyes only when the life of a new week had begun noisily in Walworth Road.

# CHAPTER VI - A CAMP OF THE RESERVE

In consequence of letters exchanged during the week, next Sunday brought the three Miss Maddens to Queen's Road to lunch with Miss Barfoot. Alice had recovered from her cold, but was still ailing, and took rather a gloomy view of the situation she had lately reviewed with such courage. Virginia maintained her enthusiastic faith in Miss Nunn, and was prepared to reverence Miss Barfoot with hardly less fervour. Both of them found it difficult to understand their young sister, who, in her letters, had betrayed distaste for the change of career proposed to her. They were received with the utmost kindness, and all greatly enjoyed their afternoon, for not even Monica's prejudice against a house, which in her own mind she had stigmatized as 'an old-maid factory,' could resist the charm of the hostess.

Though Miss Barfoot had something less than a woman's average stature, the note of her presence was personal dignity. She was handsome, and her carriage occasionally betrayed a consciousness of the fact. According to circumstances, she bore herself as the lady of aristocratic tastes, as a genial woman of the world, or as a fervid prophetess of female emancipation, and each character was supported with a spontaneity, a good-natured confidence, which inspired liking and respect. A brilliant complexion and eyes that sparkled with habitual cheerfulness gave her the benefit of doubt when her age was in question; her style of dress, gracefully ornate, would have led a stranger to presume her a wedded lady of some distinction. Yet Mary Barfoot had known many troubles, poverty among them. Her experiences and struggles bore a close resemblance to those which Rhoda Nunn had gone through, and the time of trial had lasted longer. Mental and moral stamina would have assured her against such evils of celibacy as appeared in the elder Maddens, but it was to a change of worldly fortune that she owed this revival of youthful spirit and energy in middle life.

'You and I must be friends,' she said to Monica, holding the girl's soft little hand. 'We are both black but comely.'

The compliment to herself seemed the most natural thing in the world. Monica blushed with pleasure, and could not help laughing.

It was all but decided that Monica should become a pupil at the school in Great Portland Street. In a brief private conversation, Miss Barfoot offered to lend her the money that might be needful.

'Nothing but a business transaction, Miss Madden. You can give me security; you will repay me at your convenience. If, in the end, this occupation doesn't please you, you will at all events have regained health. It is clear to me that you mustn't go on in that dreadful place you described to Miss Nunn.'

The visitors took their leave at about five o'clock.

'Poor things! Poor things!' sighed Miss Barfoot, when she was alone with her friend. 'What can we possibly do for the older ones?'

'They are excellent creatures,' said Rhoda; 'kind, innocent women; but useful for nothing except what they have done all their lives. The eldest can't teach seriously, but she can keep young children out of mischief and give them a nice way of speaking. Her health is breaking down, you can see.'

'Poor woman! One of the saddest types.'

'Decidedly. Virginia isn't quite so depressing—but how childish!'

'They all strike me as childish. Monica is a dear little girl; it seemed a great absurdity to talk to her about business. Of course she must find a husband.'

'I suppose so.'

Rhoda's tone of slighting concession amused her companion.

'My dear, after all we don't desire the end of the race.'

'No, I suppose not,' Rhoda admitted with a laugh.

'A word of caution. Your zeal is eating you up. At this rate, you will hinder our purpose. We have no mission to prevent girls from marrying suitably—only to see that those who can't shall have a means of living with some satisfaction.'

'What chance is there that this girl will marry suitably?'

'Oh, who knows? At all events, there will be more likelihood of it if she comes into our sphere.'

'Really? Do you know any man that would dream of marrying her?'

'Perhaps not, at present.'

It was clear that Miss Barfoot stood in some danger of becoming subordinate to her more vehement friend. Her little body, for all its natural dignity, put her at a disadvantage in the presence of Rhoda, who towered above her with rather imperious stateliness. Her suavity was no match for Rhoda's vigorous abruptness. But the two were very fond of each other, and by this time thought themselves able safely to dispense with the forms at first imposed by their mutual relations.

'If she marry at all,' declared Miss Nunn, 'she will marry badly. The family is branded. They belong to the class we know so well—with no social position, and unable to win an individual one. I must find a name for that ragged regiment.'

Miss Barfoot regarded her friend thoughtfully.

'Rhoda, what comfort have you for the poor in spirit?'

'None whatever, I'm afraid. My mission is not to them.'

After a pause, she added,—

'They have their religious faith, I suppose; and it's answerable for a good deal.'

'It would be a terrible responsibility to rob them of it,' remarked the elder woman gravely.

Rhoda made a gesture of impatience.

'It's a terrible responsibility to do anything at all. But I'm glad'—she laughed scornfully—'that it's not my task to release them.'

Mary Barfoot mused, a compassionate shadow on her fine face.

'I don't think we can do without the spirit of that religion,' she said at length—'the essential human spirit. These poor women—one ought to be very tender with them. I don't like your "ragged regiment" phrase. When I grow old and melancholy, I think I shall devote myself to poor hopeless and purposeless women—try to warm their hearts a little before they go hence.'

'Admirable!' murmured Rhoda, smiling. 'But in the meantime they cumber us; we have to fight.'

She threw forward her arms, as though with spear and buckler. Miss Barfoot was smiling at this Palladin attitude when a servant announced two ladies—Mrs. Smallbrook and Miss Haven. They were aunt and niece; the former a tall, ungainly, sharp-featured widow; the later a sweet-faced, gentle, sensible-looking girl of five-and-twenty.

'I am so glad you are back again,' exclaimed the widow, as she shook hands with Miss Barfoot, speaking in a hard, unsympathetic voice. 'I do so want to ask your advice about an interesting girl who has applied to me. I'm afraid her past won't bear looking into, but most certainly she is a reformed character. Winifred is most favourably impressed with her—'

Miss Haven, the Winifred in question, began to talk apart with Rhoda Nunn.

'I do wish my aunt wouldn't exaggerate so,' she said in a subdued voice, whilst Mrs. Smallbrook still talked loudly and urgently. 'I never said that I was favourably impressed. The girl protests far too much; she has played on aunt's weaknesses, I fear.'

'But who is she?'

'Oh, some one who lost her character long ago, and lives, I should say, on charitable people. Just because I said that she must once have had a very nice face, aunt misrepresents me in this way—it's too bad.'

'Is she an educated person?' Miss Barfoot was heard to ask.

'Not precisely well educated.'

'Of the lower classes, then?'

'I don't like that term, you know. Of the *poorer* classes.'

'She never was a lady,' put in Miss Haven quietly but decidedly.

'Then I fear I can be of no use,' said the hostess, betraying some of her secret satisfaction in being able thus to avoid Mrs. Smallbrook's request. Winifred, a pupil at Great Portland Street, was much liked by both her teachers; but the aunt, with her ceaseless philanthropy at other people's expense, could only be considered a bore.

'But surely you don't limit your humanity, Miss Barfoot, by the artificial divisions of society.'

'I think those divisions are anything but artificial,' replied the hostess good-humouredly. 'In the uneducated classes I have no interest whatever. You have heard me say so.

'Yes, but I cannot think—isn't that just a little narrow?'

'Perhaps so. I choose my sphere, that's all. Let those work for the lower classes (I must call them lower, for they are, in every sense), let those work for them who have a call to do so. I have none. I must keep to my own class.'

'But surely, Miss Nunn,' cried the widow, turning to Rhoda, 'we work for the abolition of all unjust privilege? To us, is not a woman a woman?'

'I am obliged to agree with Miss Barfoot. I think that as soon as we begin to meddle with uneducated people, all our schemes and views are unsettled. We have to learn a new language, for one thing. But your missionary enterprise is admirable.'

'For my part,' declared Mrs. Smallbrook, 'I aim at the solidarity of woman. You, at all events, agree with me, Winifred?'

'I really don't think, aunt, that there can be any solidarity of ladies with servant girls,' responded Miss Haven, encouraged by a look from Rhoda.

'Then I grieve that your charity falls so far below the Christian standard.'

## CHAPTER VI - A CAMP OF THE RESERVE

Miss Barfoot firmly guided the conversation to a more hopeful subject.

Not many people visited this house. Every Wednesday evening, from half-past eight to eleven, Miss Barfoot was at home to any of her acquaintances, including her pupils, who chose to call upon her; but this was in the nature of an association with recognized objects. Of society in the common sense Miss Barfoot saw very little; she had no time to sacrifice in the pursuit of idle ceremonies. By the successive deaths of two relatives, a widowed sister and an uncle, she had come into possession of a modest fortune; but no thought of a life such as would have suggested itself to most women in her place ever tempted her. Her studies had always been of a very positive nature; her abilities were of a kind uncommon in women, or at all events very rarely developed in one of her sex. She could have managed a large and complicated business, could have filled a place on a board of directors, have taken an active part in municipal government—nay, perchance in national. And this turn of intellect consisted with many traits of character so strongly feminine that people who knew her best thought of her with as much tenderness as admiration. She did not seek to become known as the leader of a 'movement,' yet her quiet work was probably more effectual than the public career of women who propagandize for female emancipation. Her aim was to draw from the overstocked profession of teaching as many capable young women as she could lay hands on, and to fit them for certain of the pursuits nowadays thrown open to their sex. She held the conviction that whatever man could do, woman could do equally well—those tasks only excepted which demand great physical strength. At her instance, and with help from her purse, two girls were preparing themselves to be pharmaceutical chemists; two others had been aided by her to open a bookseller's shop; and several who had clerkships in view received an admirable training at her school in Great Portland Street.

Thither every weekday morning Miss Barfoot and Rhoda repaired; they arrived at nine o'clock, and with an hour's interval work went on until five.

Entering by the private door of a picture-cleaner's shop, they ascended to the second story, where two rooms had been furnished like comfortable offices; two smaller on the floor above served for dressing-rooms. In one of the offices, typewriting and occasionally other kinds of work that demanded intelligence were carried on by three or four young women regularly employed. To superintend this department was Miss Nunn's chief duty, together with business correspondence under the principal's direction. In the second room Miss Barfoot instructed her pupils, never more than three being with her at a time. A bookcase full of works on the Woman Question and allied topics served as a circulating library; volumes were lent without charge to the members of this little society. Once a month Miss Barfoot or Miss Nunn, by turns, gave a brief address on some set subject; the hour was four o'clock, and about a dozen hearers generally assembled. Both worked very hard. Miss Barfoot did not look upon her enterprise as a source of pecuniary profit, but she had made the establishment more than self-supporting. Her pupils increased in number, and the working department promised occupation for a larger staff than was at present engaged. The young women in general answered their friend's expectations, but of course there were disappointing instances. One of these had caused Miss Barfoot special distress. A young girl whom she had released from a life of much hardship, and who, after a couple of months' trial, bade fair to develop noteworthy ability, of a sudden disappeared. She was without relatives in London, and Miss Barfoot's endeavours to find her proved for several weeks very futile. Then came news of her; she was living as the mistress of a married man. Every effort was made to bring her back, but the girl resisted; presently she again passed out of sight, and now more than a year had elapsed since Miss Barfoot's last interview with her.

This Monday morning, among letters delivered at the house, was one from the strayed girl. Miss Barfoot read it in private, and throughout the day remained unusually grave. At five o'clock, when staff and pupils had all departed, she sat for a while in meditation, then spoke to Rhoda, who was glancing over a book by the window.

'Here's a letter I should like you to read.'

'Something that has been troubling you since morning, isn't it?'

'Yes.'

Rhoda took the sheet and quickly ran through its contents. Her face hardened, and she threw down the letter with a smile of contempt.

'What do you advise?' asked the elder woman, closely observing her.

'An answer in two lines—with a cheque enclosed, if you see fit.'

'Does that really meet the case?'

'More than meets it, I should say.'

Miss Barfoot pondered.

'I am doubtful. That is a letter of despair, and I can't close my ears to it.'

'You had an affection for the girl. Help her, by all means, if you feel compelled to. But you would hardly dream of taking her back again?'

'That's the point. Why shouldn't I?'

'For one thing,' replied Rhoda, looking coldly down upon her friend, 'you will never do any good with her. For another, she isn't a suitable companion for the girls she would meet here.'

'I can't be sure of either objection. She acted with deplorable rashness, with infatuation, but I never discovered any sign of evil in her. Did you?'

'Evil? Well, what does the word mean? I am not a Puritan, and I don't judge her as the ordinary woman would. But I think she has put herself altogether beyond our sympathy. She was twenty-two years old—no child—and she acted with her eyes open. No deceit was practised with her. She knew the man had a wife, and she was base enough to accept a share of his attentions. Do you advocate polygamy? That is an intelligible position, I admit. It is one way of meeting the social difficulty. But not mine.'

'My dear Rhoda, don't enrage yourself.'

'I will try not to.'

'But I can't see the temptation to do so. Come and sit down, and talk quietly. No, I have no fondness for polygamy. I find it very hard to understand how she could act as she did. But a mistake, however wretched, mustn't condemn a woman for life. That's the way of the world, and decidedly it mustn't be ours.'

'On this point I practically agree with the world.'

'I see you do, and it astonishes me. You are going through curious changes, in several respects. A year ago you didn't speak of her like this.'

'Partly because I didn't know you well enough to speak my mind. Partly yes, I have changed a good deal, no doubt. But I should never have proposed to take her by the hand and let bygones be bygones. That is an amiable impulse, but anti-social.'

'A favourite word on your lips just now, Rhoda. Why is it anti-social?'

'Because one of the supreme social needs of our day is the education of women in self-respect and self-restraint. There are plenty of people—men chiefly, but a few women also of a certain temperament—who cry for a reckless individualism in these matters. They would tell you that she behaved laudably, that she was *living out herself*—and things of that kind. But I didn't think you shared such views.'

'I don't, altogether. "The education of women in self-respect." Very well. Here is a poor woman whose self-respect has given way under grievous temptation. Circumstances have taught her that she made a wild mistake. The man gives her up, and bids her live as she can; she is induced to beggary. Now, in that position a girl is tempted to sink still further. The letter of two lines and an enclosed cheque would as likely as not plunge her into depths from which she could never be rescued. It would assure her that there was no hope. On the other hand, we have it in our power to attempt that very education of which you speak. She has brains, and doesn't belong to the vulgar. It seems to me that you are moved by illogical impulses—and certainly anything but kind ones.'

Rhoda only grew more stubborn.

'You say she yielded to a grievous temptation. What temptation? Will it bear putting into words?'

'Oh yes, I think it will,' answered Miss Barfoot, with her gentlest smile. 'She fell in love with the man.

'Fell in love!' Concentration of scorn was in this echo. 'Oh, for what isn't that phrase responsible!'

'Rhoda, let me ask you a question on which I have never ventured. Do you know what it is to be in love?'

Miss Nunn's strong features were moved as if by a suppressed laugh; the colour of her cheeks grew very slightly warm.

'I am a normal human being,' she answered, with an impatient gesture. 'I understand perfectly well what the phrase signifies.'

'That is no answer, my dear. Have you ever been in love with any man?'

'Yes. When I was fifteen.'

'And not since,' rejoined the other, shaking her head and smiling. 'No, not since?'

'Thank Heaven, no!'

'Then you are not very well able to judge this case. I, on the other hand, can judge it with the very largest understanding. Don't smile so witheringly, Rhoda. I shall neglect your advice for once.'

'You will bring this girl back, and continue teaching her as before?'

'We have no one here that knows her, and with prudence she need never be talked about by those of our friends who did.'

'Oh, weak—weak—weak!'

'For once I must act independently.'

'Yes, and at a stroke change the whole character of your work. You never proposed keeping a reformatory. Your aim is to help chosen girls, who promise to be of some use in the world. This Miss Royston represents the profitless average—no, she is below the average. Are you so blind as to imagine that any good will ever come of such a person? If you wish to save her from the streets, do so by all means. But to put her among your chosen pupils is to threaten your whole undertaking. Let it once become known—and it *would* become known—that a girl of that character came here, and your usefulness is at an end. In a year's time you will have to choose between giving up the school altogether and making it a refuge for outcasts.'

Miss Barfoot was silent. She tapped with her fingers on the table.

'Personal feeling is misleading you,' Rhoda pursued. 'Miss Royston had a certain cleverness, I grant; but do you think I didn't know that she would never become what you hoped? All her spare time was given to novel-reading. If every novelist could be strangled and thrown into the sea we should have some chance of reforming women. The girl's nature was corrupted with sentimentality, like that of all but every woman who is intelligent enough to read what is called the best fiction, but not intelligent enough to understand its vice. Love—love—love; a sickening sameness of vulgarity. What is more vulgar than the ideal of novelists? They won't represent the actual world; it would be too dull for their readers. In real life, how many men and women *fall in love*? Not one in every ten thousand, I am convinced. Not one married pair in ten thousand have felt for each other as two or three couples do in every novel. There is the sexual instinct, of course, but that is quite a different thing; the novelists daren't talk about that. The paltry creatures daren't tell the one truth that would be profitable. The result is that women imagine themselves noble and glorious when they are most near the animals. This Miss Royston—when she rushed off to perdition, ten to one she had in mind some idiot heroine of a book. Oh, I tell you that you are losing sight of your first duty. There are people enough to act the good Samaritan; *you* have quite another task in life. It is your work to train and encourage girls in a path as far as possible from that of the husband-hunter. Let them marry later, if they must; but at all events you will have cleared their views on the subject of marriage, and put them in a position to judge the man who offers himself. You will have taught them that marriage is an alliance of intellects—not a means of support, or something more ignoble still. But to do this with effect you must show yourself relentless to female imbecility. If a girl gets to know that you have received back such a person as Miss Royston she will be corrupted by your spirit of charity—corrupted, at all events, for our purposes. The endeavour to give women a new soul is so difficult that we can't be cumbered by side-tasks, such as fishing foolish people out of the mud they have walked into. Charity for human weakness is all very well in its place, but it is precisely one of the virtues that you must *not* teach. You have to set an example of the sterner qualities—to discourage anything that resembles sentimentalism. And think if you illustrate in your own behaviour a sympathy for the very vice of character we are trying our hardest to extirpate!'

'This is a terrible harangue,' said Miss Barfoot, when the passionate voice had been silent for a few ticks of the clock. 'I quite enter into your point of view, but I think you go beyond practical zeal. However, I will help the girl in some other way, if possible.'

'I have offended you.'

'Impossible to take offence at such obvious sincerity.'

'But surely you grant the force of what I say?'

'We differ a good deal, Rhoda, on certain points which as a rule would never come up to interfere with our working in harmony. You have come to dislike the very thought of marriage—and everything of that kind. I think it's a danger you ought to have avoided. True, we wish to prevent girls from marrying just for the sake of being supported, and from degrading themselves as poor Bella Royston has done; but surely between ourselves we can admit that the vast majority of women would lead a wasted life if they did not marry.'

'I maintain that the vast majority of women lead a vain and miserable life because they *do* marry.'

'Don't you blame the institution of marriage with what is chargeable to human fate? A vain and miserable life is the lot of nearly all mortals. Most women, whether they marry or not, will suffer and commit endless follies.'

'Most women—as life is at present arranged for them. Things are changing, and we try to have our part in hastening a new order.'

'Ah, we use words in a different sense. I speak of human nature, not of the effect of institutions.'

'Now it is you who are unpractical. Those views lead only to pessimism and paralysis of effort.'

Miss Barfoot rose.

'I give in to your objection against bringing the girl back to work here. I will help her in other ways. It's quite true that she isn't to be relied upon.'

'Impossible to trust her in any detail of life. The pity is that her degradation can't be used as an object lesson for our other girls.'

'There again we differ. You are quite mistaken in your ideas of how the mind is influenced. The misery of Bella Royston would not in the least affect any other girl's way of thinking about the destiny of her sex. We must avoid exaggeration. If our friends get to think of us as fanatics, all our usefulness is over. The ideal we set up must be human. Do you think now that we know one single girl who in her heart believes it is better never to love and never to marry?'

'Perhaps not,' admitted Rhoda, more cheerful now that she had gained her point. 'But we know several who will not dream of marrying unless reason urges them as strongly as inclination.'

Miss Barfoot laughed.

'Pray, who ever distinguished in such a case between reason and inclination?'

'You are most unusually sceptical to-day,' said Rhoda, with an impatient laugh.

'No, my dear. We happen to be going to the root of things, that's all. Perhaps it's as well to do so now and then. Oh, I admire you immensely, Rhoda. You are the ideal adversary of those care-nothing and believe-nothing women who keep the world back. But don't prepare for yourself a woeful disillusion.'

'Take the case of Winifred Haven,' urged Miss Nunn. 'She is a good-looking and charming girl, and some one or other will want to marry her some day, no doubt.'

'Forgive my interrupting you. There is great doubt. She has no money but what she can earn, and such girls, unless they are exceptionally beautiful, are very likely indeed to remain unsought.'

'Granted. But let us suppose she has an offer. Should you fear for her prudence?'

'Winifred has much good sense,' admitted the other. 'I think she is in as little danger as any girl we know. But it wouldn't startle me if she made the most lamentable mistake. Certainly I don't fear it. The girls of our class are not like the uneducated, who, for one reason or another, will marry almost any man rather than remain single. They have at all events personal delicacy. But what I insist upon is, that Winifred would rather marry than not. And we must carefully bear that fact in mind. A strained ideal is as bad, practically, as no ideal at all. Only the most exceptional girl will believe it her duty to remain single as an example and support to what we call the odd women; yet *that* is the most human way of urging what you desire. By taking up the proud position that a woman must be altogether independent of sexual things, you damage your cause. Let us be glad if we put a few of them in the way of living single with no more discontent than an unmarried man experiences.'

'Surely that's an unfortunate comparison,' said Rhoda coldly. 'What man lives in celibacy? Consider that unmentionable fact, and then say whether I am wrong in refusing to forgive Miss Royston. Women's battle is not only against themselves. The necessity of the case demands what you call a strained ideal. I am seriously convinced that before the female sex can be raised from its low level there will have to be a widespread revolt against sexual instinct. Christianity couldn't spread over the world without help of the ascetic ideal, and this great movement for woman's emancipation must also have its ascetics.'

'I can't declare that you are wrong in that. Who knows? But it isn't good policy to preach it to our young disciples.'

'I shall respect your wish; but—'

Rhoda paused and shook her head.

'My dear,' said the elder woman gravely, 'believe me that the less we talk or think about such things the better for the peace of us all. The odious fault of working-class girls, in town and country alike, is that they are absorbed in preoccupation with their animal nature. We, thanks to our education and the tone of our society, manage to keep that in the background. Don't interfere with this satisfactory state of things. Be content to show our girls that it is their duty to lead a life of effort—to earn their bread and to cultivate their minds. Simply ignore marriage—that's the wisest. Behave as if the thing didn't exist. You will do positive harm by taking the other course—the aggressive course.'

'I shall obey you.'

'Good, humble creature!' laughed Miss Barfoot. 'Come, let us be off to Chelsea. Did Miss Grey finish that copy for Mr. Houghton?'

'Yes, it has gone to post.'

'Look, here's a big manuscript from our friend the antiquary. Two of the girls must get to work on it at once in the morning.'

Manuscripts entrusted to them were kept in a fire-proof safe. When this had been locked up, the ladies went to their dressing-room and prepared for departure. The people who lived on the premises were responsible for cleaning the rooms and other care; to them Rhoda delivered the door-keys.

Miss Barfoot was grave and silent on the way home. Rhoda, annoyed at the subject that doubtless occupied her friend's thoughts, gave herself up to reflections of her own.

# CHAPTER VII - A SOCIAL ADVANCE

A week's notice to her employers would release Monica from the engagement in Walworth Road. Such notice must be given on Monday, so that, if she could at once make up her mind to accept Miss Barfoot's offer, the coming week would be her last of slavery behind the counter. On the way home from Queen's Road, Alice and Virginia pressed for immediate decision; they were unable to comprehend how Monica could hesitate for another moment. The question of her place of abode had already been discussed. One of Miss Barfoot's young women, who lived at a convenient distance from Great Portland Street, would gladly accept a partner in her lodging—an arrangement to be recommended for its economy. Yet Monica shrank from speaking the final word.

'I don't know whether it's worth while,' she said, after a long silence, as they drew near to York Road Station, whence they were to take train for Clapham Junction.

'Not worth while?' exclaimed Virginia. 'You don't think it would be an improvement?'

'Yes, I suppose it would. I shall see how I feel about it tomorrow morning.'

She spent the evening at Lavender Hill, but without change in the mood thus indicated. A strange inquietude appeared in her behaviour. It was as though she were being urged to undertake something hard and repugnant.

On her return to Walworth Road, just as she came within sight of the shop, she observed a man's figure some twenty yards distant, which instantly held her attention. The dim gaslight occasioned some uncertainty, but she believed the figure was that of Widdowson. He was walking on the other side of the street, and away from her. When the man was exactly opposite Scotcher's establishment he gazed in that direction, but without stopping. Monica hastened, fearing to be seen and approached. Already she had reached the door, when Widdowson—yes, he it was—turned abruptly to walk back again. His eye was at once upon her; but whether he recognized her or not Monica could not know. At that moment she opened the door and passed in.

A fit of trembling seized her, as if she had barely escaped some peril. In the passage she stood motionless, listening with the intensity of dread. She could hear footsteps on the pavement; she expected a ring at the door-bell. If he were so thoughtless as to come to the door, she would on no account see him.

But there was no ring, and after a few minutes' waiting she recovered her self-command. She had not made a mistake; even his features had been discernible as he turned towards her. Was this the first time that he had come to look at the place where she lived—possibly to spy upon her? She resented this behaviour, yet the feeling was confused with a certain satisfaction.

From one of the dormitories there was a view of Walworth Road. She ran upstairs, softly opened the door of that room, and peeped in. The low burning gas showed her that only one bed had an occupant, who appeared to be asleep. Softly she went to the window, drew the blind aside, and looked down into the street. But Widdowson had disappeared. He might of course be on this side of the way.

'Who's that?' suddenly asked a voice from the occupied bed.

The speaker was Miss Eade. Monica looked at her, and nodded.

'You? What are you doing here?'

'I wanted to see if some one was standing outside.'

'You mean *him*?'

The other nodded.

'I've got a beastly headache. I couldn't hold myself up, and I had to come home at eight o'clock. There's such pains all down my back too. I shan't stay at this beastly place much longer. I don't want to get ill, like Miss Radford. Somebody went to see her at the hospital this afternoon, and she's awfully bad. Well, have you seen him?'

'He's gone. Good-night.'

And Monica left the room.

Next day she notified her intention of leaving her employment. No questions were asked; she was of no particular importance; fifty, or, for the matter of that, five score, young women equally capable could be found to fill her place.

On Tuesday morning there came a letter from Virginia—a few lines requesting her to meet her sisters, as soon as possible after closing time that evening, in front of the shop. 'We have something *very delightful* to tell you. We *do hope* you gave notice to-day, as things are getting so bright in every direction.'

At a quarter to ten she was able to run out, and close at hand were the two eagerly awaiting her.

'Mrs. Darby has found a place for Alice,' began Virginia. 'We heard by the afternoon post yesterday. A lady at Yatton wants a governess for two young children. Isn't it fortunate?'

'So delightfully convenient for what we were thinking of,' put in the eldest, with her croaking voice. 'Nothing could have been better.'

'You mean about the school?' said Monica dreamily.

'Yes, the school,' Virginia replied, with trembling earnestness. 'Yatton is convenient both for Clevedon and Weston. Alice will be able to run over to both places and make enquiries, and ascertain where the best opening would be.'

Miss Nunn's suggestion, hitherto but timidly discussed, had taken hold upon their minds as soon as Alice received the practical call to her native region. Both were enthusiastic for the undertaking. It afforded them a novel subject of conversation, and inspirited them by seeming to restore their self-respect. After all, they might have a mission, a task in the world. They pictured themselves the heads of a respectable and thriving establishment, with subordinate teachers, with pleasant social relations; they felt young again, and capable of indefinite activity. Why had they not thought of this long ago? and thereupon they reverted to antistrophic laudation of Rhoda Nunn.

'Is it a good place?' their younger sister inquired.

'Oh, pretty good. Only twelve pounds a year, but nice people, Mrs. Darby says. They want me at once, and it is very likely that in a few weeks I shall go with them to the seaside.'

'What *could* have been better?' cried Virginia. 'Her health will be established, and in half a year, or less, we shall be able to come to a decision about the great step. Oh, and have you given notice, darling?'

'Yes, I have.'

Both clapped their hands like children. It was an odd little scene on the London pavement at ten o'clock at night; so intimately domestic amid surroundings the very antithesis of domesticity. Only a few yards away, a girl, to whom the pavement was a place of commerce, stood laughing with two men. The sound of her voice hinted to Monica the advisability of walking as they conversed, and they moved towards Walworth Road Station.

'We thought at first,' said Virginia, 'that when Alice had gone you might like to share my room; but then the distance from Great Portland

Street would be a decided objection. I might move, but we doubt whether that would be worth while. It is so comfortable with Mrs. Conisbee, and for the short remaining time—Christmas, I should think, would be a very good time for opening. If it were possible to decide upon dear old Clevedon, of course we should prefer it; but perhaps Weston will offer more scope. Alice will weigh all the arguments on the spot. Don't you envy her, Monica? Think of being *there* in this summer weather!'

'Why don't you go as well?' Monica asked.

'I? And take lodgings, you mean? We never thought of that. But we still have to consider expenditure very seriously, you know. If possible, I must find employment for the rest of the year. Remember how very likely it is that Miss Nunn will have something to suggest for me. And when I think it will be of so much practical use for me to see her frequently for a few weeks. Already I have learnt so much from her and from Miss Barfoot. Their conversation is so encouraging. I feel that it is a training of the mind to be in contact with them.'

'Yes, I quite share that view,' said Alice, with tremulous earnestness. 'Virginia can reap much profit from intercourse with them. They have the new ideas in education, and it would be so good if our school began with the advantage of quite a modern system.'

Monica became silent. When her sisters had talked in the same strain for a quarter of an hour, she said absently,—

'I wrote to Miss Barfoot last night, so I suppose I shall be able to move to those lodgings next Sunday.'

It was eleven o'clock before they parted. Having taken leave of her sisters near the station, Monica turned to walk quickly home. She had gone about half the way, when her name was spoken just behind her, in Widdowson's voice. She stopped, and there stood the man, offering his hand.

'Why are you here at this time?' she asked in an unsteady voice.

'Not by chance. I had a hope that I might see you.'

He was gloomy, and looked at her searchingly.

'I mustn't wait to talk now, Mr. Widdowson. It's very late.'

'Very late indeed. It surprised me to see you.'

'Surprised you? Why should it?'

'I mean that it seemed so very unlikely—at this hour.'

'Then how could you have hoped to see me?'

Monica walked on, with an air of displeasure, and Widdowson kept beside her, incessantly eyeing her countenance.

'No, I didn't really think of seeing you, Miss Madden. I wished to be near the place where you were, that was all.'

'You saw me come out I dare say.'

'No.'

'If you had done, you would have known that I came to meet two ladies, my sisters. I walked with them to the station, and now I am going home. You seem to think an explanation necessary—'

'Do forgive me! What right have I to ask anything of the kind? But I have been very restless since Sunday. I wished so to meet you, if only for a few minutes. Only an hour or two ago I posted a letter to you.'

Monica said nothing.

'It was to ask you to meet me next Sunday, as we arranged. Shall you be able to do so?'

'I'm afraid I can't. At the end of this week I leave my place here, and on Sunday I shall be moving to another part of London.'

'You are leaving? You have decided to make the change you spoke of?'

'Yes.'

'And will you tell me where you are going to live?'

'In lodgings near Great Portland Street. I must say good-night, Mr. Widdowson. I must, indeed.'

'Please—do give me one moment!'

'I can't stay—I can't—good-night!'

It was impossible for him to detain her. Ungracefully he caught at his hat, made the salute, and moved away with rapid, uneven strides. In less than half an hour he was back again at this spot. He walked past the shop many times without pausing; his eyes devoured the front of the building, and noted those windows in which there was a glimmer of light. He saw girls enter by the private door, but Monica did not again show herself. Some time after midnight, when the house had long been dark and perfectly quiet, the uneasy man took a last look, and then sought a cab to convey him home.

The letter of which he had spoken reached Monica's hands next morning. It was a very respectful invitation to accompany the writer on a drive in Surrey. Widdowson proposed to meet her at Herne Hill railway station, where his vehicle would be waiting. 'In passing, I shall be able to point out to you the house which has been my home for about a year.'

As circumstances were, it would be hardly possible to accept this invitation without exciting curiosity in her sisters. The Sunday morning would be occupied, probably, in going to the new lodgings and making the acquaintance of her future companion there; in the afternoon, her sisters were to pay her a visit, as Alice had decided to start for Somerset on the Monday. She must write a refusal, but it was by no means her wish to discourage Widdowson altogether. The note which at length satisfied her ran thus:

'DEAR MR. WIDDOWSON—I am very sorry that it will be impossible for me to see you next Sunday. All day I shall be occupied. My eldest sister is leaving London, and Sunday will be my last day with her, perhaps for a long time. Please do not think that I make light of your kindness. When I am settled in my new life, I hope to be able to let you know how it suits me.—Sincerely yours,
MONICA MADDEN.'

In a postscript she mentioned her new address. It was written in very small characters—perhaps an unpurposed indication of the misgiving with which she allowed herself to pen the words.

Two days went by, and again a letter from Widdowson was delivered,

'DEAR MISS MADDEN—My chief purpose in writing again so soon is to apologize sincerely for my behaviour on Tuesday evening. It was quite unjustifiable. The best way of confessing my fault is to own that I had a foolish dislike of your walking in the streets unaccompanied at so late an hour. I believe that any man who had newly made your acquaintance, and had thought as much about you as I have, would have experienced the same feeling. The life which made it impossible for you to see friends at any other time of the day was so evidently unsuited to one of your refinement that I was made angry by the thought of it. Happily it is coming to an end, and I shall be greatly relieved when I know that you have left the house of business.

'You remember that we are to be friends. I should be much less than your friend if I did not desire for you a position very different from that which necessity forced upon you. Thank you very much for the promise to tell me how you like the new employment and your new friends. Shall you not henceforth be at leisure on other days besides Sunday? As you will now be near Regent's Park, perhaps I may hope to meet you there some evening before long. I would go any distance to see you and speak with you for only a few minutes.

'Do forgive my impertinence, and believe me, dear Miss Madden.— Ever yours,

EDMUND WIDDOWSON.'

Now this undoubtedly might be considered a love-letter, and it was the first of its kind that Monica had ever received. No man had ever written to her that he was willing to go 'any distance' for the reward of looking on her face. She read the composition many times, and with many thoughts. It did not enchant her; presently she felt it to be dull and prosy—anything but the ideal of a love-letter, even at this early stage.

The remarks concerning Widdowson made in the bedroom by the girl who fancied her asleep had greatly disturbed her conception of him. He was old, and looked still older to a casual eye. He had a stiff dry way, and already had begun to show how precise and exacting he could be. A year or two ago the image of such a man would have repelled her. She did not think it possible to regard him with warm feelings; yet, if he asked her to marry him—and that seemed likely to happen very soon—almost certainly her answer would be yes. Provided, of course, that all he had told her about himself could be in some satisfactory way confirmed.

Her acquaintance with him was an extraordinary thing. With what amazement and rapture would any one of her shop companions listen to the advances of a man who had six hundred a year! Yet Monica did not doubt this truthfulness and the honesty of his intentions. His life-story sounded credible enough, and the very dryness of his manner inspired confidence. As things went in the marriage war, she might esteem herself a most fortunate young woman. It seemed that he had really fallen in love with her; he might prove a devoted husband. She felt no love in return; but between the prospect of a marriage of esteem and that of no marriage at all there was little room for hesitation. The chances were that she might never again receive an offer from a man whose social standing she could respect.

In the meantime there had come a civil little note from the girl whose rooms she was to share. 'Miss Barfoot has spoken of you so favourably that I did not think it necessary to see you before consenting to what she suggested. Perhaps she has told you that I have my own furniture; it is very plain, but, I think, comfortable. For the two rooms, with attendance, I pay eight and sixpence a week; my landlady will ask eleven shillings when there are two of us, so that your share would be five-and-six. I hope you won't think this is too much. I am a quiet and I think a very reasonable person.' The signature was 'Mildred H. Vesper.'

The day of release arrived. As it poured with rain all the morning, Monica the less regretted that she had been obliged to postpone her meeting with Widdowson. At breakfast-time she said good-bye to the three or four girls in whom she had any interest. Miss Eade was delighted to see her go. This rival finally out of the way, Mr. Bullivant might perchance turn his attention to the faithful admirer who remained.

She went by train to Great Portland Street, and thence by cab, with her two boxes, to Rutland Street, Hampstead Road—an uphill little street of small houses. When the cab stopped, the door of the house she sought at once opened, and on the threshold appeared a short, prim, plain-featured girl, who smiled a welcome.

'You are Miss Vesper?' Monica said, approaching her.

'Yes—very pleased to see you, Miss Madden. As London cabmen have a narrow view of their duties, I'll help you to get the boxes in.'

Monica liked the girl at once. Jehu condescending to hand down the luggage, they transferred it to the foot of the staircase, then, the fare having been paid, went up to the second floor, which was the top of the house. Miss Vesper's two rooms were very humble, but homely. She looked at Monica to remark the impression produced by them.

'Will it do?'

'Oh, very nicely indeed. After my quarters in Walworth Road! But I feel ashamed to intrude upon you.'

'I have been trying to find someone to share my rent,' said the other, with a simple frankness that was very agreeable. 'Miss Barfoot was full of your praises—and indeed I think we may suit each other.'

'I shall try to be as little disturbance to you as possible.'

'And I to you. The street is a very quiet one. Up above here is Cumberland Market; a hay and straw market. Quite pleasant odours—country odours—reach us on market day. I am country-bred; that's why I speak of such a trifle.'

'So am I,' said Monica. 'I come from Somerset.'

'And I from Hampshire. Do you know, I have a strong suspicion that all the really nice girls in London *are* country girls.'

Monica had to look at the speaker to be sure that this was said in pleasantry. Miss Vesper was fond of making dry little jokes in the gravest tone; only a twinkle of her eyes and a movement of her tight little lips betrayed her.

'Shall I ask the landlady to help me up with the luggage?'

'You are rather pale, Miss Madden. Better let me see to that. I have to go down to remind Mrs. Hocking to put salt into the saucepan with the potatoes. She cooks for me only on Sunday, and if I didn't remind her every week she would boil the potatoes without salt. Such a state of mind is curious, but one ends by accepting it as a fact in nature.'

They joined in merry laughter. When Miss Vesper gave way to open mirth, she enjoyed it so thoroughly that it was a delight to look at her.

By the time dinner was over they were on excellent terms, and had exchanged a great deal of personal information. Mildred Vesper seemed to be one of the most contented of young women. She had sisters and brothers, whom she loved, all scattered about England in pursuit of a livelihood; it was rare for any two of them to see each other, but she spoke of this as quite in the order of things. For Miss Barfoot her respect was unbounded.

'She had made more of me than any one else could have done. When I first met her, three years ago, I was a simpleton; I thought myself ill-used because I had to work hard for next to no payment and live in solitude. Now I should be ashamed to complain of what falls to the lot of thousands of girls.'

'Do you like Miss Nunn?' asked Monica.

'Not so well as Miss Barfoot, but I think very highly of her. Her zeal makes her exaggerate a little now and then, but then the zeal is so splendid. I haven't it myself—not in that form.'

'You mean—'

'I mean that I feel a shameful delight when I hear of a girl getting married. It's very weak, no doubt; perhaps I shall improve as I grow older. But I have half a suspicion, do you know, that Miss Barfoot is not without the same weakness.'

Monica laughed, and spoke of something else. She was in good spirits; already her companion's view of life began to have an effect upon her; she thought of people and things in a more lightsome way, and was less disposed to commiserate herself.

The bedroom which both were to occupy might with advantage have been larger, but they knew that many girls of instinct no less delicate than their own had to endure far worse accommodation in London—where poverty pays for its sheltered breathing-space at so much a square foot. It was only of late that Miss Vesper had been able to buy furniture (four sovereigns it cost in all), and thus to allow herself the luxury of two rooms at the rent she previously paid for one.

Miss Barfoot did not remunerate her workers on a philanthropic scale, but strictly in accordance with market prices; common sense dictated this principle. In talking over their arrangements, Monica decided to expend a few shillings on the purchase of a chair-bedstead for her own use.

'I often have nightmares,' she remarked, 'and kick a great deal. It wouldn't be nice to give you bruises.'

A week passed. Alice had written from Yatton, and in a cheerful tone. Virginia, chronically excited, had made calls at Rutland Street and at Queen's Road; she talked like one who had suddenly received a great illumination, and her zeal in the cause of independent womanhood rivalled Miss Nunn's. Without enthusiasm, but seemingly contented, Monica worked at the typewriting machine, and had begun certain studies which her friends judged to be useful. She experienced a growth of self-respect. It was much to have risen above the status of shop-girl, and the change of moral atmosphere had a very beneficial effect upon her.

Mildred Vesper was a studious little person, after a fashion of her own. She possessed four volumes of Maunder's 'Treasuries', and to one or other of these she applied herself for at least an hour every evening.

'By nature,' she said, when Monica sought an explanation of this study, 'my mind is frivolous. What I need is a store of solid information, to reflect upon. No one could possibly have a worse memory, but by persevering I manage to learn one or two facts a day.'

Monica glanced at the books now and then, but had no desire to cultivate Maunder's acquaintance. Instead of reading, she meditated the problems of her own life.

Edmund Widdowson, of course, wrote to her at the new address. In her reply she again postponed their meeting. Whenever she went out in the evening, it was with expectation of seeing him somewhere in the neighbourhood; she felt assured that he had long ago come to look at the house, and more likely than not his eyes had several times been upon her. That did not matter; her life was innocent, and Widdowson might watch her coming and going as much as he would.

At length, about nine o'clock one evening, she came face to face with him. It was in Hampstead Road; she had been buying at a draper's, and carried the little parcel. At the moment of recognition, Widdowson's face so flushed and brightened that Monica could not help a sympathetic feeling of pleasure.

'Why are you so cruel to me?' he said in a low voice, as she gave her hand. 'What a time since I saw you!'

## CHAPTER VII - A SOCIAL ADVANCE

'Is that really true?' she replied, with an air more resembling coquetry than any he had yet seen in her.

'Since I spoke to you, then.'

'When did you see me?'

'Three evenings ago. You were walking in Tottenham Court Road with a young lady.'

'Miss Vesper, the friend I live with.'

'Will you give me a few minutes now?' he asked humbly. 'Is it too late?'

For reply Monica moved slowly on. They turned up one of the ways parallel with Rutland Street, and so came into the quiet district that skirts Regent's Park, Widdowson talking all the way in a strain of all but avowed tenderness, his head bent towards her and his voice so much subdued that occasionally she lost a few words.

'I can't live without seeing you,' he said at length. 'If you refuse to meet me, I have no choice but to come wandering about the places where you are. Don't, pray don't think I spy upon you. Indeed, it is only just to see your face or your form as you walk along. When I have had my journey in vain I go back in misery. You are never out of my thoughts—never.'

'I am sorry for that, Mr. Widdowson.'

'Sorry? Are you really sorry? Do you think of me with less friendliness than when we had our evening on the river?'

'Oh, not with less friendliness. But if I only make you unhappy—'

'In one way unhappy, but as no one else ever had the power to. If you would let me meet you at certain times my restlessness would be at an end. The summer is going so quickly. Won't you come for that drive with me next Sunday? I will be waiting for you at any place you like to appoint. If you could imagine what joy it would give me!'

Presently Monica assented. If it were fine, she would be by the southeast entrance to Regent's Park at two o'clock. He thanked her with words of the most submissive gratitude, and then they parted.

The day proved doubtful, but she kept her appointment. Widdowson was on the spot with horse and trap. These were not, as he presently informed Monica, his own property, but hired from a livery stable, according to his custom.

'It won't rain,' he exclaimed, gazing at the sky. 'It *shan't* rain! These few hours are too precious to me.'

'It would be very awkward if it *did*,' Monica replied, in merry humour, as they drove along.

The sky threatened till sundown, but Widdowson was able to keep declaring that rain would not come. He took a south-westward course, crossed Waterloo Bridge, and thence by the highways made for Herne Hill. Monica observed that he made a short detour to avoid Walworth Road. She asked his reason.

'I hate the road!' Widdowson answered, with vehemence.

'You hate it?'

'Because you slaved and suffered there. If I had the power, I would destroy it—every house. Many a time,' he added, in a lower voice, 'when you were lying asleep, I walked up and down there in horrible misery.'

'Just because I had to stand at a counter?'

'Not only that. It wasn't fit for you to work in that way—but the people about you! I hated every face of man or woman that passed along the street.'

'I didn't like the society.'

'I should hope not. Of course, I know you didn't. Why did you ever come to such a place?'

There was severity rather than sympathy in his look.

'I was tired of the dull country life,' Monica replied frankly. 'And then I didn't know what the shops and the people were like.'

'Do you need a life of excitement?' he asked, with a sidelong glance.

'Excitement? No, but one must have change.'

When they reached Herne Hill, Widdowson became silent, and presently he allowed the horse to walk.

'That is my house, Miss Madden—the right-hand one.'

Monica looked, and saw two little villas, built together with stone facings, porches at the doors and ornamented gables.

'I only wanted to show it you,' he added quickly. 'There's nothing pretty or noticeable about it, and it isn't at all grandly furnished. My old housekeeper and one servant manage to keep it in order.'

They passed, and Monica did not allow herself to look back.

'I think it's a nice house,' she said presently.

'All my life I have wished to have a house of my own, but I didn't dare to hope I ever should. Men in general don't seem to care so long as they have lodgings that suit them—I mean unmarried men. But I always wanted to live alone—without strangers, that is to say. I told you that I am not very sociable. When I got my house, I was like a child with a toy; I couldn't sleep for satisfaction. I used to walk all over it, day after day, before it was furnished. There was something that delighted me in the sound of my footsteps on the staircases and the bare floors. Here I shall live and die, I kept saying to myself. Not in solitude, I hoped. Perhaps I might meet some one—'

Monica interrupted him to ask a question about some object in the landscape. He answered her very briefly, and for a long time neither spoke. Then the girl, glancing at him with a smile of apology, said in a gentle tone—

'You were telling me how the house pleased you. Have you still the same pleasure in living there?'

'Yes. But lately I have been hoping—I daren't say more. You will interrupt me again.'

'Which way are we going now, Mr. Widdowson?'

'To Streatham, then on to Carshalton. At five o'clock we will use our right as travellers, and get some innkeeper to make tea for us. Look, the sun is trying to break through; we shall have a fine evening yet. May I, without rudeness, say that you look better since you left that abominable place.'

'Oh, I feel better.'

After keeping his look fixed for a long time on the horse's ears, Widdowson turned gravely to his companion.

'I told you about my sister-in-law. Would you be willing to make her acquaintance?'

'I don't feel able to do that, Mr. Widdowson,' Monica answered with decision.

Prepared for this reply, he began a long and urgent persuasion. It was useless; Monica listened quietly, but without sign of yielding. The subject dropped, and they talked of indifferent things.

On the homeward drive, when the dull sky grew dusk about them, and the suburban street-lamps began to show themselves in long glimmering lines, Widdowson returned with shamefaced courage to the subject which for some hours had been in abeyance.

'I can't part from you this evening without a word of hope to remember. You know that I want you to be my wife. Will you tell me if there is anything I can say or do to make your consent possible? Have you any doubt of me?'

'No doubt whatever of your sincerity.'

'In one sense, I am still a stranger to you. Will you give me the opportunity of making things between us more regular? Will you allow me to meet some friend of yours whom you trust?'

'I had rather you didn't yet.'

'You wish to know still more of me, personally?'

'Yes—I think I must know you much better before I can consent to any step of that kind.'

'But,' he urged, 'if we became acquaintances in the ordinary way, and knew each other's friends, wouldn't that be most satisfactory to you?'

'It might be. But you forget that so much would have to be explained. I have behaved very strangely. If I told everything to my friends I should leave myself no choice.'

'Oh, why not? You would be absolutely free. I could no more than try to recommend myself to you. If I am so unhappy as to fail, how would you be anything but quite free?'

'But surely you must understand me. In this position, I must either not speak of you at all, or make it known that I am engaged to you. I can't have it taken for granted that I am engaged to you when I don't wish to be.'

Widdowson's head drooped; he set his lips in a hard gloomy expression.

'I have behaved very imprudently,' continued the girl. But I don't see—I can't see—what else I could have done. Things are so badly arranged. It wasn't possible for us to be introduced by any one who knew us both, so I had either to break off your acquaintance after that first conversation, or conduct myself as I have been doing. I think it's a very hard position. My sisters would call me an immodest girl, but I don't think it is true. I may perhaps come to feel you as a girl ought to when she marries, and how else can I tell unless I meet you and talk with you? And your position is just the same. I don't blame you for a moment; I think it would be ridiculous to blame you. Yet we have gone against the ordinary rule, and people would make us suffer for it—or me, at all events.

Her voice at the close was uncertain. Widdowson looked at her with eyes of passionate admiration.

'Thank you for saying that—for putting it so well, and so kindly for me. Let us disregard people, then. Let us go on seeing each other. I love you with all my soul'—he choked a little at this first utterance of the solemn word—'and your rules shall be mine. Give me a chance of winning you. Tell me if I offend you in anything—if there's anything you dislike in me.'

'Will you cease coming to look for me when I don't know of it?'

'I promise you. I will never come again. And you will meet me a little oftener?'

'I will see you once every week. But I must still be perfectly free.'

'Perfectly! I will only try to win you as any man may who loves a woman.'

The tired horse clattered upon the hard highway and clouds gathered for a night of storm.

## CHAPTER VIII - COUSIN EVERARD

As Miss Barfoot's eye fell on the letters brought to her at breakfast-time, she uttered an exclamation, doubtful in its significance. Rhoda Nunn, who rarely had a letter from any one, looked up inquiringly.

'I am greatly mistaken if that isn't my cousin Everard's writing. I thought so. He is in London.'

Rhoda made no remark.

'Pray read it,' said the other, handing her friend the epistle after she had gone through it.

The handwriting was remarkably bold, but careful. Punctuation was strictly attended to, and in places a word had been obliterated with a circular scrawl which left it still legible.

> 'DEAR COUSIN MARY,—I hear that you are still active in an original way, and that civilization is more and more indebted to you. Since my arrival in London a few weeks ago, I have several times been on the point of calling at your house, but scruples withheld me. Our last interview was not quite friendly on your side, you will remember, and perhaps your failure to write to me means continued displeasure; in that case I might be rejected at your door, which I shouldn't like, for I am troubled with a foolish sense of personal dignity. I have taken a flat, and mean to stay in London for at least half a year. Please let me know whether I may see you. Indeed I should like to. Nature meant us for good friends, but prejudice came between us. Just a line, either of welcome or "get thee behind me!" In spite of your censures, I always was, and still am, affectionately yours,
>
> EVERARD BARFOOT.'

Rhoda perused the sheet very attentively.

'An impudent letter,' said Miss Barfoot. 'Just like him.'

'Where does he appear from?'

'Japan, I suppose. "But prejudice came between us." I like that! Moral conviction is always prejudice in the eyes of these advanced young men. Of course he must come. I am anxious to see what time has made of him.'

'Was it really moral censure that kept you from writing to him?' inquired Rhoda, with a smile.

'Decidedly. I didn't approve of him at all, as I have frequently told you.'

'But I gather that he hasn't changed much.'

'Not in theories,' replied Miss Barfoot. 'That isn't to be expected. He is far too stubborn. But in mode of life he may possibly be more tolerable.'

'After two or three years in Japan,' rejoined Rhoda, with a slight raising of the eyebrows.

'He is about three-and-thirty, and before he left England I think he showed possibilities of future wisdom. Of course I disapprove of him, and, if necessary, shall let him understand that quite as plainly as before. But there's no harm in seeing if he has learnt to behave himself.'

Everard Barfoot received an invitation to dine. It was promptly accepted, and on the evening of the appointment he arrived at half-past seven. His cousin sat alone in the drawing-room. At his entrance she regarded him with keen but friendly scrutiny.

He had a tall, muscular frame, and a head of striking outline, with large nose, full lips, deep-set eyes, and prominent eyebrows. His hair was the richest tone of chestnut; his moustache and beard—the latter peaking slightly forward—inclined to redness. Excellent health manifested itself in the warm purity of his skin, in his cheerful aspect, and the lightness of his bearing. The lower half of his forehead was wrinkled, and when he did not fix his look on anything in particular, his eyelids drooped, giving him for the moment an air of languor. On sitting down, he at once abandoned himself to a posture of the completest ease, which his admirable proportions made graceful. From his appearance one would have expected him to speak in rather loud and decided tones; but he had a soft voice, and used it with all the discretion of good-breeding, so that at times it seemed to caress the ear. To this mode of utterance corresponded his smile, which was frequent, but restrained to the expression of a delicate, good-natured irony.

'No one had told me of your return,' were Miss Barfoot's first words as she shook hands with him.

'I fancy because no one knew. You were the first of my kinsfolk to whom I wrote.'

'Much honour, Everard. You look very well.'

'I am glad to be able to say the same of you. And yet I hear that you work harder than ever.'

'Who is the source of your information about me?'

'I had an account of you from Tom, in a letter that caught me at Constantinople.'

'Tom? I thought he had forgotten my existence. Who told him about me I can't imagine. So you didn't come straight home from Japan?'

Barfoot was nursing his knee, his head thrown back.

'No; I loitered a little in Egypt and Turkey. Are you living quite alone?'

He drawled slightly on the last word, its second vowel making quite a musical note, of wonderful expressiveness. The clear decision of his cousin's reply was a sharp contrast.

'A lady lives with me—Miss Nunn. She will join us in a moment.'

'Miss Nunn?' He smiled. 'A partner in your activity?'

'She gives me valuable help.'

'I must hear all about it—if you will kindly tell me some day. It will interest me greatly. You always were the most interesting of our family. Brother Tom promised to be a genius, but marriage has blighted the hope, I fear.'

'The marriage was a very absurd one.'

'Was it? I feared so; but Tom seems satisfied. I suppose they will stay at Madeira.'

'Until his wife is tired of her imaginary phthisis, and amuses herself with imagining some other ailment that requires them to go to Siberia.'

'Ah, that kind of person, is she?' He smiled indulgently, and played for a moment with the lobe of his right ear. His ears were small, and of the ideal contour; the hand, too, thus displayed, was a fine example of blended strength and elegance.

Rhoda came in, so quietly that she was able to observe the guest before he had detected her presence. The movement of Miss Barfoot's eyes first informed him that another person was in the room. In the quietest possible way the introduction was performed, and all seated themselves.

Dressed, like the hostess, in black, and without ornaments of any kind save a silver buckle at her waist, Rhoda seemed to have endeavoured to liken herself to the suggestion of her name by the excessive plainness with which she had arranged her hair; its tight smoothness was nothing like so becoming as the mode she usually adopted, and it made her look older. Whether by accident or design, she took an upright chair, and sat upon it in a stiff attitude. Finding it difficult to suspect Rhoda of shyness, Miss Barfoot once or twice glanced at her with curiosity. For settled conversation there was no time; a servant announced dinner almost immediately.

'There shall be no forms, cousin Everard,' said the hostess. 'Please to follow us.'

Doing so, Everard examined Miss Nunn's figure, which in its way was strong and shapely as his own. A motion of his lips indicated amused approval, but at once he commanded himself, and entered the dining-room with exemplary gravity. Naturally, he sat opposite Rhoda, and his eyes often skimmed her face; when she spoke, which was very seldom, he gazed at her with close attention.

During the first part of the meal, Miss Barfoot questioned her relative concerning his Oriental experiences. Everard spoke of them in a light, agreeable way, avoiding the tone of instruction, and, in short, giving evidence of good taste. Rhoda listened with a look of civil interest, but asked no question, and smiled only when it was unavoidable. Presently the talk turned to things of home.

'Have you heard of your friend Mr. Poppleton?' the hostess asked.

'Poppleton? Nothing whatever. I should like to see him.'

'I'm sorry to tell you he is in a lunatic asylum.'

As Barfoot kept the silence of astonishment, his cousin went on to tell him that the unhappy man seemed to have lost his wits among business troubles.

'Yet I should have suggested another explanation,' remarked the young man, in his most discreet tone, 'You never met Mrs. Poppleton?'

Seeing that Miss Nunn had looked up with interest, he addressed himself to her.

'My friend Poppleton was one of the most delightful men—perhaps the best and kindest I ever knew, and so overflowing with natural wit and humour that there was no resisting his cheerful influence. To the amazement of every one who knew him, he married perhaps the dullest woman he could have found. Mrs. Poppleton not only never made a joke, but couldn't understand what joking meant. Only the flattest literalism was intelligible to her; she could follow nothing but the very macadam of conversation—had no palate for anything but the suet-pudding of talk.'

Rhoda's eyes twinkled, and Miss Barfoot laughed. Everard was allowing himself a freedom in expression which hitherto he had sedulously avoided.

'Yes,' he continued, 'she was by birth a lady—which made the infliction harder to bear. Poor old Poppleton! Again and again I have heard him—what do you think?—laboriously *explaining* jests to her. That was a trial, as you may imagine. There we sat, we three, in the unbeautiful little parlour—for they were anything but rich. Poppleton would say something that convulsed me with laughter—in spite of my efforts, for I always dreaded the result so much that I strove my hardest to do no more than smile appreciation. My laugh compelled Mrs. Poppleton to stare at me—oh, her eyes! Thereupon, her husband began his dread performance. The patience, the heroic patience, of that dear, good fellow! I have known him explain, and re-explain, for a quarter of an hour, and invariably without success. It might be a mere pun; Mrs. Poppleton no more understood the nature of a pun than of the binomial theorem. But worse was when the jest involved some allusion. When I heard Poppleton begin to elucidate, to expound, the perspiration already on his forehead, I looked at him with imploring anguish. Why *would* he attempt the impossible? But the kind fellow couldn't disregard his wife's request. Shall I ever forget her. "Oh—yes—I see"?—when obviously she saw nothing but the wall at which she sat staring.'

'I have known her like,' said Miss Barfoot merrily.

'I am convinced his madness didn't come from business anxiety. It was the necessity, ever recurring, ever before him, of expounding jokes to his wife. Believe me, it was nothing but that.'

'It seems very probable,' asserted Rhoda dryly.

'Then there's another friend of yours whose marriage has been unfortunate,' said the hostess. 'They tell me that Mr. Orchard has forsaken his wife, and without intelligible reason.'

'There, too, I can offer an explanation,' replied Barfoot quietly, 'though you may doubt whether it justifies him. I met Orchard a few months ago in Alexandria, met him by chance in the street, and didn't recognize him until he spoke to me. He was worn to skin and bone. I found that he had abandoned all his possessions to Mrs. Orchard, and just kept himself alive on casual work for the magazines, wandering about the shores of the Mediterranean like an uneasy spirit. He showed me the thing he had last written, and I see it is published in this month's *Macmillan.* Do read it. An exquisite description of a night in Alexandria. One of these days he will starve to death. A pity; he might have done fine work.'

'But we await your explanation. What business has he to desert his wife and children?'

'Let me give an account of a day I spent with him at Tintern, not long before I left England. He and his wife were having a holiday there, and I called on them. We went to walk about the Abbey. Now, for some two hours—I will be strictly truthful—whilst we were in the midst of that lovely scenery, Mrs. Orchard discoursed unceasingly of one subject—the difficulty she had with her domestic servants. Ten or twelve of these handmaidens were marshalled before our imagination; their names, their ages, their antecedents, the wages they received, were carefully specified. We listened to a *catalogue raisonne* of the plates, cups, and other utensils that they had broken. We heard of the enormities which in each case led to their dismissal. Orchard tried repeatedly to change the subject, but only with the effect of irritating his wife. What could he or I do but patiently give ear? Our walk was ruined, but there was no help for it. Now, be good enough to extend this kind of thing over a number of years. Picture Orchard sitting down in his home to literary work, and liable at any moment to an invasion from Mrs. Orchard, who comes to tell him, at great length, that the butcher has charged for a joint they have not consumed—or something of that kind. He assured me that his choice lay between flight and suicide, and I firmly believed him.'

As he concluded, his eyes met those of Miss Nunn, and the latter suddenly spoke.

'Why will men marry fools?'

Barfoot was startled. He looked down into his plate, smiling.

'A most sensible question,' said the hostess, with a laugh. 'Why, indeed?'

'But a difficult one to answer,' remarked Everard, with his most restrained smile. 'Possibly, Miss Nunn, narrow social opportunity has something to do with it. They must marry some one, and in the case of most men choice is seriously restricted.'

'I should have thought,' replied Rhoda, elevating her eyebrows, 'that to live alone was the less of two evils.'

'Undoubtedly. But men like these two we have been speaking of haven't a very logical mind.'

Miss Barfoot changed the topic.

When, not long after, the ladies left him to meditate over his glass of wine, Everard curiously surveyed the room. Then his eyelids drooped, he smiled absently, and a calm sigh seemed to relieve his chest. The claret had no particular quality to recommend it, and in any case he would have drunk very little, for as regards the bottle his nature was abstemious.

'It is as I expected,' Miss Barfoot was saying to her friend in the drawing-room. 'He has changed very noticeably.'

'Mr. Barfoot isn't quite the man your remarks had suggested to me,' Rhoda replied.

'I fancy he is no longer the man I knew. His manners are wonderfully improved. He used to assert himself in rather alarming ways. His letter, to be sure, had the old tone, or something of it.'

'I will go to the library for an hour,' said Rhoda, who had not seated herself. 'Mr. Barfoot won't leave before ten, I suppose?'

'I don't think there will be any private talk.'

'Still, if you will let me—'

So, when Everard appeared, he found his cousin alone.

'What are you going to do?' she asked of him good-naturedly.

'To do? You mean, how do I propose to employ myself? I have nothing whatever in view, beyond enjoying life.'

'At your age?'

'So young? Or so old? Which?'

'So young, of course. You deliberately intend to waste your life?'

'To enjoy it, I said. I am not prompted to any business or profession; that's all over for me; I have learnt all I care to of the active world.'

'But what do you understand by enjoyment?' asked Miss Barfoot, with knitted brows.

'Isn't the spectacle of existence quite enough to occupy one through a lifetime? If a man merely travelled, could he possibly exhaust all the beauties and magnificences that are offered to him in every country? For ten years and more I worked as hard as any man; I shall never regret it, for it has given me a feeling of liberty and opportunity such as I should not have known if I had always lived at my ease. It taught me a great deal, too; supplemented my so-called education as nothing else could have done. But to work for ever is to lose half of life. I can't understand those people who reconcile themselves to quitting the world without having seen a millionth part of it.'

'I am quite reconciled to that. An infinite picture gallery isn't my idea of enjoyment.'

'Nor mine. But an infinite series of modes of living. A ceaseless exercise of all one's faculties of pleasure. That sounds shameless to you? I can't understand why it should. Why is the man who toils more meritorious than he who enjoys? What is the sanction for this judgment?'

'Social usefulness, Everard.'

'I admit the demand for social usefulness, up to a certain point. But, really, I have done my share. The mass of men don't toil with any such ideal, but merely to keep themselves alive, or to get wealth. I think there is a vast amount of unnecessary labour.'

'There is an old proverb about Satan and idle hands. Pardon me; you alluded to that personage in your letter.'

'The proverb is a very true one, but, like other proverbs, it applies to the multitude. If I get into mischief, it will not be because I don't perspire for so many hours every day, but simply because it is human to err. I have no intention whatever of getting into mischief.'

The speaker stroked his beard, and smiled with a distant look.

'Your purpose is intensely selfish, and all indulged selfishness reacts on the character,' replied Miss Barfoot, still in a tone of the friendliest criticism.

'My dear cousin, for anything to be selfish, it must be a deliberate refusal of what one believes to be duty. I don't admit that I am neglecting any duty to others, and the duty to myself seems very clear indeed.'

'Of *that* I have no doubt,' exclaimed the other, laughing. 'I see that you have refined your arguments.'

'Not my arguments only, I hope,' said Everard modestly. 'My time has been very ill spent if I haven't in some degree, refined my nature.'

'That sounds very well, Everard. But when it comes to degrees of self-indulgence—'

She paused and made a gesture of dissatisfaction.

'It comes to that, surely, with every man. But we certainly shall not agree on this subject. You stand at the social point of view; I am an individualist. You have the advantage of a tolerably consistent theory; whilst I have no theory at all, and am full of contradictions. The only thing clear to me is that I have a right to make the most of my life.'

'No matter at whose expense?'

'You are quite mistaken. My conscience is a tender one. I dread to do any one an injury. That has always been true of me, in spite of your sceptical look; and the tendency increases as I grow older. Let us have done with so unimportant a matter. Isn't Miss Nunn able to rejoin us?'

'She will come presently, I think.'

'How did you make this lady's acquaintance?'

Miss Barfoot explained the circumstances.

'She makes an impression,' resumed Everard. 'A strong character, of course. More decidedly one of the new women than you yourself—isn't she?'

'Oh, *I* am a very old-fashioned woman. Women have thought as I do at any time in history. Miss Nunn has much more zeal for womanhood militant.'

'I should delight to talk with her. Really, you know, I am very strongly on your side.'

Miss Barfoot laughed.

'Oh, sophist! You despise women.'

'Why, yes, the great majority of women—the typical woman. All the more reason for my admiring the exceptions, and wishing to see them become more common. You, undoubtedly, despise the average woman.'

'I despise no human being, Everard.'

'Oh, in a sense! But Miss Nunn, I feel sure, would agree with me.'

'I am very sure Miss Nunn wouldn't. She doesn't admire the feebler female, but that is very far from being at one with *your* point of view, my cousin.'

Everard mused with a smile.

'I must get to understand her line of thought. You permit me to call upon you now and then?'

'Oh, whenever you like, in the evening. Except,' Miss Barfoot added, 'Wednesday evening. Then we are always engaged.'

'Summer holidays are unknown to you, I suppose?'

'Not altogether. I had mine a few weeks ago. Miss Nunn will be going away in a fortnight, I think.'

Just before ten o'clock, when Barfoot was talking of some acquaintances he had left in Japan, Rhoda entered the room. She seemed little disposed for conversation, and Everard did not care to assail her taciturnity this evening. He talked on a little longer, observing her as she listened, and presently took an opportunity to rise for departure.

'Wednesday is the forbidden evening, is it not?' he said to his cousin.

'Yes, that is devoted to business.'

As soon as he had gone, the friends exchanged a look. Each understood the other as referring to this point of Wednesday evening, but neither made a remark. They were silent for some time. When Rhoda at length spoke it was in a tone of half-indifferent curiosity.

'You are sure you haven't exaggerated Mr. Barfoot's failings?'

The reply was delayed for a moment.

'I was a little indiscreet to speak of him at all. But no, I didn't exaggerate.'

'Curious,' mused the other dispassionately, as she stood with one foot on the fender. 'He hardly strikes one as that kind of man.'

'Oh, he has certainly changed a great deal.'

Miss Barfoot went on to speak of her cousin's resolve to pursue no calling.

'His means are very modest. I feel rather guilty before him; his father bequeathed to me much of the money that would in the natural course have been Everard's. But he is quite superior to any feeling of grudge on that score.'

'Practically, his father disinherited him?'

'It amounted to that. From quite a child, Everard was at odds with his father. A strange thing, for in so many respects they resembled each other very closely. Physically, Everard is his father walking the earth again. In character, too, I think they must be very much alike. They couldn't talk about the simplest thing without disagreeing. My uncle had risen from the ranks but he disliked to be reminded of it. He disliked the commerce by which he made his fortune. His desire was to win social position; if baronetcies could be purchased in our time, he would have given a huge sum to acquire one. But he never distinguished himself, and one of the reasons was, no doubt, that he married too soon. I have heard him speak bitterly, and very indiscreetly, of early marriages; his wife was dead then, but every one knew what he meant. Rhoda, when one thinks how often a woman is a clog upon a man's ambition, no wonder they regard us as they do.'

'Of course, women are always retarding one thing or another. But men are intensely stupid not to have remedied that long ago.'

'He determined that his boys should be gentlemen. Tom, the elder, followed his wishes exactly; he was remarkably clever, but idleness spoilt him, and now he has made that ridiculous marriage—the end of poor Tom. Everard went to Eton, and the school had a remarkable effect upon him; it made him a furious Radical. Instead of imitating the young aristocrats he hated and scorned them. There must have been great force of originality in the boy. Of course I don't know whether any Etonians of his time preached Radicalism, but it seems unlikely. I think it was sheer vigour of character, and the strange desire to oppose his father in everything. From Eton he was of course to pass to Oxford, but at that stage came practical rebellion. No, said the boy; he wouldn't go to a university, to fill his head with useless learning; he had made up his mind to be an engineer. This was an astonishment to every one; engineering didn't seem at all the thing for him; he had very little ability in mathematics, and his bent had always been to liberal studies. But nothing could shake his idea. He had got it into his head that only some such work as engineering—something of a practical kind, that called for strength and craftsmanship—was worthy of a man with his opinions. He would rank with the classes that keep the world going with their sturdy toil: that was how he spoke. And, after a great fight, he had his way. He left Eton to study civil engineering.'

Rhoda was listening with an amused smile.

'Then,' pursued her friend, 'came another display of firmness or obstinacy, whichever you like to call it. He soon found out that he had made a complete mistake. The studies didn't suit him at all, as others had foreseen. But he would have worked himself to death rather than confess his error; none of us knew how he was feeling till long after. Engineering he had chosen, and an engineer he would be, cost him what effort it might. His father shouldn't triumph over him. And from the age of eighteen till nearly thirty he stuck to a profession which I am sure he loathed. By force of resolve he even got on to it, and reached a good position with the firm he worked for. Of course his father wouldn't assist him with money after he came of age; he had to make his way just like any young man who has no influence.'

'All this puts him in quite another light,' remarked Rhoda.

'Yes, it would be all very well, if there were no vices to add to the picture. I never experienced such a revulsion of feeling as the day when I learnt shameful things about Everard. You know, I always regarded him as a boy, and very much as if he had been my younger brother; then came the shock—a shock that had a great part in shaping my life thenceforward. Since, I have thought of him as I have spoken of him to you—as an illustration of evils we have to combat. A man of the world would tell you that I grossly magnified trifles; it is very likely that Everard was on a higher moral level than most men. But I shall never forgive him for destroying my faith in his honour and nobility of feeling.'

Rhoda had a puzzled look.

'Perhaps even now you are unintentionally misleading me,' she said. 'I have supposed him an outrageous profligate.'

'He was vicious and cowardly—I can't say any more.'

'And that was the immediate cause of his father's leaving him poorly provided for?'

'It had much to do with it, I have no doubt.'

'I see. I imagined that he was cast out of all decent society.'

'If society were really decent, he would have been. It's strange how completely his Radicalism has disappeared. I believe he never had a genuine sympathy with the labouring classes. And what's more, I fancy he had a great deal of his father's desire for command and social distinction. If he had seen his way to become a great engineer, a director of vast enterprises, he wouldn't have abandoned his work. An incredible stubbornness has possibly spoilt his whole life. In a congenial pursuit he might by this time have attained to something noteworthy. It's too late now, I fear.'

Rhoda meditated.

'Does he aim at nothing whatever?'

'He won't admit any ambition. He has no society. His friends are nearly all obscure people, like those you heard him speak of this evening.'

'After all, what ambition should he have?' said Rhoda, with a laugh. 'There's one advantage in being a woman. A woman with brains and will may hope to distinguish herself in the greatest movement of our time—that of emancipating her sex. But what can a man do, unless he has genius?'

'There's the emancipation of the working classes. That is the great sphere for men; and Everard cares no more for the working classes than I do.'

'Isn't it enough to be free oneself?'

'You mean that he has task enough in striving to be an honourable man?'

'Perhaps. I hardly know what I meant.'

Miss Barfoot mused, and her face lighted up with a glad thought.

'You are right. It's better to be a woman, in our day. With us is all the joy of advance, the glory of conquering. Men have only material progress to think about. But we—we are winning souls, propagating a new religion, purifying the earth!'

Rhoda nodded thrice.

'My cousin is a fine specimen of a man, after all, in body and mind. But what a poor, ineffectual creature compared with *you*, Rhoda! I don't flatter you, dear. I tell you bluntly of your faults and extravagances. But I am proud of your magnificent independence, proud of your pride, dear, and of your stainless heart. Thank Heaven we are women!'

It was rare indeed for Miss Barfoot to be moved to rhapsody. Again Rhoda nodded, and then they laughed together, with joyous confidence in themselves and in their cause.

## CHAPTER IX - THE SIMPLE FAITH

Seated in the reading-room of a club to which he had newly procured admission, Everard Barfoot was glancing over the advertisement columns of a literary paper. His eye fell on an announcement that had a personal interest to him, and at once he went to the writing-table to pen a letter.

> 'DEAR MICKLETHWAITE,—I am back in England, and ought before this to have written to you. I see you have just published a book with an alarming title, "A Treatise on Trilinear Co-ordinates." My hearty congratulations on the completion of such a labour; were you not the most disinterested of mortals, I would add a hope that it may somehow benefit you financially. I presume there *are* people who purchase such works. But of course the main point with you is to have delivered your soul on Trilinear Co-ordinates. Shall I run down to Sheffield to see you, or is there any chance of the holidays bringing you this way? I have found a cheap flat, poorly furnished, in Bayswater; the man who let it to me happens to be an engineer, and is absent on Italian railway work for a year or so. My stay in London won't, I think, be for longer than six months, but we must see each other and talk over old times,' etc.

This he addressed to a school at Sheffield. The answer, directed to the club, reached him in three days.

> 'My DEAR BARFOOT,—I also am in London; your letter has been forwarded from the school, which I quitted last Easter. Disinterested or not, I am happy to tell you that I have got a vastly better appointment. Let me know when and where to meet you; or if you like, come to these lodgings of mine. I don't enter upon duties till end of Oc-

tober, and am at present revelling in mathematical freedom. There's a great deal to tell.—Sincerely yours,
THOMAS MICKLETHWAITE.'

Having no occupation for his morning, Barfoot went at once to the obscure little street by Primrose Hill where his friend was lodging. He reached the house about noon, and, as he had anticipated, found the mathematician deep in study. Micklethwaite was a man of forty, bent in the shoulders, sallow, but not otherwise of unhealthy appearance; he had a merry countenance, a great deal of lank, disorderly hair, and a beard that reached to the middle of his waistcoat. Everard's acquaintance with him dated from ten years ago, when Micklethwaite had acted as his private tutor in mathematics.

The room was a musty little back-parlour on the ground floor.

'Quiet, perfectly quiet,' declared its occupant, 'and that's all I care for. Two other lodgers in the house; but they go to business every morning at half-past eight, and are in bed by ten at night. Besides, it's only temporary. I have great things in view—portentous changes! I'll tell you all about it presently.'

He insisted, first of all, on hearing a full account of Barfoot's history since they both met. They had corresponded about twice a year, but Everard was not fond of letter-writing, and on each occasion gave only the briefest account of himself. In listening, Micklethwaite assumed extraordinary positions, the result, presumably, of a need of physical exercise after hours spent over his work. Now he stretched himself at full length on the edge of his chair, his arms extended above him; now he drew up his legs, fixed his feet on the chair, and locked his hands round his knees; thus perched, he swayed his body backwards and forwards, till it seemed likely that he would pitch head foremost on to the floor. Barfoot knew these eccentricities of old, and paid no attention to them.

'And what is the appointment you have got?' he asked at length, dismissing his own affairs with impatience.

It was that of mathematical lecturer at a London college.

'I shall have a hundred and fifty a year, and be able to take private pupils. On two hundred, at least, I can count, and there are possibilities I won't venture to speak of, because it doesn't do to be too hopeful. Two hundred a year is a great advance for me.'

'Quite enough, I suppose,' said Everard kindly.

'Not—not enough. I must make a little more somehow.'

'Hollo! Why this spirit of avarice all at once?'

The mathematician gave a shrill, cackling laugh, and rolled upon his chair.

'I must have more than two hundred. I should be satisfied with *three* hundred, but I'll take as much more as I can get.'

'My revered tutor, this is shameless. I came to pay my respects to a philosopher, and I find a sordid worldling. Look at me! I am a man of the largest needs, spiritual and physical, yet I make my pittance of four hundred and fifty suffice, and never grumble. Perhaps you aim at an income equal to my own?'

'I do! What's four hundred and fifty? If you were a man of enterprise you would double or treble it. I put a high value on money. I wish to be *rich*!'

'You are either mad or are going to get married.'

Micklethwaite cackled louder than ever.

'I am planning a new algebra for school use. If I'm not much mistaken, I can turn out something that will supplant all the present books. Think! If Micklethwaite's Algebra got accepted in all the schools, what would that mean to Mick? Hundreds a year, my boy—hundreds.'

'I never knew you so indecent.'

'I am renewing my youth. Nay, for the first time I am youthful. I never had time for it before. At the age of sixteen I began to teach in a school, and ever since I have pegged away at it, school and private. Now luck has come to me, and I feel five-and-twenty. When I was really five-and-twenty, I felt forty.'

'Well, what has that to do with money-making?'

'After Mick's Algebra would follow naturally Mick's Arithmetic, Mick's Euclid, Mick's Trigonometry. Twenty years hence I should have an income of thousands—thousands! I would then cease to teach (resign my professorship—that is to say, for of course I should be professor), and devote myself to a great work on Probability. Many a man has begun the best of his life at sixty—the most enjoyable part of it, I mean.'

Barfoot was perplexed. He knew his friend's turn for humorous exaggeration, but had never once heard him scheme for material advancement, and evidently this present talk meant something more than a jest.

'Am I right or not? You are going to get married?'

Micklethwaite glanced at the door, then said in a tone of caution,—

'I don't care to talk about it here. Let us go somewhere and eat together. I invite you to have dinner with me—or lunch, as I suppose you would call it, in your aristocratic language.'

'No, you had better have lunch with me. Come to my club.'

'Confound your impudence! Am I not your father in mathematics?'

'Be so good as to put on a decent pair of trousers, and brush your hair. Ah, here is your Trilinear production. I'll look over it whilst you make yourself presentable.'

'There's a bad misprint in the Preface. Let me show you—'

'It's all the same to me, my dear fellow.'

But Micklethwaite was not content until he had indicated the error, and had talked for five minutes about the absurdities that it involved.

'How do you suppose I got the thing published?' he then asked. 'Old Bennet, the Sheffield headmaster, is security for loss if the book doesn't pay for itself in two years' time. Kind of him, wasn't it? He pressed the offer upon me, and I think he's prouder of the book than I am myself. But it's quite remarkable how kind people are when one is fortunate. I fancy a great deal of nonsense is talked about the world's enviousness. Now as soon as it got known that I was coming to this post in London, people behaved to me with surprising good nature all round. Old Bennet talked in quite an affectionate strain. "Of course," he said, "I have long known that you ought to be in a better place than this; your payment is altogether inadequate; if it had depended upon *me*, I should long ago have increased it. I truly rejoice that you have found a more fitting sphere for your remarkable abilities." No; I maintain that the world is always ready to congratulate you with sincerity, if you will only give it a chance.'

'Very gracious of you to give it the chance. But, by-the-bye, how did it come about?'

'Yes, I ought to tell you that. Why, about a year ago, I wrote an answer to a communication signed by a Big Gun in one of the scientific papers. It was a question in Probability—you wouldn't understand it. My answer was printed, and the Big Gun wrote privately to me—a very flattering letter. That correspondence led to my appointment; the Big Gun exerted himself on my behalf. The fact is, the world is bursting with good nature.'

'Obviously. And how long did it take you to write this little book?'

'Oh, only about seven years—the actual composition. I never had much time to myself, you must remember.'

'You're a good soul, Thomas. Go and equip yourself for civilized society.'

To the club they repaired on foot. Micklethwaite would talk of anything but that which his companion most desired to hear.

'There are solemnities in life,' he answered to an impatient question, 'things that can't be spoken of in the highway. When we have eaten, let us go to your flat, and there I will tell you everything.'

They lunched joyously. The mathematician drank a bottle of excellent hock, and did corresponding justice to the dishes. His eyes gleamed with happiness; again he enlarged upon the benevolence of mankind, and the admirable ordering of the world. From the club they drove to Bayswater, and made themselves comfortable in Barfoot's flat, which was very plainly, but sufficiently, furnished. Micklethwaite, cigar in mouth, threw his legs over the side of the easy-chair in which he was sitting.

'Now,' he began gravely, 'I don't mind telling you that your conjecture was right. I *am* going to be married.'

'Well,' said the other, 'you have reached the age of discretion. I must suppose that you know what you are about.'

'Yes, I think I do. The story is unexciting. I am not a romantic person, nor is my future wife. Now, you must know that when I was about twenty-three years old I fell in love. You never suspected me of that, I dare say?'

'Why not?'

'Well, I did fall in love. The lady was a clergyman's daughter at Hereford, where I had a place in a school; she taught the infants in an elementary school connected with ours; her age was exactly the same as my own. Now, the remarkable thing was that she took a liking for me, and when I was scoundrel enough to tell her of my feeling, she didn't reject me.'

'Scoundrel enough? Why scoundrel?'

'Why? But I hadn't a penny in the world. I lived at the school, and received a salary of thirty pounds, half of which had to go towards the support of my mother. What could possibly have been more villainous? What earthly prospect was there of my being able to marry?'

'Well, grant the monstrosity of it.'

'This lady—a very little lower than the angels—declared that she was content to wait an indefinite time. She believed in me, and hoped for my future. Her father—the mother was dead—sanctioned our engagement. She had three sisters, one of them a governess, another keeping house, and the third a blind girl. Excellent people, all of them. I was at their house as often as possible, and they made much of me. It was a pity, you know, for in those few leisure hours I ought to have been working like a nigger.'

'Plainly you ought.'

'Fortunately, I left Hereford, and went to a school at Gloucester, where I had thirty-five pounds. How we gloried over that extra five pounds! But it's no use going on with the story in this way; it would take me till to-morrow morning. Seven years went by; we were thirty years old, and no prospect whatever of our engagement coming to anything. I had worked pretty hard; I had taken my London degree; but not a penny had I saved, and all I could spare was still needful to my mother. It struck me all at once that I had no right to continue the engagement. On my thirtieth birthday I wrote a letter to Fanny—that is her name—and begged her to be free. Now, would you have done the same, or not?'

'Really, I am not imaginative enough to put myself in such a position. It would need a stupendous effort, at all events.'

'But was there anything gross in the proceeding?'

'The lady took it ill?'

'Not in the sense of being offended. But she said it had caused her much suffering. She begged me to consider *myself* free. She would remain Faithful, and if, in time to come, I cared to write to her again—After all these years, I can't speak of it without huskiness. It seemed to me that I had behaved more like a scoundrel than ever. I thought I had better kill myself, and even planned ways of doing it—I did indeed. But after all we decided that our engagement should continue.'

'Of course.'

'You think it natural? Well, the engagement has continued till this day. A month ago I was forty, so that we have waited for seventeen years.'

Micklethwaite paused on a note of awe.

'Two of Fanny's sisters are dead; they never married. The blind one Fanny has long supported, and she will come to live with us. Long, long ago we had both of us given up thought of marriage. I have never spoken to any one of the engagement; it was something too absurd, and also too sacred.'

The smile died from Everard's face, and he sat in thought.

'Now, when are *you* going to marry?' cried Micklethwaite, with a revival of his cheerfulness.

'Probably never.'

'Then I think you will neglect a grave duty. Yes. It is the duty of every man, who has sufficient means, to maintain a wife. The life of unmarried women is a wretched one; every man who is able ought to save one of them from that fate.'

'I should like my cousin Mary and her female friends to hear you talk in that way. They would overwhelm you with scorn.'

'Not sincere scorn, is my belief. Of course I have heard of that kind of woman. Tell me something about them.'

Barfoot was led on to a broad expression of his views.

'I admire your old-fashioned sentiment, Micklethwaite. It sits well on you, and you're a fine fellow. But I have much more sympathy with the new idea that women should think of marriage only as men do—I mean, not to grow up in the thought that they must marry or be blighted creatures. My own views are rather extreme, perhaps; strictly, I don't believe in marriage at all. And I haven't anything like the respect for women, as women, that you have. You belong to the Ruskin school; and I—well, perhaps my experience has been unusual, though I don't think so. You know, by-the-bye, that my relatives consider me a blackguard?'

'That affair you told me about some years ago?'

'Chiefly that. I have a good mind to tell you the true story; I didn't care to at the time. I accepted the charge of black-guardism; it didn't matter much. My cousin will never forgive me, though she has an air of friendliness once more. And I suspect she had told her friend Miss Nunn all about me. Perhaps to put Miss Nunn on her guard—Heaven knows!'

He laughed merrily.

'Miss Nunn, I dare say, needs no protection against you.'

'I had an odd thought whilst I was there.' Everard leaned his head back, and half closed his eyes. 'Miss Nunn, I warrant, considers herself proof against any kind of wooing. She is one of the grandly severe women; a terror, I imagine, to any young girl at their place who betrays weak thoughts of matrimony. Now, it's rather a temptation to a man of my kind. There would be something piquant in making vigorous love to Miss Nunn, just to prove her sincerity.'

Micklethwaite shook his head.

'Unworthy of you, Barfoot. Of course you couldn't really do such a thing.'

'But such women really challenge one. If she were rich, I think I could do it without scruple.'

'You seem to be taking it for granted,' said the mathematician, smiling, 'that this lady would—would respond to your lovemaking.'

'I confess to you that women have spoilt me. And I am rather resentful when any one cries out against me for lack of respect to womanhood. I have been the victim of this groundless veneration for females. Now you shall hear the story; and bear in mind that you are the only person to whom I have ever told it. I never tried to defend myself when I was vilified on all hands. Probably the attempt would have been useless; and then it would certainly have increased the odium in which I stood. I think I'll tell cousin Mary the truth some day; it would be good for her.'

The listener looked uneasy, but curious.

'Well now, I was staying in the summer with some friends of ours at a little place called Upchurch, on a branch line from Oxford. The people were well-to-do—Goodall their name—and went in for philanthropy. Mrs. Goodall always had a lot of Upchurch girls about her, educated and not; her idea was to civilize one class by means of the other, and to give a new spirit to both. My cousin Mary was staying at the house whilst I was there. She had more reasonable views than Mrs. Goodall, but took a great interest in what was going on.

'Now one of the girls in process of spiritualization was called Amy Drake. In the ordinary course of things I shouldn't have met her, but she served in a shop where I went two or three times to get a newspaper; we talked a little—with absolute propriety on my part, I assure you—and she knew that I was a friend of the Goodalls. The girl had no parents, and she was on the point of going to London to live with a married sister.

'It happened that by the very train which took me back to London, when my visit was over, this girl also travelled, and alone. I saw her at Upchurch Station, but we didn't speak, and I got into a smoking carriage. We had to change at Oxford, and there, as I walked about the platform, Amy put herself in my way, so that I was obliged to begin talking with her. This behaviour rather surprised me. I wondered what Mrs. Goodall would think of it. But perhaps it was a sign of innocent freedom in the intercourse of men and women. At all events, Amy managed to get me into the same carriage with herself, and on the way to London we were alone. You foresee the end of it. At Paddington Station the girl and I went off together, and she didn't get to her sister's till the evening.

'Of course I take it for granted that you believe my account of the matter. Miss Drake was by no means the spiritual young person that Mrs. Goodall thought her, or hoped to make her; plainly, she was a reprobate of experience. This, you will say, doesn't alter the fact that I also behaved like a reprobate. No; from the moralist's point of view I was to blame. But I had no moral pretentions, and it was too much to expect that I should rebuke the young woman and preach her a sermon. You admit that, I dare say?'

The mathematician, frowning uncomfortably, gave a nod of assent.

'Amy was not only a reprobate, but a rascal. She betrayed me to the people at Upchurch, and, I am quite sure, meant from the first to do so. Imagine the outcry. I had committed a monstrous crime—had led astray an innocent maiden, had outraged hospitality—and so on. In Amy's case there were awkward results. Of course I must marry the girl forthwith. But of course I was determined to do no such thing. For the reasons I have explained, I let the storm break upon me. I had been a fool, to be sure, and couldn't help myself. No one would have believed my plea—no one would have allowed that the truth was an excuse. I was abused on all hands. And when, shortly after, my father made his will and died, doubtless he cut me off with my small annuity on this very account. My cousin Mary got a good deal of the money that would otherwise have been mine. The old man had been on rather better terms with me just before that; in a will that he destroyed I believe he had treated me handsomely.'

'Well, well,' said Micklethwaite, 'every one knows there are detestable women to be found. But you oughtn't to let this affect your view of women in general. What became of the girl?'

'I made her a small allowance for a year and a half. Then her child died, and the allowance ceased. I know nothing more of her. Probably she has inveigled some one into marriage.'

'Well, Barfoot,' said the other, rolling about in his chair, 'my opinion remains the same. You are in debt to some worthy woman to the extent of half your income. Be quick and find her. It will be better for you.'

'And do you suppose,' asked Everard, with a smile of indulgence, 'that I could marry on four hundred and fifty a year.'

'Heavens! Why not?'

'Quite impossible. A wife *might* be acceptable to me; but marriage with poverty—I know myself and the world too well for that.'

'Poverty!' screamed the mathematician. 'Four hundred and fifty pounds!'

'Grinding poverty—for married people.'

Micklethwaite burst into indignant eloquence, and Everard sat listening with the restrained smile on his lips.

# CHAPTER X - FIRST PRINCIPLES

Having allowed exactly a week to go by, Everard Barfoot made use of his cousin's permission, and called upon her at nine in the evening. Miss Barfoot's dinner-hour was seven o'clock; she and Rhoda, when alone, rarely sat for more than half an hour at table, and in this summer season they often went out together at sunset to enjoy a walk along the river. This evening they had returned only a few minutes before Everard's ring sounded at the door. Miss Barfoot (they were just entering the library) looked at her friend and smiled.

'I shouldn't wonder if that is the young man. Very flattering if he has come again so soon.'

The visitor was in mirthful humour, and met with a reception of corresponding tone. He remarked at once that Miss Nunn had a much pleasanter aspect than a week ago; her smile was ready and agreeable; she sat in a sociable attitude and answered a jesting triviality with indulgence.

'One of my reasons for coming to-day,' said Everard, 'was to tell you a remarkable story. It connects'—he addressed his cousin—'with our talk about the matrimonial disasters of those two friends of mine. Do you remember the name of Micklethwaite—a man who used to cram me with mathematics? I thought you would. He is on the point of marrying, and his engagement has lasted just seventeen years.'

'The wisest of your friends, I should say.'

'An excellent fellow. He is forty, and the lady the same. An astonishing case of constancy.'

'And how is it likely to turn out?'

'I can't predict, as the lady is unknown to me. But,' he added with facetious gravity, 'I think it likely that they are tolerably well acquainted with each other. Nothing but sheer poverty has kept them apart. Pathetic, don't you think? I have a theory that when an engagement has lasted ten years, with constancy on both sides, and poverty still prevents marriage, the State ought to make provision for a man in some way, according to his social standing. When one thinks of it, a whole socialistic system lies in that suggestion.'

'If,' remarked Rhoda, 'it were first provided that no marriage should take place until *after* a ten years' engagement.'

'Yes,' Barfoot assented, in his smoothest and most graceful tone. 'That completes the system. Unless you like to add that no engagement is permitted except between people who have passed a certain examination; equivalent, let us say, to that which confers a university degree.'

'Admirable. And no marriage, except where both, for the whole decennium, have earned their living by work that the State recognizes.'

'How would that affect Mr. Micklethwaite's betrothed?' asked Miss Barfoot.

'I believe she has supported herself all along by teaching.'

'Of course!' exclaimed the other impatiently. 'And more likely than not, with loathing of her occupation. The usual kind of drudgery, was it?'

'After all, there must be some one to teach children to read and write.'

'Yes; but people who are thoroughly well trained for the task, and who take a pleasure in it. This lady may be an exception; but I picture her as having spent a lifetime of uncongenial toil, longing miserably for the day when poor Mr. Micklethwaite was able to offer her a home. That's the ordinary teacher-woman, and we must abolish her altogether.'

'How are you to do that?' inquired Everard suavely. 'The average man labours that he may be able to marry, and the average woman certainly has the same end in view. Are female teachers to be vowed to celibacy?'

'Nothing of the kind. But girls are to be brought up to a calling in life, just as men are. It's because they have no calling that, when need comes, they all offer themselves as teachers. They undertake one of the most difficult and arduous pursuits as if it were as simple as washing up dishes. We can't earn money in any other way, but we can teach children! A man only becomes a schoolmaster or tutor when he has gone through laborious preparation—anything but wise or adequate, of course, but still conscious preparation; and only a very few men, comparatively, choose that line of work. Women must have just as wide a choice.'

'That's plausible, cousin Mary. But remember that when a man chooses his calling he chooses it for life. A girl cannot but remember that if she marries her calling at once changes. The old business is thrown aside—henceforth profitless.'

'No. Not henceforth profitless! There's the very point I insist upon. So far is it from profitless, that it has made her a wholly different woman from what she would otherwise have been. Instead of a moping, mawkish creature, with—in most instances—a very unhealthy mind, she is a complete human being. She stands on an equality with the man. He can't despise her as he now does.'

'Very good,' assented Everard, observing Miss Nunn's satisfied smile. 'I like that view very much. But what about the great number of girls who are claimed by domestic duties? Do you abandon them, with a helpless sigh, to be moping and mawkish and unhealthy?'

'In the first place, there needn't be a great number of unmarried women claimed by such duties. Most of those you are thinking of are not fulfilling a duty at all; they are only pottering about the house, because they have nothing better to do. And when the whole course of female education is altered; when girls are trained as a matter of course to some definite pursuit; then those who really are obliged to remain at home will do their duty there in quite a different spirit. Home work will be their serious business, instead of a disagreeable drudgery, or a way of getting through the time till marriage offers. I would have no girl, however wealthy her parent, grow up without a profession. There should be no such thing as a class of females vulgarized by the necessity of finding daily amusement.'

'Nor of males either, of course,' put in Everard, stroking his beard.

'Nor of males either, cousin Everard.'

'You thoroughly approve all this, Miss Nunn?'

'Oh yes. But I go further. I would have girls taught that marriage is a thing to be avoided rather than hoped for. I would teach them that for the majority of women marriage means disgrace.'

'Ah! Now do let me understand you. Why does it mean disgrace?'

'Because the majority of men are without sense of honour. To be bound to them in wedlock is shame and misery.'

Everard's eyelids drooped, and he did not speak for a moment.

'And you seriously think, Miss Nunn, that by persuading as many woman as possible to abstain from marriage you will improve the character of men?'

'I have no hope of sudden results, Mr. Barfoot. I should like to save as many as possible of the women now living from a life of dishonour; but the spirit of our work looks to the future. When *all* women, high and low alike, are trained to self-respect, then men will regard them in a different light, and marriage may be honourable to both.'

Again Everard was silent, and seemingly impressed.

'We'll go on with this discussion another time,' said Miss Barfoot, with cheerful interruption. 'Everard, do you know Somerset at all?'

'Never was in that part of England.'

'Miss Nunn is going to take her holiday at Cheddar and we have been looking over some photographs of that district taken by her brother.'

From the table she reached a scrapbook, and Everard turned it over with interest. The views were evidently made by an amateur, but in general had no serious faults. Cheddar cliffs were represented in several aspects.

'I had no idea the scenery was so fine. Cheddar cheese has quite overshadowed the hills in my imagination. This might be a bit of Cumberland, or of the Highlands.'

'It was my playground when I was a child,' said Rhoda.

'You were born at Cheddar?'

'No; at Axbridge, a little place not far off. But I had an uncle at Cheddar, a farmer, and very often stayed with him. My brother is farming there now.'

'Axbridge? Here is a view of the market-place. What a delightful old town!'

'One of the sleepiest spots in England, I should say. The railway goes through it now, but hasn't made the slightest difference. Nobody pulls down or builds; nobody opens a new shop; nobody thinks of extending his trade. A delicious place!'

'But surely you find no pleasure in that kind of thing, Miss Nunn?'

'Oh yes—at holiday time. I shall doze there for a fortnight, and forget all about the "so-called nineteenth century."'

'I can hardly believe it. There will be a disgraceful marriage at this beautiful old church, and the sight of it will exasperate you.'

Rhoda laughed gaily.

'Oh, it will be a marriage of the golden age! Perhaps I shall remember the bride when she was a little girl; and I shall give her a kiss, and pat her on the rosy cheek, and wish her joy. And the bridegroom will be such a good-hearted simpleton, unable to pronounce *f* and *s*. I don't mind that sort of marriage a bit!'

The listeners were both regarding her—Miss Barfoot with an affectionate smile, Everard with a puzzled, searching look, ending in amusement.

'I must run down into that country some day,' said the latter.

He did not stay much longer, but left only because he feared to burden the ladies with too much of his company.

Again a week passed, and the same evening found Barfoot approaching the house in Queen's Road. To his great annoyance he learnt that Miss Barfoot was not at home; she had dined, but afterwards had gone out. He did not venture to ask for Miss Nunn, and was moving disappointedly away, when Rhoda herself, returning from a walk, came up to the door. She offered her hand gravely, but with friendliness.

'Miss Barfoot, I am sorry to say, has gone to visit one of our girls who is ill. But I think she will very soon be back. Will you come in?'

'Gladly. I had so counted on an hour's talk.'

Rhoda led him to the drawing-room, excused herself for a few moments, and came back in her ordinary evening dress. Barfoot noticed that her hair was much more becomingly arranged than when he first saw her; so it had been on the last occasion, but for some reason its appearance attracted his eyes this evening. He scrutinized her, at discreet intervals, from head to foot. To Everard, nothing female was alien; woman, merely as woman, interested him profoundly. And this example of her sex had excited his curiosity in no common degree. His concern with her was purely intellectual; she had no sensual attraction for him, but he longed to see further into her mind, to probe the sincerity of the motives she professed, to understand her mechanism, her process of growth. Hitherto he had enjoyed no opportunity of studying this type. For his cousin was a very different person; by habit he regarded her as old, whereas Miss Nunn, in spite of her thirty years, could not possibly be considered past youth.

He enjoyed her air of equality; she sat down with him as a male acquaintance might have done, and he felt sure that her behaviour would be the same under any circumstances. He delighted in the frankness of her speech; it was doubtful whether she regarded any subject as improper for discussion between mature and serious people. Part cause of this, perhaps, was her calm consciousness that she had not a beautiful face. No, it was not beautiful; yet even at the first meeting it did not repel him. Studying her features, he saw how fine was their expression. The prominent forehead, with its little unevenness that meant brains; the straight eyebrows, strongly marked, with deep vertical furrows generally drawn between them; the chestnut-brown eyes, with long lashes; the high-bridged nose, thin and delicate; the intellectual lips, a protrusion of the lower one, though very slight, marking itself when he caught her profile; the big, strong chin; the shapely neck—why, after all, it was a kind of beauty. The head might have been sculptured with fine effect. And she had a well-built frame. He observed her strong wrists, with exquisite vein-tracings on the pure white. Probably her constitution was very sound; she had good teeth, and a healthy brownish complexion.

With reference to the sick girl whom Miss Barfoot was visiting, Everard began what was practically a resumption of their last talk.

'Have you a formal society, with rules and so on?'

'Oh no; nothing of the kind.'

'But you of course select the girls whom you instruct or employ?'

'Very carefully.'

'How I should like to see them all!—I mean,' he added, with a laugh, 'it would be so very interesting. The truth is, my sympathies are strongly with you in much of what you said the other day about women and marriage. We regard the matter from different points of view, but our ends are the same.'

Rhoda moved her eyebrows, and asked calmly,—

'Are you serious?'

'Perfectly. You are absorbed in your present work, that of strengthening women's minds and character; for the final issue of this you can't care much. But to me that is the practical interest. In my mind, you are working for the happiness of men.'

'Indeed?' escaped Rhoda's lips, which had curled in irony.

'Don't misunderstand me. I am not speaking cynically or trivially. The gain of women is also the gain of men. You are bitter against the average man for his low morality; but that fault, on the whole, is directly traceable to the ignobleness of women. Think, and you will grant me this.'

'I see what you mean. Men have themselves to thank for it.'

'Assuredly they have. I say that I am on your side. Our civilization in this point has always been absurdly defective. Men have kept women at a barbarous stage of development, and then complain that they are barbarous. In the same way society does its best to create a criminal class, and then rages against the criminals. But, you see, I am one of the men, and an impatient one too. The mass of women I see about me are so contemptible that, in my haste, I use unjust language. Put yourself in the man's place. Say that there are a million or so of us very intelligent and highly educated. Well, the women of corresponding mind number perhaps a few thousands. The vast majority of men must make a marriage that is doomed to be a dismal failure. We fall in love it is true; but do we really deceive ourselves about the future? A very young man may; why, we know of very young men who are so frantic as to marry girls of the working class—mere lumps of human flesh. But most of us know that our marriage is a *pis aller*. At first we are sad about it; then we grow cynical, and snap our fingers at moral obligation.'

'Making a bad case very much worse, instead of bravely bettering it.'

'Yes, but human nature is human nature. I am only urging to you the case of average intelligent men. As likely as not—so preposterous are our conventions—you have never heard it put honestly. I tell you the simple truth when I say that more than half these men regard their wives with active disgust. They will do anything to be relieved of the sight of them for as many hours as possible at a time. If circumstances allowed, wives would be abandoned very often indeed.'

Rhoda laughed.

'You regret that it isn't done?'

'I prefer to say that I approve it when it is done without disregard of common humanity. There's my friend Orchard. With him it was suicide or freedom from his hateful wife. Most happily, he was able to make provision for her and the children, and had strength to break his bonds. If he had left them to starve, I should have *understood* it, but couldn't have approved it. There are men who might follow his example, but prefer to put up with a life of torture. Well, they *do* prefer it, you see. I may think that they are foolishly weak, but I can only recognize that they make a choice between two forms of suffering. They have tender consciences; the thought of desertion is too painful to them. And in a great number of cases, mere considerations of money and the like keep a man bound. But conscience and habit—detestable habit—and fear of public opinion generally hold him.'

'All this is very interesting,' said Rhoda, with grave irony. 'By-the-bye, under the head of detestable habit you would put love of children?'

Barfoot hesitated.

'That's a motive I oughtn't to have left out. Yet I believe, for most men, it is represented by conscience. The love of children would not generally, in itself, be strong enough to outweigh matrimonial wretchedness. Many an intelligent and kind-hearted man has been driven from his wife notwithstanding thought for his children. He provides for them as well as he can—but, and even for their sakes, he must save himself.'

The expression of Rhoda's countenance suddenly changed. An extreme mobility of facial muscles was one of the things in her that held Everard's attention.

'There's something in your way of putting it that I don't like,' she said, with much frankness; 'but of course I agree with you in the facts. I am convinced that most marriages are hateful, from every point of view. But there will be no improvement until women have revolted against marriage, from a reasonable conviction of its hatefulness.'

'I wish you all success—most sincerely I do.'

He paused, looked about the room, and stroked his ear. Then, in a grave tone,—

'My own ideal of marriage involves perfect freedom on both sides. Of course it could only be realized where conditions are favourable; poverty and other wretched things force us so often to sin against our best beliefs. But there are plenty of people who might marry on these ideal terms. Perfect freedom, sanctioned by the sense of intelligent society, would abolish most of the evils we have in mind. But women must first be civilized; you are quite right in that.'

The door opened, and Miss Barfoot came in. She glanced from one to the other, and without speaking gave her hand to Everard.

'How is your patient?' he asked.

'A little better, I think. It is nothing dangerous. Here's a letter from your brother Tom. Perhaps I had better read it at once; there may be news you would like to hear.'

She sat down and broke the envelope. Whilst she was reading the letter to herself, Rhoda quietly left the room.

'Yes, there is news,' said Miss Barfoot presently, 'and of a disagreeable kind. A few weeks ago—before writing, that is—he was thrown off a horse and had a rib fractured.'

'Oh? How is he going on?'

'Getting right again, he says. And they are coming back to England; his wife's consumptive symptoms have disappeared, of course, and she is very impatient to leave Madeira. It is to be hoped she will allow poor Tom time to get his rib set. Probably that consideration doesn't weigh much with her. He says that he is writing to you by the same mail.'

'Poor old fellow!' said Everard, with feeling. 'Does he complain about his wife?'

'He never has done till now, but there's a sentence here that reads doubtfully. "Muriel," he says, "has been terribly upset about my accident. I can't persuade her that I didn't get thrown on purpose; yet I assure you I didn't.'"

Everard laughed.

'If old Tom becomes ironical, he must be hard driven. I have no great longing to meet Mrs. Thomas.'

'She's a silly and a vulgar woman. But I told him that in plain terms before he married. It says much for his good nature that he remains so friendly with me. Read the letter, Everard.'

He did so.

'H'm—very kind things about me. Good old Tom! Why don't I marry? Well, now, one would have thought that his own experience—'

Miss Barfoot began to talk about something else. Before very long Rhoda came back, and in the conversation that followed it was mentioned that she would leave for her holiday in two days.

'I have been reading about Cheddar,' exclaimed Everard, with animation. 'There's a flower grows among the rocks called the Cheddar pink. Do you know it?'

'Oh, very well,' Rhoda answered. 'I'll bring you some specimens.'

'Will you? That's very kind.'

'Bring *me* a genuine pound or two of the cheese, Rhoda,' requested Miss Barfoot gaily.

'I will. What they sell in the shops there is all sham, Mr. Barfoot—like so much else in this world.'

'I care nothing about the cheese. That's all very well for a matter-of-fact person like cousin Mary, but *I* have a strong vein of poetry; you must have noticed it?'

When they shook hands,—

'You will really bring me the flowers?' Everard said in a voice sensibly softened.

'I will make a note of it,' was the reassuring answer.

## CHAPTER XI - AT NATURE'S BIDDING

The sick girl whom Miss Barfoot had been to see was Monica Madden.

With strange suddenness, after several weeks of steady application to her work, in a cheerful spirit which at times rose to gaiety, Monica became dull, remiss, unhappy; then violent headaches attacked her, and one morning she declared herself unable to rise. Mildred Vesper went to Great Portland Street at the usual hour, and informed Miss Barfoot of her companion's illness. A doctor was summoned; to him it seemed probable that the girl was suffering from consequences of overstrain at her old employment; there was nervous collapse, hysteria, general disorder of the system. Had the patient any mental disquietude? Was trouble of any kind (the doctor smiled) weighing upon her? Miss Barfoot, unable to answer these questions, held private colloquy with Mildred; but the latter, though she pondered a good deal with corrugated brows, could furnish no information.

In a day or two Monica was removed to her sister's lodgings at Lavender Hill. Mrs. Conisbee managed to put a room at her disposal, and Virginia tended her. Thither Miss Barfoot went on the evening when Everard found her away; she and Virginia, talking together after being with the invalid for a quarter of an hour, agreed that there was considerable improvement, but felt a like uneasiness regarding Monica's state of mind.

'Do you think,' asked the visitor, 'that she regrets the step I persuaded her to take?'

'Oh, I *can't* think that! She has been so delighted with her progress each time I have seen her. No, I feel sure it's only the results of what she suffered at Walworth Road. In a very short time we shall have her at work again, and brighter than ever.'

Miss Barfoot was not convinced. After Everard's departure that evening she talked of the matter with Rhoda.

# CHAPTER XI - AT NATURE'S BIDDING

'I'm afraid,' said Miss Nunn, 'that Monica is rather a silly girl. She doesn't know her own mind. If this kind of thing is repeated, we had better send her back to the country.'

'To shop work again?'

'It might be better.'

'Oh, I don't like the thought of that.'

Rhoda had one of her fits of wrathful eloquence.

'Now could one have a better instance than this Madden family of the crime that middle-class parents commit when they allow their girls to go without rational training? Of course I know that Monica was only a little child when they were left orphans; but her sisters had already grown up into uselessness, and their example has been harmful to her all along. Her guardians dealt with her absurdly; they made her half a lady and half a shop-girl. I don't think she'll ever be good for much. And the elder ones will go on just keeping themselves alive; you can see that. They'll never start the school that there's so much talk of. That poor, helpless, foolish Virginia, alone there in her miserable lodging! How can we hope that any one will take her as a companion? And yet they are capitalists; eight hundred pounds between them. Think what capable women might do with eight hundred pounds.'

'I am really afraid to urge them to meddle with the investments.'

'Of course; so am I. One is afraid to do or propose anything. Virginia is starving, *must* be starving. Poor creature! I can never forget how her eyes shone when I put that joint of meat before her.'

'I do, do wish,' sighed Miss Barfoot, with a pained smile, 'that I knew some honest man who would be likely to fall in love with little Monica! In spite of you, my dear, I would devote myself to making the match. But there's no one.'

'Oh, I would help,' laughed Rhoda, not unkindly. 'She's fit for nothing else, I'm afraid. We mustn't look for any kind of heroism in Monica.'

Less than half an hour after Miss Barfoot had left the house at Lavender Hill, Mildred Vesper made a call there. It was about half-past nine; the invalid, after sitting up since midday, had gone to bed, but could not sleep. Summoned to the house-door, Virginia acquainted Miss Vesper with the state of affairs.

'I think you might see her for a few minutes.'

'I should like to, if you please, Miss Madden,' replied Mildred, who had a rather uneasy look.

She went upstairs and entered the bedroom, where a lamp was burning. At the sight of her friend Monica showed much satisfaction; they kissed each other affectionately.

'Good old girl! I had made up my mind to come back tomorrow, or at all events the day after. It's so frightfully dull here. Oh, and I wanted to know if anything—any letter—had come for me.'

'That's just why I came to see you to-night.'

Mildred took a letter from her pocket, and half averted her face as she handed it.

'It's nothing particular,' said Monica, putting it away under her pillow. 'Thank you, dear.'

But her cheeks had become hot, and she trembled.

'Monica—'

'Well?'

'You wouldn't care to tell me about—anything? You don't think it would make your mind easier?'

For a minute Monica lay back, gazing at the wall, then she looked round quickly, with a shamefaced laugh.

'It's very silly of me not to have told you long before this. But you're so sensible; I was afraid. I'll tell you everything. Not now, but as soon as I get to Rutland Street. I shall come to-morrow.'

'Do you think you can? You look dreadfully bad still.'

'I shan't get any better here,' replied the invalid in a whisper. 'Poor Virgie does depress me so. She doesn't understand that I can't bear to hear her repeating the kind of things she has heard from Miss Barfoot and Miss Nunn. She tries so hard to look forward hopefully—but I *know* she is miserable, and it makes me more miserable still. I oughtn't to have left you; I should have been all right in a day or two, with you to help me. You don't make-believe, Milly; it's all real and natural good spirits. It has done me good only to see your dear old face.'

'Oh, you're a flatterer. And do you really feel better?'

'Very much better. I shall go to sleep very soon.'

The visitor took her leave. When, a few minutes after, Monica had bidden good-night to her sister (requesting that the lamp might be left), she read what Mildred had brought.

> 'MY DEAREST MONICA,'—the missive began—'Why have you not written before this? I have been dreadfully uneasy ever since receiving your last letter. Your headache soon went away, I hope? Why haven't you made another appointment? It is all I can do to keep from breaking my promise and coming to ask about you. Write at

once, I implore you, my dearest. It's no use telling me that I must not use these words of affection; they come to my lips and to my pen irresistibly. You know so well that I love you with all my heart and soul; I can't address you like I did when we first corresponded. My darling! My dear, sweet, beautiful little girl—'

Four close pages of this, with scarce room at the end for 'E.W.' When she had gone through it, Monica turned her face upon the pillow and lay so for a long time. A clock in the house struck eleven; this roused her, and she slipped out of the bed to hide the letter in her dress-pocket. Not long after she was asleep.

The next day, on returning from her work and opening the sitting-room door, Mildred Vesper was greeted with a merry laugh. Monica had been here since three o'clock, and had made tea in readiness for her friend's arrival. She looked very white, but her eyes gleamed with pleasure, and she moved about the room as actively as before.

'Virgie came with me, but she wouldn't stay. She says she has a most important letter to write to Alice—about the school, of course. Oh, that school! I do wish they could make up their minds. I've told them they may have all my money, if they like.'

'Have you? I should like the sensation of offering hundreds of pounds to some one. It must give a strange feeling of dignity and importance.'

'Oh, only *two* hundred! A wretched little sum.'

'You are a person of large ideas, as I have often told you. Where did you get them, I wonder?'

'Don't put on that face! It's the one I like least of all your many faces. It's suspicious.'

Mildred went to take off her things, and was quickly at the tea-table. She had a somewhat graver look than usual, and chose rather to listen than talk.

Not long after tea, when there had been a long and unnatural silence, Mildred making pretence of absorption in a 'Treasury' and her companion standing at the window, whence she threw back furtive glances, the thunder of a postman's knock downstairs caused both of them to start, and look at each other in a conscience-stricken way.

'That may be for me,' said Monica, stepping to the door. 'I'll go and look.'

Her conjecture was right. Another letter from Widdowson, still more alarmed and vehement than the last. She read it rapidly on the staircase, and entered the room with sheet and envelope squeezed together in her hand.

'I'm going to tell you all about this, Milly.'

The other nodded and assumed an attitude of sober attention. In relating her story, Monica moved hither and thither; now playing with objects on the mantlepiece, now standing in the middle of the floor, hands locked nervously behind her. Throughout, her manner was that of defence; she seemed doubtful of herself, and anxious to represent the case as favourably as possible; not for a moment had her voice the ring of courageous passion, nor the softness of tender feeling. The narrative hung together but awkwardly, and in truth gave a very indistinct notion of how she had comported herself at the various stages of the irregular courtship. Her behaviour had been marked by far more delicacy and scruple than she succeeded in representing. Painfully conscious of this, she exclaimed at length,—

'I see your opinion of me has suffered. You don't like this story. You wonder how I could do such things.'

'Well, dear, I certainly wonder how you could begin,' Mildred made answer, with her natural directness, but gently. 'Afterwards, of course, it was different. When you had once got to be sure that he was a gentleman—'

'I was sure of that so soon,' exclaimed Monica, her cheeks still red. 'You will understand it much better when you have seen him.'

'You wish me to?'

'I am going to write now, and say that I will marry him.'

They looked long at each other.

'You are—really?'

'Yes. I made up my mind last night.'

'But, Monica—you mustn't mind my speaking plainly—I don't think you love him.'

'Yes, I love him well enough to feel that I am doing right in marrying him.' She sat down by the table, and propped her head on her hand. 'He loves me; I can't doubt that. If you could read his letters, you would see how strong his feeling is.'

She shook with the cold induced by excitement; her voice was at moments all but choked.

'But, putting love aside,' went on the other, very gravely, 'what do you really know of Mr. Widdowson? Nothing whatever but what he has told you himself. Of course you will let your friends make inquiries for you?'

'Yes. I shall tell my sisters, and no doubt they will go to Miss Nunn at once. I don't want to do anything rash. But it will be all right—I mean, he has told me the truth about everything. You would be sure of that if you knew him.'

Mildred, with hands before her on the table, made the tips of her fingers meet. Her lips were drawn in; her eyes seemed looking for something minute on the cloth.

'You know,' she said at length, 'I suspected what was going on. I couldn't help.'

'Of course you couldn't.'

'Naturally I thought it was some one whose acquaintance you had made at the shop.'

'How *could* I think of marrying any one of that kind?'

'I should have been grieved.'

'You may believe me, Milly; Mr. Widdowson is a man you will respect and like as soon as you know him. He couldn't have behaved to me with more delicacy. Not a word from him, spoken or written, has ever pained me—except that he tells me he suffers so dreadfully, and of course I can't hear that without pain.'

'To respect, and even to like, a man, isn't at all the same as loving him.'

'I said *you* would respect and like him,' exclaimed Monica, with humorous impatience. 'I don't want *you* to love him.'

Mildred laughed, with constraint.

'I never loved any one yet, dear, and it's very unlikely I ever shall. But I think I know the signs of the feeling.'

Monica came behind her, and leaned upon her shoulder.

'He loves me so much that he has made me think I *must* marry him. And I am glad of it. I'm not like you, Milly; I can't be contented with this life. Miss Barfoot and Miss Nunn are very sensible and good people, and I admire them very much, but I *can't* go their way. It seems to me that it would be dreadful, dreadful, to live one's life alone. Don't turn round and snap at me; I want to tell you the truth whilst you can't see me. Whenever I think of Alice and Virginia, I am frightened; I had rather, oh, far rather, kill myself than live such a life at their age. You can't imagine how miserable they are, really. And I have the same nature as theirs, you know. Compared with you and Miss Haven I'm very weak and childish.'

After drumming on the table for a moment, with wrinkled brows, Mildred made grave response.

'You must let *me* tell the truth as well. I think you're going to marry with altogether wrong ideas. I think you'll do an injustice to Mr. Widdowson. You will marry him for a comfortable home—that's what it amounts to. And you'll repent it bitterly some day—you'll repent.'

Monica raised herself and stood apart.

'For one thing,' pursued Mildred, with nervous earnestness, 'he's too old. Your habits and his won't suit.'

'He has assured me that I shall live exactly the kind of life I please. And that will be what *he* pleases. I feel his kindness to me very much, and I shall do my utmost to repay him.'

'That's a very nice spirit; but I believe married life is no easy thing even when the people are well matched. I have heard the most dreadful stories of quarrelling and all sorts of unhappiness between people I thought safe from any such dangers. You *may* be fortunate; I only say that the chances are very much against it, marrying from such motives as you confess.'

Monica drew herself up.

'I haven't confessed any motive to be ashamed of, Milly.'

'You say you have decided to marry now because you are afraid of never having another chance.'

'No; that's turning it very unkindly. I only said that *after* I had told you that I did love him. And I do love him. He has made me love him.'

'Then I have no right to say any more. I can only wish you happiness.'

Mildred heaved a sigh, and pretended to give her attention to Maunder.

After waiting irresolutely for some minutes, Monica looked for notepaper, and took it, together with her inkstand, into the bedroom. She was absent half an hour. On her return there was a stamped letter in her hand.

'It is going, Milly.'

'Very well, dear. I have nothing more to say.'

'You give me up for lost. We shall see.'

It was spoken light-heartedly. Again she left the room, put on her out-of-door things, and went to post the letter. By this time she began to feel the results of exertion and excitement; headache and tremulous failing of her strength obliged her to go to bed almost as soon as she returned. Mildred waited upon her with undiminished kindness.

'It's all right,' Monica murmured, as her head sank on the pillow. 'I feel so relieved and so glad—so happy—now I have done it.'

'Good-night, dear,' replied the other, with a kiss, and went back to her semblance of reading.

Two days later Monica called unexpectedly at Mrs. Conisbee's. Being told by that worthy woman that Miss Madden was at home, she ran upstairs and tapped at the door. Virginia's voice inquired hurriedly who was there, and on Monica's announcing herself there followed a startled exclamation.

'Just a minute, my love! Only a minute.'

When the door opened Monica was surprised by a disorder in her sister's appearance. Virginia had flushed cheeks, curiously vague eyes, and hair ruffled as if she had just risen from a nap. She began to talk in a hurried, disconnected way, trying to explain that she had not been quite well, and was not yet properly dressed.

'What a strange smell!' Monica exclaimed, looking about the room. 'It's like brandy.'

'You notice it? I have—I was obliged to get—to ask Mrs. Conisbee for—I don't want to alarm you, dear, but I felt rather faint. Indeed, I thought I should have a fainting fit. I was obliged to call Mrs. Conisbee—But don't think anything about it. It's all over. The weather is very trying—'

She laughed nervously and began to pat Monica's hand. The girl was not quite satisfied, and pressed many questions, but in the end she accepted Virginia's assurances that nothing serious had happened. Then her own business occupied her; she sat down, and said with a smile,—

'I have brought you astonishing news. If you didn't faint before you'll be very likely to do so now.'

Her sister exhibited fresh agitation, and begged not to be kept in suspense.

'My nerves are in a shocking state to-day. It *must* be the weather. What *can* you have to tell me, Monica?'

'I think I shan't need to go on with typewriting.'

'Why? What are you going to do, child?' the other asked sharply.

'Virgie—I am going to be married.'

The shock was a severe one. Virginia's hands fell, her eyes started, her mouth opened; she became the colour of clay, even her lips losing for the moment all their colour.

'Married?' she at length gasped. 'Who—who is it?'

'Some one you have never heard of. His name is Mr. Edmund Widdowson. He is very well off, and has a house at Herne Hill.'

'A private gentleman?'

'Yes. He used to be in business, but is retired. Now, I am not going to tell you much more about him until you have made his acquaintance. Don't ask a lot of questions. You are to come with me this after-afternoon to his house. He lives alone, but a relative of his, his sister-in-law, is going to be with him to meet us.'

'Oh, but it's so sudden! I can't go to pay a call like that at a moment's notice. Impossible, darling! What *does* it all mean? You are going to be married, Monica? I can't understand it. I can't realize it. Who is this gentleman? How long—'

'No; you won't get me to tell you more than I have done, till you have seen him.'

'But what *have* you told me? I couldn't grasp it. I am quite confused. Mr.—what was the name?'

It took half an hour to familiarize Virginia with the simple fact. When she was convinced of its truth, a paroxysm of delight appeared in her. She laughed, uttered cries of joy, even clapped her hands.

'Monica to be married! A private gentleman—a large fortune! My darling, how shall I ever believe it? Yet I felt so sure that the day would come. What *will* Alice say? And Rhoda Nunn? Have you—have you ventured to tell her?'

'No, that I haven't. I want you to do that You shall go and see them to-morrow, as it's Sunday.'

'Oh, the delight! Alice won't be able to contain herself. We always said the day would come.'

'You won't have any more anxieties, Virgie. You can take the school or not, as you like. Mr. Widdowson—'

'Oh, my dear,' interposed Virginia, with sudden dignity, 'we shall certainly open the school. We have made up our minds; that is to be our life's work. It is far, far more than a mere means of subsistence. But perhaps we shall not need to hurry. Everything can be matured at our leisure. If you would only just tell me, darling, when you were first introduced?'

Monica laughed gaily, and refused to explain. It was time for Virginia to make herself ready, and here arose a new perturbation; what had she suitable for wear under such circumstances? Monica had decked herself a little, and helped the other to make the best of her narrow resources. At four o'clock they set out.

# CHAPTER XII - WEDDINGS

When they reached the house at Herne Hill the sisters were both in a state of nervous tremor. Monica had only the vaguest idea of the kind of person Mrs. Luke Widdowson would prove to be, and Virginia seemed to herself to be walking in a dream.

'Have you been here often?' whispered the latter, as soon as they came in view of the place. Its aspect delighted her, but the conflict of her emotions was so disturbing that she had to pause and seek the support of her sister's arm.

'I've never been inside,' Monica answered indistinctly. 'Come; we shall be unpunctual.'

'I do wish you would tell me, dear—'

'I can't talk, Virgie. Try and keep quiet, and behave as if it were all quite natural.'

This was altogether beyond Virginia's power. It happened most luckily, though greatly to Widdowson's annoyance, that the sister-in-law, Mrs. Luke Widdowson, arrived nearly half an hour later than the time she had appointed. Led by the servant into a comfortable drawing-room, the visitors were received by the master of the house alone; with a grim smile, the result of his embarrassment, with profuse apologies and a courtesy altogether excessive, Widdowson did his best to put them at their ease—of course with small result. The sisters side by side on a settee at one end of the room, and the host seated far away from them, they talked with scarcely any understanding of what was said on either side—the weather and the vastness of London serving as topics—until of a sudden the door was thrown open, and there appeared a person of such imposing presence that Virginia gave a start and Monica gazed in painful fascination. Mrs. Luke was a tall and portly woman in the prime of life, with rather a high colour; her features were handsome, but without much refinement, their expression a condescending good-humour. Her mourning garb, if mourning it could be called, represented an extreme of the prevailing fashion; its glint and rustle inspired awe in the female observer. A moment ago the drawing-room had seemed empty; Mrs. Luke, in her sole person, filled and illumined it.

Widdowson addressed this resplendent personage by her Christian name, his familiarity exciting in Monica an irrational surprise. He presented the sisters to her, and Mrs. Luke, bowing grandly at a distance, drew from her bosom a gold-rimmed *pince-nez*, through which she scrutinized Monica. The smile which followed might have been interpreted in several senses; Widdowson, alone capable of remarking it, answered with a look of severe dignity.

Mrs. Luke had no thought of apologizing for the lateness of her arrival, and it was evident that she did not intend to stay long. Her purpose seemed to be to make the occasion as informal as possible.

'Do you, by chance, know the Hodgson Bulls?' she asked of her relative, interrupting him in the nervous commonplaces with which he was endeavouring to smooth the way to a general conversation. She had the accent of cultivation, but spoke rather imperiously.

'I never heard of them,' was the cold reply.

'No? They live somewhere about here. I have to make a call on them. I suppose my coachman will find the place.'

There was an awkward silence. Widdowson was about to say something to Monica, when Mrs. Luke, who had again closely observed the girl through the glasses, interposed in a gentle tone.

'Do you like this neighbourhood, Miss Madden?'

Monica gave the expected answer, her voice sounding very weak and timid by comparison. And so, for some ten minutes, an appearance of dialogue was sustained. Mrs. Luke, though still condescending, evinced a desire to be agreeable; she smiled and nodded in reply to the girl's remarks, and occasionally addressed Virginia with careful civility, conveying the impression, perhaps involuntarily, that she commiserated the shy and shabbily-dressed person. Tea was brought in, and after pretending to take a cup, she rose for departure.

'Perhaps you will come and see me some day, Miss Madden,' fell from her with unanticipated graciousness, as she stepped forward to the girl and offered her hand. 'Edmund must bring you—at some quiet time when we can talk. Very glad to have met you—very glad indeed.'

And the personage was gone; they heard her carriage roll away from beneath the window. All three drew a breath of relief, and Widdowson, suddenly quite another man, took a place near to Virginia, with whom in a few minutes he was conversing in the friendliest way. Virginia, experiencing a like relief, also became herself; she found courage to ask needful questions, which in every case were satisfactorily met. Of Mrs. Luke there was no word, but when they had taken their leave—the visit lasted altogether some two hours—Monica and her sister discussed that great lady with the utmost freedom. They agreed that she was personally detestable.

'But very rich, my dear,' said Virginia in a murmuring voice. 'You can see that. I have met such people before; they have a manner—oh! Of course Mr. Widdowson will take you to call upon her.'

'When nobody else is likely to be there; that's what she meant,' remarked Monica coldly.

'Never mind, my love. You don't wish for grand society. I am very glad to tell you that Edmund impresses me very favourably. He is reserved, but that is no fault. Oh, we must write to Alice at once! Her surprise! Her delight!'

When, on the next day, Monica met her betrothed in Regent's Park—she still lived with Mildred Vesper, but no longer went to Great Portland Street—their talk was naturally of Mrs. Luke. Widdowson speedily led to the topic.

'I had told you,' he said, with careful accent, 'that I see very little of her. I can't say that I like her, but she is a very difficult person to understand, and I fancy she often gives offence when she doesn't at all mean it. Still, I hope you were not—displeased?'

Monica avoided a direct answer.

'Shall you take me to see her?' were her words.

'If you will go, dear. And I have no doubt she will be present at our wedding. Unfortunately, she's my only relative; or the only one I know anything about. After our marriage I don't think we shall see much of her—'

'No, I dare say not,' was Monica's remark. And thereupon they turned to pleasanter themes.

That morning Widdowson had received from his sister-in-law a scribbled post-card, asking him to call upon Mrs. Luke early the day that followed. Of course this meant that the lady was desirous of further talk concerning Miss Madden. Unwillingly, but as a matter of duty, he kept the appointment. It was at eleven in the morning, and, when admitted to the flat in Victoria Street which was his relative's abode, he had to wait a quarter of an hour for the lady's appearance.

Luxurious fashion, as might have been expected, distinguished Mrs. Luke's drawing-room. Costly and beautiful things superabounded; perfume soothed the air. Only since her bereavement had Mrs. Widdowson been able to indulge this taste for modern exuberance in domestic adornment. The deceased Luke was a plain man of business, who clung to the fashions which had been familiar to him in his youth; his second wife found a suburban house already furnished, and her influence with him could not prevail to banish the horrors amid which he chose to live: chairs in maroon rep, Brussels carpets of red roses on a green ground, horse-hair sofas of the most uncomfortable shape ever designed, antimacassars everywhere, chimney ornaments of cut glass trembling in sympathy with the kindred chandeliers. She belonged to an obscure branch of a house that culminated in an obscure baronetcy; penniless and ambitious, she had to thank her imposing physique for rescue at a perilous age, and though despising Mr. Luke Widdowson for his plebeian tastes, she shrewdly retained the good-will of a husband who seemed no candidate for length of years. The money-maker died much sooner than she could reasonably have hoped, and left her an income of four thousand pounds. Thereupon began for Mrs. Luke a life of feverish aspiration. The baronetcy to which she was akin had inspired her, even from childhood, with an aristocratic ideal; a handsome widow of only eight-and-thirty, she resolved that her wealth should pave the way for her to a titled alliance. Her acquaintance lay among City people, but with the opportunities of freedom it was soon extended to the sphere of what is known as smart society; her flat in Victoria Street attracted a heterogeneous cluster of pleasure-seekers and fortune-hunters, among them one or two vagrant members of the younger aristocracy. She lived at the utmost pace compatible with technical virtue. When, as shortly happened, it became evident that her income was not large enough for her serious purpose, she took counsel with an old friend great in finance, and thenceforth the excitement of the gambler gave a new zest to her turbid existence. Like most of her female associates, she had free recourse to the bottle; but for such stimulus the life of a smart woman would be physically impossible. And Mrs. Luke enjoyed life, enjoyed it vastly. The goal of her ambition, if all went well in the City, was quite within reasonable hope. She foretasted the day when a vulgar prefix would no longer attach to her name, and when the journals of society would reflect her rising effulgence.

Widdowson was growing impatient, when his relative at length appeared. She threw herself into a deep chair, crossed her legs, and gazed at him mockingly.

'Well, it isn't quite so bad as I feared, Edmund.'

'What do you mean?'

'Oh, she's a decent enough little girl, I can see. But you're a silly fellow for all that. You couldn't have deceived me, you know. If there'd been anything—you understand?—I should have spotted it at once.'

'I don't relish this kind of talk,' observed Widdowson acidly. 'In plain English, you supposed I was going to marry some one about whom I couldn't confess the truth.'

'Of course I did. Now come; tell me how you got to know her.'

The man moved uneasily, but in the end related the whole story. Mrs. Luke kept nodding, with an amused air.

'Yes, yes; she managed it capitally. Clever little witch. Fetching eyes she has.'

'If you sent for me to make insulting remarks—'

'Bosh! I'll come to the wedding gaily. But you're a silly fellow. Now, why didn't you come and ask me to find you a wife? Why, I know two or three girls of really good family who would have jumped, simply jumped, at a man with your money. Pretty girls too. But you always were so horribly unpractical. Don't you know, my dear boy, that there are heaps of ladies, real ladies, waiting the first decent man who offers them five or six hundred a year? Why haven't you used the opportunities that you knew I could put in your way?'

Widdowson rose from his seat and stood stiffly.

'I see you don't understand me in the least. I am going to marry because, for the first time in my life, I have met the woman whom I can respect and love.'

'That's very nice and proper. But why shouldn't you respect and love a girl who belongs to good society?'

'Miss Madden is a lady,' he replied indignantly.

'Oh—yes—to be sure,' hummed the other, letting her head roll back. 'Well, bring her here some day when we can lunch quietly together. I see it's no use. You're not a sharp man, Edmund.'

'Do you seriously tell me,' asked Widdowson, with grave curiosity, 'that there are ladies in good society who would have married me just because I have a few hundreds a year?'

'My dear boy, I would get together a round dozen in two or three days. Girls who would make good, faithful wives, in mere gratitude to the man who saved them from—horrors.'

'Excuse me if I say that I don't believe it.'

Mrs. Luke laughed merrily, and the conversation went on in this strain for another ten minutes. At the end, Mrs. Luke made herself very agreeable, praised Monica for her sweet face and gentle manners, and so dismissed the solemn man with a renewed promise to countenance the marriage by her gracious presence.

When Rhoda Nunn returned from her holiday it wanted but a week to Monica's wedding, so speedily had everything been determined and arranged. Miss Barfoot, having learnt from Virginia all that was to be known concerning Mr. Widdowson, felt able to hope for the best; a grave husband, of mature years, and with means more than sufficient, seemed, to the eye of experience, no unsuitable match for a girl such as Monica. This view of the situation caused Rhoda to smile with contemptuous tolerance.

'And yet,' she remarked, 'I have heard you speak severely of such marriages.'

'It isn't the ideal wedlock,' replied Miss Barfoot. 'But so much in life is compromise. After all, she may regard him more affectionally than we imagine.'

'No doubt she has weighed advantages. If the prospects you offered her had proved more to her taste she would have dismissed this elderly admirer. His fate has been decided during the last few weeks. It's probable that the invitation to your Wednesday evenings gave her a hope of meeting young men.'

'I see no harm if it did,' said Miss Barfoot, smiling. 'But Miss Vesper would very soon undeceive her on that point.'

'I hardly thought of her as a girl likely to make chance friendships with men in highways and by-ways.'

'No more did I; and that makes all the more content with what has come about. She ran a terrible risk, poor child. You see, Rhoda, nature is too strong for us.'

Rhoda threw her head back.

'And the delight of her sister! It is really pathetic. The mere fact that Monica is to be married blinds the poor woman to every possibility of misfortune.' In the course of the same conversation, Rhoda remarked thoughtfully,—

'It strikes me that Mr. Widdowson must be of a confiding nature. I don't think men in general, at all events those with money, care to propose marriage to girls they encounter by the way.'

'I suppose he saw that the case was exceptional.'

'How was he to see that?'

'You are severe. Her shop training accounts for much. The elder sisters could never have found a husband in this way. The revelation must have shocked them at first.'

Rhoda dismissed the subject lightly, and henceforth showed only the faintest interest in Monica's concerns.

# CHAPTER XII - WEDDINGS

Monica meanwhile rejoiced in her liberation from the work and philosophic severities of Great Portland Street. She saw Widdowson somewhere or other every day, and heard him discourse on the life that was before them, herself for the most part keeping silence. Together they called upon Mrs. Luke, and had luncheon with her. Monica was not displeased with her reception, and began secretly to hope that more than a glimpse of that gorgeous world might some day be vouchsafed to her.

Apart from her future husband, Monica was in a sportive mood, with occasional fits of exhilaration which seemed rather unnatural. She had declared to Mildred her intention of inviting Miss Nunn to the wedding, and her mind was evidently set on carrying out this joke, as she regarded it. When the desire was intimated by letter, Rhoda replied with a civil refusal: she would be altogether out of place at such a ceremony, but hoped that Monica would accept her heartiest good wishes. Virginia was then dispatched to Queen's Road, and appealed so movingly that the prophetess at length yielded. On hearing this Monica danced with delight, and her companion in Rutland Street could not help sharing her merriment.

The ceremony was performed at a church at Herne Hill. By an odd arrangement—like everything else in the story of this pair, a result of social and personal embarrassments—Monica's belongings, including her apparel for the day, were previously dispatched to the bridegroom's house, whither, in company with Virginia, the bride went early in the morning. It was one of the quietest of weddings, but all ordinary formalities were complied with, Widdowson having no independent views on the subject. Present were Virginia (to give away the bride), Miss Vesper (who looked decidedly odd in a pretty dress given her by Monica), Rhoda Nunn (who appeared to advantage in a costume of quite unexpected appropriateness), Mrs. Widdowson (an imposing figure, evidently feeling that she had got into strange society), and, as friend of the bridegroom, one Mr. Newdick, a musty and nervous City clerk. Depression was manifest on every countenance, not excepting Widdowson's; the man had such a stern, gloomy look, and held himself with so much awkwardness, that he might have been imagined to stand here on compulsion. For an hour before going to the church, Monica cried and seemed unutterably doleful; she had not slept for two nights; her face was ghastly. Virginia's gladness gave way just before the company assembled, and she too shed many tears.

There was a breakfast, more dismal fooling than even this species of fooling is wont to be. Mr. Newdick, trembling and bloodless, proposed Monica's health; Widdowson, stern and dark as ever, gloomily responded; and then, *that* was happily over. By one o'clock the gathering began to disperse. Monica drew Rhoda Nunn aside.

'It was very kind of you to come,' she whispered, with half a sob. 'It all seems very silly, and I'm sure you have wished yourself away a hundred times. I am really, seriously, grateful to you.'

Rhoda put a hand on each side of the girl's face, and kissed her, but without saying a word; and thereupon left the house. Mildred Vesper, after changing her dress in the room used by Monica, as she had done on arriving, went off by train to her duties in Great Portland Street. Virginia alone remained to see the married couple start for their honeymoon. They were going into Cornwall, and on the return journey would manage to see Miss Madden at her Somerset retreat. For the present, Virginia was to live on at Mrs. Conisbee's, but not in the old way; henceforth she would have proper attendance, and modify her vegetarian diet—at the express bidding of the doctor, as she explained to her landlady.

Though that very evening Everard Barfoot made a call upon his friends in Chelsea, the first since Rhoda's return from Cheddar, he heard nothing of the event that marked the day. But Miss Nunn appeared to him unlike herself; she was absent, had little to say, and looked, what he had never yet known her, oppressed by low spirits. For some reason or other Miss Barfoot left the room.

'You are thinking with regret of your old home,' Everard remarked, taking a seat nearer to Miss Nunn.'

'No. Why should you fancy that?'

'Only because you seem rather sad.'

'One is sometimes.'

'I like to see you with that look. May I remind you that you promised me some flowers from Cheddar?'

'Oh, so I did,' exclaimed the other in a tone of natural recollection. 'I have brought them, scientifically pressed between blotting-paper. I'll fetch them.'

When she returned it was together with Miss Barfoot, and the conversation became livelier.

A day or two after this Everard left town, and was away for three weeks, part of the time in Ireland.

'I left London for a while,' he wrote from Killarney to his cousin, 'partly because I was afraid I had begun to bore you and Miss Nunn. Don't you regret giving me permission to call upon you? The fact is, I can't live without intelligent female society; talking with women, as I talk with you two, is one of my chief enjoyments. I hope you won't get tired of my visits; in fact, they are all but a necessity to me, as I have discovered since coming away. But it was fair that you should have a rest.'

'Don't be afraid,' Miss Barfoot replied to this part of his letter. 'We are not at all weary of your conversation. The truth is, I like it much better than in the old days. You seem to me to have a healthier mind, and I am quite sure that the society of intelligent women (we affect no foolish self-depreciation, Miss Nunn and I) is a good thing for you. Come back to us as soon as you like; I shall welcome you.'

It happened that his return to England was almost simultaneous with the arrival from Madeira of Mr. and Mrs. Thomas Barfoot. Everard at once went to see his brother, who for the present was staying at Torquay. Ill-health dictated his choice of residence; Thomas was still suffering from the results of his accident; his wife had left him at a hotel, and was visiting relatives in different parts of England. The brothers exhibited much affectionate feeling after their long separation; they spent a week together, and planned for another meeting when Mrs. Thomas should have returned to her husband.

An engagement called Everard back to town. He was to be present at the wedding of his friend Micklethwaite, now actually on the point of taking place. The mathematician had found a suitable house, very small and of very low rental, out at South Tottenham, and thither was transferred the furniture which had been in his bride's possession since the death of her parents; Micklethwaite bought only a few new things. By discreet inquiry, Barfoot had discovered that 'Fanny,' though musically inclined, would not possess a piano, her old instrument being quite worn out and not worth the cost of conveyance; thus it came to pass that, a day or two before the wedding, Micklethwaite was astonished by the arrival of an instrument of the Cottage species, mysteriously addressed to a person not yet in existence, Mrs. Micklethwaite.

'You scoundrel!' he cried, when, on the next day, Barfoot presented himself at the house. 'This is *your* doing. What the deuce do you mean? A man who complains of poverty! Well, it's the greatest kindness I ever received, that's all. Fanny will be devoted to you. With music in the house, our blind sister will lead quite a different life. Confound it! I want to begin crying. Why, man, I'm not accustomed to receive presents, even as a proxy; I haven't had one since I was a schoolboy.'

'That's an audacious statement. When you told me that Miss Wheatley never allowed your birthday to pass without sending something.'

'Oh, Fanny! But I have never thought of Fanny as a separate person. Upon my word, now I think of it, I never have. Fanny and I have been one for ages.'

That evening the sisters arrived from their country home. Micklethwaite gave up the house to them, and went to a lodging.

It was with no little curiosity that, on the appointed morning, Barfoot repaired to South Tottenham. He had seen a photograph of Miss Wheatley, but it dated from seventeen years ago. Standing in her presence, he was moved with compassion, and with another feeling more rarely excited in him by a women's face, that of reverential tenderness. Impossible to recognize in this countenance the features known to him from the portrait. At three-and-twenty she had possessed a sweet, simple comeliness on which any man's eye would have rested with pleasure; at forty she was wrinkled, hollow-cheeked, sallow, indelible weariness stamped upon her brow and lips. She looked much older than Mary Barfoot, though they were just of an age. And all this for want of a little money. The life of a pure, gentle, tender-hearted woman worn away in hopeless longing and in hard struggle for daily bread. As she took his hand and thanked him with an exquisite modesty for the present she had received, Everard felt a lump rise in his throat. He was ashamed to notice that the years had dealt so unkindly with her; fixing his look upon her eyes, he gladdened at the gladness which shone in them, at the soft light which they could still shed forth.

Micklethwaite was probably unconscious of the poor woman's faded appearance. He had seen her from time to time, and always with the love which idealizes. In his own pathetic phrase, she was simply a part of himself; he no more thought of criticizing her features than of standing before the glass to mark and comment upon his own. It was enough to glance at him as he took his place beside her, the proudest and happiest of men. A miracle had been wrought for him; kind fate, in giving her to his arms, had blotted out those long years of sorrow, and to-day Fanny was the betrothed of his youth, beautiful in his sight as when first he looked upon her.

Her sister, younger by five years, had more regular lineaments, but she too was worn with suffering, and her sightless eyes made it more distressing to contemplate her. She spoke cheerfully, however, and laughed with joy in Fanny's happiness. Barfoot pressed both her hands with the friendliest warmth.

One vehicle conveyed them all to the church, and in half an hour the lady to whom the piano was addressed had come into being. The simplest of transformations; no bridal gown, no veil, no wreath; only the gold ring for symbol of union. And it might have happened nigh a score of years ago; nigh a score of years lost from the span of human life—all for want of a little money.

'I will say good-bye to you here,' muttered Everard to his friend at the church door.

The married man gripped him by the arm.

'You will do nothing of the kind.—Fanny, he wants to be off at once!—You won't go until you have heard my wife play something on that blessed instrument.'

So all entered a cab again and drove back to the house. A servant who had come with Fanny from the country, a girl of fifteen, opened the door to them, smiling and curtseying. And all sat together in happy talk, the blind woman gayest among them; she wished to have the clergyman described to her, and the appearance of the church. Then Mrs. Micklethwaite placed herself at the piano, and played simple, old-fashioned music, neither well nor badly, but to the infinite delight of two of her hearers.

'Mr. Barfoot,' said the sister at length, 'I have known your name for a long time, but I little thought to meet you on such a day as this, and to owe you such endless thanks. So long as I can have music I forget that I can't see.

'Barfoot is the finest fellow on earth,' exclaimed Micklethwaite. 'At least, he would be if he understood Trilinear Co-ordinates.'

'Are *you* strong in mathematics, Mrs. Micklethwaite?' asked Everard.

'I? Oh dear, no! I never got much past the Rule of Three. But Tom has forgiven me that long ago.'

'I don't despair of getting you into plane trigonometry, Fanny. We will gossip about sines and co-sines before we die.'

It was said half-seriously, and Everard could not but burst into laughter.

He sat down with them to their plain midday meal, and early in the afternoon took his leave. He had no inclination to go home, if the empty flat could be dignified with such a name. After reading the papers at his club, he walked aimlessly about the streets until it was time to return to the same place for dinner. Then he sat with a cigar, dreaming, and at half-past eight went to the Royal Oak Station, and journeyed to Chelsea.

# CHAPTER XIII - DISCORD OF LEADERS

A disappointment awaited him. Miss Barfoot was not well enough to see any one. Had she been suffering long? he inquired. No; it was only this evening; she had not dined, and was gone to her room. Miss Nunn could not receive him.

He went home, and wrote to his cousin.

The next morning he came upon a passage in the newspaper which seemed to suggest a cause for Miss Barfoot's indisposition. It was the report of an inquest. A girl named Bella Royston had poisoned herself. She was living alone, without occupation, and received visits only from one lady. This lady, her name Miss Barfoot, had been supplying her with money, and had just found her a situation in a house of business; but the girl appeared to have gone through troubles which had so disturbed her mind that she could not make the effort required of her. She left a few lines addressed to her benefactress, just saying that she chose death rather than the struggle to recover her position.

It was Saturday. He decided to call in the afternoon and see whether Mary had recovered.

Again a disappointment. Miss Barfoot was better, and had been away since breakfast; Miss Nunn was also absent.

Everard sauntered about the neighbourhood, and presently found himself in the gardens of Chelsea Hospital. It was a warm afternoon, and so still that he heard the fall of yellow leaves as he walked hither and thither along the alleys. His failure to obtain an interview with Miss Nunn annoyed him; but for her presence in the house he would not have got into this habit of going there. As far as ever from harbouring any serious thoughts concerning Rhoda, he felt himself impelled along the way which he had jokingly indicated in talk with Micklethwaite; he was tempted to make love to her as an interesting pastime, to observe how so strong-minded a woman would conduct herself under such circumstances. Had she or not a vein of sentiment in her character? Was it impossible to move her as other women are moved? Meditating thus, he looked up and saw the subject of his thoughts. She was seated a few yards away, and seemingly had not yet become aware of him, her eyes were on the ground, and troubled reverie appeared in her countenance.

'I have just called at the house, Miss Nunn. How is my cousin today?'

She had looked up only a moment before he spoke, and seemed vexed at being thus discovered.

'I believe Miss Barfoot is quite well,' she answered coldly, as they shook hands.

'But yesterday she was not so.'

'A headache, or something of the kind.'

He was astonished. Rhoda spoke with a cold indifference. She has risen, and showed her wish to move from the spot.

'She had to attend an inquest yesterday. Perhaps it rather upset her?'

'Yes, I think it did.'

Unable to adapt himself at once to this singular mood of Rhoda's, but resolved not to let her go before he had tried to learn the cause of it, he walked along by her side. In this part of the gardens there were only a few nursemaids and children; it would have been a capital place and time for improving his intimacy with the remarkable woman. But possibly she was determined to be rid of him. A contest between his will and hers would be an amusement decidedly to his taste.

'You also have been disturbed by it, Miss Nunn.'

'By the inquest?' she returned, with barely veiled scorn. 'Indeed I have not.'

'Did you know that poor girl?'

'Some time ago.'

'Then it is only natural that her miserable fate should sadden you.'

He spoke as if with respectful sympathy, ignoring what she had said.

'It has no effect whatever upon me,' Rhoda answered, glancing at him with surprise and displeasure.

'Forgive me if I say that I find it difficult to believe that. Perhaps you—'

She interrupted him.

'I don't easily forgive anyone who charges me with falsehood, Mr. Barfoot.'

'Oh, you take it too seriously. I beg your pardon a thousand times. I was going to say that perhaps you won't allow yourself to acknowledge any feeling of compassion in such a case.'

'I don't acknowledge what I don't feel. I will bid you good-afternoon.'

He smiled at her with all the softness and persuasiveness of which he was capable. She had offered her hand with cold dignity, and instead of taking it merely for good-bye he retained it.

'You must, you shall forgive me! I shall be too miserable if you dismiss me in this way. I see that I was altogether wrong. You know all the particulars of the case, and I have only read a brief newspaper account. I am sure the girl didn't deserve your pity.'

She was trying to draw her hand away. Everard felt the strength of her muscles, and the sensation was somehow so pleasant that he could not at once release her.

'You do pardon me, Miss Nunn?'

'Please don't be foolish. I will thank you to let my hand go.'

Was it possible? Her cheek had coloured, ever so slightly. But with indignation, no doubt, for her eyes flashed sternly at him. Very unwillingly, Everard had no choice but to obey the command.

'Will you have the kindness to tell me,' he said more gravely, 'whether my cousin was suffering only from that cause?'

'I can't say,' she added after a pause. 'I haven't spoken with Miss Barfoot for two or three days.'

He looked at her with genuine astonishment.

'You haven't seen each other?'

'Miss Barfoot is angry with me. I think we shall be obliged to part.'

'To part? What can possibly have happened? Miss Barfoot angry with *you*?'

'If I *must* satisfy your curiosity, Mr. Barfoot, I had better tell you at once that the subject of our difference is the girl you mentioned. Not very long ago she tried to persuade your cousin to receive her again—to give her lessons at the place in Great Portland Street, as before she disgraced herself. Miss Barfoot, with too ready good-nature, was willing to do this, but I resisted. It seemed to me that it would be a very weak and wrong thing to do. At the time she ended by agreeing with me. Now that the girl has killed herself, she throws the blame upon my interference. We had a painful conversation, and I don't think we can continue to live together.'

Barfoot listened with gratification. It was much to have compelled Rhoda to explain herself, and on such a subject.

'Nor even to work together?' he asked.

'It is doubtful.'

Rhoda still moved forward, but very slowly, and without impatience.

'You will somehow get over this difficulty, I am sure. Such friends as you and Mary don't quarrel like ordinary unreasonable women. Won't you let me be of use?'

'How?' asked Rhoda with surprise.

'I shall make my cousin see that she is wrong.'

'How do you know that she is wrong?'

'Because I am convinced that *you* must be right. I respect Mary's judgment, but I respect yours still more.'

Rhoda raised her head and smiled.

'That compliment,' she said, 'pleases me less than the one you have uttered without intending it.'

'You must explain.'

'You said that by making Miss Barfoot see she was wrong you could alter her mind towards me. The world's opinion would hardly support you in that, even in the case of men.'

Everard laughed.

'Now this is better. Now we are talking in the old way. Surely you know that the world's opinion has no validity for me.'

She kept silence.

'But, after all, *is* Mary wrong? I'm not afraid to ask the question now that your face has cleared a little. How angry you were with me! But surely I didn't deserve it. You would have been much more forbearing if you had known what delight I felt when I saw you sitting over there. It is nearly a month since we met, and I couldn't keep away any longer.'

Rhoda swept the distance with indifferent eyes.

'Mary was fond of this girl?' he inquired, watching her.

'Yes, she was.'

'Then her distress, and even anger, are natural enough. We won't discuss the girl's history; probably I know all that I need to. But whatever her misdoing, you certainly didn't wish to drive her to suicide.'

Rhoda deigned no reply.

'All the same,' he continued in his gentlest tone, 'it turns out that you have practically done so. If Mary had taken the girl back that despair would most likely never have come upon her. Isn't it natural that Mary should repent of having been guided by you, and perhaps say rather severe things?'

'Natural, no doubt. But it is just as natural for me to resent blame where I have done nothing blameworthy.'

'You are absolutely sure that this is the case?'

'I thought you expressed a conviction that I was in the right?'

There was no smile, but Everard believed that he detected its possibility on the closed lips.

'I have got into the way of always thinking so—in questions of this kind. But perhaps you tend to err on the side of severity. Perhaps you make too little allowance for human weakness.'

'Human weakness is a plea that has been much abused, and generally in an interested spirit.'

This was something like a personal rebuke. Whether she so meant it, Barfoot could not determine. He hoped she did, for the more personal their talk became the better he would be pleased.

'I, for one,' he said, 'very seldom urge that plea, whether in my own defence or another's. But it answers to a spirit we can't altogether dispense with. Don't you feel ever so little regret that your severe logic prevailed?'

'Not the slightest regret.'

Everard thought this answer magnificent. He had anticipated some evasion. However inappropriately, he was constrained to smile.

'How I admire your consistency! We others are poor halting creatures in comparison.'

'Mr. Barfoot,' said Rhoda suddenly, 'I have had enough of this. If your approval is sincere, I don't ask for it. If you are practising your powers of irony, I had rather you chose some other person. I will go my way, if you please.'

She just bent her head, and left him.

Enough for the present. Having raised his hat and turned on his heels, Barfoot strolled away in a mood of peculiar satisfaction. He laughed to himself. She was certainly a fine creature—yes, physically as well. Her out-of-door appearance on the whole pleased him; she could dress very plainly without disguising the advantages of figure she possessed. He pictured her rambling about the hills, and longed to be her companion on such an expedition; there would be no consulting with feebleness, as when one sets forth to walk with the everyday woman. What daring topics might come up in the course of a twenty-mile stretch across country! No Grundyism in Rhoda Nunn; no simpering, no mincing of phrases. Why, a man might do worse than secure her for his comrade through the whole journey of life.

Suppose he pushed his joke to the very point of asking her to marry him? Undoubtedly she would refuse; but how enjoyable to watch the proud vigour of her freedom asserting itself! Yet would not an offer of marriage be too commonplace? Rather propose to her to share his life in a free union, without sanction of forms which neither for her nor him were sanction at all. Was it too bold a thought?

Not if he really meant it. Uttered insincerely, such words would be insult; she would see through his pretence of earnestness, and then farewell to her for ever. But if his intellectual sympathy became tinged with passion—and did he discern no possibility of that? An odd thing were he to fall in love with Rhoda Nunn. Hitherto his ideal had been a widely different type of woman; he had demanded rare beauty of face, and the charm of a refined voluptuousness. To be sure, it was but an ideal; no woman that approached it had ever come within his sphere. The dream exercised less power over him than a few years ago; perhaps because his youth was behind him. Rhoda might well represent the desire of a mature man, strengthened by modern culture and with his senses fairly subordinate to reason. Heaven forbid that he should ever tie himself to the tame domestic female; and just as little could he seek for a mate among the women of society, the creatures all surface, with empty pates and vitiated blood. No marriage for him, in the common understanding of the word. He wanted neither offspring nor a 'home'. Rhoda Nunn, if she thought of such things at all, probably desired a union which would permit her to remain an intellectual being; the kitchen, the cradle, and the work-basket had no power over her imagination. As likely as not, however, she was perfectly content with single life—even regarded it as essential to her purposes. In her face he read chastity; her eye avoided no scrutiny; her palm was cold.

One does not break the heart of such a woman. Heartbreak is a very old-fashioned disorder, associated with poverty of brain. If Rhoda were what he thought her, she enjoyed this opportunity of studying a modern male, and cared not how far he proceeded in his own investigations, sure that at any moment she could bid him fall back. The amusement was only just beginning. And if for him it became earnest, why what did he seek but strong experiences?

Rhoda, in the meantime, had gone home. She shut herself in her bedroom, and remained there until the bell rang for dinner.

Miss Barfoot entered the dining-room just before her; they sat down in silence, and through the meal exchanged but a few sentences, relative to a topic of the hour which interested neither of them.

The elder woman had a very unhappy countenance; she looked worn out; her eyes never lifted themselves from the table.

Dinner over, Miss Barfoot went to the drawing-room alone. She had sat there about half an hour, brooding, unoccupied, when Rhoda came in and stood before her.

'I have been thinking it over. It isn't right for me to remain here. Such an arrangement was only possible whilst we were on terms of perfect understanding.'

'You must do what you think best, Rhoda,' the other replied gravely, but with no accent of displeasure.

'Yes, I had better take a lodging somewhere. What I wish to know is, whether you can still employ me with any satisfaction?'

'I don't employ you. That is not the word to describe your relations with me. If we must use business language, you are simply my partner.'

'Only your kindness put me into that position. When you no longer regard me as a friend, I am only in your employment.'

'I haven't ceased to regard you as a friend. The estrangement between us is entirely of your making.'

Seeing that Rhoda would not sit down, Miss Barfoot rose and stood by the fireplace.

'I can't bear reproaches,' said the former; 'least of all when they are irrational and undeserved.'

'If I reproached you, it was in a tone which should never have given you offence. One would think that I had rated you like a disobedient servant.'

'If *that* had been possible,' answered Rhoda, with a faint smile, 'I should never have been here. You said that you bitterly repented having given way to me on a certain occasion. That was unreasonable; in giving way, you declared yourself convinced. And the reproach I certainly didn't deserve, for I had behaved conscientiously.'

'Isn't it allowed me to disapprove of what your conscience dictates?'

'Not when you have taken the same view, and acted upon it. I don't lay claim to many virtues, and I haven't that of meekness. I could never endure anger; my nature resents it.'

'I did wrong to speak angrily, but indeed I hardly knew what I was saying. I had suffered a terrible shock. I loved that poor girl; I loved her all the more for what I had seen of her since she came to implore my help. Your utter coldness—it seemed to me inhuman—I shrank from you. If your face had shown ever so little compassion—'

'I *felt* no compassion.'

'No. You have hardened your heart with theory. Guard yourself, Rhoda! To work for women one must keep one's womanhood. You are becoming—you are wandering as far from the true way—oh, much further than Bella did!'

'I can't answer you. When we argued about our differences in a friendly spirit, all was permissible; now if I spoke my thought it would be mere harshness and cause of embitterment. I fear all is at an end between us. I should perpetually remind you of this sorrow.'

There was a silence of some length. Rhoda turned away, and stood in reflection.

'Let us do nothing hastily,' said Miss Barfoot. 'We have more to think of than our own feelings.'

'I have said that I am quite willing to go on with my work, but it must be on a different footing. The relation between us can no longer be that of equals. I am content to follow your directions. But your dislike of me will make this impossible.'

'Dislike? You misunderstand me wretchedly. I think rather it is you who dislike me, as a weak woman with no command of her emotions.'

Again they ceased from speech. Presently Miss Barfoot stepped forward.

'Rhoda, I shall be away all to-morrow; I may not return to London until Monday morning. Will you think quietly over it all? Believe me, I am not angry with you, and as for disliking you—what nonsense are we talking! But I can't regret that I let you see how painfully your behaviour impressed me. That hardness is not natural to you. You have encouraged yourself in it, and you are warping a very noble character.'

'I wish only to be honest. Where you felt compassion I felt indignation.'

'Yes; we have gone through all that. The indignation was a forced, exaggerated sentiment. You can't see it in that light perhaps. But try to imagine for a moment that Bella had been your sister—'

'That is confusing the point at issue,' Rhoda exclaimed irritably. 'Have I ever denied the force of such feelings? My grief would have blinded me to all larger considerations, of course. But she was happily *not* my sister, and I remained free to speak the simple truth about her case. It isn't personal feeling that directs a great movement in civilization. If you were right, I also was right. You should have recognized the inevitable discord of our Opinions at that moment.'

'It didn't seem to me inevitable.'

'I should have despised myself if I could have affected sympathy.'

'Affected—yes.'

'Or have really felt it. That would have meant that I did not know myself. I should never again have dared to speak on any grave subject.'

Miss Barfoot smiled sadly.

'How young you are! Oh, there is far more than ten years between our ages, Rhoda! In spirit you are a young girl, and I an old woman. No, no; we *will not* quarrel. Your companionship is far too precious to me, and I dare to think that mine is not without value for you. Wait till my grief has had its course; then I shall be more reasonable and do you more justice.'

Rhoda turned towards the door, lingered, but without looking back, and so left the room.

Miss Barfoot was absent as she had announced, returning only in time for her duties in Great Portland Street on Monday morning. She and Rhoda then shook hands, but without a word of personal reference. They went through the day's work as usual.

This was the day of the month on which Miss Barfoot would deliver her four o'clock address. The subject had been announced a week ago: 'Woman as an Invader.' An hour earlier than usual work was put aside, and seats were rapidly arranged for the small audience; it numbered only thirteen—the girls already on the premises and a few who came specially. All were aware of the tragedy in which Miss Barfoot had recently been concerned; her air of sadness, so great a contrast to that with which she was wont to address them, they naturally attributed to this cause.

As always, she began in the simplest conversational tone. Not long since she had received an anonymous letter, written by some clerk out of employment, abusing her roundly for her encouragement of female competition in the clerkly world. The taste of this epistle was as bad as its grammar, but they should hear it; she read it all through. Now, whoever the writer might be, it seemed pretty clear that he was not the kind of person with whom one could profitably argue; no use in replying to him, even had he given the opportunity. For all that, his uncivil attack had a meaning, and there were plenty of people ready to urge his argument in more respectable terms. 'They will tell you that, in entering the commercial world, you not only unsex yourselves, but do a grievous wrong to the numberless men struggling hard for bare sustenance. You reduce salaries, you press into an already overcrowded field, you injure even your own sex by making it impossible for men to marry, who, if they earned enough, would be supporting a wife.' Today, continued Miss Barfoot, it was not her purpose to debate the economic aspects of the question. She would consider it from another point of view, repeating, perhaps, much that she had already said to them on other occasions, but doing so because these thoughts had just now very strong possession of her mind.

This abusive correspondent, who declared that he was supplanted by a young woman who did his work for smaller payment, doubtless had a grievance. But, in the miserable disorder of our social state, one grievance had to be weighed against another, and Miss Barfoot held that there was much more to be urged on behalf of women who invaded what had been exclusively the men's sphere, than on behalf of the men who began to complain of this invasion.

'They point to half a dozen occupations which are deemed strictly suitable for women. Why don't we confine ourselves to this ground? Why don't I encourage girls to become governesses, hospital nurses, and so on? You think I ought to reply that already there are too many applicants for such places. It would be true, but I don't care to make use of the argument, which at once involves us in a debate with the out-crowded clerk. No; to put the truth in a few words, I am not chiefly anxious that you should *earn money*, but that women in general shall become *rational and responsible human beings*.

'Follow me carefully. A governess, a nurse, may be the most admirable of women. I will dissuade no one from following those careers who is distinctly fitted for them. But these are only a few out of the vast number of girls who must, if they are not to be despicable persons, somehow find serious work. Because I myself have had an education in clerkship, and have most capacity for such employment, I look about for girls of like mind, and do my best to prepare them for work in offices. And (here I must become emphatic once more) I am *glad* to have entered on this course. I am *glad* that I can show girls the way to a career which my opponents call unwomanly.

'Now see why. Womanly and womanish are two very different words; but the latter, as the world uses it, has become practically synonymous with the former. A womanly occupation means, practically, an occupation that a man disdains. And here is the root of the matter. I repeat that I am not first of all anxious to keep you supplied with daily bread. I am a troublesome, aggressive, revolutionary person. I want to do away with that common confusion of the words womanly and womanish, and I see very clearly that this can only be effected by an armed movement, an invasion by women of the spheres which men have always forbidden us to enter. I am strenuously opposed to that view of us set forth in such charming language by Mr. Ruskin—for it tells on the side of those men who think and speak of us in a way the reverse of charming. Were we living in an ideal world, I think women would not go to sit all day in offices. But the fact is that we live in a world as far from ideal as can be conceived. We live in a time of warfare, of revolt. If woman is no longer to be womanish, but a human being of powers and responsibilities, she must become militant, defiant. She must push her claims to the extremity.

'An excellent governess, a perfect hospital nurse, do work which is invaluable; but for our cause of emancipation they are no good—nay, they are harmful. Men point to them, and say: Imitate these, keep to your proper world. Our proper world is the world of intelligence, of honest effort, of moral strength. The old types of womanly perfection are no longer helpful to us. Like the Church service, which to all but one person in a thousand has become meaningless gabble by dint of repetition, these types have lost their effect. They are no longer educational. We have to ask ourselves: What course of training will wake women up, make them conscious of their souls, startle them into healthy activity?'

'It must be something new, something free from the reproach of womanliness. I don't care whether we crowd out the men or not. I don't care *what* results, if only women are made strong and self-reliant and nobly independent! The world must look to its concerns. Most likely we shall have a revolution in the social order greater than any that yet seems possible. Let it come, and let us help its coming. When I think of the contemptible wretchedness of women enslaved by custom, by their weakness, by their desires, I am ready to cry, Let the world perish in tumult rather than things go on in this way!'

For a moment her voice failed. There were tears in her eyes. The hearers, most of them, understood what made her so passionate; they exchanged grave looks.

'Our abusive correspondent shall do as best he can. He suffers for the folly of men in all ages. We can't help it. It is very far from our wish to cause hardship to any one, but we ourselves are escaping from a hardship that has become intolerable. We are educating ourselves. There must be a new type of woman, active in every sphere of life: a new worker out in the world, a new ruler of the home. Of the old ideal virtues we can retain many, but we have to add to them those which have been thought appropriate only in men. Let a woman be gentle, but at the same time let her be strong; let her be pure of heart, but none the less wise and instructed. Because we have to set an example to the sleepy of our sex, we must carry on an active warfare—must be invaders. Whether woman is the equal of man I neither know nor care. We are not his equal in size, in weight, in muscle, and, for all I can say, we may have less power of brain. That has nothing to do with it. Enough for us to know that our natural growth has been stunted. The mass of women have always been paltry creatures, and their paltriness has proved a curse to men. So, if you like to put it in this way, we are working for the advantage of men as well as for our own. Let the responsibility for disorder rest on those who have made us despise our old selves. At any cost—at any cost—we will free ourselves from the heritage of weakness and contempt!'

The assembly was longer than usual in dispersing. When all were gone, Miss Barfoot listened for a footstep in the other room. As she could detect no sound, she went to see if Rhoda was there or not.

Yes; Rhoda was sitting in a thoughtful attitude. She looked up, smiled, and came a few paces forward.

'It was very good.'

'I thought it would please you.'

Miss Barfoot drew nearer, and added,—

'It was addressed to you. It seemed to me that you had forgotten how I really thought about these things.'

'I have been ill-tempered,' Rhoda replied. 'Obstinacy is one of my faults.'

'It is.'

Their eyes met.

'I believe,' continued Rhoda, 'that I ought to ask your pardon. Right or wrong, I behaved in an unmannerly way.'

'Yes, I think you did.'

Rhoda smiled, bending her head to the rebuke.

'And there's the last of it,' added Miss Barfoot. 'Let us kiss and be friends.'

## CHAPTER XIV - MOTIVES MEETING

When Barfoot made his next evening call Rhoda did not appear. He sat for some time in pleasant talk with his cousin, no reference whatever being made to Miss Nunn; then at length, beginning to fear that he would not see her, he inquired after her health. Miss Nunn was very well, answered the hostess, smiling.

'Not at home this evening?'

'Busy with some kind of study, I think.'

Plainly, the difference between these women had come to a happy end, as Barfoot foresaw that it would. He thought it better to make no mention of his meeting with Rhoda in the gardens.

'That was a very unpleasant affair that I saw your name connected with last week,' he said presently.

'It made me very miserable—ill indeed for a day or two.'

'That was why you couldn't see me?'

'Yes.'

'But in your reply to my note you made no mention of the circumstances.'

Miss Barfoot kept silence; frowning slightly, she looked at the fire near which they were both sitting, for the weather had become very cold.

'No doubt,' pursued Everard, glancing at her, 'you refrained out of delicacy—on my account, I mean.'

'Need we talk of it?'

'For a moment, please. You are very friendly with me nowadays, but I suppose your estimate of my character remains very much the same as years ago?'

'What is the use of such questions?'

'I ask for a distinct purpose. You can't regard me with any respect?'

'To tell you the truth, Everard, I know nothing about you. I have no wish to revive disagreeable memories, and I think it quite possible that you may be worthy of respect.'

'So far so good. Now, in justice, please answer me another question. How have you spoken of me to Miss Nunn?'

'How can it matter?'

'It matters a good deal. Have you told her any scandal about me?'

'Yes, I have.'

Everard looked at her with surprise.

'I spoke to Miss Nunn about you,' she continued, 'before I thought of your coming here. Frankly, I used you as an illustration of the evils I abominate.'

'You are a courageous and plain-spoken woman, cousin Mary,' said Everard, laughing a little. 'Couldn't you have found some other example?'

There was no reply.

'So,' he proceeded, 'Miss Nunn regards me as a proved scoundrel?'

'I never told her the story. I made known the general grounds of my dissatisfaction with you, that was all.'

'Come, that's something. I'm glad you didn't amuse her with that unedifying bit of fiction.'

'Fiction?'

'Yes, fiction,' said Everard bluntly. 'I am not going into details; the thing's over and done with, and I chose my course at the time. But it's as well to let you know that my behaviour was grossly misrepresented. In using me to point a moral you were grievously astray. I shall say no more. Ii you can believe me, do; if you can't, dismiss the matter from your mind.'

There followed a silence of some moments. Then, with a perfectly calm manner, Miss Barfoot began to speak of a new subject. Everard followed her lead. He did not stay much longer, and on leaving asked to be remembered to Miss Nunn.

A week later he again found his cousin alone. He now felt sure that Miss Nunn was keeping out of his way. Her parting from him in the gardens had been decidedly abrupt, and possibly it signified more serious offence than at the time he attributed to her. It was so difficult to be sure of anything in regard to Miss Nunn. If another woman had acted thus he would have judged it coquetry. But perhaps Rhoda was quite incapable of anything of that kind. Perhaps she took herself so very seriously that the mere suspicion of banter in his talk had moved her to grave resentment. Or again, she might be half ashamed to meet him after confessing her disagreement with Miss Barfoot; on recovery from ill-temper (unmistakable ill-temper it was), she had seen her behaviour in an embarrassing light. Between these various conjectures he wavered whilst talking with Mary. But he did not so much as mention Miss Nunn's name.

Some ten days went by, and he paid a call at the hour sanctioned by society, five in the afternoon; it being Saturday. One of his reasons for coming at this time was the hope that he might meet other callers, for he felt curious to see what sort of people visited the house. And this wish was gratified. On entering the drawing-room, whither he was led by the servant straightway, after the manner of the world, he found not only his cousin and her friend, but two strangers, ladies. A glance informed him that both of these were young and good-looking, one being a type that particularly pleased him—dark, pale, with very bright eyes.

Miss Barfoot received him as any hostess would have done. She was her cheerful self once more, and in a moment introduced him to the lady with whom she had been talking—the dark one, by name Mrs. Widdowson. Rhoda Nunn, sitting apart with the second lady, gave him her hand, but at once resumed her conversation.

With Mrs. Widdowson he was soon chatting in his easy and graceful way, Miss Barfoot putting in a word now and then. He saw that she had not long been married; a pleasant diffidence and the maidenly glance of her bright eyes indicated this. She was dressed very prettily, and seemed aware of it.

'We went to hear the new opera at the Savoy last night,' she said to Miss Barfoot, with a smile of remembered enjoyment.

'Did you? Miss Nunn and I were there.'

Everard gazed at his cousin with humorous incredulity.

'Is it possible?' he exclaimed. 'You were at the Savoy?'

'Where is the impossibility? Why shouldn't Miss Nunn and I go to the theatre?'

'I appeal to Mrs. Widdowson. She also was astonished.'

'Yes, indeed I was, Miss Barfoot!' exclaimed the younger lady, with a merry little laugh. 'I hesitated before speaking of such a frivolous entertainment.'

Lowering her voice, and casting a smile in Rhoda's direction, Miss Barfoot replied,—

'I have to make a concession occasionally on Miss Nunn's account. It would be unkind never to allow her a little recreation.'

The two at a distance were talking earnestly, with grave countenances. In a few moments they rose, and the visitor came towards Miss Barfoot to take her leave. Thereupon Everard crossed to Miss Nunn.

'Is there anything very good in the new Gilbert and Sullivan opera?' he asked.

'Many good things. You really haven't been yet?'

'No—I'm ashamed to say.'

'Do go this evening, if you can get a seat. Which part of the theatre do you prefer?'

His eye rested on her, but he could detect no irony.

'I'm a poor man, you know. I have to be content with the cheap places. Which do you like best, the Savoy operas or the burlesques at the Gaiety?'

A few more such questions and answers, of laboured commonplace or strained flippancy, and Everard, after searching his companion's face, broke off with a laugh.

'There now,' he said, 'we have talked in the approved five o'clock way. Precisely the dialogue I heard in a drawing-room yesterday. It goes on day after day, year after year, through the whole of people's lives.'

'You are on friendly terms with such people?'

'I am on friendly terms with people of every kind.' He added, in an undertone, 'I hope I may include you, Miss Nunn?'

But to this she paid no attention. She was looking at Monica and Miss Barfoot, who had just risen from their seats. They approached, and presently Barfoot found himself alone with the familiar pair.

'Another cup of tea, Everard?' asked his cousin.

'Thank you. Who was the young lady you didn't introduce me to?'

'Miss Haven—one of our pupils.'

'Does she think of going into business?'

'She has just got a place in the publishing department of a weekly paper.'

'But really—from the few words of her talk that fell upon my ear I should have thought her a highly educated girl.'

'So she is,' replied Miss Barfoot. 'What is your objection?'

'Why doesn't she aim at some better position?'

Miss Barfoot and Rhoda exchanged smiles.

'But nothing could be better for her. Some day she hopes to start a paper of her own, and to learn all the details of such business is just what she wants. Oh, you are still very conventional, Everard. You meant she ought to take up something graceful and pretty—something ladylike.'

'No, no. It's all right. I thoroughly approve. And when Miss Haven starts her paper, Miss Nunn will write for it.'

'I hope so,' assented his cousin.

'You make me feel that I am in touch with the great movements of our time. It's delightful to know you. But come now, isn't there any way in which I could help?'

Mary laughed.

'None whatever, I'm afraid.'

'Well,—"They also serve who only stand and wait."'

If Everard had pleased himself he would have visited the house in Queen's Road every other day. As this might not be, he spent a good deal of his time in other society, not caring to read much, or otherwise occupy his solitude. Starting with one or two acquaintances in London, people of means and position, he easily extended his social sphere. Had he cared to marry, he might, notwithstanding his poverty, have wooed with fair chance in a certain wealthy family, where two daughters, the sole children, plain but well-instructed girls, waited for the men of brains who should appreciate them. So rare in society, these men of brains, and, alas! so frequently deserted by their wisdom when it comes to choosing a wife. It being his principle to reflect on every possibility, Barfoot of course asked himself whether it would not be reasonable to approach one or other of these young women—the Miss Brissendens. He needed a larger income; he wanted to travel in a more satisfactory way than during his late absence. Agnes Brissenden struck him as a very calm and sensible girl; not at all likely to marry any one but the man who would be a suitable companion for her, and probably disposed to look on marriage as a permanent friendship, which must not be endangered by feminine follies. She had no beauty, but mental powers above the average—superior, certainly, to her sister's.

It was worth thinking about, but in the meantime he wanted to see much more of Rhoda Nunn. Rhoda he was beginning to class with women who are attractive both physically and mentally. Strange how her face had altered to his perception since the first meeting. He smiled now when he beheld it—smiled as a man does when his senses are pleasantly affected. He was getting to know it so well, to be prepared for its constant changes, to watch for certain movements of brows or lips when he had said certain things. That forcible holding of her hand had marked a stage in progressive appreciation; since then he felt a desire to repeat the experiment.

'Or if thy mistress some rich anger shows, Imprison her soft hand, and let her rave—'

The lines occurred to his memory, and he understood them better than heretofore. It would delight him to enrage Rhoda, and then to detain her by strength, to overcome her senses, to watch her long lashes droop over the eloquent eyes. But this was something very like being in love, and he by no means wished to be seriously in love with Miss Nunn.

It was another three weeks before he had an opportunity of private talk with her. Trying a Sunday afternoon, about four, he found Rhoda alone in the drawing-room; Miss Barfoot was out of town. Rhoda's greeting had a frank friendliness which she had not bestowed upon him for a long time; not, indeed, since they met on her return from Cheddar. She looked very well, readily laughed, and seemed altogether in a coming-on disposition. Barfoot noticed that the piano was open.

'Do you play?' he inquired. 'Strange that I should still have to ask the question.'

'Oh, only a hymn on Sunday,' she answered off-hand.

'A hymn?'

'Why not? I like some of the old tunes very much. They remind me of the golden age.'

'In your own life, you mean?'

She nodded.

'You have once or twice spoken of that time as if you were not quite happy in the present.'

'Of course I am not quite happy. What woman is? I mean, what woman above the level of a petted pussy-cat?'

Everard was leaning towards her on the head of the couch where he sat. He gazed into her face fixedly.

'I wish it were in my power to remove some of your discontents. I would, more gladly than I can tell you.'

'You abound in good nature, Mr. Barfoot,' she replied laughing. 'But unfortunately you can't change the world.'

'Not the world at large. But might I not change your views of it—in some respects?'

'Indeed I don't see how you could. I think I had rather have my own view than any you might wish to substitute for it.'

In this humour she seemed more than ever a challenge to his manhood. She was armed at all points. She feared nothing that he might say. No flush of apprehension; no nervous tremor; no weak self-consciousness. Yet he saw her as a woman, and desirable.

'My views are not ignoble,' he murmured.

'I hope not. But they are the views of a man.'

'Man and woman ought to see life with much the same eyes.'

'Ought they? Perhaps so. I am not sure. But they never will in our time.'

'Individuals may. The man and woman who have thrown away prejudice and superstition. You and I, for instance.'

'Oh, those words have such different meanings. In your judgment I should seem full of idle prejudice.'

She liked this conversation; he read pleasure in her face, saw in her eyes a glint of merry defiance. And his pulses throbbed the quicker for it.

'You have a prejudice against *me*, for instance.'

'Pray, did you go to the Savoy?' inquired Rhoda absently.

'I have no intention of talking about the Savoy, Miss Nunn. It is teacup time, but as yet we have the room to ourselves.'

Rhoda went and rang the bell.

'The teacups shall come at once.'

He laughed slightly, and looked at her from beneath drooping lids. Rhoda went on with talk of trifles, until the tea was brought and she had given a cup. Having emptied it at two draughts, he resumed his former leaning position.

'Well, you were saying that you had a prejudice against me. Of course my cousin Mary is accountable for that. Mary has used me rather ill. Before ever you saw me, I represented to your mind something very disagreeable indeed. That was too bad of my cousin.'

Rhoda, sipping her tea, had a cold, uninterested expression.

'I didn't know of this,' he proceeded, 'when we met that day in the gardens, and when I made you so angry.'

'I wasn't disposed to jest about what had happened.'

'But neither was I. You quite misunderstood me. Will you tell me how that unpleasantness came to an end?'

'Oh yes. I admitted that I had been ill-mannered and obstinate.'

'How delightful! Obstinate? I have a great deal of that in my character. All the active part of my life was one long fit of obstinacy. As a lad I determined on a certain career, and I stuck to it in spite of conscious unfitness, in spite of a great deal of suffering, out of sheer obstinacy. I wonder whether Mary ever told you that.'

'She mentioned something of the kind once.'

'You could hardly believe it, I dare say? I am a far more reasonable being now. I have changed in so many respects that I hardly know my old self when I look back on it. Above all, in my thoughts about women. If I had married during my twenties I should have chosen, as the average man does, some simpleton—with unpleasant results. If I marry now, it will be a woman of character and brains. Marry in the legal sense I never shall. My companion must be as independent of forms as I am myself.'

Rhoda looked into her teacup for a second or two, then said with a smile,—

'You also are a reformer?'

'In that direction.'

He had difficulty in suppressing signs of nervousness. The bold declaration had come without forethought, and Rhoda's calm acceptance of it delighted him.

'Questions of marriage,' she went on to say, 'don't interest me much; but this particular reform doesn't seem very practical. It is trying to bring about an ideal state of things whilst we are yet struggling with elementary obstacles.'

'I don't advocate this liberty for all mankind. Only for those who are worthy of it.'

'And what'—she laughed a little—'are the sure signs of worthiness? I think it would be very needful to know them.'

Everard kept a grave face.

'True. But a free union presupposes equality of position. No honest man would propose it, for instance, to a woman incapable of understanding all it involved, or incapable of resuming her separate life if that became desirable. I admit all the difficulties. One must consider those of feeling, as well as the material. If my wife should declare that she must be released, I might suffer grievously, but being a man of some intelligence, I should admit that the suffering couldn't be helped; the brutality of enforced marriage doesn't seem to me an alternative worth considering. It wouldn't seem so to any woman of the kind I mean.'

Would she have the courage to urge one grave difficulty that he left aside? No. He fancied her about to speak, but she ended by offering him another cup of tea.

'After all, that is *not* your ideal?' he said.

'I haven't to do with the subject at all,' Rhoda answered, with perhaps a trace of impatience. 'My work and thought are for the women who do not marry—the 'odd women' I call them. They alone interest me. One mustn't undertake too much.'

'And you resolutely class yourself with them?'

'Of course I do.'

'And therefore you have certain views of life which I should like to change. You are doing good work, but I had rather see any other woman in the world devote her life to it. I am selfish enough to wish—'

The door opened, and the servant announced,—

'Mr. and Mrs. Widdowson.'

With perfect self-command Miss Nunn rose and stepped forward. Barfoot, rising more slowly, looked with curiosity at the husband of the pretty, black-browed woman whom he had already met. Widdowson surprised and amused him. How had this stiff, stern fellow with the grizzled beard won such a wife? Not that Mrs. Widdowson seemed a remarkable person, but certainly it was an ill-assorted union.

She came and shook hands. As he spoke a few natural words, Everard chanced to notice that the husband's eye was upon him, and with what a look! If ever a man declared in his countenance the worst species of jealous temper, Mr. Widdowson did so. His fixed smile became sardonic.

Presently Barfoot and he were introduced. They had nothing to say to each other, but Everard maintained a brief conversation just to observe the man. Turning at length, he began to talk with Mrs. Widdowson, and, because he was conscious of the jealous eye, assumed an especial sprightliness, an air of familiar pleasantry, to which the lady responded, but with a nervous hesitation.

The arrival of these people was an intense annoyance to him. Another quarter of an hour and things would have come to an exciting pass between Rhoda and himself; he would have heard how she received a declaration of love. Rhoda's self-possession notwithstanding, he believed that he was not without power over her. She liked to talk with him, enjoyed the freedom he allowed himself in choice of subject. Perhaps no man before had ever shown an appreciation of her qualities as woman. But she would not yield, was in no real danger from his love-making. Nay, the danger was to his own peace. He felt that resistance would intensify the ardour of his wooing, and possibly end by making him a victim of genuine passion. Well, let her enjoy that triumph, if she were capable of winning it.

He had made up his mind to outstay the Widdowsons, who clearly would not make a long call. But the fates were against him. Another visitor arrived, a lady named Cosgrove, who settled herself as if for at least an hour. Worse than that, he heard her say to Rhoda,—

'Oh, then do come and dine with us. Do, I beg!'

'I will, with pleasure,' was Miss Nunn's reply. 'Can you wait and take me with you?'

Useless to stay longer. As soon as the Widdowsons had departed he went up to Rhoda and silently offered his hand. She scarcely looked at him, and did not in the least return his pressure.

Rhoda dined at Mrs. Cosgrove's, and was home again at eleven o'clock. When the house was locked up, and the servants had gone to bed, she sat in the library, turning over a book that she had brought from her friend's house. It was a volume of essays, one of which dealt with the relations between the sexes in a very modern spirit, treating the subject as a perfectly open one, and arriving at unorthodox conclusions. Mrs. Cosgrove had spoken of this dissertation with lively interest. Rhoda perused it very carefully, pausing now and then to reflect.

In this reading of her mind, Barfoot came near the truth.

No man had ever made love to her; no man, to her knowledge, had ever been tempted to do so. In certain moods she derived satisfaction from this thought, using it to strengthen her life's purpose; having passed her thirtieth year, she might take it as a settled thing that she would never be sought in marriage, and so could shut the doors on every instinct tending to trouble her intellectual decisions. But these instincts sometimes refused to be thus treated. As Miss Barfoot told her, she was very young for her years, young in physique, young in emotion. As a girl she had dreamt passionately, and the fires of her nature, though hidden beneath aggregations of moral and mental attainment, were not yet smothered. An hour of lassitude filled her with despondency, none the less real because she was ashamed of it. If only she had once been loved, like other women—if she had listened to an offer of devotion, and rejected it—her heart would be more securely at peace. So she thought. Secretly she deemed it a hard thing never to have known that common triumph of her sex. And, moreover, it took away from the merit of her position as a leader and encourager of women living independently. There might be some who said, or thought, that she made a virtue of necessity.

Everard Barfoot's advances surprised her not a little. Judging him as a man wholly without principle, she supposed at first that this was merely his way with all women, and resented it as impertinence. But even then she did not dislike the show of homage; what her mind regarded with disdain, her heart was all but willing to feed upon, after its long hunger. Barfoot interested her, and not the less because of his evil reputation. Here was one of the men for whom women—doubtless more than one—had sacrificed themselves; she could not but regard him with sexual curiosity. And her interest grew, her curiosity was more haunting, as their acquaintance became a sort of friendship; she found that her moral disapprobation wavered, or was altogether forgotten. Perhaps it was to compensate for this that she went the length of outraging Miss Barfoot's feelings on the death of Bella Royston.

Certainly she thought with much frequency of Barfoot, and looked forward to his coming. Never had she wished so much to see him again as after their encounter in Chelsea Gardens, and on that account she forced herself to hold aloof when he came. It was not love, nor the beginning of love; she judged it something less possible to avow. The man's presence affected her with a perturbation which she had no difficulty in concealing at the time, though afterwards it distressed and shamed her. She took refuge in the undeniable fact that the quality of his mind made an impression upon her, that his talk was sympathetic. Miss Barfoot submitted to this influence; she confessed that her cousin's talk had always had a charm for her.

Could it be that this man reciprocated, and more than reciprocated, her complex feeling? To-day only accident had prevented him from making an avowal of love—unless she strangely mistook him. All the evening she had dwelt on this thought; it grew more and more astonishing. Was he worse than she had imagined? Under cover of independent thought, of serious moral theories, did he conceal mere profligacy and heartlessness? It was an extraordinary thing to have to ask such questions in relation to herself. It made her feel as if she had to learn herself anew, to form a fresh conception of her personality. She the object of a man's passion!

And the thought was exultant. Even thus late, then, the satisfaction of vanity had been granted her—nay, not of vanity alone.

He must be sincere. What motive could he possibly have for playing a part? Might it not be true that he was a changed man in certain respects, and that a genuine emotion at length had control of him? If so, she had only to wait for his next speech with her in private; she could not misjudge a lover's pleading.

The interest would only be that of comedy. She did not love Everard Barfoot, and saw no likelihood of ever doing so; on the whole, a subject for thankfulness. Nor could he seriously anticipate an assent to his proposal for a free union; in declaring that legal marriage was out of the question for him, he had removed his love-making to the region of mere ideal sentiment. But, if he loved her, these theories would sooner or later be swept aside; he would plead with her to become his legal wife.

To that point she desired to bring him. Offer what he might, she would not accept it; but the secret chagrin that was upon her would be removed. Love would no longer be the privilege of other women. To reject a lover in so many respects desirable, whom so many women might envy her, would fortify her self-esteem, and enable her to go forward in the chosen path with firmer tread.

It was one o'clock; the fire had died out and she began to shiver with cold. But a trembling of joy at the same time went through her limbs; again she had the sense of exultation, of triumph. She would not dismiss him peremptorily. He should prove the quality of his love, if love it were. Coming so late, the experience must yield her all it had to yield of delight and contentment.

## CHAPTER XV - THE JOYS OF HOME

Monica and her husband, on leaving the house in Queen's Road, walked slowly in the eastward direction. Though night had fallen, the air was not unpleasant; they had no object before them, and for five minutes they occupied themselves with their thoughts. Then Widdowson stopped.

'Shall we go home again?' he asked, just glancing at Monica, then letting his eyes stray vaguely in the gloom.

'I should like to see Milly, but I'm afraid I can hardly take you there to call with me.'

'Why not?'

'It's a very poor little sitting-room, you know, and she might have some friend. Isn't there anywhere you could go, and meet me afterwards?'

Frowning, Widdowson looked at his watch.

'Nearly six o'clock. There isn't much time.'

'Edmund, suppose you go home, and let me come back by myself? You wouldn't mind, for once? I should like so much to have a talk with Milly. If I got back about nine or half-past, I could have a little supper, and that's all I should want.'

He answered abruptly,—

'Oh, but I can't have you going about alone at night.'

'Why not?' answered Monica, with a just perceptible note of irritation. 'Are you afraid I shall be robbed or murdered?'

'Nonsense. But you mustn't be alone.'

'Didn't I always use to be alone?'

He made an angry gesture.

'I have begged you not to speak of that. Why do you say what you know is disagreeable to me? You used to do all sorts of things that you never ought to have been obliged to do, and it's very painful to remember it.'

Monica, seeing that people were approaching, walked on, and neither spoke until they had nearly reached the end of the road.

'I think we had better go home,' Widdowson at length remarked.

'If you wish it; but I really don't see why I shouldn't call on Milly, now that we are here.'

'Why didn't you speak of it before we left home? You ought to be more methodical, Monica. Each morning I always plan how my day is to be spent, and it would be much better if you would do the same. Then you wouldn't be so restless and uncertain.'

'If I go to Rutland Street,' said Monica, without heeding this admonition, 'couldn't you leave me there for an hour?'

'What in the world am I to do?'

'I should have thought you might walk about. It's a pity you don't know more people, Edmund. It would make things so much pleasanter for you.'

In the end he consented to see her safely as far as Rutland Street, occupy himself for an hour, and come back for her. They went by cab, which was dismissed in Hampstead Road. Widdowson did not turn away until he had ocular proof of his wife's admittance to the house where Miss Vesper lived, and even then he walked no farther than the neighbouring streets, returning about every ten minutes to watch the house from a short distance, as though he feared Monica might have some project of escape. His look was very bilious; trudging mechanically hither and thither where fewest people were to be met, he kept his eyes on the ground, and clumped to a dismal rhythm with the end of his walking-stick. In the three or four months since his marriage, he seemed to have grown older; he no longer held himself so upright.

At the very moment agreed upon he was waiting close by the house. Five minutes passed; twice he had looked at his watch, and he grew excessively impatient, stamping as if it were necessary to keep himself warm. Another five minutes, and he uttered a nervous ejaculation. He had all but made up his mind to go and knock at the door when Monica came forth.

'You haven't been waiting here long, I hope?' she said cheerfully.

'Ten minutes. But it doesn't matter.'

'I'm very sorry. We were talking on—'

'Yes, but one must always be punctual. I wish I could impress that upon you. Life without punctuality is quite impossible.'

'I'm very sorry, Edmund. I will be more careful. Please don't lecture me, dear. How shall we go home?'

'We had better take a cab to Victoria. No knowing how long we may have to wait for a train when we get there.'

'Now don't be so grumpy. Where have you been all the time?'

'Oh, walking about. What else was I to do?'

On the drive they held no conversation. At Victoria they were delayed about half an hour before a train started for Herne Hill; Monica sat in a waiting-room, and her husband trudged about the platform, still clumping rhythmically with his stick.

Their Sunday custom was to dine at one o'clock, and at six to have tea. Widdowson hated the slightest interference with domestic routine, and he had reluctantly indulged Monica's desire to go to Chelsea this afternoon. Hunger was now added to his causes of discontent.

'Let us have something to eat at once,' he said on entering the house. 'This disorder really won't do: we must manage better somehow.'

Without replying, Monica rang the dining-room bell, and gave orders.

Little change had been made in the interior of the house since its master's marriage. The dressing-room adjoining the principal bedchamber was adapted to Monica's use, and a few ornaments were added to the drawing-room. Unlike his deceased brother, Widdowson had the elements of artistic taste; in furnishing his abode he took counsel with approved decorators, and at moderate cost had made himself a home which presented no original features, but gave no offence to a cultivated eye. The first sight of the rooms pleased Monica greatly. She declared that all was perfect, nothing need be altered. In those days, if she had bidden him spend a hundred pounds on reconstruction, the lover would have obeyed, delighted to hear her express a wish.

Though competence had come to him only after a lifetime of narrow means, Widdowson felt no temptation to parsimony. Secure in his all-sufficing income, he grudged no expenditure that could bring himself or his wife satisfaction. On the wedding-tour in Cornwall, Devon, and Somerset—it lasted about seven weeks—Monica learnt, among other things less agreeable, that her husband was generous with money.

He was anxious she should dress well, though only, as Monica soon discovered, for his own gratification. Soon after they had settled down at home she equipped herself for the cold season, and Widdowson cared little about the price so long as the effect of her new costumes was pleasing to him.

'You are making a butterfly of me,' said Monica merrily, when he expressed strong approval of a bright morning dress that had just come home.

'A beautiful woman,' he replied, with the nervous gravity which still possessed him when complimenting her, or saying tender things, 'a beautiful woman ought to be beautifully clad.'

At the same time he endeavoured to impress her with the gravest sense of a married woman's obligations. His raptures, genuine enough, were sometimes interrupted in the oddest way if Monica chanced to utter a careless remark of which he could not strictly approve, and such interruptions frequently became the opportunity for a long and solemn review of the wifely status. Without much trouble he had brought her into a daily routine which satisfied him. During the whole of the morning she was to be absorbed in household cares. In the afternoon he would take her to walk or drive, and the evening he wished her to spend either in drawing-room or library, occupied with a book. Monica soon found that his idea of wedded happiness was that they should always be together. Most reluctantly he consented to her going any distance alone, for whatever purpose. Public entertainments he regarded with no great favour, but when he saw how Monica enjoyed herself at concert or theatre, he made no objection to indulging her at intervals of a fortnight or so; his own fondness for music made this compliance easier. He was jealous of her forming new acquaintances; indifferent to society himself, he thought his wife should be satisfied with her present friends, and could not understand why she wished to see them so often.

The girl was docile, and for a time he imagined that there would never be conflict between his will and hers. Whilst enjoying their holiday they naturally went everywhere together, and were scarce an hour out of each other's presence, day or night. In quiet spots by the seashore, when they sat in solitude, Widdowson's tongue was loosened, and he poured forth his philosophy of life with the happy assurance that Monica would listen passively. His devotion to her proved itself in a thousand ways; week after week he grew, if anything, more kind, more tender; yet in his view of their relations he was unconsciously the most complete despot, a monument of male autocracy. Never had it occurred to Widdowson that a wife remains an individual, with rights and obligations independent of her wifely condition. Everything he said presupposed his own supremacy; he took for granted that it was his to direct, hers to be guided. A display of energy, purpose, ambition, on Monica's part, which had no reference to domestic pursuits, would have gravely troubled him; at once he would have set himself to subdue, with all gentleness, impulses so inimical to his idea of the married state. It rejoiced him that she spoke with so little sympathy of the principles supported by Miss Barfoot and Miss Nunn; these persons seemed to him well-meaning, but grievously mistaken. Miss Nunn he judged 'unwomanly,' and hoped in secret that Monica would not long remain on terms of friendship with her. Of course his wife's former pursuits were an abomination to him; he could not bear to hear them referred to.

'Woman's sphere is the home, Monica. Unfortunately girls are often obliged to go out and earn their living, but this is unnatural, a necessity which advanced civilization will altogether abolish. You shall read John Ruskin; every word he says about women is good and precious. If a woman can neither have a home of her own, nor find occupation in any one else's she is deeply to be pitied; her life is bound to be unhappy. I sincerely believe that an educated woman had better become a domestic servant than try to imitate the life of a man.'

Monica seemed to listen attentively, but before long she accustomed herself to wear this look whilst in truth she was thinking her own thoughts. And as often as not they were of a nature little suspected by her prosing companion.

He believed himself the happiest of men. He had taken a daring step, but fortune smiled upon him, Monica was all he had imagined in his love-fever; knowledge of her had as yet brought to light no single untruth, not trait of character that he could condemn. That she returned his love he would not and could not doubt. And something she said to him one day, early in their honeymoon, filled up the measure of his bliss.

'What a change you have made in my life, Edmund! How much I have to thank you for!'

That was what he had hoped to hear. He had thought it himself; had wondered whether Monica saw her position in this light. And when the words actually fell from her lips he glowed with joy. This, to his mind, was the perfect relation of wife to husband. She must look up to him as her benefactor, her providence. It would have pleased him still better if she had not possessed a penny of her own, but happily Monica seemed never to give a thought to the sum at her disposal.

Surely he was the easiest of men to live with. When he first became aware that Monica suffered an occasional discontent, it caused him troublous surprise. As soon as he understood that she desired more freedom of movement, he became anxious, suspicious irritable. Nothing like a quarrel had yet taken place between them, but Widdowson began to perceive that he must exert authority in a way he had imagined would never be necessary. All his fears, after all, were not groundless. Monica's undomestic life, and perhaps the association with those Chelsea people, had left results upon her mind. By way of mild discipline, he first of all suggested a closer attention to the affairs of the house. Would it not be well if she spent an hour a day in sewing or fancy work? Monica so far obeyed as to provide herself with some plain needlework, but Widdowson, watching with keen eye, soon remarked that her use of the needle was only a feint. He lay awake o' nights, pondering darkly.

On the present evening he was more decidedly out of temper than ever hitherto. He satisfied his hunger hurriedly and in silence. Then, observing that Monica ate only a few morsels, he took offence at this.

'I'm afraid you are not well, dear. You have had no appetite for several days.'

'As much as usual, I think,' she replied absently.

They went into the library, commonly their resort of an evening. Widdowson possessed several hundred volumes of English literature, most of them the works which are supposed to be indispensible to a well-informed man, though very few men even make a pretence of reading them. Self-educated, Widdowson deemed it his duty to make acquaintance with the great, the solid authors. Nor was his study of them affectation. For the poets he had little taste; the novelists he considered only profitable in intervals of graver reading; but history, political economy, even metaphysics, genuinely appealed to him. He had always two or three solid books on hand, each with its marker; he studied them at stated hours, and always sitting at a table, a notebook open beside him. A little work once well-known, Todd's 'Student's Manual,' had formed his method and inspired him with zeal.

To-night, it being Sunday, he took down a volume of Barrow's Sermons. Though not strictly orthodox in religious faith, he conformed to the practices of the Church of England, and since his marriage had been more scrupulous on this point than before. He abhorred unorthodoxy in a woman, and would not on any account have suffered Monica to surmise that he had his doubts concerning any article of the Christian faith. Like most men of his kind, he viewed religion as a precious and powerful instrument for directing the female conscience. Frequently he read aloud to his wife, but this evening he showed no intention of doing so. Monica, however, sat unoccupied. After glancing at her once or twice, he said reprovingly,—

'Have you finished your Sunday book?'

'Not quite. But I don't care to read just now.'

The silence that followed was broken by Monica herself.

'Have you accepted Mrs. Luke's invitation to dinner?' she asked.

'I have declined it,' was the reply, carelessly given.

Monica bit her lip.

'But why?'

'Surely we needn't discuss that over again, Monica.'

His eyes were still on the book, and he stirred impatiently.

'But,' urged his wife, 'do you mean to break with her altogether? If so, I think it's very unwise, Edmund. What an opinion you must have of me, if you think I can't see people's faults! I know it's very true, all you say about her. But she wishes to be kind to us, I'm sure—and I like to see something of a life so different from our own.'

Widdowson drummed on the floor with his foot. In a few moments, ignoring Monica's remarks, he stroked his beard, and asked, with a show of casual interest—

'How was it you knew that Mr. Barfoot?'

'I had met him before—when I went there on the Saturday.'

Widdowson's eyes fell; his brow was wrinkled.

'He's often there, then?'

'I don't know. Perhaps he is. He's Miss Barfoot's cousin, you know.'

'You haven't seen him more than once before?'

'No. Why do you ask?'

'Oh, it was only that he seemed to speak as if you were old acquaintances.'

'That's his way, I suppose.'

Monica had already learnt that the jealousy which Widdowson so often betrayed before their manage still lurked in his mind. Perceiving why he put these questions, she could not look entirely unconcerned, and the sense of his eye being upon her caused her some annoyance.

'You talked to him, didn't you?' she said, changing her position in the deep chair.

'Oh, the kind of talk that is possible with a perfect stranger. I suppose he is in some profession?'

'I really don't know. Why, Edmund? Does he interest you?'

'Only that one likes to know something about the people that are introduced to one's wife,' Widdowson answered rather acridly.

Their bedtime was half-past ten. Precisely at that moment Widdowson closed his book—glad to be relieved from the pretence of reading—and walked over the lower part of the house to see that all was right. He had a passion for routine. Every night, before going upstairs, he did a number of little things in unvarying sequence—changed the calendar for next day, made perfect order on his writing-table, wound lip his watch, and so on. That Monica could not direct her habits with like exactitude was frequently a distress to him; if she chanced to forget any most trivial detail of daily custom he looked very solemn, and begged her to be more vigilant.

Next morning after breakfast, as Monica stood by the dining-room window and looked rather cheerlessly at a leaden sky, her husband came towards her as if he had something to say. She turned, and saw that his face no longer wore the austere expression which had made her miserable last night, and even during the meal this morning.

'Are we friends?' he said, with the attempt at playfulness which always made him look particularly awkward.

'Of course we are,' Monica answered, smiling, but not regarding him.

'Didn't he behave gruffly last night to his little girl?'

'Just a little.'

'And what can the old bear do to show that he's sorry?'

'Never be gruff again.'

'The old bear is sometimes an old goose as well, and torments himself in the silliest way. Tell him so, if ever he begins to behave badly. Isn't it account-book morning?'

'Yes. I'll come to you at eleven.'

'And if we have a nice, quiet, comfortable week, I'll take you to the Crystal Palace concert next Saturday.'

Monica nodded cheerfully, and went off to look after her housekeeping.

The week was in all respects what Widdowson desired. Not a soul came to the house; Monica went to see no one. Save on two days, it rained, sleeted, drizzled, fogged; on those two afternoons they had an hour's walk. Saturday brought no improvement of the atmosphere, but Widdowson was in his happiest mood; he cheerfully kept his promise about the concert. As they sat together at night, his contentment overflowed in tenderness like that of the first days of marriage.

'Now, why can't we always live like this? What have we to do with other people? Let us be everything to each other, and forget that any one else exists.'

'I can't help thinking that's a mistake,' Monica ventured to reply. 'For one thing, if we saw more people, we should have so much more to talk about when we are alone.'

'It's better to talk about ourselves. I shouldn't care if I never again saw any living creature but you. You see, the old bear loves his little girl better than she loves him.'

Monica was silent.

'Isn't it true? You don't feel that my company would be enough for you?'

'Would it be right if I ceased to care for every one else? There are my sisters. I ought to have asked Virginia to come to-morrow; I'm sure she thinks I neglect her, and it must be dreadful living all alone like she does.'

'Haven't they made up their mind yet about the school? I'm sure it's the right thing for them to do. If the venture were to fail, and they lost money, we would see that they never came to want.'

'They're so timid about it. And it wouldn't be nice, you know, to feel they were going to be dependent upon us for the rest of their lives. I had better go and see Virgie to-morrow morning, and bring her back for dinner.

'If you like,' Widdowson assented slowly. 'But why not send a message, and ask her to come here?'

'I had rather go. It makes a change for me.'

This was a word Widdowson detested. Change, on Monica's lips, always seemed to mean a release from his society. But he swallowed his dissatisfaction, and finally consented to the arrangement.

Virginia came to dinner, and stayed until nightfall. Thanks to her sister's kindness, she was better clad than in former days, but her face signified no improvement of health. The enthusiasm with which Rhoda Nunn had inspired her appeared only in fitful affectations of interest when Monica pressed her concerning the projected undertaking down in Somerset. In general she had a dreamy, reticent look, and became uncomfortable when any one gazed at her inquiringly. Her talk was of the most insignificant things; this afternoon she spent nearly half an hour in describing a kitten which Mrs. Conisbee had given her; care of the little animal appeared to have absorbed her whole attention for many days past.

Another visitor to-day was Mr. Newdick, the City clerk who had been present at Monica's wedding. He and Mrs. Luke Widdowson were the sole friends of her husband that Monica had seen. Mr. Newdick enjoyed coming to Herne Hill. Always lugubrious to begin with, he gradually cheered up, and by the time for departure was loquacious. But he had the oddest ideas of talk suitable to a drawing-room. Had he been permitted, he would have held forth to Monica by the hour on the history of the business firm which he had served for a quarter of a century. This subject alone could animate him. His anecdotes were as often as not quite unintelligible, save to people of City experience. For all that Monica did not dislike the man; he was a good, simple, unselfish fellow, and to her he behaved with exaggeration of respect.

A few days later Monica had a sudden fit of illness. Her marriage, and the long open-air holiday, had given her a much healthier appearance than when she was at the shop; but this present disorder resembled the attack she had suffered in Rutland Street. Widdowson hoped that it signified a condition for which he was anxiously waiting. That, however, did not seem to be the case. The medical man who was called in asked questions about the patient's mode of life. Did she take enough exercise? Had she wholesome variety of occupation? At these inquiries Widdowson inwardly raged. He was tormented with a suspicion that they resulted from something Monica had said to the doctor.

She kept her bed for three or four days, and on rising could only sit by the fireside, silent, melancholy. Widdowson indulged his hope, though Monica herself laughed it aside, and even showed annoyance if he return to the subject. Her temper was strangely uncertain; some chance word in a conversation would irritate her beyond endurance, and after an outburst of petulant displeasure she became obstinately mute. At other times she behaved with such exquisite docility and sweetness that Widdowson was beside himself with rapture.

After a week of convalescence, she said one morning,—

'Couldn't we go away somewhere? I don't think I shall ever be quite well staying here.'

'It's wretched weather,' replied her husband.

'Oh, but there are places where it wouldn't be like this. You don't mind the expense, do you, Edmund?'

'Expense? Not I, indeed! But—were you thinking of abroad?'

She looked at him with eyes that had suddenly brightened.

'Oh! would it be possible? People do go out of England in the winter.'

Widdowson plucked at his grizzled beard and fingered his watch-chain. It was a temptation. Why not take her away to some place where only foreigners and strangers would be about them? Yet the enterprise alarmed him.

'I have never been out of England,' he said, with misgiving.

'All the more reason why we should go. I think Miss Barfoot could advise us about it. She has been abroad, I know, and she has so many friends.'

'I don't see any need to consult Miss Barfoot,' he replied stiffly. 'I am not such a helpless man, Monica.'

Yet a feeling of inability to grapple with such an undertaking as this grew on him the more he thought of it. Naturally, his mind busied itself with such vague knowledge as he had gathered of those places in the South of France, where rich English people go to escape their own climate: Nice, Cannes. He could not imagine himself setting forth to these regions. Doubtless it was possible to travel thither, and live there when one arrived, without a knowledge of French; but he pictured all sorts of humiliating situations resulting from his ignorance. Above everything he dreaded humiliation in Monica's sight; it would be intolerable to have her comparing him with men who spoke foreign languages, and were at home on the Continent.

Nevertheless, he wrote to his friend Newdick, and invited him to dine, solely for the purpose of talking over this question with him in private. After dinner he broached the subject. To his surprise, Newdick had ideas concerning Nice and Cannes and such places. He had heard about them from the junior partner of his firm, a young gentleman who talked largely of his experiences abroad.

'An immoral lot there,' he said, smiling and shaking his head. 'Queer goings on.'

'Oh, but that's among the foreigners, isn't it?'

Thereupon Mr. Newdick revealed his acquaintance with English literature.

'Did you ever read any of Ouida's novels?'

'No, I never did.'

'I advise you to before you think of taking your wife over there. She writes a great deal about those parts. People get mixed up so, it seems. You couldn't live by yourself. You have to eat at public tables, and you'd have all sorts of people trying to make acquaintance with Mrs. Widdowson. They're a queer lot, I believe.'

He abandoned the thought, at once and utterly. When Monica learnt this—he gave only vague and unsatisfactory reasons—she fell back into her despondent mood. For a whole day she scarcely uttered a word.

On the next day, in the dreary afternoon, they were surprised by a call from Mrs. Luke. The widow—less than ever a widow in externals—came in with a burst of exuberant spirits, and began to scold the moping couple like an affectionate parent.

'When are you silly young people coming to an end of your honeymoon? Do you sit here day after day and call each other pretty names? Really it's very charming in its way. I never knew such an obstinate case.—Monica, my black-eyed beauty, change your frock, and come with me to look up the Hodgson Bulls. They're quite too awful; I can't face them alone; but I'm bound to keep in with them. Be off, and let me pitch into your young man for daring to refuse my dinner. Don't you know, sir, that my invitations are like those of Royalty—polite commands?'

Widdowson kept silence, waiting to see what his wife would do. He could not with decency object to her accompanying Mrs. Luke, yet hated the thought of such a step. A grim smile on his face, he sat stiffly, staring at the wall. To his inexpressible delight, Monica, after a short hesitation, excused herself; she was not well; she did not feel able—

'Oh!' laughed the visitor. 'I see, I see! Do just as you like, of course. But if Edmund has any *nous*'—this phrase she had learnt from a young gentleman, late of Oxford, now of Tattersall's and elsewhere—'he won't let you sit here in the dumps. You *are* in the dumps, I can see.'

The vivacious lady did not stay long. When she had rustled forth again to her carriage, Widdowson broke into a paean of amorous gratitude. What could he do to show how he appreciated Monica's self-denial on his behalf? For a day or two he was absent rather mysteriously, and in the meantime made up his mind, after consultation with Newdick, to take his wife for a holiday in Guernsey.

Monica, when she heard of this project, was at first moderately grateful, but in a day or two showed by reviving strength and spirits that she looked forward eagerly to the departure. Her husband advertised for lodgings in St. Peter Port; he would not face the disagreeable chances of a hotel. In a fortnight's time all their preparations were made. During their absence, which might extend over a month, Virginia was to live at Herne Hill, in supervision of the two servants.

On the last Sunday Monica went to see her friends in Queen's Road. Widdowson was ashamed to offer an objection; he much disliked her going there alone, but disliked equally the thought of accompanying her, for at Miss Barfoot's he could not pretend to sit, stand, or converse with ease.

It happened that Mrs. Cosgrove was again calling. On the first occasion of meeting with Monica this lady paid her no particular attention; to-day she addressed her in a friendly manner, and their conversation led to the discovery that both of them were about to spend the ensuing month in the same place. Mrs. Cosgrove hoped they might occasionally see each other.

Of this coincidence Monica thought better to say nothing on her return home. She could not be sure that her husband might not, at the last moment, decide to stay at Herne Hill rather than incur the risk of her meeting an acquaintance in Guernsey. On this point he could not be trusted to exercise common sense. For the first time Monica had a secret she desired to keep from him, and the necessity was one which could not but have an unfavourable effect on her manner of regarding Widdowson. They were to start on Monday evening. Through the day her mind was divided between joy in the thought of seeing a new part of the world and a sense of weary dislike for her home. She had not understood until now how terrible would be the prospect of living here for a long time with no companionship but her husband's. On the return that prospect would lie before her. But no; their way of life must somehow be modified; on that she was resolved.

## CHAPTER XVI - HEALTH FROM THE SEA

From Herne Hill to St. Peter Port was a change which made of Monica a new creature. The weather could not have been more propitious; day after day of still air and magnificent sky, with temperature which made a brisk walk at any hour thoroughly enjoyable, yet allowed one to sit at ease in the midday sunshine. Their lodgings were in the best part of the town, high up, looking forth over blue sea to the cliffs of Sark. Widdowson congratulated himself on having taken this step; it was like a revival of his honeymoon; never since their settling down at home had Monica been so grateful, so affectionate. Why, his wife was what he had thought her from the first, perfect in every wifely attribute. How lovely she looked as she sat down to the breakfast-table, after breathing sea air at the open windows, in her charming dress, her black hair arranged in some new fashion just to please him! Or when she walked with him about the quays, obviously admired by men who passed them. Or when she seated herself in the open carriage for a drive which would warm her cheeks and make her lips redder and sweeter.

'Edmund,' she said to him one evening, as they talked by the fireside, 'don't you think you take life rather too gravely?'

He laughed.

'Gravely? Don't I seem to enjoy myself?'

'Oh yes; just now. But—still in a rather serious way. One would think you always had cares on your mind, and were struggling to get rid of them.'

'I haven't a care in the world. I am the most blessed of mortals.'

'So you ought to think yourself. But when we get back again, how will it be? You won't be angry with me? I really don't think I can live again as we were doing.'

'Not live as—'

His brow darkened; he looked at her in astonishment.

'We ought to have more enjoyment,' she pursued courageously. 'Think of the numbers of people who live a dull, monotonous life just because they can't help it. How they would envy us, with so much money to spend, free to do just what we like! Doesn't it seem a pity to sit there day after day alone—'

'Don't, my darling!' he implored. 'Don't! That makes me think you don't really love me.

'Nonsense! I want you to see what I mean. I am not one of the silly people who care for nothing but amusement, but I do think we might enjoy our lives more when we are in London. We shan't live for ever, you know. Is it right to spend day after day sitting there in the house—'

'But come, come; we have our occupations. Surely it ought to be a pleasure to you to see that the house is kept in order. There are duties—'

'Yes, I know. But these duties I could perform in an hour or two.'

'Not thoroughly.'

'Quite thoroughly enough.'

'In my Opinion, Monica, a woman ought never to be so happy as when she is looking after her home.'

It was the old pedantic tone. His figure, in sympathy with it, abandoned an easy attitude and became awkward. But Monica would not allow herself to be alarmed. During the past week she had conducted herself so as to smooth the way for this very discussion. Unsuspecting husband!

'I wish to do my duty,' she said in a firm tone, 'but I don't think it's right to make dull work for oneself, when one might be living. I don't think it *is* living to go on week after week like that. If we were poor, and I had a lot of children to look after as well as all the housework to do, I believe I shouldn't grumble—at least, I hope I shouldn't. I should know that I ought to do what there was no one else to do, and make the best of it. But——'

'Make the best of it!' he interrupted indignantly. 'What an expression to use! It would not only be your duty, dear, but your privilege!'

'Wait a moment, Edmund. If you were a shopman earning fifteen shillings a week, and working from early morning to late at night, should you think it not Only your duty but your privilege?'

He made a wrathful gesture.

'What comparison is there? I should be earning a hard livelihood by slaving for other people. But a married woman who works in her own home, for her husband's children—'

'Work is work, and when a woman is overburdened with it she must find it difficult not to weary of home and husband and children all together. But of course I don't mean to say that my work is too hard. All I mean is, that I don't see why any one should *make* work, and why life shouldn't be as full of enjoyment as possible.'

'Monica, you have got these ideas from those people at Chelsea. That is exactly why I don't care for you to see much of them. I utterly disapprove of—'

'But you are mistaken. Miss Barfoot and Miss Nunn are all for work. They take life as seriously as you do.'

'Work? What kind of work? They want to make women unwomanly, to make them unfit for the only duties women ought to perform. You know very well my opinions about that kind of thing.'

He was trembling with the endeavour to control himself, to speak indulgently.

'I don't think, Edmund, there's much real difference between men and women. That is, there wouldn't be, if women had fair treatment.'

'Not much difference? Oh, come; you are talking nonsense. There's as much difference between their minds as between their bodies. They are made for entirely different duties.'

Monica sighed.

'Oh, that word Duty!'

Pained unutterably, Widdowson bent forward and took her hand. He spoke in a tone of the gravest but softest rebuke. She was giving entertainment to thoughts that would lead her who knew whither, that would undermine her happiness, would end by making both of them miserable. He besought her to put all such monstrous speculations out of her mind.

'Dear, good little wife! Do be guided by your husband. He is older than you, darling, and has seen so much more of the world.'

'I haven't said anything dreadful, dear. My thoughts don't come from other people; they rise naturally in my own head.'

'Now, what do you really want? You say you can't live as we were doing. What change would you make?'

'I should like to make more friends, and to see them often. I want to hear people talk, and know what is going on round about me. And to read a different kind of books; books that would really amuse me, and give me something I could think about with pleasure. Life will be a burden to me before long if I don't have more freedom.'

'Freedom?'

'Yes, I don't think there's any harm in saying that.'

'Freedom?' He glared at her. 'I shall begin to think that you wish you had never married me.'

'I should only wish that if I were made to feel that you shut me up in a house and couldn't trust me to go where I chose. Suppose the thought took you that you would go and walk about the City some afternoon, and you wished to go alone, just to be more at ease, should I have a right to forbid you, or grumble at you? And yet you are very dissatisfied if I wish to go anywhere alone.'

'But here's the old confusion. I am a man; you are a woman.'

'I can't see that that makes any difference. A woman ought to go about just as freely as a man. I don't think it's just. When I have done my work at home I think I ought to be every bit as free as you are—every bit as free. And I'm sure, Edmund, that love needs freedom if it is to remain love in truth.'

He looked at her keenly.

'That's a dreadful thing for you to say. So, if I disapprove of your becoming the kind of woman that acknowledges no law, you will cease to love me?'

'What law do you mean?'

'Why, the natural law that points out a woman's place, and'—he added, with shaken voice—'commands her to follow her husband's guidance.'

'Now you are angry. We mustn't talk about it any more just now.'

She rose and poured out a glass of water. Her hand trembled as she drank. Widdowson fell into gloomy abstraction. Later, as they lay side by side, he wished to renew the theme, but Monica would not talk; she declared herself too sleepy, turned her back to him, and soon slept indeed.

That night the weather became stormy; a roaring wind swept the Channel, and when day broke nothing could be seen but cloud and rain. Widdowson, who had rested little, was in a heavy, taciturn mood; Monica, on the other hand, talked gaily, seeming not to observe her companion's irresponsiveness. She was glad of the wild sky; now they would see another aspect of island life—the fierce and perilous surges beating about these granite shores.

They had brought with them a few books, and Widdowson, after breakfast, sat down by the fire to read. Monica first of all wrote a letter to her sister; then, as it was still impossible to go out, she took up one of the volumes that lay on a side-table in their sitting-room, novels left by former lodgers. Her choice was something or other with yellow back. Widdowson, watching all her movements furtively, became aware of the pictured cover.

'I don't think you'll get much good out of that,' he remarked, after one or two efforts to speak.

'No harm, at all events,' she replied good-humouredly.

'I'm not so sure. Why should you waste your time? Take "Guy Mannering," if you want a novel.'

'I'll see how I like this first.'

He felt himself powerless, and suffered acutely from the thought that Monica was in rebellion against him. He could not understand what had brought about this sudden change. Fear of losing his wife's love restrained him from practical despotism, yet he was very near to uttering a definite command.

In the afternoon it no longer rained, and the wind had less violence. They went out to look at the sea. Many people were gathered about the harbour, whence was a fine view of the great waves that broke into leaping foam and spray against the crags of Sark. As they stood thus Occupied, Monica heard her name spoken in a friendly voice—that of Mrs. Cosgrove.

'I have been expecting to see you,' said the lady. 'We arrived three days ago.'

Widdowson, starting with surprise, turned to examine the speaker. He saw a woman of something less than middle age, unfashionably attired, good-looking, with an air of high spirits; only when she offered her hand to him did he remember having met her at Miss Barfoot's. To be graceful in a high wind is difficult for any man; the ungainliness with which he returned Mrs. Cosgrove's greeting could not have been surpassed, and probably would have been much the same even had he not, of necessity, stood clutching at his felt hat.

The three talked for a few minutes. With Mrs. Cosgrove were two persons, a younger woman and a man of about thirty—the latter a comely and vivacious fellow, with rather long hair of the orange-tawny hue. These looked at Monica, but Mrs. Cosgrove made no introduction.

'Come and see me, will you?' she said, mentioning her address. 'One can't get much in the evenings; I shall be nearly always at home after dinner, and we have music—of a kind.'

Monica boldly accepted the invitation, said she would be glad to come. Then Mrs. Cosgrove took leave of them, and walked landwards with her companions.

Widdowson stood gazing at the sea. There was no misreading his countenance. When Monica had remarked it, she pressed her lips together, and waited for what he would say or do. He said nothing, but presently turned his back upon the waves and began to walk on. Neither spoke until they were in the shelter of the streets; then Widdowson asked suddenly,—

'Who *is* that person?'

'I only know her name, and that she goes to Miss Barfoot's.'

'It's a most extraordinary thing,' he exclaimed in high irritation. 'There's no getting out of the way of those people.'

Monica also was angry; her cheeks, reddened by the wind, grew hotter.

'It's still more extraordinary that you should object so to them.'

'Whether or no—I *do* object, and I had rather you didn't go to see that woman.'

'You are unreasonable,' Monica answered sharply. 'Certainly I shall go and see her.'

'I forbid you to do so! If you go, it will be in defiance of my wish.'

'Then I am obliged to defy your wish. I shall certainly go.'

His face was frightfully distorted. Had they been in a lonely spot, Monica would have felt afraid of him. She moved hurriedly away in the direction of their lodgings, and for a few paces he followed; then he checked himself, turned round about, took an opposite way.

With strides of rage he went along by the quay, past the hotels and the smaller houses that follow, on to St. Sampson. The wind, again preparing for a tempestuous night, beat and shook and at moments all but stopped him; he set his teeth like a madman, and raged on. Past the granite quarries at Bordeaux Harbour, then towards the wild north extremity of the island, the sandy waste of L'Ancresse. When darkness began to fall, no human being was in his range of sight. He stood on one spot for nearly a quarter of an hour, watching, or appearing to watch, the black, low-flying scud.

Their time for dining was seven. Shortly before this Widdowson entered the house and went to the sitting-room; Monica was not there. He found her in the bed-chamber, before the looking-glass. At the sight of his reflected face she turned instantly.

'Monica!' He put his hands on her shoulders, whispering hoarsely, 'Monica! don't you love me?'

She looked away, not replying.

'Monica!'

And of a sudden he fell on his knees before her, clasped her about the waist, burst into choking sobs.

'Have you no love for me? My darling! My dear, beautiful wife! Have you begun to hate me?'

Tears came to her eyes. She implored him to rise and command himself.

'I was so violent, so brutal with you. I spoke without thinking—'

'But *why* should you speak like that? Why are you so unreasonable? If you forbid me to do simple things, with not the least harm in them, you can't expect me to take it like a child. I shall resist; I can't help it.'

He had risen and was crushing her in his arms, his hot breath on her neck, when he began to whisper,—

'I want to keep you all to myself. I don't like these people—they think so differently—they put such hateful ideas into your mind—they are not the right kind of friends for you—'

'You misunderstand them, and you don't in the least understand me. Oh, you hurt me, Edmund!'

He released her body, and took her head between his hands.

'I had rather you were dead than that you should cease to love me! You shall go to see her; I won't say a word against it. But, Monica, be faithful, be faithful to me!'

'Faithful to you?' she echoed in astonishment. 'What have I said or done to put you in such a state? Because I wish to make a few friends as all women do—'

'It's because I have lived so much alone. I have never had more than one or two friends, and I am absurdly jealous when you want to get away from me and amuse yourself with strangers. I can't talk to such people. I am not suited for society. If I hadn't met you in that strange way, by miracle, I should never have been able to marry. If I allow you to have these friends—'

'I don't like to hear that word. Why should you say *allow*? Do you think of me as your servant, Edmund?'

'You know how I think of you. It is I who am your servant, your slave.'

'Oh, I can't believe that!' She pressed her handkerchief to her cheeks, and laughed unnaturally. 'Such words don't mean anything. It is you who forbid and allow and command, and—'

'I will never again use such words. Only convince me that you love me as much as ever.'

'It is so miserable to begin quarrelling—'

'Never again! Say you love me! Put your arms round my neck—press closer to me—'

She kissed his cheek, but did not utter a word.

'You can't say that you love me?'

'I think I am always showing it. Do get ready for dinner now; it's past seven. Oh, how foolish you have been!'

Of course their talk lasted half through the night. Monica held with remarkable firmness to the position she had taken; a much older woman might have envied her steadfast yet quite rational assertion of the right to live a life of her Own apart from that imposed upon her by the duties of wedlock. A great deal of this spirit and the utterance it found was traceable to her association with the women whom Widdowson so deeply suspected; prior to her sojourn in Rutland Street she could not even have made clear to herself the demands which she now very clearly formulated. Believing that she had learnt nothing from them, and till of late instinctively opposing the doctrines held by Miss Barfoot and Rhoda Nunn, Monica in truth owed the sole bit of real education she had ever received to those few weeks of attendance in Great Portland Street. Circumstances were now proving how apt a pupil she had been, even against her will. Marriage, as is always the case with women capable of development, made for her a new heaven and a new earth; perhaps on no single subject did she now think as on the morning of her wedding-day.

'You must either trust me completely,' she said, 'or not at all. If you can't and won't trust me, how can I possibly love you?'

'Am I never to advise?' asked her husband, baffled, and even awed, by this extraordinary revelation of a woman he had supposed himself to know thoroughly.

'Oh, that's a very different thing from forbidding and commanding!' she laughed. 'There was that novel this morning. Of course I know as well as you do that "Guy Mannering" is better; but that doesn't say I am not to form my opinion of other books. You mustn't be afraid to leave me the same freedom you have yourself.'

The result of it all was that Widdowson felt his passionate love glow with new fire. For a moment he thought himself capable of accepting this change in their relations. The marvellous thought of equality between man and wife, that gospel which in far-off days will refashion the world, for an instant smote his imagination and exalted him above his native level.

Monica paid for the energy she had put forth by a day of suffering. Her head ached intolerably; she had feverish symptoms, and could hardly raise herself from the bed. It passed, and she was once more eager to go forth under the blue sky that followed the tempest.

'Will you go with me to Mrs. Cosgrove's this evening?' she asked of her husband.

He consented, and after dinner they sought the hotel where their acquaintance was staying. Widdowson was in extreme discomfort, partly due to the fact that he had no dress clothes to put on; for far from anticipating or desiring any such intercourse in Guernsey, he had never thought of packing an evening suit. Had he known Mrs. Cosgrave this uneasiness would have been spared him. That lady was in revolt against far graver institutions than the swallow-tail; she cared not a button in what garb her visitors came to her. On their arrival, they found, to Widdowson's horror, a room full of women. With the hostess was that younger lady they had seen on the quay, Mrs. Cosgrove's unmarried sister; Miss Knott's health had demanded this retreat from the London winter. The guests were four—a Mrs. Bevis and her three daughters—all invalidish persons, the mother somewhat lackadaisical, the girls with a look of unwilling spinsterhood.

Monica, noteworthy among the gathering for her sweet, bright prettiness, and the finish of her dress, soon made herself at home; she chatted gaily with the girls—wondering indeed at her own air of maturity, which came to her for the first time. Mrs. Cosgrove, an easy woman of the world when circumstances required it, did her best to get something out of Widdowson who presently thawed a little.

Then Miss Knott sat down to the piano, and played more than tolerably well; and the youngest Miss Bevis sang a song of Schubert, with passable voice but in very distressing German—the sole person distressed by it being the hostess.

Meanwhile Monica had been captured by Mrs. Bevis, who discoursed to her on a subject painfully familiar to all the old lady's friends.

'Do you know my son, Mrs. Widdowson? Oh, I thought you had perhaps met him. You will do so this evening, I hope. He is over here on a fortnight's holiday.'

'Do you live in Guernsey?' Monica inquired.

'*I* practically live here, and one of my daughters is always with me. The other two live with their brother in a flat in Bayswater. Do you care for flats, Mrs. Widdowson?'

Monica could only say that she had no experience of that institution.

'I do think them such a boon,' pursued Mrs. Bevis. 'They are expensive but the advantages and comforts are so many. My son wouldn't on any consideration give up his flat. As I was saying, he always has two of his sisters to keep house for him. He is quite a young man, not yet thirty, but—would you believe it?—we are all dependent upon him!

My son has supported the *whole* of the family for the last six or seven years, and that by his own work. It sounds incredible, doesn't it? But for him we should be quite unable to live. The dear girls have very delicate health; simply impossible for them to exert themselves in any way. My son has made extraordinary sacrifices on our account. His desire was to be a professional musician, and every one thinks he would have become eminent; myself, I am convinced of it—perhaps that is only natural. But when our circumstances began to grow very doubtful, and we really didn't know what was before us, my son consented to follow a business career—that of wine merchant, with which his father was connected. And he exerted himself so nobly, and gave proof of such ability, that very soon all our fears were at an end; and now, before he is thirty, his position is quite assured. We have no longer a care. I live here very economically—really sweet lodgings on the road to St. Martin's; I *do* hope you will come and see me. And the girls go backwards and forwards. You see we are *all* here at present. When my son returns to London he will take the eldest and the youngest with him. The middle girl, dear Grace—she is thought very clever in water-colours, and I am quite sure, if it were necessary, she could pursue the arts in a professional spirit.'

Mr. Bevis entered the room, and Monica recognized the sprightly young man whom she had seen on the quay. The hostess presented him to her new friends, and he got into talk with Widdowson. Requested to make music for the company, he sang a gay little piece, which, to Monica at all events, seemed one of the most delightful things she had ever heard.

'His own composition,' whispered Miss Grace Bevis, then sitting by Mrs. Widdowson.

That increased her delight. Foolish as Mrs. Bevis undoubtedly was, she perchance had not praised her son beyond his merits. He looked the best of good fellows; so kind and merry and spirited; such a capable man, too. It struck Monica as a very hard fate that he should have this family on his hands. What they must cost him! Probably he could not think of marrying, just on their account.

Mr. Bevis came and took a place by her side.

'Thank you so very much,' she said, 'for that charming song. Is it published?'

'Oh dear, no!' He laughed and shook his thick hair about. 'It's one of two or three that I somehow struck out when I was studying in Germany, ages ago. You play, I hope?'

Monica gave a sad negative.

'Oh, what does it matter? There are hosts of people who will always be overjoyed to play when you ask them. It would be a capital thing if only those children were allowed to learn an instrument who showed genuine talent for music.'

'In that case,' said Monica, 'there certainly wouldn't be hosts of people ready to play for me.'

'No.' His merry laugh was repeated. 'You mustn't mind when I contradict myself; it's one of my habits. Are you here for the whole winter?'

'Only a few weeks, unfortunately.'

'And do you dread the voyage back?'

'To tell the truth, I do. I had a very unpleasant time coming.'

'As for myself, how I ever undertake the thing I really don't know. One of these times I shall die; there's not a shadow of doubt of that. The girls always have to carry me ashore, one holding me by the hair and one by the boots. Happily, I am so emancipated that my weight doesn't distress them. I pick up flesh in a day or two, and then my health is stupendous—as at present. You see how marvellously *fit* I look.'

'Yes, you look very well,' replied Monica, glancing at the fair, comely face.

'It's deceptive. All our family have wretched constitutions. If I go to work regularly for a couple of months without a holiday, I sink into absolute decrepitude. An office-chair has been specially made for me, to hold me up at the desk.—I beg your pardon for this clowning, Mrs. Widdowson,' he suddenly added in another voice. 'The air puts me in such spirits. What air it is! Speaking quite seriously, my mother was saved by coming to live here. We believed her to be dying, and now I have hopes that she will live ever so many years longer.'

He spoke of his mother with evident affection, glancing kindly towards her with his blue eyes.

Only once or twice had Monica ventured to exchange a glance with her husband. It satisfied her that he managed to converse; what his mood really was could not be determined until afterwards. When they were about to leave she saw him, to her surprise, speaking quite pleasantly with Mr. Bevis. A carriage was procured to convey them home, and as soon as they had started, Monica asked her husband, with a merry look, how he had enjoyed himself.

'There is not much harm in it,' he replied dryly.

'Harm? How like you, Edmund, to put it that way! Now confess you will be glad to go again.'

'I shall go if you wish.'

'Unsatisfactory man! You can't bring yourself to admit that it was pleasant to be among new people. I believe, in your heart, you think all enjoyment is wrong. The music was nice, wasn't it?'

'I didn't think much of the girl's singing, but that fellow Bevis wasn't bad.'

Monica examined him as he spoke, and seemed to suppress a laugh.

'No, he wasn't at all bad. I saw you talking with Mrs. Bevis. Did she tell you anything about her wonderful son?'

'Nothing particular.'

'Oh, then I must tell you the whole story.'

And she did so, in a tone half of jest, half of serious approval.

'I don't see that he has done anything more than his duty,' remarked Widdowson at the end. 'But he isn't a bad fellow.'

For private reasons, Monica contrasted this attitude towards Bevis with the disfavour her husband had shown to Mr. Barfoot, and was secretly much amused.

Two or three days after they went to spend the morning at Petit Bot Bay, and there encountered with Bevis and his three sisters. The result was an invitation to go back and have lunch at Mrs. Bevis's lodgings; they accepted it, and remained with their acquaintances till dusk. The young man's holiday was at an end; next morning he would face the voyage which he had depicted so grotesquely.

'And alone!' he lamented to Monica. 'Only think of it. The girls are all rather below par just now; they had better stay here for the present.'

'And in London you will be alone too?'

'Yes. It's very sad. I must bear up under it. The worst of it is, I am naturally subject to depression. In solitude I sink, sink. But the subject is too painful. Don't let us darken the last hours with such reflections.'

Widdowson retained his indulgent opinion of the facetious young wine merchant. He even laughed now and then in recalling some phrase or other that Bevis had used to him.

Subsequently, Monica had several long conversations with the old lady. Impelled to gossipy frankness about all her affairs, Mrs. Bevis allowed it to be understood that the chief reason for two of the girls always being with their brother was the possibility thus afforded of their 'meeting people'—that is to say, of their having a chance of marriage. Mrs. Cosgrove and one or two other ladies did them social service.

'They never *will* marry!' said Monica to her husband, rather thoughtfully than with commiseration.

'Why not? They are nice enough girls.'

'Yes, but they have no money; and'—she smiled—'people see that they want to find husbands.'

'I don't see that the first matters; and the second is only natural.'

Monica attempted no rejoinder, but said presently—

'Now they are just the kind of women who ought to find something to do.'

'Something to do? Why, they attend to their mother and their brother. What could be more proper?'

'Very proper, perhaps. But they are miserable, and always will be.'

'Then they have no *right* to be miserable. They are doing their duty, and that ought to keep them cheerful.'

Monica could have said many things, but she overcame the desire, and laughed the subject aside.

## CHAPTER XVII - THE TRIUMPH

Nor till mid-winter did Barfoot again see his friends the Micklethwaites. By invitation he went to South Tottenham on New Year's Eve, and dined with them at seven o'clock. He was the first guest that had entered the house since their marriage.

From the very doorstep Everard became conscious of a domestic atmosphere that told soothingly upon his nerves. The little servant who opened to him exhibited a gentle, noiseless demeanour which was no doubt the result of careful discipline. Micklethwaite himself, who at once came out into the passage, gave proof of a like influence; his hearty greeting was spoken in soft tones; a placid happiness beamed from his face. In the sitting-room (Micklethwaite's study, used for reception because the other had to serve as dining-room) tempered lamplight and the glow of a hospitable fire showed the hostess and her blind sister standing in expectation; to Everard's eyes both of them looked far better in health than a few months ago. Mrs. Micklethwaite was no longer so distressingly old; an expression that resembled girlish pleasure lit up her countenance as she stepped forward; nay, if he mistook not, there came a gentle warmth to her cheek, and the momentary downward glance was as graceful and modest as in a youthful bride. Never had Barfoot approached a woman with more finished courtesy, the sincere expression of his feeling. The blind sister he regarded in like spirit; his voice touched its softest note as he held her hand for a moment and replied to her pleasant words.

No undue indication of poverty disturbed him. He saw that the house had been improved in many ways since Mrs. Micklethwaite had taken possession of it; pictures, ornaments, pieces of furniture were added, all in simple taste, but serving to heighten the effect of refined comfort. Where the average woman would have displayed pretentious emptiness, Mrs. Micklethwaite had made a home which in its way was beautiful. The dinner, which she herself had cooked, and which she assisted in serving, aimed at being no more than a simple; decorous meal, but the guest unfeignedly enjoyed it; even the vegetables and the bread seemed to him to have a daintier flavour than at many a rich table. He could not help noticing and admiring the skill with which Miss Wheatley ate without seeing what was before her; had he not known her misfortune, he would hardly have become aware of it by any peculiarity as she sat opposite to him.

The mathematician had learnt to sit upon a chair like ordinary mortals. For the first week or two it must have cost him severe restraint; now he betrayed no temptation to roll and jerk and twist himself. When the ladies retired, he reached from the sideboard a box which Barfoot viewed with uneasiness.

'Do you smoke here—in this room?'

'Oh, why not?'

Everard glanced at the pretty curtains before the windows.

'No, my boy, you do *not* smoke here. And, in fact, I like your claret; I won't spoil the flavour of it.'

'As you please; but I think Fanny will be distressed.'

'You shall say that I have abandoned the weed.'

Emotions were at conflict in Micklethwaite's mind, but finally he beamed with gratitude.

'Barfoot'—he bent forward and touched his friend's arm—'there are angels walking the earth in this our day. Science hasn't abolished them, my dear fellow, and I don't think it ever will.'

'It falls to the lot of but few men to encounter them, and of fewer still to entertain them permanently in a cottage at South Tottenham.'

'You are right.' Micklethwaite laughed in a new way, with scarcely any sound; a change Everard had already noticed. 'These two sisters—but I had better not speak about them. In my old age I have become a worshipper, a mystic, a man of dream and vision.'

'How about worship in a parochial sense?' inquired Barfoot, smiling. 'Any difficulty of that point?'

'I conform, in moderation. Nothing would be asked of me. There is no fanaticism, no intolerance. It would be brutal if I declined to go to church on a Sunday morning. You see, my strictly scientific attitude helps in avoiding offence. Fanny can't understand it, but my lack of dogmatism vastly relieves her. I have been trying to explain to her that the scientific mind can have nothing to do with materialism. The new order of ideas is of course very difficult for her to grasp; but in time, in time.'

'For heaven's sake, don't attempt conversion!'

'On no account whatever. But I *should* like her to see what is meant by perception and conception, by the relativity of time and space—and a few simple things of that kind!'

Barfoot laughed heartily.

'By-the-bye,' he said, shifting to safer ground, 'my brother Tom is in London, and in wretched health. *His* angel is from the wrong quarter, from the nethermost pit. I seriously believe that she has a plan for killing her husband. You remember my mentioning in a letter his horse-accident? He has never recovered from that, and as likely as not never will. His wife brought him away from Madeira just when he ought to have stopped there to get well. He settled himself at Torquay, whilst that woman ran about to pay visits. It was understood that she should go back to him at Torquay, but this she at length refused to do. The place was too dull; it didn't suit her extremely delicate health; she must live in London, her pure native air. If Tom had taken any advice, he would have let her live just where she pleased, thanking Heaven that she was at a distance from him. But the poor fellow can't be away from her. He has come up, and here I feel convinced he will die. It's a very monstrous thing, but uncommonly like women in general who have got a man into their power.'

Micklethwaite shook his head.

'You are too hard upon them. You have been unlucky. You know my view of your duty.'

'I begin to think that marriage isn't impossible for me,' said Barfoot, with a grave smile.

'Ha! Capital!'

'But as likely as not it will be marriage without forms—imply a free union.'

The mathematician was downcast.

'I'm sorry to hear that. It won't do. We must conform. Besides, in that case the person decidedly isn't suitable to you. You of all men must marry a lady.'

'I should never think of any one that wasn't a lady.'

'Is emancipation getting as far as that? Do ladies enter into that kind of union?'

'I don't know of any example. That's just why the idea tempts me.' Barfoot would go no further in explanation.

'How about your new algebra?'

'Alas! My dear boy, the temptation is so frightful—when I get back home. Remember that I have never known what it was to sit and talk through the evening with ordinary friends, let alone—It's too much for me just yet. And, you know, I don't venture to work on Sundays. That will come; all in good time. I must grant myself half a year of luxury after such a life as mine has been.'

'Of course you must. Let algebra wait.'

'I think it over, of course, at odd moments. Church on Sunday morning is a good opportunity.'

Barfoot could not stay to see the old year out, but good wishes were none the less heartily exchanged before he went. Micklethwaite walked with him to the railway station; at a few paces' distance from his house he stood and pointed back to it.

'That little place, Barfoot, is one of the sacred spots of the earth. Strange to think that the house has been waiting for me there through all the years of my hopelessness. I feel that a mysterious light ought to shine about it. It oughtn't to look just like common houses.'

On his way home Everard thought over what he had seen and heard, smiling good-naturedly. Well, that was one ideal of marriage. Not *his* ideal; but very beautiful amid the vulgarities and vileness of ordinary experience. It was the old fashion in its purest presentment; the consecrated form of domestic happiness, removed beyond reach of satire, only to be touched, if touched at all, with the very gentlest irony.

A life by no means for him. If he tried it, even with a woman so perfect, he would perish of *ennui*. For him marriage must not mean repose, inevitably tending to drowsiness, but the mutual incitement of vigorous minds. Passion—yes, there must be passion, at all events to begin with; passion not impossible of revival in days subsequent to its first indulgence. Beauty in the academic sense he no longer demanded; enough that the face spoke eloquently, that the limbs were vigorous. Let beauty perish if it cannot ally itself with mind; be a woman what else she may, let her have brains and the power of using them! In that demand the maturity of his manhood expressed itself. For casual amour the odalisque could still prevail with him; but for the life of wedlock, the durable companionship of man and woman, intellect was his first requirement.

A woman with man's capability of understanding and reasoning; free from superstition, religious or social; far above the ignoble weaknesses which men have been base enough to idealize in her sex. A woman who would scorn the vulgarism of jealousy, and yet know what it is to love. This was asking much of nature and civilization; did he grossly deceive himself in thinking he had found the paragon?

For thus far had he advanced in his thoughts of Rhoda Nunn. If the phrase had any meaning, he was in love with her; yet, strange complex of emotions, he was still only half serious in his desire to take her for a wife, wishing rather to amuse and flatter himself by merely inspiring her with passion. Therefore he refused to entertain a thought of formal marriage. To obtain her consent to marriage would mean nothing at all; it would afford him no satisfaction. But so to play upon her emotions that the proud, intellectual, earnest woman was willing to defy society for his sake—ah! that would be an end worth achieving.

Ever since the dialogue in which he frankly explained his position, and all but declared love, he had not once seen Rhoda in private. She shunned him purposely beyond a doubt, and did not that denote a fear of him justified by her inclination? The postponement of what must necessarily come to pass between them began to try his patience, as assuredly it inflamed his ardour. If no other resource offered, he would be obliged to make his cousin an accomplice by requesting her beforehand to leave him alone with Rhoda some evening when he had called upon them.

But it was time that chance favoured him, and his interview with Miss Nunn came about in a way he could not have foreseen.

At the end of the first week of January he was invited to dine at Miss Barfoot's. The afternoon had been foggy, and when he set forth there seemed to be some likelihood of a plague of choking darkness such as would obstruct traffic. As usual, he went by train to Sloane Square, purposing (for it was dry under foot, and he could not disregard small economies) to walk the short distance from there to Queen's Road. On coming out from the station he found the fog so dense that it was doubtful whether he could reach his journey's end. Cabs were not to be had; he must either explore the gloom, with risk of getting nowhere at all, or give it up and take a train back. But he longed too ardently for the sight of Rhoda to abandon his evening without an effort. Having with difficulty made his way into King's Road, he found progress easier on account of the shop illuminations; the fog, however, was growing every moment more fearsome, and when he had to turn out of the highway his case appeared desperate. Literally he groped along, feeling the fronts of the houses. As under ordinary circumstances he would have had only just time enough to reach his cousin's punctually, he must be very late: perhaps they would conclude that he had not ventured out on such a night, and were already dining without him. No matter; as well go one way as another now. After abandoning hope several times, and all but asphyxiated, he found by inquiry of a man with whom he collided that he was actually within a few doors of his destination. Another effort and he rang a joyous peal at the bell.

A mistake. It was the wrong house, and he had to go two doors farther on.

This time he procured admittance to the familiar little hall. The servant smiled at him, but said nothing. He was led to the drawing-room, and there found Rhoda Nunn alone. This fact did not so much surprise him as Rhoda's appearance. For the first time since he had known her, her dress was not uniform black; she wore a red silk blouse with a black skirt, and so admirable was the effect of this costume that he scarcely refrained from a delighted exclamation.

Some concern was visible in her face.

'I am sorry to say,' were her first words, 'that Miss Barfoot will not be here in time for dinner. She went to Faversham this morning, and ought to have been back about half-past seven. But a telegram came some time ago. A thick fog caused her to miss the train, and the next doesn't reach Victoria till ten minutes past ten.'

It was now half-past eight; dinner had been appointed for the hour. Barfoot explained his lateness in arriving.

'Is it so bad as that? I didn't know.'

The situation embarrassed both of them. Barfoot suspected a hope on Miss Nunn's part that he would relieve her of his company, but, even had there been no external hindrance, he could not have relinquished the happy occasion. To use frankness was best.

'Out of the question for me to leave the house,' he said, meeting her eyes and smiling. 'You won't be hard upon a starving man?'

At once Rhoda made a pretence of having felt no hesitation.

'Oh, of course we will dine immediately.' She rang the bell. 'Miss Barfoot took it for granted that I would represent her. Look, the fog is penetrating even to our fireside.'

'Cheerful, very. What is Mary doing at Faversham?'

'Some one she has been corresponding with for some time begged her to go down and give an address to a number of ladies on—a certain subject.'

'Ah! Mary is on the way to become a celebrity.'

'Quite against her will, as you know.'

They went to dinner, and Barfoot, thoroughly enjoying the abnormal state of things, continued to talk of his cousin.

'It seems to me that she can't logically refuse to put herself forward. Work of her kind can't be done in a corner. It isn't a case of "Oh teach the orphan girl to sew."'

'I have used the same argument to her,' said Rhoda.

Her place at the head of the table had its full effect upon Everard's imagination. Why should he hold by a resolve of which he did not absolutely approve the motive? Why not ask her simply to be his wife, and so remove one element of difficulty from his pursuit? True, he was wretchedly poor. Marrying on such an income, he would at once find his freedom restricted in every direction. But then, more likely than not, Rhoda had determined against marriage, and of him, especially, never thought for a moment as a possible husband. Well, that was what he wanted to ascertain.

They conversed naturally enough till the meal was over. Then their embarrassment revived, but this time it was Rhoda who took the initiative.

'Shall I leave you to your meditations?' she asked, moving a few inches from the table.

'I should much prefer your society, if you will grant it me for a little longer.'

Without speaking, she rose and led the way to the drawingroom. There, sitting at a formal distance from each other, they talked—of the fog. Would Miss Barfoot be able to get back at all?

'*A propos*,' said Everard, 'did you ever read "The City of Dreadful Night"?'

'Yes, I have read it.'

'Without sympathy, of course?'

'Why "of course"? Do I seem to you a shallow optimist?'

'No. A vigorous and rational optimist—such as I myself aim at being.'

'Do you? But optimism of that kind must be proved by some effort on behalf of society.'

'Precisely the effort I am making. If a man works at developing and fortifying the best things in his own character, he is surely doing society a service.'

She smiled sceptically.

'Yes, no doubt. But how do you develop and fortify yourself?'

She was meeting him half-way, thought Everard. Foreseeing the inevitable, she wished to have it over and done with. Or else—

'I live very quietly,' was his reply, 'thinking of grave problems most of my time. You know I am a great deal alone.'

'Naturally.'

'No; anything but naturally.'

Rhoda said nothing. He waited a moment, then moved to a seat much nearer hers. Her face hardened, and he saw her fingers lock together.

'Where a man is in love, solitude seems to him the most unnatural of conditions.'

'Please don't make me your confidante, Mr. Barfoot,' Rhoda with well-assumed pleasantry. 'I have no taste for that kind of thing.'

'But I can't help doing so. It is you that I am in love with.'

'I am very sorry to hear it. Happily, the sentiment will not long trouble you.'

He read in her eyes and on her lips a profound agitation. She glanced about the room, and, before he could again speak, had risen to ring the bell.

'You always take coffee, I think?'

Without troubling to give any assent, he moved apart and turned over some books on the table. For full five minutes there was silence. The coffee was brought; he tasted it and put his cup down. Seeing that Rhoda had, as it were, entrenched herself behind the beverage, and would continue to sip at is as long as might be necessary, he went and stood in front of her.

'Miss Nunn, I am more serious than you will give me credit for being. The sentiment, as you call it, has troubled me for some time, and will last.'

Her refuge failed her. The cup she was holding began to shake a little.

'Please let me put it aside for you.'

Rhoda allowed him to do so, and then locked her fingers.

'I am so much in love with you that I can't keep away from this house more than a few days at a time. Of course you have known it; I haven't tried to disguise why I came here so often. It's so seldom that I see you alone; and now that fortune is kind to me I must speak as best I can. I won't make myself ridiculous in your eyes—if I can help it. You despise the love-making of ballrooms and garden parties; so do I, most heartily. Let me speak like a man who has few illusions to overcome. I want you for the companion of my life; I don't see very well how I am to do without you. You know, I think, that I have only a moderate competence; it's enough to live upon without miseries, that's all one can say. Probably I shall never be richer, for I can't promise to exert myself to earn money; I wish to live for other things. You can picture the kind of life I want you to share. You know me well enough to understand that my wife—if we use the old word—would be as free to live in her own way as I to live in mine. All the same, it is love that I am asking for. Think how you may about man and woman, you know that there is such a thing as love between them, and that the love of a man and a woman who can think intelligently may be the best thing life has to offer them.'

He could not see her eyes, but she was smiling in a forced way, with her lips close set.

'As you insisted on speaking,' she said at length, 'I had no choice but to listen. It is usual, I think—if one may trust the novels—for a woman to return thanks when an offer of this kind has been made to her. So—thank you very much, Mr. Barfoot.'

Everard seized a little chair that was close by, planted it beside Rhoda's, there seated himself and took possession of one of her hands. It was done so rapidly and vehemently that Rhoda started back, her expression changing from sportive mockery to all but alarm.

'I will have no such thanks,' he uttered in a low voice, much moved, a smile making him look strangely stern. 'You shall understand what it means when a man says that he loves you. I have come to think your face so beautiful that I am in torment with the desire to press my lips upon yours. Don't be afraid that I shall be brutal enough to do it without your consent; my respect for you is stronger even than my passion. When I first saw you, I thought you interesting because of your evident intelligence—nothing more; indeed you were not a woman to me. Now you are the one woman in the world; no other can draw my eyes from you. Touch me with your fingers and I shall tremble—that is what my love means.'

She was colourless; her lips, just parted, quivered as the breath panted between them. She did not try to withdraw her hand.

'Can you love me in return?' Everard went on, his face still nearer. 'Am I anything like this to *you*? Have the courage you boast of. Speak to me as one human being to another, plain, honest words.'

'I don't love you in the least. And if I did I would never share your life.'

The voice was very unlike her familiar tones. It seemed to hurt her to speak.

'The reason.—Because you have no faith in me?'

'I can't say whether I have or not. I know absolutely nothing of your life. But I have my work, and no one shall ever persuade me to abandon it.'

'Your work? How do you understand it? What is its importance to you?'

'Oh, and you pretend to know me so well that you wish me to be your companion at every moment!'

She laughed mockingly, and tried to draw away her hand, for it was burnt by the heat of his. Barfoot held her firmly.

'What *is* your work? Copying with a type-machine, and teaching others to do the same—isn't that it?'

'The work by which I earn money, yes. But if it were no more than that—'

'Explain, then.'

Passion was overmastering him as he watched the fine scorn in her eyes. He raised her hand to his lips.

'No!' Rhoda exclaimed with sudden wrath. 'Your respect—oh, I appreciate your respect!'

She wrenched herself from his grasp, and went apart. Barfoot rose, gazing at her with admiration.

'It is better I should be at a distance from you,' he said. 'I want to know your mind, and not to be made insensate.'

'Wouldn't it be better still if you left me?' Rhoda suggested, mistress of herself again.

'If you really wish it.' He remembered the circumstances and spoke submissively. 'Yet the fog gives me such a good excuse for begging your indulgence. The chances are I should only lose myself in an inferno.'

'Doesn't it strike you that you take an advantage of me, as you did once before? I make no pretence of equalling you in muscular strength, yet you try to hold me by force.'

He divined in her pleasure akin to his own, the delight of conflict. Otherwise, she would never have spoken thus.

'Yes, it is true. Love revives the barbarian; it wouldn't mean much if it didn't. In this one respect I suppose no man, however civilized, would wish the woman he loves to be his equal. Marriage by capture can't quite be done away with. You say you have not the least love for me; if you had, should I like you to confess it instantly? A man must plead and woo; but there are different ways. I can't kneel before you and exclaim about my miserable unworthiness—for I am not unworthy of you. I shall never call you queen and goddess—unless in delirium, and I think I should soon weary of the woman who put her head under my foot. Just because I am stronger than you, and have stronger passions, I take that advantage—try to overcome, as I may, the womanly resistance which is one of your charms.

'How useless, then, for us to talk. If you are determined to remind me again and again that your strength puts me at your mercy—'

'Oh, not that! I will come no nearer to you. Sit down, and tell me what I asked.'

Rhoda hesitated, but at length took the chair by which she was standing.

'You are resolved never to marry?'

'I never shall,' Rhoda replied firmly.

'But suppose marriage in no way interfered with your work?'

'It would interfere hopelessly with the best part of my life. I thought you understood this. What would become of the encouragement I am able to offer our girls?'

'Encouragement to refuse marriage?'

'To scorn the old idea that a woman's life is wasted if she does not marry. My work is to help those women who, by sheer necessity, must live alone—woman whom vulgar opinion ridicules. How can I help them so effectually as by living among them, one of them, and showing that my life is anything but weariness and lamentation? I am fitted for this. It gives me a sense of power and usefulness which I enjoy. Your cousin is doing the same work admirably. If I deserted I should despise myself.'

'Magnificent! If I could bear the thought of living without you, I should bid you persevere and be great.'

'I need no such bidding to persevere.'

'And for that very reason, because you are capable of such things, I love you only the more.'

There was triumph in her look, though she endeavoured to disguise it.

'Then, for your own peace,' she said, 'I must hope that you will avoid me. It is so easily done. We have nothing in common, Mr. Barfoot.'

'I can't agree with that. For one thing, there are perhaps not half a dozen women living with whom I could talk as I have talked with you. It isn't likely that I shall ever meet one. Am I to make my bow, and abandon in resignation the one chance of perfecting my life?'

'You don't know me. We differ profoundly on a thousand essential points.'

'You think so because you have a very wrong idea of me.'

Rhoda glanced at the clock on the mantelpiece.

'Mr. Barfoot,' she said in a changed voice, 'you will forgive me if I remind you that it is past ten o'clock.'

He sighed and rose.

'The fog certainly cannot be so thick now. Shall I ask them to try and get you a cab?'

'I shall walk to the station.'

'Only one more word.' She assumed a quiet dignity which he could not disregard. 'We have spoken in this way for the last time. You will not oblige me to take all sorts of trouble merely to avoid useless and painful conversations?'

'I love you, and I can't abandon hope.'

'Then I *must* take that trouble.' Her face darkened, and she stood in expectation of his departure.

'I mustn't offer to shake hands,' said Everard, drawing a step nearer.

'I hope you can remember that I had no choice but to be your hostess.'

The face and tone affected him with a brief shame. Bending his head, he approached her, and held her offered hand, without pressure, only for an instant.

Then he left the room.

There was a little improvement in the night; he could make his way along the pavement without actual groping, and no unpleasant adventure checked him before he reached the station. Rhoda's face and figure went before him. He was not downcast; for all that she had said, this woman, soon or late, would yield herself; he had a strange, unreasoning assurance of it. Perhaps the obstinacy of his temper supplied him with that confident expectation. He no longer cared on what terms he obtained her—legal marriage or free union—it was indifferent to him. But her life should be linked with his if fierce energy of will meant anything.

Miss Barfoot arrived at half-past eleven, after many delays on her journey. She was pierced with cold, choked with the poisonous air, and had derived very little satisfaction from her visit to Faversham.

'What happened?' was her first question, as Rhoda came out into the hall with sympathy and solicitude. 'Did the fog keep our guest away?'

'No; he dined here.'

'It was just as well. You haven't been lonely.'

They spoke no more on the subject until Miss Barfoot recovered from her discomfort, and was enjoying a much needed supper.

'Did he offer to go away?'

'It was really impossible. It took him more than half an hour to get here from Sloane Square.'

'Foolish fellow! Why didn't he take a train back at once?'

There was a peculiar brightness in Rhoda's countenance, and Miss Barfoot had observed it from the first.

'Did you quarrel much?'

'Not more than was to be expected.'

'He didn't think of staying for my return?'

'He left about ten o'clock.'

'Of course. Quite late enough, under the circumstances. It was very unfortunate, but I don't suppose Everard cared much. He would enjoy the opportunity of teasing you.'

A glance told her that Everard was not alone in his enjoyment of the evening. Rhoda led the talk into other channels, but Miss Barfoot continued to reflect on what she had perceived.

A few evenings after, when Miss Barfoot had been sitting alone for an hour or two, Rhoda came to the library and took a place near her. The elder woman glanced up from her book, and saw that her friend had something special to say.

'What is it, dear?'

'I am going to tax your good-nature, to ask you about unpleasant things.'

Miss Barfoot knew immediately what this meant. She professed readiness to answer, but had an uneasy look.

'Will you tell me in plain terms what it was that your cousin did when he disgraced himself?'

'Must you really know?'

'I wish to know.'

There was a pause. Miss Barfoot kept her eyes on the page open before her.

'Then I shall take the liberty of an old friend, Rhoda. Why do you wish to know?'

'Mr. Barfoot,' answered the other dryly, 'has been good enough to say that he is in love with me.'

Their eyes met.

'I suspected it. I felt sure it was coming. He asked you to marry him?'

'No, he didn't,' replied Rhoda in purposely ambiguous phrase.

'You wouldn't allow him to?'

'At all events, it didn't come to that. I should be glad if you would let me know what I asked.'

Miss Barfoot deliberated, but finally told the story of Amy Drake. Her hands supporting one knee, her head bent, Rhoda listened without comment, and, to judge from her features, without any emotion of any kind.

'That,' said her friend at the close, 'is the story as it was understood at the time—disgraceful to him in every particular. He knew what was said of him, and offered not a word of contradiction. But not very long ago he asked me one evening if you had been informed of this scandal. I told him that you knew he had done something which I thought very base. Everard was hurt, and thereupon he declared that neither I nor any other of his acquaintances knew the truth—that he had been maligned. He refused to say more, and what am I to believe?'

Rhoda was listening with livelier attention.

'He declared that he wasn't to blame?'

'I suppose he meant that. But it is difficult to see—'

'Of course the truth can never be known,' said Rhoda, with sudden indifference. 'And it doesn't matter. Thank you for satisfying my curiosity.'

Miss Barfoot waited a moment, then laughed.

'Some day, Rhoda, you shall satisfy mine.'

'Yes—if we live long enough.'

What degree of blame might have attached to Barfoot, Rhoda did not care to ask herself; she thought no more of the story. Of course there must have been other such incidents in his career; morally he was neither better nor worse than men in general. She viewed with contempt the women who furnished such opportunities; in her judgment of the male offenders she was more lenient, more philosophical, than formerly.

She had gained her wish, had enjoyed her triumph. A raising of the finger and Everard Barfoot would marry her. Assured of that, she felt a new contentment in life; at times when she was occupied with things as far as possible from this experience, a rush of joy would suddenly fill her heart, and make her cheek glow. She moved among people with a conscious dignity quite unlike that which had only satisfied her need of distinction. She spoke more softly, exercised more patience, smiled where she had been wont to scoff. Miss Nunn was altogether a more amiable person.

Yet, she convinced herself, essentially quite unchanged. She pursued the aim of her life with less bitterness, in a larger spirit, that was all. But pursued it, and without fear of being diverted from the generous path.

# CHAPTER XVIII - A REINFORCEMENT

Throughout January, Barfoot was endeavouring to persuade his brother Tom to leave London, where the invalid's health perceptibly grew worse. Doctors were urgent to the same end, but ineffectually; for Mrs. Thomas, though she professed to be amazed at her husband's folly in remaining where he could not hope for recovery, herself refused to accompany him any whither. This pair had no children. The lady always spoke of herself as a sad sufferer from mysterious infirmities, and had, in fact, a tendency to hysteria, which confused itself inextricably with the results of evil nurture and the impulses of a disposition originally base; nevertheless she made a figure in a certain sphere of vulgar wealth, and even gave opportunity to scandalous tongues. Her husband, whatever his secret thought, would hear nothing against her; his temper, like Everard's, was marked with stubbornness, and after a good deal of wrangling he forbade his brother to address him again on the subject of their disagreement.

'Tom is dying,' wrote Everard, early in February, to his cousin in Queen's Road. 'Dr. Swain assures me that unless he be removed he cannot last more than a month or two. This morning I saw the woman'—it was thus he always referred to his sister-in-law—'and talked to her in what was probably the plainest language she ever had the privilege of hearing. It was a tremendous scene, brought to a close only by her flinging herself on the sofa with shrieks which terrified the whole household. My idea is that we must carry the poor fellow away by force. His infatuation makes me rage and curse, but I am bent on trying to save his life. Will you come and give your help?'

A week later they succeeded in carrying the invalid back to Torquay. Mrs. Barfoot had abandoned him to his doctors, nurses, and angry relatives; she declared herself driven out of the house, and went to live at a fashionable hotel. Everard remained in Devon for more than a month, devoting himself with affection, which the trial of his temper seemed only to increase, to his brother's welfare. Thomas improved a little; once more there was hope. Then on a sudden frantic impulse, after writing fifty letters which elicited no reply, he travelled in pursuit of his wife; and three days after his arrival in London he was dead.

By a will, executed at Torquay, he bequeathed to Everard about a quarter of his wealth. All the rest went to Mrs. Barfoot, who had declared herself too ill to attend the funeral, but in a fortnight was sufficiently recovered to visit one of her friends in the country.

Everard could now count upon an income of not much less than fifteen hundred a year. That his brother's death would enrich him he had always foreseen, but no man could have exerted himself with more ardent energy to postpone that advantage. The widow charged him, wherever she happened to be, with deliberate fratricide; she vilified his reputation, by word of mouth or by letter, to all who knew him, and protested that his furious wrath at not having profited more largely by the will put her in fear of her life. This last remarkable statement was made in a long and violent epistle to Miss Barfoot, which the recipient showed to her cousin on the first opportunity. Everard had called one Sunday morning—it was the end of March—to say good-bye on his departure for a few weeks' travel. Having read the letter, he laughed with a peculiar fierceness.

'This kind of thing,' said Miss Barfoot, 'may necessitate your prosecuting her. There is a limit, you know, even to a woman's licence.'

'I am far more likely,' he replied, 'to purchase a very nice little cane, and give her an exemplary thrashing.'

'Oh! Oh!'

'Upon my word, I see no reason against it! That's how I should deal with a man who talked about me in this way, and none the less if he were a puny creature quite unable to protect himself. In that furious scene before we got Tom away I felt most terribly tempted to beat her. There's a great deal to be said for woman-beating. I am quite sure that many a labouring man who pommels his wife is doing exactly the right thing; no other measure would have the least result. You see what comes of impunity. If this woman saw the possibility that I should give her a public caning she would be far more careful how she behaved herself. Let us ask Miss Nunn's opinion.'

Rhoda had that moment entered the room. She offered her hand frankly, and asked what the subject was.

'Glance over this letter,' said Barfoot. 'Oh, you have seen it. I propose to get a light, supple, dandyish cane, and to give Mrs. Thomas Barfoot half a dozen smart cuts across the back in her own drawing-room, some afternoon when people were present. What have you to say to it?'

He spoke with such show of angry seriousness that Rhoda paused before replying.

'I sympathized with you,' she said at length, 'but I don't think I would go to that extremity.'

Everard repeated the argument he had used to his cousin.

'You are quite right,' Rhoda assented. 'I think many women deserve to be beaten, and ought to be beaten. But public Opinion would be so much against *you*.'

'What do I care? So is public opinion against you.'

'Very well. Do as you like. Miss Barfoot and I will come to the police court and give strong evidence in your favour.'

'Now there's a woman!' exclaimed Everard, not all in jest, for Rhoda's appearance had made his nerves thrill and his pulse beat. 'Look at her, Mary. Do you wonder that I would walk the diameter of the globe to win her love?'

Rhoda flushed scarlet, and Miss Barfoot was much embarrassed. Neither could have anticipated such an utterance as this. 'That's the simple truth,' went on Everard recklessly, 'and she knows it, and yet won't listen to me. Well, good-bye to you both! Now that I have so grossly misbehaved myself, she has a good excuse for refusing even to enter the room when I am here. But do speak a word for me whilst I am away, Mary.'

He shook hands with them, scarcely looking at their faces, and abruptly departed.

The women stood for a moments at a distance from each other. Then Miss Barfoot glanced at her friend and laughed.

'Really my poor cousin is not very discreet.'

'Anything but,' Rhoda answered, resting on the back of a chair, her eyes cast down. 'Do you think he will really cane his sister-in-law?'

'How can you ask such a question?'

'It would be amusing. I should think better of him for it.'

'Well, make it a condition. We know the story of the lady and her glove. I can see you sympathize with her.'

Rhoda laughed and went away, leaving Miss Barfoot with the impression that she had revealed a genuine impulse. It seemed not impossible that Rhoda might wish to say to her lover: 'Face this monstrous scandal and I am yours.

A week passed and there arrived a letter, with a foreign stamp, addressed to Miss Nunn. Happening to receive it before Miss Barfoot had come down to breakfast, she put in away in a drawer till evening leisure, and made no mention of its arrival. Exhilaration appeared in her behaviour through the day. After dinner she disappeared, shutting herself up to read the letter.

> 'DEAR MISS NUNN,—I am sitting at a little marble table outside a cafe on the Cannibiere. Does that name convey anything to you? The Cannibiere is the principal street of Marseilles, street of gorgeous cafe's and restaurants, just now blazing with electric light. You, no doubt, are shivering by the fireside; here it is like an evening of summer. I have dined luxuriously, and I am taking my coffee whilst I write. At a table near to me sit two girls, engaged in the liveliest possible conversation, of which I catch a few words now and then, pretty French phrases that caress the ear. One of them is so strikingly beautiful that I cannot take my eyes from her when they have been tempted to that quarter. She speaks with indescribable grace and animation, has the sweetest eyes and lips—
>
> 'And all the time I am thinking of some one else. Ah, if *you* were here! How we would enjoy ourselves among these southern scenes! Alone, it is delightful; but with you for a companion, with you to talk about everything in your splendidly frank way! This French girl's talk is of course only silly chatter; it makes me long to hear a few words from your lips—strong, brave, intelligent.
>
> 'I dream of the ideal possibility. Suppose I were to look up and see you standing just in front of me, there on the pavement. You have come in a few hours straight from London. Your eyes glow with delight. To-morrow we shall travel on to Genoa, you and I, more than friends, and infinitely more than the common husband and wife! We have bidden the world go round for *our* amusement; henceforth it is our occupation to observe and discuss and make merry.

'Is it all in vain? Rhoda, if you never love me, my life will be poor to what it might have been; and you, you also, will lose something. In imagination I kiss your hands and your lips.

EVERARD BARFOOT.'

There was an address at the head of this letter, but certainly Barfoot expected no reply, and Rhoda had no thought of sending one. Every night, however, she unfolded the sheet of thin foreign paper, and read, more than once, what was written upon it. Read it with external calm, with a brow of meditation, and afterwards sat for some time in absent mood.

Would he write again? Her daily question was answered in rather more than a fortnight. This time the letter came from Italy; it was lying on the hall table when Rhoda returned from Great Portland Street, and Miss Barfoot was the first to read the address. They exchanged no remark. On breaking the envelope—she did so at once—Rhoda found a little bunch of violets crushed but fragrant.

'These in return for your Cheddar pinks,' began the informal note accompanying the flowers. 'I had them an hour ago from a pretty girl in the streets of Parma. I didn't care to buy, and walked on, but the pretty girl ran by me, and with gentle force fixed the flowers in my button-hole, so that I had no choice but to stroke her velvety cheek and give her a lira. How hungry I am for the sight of your face! Think of me sometimes, dear friend.'

She laughed, and laid the letter and its violets away with the other.

'I must depend on you, it seems, for news of Everard,' said Miss Barfoot after dinner.

'I can only tell you,' Rhoda answered lightly, 'that he has travelled from the south of France to the north of Italy, with much observation of female countenances.'

'He informs you of that?'

'Very naturally. It is his chief interest. One likes people to tell the truth.'

Barfoot was away until the end of April, but after that note from Parma he did not write. One bright afternoon in May, a Saturday, he presented himself at his cousin's house, and found two or three callers in the drawing-room, ladies as usual; one of them was Miss Winifred Haven, another was Mrs. Widdowson. Mary received him without effusiveness, and after a few minutes' talk with her he took a place by Mrs. Widdowson, who, it struck him, looked by no means in such good spirits as during the early days of her marriage. As soon as she began to converse, his impression of a change in her was confirmed; the girlishness so pleasantly noticeable when first he knew her had disappeared, and the gravity substituted for it was suggestive of disillusion, of trouble.

She asked him if he knew some people named Bevis, who occupied a flat just above his own.

'Bevis? I have seen the name on the index at the foot of the stairs; but I don't know them personally.'

'That was how I came to know that *you* live there,' said Monica. 'My husband took me to call upon the Bevises, and there we saw your name. At least, we supposed it was you, and Miss Barfoot tells me we were right.'

'Oh yes; I live there all alone, a gloomy bachelor. How delightful if you knocked at my door some day, when you and Mr. Widdowson are again calling on your friends.'

Monica smiled, and her eyes wandered restlessly.

'You have been away—out of England?' she next said.

'Yes; in Italy.'

'I envy you.'

'You have never been there?'

'No—not yet.'

He talked a little of the agreeables and disagreeables of life in that country. But Mrs. Widdowson had become irresponsive; he doubted at length whether she was listening to him, so, as Miss Haven stepped this way, he took an opportunity of a word aside with his cousin.

'Miss Nunn not at home?'

'No. Won't be till dinner-time.'

'Quite well?'

'Never was better. Would you care to come back and dine with us at half-past seven?'

'Of course I should.'

With this pleasant prospect he took his leave. The afternoon being sunny, instead of walking straight to the station, to return home, he went out on to the Embankment, and sauntered round by Chelsea Bridge Road. As he entered Sloane Square he saw Mrs. Widdowson, who was coming towards the railway; she walked rather wearily, with her eyes on the ground, and did not become aware of him until he addressed her.

'Are we travelling the same way?' he asked. 'Westward?'

'Yes. I am going all the way round to Portland Road.'

They entered the station, Barfoot chatting humorously. And, so intent was he on the expression of his companion's downcast face, that he allowed an acquaintance to pass close by him unobserved. It was Rhoda Nunn, returning sooner than Miss Barfoot had expected. She saw the pair, regarded them with a moment's keen attentiveness, and went on, out into the street.

In the first-class carriage which they entered there was no other passenger as far as Barfoot's station. He could not resist the temptation to use rather an intimate tone, though one that was quite conventional, in the hope that he might discover something of Mrs. Widdowson's mind. He began by asking whether she thought it a good Academy this year. She had not yet visited it, but hoped to do so on Monday. Did she herself do any kind of artistic work? Oh, nothing whatever; she was a very useless and idle person. He believed she had been a pupil of Miss Barfoot's at one time? Yes, for a very short time indeed, just before her marriage. Was she not an intimate friend of Miss Nunn? Hardly intimate. They knew each other a few years ago, but Miss Nunn did not care much about her now.

'Probably because I married,' she added with a smile.

'Is Miss Nunn really such a determined enemy of marriage?'

'She thinks it pardonable in very weak people. In my case she was indulgent enough to come to the wedding.'

This piece of news surprised Barfoot.

'She came to your wedding? And wore a wedding garment?'

'Oh yes. And looked very nice.'

'Do describe it to me. Can you remember?'

Seeing that no woman ever forgot the details of another's dress, on however trivial an occasion, and at whatever distance of time, Monica was of course able to satisfy the inquirer. Her curiosity excited, she ventured in turn upon one or two insidious questions.

'You couldn't imagine Miss Nunn in such a costume?'

'I should very much like to have seen her.'

'She has a very striking face—don't you think so?'

'Indeed I do. A wonderful face.'

Their eyes met. Barfoot bent forward from his place opposite Monica.

'To me the most interesting of all faces,' he said softly.

His companion blushed with surprise and pleasure.

'Does it seem strange to you, Mrs. Widdowson?'

'Oh—why? Not at all.'

All at once she had brightened astonishingly. This subject was not pursued, but for the rest of the time they talked with a new appearance of mutual confidence and interest, Monica retaining her pretty, half-bashful smile. And when Barfoot alighted at Bayswater they shook hands with an especial friendliness, both seeming to suggest a wish that they might soon meet again.

## CHAPTER XVIII - A REINFORCEMENT

They did so not later than the following Monday. Remembering what Mrs. Widdowson had said of her intention to visit Burlington House, Barfoot went there in the afternoon. If he chanced to encounter the pretty little woman it would not be disagreeable. Perhaps her husband might be with her, and in that case he could judge of the terms on which they stood. A surly fellow, Widdowson; very likely to play the tyrant, he thought. If he were not mistaken, she had wearied of him and regretted her bondage—the old story. Thinking thus, and strolling through the rooms with casual glances at a picture, he discovered his acquaintance, catalogue in hand, alone for the present. Her pensive face again answered to his smile. They drew back from the pictures and sat down.

'I dined with our friends at Chelsea on Saturday evening,' said Barfoot.

'On Saturday? You didn't tell me you were going back again.'

'I wasn't thinking of it just at the time.'

Monica hinted an amused surprise.

'You see,' he went on, 'I expected nothing, and happy for me that it was so. Miss Nunn was in her severest mood; I think she didn't smile once through the evening. I will confess to you I wrote her a letter whilst I was abroad, and it offended her, I suppose.'

'I don't think you can always judge of her thoughts by her face.'

'Perhaps not. But I have studied her face so often and so closely. For all that, she is more a mystery to me than any woman I have ever known. That, of course, is partly the reason of her power over me. I feel that if ever—if ever she should disclose herself to me, it would be the strangest revelation. Every woman wears a mask, except to one man; but Rhoda's—Miss Nunn's—is, I fancy, a far completer disguise than I ever tried to pierce.'

Monica had a sense of something perilous in this conversation. It arose from a secret trouble in her own heart, which she might, involuntarily, be led to betray. She had never talked thus confidentially with any man; not, in truth, with her husband. There was no fear whatever of her conceiving an undue interest in Barfoot; certain reasons assured her of that; but talk that was at all sentimental gravely threatened her peace—what little remained to her. It would have been better to discourage this man's confidences; yet they flattered her so pleasantly, and afforded such a fruitful subject for speculation, that she could not obey the prompting of prudence.

'Do you mean,' she said, 'that Miss Nunn seems to disguise her feelings?'

'It is supposed to be wrong—isn't it?—for a man to ask one woman her opinion of another.'

'I can't be treacherous if I wished,' Monica replied. 'I don't feel that I understand her.'

Barfoot wondered how much intelligence he might attribute to Mrs. Widdowson. Obviously her level was much below that of Rhoda. Yet she seemed to possess delicate sensibilities, and a refinement of thought not often met with in women of her position. Seriously desiring her aid, he looked at her with a grave smile, and asked,—

'Do you believe her capable of falling in love?'

Monica showed a painful confusion. She overcame it, however, and soon answered.

'She would perhaps try not—not to acknowledge it to herself.'

'When, in fact, it had happened?'

'She thinks it so much nobler to disregard such feelings.'

'I know. She is to be an inspiring example to the women who cannot hope to marry.' He laughed silently. 'And I suppose it is quite possible that mere shame would withhold her from taking the opposite course.'

'I think she is very strong. But—'

'But?'

He looked eagerly into her face.

'I can't tell. I don't really know her. A woman may be as much a mystery to another woman as she is to a man.'

'On the whole, I am glad to hear you say that. I believe it. It is only the vulgar that hold a different opinion.'

'Shall we look at the pictures, Mr. Barfoot?'

'Oh, I am so sorry. I have been wasting your time—'

Nervously disclaiming any such thought, Monica, rose and drew near to the canvases. They walked on together for some ten minutes, until Barfoot, who had turned to look at a passing figure, said in his ordinary voice—

'I think that is Mr. Widdowson on the other side of the room.'

Monica looked quickly round, and saw her husband, as if occupied with the pictures, glancing in her direction.

## CHAPTER XIX - THE CLANK OF THE CHAINS

Since Saturday evening Monica and her husband had not been on speaking terms. A visit she paid to Mildred Vesper, after her call at Miss Barfoot's, prolonged itself so that she did not reach home until the dinner-hour was long past. On arriving, she was met with an outburst of tremendous wrath, to which she opposed a resolute and haughty silence; and since then the two had kept as much apart as possible.

Widdowson knew that Monica was going to the Academy. He allowed her to set forth alone, and even tried to persuade himself that he was indifferent as to the hour of her return; but she had not long been gone before he followed. Insufferable misery possessed him. His married life threatened to terminate in utter wreck, and he had the anguish of recognizing that to a great extent this catastrophe would be his own fault. Resolve as he might, he found it impossible to repress the impulses of jealousy which, as soon as peace had been declared between them, brought about a new misunderstanding. Terrible thoughts smouldered in his mind; he felt himself to be one of those men who are driven by passion into crime. Deliberately he had brooded over a tragic close to the wretchedness of his existence; he would kill himself, and Monica should perish with him. But an hour of contentment sufficed to banish such visions as sheer frenzy. He saw once more how harmless, how natural, were Monica's demands, and how peacefully he might live with her but for the curse of suspicion from which he could not free himself. Any other man would deem her a model wifely virtue. Her care of the house was all that reason could desire. In her behaviour he had never detected the slightest impropriety. He believed her chaste as any woman living She asked only to be trusted, and that, in spite of all, was beyond his power.

In no woman on earth could he have put perfect confidence. He regarded them as born to perpetual pupilage. Not that their inclinations were necessarily wanton; they were simply incapable of attaining maturity, remained throughout their life imperfect beings, at the mercy of craft, ever liable to be misled by childish misconceptions. Of course he was right; he himself represented the guardian male, the wife-proprietor, who from the dawn of civilization has taken abundant care that woman shall not outgrow her nonage. The bitterness of his situation lay in the fact that he had wedded a woman who irresistibly proved to him her claims as a human being. Reason and tradition contended in him, to his ceaseless torment.

And again, he feared that Monica did not love him. Had she ever loved him? There was too much ground for suspecting that she had only yielded to the persistence of his entreaties, with just liking enough to permit a semblance of tenderness, and glad to exchange her prospect of distasteful work for a comfortable married life. Her liking he might have fostered; during those first happy weeks, assuredly he had done so, for no woman could be insensible to the passionate worship manifest in his every look, his every word. Later, he took the wrong path, seeking to oppose her instincts, to reform her mind, eventually to become her lord and master. Could he not even now retrace his steps? Supposing her incapable of bowing before him, of kissing his feet, could he not be content to make of her a loyal friend, a delightful companion?

In that mood he hastened towards Burlington House. Seeking Monica through the galleries, he saw her at length—sitting side by side with that man Barfoot. They were in closest colloquy. Barfoot bent towards her as if speaking in an undertone, a smile on his face. Monica looked at once pleased and troubled.

The blood boiled in his veins. His first impulse was to walk straight up to Monica and bid her follow him. But the ecstasy of jealous suffering kept him an observer. He watched the pair until he was descried.

There was no help for it. Though his brain whirled, and his flesh was stabbed, he had no choice but to take the hand Barfoot offered him. Smile he could not, nor speak a word.

'So you have come after all?' Monica was saying to him.

He nodded. On her countenance there was obvious embarrassment, but this needed no explanation save the history of the last day or two. Looking into her eyes, he knew not whether consciousness of wrong might be read there. How to get at the secrets of this woman's heart?

Barfoot was talking, pointing at this picture and that, doing his best to smooth what he saw was an awkward situation. The gloomy husband, more like a tyrant than ever, muttered incoherent phrases. In a minute or two Everard freed himself and moved out of sight.

Monica turned from her husband and affected interest in the pictures. They reached the end of the room before Widdowson spoke.

'How long do you want to stay here?'

'I will go whenever you like,' she answered, without looking at him.

'I have no wish to spoil your pleasure.'

'Really, I have very little pleasure in anything. Did you come to keep me in sight?'

'I think we will go home now, and you can come another day.'

Monica assented by closing her catalogue and walking on.

Without a word, they made the journey back to Herne Hill. Widdowson shut himself in the library, and did not appear till dinner-time. The meal was a pretence for both of them, and as soon as they could rise from the table they again parted.

About ten o'clock Monica was joined by her husband in the drawing-room.

'I have almost made up my mind,' he said, standing near her, 'to take a serious step. As you have always spoken with pleasure of your old home, Clevedon, suppose we give up this house and go and live there?'

'It is for you to decide.'

'I want to know whether you would have any objection.'

'I shall do as you wish.'

'No, that isn't enough. The plan I have in mind is this. I should take a good large house—no doubt rents are low in the neighbourhood—and ask your sisters to come and live with us. I think it would be a good thing both for them and for you.'

'You can't be sure that they would agree to it. You see that Virginia prefers her lodgings to living here.'

Oddly enough, this was the case. On their return from Guernsey they had invited Virginia to make a permanent home with them, and she refused. Her reasons Monica could not understand; those which she alleged—vague arguments as to its being better for a wife's relatives not to burden the husband—hardly seemed genuine. It was possible that Virginia had a distaste for Widdowson's society.

'I think they both would be glad to live at Clevedon,' he urged, 'judging from your sisters' talk. It's plain that they have quite given up the idea of the school, and Alice, you tell me, is getting dissatisfied with her work at Yatton. But I must know whether you will enter seriously into this scheme.'

Monica kept silence.

'Please answer me.'

'Why have you thought of it?'

'I don't think I need explain. We have had too many unpleasant conversations, and I wish to act for the best without saying things you would misunderstand.'

'There is no fear of my misunderstanding. You have no confidence in me, and you want to get me away into a quiet country place where I shall be under your eyes every moment. It's much better to say that plainly.'

'That means you would consider it going to prison.'

'How could I help? What other motive have you?'

He was prompted to make brutal declaration of authority, and so cut the knot. Monica's unanswerable argument merely angered him. But he made an effort over himself.

'Don't you think it best that we should take some step before our happiness is irretrievably ruined?'

'I see no need for its ruin. As I have told you before, in talking like that you degrade yourself and insult me.'

'I have my faults; I know them only too well. One of them is that I cannot bear you to make friends with people who are not of my kind. I shall never be able to endure that.'

'Of course you are speaking of Mr. Barfoot.'

'Yes,' he avowed sullenly. 'It was a very unfortunate thing that I happened to come up just as he was in your company.'

'You are so very unreasonable,' exclaimed Monica tartly. 'What possible harm is there in Mr. Barfoot, when he meets me by chance in a public place, having a conversation with me? I wish I knew twenty such men. Such conversation gives me a new interest in life. I have every reason to think well of Mr. Barfoot.'

Widdowson was in anguish.

'And I,' he replied, in a voice shaken with angry feeling, 'feel that I have every reason to dislike and suspect him. He is not an honest man; his face tells me that. I know his life wouldn't bear inspection. You can't possibly be as good a judge as I am in such a case. Contrast him with Bevis. No, Bevis is a man one can trust; one talk with him produces a lasting favourable impression.'

Monica, silent for a brief space, looked fixedly before her, her features all but expressionless.

'Yet even with Mr. Bevis,' she said at length, 'you don't make friends. That is the fault in you which causes all this trouble. You haven't a sociable spirit. Your dislike of Mr. Barfoot only means that you don't know him, and don't wish to. And you are completely wrong in your judgment of him. I have every reason for being sure that you are wrong.'

'Of course you think so. In your ignorance of the world—'

'Which you think very proper in a woman,' she interposed caustically.

'Yes, I do! That kind of knowledge is harmful to a woman.'

'Then, please, how is she to judge her acquaintances?'

'A married woman must accept her husband's opinion, at all events about men.' He plunged on into the ancient quagmire. 'A man may know with impunity what is injurious if it enters a woman's mind.'

'I don't believe that. I can't and won't believe it.'

He made a gesture of despair.

'We differ hopelessly. It was all very well to discuss these things when you could do so in a friendly spirit. Now you say whatever you know will irritate me, and you say it on purpose to irritate me.'

'No; indeed I do not. But you are quite right that I find it hard to be friendly with you. Most earnestly I wish to be your friend—your true and faithful friend. But you won't let me.'

'Friend!' he cried scornfully. 'The woman who has become my wife ought to be something more than a friend, I should think. You have lost all love for me—there's the misery.'

Monica could not reply. That word 'love' had grown a weariness to her upon his lips. She did not love him; could not pretend to love him. Every day the distance between them widened, and when he took her in his arms she had to struggle with a sense of shrinking, of disgust. The union was unnatural; she felt herself constrained by a hateful force when he called upon her for the show of wifely tenderness. Yet how was she to utter this? The moment such a truth had passed her lips she must leave him. To declare that no trace of love remained in her heart, and still to live with him—that was impossible! The dark foresight of a necessity of parting from him corresponded in her to those lurid visions which at times shook Widdowson with a horrible temptation.

'You don't love me,' he continued in harsh, choking tones. 'You wish to be my *friend*. That's how you try to compensate me for the loss of your love.'

He laughed with bitterness.

'When you say that,' Monica answered, 'do you ever ask yourself whether you try to make me love you? Scenes like this are ruining my health. I have come to dread your talk. I have almost forgotten the sound of your voice when it isn't either angry or complaining.'

Widdowson walked about the room, and a deep moan escaped him.

'That is why I have asked you to go away from here, Monica. We must have a new home if our life is to begin anew.'

'I have no faith in mere change of place. You would be the same man. If you cannot command your senseless jealousy here, you never would anywhere else.'

He made an effort to say something; seemed to abandon it; again tried, and spoke in a thick, unnatural voice.

'Can you honestly repeat to me what Barfoot was saying to-day, when you were on the seat together?'

Monica's eyes flashed.

'I could; every word. But I shall not try to do so.'

'Not if I beseech you to, Monica? To put my mind at rest—'

'No. When I tell you that you might have heard every syllable, I have said all that I shall.'

It mortified him profoundly that he should have been driven to make so humiliating a request. He threw himself into a chair and hid his face, sitting thus for a long time in the hope that Monica would be moved to compassion. But when she rose it was only to retire for the night. And with wretchedness in her heart, because she must needs go to the same chamber in which her husband would sleep. She wished so to be alone. The poorest bed in a servant's garret would have been thrice welcome to her; liberty to lie awake, to think without a disturbing presence, to shed tears of need be—that seemed to her a precious boon. She thought with envy of the shop-girls in Walworth Road; wished herself back there. What unspeakable folly she had committed! And how true was everything she had heard from Rhoda Nunn on the subject of marriage! The next day Widdowson resorted to an expedient which he had once before tried in like circumstances. He wrote his wife a long letter, eight close pages, reviewing the cause of their troubles, confessing his own errors, insisting gently on those chargeable to her, and finally imploring her to cooperate with him in a sincere endeavour to restore their happiness. This he laid on the table after lunch, and then left Monica alone that she might read it. Knowing beforehand all that the letter contained, Monica glanced over it carelessly. An answer was expected, and she wrote one as briefly as possible.

'Your behaviour seems to me very weak, very unmanly. You make us both miserable, and quite without cause. I can only say as I have said before, that things will never be better until you come to think of me as your free companion, not as your bond-woman. If you can't do this, you will make me wish that I had never met you, and in the end I am sure it won't be possible for us to go on living together.'

## CHAPTER XIX - THE CLANK OF THE CHAINS

She left this note, in a blank envelope, on the hall table, and went out to walk for an hour.

It was the end of one more acute stage in their progressive discord. By keeping at home for a fortnight. Monica soothed her husband and obtained some repose for her own nerves. But she could no longer affect a cordial reconciliation; caresses left her cold, and Widdowson saw that his company was never so agreeable to her as solitude. When they sat together, both were reading. Monica found more attraction in books as her life grew more unhappy. Though with reluctance Widdowson had consented to a subscription at Mudie's, and from the new catalogues she either chose for herself, necessarily at random, or by the advice of better-read people, such as she met at Mrs. Cosgrove's. What modern teaching was to be got from these volumes her mind readily absorbed. She sought for opinions and arguments which were congenial to her mood of discontent, all but of revolt.

Sometimes the perusal of a love-story embittered her lot to the last point of endurance. Before marriage, her love-ideal had been very vague, elusive; it found scarcely more than negative expression, as a shrinking from the vulgar or gross desires of her companions in the shop. Now that she had a clearer understanding of her own nature, the type of man correspondent to her natural sympathies also became clear. In every particular he was unlike her husband. She found a suggestion of him in books; and in actual life, already, perhaps something more than a suggestion. Widdowson's jealousy, in so far as it directed itself against her longing for freedom, was fully justified; this consciousness often made her sullen when she desired to express a nobler indignation; but his special prejudice led him altogether astray, and in free resistance on this point she found the relief which enabled her to bear a secret self-reproach. Her refusal to repeat the substance of Barfoot's conversation was, in some degree, prompted by a wish for the continuance of his groundless fears. By persevering in suspicion of Barfoot, he afforded her a firm foothold in their ever-renewed quarrels.

A husband's misdirected jealousy excites in the wife derision and a sense of superiority; more often than not, it fosters an unsuspected attachment, prompts to a perverse pleasure in misleading. Monica became aware of this; in her hours of misery she now and then gave a harsh laugh, the result of thoughts not seriously entertained, but tempting the fancy to recklessness. What, she asked herself again, would be the end of it all? Ten years hence, would she have subdued her soul to a life of weary insignificance, if not of dishonour? For it was dishonour to live with a man she could not love, whether her heart cherished another image or was merely vacant. A dishonour to which innumerable women submitted, a dishonour glorified by social precept, en-enforced under dread penalties.

But she was so young, and life abounds in unexpected changes.

# CHAPTER XX - THE FIRST LIE

Mrs. Cosgrove was a childless widow, with sufficient means and a very mixed multitude of acquaintances. In the general belief her marriage had been a happy one; when she spoke of her deceased husband it was with respect, and not seldom with affection. Yet her views on the matrimonial relation were known to be of singular audacity. She revealed them only to a small circle of intimates; most of the people who frequented her house had no startling theories to maintain, and regarded their hostess as a good-natured, rather eccentric woman, who loved society and understood how to amuse her guests.

Wealth and position were rarely represented in her drawing-room; nor, on the other hand, was Bohemianism. Mrs. Cosgrove belonged by birth and marriage to the staid middle class, and it seemed as if she made it her object to provide with social entertainment the kind of persons who, in an ordinary way, would enjoy very little of it. Lonely and impecunious girls or women were frequently about her; she tried to keep them in good spirits, tried to marry them if marriage seemed possible, and, it was whispered, used a good deal of her income for the practical benefit of those who needed assistance. A sprinkling of maidens who were neither lonely nor impecunious served to attract young men, generally strugglers in some profession or other, on the lookout for a wife. Intercourse went on with a minimum of formalities. Chaperonage—save for that represented by the hostess herself—was as often as not dispensed with.

'We want to get rid of a lot of sham propriety'—so she urged to her closer friends. 'Girls must learn to trust themselves, and look out for dangers. If a girl can only be kept straight by incessant watchfulness, why, let her go where she will, and learn by experience. In fact, I want to see experience substituted for precept.'

Between this lady and Miss Barfoot there were considerable divergences of opinion, yet they agreed on a sufficient number of points to like each other very well. Occasionally one of Mrs. Cosgrove's *protegees* passed into Miss Barfoot's hands, abandoning the thought of matrimony for study in Great Portland Street. Rhoda Nunn, also, had a liking for Mrs. Cosgrove, though she made no secret of her opinion that Mrs. Cosgrove's influence was on the whole decidedly harmful.

'That house,' she once said to Miss Barfoot, 'is nothing more than a matrimonial agency.'

'But so is every house where many people are entertained.'

'Not in the same way. Mrs. Cosgrove was speaking to me of some girl who has just accepted an offer of marriage. "I don't think they'll suit each other," she said, "but there's no harm in trying."'

Miss Barfoot could not restrain a laugh.

'Who knows? Perhaps she is right in that view of things. After all, you know, it's only putting into plain words what everybody thinks on all but every such occasion.'

'The first part of her remark—yes,' said Rhoda caustically. 'But as for the "no harm in trying," well, let us ask the wife's opinion in a year's time.'

Midway in the London season on Sunday afternoon, about a score of visitors were assembled in Mrs. Cosgrove's drawing-rooms—there were two of them, with a landing between. As usual, some one sat at the piano, but a hum of talk went on as undercurrent to the music. Downstairs, in the library, half a dozen people found the quietness they preferred, and among these was Mrs. Widdowson. She had an album of portraits on her lap; whilst turning them over, she listened to a chat going on between the sprightly Mr. Bevis and a young married woman who laughed ceaselessly at his jokes. It was only a few minutes since she had come down from the drawing-room. Presently her eyes encountered a glance from Bevis, and at once he stepped over to a seat beside her.

'Your sisters are not here to-day?' she said.

'No. They have guests of their own. And when are you coming to see them again?'

'Before long, I hope.'

Bevis looked away and seemed to reflect.

'Do come next Saturday—could you?'

'I had better not promise.'

'Do try, and'—he lowered his voice—'come alone. Forgive me for saying that. The girls are rather afraid of Mr. Widdowson, that's the truth. They would so like a free gossip with you. Let me tell them to expect you about half-past three or four. They will rise up and call me blessed.'

## CHAPTER XX - THE FIRST LIE

Laughing, Monica at length agreed to come if circumstances were favourable. Her talk with Bevis continued for a long time, until people had begun to leave. Some other acquaintance then claimed her, but she was now dull and monosyllabic, as if conversation had exhausted her energies. At six o'clock she stole away unobserved, and went home.

Widdowson had resigned himself, in appearance at all events, to these absences. It was several weeks since he had accompanied his wife to call upon any one; a sluggishness was creeping over him, strengthening his disinclination for society. The futile endeavour to act with decision, to carry Monica away into Somerset, resulted, as futile efforts of that kind are wont to do, in increased feebleness of the will; he was less capable than ever of exerting the authority which he still believed himself to keep for the last resort. Occasionally some days went by without his leaving the house. Instead of the one daily newspaper he had been used to take he now received three; after breakfast he sometimes spent a couple of hours over the *Times*, and the evening papers often occupied him from dinner to bedtime. Monica noticed, with a painful conflict of emotions, that his hair had begun to lose its uniform colour, and to show streaks that matched with his grizzled beard. Was *she* responsible for this?

On the Saturday when she was to visit the Bevises she feared lest he should propose to go with her. She wished even to avoid the necessity of telling him where she was going. As she rose from luncheon Widdowson glanced at her.

'I've ordered the trap, Monica. Will you come for a drive?'

'I have promised to go into the town. I'm very sorry.'

'It doesn't matter.'

This was his latest mode of appealing to her—with an air of pained resignation.

'For a day or two I haven't felt at all well,' he continued gloomily. 'I thought a drive might do me good.'

'Certainly. I hope it will. When would you like to have dinner?'

'I never care to alter the hours. Of course I shall be back at the usual time. Shall *you* be?'

'Oh yes—long before dinner.'

So she got away without any explanation. At a quarter to four she reached the block of flats in which the Bevises (and Everard Barfoot) resided. With a fluttering of the heart, she went very quietly upstairs, as if anxious that her footsteps should not be heard; her knock at the door was timid.

Bevis in person opened to her.

'Delighted! I thought it *might* be—'

She entered, and walked into the first room, where she had been once before. But to her surprise it was vacant. She looked round and saw Bevis's countenance gleaming with satisfaction.

'My sisters will be here in a few minutes,' he said. 'A few minutes at most. Will you take this chair, Mrs. Widdowson? How delighted I am that you were able to come!'

So perfectly natural was his manner, that Monica, after the first moment of consternation, tried to forget that there was anything irregular in her presence here under these circumstances. As regards social propriety, a flat differs in many respects from a house. In an ordinary drawing-room, it could scarcely have mattered if Bevis entertained her for a short space until his sisters' arrival; but in this little set of rooms it was doubtfully permissible for her to sit *tete-a-tete* with a young man, under any excuse. And the fact of his opening the front door himself seemed to suggest that not even a servant was in the flat. A tremor grew upon her as she talked, due in part to the consciousness that she was glad to be thus alone with Bevis.

'A place like this must seem to you to be very unhomelike,' he was saying, as he lounged on a low chair not very far from her. 'The girls didn't like it at all at first. I suppose it's a retrograde step in civilization. Servants are decidedly of that opinion; we have a great difficulty in getting them to stay here. The reason seems to me that they miss the congenial gossip of the area door. At this moment we are without a domestic. I found she compensated herself for disadvantages by stealing my tobacco and cigars. She went to work with such a lack of discretion—abstracting half a pound of honeydew at a time—that I couldn't find any sympathy for her. Moreover, when charged with the delinquency, she became abusive, so very abusive that we were obliged to insist upon her immediate departure.'

'Do you think she smoked?' asked Monica laughingly.

'We have debated that point with much interest. She was a person of advanced ideas, as you see; practically a communist. But I doubt whether honeydew had any charms for her personally. It seems more probable that some milkman, or baker's assistant, or even metropolitan policeman, benefited by her communism.'

Indifferent to the progress of time, Bevis talked on with his usual jocoseness, now and then shaking his tawny hair in a fit of laughter the most contagious.

'But I have something to tell you,' he said at length more seriously. 'I am going to leave England. They want me to live at Bordeaux for a tune, two or three years perhaps. It's a great bore, but I shall have to go. I am not my own master.'

'Then your sisters will go to Guernsey?'

'Yes. I dare say I shall leave about the end of July.'

He became silent, looking at Monica with humorous sadness.

'Do you think your sisters will soon be here, Mr. Bevis?' Monica asked, with a glance round the room.

'I think so. Do you know, I did a very silly thing. I wanted your visit (if you came) to be a surprise for them, and so—in fact, I said nothing about it. When I got here from business, a little before three, they were just going out. I asked them if they were sure they would be back in less than an hour. Oh, they were quite sure—not a doubt about it. I do hope they haven't altered their mind, and gone to call somewhere. But, Mrs. Widdowson, I am going to make you a cup of tea—with my own fair hands, as the novelist say.'

Monica begged that he would not trouble. Under the circumstances she had better not stay. She would come again very soon.

'No, I can't, I can't let you go!' Bevis exclaimed, softening his gay tone as he stood before her. 'How shall I entreat you? If you knew what an unforgettable delight it will be to me to make you a cup of tea! I shall think of it at Bordeaux every Saturday.'

She had risen, but exhibited no immutable resolve.

'I really must go, Mr. Bevis—!'

'Don't drive me to despair. I am capable of turning my poor sisters out of house and home—flat and home, I mean—in anger at their delay. On their account, in pity for their youth, do stay, Mrs. Widdowson! Besides, I have a new song that I want you to bear—words and music my own. One little quarter of an hour! And I know the girls will be here directly.'

His will, and her inclination, prevailed. Monica sat down again, and Bevis disappeared to make the tea. Water must have been already boiling, for in less than five minutes the young man returned with a tray, on which all the necessaries were neatly arranged. With merry homage he waited upon his guest. Monica's cheeks were warm. After the vain attempt to release herself from what was now distinctly a compromising situation, she sat down in an easier attitude than before, as though resolved to enjoy her liberty whilst she might. There was a suspicion in her mind that Bevis had arranged this interview; she doubted the truth of his explanation. And indeed she hoped that his sisters would not return until after her departure; it would be very embarrassing to meet them.

Whilst talking and listening, she silently defended herself against the charge of impropriety. What wrong was she committing? What matter that they were alone? Their talk was precisely what it might have been in other people's presence. And Bevis, such a frank, good-hearted fellow, could not by any possibility fail in respect to her. The objections were all cant, and cant of the worst kind. She would not be a slave of such ignoble prejudices.

'You haven't made Mr. Barfoot's acquaintance yet?' she asked.

'No, I haven't. There seems to have been no opportunity. Did you seriously wish me to know him?'

'Oh, I had no wish in the matter at all.'

'You like Mr. Barfoot?'

'I think him very pleasant.'

'How delightful to be praised by you, Mrs. Widdowson! Now if any one speaks to you about *me*, when I have left England, will you find some nice word? Don't think me foolish. I do so desire the good opinion of my friends. To know that you spoke of me as you did for Mr. Barfoot would give me a whole day of happiness.'

'How enviable! To be so easily made happy.'

'Now let me sing you this song of mine. It isn't very good; I haven't composed for years. But—'

He sat down and rattled over the keys. Monica was expecting a lively air and spirited words, as in the songs she had heard at Guernsey; but this composition told of sadness and longing and the burden of a lonely heart. She thought it very beautiful, very touching. Bevis looked round to see the effect it produced upon her, and she could not meet his eyes.

'Quite a new sort of thing for me, Mrs. Widdowson. Does it strike you as so very bad?'

'No—not at all.'

'But you can't honestly praise it?' He sighed, in dejection. 'I meant to give you a copy. I made this one specially for you, and—if you will forgive me—I have taken the liberty of dedicating it to you. Songwriters do that, you know. Of course it is altogether unworthy of your acceptance—'

'No—no—indeed I am very grateful to you, Mr. Bevis. Do give it to me—as you meant to.'

'You will have it?' he cried delightedly. 'Now for a triumphal march!'

Whilst he played, with look corresponding to the exultant strain, Monica rose from her chair. She stood with eyes downcast and lips pressed together. When the last chord had sounded,—

'Now I must say good-bye, Mr. Bevis. I am so sorry your sisters haven't come.'

'So am I—and yet I am not. I have enjoyed the happiest half-hour of my life.'

'Will you give me the piece of music?'

'Let me roll it up. There; it won't be very awkward to carry. But of course I shall see you again before the end of July? You will come some other afternoon?'

'If Miss Bevis will let me know when she is quite sure—'

'Yes, she shall. Do you know, I don't think I shall say a word about what has happened this afternoon. Will you allow me to keep silence about your call, Mrs. Widdowson? They would be so annoyed—and really it was a silly thing not to tell them—'

Monica gave no verbal reply. She looked towards the door. Bevis stepped forward, and held it open.

'Good-bye, then. You know what I told you about my tendency to low spirits. I'm going to have a terrible turn—down, down, down!'

She laughed, and offered her hand. He held it very lightly, looking at her with his blue eyes, which indeed expressed a profound melancholy.

'Thank you,' he murmured. 'Thank you for your great kindness.'

And thereupon he opened the front door for her. Without another look Monica went quickly down the stairs; she appreciated his motive for not accompanying her to the exit.

Before entering the house she had managed to conceal the sheet of music which she was carrying. But, happily, Widdowson was still absent. Half an hour passed—half an hour of brooding and reverie—before she heard his footstep ascending the stairs. On the landing she met him with a pleasant smile.

'Have you enjoyed your drive?'

'Pretty well.'

'And do you feel better?'

'Not much, dear. But it isn't worth talking about.'

Later, he inquired where she had been.

'I had an appointment with Milly Vesper.'

The first falsehood she had ever told him, and yet uttered with such perfect assumption of sincerity as would have deceived the acutest observer. He nodded, discontented as usual, but entertaining no doubt.

And from that moment she hated him. If he had plied her with interrogations, if he had seemed to suspect anything, the burden of untruth would have been more endurable. His simple acceptance of her word was the sternest rebuke she could have received. She despised herself, and hated him for the degradation which resulted from his lordship over her.

# CHAPTER XXI - TOWARDS THE DECISIVE

Mary Barfoot had never suffered from lack of interest in life. Many a vivid moment dwelt in her memory; joys and sorrows, personal or of larger scope, affected her the more deeply because of that ruling intelligence which enabled her to transmute them into principles. No longer anticipating or desiring any great change in her own environment, in the modes and motives of her activity, she found it a sufficient happiness to watch, and when possible to direct, the tendency of younger lives. So kindly had nature tempered her disposition, that already she had been able to outlive those fervours of instinct which often make the middle life of an unwedded woman one long repining; but her womanly sympathies remained. And at present there was going forward under her own roof, within her daily observation, a comedy, a drama, which had power to excite all her disinterested emotions. It had been in progress for twelve months, and now, unless she was strangely mistaken, the *denouement* drew very near.

For all her self-study, her unflinching recognition of physical and psychical facts which the average woman blinks over, Mary deceived herself as to the date of that final triumph which permitted her to observe Rhoda Nunn with perfect equanimity. Her outbreak of angry feeling on the occasion of Bella Royston's death meant something more than she would acknowledge before the inquisition of her own mind. It was just then that she had become aware of Rhoda's changing attitude towards Everard Barfoot; trifles such as only a woman would detect had convinced her that Everard's interest in Rhoda was awakening a serious response; and this discovery, though it could not surprise her, caused an obscure pang which she attributed to impersonal regret, to mere natural misgiving. For some days she thought of Rhoda in an ironic, half-mocking spirit. Then came Bella's suicide, and the conversation in which Rhoda exhibited a seeming heartlessness, the result, undoubtedly, of grave emotional disturbance. To her own astonishment, Mary was overcome with an impulse of wrathful hostility, and spoke words which she regretted as soon as they had passed her lips.

Poor Bella had very little to do with this moment of discord between two women who sincerely liked and admired each other. She only offered the occasion for an outburst of secret feeling which probably could not have been avoided. Mary Barfoot had loved her cousin Everard; it began when he was one-and-twenty; she, so much older, had never allowed Everard or any one else to suspect her passion, which made her for two or three years more unhappy than she had ever been, or was ever to be when once her strong reason had prevailed. The scandal of Amy Drake, happening long after, revived her misery, which now took the form of truly feminine intolerance; she tried to believe that Everard was henceforth of less than no account to her, that she detested him for his vices. Amy Drake, however, she detested much more.

When her friendship with Rhoda Nunn had progressed to intimacy, she could not refrain from speaking of her cousin Everard, absent at the ends of the earth, and perchance lost to her sight for ever. Her mention of him was severe, yet of a severity so obviously blended with other feeling, that Rhoda could not but surmise the truth. Sentimental confession never entered Miss Barfoot's mind; she had conquered her desires, and was by no means inclined to make herself ridiculous; Rhoda Nunn, of all women, seemed the least likely to make remarks, or put questions, such as would endanger a betrayal of the buried past. Yet, at a later time, when pressing the inquiry whether Rhoda had ever been in love, Mary did not scruple to suggest that her own knowledge in that direction was complete. She did it in lightness of heart, secure under the protection of her forty years. Rhoda, of course, understood her as referring to Everard.

So the quarrel was one of jealousy. But no sooner had it taken place when Mary Barfoot experienced a shame, a distress, which in truth signified the completion of self-conquest. She thought herself ashamed of being angry where anger was uncalled for; in reality, she chastised herself for the last revival of a conflict practically over and done with so many years ago. And on this very account, precisely because she was deceiving herself as to her state of mind, she prolonged the painful situation. She said to herself that Rhoda had behaved so wrongly that displeasure was justified, that to make up the quarrel at once would be unwise, for Miss Nunn needed a little discipline. This insistence upon the side issue helped her to disregard the main one, and when at length she offered Rhoda the kiss of reconcilement, that also signified something other than was professed. It meant a hope that Rhoda might know the happiness which to her friend had been denied.

## CHAPTER XXI - TOWARDS THE DECISIVE

Everard's announcement of his passion for Miss Nunn seemed to Mary a well-calculated piece of boldness. If he seriously sought Rhoda for his wife, this frank avowal of the desire before a third person might remove some of the peculiar difficulties of the case. Whether willing or not to be wooed, Rhoda, in mere consistency with her pronounced opinions, must needs maintain a scornful silence on the subject of Everard's love-making; by assailing this proud reserve, this dignity which perchance had begun to burden its supporter, Everard made possible, if not inevitable, a discussion of his suit between the two women. She who talks of her lover will be led to think of him.

Miss Barfoot knew not whether to hope for the marriage of this strange pair. She was distrustful of her cousin, found it hard to imagine him a loyal husband, and could not be sure whether Rhoda's qualities were such as would ultimately retain or repel him. She inclined to think this wooing a mere caprice. But Rhoda gave ear to him, of that there could be little doubt; and since his inheritance of ample means the affair began to have a new aspect. That Everard persevered, though the world of women was now open to him—for, on a moderate computation, any man with Barfoot's personal advantages, and armed with fifteen hundred a year, may choose among fifty possible maidens—seemed to argue that he was really in love. But what it would cost Rhoda to appear before her friends in the character of a bride! What a humbling of her glory!

Was she capable of the love which defies all humiliation? Or, loving ardently, would she renounce a desired happiness from dread of female smiles and whispers? Or would it be her sufficient satisfaction to reject a wealthy suitor, and thus pose more grandly than ever before the circle who saw in her an example of woman's independence? Powerful was the incitement to curiosity in a situation which, however it ended, would afford such matter for emotional hypothesis.

They did not talk of Everard. Whether Rhoda replied to his letters from abroad Miss Barfoot had no means of ascertaining. But after his return he had a very cold reception—due, perhaps, to some audacity he had allowed himself in his correspondence. Rhoda again avoided meeting with him, and, as Miss Barfoot noticed, threw herself with increased energy into all her old pursuits.

'What about your holiday this year?' Mary asked one evening in June. 'Shall you go first, or shall I?'

'Please make whatever arrangements you like.'

Miss Barfoot had a reason for wishing to postpone her holiday until late in August. She said so, and proposed that Rhoda should take any three weeks she liked prior to that.

'Miss Vesper,' she added, 'can manage your room very well. We shall be much more at ease in that respect than last year.'

'Yes. Miss Vesper is getting to be very useful and trustworthy.'

Rhoda mused when she had made this remark.

'Do you know,' she asked presently, 'whether she sees much of Mrs. Widdowson?'

'I have no idea.'

They decided that Rhoda should go away at the close of July. Where was her holiday to be spent? Miss Barfoot suggested the lake country.

'I was thinking of it myself,' said Rhoda. 'I should like to have some sea-bathing, though. A week by the shore, and then the rest of the time spent in vagabondage among the mountains, would suit me very well. Mrs. Cosgrove is at home in Cumberland; I must ask her advice.'

This was done, and there resulted a scheme which seemed to excite Rhoda with joyous anticipation. On the coast of Cumberland, a few miles south of St. Bees, is a little place called Seascale, unknown to the ordinary tourist, but with a good hotel and a few scattered houses where lodgings can be obtained. Not far away rise the mountain barriers of lake-land, Wastdale clearly discernible. At Seascale, then, Rhoda would spend her first week, the quiet shore with its fine stretch of sand affording her just the retreat that she desired.

'There are one or two bathing-machines, Mrs. Cosgrove says, but I hope to avoid such abominations. How delicious it was in one's childhood, when one ran into the sea naked! I will enjoy that sensation once more, if I have to get up at three in the morning.'

About this time Barfoot made one of his evening calls. He had no hope of seeing Rhoda, and was agreeably surprised by her presence in the drawing-room. Just as happened a year ago, the subject of Miss Barfoot making a direct inquiry. With lively interest, Mary waited for the reply, and was careful not to smile when Rhoda made known her intentions.

'Have you planned a route after your stay at Seascale?' Barfoot asked.

'No. I shall do that when I am there.'

Whether or not he intended a contrast to these homely projects, Barfoot presently began to talk of travel on a grander scale. When he next left England, he should go by the Orient Express right away to

Constantinople. His cousin asked questions about the Orient Express, and he supplied her with details very exciting to the imagination of any one who longs to see the kingdoms of the earth—as undoubtedly Rhoda did. The very name, Orient Express, has a certain sublimity, such as attaches, more or less, to all the familiar nomenclature of world-transits. He talked himself into fervour, and kept a watch on Rhoda's countenance. As also did Miss Barfoot. Rhoda tried to appear unaffected, but her coldness betrayed its insincerity.

The next day, when work at Great Portland Street was just finished, she fell into conversation with Mildred Vesper. Miss Barfoot had an engagement to dine out that evening, and Rhoda ended by inviting Milly to come home with her to Chelsea. To Milly this was a great honour; she hesitated because of her very plain dress, but easily allowed herself to be persuaded when she saw that Miss Nunn really desired her company.

Before dinner they had a walk in Battersea Park. Rhoda had never been so frank and friendly; she induced the quiet, unpretending girl to talk of her early days, her schools, her family. Remarkable was Milly's quiet contentedness; not long ago she had received an increase of payment from Miss Barfoot, and one would have judged that scarcely a wish now troubled her, unless it were that she might see her scattered brothers and sisters, all of whom, happily, were doing pretty well in the struggle for existence.

'You must feel rather lonely in your lodgings sometimes?' said Rhoda.

'Very rarely. In future I shall have music in the evening. Our best room has been let to a young man who has a violin, and he plays "The Blue Bells of Scotland"—not badly.'

Rhoda did not miss the humorous intention, veiled, as usual, under a manner of extreme sedateness.

'Does Mrs. Widdowson come to see you?'

'Not often. She came a few days ago.'

'You go to her house sometimes?'

'I haven't been there for several months. At first I used to go rather frequently, but—it's a long way.'

To this subject Rhoda returned after dinner, when they were cosily settled in the drawing-room.

'Mrs. Widdowson comes here now and then, and we are always very glad to see her. But I can't help thinking she looks rather unhappy.'

'I'm afraid she does,' assented the other gravely.

'You and I were both at her wedding. It wasn't very cheerful, was it? I had a disagreeable sense of bad omens all the time. Do you think she is sorry?'

'I'm really afraid she is.'

Rhoda observed the look that accompanied this admission.

'Foolish girl! Why couldn't she stay with us, and keep her liberty? She doesn't seem to have made any new friends. Has she spoken to you of any?'

'Only of people she has met here.'

Rhoda yielded—or seemed to yield—to an impulse of frankness. Bending slightly forward, with an anxious expression, she said in confidential tones—

'Can you help to put my mind at rest about Monica? You saw her a week ago. Did she say anything, or give any sign, that might make one really uneasy on her account?'

There was a struggle in Milly before she answered. Rhoda added—

'Perhaps you had rather not—'

'Yes, I had rather tell you. She said a good many strange things, and I *have* been uneasy about her. I wished I could speak to some one—'

'How strange that I should feel urged to ask you about this,' said Rhoda, her eyes, peculiarly bright and keen, fixed on the girl's face. 'The poor thing is very miserable, I am sure. Her husband seems to leave her entirely to herself.'

Milly looked surprised.

'Monica made quite the opposite complaint to me. She said that was a prisoner.'

'That's very odd. She certainly goes about a good deal and alone.'

'I didn't know that,' said Milly. 'She has very often talked to me about a woman's right to the same freedom as a man, and I always understood that Mr. Widdowson objected to her going anywhere without him, except just to call here, or at my lodgings.'

'Do you think she has any acquaintance that he dislikes?'

The direct answer was delayed, but it came at length.

'There is some one. She hasn't told me who it is.'

'In plain words, Mr. Widdowson thinks he has cause for jealousy?'

'Yes, I understand Monica to mean that.'

Rhoda's face had grown very dark. She moved her hands nervously.

'But—you don't think she could deceive him?'

'Oh, I can't think that!' replied Miss Vesper, with much earnestness. 'But what I couldn't help fearing, after I saw her last, was that she might almost be tempted to leave her husband. She spoke so much of freedom—and of a woman's right to release herself if she found her marriage was a mistake.'

'I am so grateful to you for telling me all this. We must try to help her. Of course I will make no mention of you, Miss Vesper. Then you are really under the impression that there's some one she—prefers to her husband?'

'I can't help thinking there is,' admitted the other very solemnly. 'I was so sorry for her, and felt so powerless. She cried a little. All I could do was to entreat her not to behave rashly. I thought her sister ought to know—'

'Oh, Miss Madden is useless. Monica cannot look to her for advice or support.'

After this conversation Rhoda passed a very unquiet night, and gloom appeared in her countenance for the next few days.

She wished to have a private interview with Monica, but doubted whether it would in any degree serve her purpose—that of discovering whether certain suspicions she entertained had actual ground. Confidence between her and Mrs. Widdowson had never existed, and in the present state of things she could not hope to probe Monica's secret feelings. Whilst she still brooded over the difficulty there came a letter for her from Everard Barfoot. He wrote formally; it had occurred to him that he might be of some slight service, in view of her approaching holiday, if he looked through the guide-books, and jotted down the outline of such a walking-tour as she had in mind. This he had done, and the results were written out on an enclosed sheet of paper. Rhoda allowed a day to intervene, then sent a reply. She thanked Mr. Barfoot sincerely for the trouble he had so kindly taken. 'I see you limit me to ten miles a day. In such scenery of course one doesn't hurry on, but I can't help informing you that twenty miles wouldn't alarm me. I think it very likely that I shall follow your itinerary, after my week of bathing and idling. I leave on Monday week.'

Barfoot did not call again. Every evening she sat in expectation of his coming. Twice Miss Barfoot was away until a late hour, and on those occasions, after dinner, Rhoda sat in complete idleness, her face declaring the troubled nature of 'her thoughts. On the Sunday before her departure she took a sudden resolve and went to call upon Monica at Herne Hill.

Mrs. Widdowson, she learnt from the servant, had left home about an hour since.

'Is Mr. Widdowson at home?'

Yes, he was. And Rhoda waited for some time in the drawing-room until he made his appearance. Of late Widdowson had grown so careless in the matter of toilet, that an unexpected visit obliged him to hurry through a change of apparel before he could present himself. Looking upon him for the first time for several months, Rhoda saw that misery was undermining the man's health. Words could not have declared his trouble more plainly than the haggard features and stiff, depressed, self-conscious manner. He fixed his sunken eyes upon the visitor, and smiled, as was plain, only for civility's sake. Rhoda did her best to seem at ease; she explained (standing, for he forgot to ask her to be seated) that she was going away on the morrow, and had hoped to see Mrs. Widdowson, who, she was told, had not been very well of late.

'No, she is not in very good health,' said Widdowson vaguely. 'She has gone this afternoon to Mrs. Cosgrove's—I think you know her.'

Less encouragement to remain could not have been offered, but Rhoda conceived a hope of hearing something significant if she persevered in conversation. The awkwardness of doing so was indifferent to her.

'Shall you be leaving town shortly, Mr. Widdowson?'

'We are not quite sure—But pray sit down, Miss Nunn. You haven't seen my wife lately?'

He took a chair, and rested his hands upon his knees, gazing at the visitor's skirt.

'Mrs. Widdowson hasn't been to see us for more than a month—if I remember rightly.'

His look expressed both surprise and doubt.

'A month? But I thought—I had an idea—that she went only a few days ago.'

'In the day time?'

'To Great Portland Street, I mean—to hear a lecture, or something of that kind, by Miss Barfoot.'

Rhoda kept silence for a moment. Then she replied hastily—

'Oh yes—very likely—I wasn't there that afternoon.'

'I see. That would explain—'

He seemed relieved, but only for the instant; then his eyes glanced hither and thither, with painful restlessness. Rhoda observed him closely. After fidgeting with his feet, he suddenly took a stiff position, and said in a louder voice—

'We are going to leave London altogether. I have decided to take a house at my wife's native place, Clevedon. Her sisters will come and live with us.'

'That is a recent decision, Mr. Widdowson?'

'I have thought about it for some time. London doesn't suit Monica's health; I'm sure it doesn't. She will be much better in the country.'

'Yes, I think that very likely.'

'As you say that you have noticed her changed looks, I shall lose no time in getting away.' He made a great show of determined energy. 'A few weeks—. We will go down to Clevedon at once and find a house. Yes, we will go to-morrow, or the day after. Miss Madden, also, is very far from well. I wish I hadn't delayed so long.'

'You are doing very wisely, I think. I had meant to suggest something of this kind to Mrs. Widdowson. Perhaps, if I went at once to Mrs. Cosgrove's, I might be fortunate enough to find her still there?'

'You might. Did I understand you to say that you go away tomorrow? For three weeks. Ah, then we may be getting ready to remove when you come back.'

The change that had come over him was remarkable. He could not keep his seat, and began to pace the end of the room. Seeing no possibility of prolonging the talk for her own purposes, Rhoda accepted this dismissal, and with the briefest leave-taking went her way to Mrs. Cosgrove's.

She was deeply agitated. Monica had not attended that lecture of Miss Barfoot's, and so, it was evident, had purposely deceived her husband. To what end? Where were those hours spent? Mildred Vesper's report supplied grounds for sombre conjecture, and the incident at Sloane Square Station, the recollection of Monica and Barfoot absorbed in talk, seemed to have a possible significance which fired Rhoda with resentment.

Her arrival at Mrs. Cosgrove's was too late. Monica had been there said the hostess, but had left nearly half an hour ago.

Rhoda's instant desire was to go on to Bayswater, and somehow keep watch near the flats where Barfoot lived. Monica might be there. Her coming forth from the building might be detected.

But the difficulty of the understanding, and, still more, a dread of being seen hovering about that quarter, checked her purpose as soon as it was formed. She returned home, and for an hour or two kept in solitude.

'What has happened?' asked Miss Barfoot, when they at length met.

'Happened? Nothing that I know of.'

'You look very strange.'

'Your imagination. I have been packing; perhaps it's from stooping over the trunk.'

This by no means satisfied Mary, who felt that things mysterious were going on about her. But she could only wait, repeating to herself that the grand *denouement* decidedly was not far off.

At nine o'clock sounded the visitor's bell. If, as she thought likely, the caller was Everard, Miss Barfoot decided that she would disregard everything but the dramatic pressure of the moment, and leave those two alone together for half an hour. Everard it was; he entered the drawing-room with an unusual air of gaiety.

'I have been in the country all day,' were his first words; and he went on to talk of trivial things—the doings of a Cockney excursion party that had come under his notice.

In a few minutes Mary made an excuse for absenting herself. When she was gone, Rhoda looked steadily at Barfoot, and asked—

'Have you really been out of town?'

'Why should you doubt it?'

'As I told you.

She averted her look. After examining her curiously, Everard came and stood before her.

'I want to ask your leave to meet you somewhere during these next three weeks. At any point on your route. We could have a day's ramble together, and then—say good-bye.'

'The lake country is free to you, Mr. Barfoot.'

'But I mustn't miss you. You will leave Seascale to-morrow week?'

'At present I think so. But I can't restrict myself by any agreement. Holiday must be a time of liberty.'

They looked at each other—she with a carelessness which was all but defiance, he with a significant smile.

'To-morrow week, then, perhaps we may meet again.'

Rhoda made no reply, beyond a movement of her eyebrows, as if to express indifference.

'I won't stay longer this evening. A pleasant journey to you!'

He shook hands, and left the room. In the hall Miss Barfoot came to meet him; they exchanged a few words, unimportant and without reference to what had passed between him and Rhoda. Nor did Rhoda speak of the matter when joined by her friend. She retired early, having settled all the arrangements for her departure by the ten o'clock express from Euston next morning.

# CHAPTER XXI - TOWARDS THE DECISIVE

Her luggage was to consist of one trunk and a wallet with a strap, which would serve the purposes of a man's knapsack. Save the indispensable umbrella, she carried no impeding trifles. A new costume, suitable for shore and mountain, was packed away in the trunk; Miss Barfoot had judged of its effect, and was of opinion that it became the wearer admirably.

But Rhoda, having adjusted everything that she was going to take with her, still had an occupation which kept her up for several hours. From a locked drawer she brought forth packets of letters, the storage of many years, and out of these selected carefully perhaps a tithe, which she bound together and deposited in a box; the remainder she burnt in the empty fireplace. Moreover, she collected from about the room a number of little objects, ornaments and things of use, which also found a place in the same big box. All her personal property which had any value for her, except books, was finally under lock and key, and in portable repositories. But still she kept moving, as if in search of trifles that might have escaped her notice; silently, in her soft slippers, she strayed hither and thither, till the short summer night had all but given place to dawn; and when at length weariness compelled her to go to bed, she was not able to sleep.

Nor did Mary Barfoot enjoy much sleep that night. She lay thinking, and forecasting strange possibilities.

On Monday evening, returned from Great Portland Street, the first thing she did was to visit Rhoda's chamber. The ashes of burnt paper had been cleared away, but a glance informed her of the needless and unprecedented care with which Miss Nunn had collected and packed most of the things that belonged to her. Again Mary had a troubled night.

## CHAPTER XXII - HONOUR IN DIFFICULTIES

At Mrs. Cosgrove's, this Sunday afternoon, Monica had eyes and thoughts for one person only. Her coming at all was practically an appointment to meet Bevis, whom she had seen twice since her visit to the flat. A day or two after that occasion, she received a call from the Bevis girls, who told her of their brother's approaching departure for Bordeaux, and thereupon she invited the trio to dine with her. A fortnight subsequently to the dinner she had a chance encounter with Bevis in Oxford Street; constraint of business did not allow him to walk beside her for more than a minute or two, but they spoke of Mrs. Cosgrove's on the following Sunday, and there, accordingly, found each other.

Tremor of self-consciousness kept Monica in dread of being watched and suspected. Few people were present to-day, and after exchanging formal words with Bevis, she moved away to talk with the hostess. Not till half an hour had passed did she venture to obey the glances which her all but avowed lover cast towards her in conversation. He was so much at ease, so like what she had always known him, that Monica asked herself whether she had not mistaken the meaning of his homage. One moment she hoped it might be so; the next, she longed for some sign of passionate devotion, and thought with anguish of the day, now so near, when he would be gone for ever. This, she ardently believed, was the man who should have been her husband. Him she could love with heart and soul, could make his will her absolute law, could live on his smiles, could devote herself to his interests. The independence she had been struggling to assert ever since her marriage meant only freedom to love. If she had understood herself as she now did, her life would never have been thus cast into bondage.

'The girls,' Bevis was saying, 'leave on Thursday. The rest of the week I shall be alone. On Monday the furniture will be stowed away at the Pantechnicon, and on Tuesday—off I go.'

A casual listener could have supposed that the prospect pleased him. Monica, with a fixed smile, looked at the other groups conversing in the room; no one was paying any attention to her. In the same moment she heard a murmur from her companion's lips; he was speaking still, but in a voice only just audible.

'Come on Friday afternoon about four o'clock.'

Her heart began to throb painfully, and she knew that a treacherous colour had risen to her checks.

'Do come—once more—for the last time. It shall be just as before—just as before. An hour's talk, and we will say good-bye to each other.'

She was powerless to breathe a word. Bevis, noticing that Mrs. Cosgrove had thrown a look in their direction, suddenly laughed as if at some jest between them, and resumed his lively strain of talk. Monica also laughed. An interval of make-believe, and again the soft murmur fell upon her ear.

'I shall expect you. I know you won't refuse me this one last kindness. Some day,' his voice was all but extinguished, 'some day—who knows?'

Dreadful hope struck through her. A stranger's eyes turned their way, and again she laughed.

'On Friday, at four. I shall expect you.'

She rose, looked for an instant about the room, then offered him her hand, uttering some commonplace word of leave-taking. Their eyes did not meet. She went up to Mrs. Cosgrove, and as soon as possible left the house.

Widdowson met her as she crossed the threshold of home. His face told her that something extraordinary had happened, and she trembled before him.

'Back already?' he exclaimed, with a grim smile. 'Be quick, and take your things off, and come to the library.'

If he had discovered anything (the lie, for instance, that she told him a month ago, or that more recent falsehood when she pretended, without serious reason, to have been at Miss Barfoot's lecture), he would not look and speak thus. Hurrying, panting, she made a change of dress, and obeyed his summons.

'Miss Nunn has been here,' were his first words.

She turned pale as death. Of course he observed it; she was now preparing for anything.

'She wanted to see you because she is going away on Monday. What's the matter?'

'Nothing. You spoke so strangely—'

'Did I? And you *look* very strangely. I don't understand you. Miss Nunn says that everybody has noticed how ill you seem. It's time we did something. To-morrow morning we are going down into Somerset, to Clevedon, to find a house.'

'I thought you had given up that idea.'

'Whether I had or not doesn't matter.'

In the determination to appear, and be, energetic, he spoke with a rough obstinacy, a doggedness that now and then became violence. 'I am decided on it now. There's a train to Bristol at ten-twenty. You will pack just a few things; we shan't be away for more than a day or two.'

Tuesday, Wednesday, Thursday—By Friday they might be back. Till now, in an anguish of uncertainty, Monica had made up her mind. She would keep the appointment on Friday, come of it what might. If she could not be back in time, she would write a letter.

'Why are you talking in this tone?' she said coldly.

'What tone? I am telling you what I have decided to do, that's all. I shall easily find a house down there, no doubt. Knowing the place, you will be able to suggest the likely localities.'

She sat down, for strength was failing her.

'It's quite true,' Widdowson went on, staring at her with inflamed eyes. 'You are beginning to look like a ghost. Oh, we'll have an end of this!' He cackled in angry laughter. 'Not a day's unnecessary delay! Write to both your sisters this evening and tell them. I wish them both to come and live with us.'

'Very well.'

'Now, won't you be glad? Won't it be better in every way?'

He came so near that she felt his feverish breath.

'I told you before,' she answered, 'to do just as you liked.'

'And you won't talk about being kept a prisoner?'

Monica laughed.

'Oh no, I won't say anything at all.'

She scarcely knew what words fell from her lips. Let him propose, let him do what he liked; to her it was indifferent. She saw something before her—something she durst not, even an hour ago, have steadily contemplated; it drew her with the force of fate.

'You know we couldn't go on living like this—don't you, Monica?'

'No, we couldn't.'

'You see!' He almost shouted in triumph, misled by the smile on her face. 'All that was needed was resolution on my part. I have been absurdly weak, and weakness in the husband means unhappiness in the wife. From today you look to me for guidance. I am no tyrant, but I shall rule you for your own good.'

Still she smiled.

'So there's an end of our misery—isn't it, darling? What misery! Good God, how I have suffered! Haven't you known it?'

'I have known it too well.'

'And now you will make up to me for it, Monica?'

Again prompted by the irresistible force, she answered mechanically,—

'I will do the best for both.'

He threw himself on the ground beside her and clasped her in his arms.

'No, that is my own dear wife once more! Your face has altogether changed. See how right it is that a husband should take the law into his own hands! Our second year of marriage shall be very different from the first. And yet we *were* happy, weren't we, my beautiful? It's only this cursed London that has come between us. At Clevedon we shall begin our life over again—like we did at Guernsey. All our trouble, I am convinced, has come of your ill-health. This air has never suited you; you have felt miserable, and couldn't be at peace in your home. Poor little girl! My poor darling!'

Through the evening he was in a state of transport, due partly to the belief that Monica really welcomed his decision, partly to the sense of having behaved at length like a resolute man. His eyes were severely bloodshot, and before bedtime headache racked him intolerably.

Everything was carried out as he had planned it. They journeyed down into Somerset, put up at a Clevedon hotel, and began house-hunting. On Wednesday the suitable abode was discovered—a house of modest pretensions, but roomy and well situated. It could be made ready for occupation in a fortnight. Bent on continuing his exhibition of vigorous promptitude, Widdowson signed a lease that same evening.

'To-morrow we will go straight home and make our preparations for removal. When all is ready, you shall come down here and live at the hotel until the house is furnished. Go to your sister Virginia and simply bid her do as you wish. Imitate me!' He laughed fatuously. 'Don't listen to any objection. When you have once got her away she will thank you.'

By Thursday afternoon they were back at Herne Hill. Widdowson still kept up the show of extravagant spirits, but he was worn out. He spoke so hoarsely that one would have thought he had contracted a severe sore throat; it resulted merely from nervous strain. After a pretence of dinner, he seated himself as if to read; glancing at him a few minutes later, Monica found that he was fast asleep.

She could not bear to gaze at him, yet her eyes turned thither again and again. His face was repulsive to her; the deep furrows, the red eyelids, the mottled skin moved her to loathing. And yet she pitied him. His frantic exultation was the cruelest irony. What would he do? What would become of him? She turned away, and presently left the room, for the sound of his uneasy breathing made her suffer too much.

When he woke up, he came in search of her, and laughed over his involuntary nap.

'Well, now, you will go and see your sister to-morrow morning.'

'In the afternoon, I think.'

'Why? Don't let us have any procrastination. The morning, the morning!'

'Please do let me have my way in such a trifle as that,' Monica exclaimed nervously. 'I have all sorts of things to see to here before I can go out.'

He caressed her.

'You shan't say that I am unreasonable. In the afternoon, then. And don't listen to any objections.'

'No, no.'

It was Friday. All the morning Widdowson had business with house agents and furniture removers, for he would not let a day go by without some practical step towards release from the life he detested. Monica seemed to be equally active in her own department; she was turning out drawers and wardrobes, and making selection of things—on some principle understood by herself. A flush remained upon her cheeks, in marked contrast to the pallor which for a long time had given her an appearance of wasting away. That and her singularly bright eyes endowed her with beauty suggestive of what she might have gained in happy marriage.

They had luncheon at one o'clock, and at a quarter to two Monica started by train for Clapham Junction. It was her purpose to have a short conversation with Virginia, who knew of the trip to Clevedon, and to speak as though she were quite reconciled to the thought of removal; after that, she would pursue her journey so as to reach Bayswater by four o'clock. But Virginia was not at home. Mrs. Conisbee said she had gone out at eleven in the morning, and with the intention of returning by teatime. After a brief hesitation Monica requested the landlady to deliver a message.

'Please ask her not to come to Herne Hill until she hears from me, as I am not likely to be at home for a day or two.'

This left more time at her disposal than she knew how to employ. She returned to the railway station, and travelled on to Victoria; there, in the corner of a waiting-room, she sat, feverishly impatient, until her watch told her that she might take the next train westward.

A possible danger was before her—though perhaps she need not trouble herself with the thought of such dangers. What if Mr. Barfoot happened to encounter her as she ascended the stairs? But most likely he had no idea that her female friends, who dwelt on the floor above him, were gone away. Did it matter what he might think? In a day or two—

She came to the street, approached the block of flats, involuntarily casting anxious glances about her. And when she was within twenty yards of the door, it opened, and forth came Barfoot. Her first sensation was unreasoning terror; her next, thankfulness that she had not been a few minutes sooner, when the very meeting she had feared, within the building itself, would have come to pass. He walked this way; he saw her; and the pleasantest smile of recognition lit up his face.

'Mrs. Widdowson! Not a minute ago you were in my thoughts. I wished I could see you.'

'I am going—to make a call in this neighbourhood—'

She could not command herself. The shock had left her trembling, and the necessity of feigning calmness was a new trial of her nerves. Barfoot, she felt certain, was reading her face like a printed page; he saw guilt there; his quickly-averted eyes, his peculiar smile, seemed to express the facile tolerance of a man of the world.

'Allow me to accompany you to the end of the street.'

His words buzzed in her ears. She walked on without conscious effort, like an automaton obedient to a touch.

'You know that Miss Nunn has gone down into Cumberland?' Barfoot was saying, his look bent upon her.

'Yes. I know.'

She tried to glance at him with a smile.

'To-morrow,' he pursued, 'I am going there myself.'

'To Cumberland?'

'I shall see her, I hope. Perhaps she will only be angry with me.'

'Perhaps. But perhaps not.'

Her confusion would not be overcome. She felt a burning in her ears, on her neck. It was an agony of shame. The words she spoke sounded imbecile mutterings, which must confirm Barfoot in his worst opinion of her.

'If it is all in vain,' he continued, 'then I shall say good-bye, and there's an end.'

'I hope not—I should think—'

Useless. She set her lips and became mute. If only he would leave her! And almost immediately he did so, with a few words of kind tone. She felt the pressure of his hand, and saw him walk rapidly away; doubtless he knew this was what she desired.

Until he had passed out of sight, Monica kept the same direction. Then she turned round and hurried back, fearful lest the detention might make her late, and Bevis might lose hope of her coming. There could be no one in the building now whom she need fear to meet. She opened the big entrance door and went up.

Bevis must have been waiting for the sound of her light footstep; his door flew open before she could knock. Without speaking, a silent laugh of joy upon his lips, he drew back to make room for her entrance, and then pressed both her hands.

In the sitting-room were beginnings of disorder. Pictures had been taken down from the walls and light ornaments removed.

'I shan't sleep here after to-night,' Bevis began, his agitation scarcely less obvious than Monica's. 'To-morrow I shall be packing what is to go with me. How I hate it all!'

Monica dropped into a chair near the door.

'Oh, not there!' he exclaimed. 'Here, where you sat before. We are going to have tea together again.'

His utterances were forced, and the laugh that came between them betrayed the quivering of his nerves.

'Tell me what you have been dòing. I have thought of you day and night.'

He brought a chair close to her, and when he had seated himself he took one of her hands. Monica, scarcely repressing a sob, the result of reaction from her fears and miseries, drew the hand away. But again he took it.

'There's the glove on it,' he said in a shaking voice. 'What harm in my holding your glove? Don't think of it, and talk to me. I love music, but no music is like your voice.'

'You go on Monday?'

It was her lips spoke the sentence, not she.

'No, on Tuesday—I think.'

'My—Mr. Widdowson is going to take me away from London.'

'Away?'

She told him the circumstances. Bevis kept his eyes upon her face, with a look of rapt adoration which turned at length to pain and woeful perplexity.

'You have been married a year,' he murmured. 'Oh, if I had met you before that! What a cruel fate that we should know each other only when there was no hope!'

The man revealed himself in this dolorous sentimentality. His wonted blitheness and facetiousness, his healthy features, his supple, well-built frame, suggested that when love awoke within him he would express it with virile force. But he trembled and blushed like a young girl, and his accents fell at last into a melodious whining.

He raised the gloved fingers to his lips. Monica bent her face away, deadly pale, with closed eyes.

'Are we to part to-day, and never again see each other?' he went on. 'Say that you love me! Only say that you love me!'

'You despise me for coming to you like this.'

'Despise you?'

In a sudden rapture he folded his arms about her.

'Say that you love me!'

He kissed away the last syllable of her whispered reply.

'Monica!—what is there before us? How can I leave you?'

Yielding herself for the moment in a faintness that threatened to subdue her, she was yet able, when his caresses grew wild with passion, to put back his arms and move suddenly away. He sprang up, and they stood speechless. Again he drew near.

'Take me away with you!' Monica then cried, clasping her hands together. 'I can't live with *him*. Let me go with you to France.'

Bevis's blue eyes widened with consternation.

'Dare you—dare you do that?' he stammered.

'Dare I? What courage is needed? How *dare* I remain with a man I hate?'

'You must leave him. Of course you must leave him.'

'Oh, before another day has passed!' sobbed Monica. 'It is wrong even to go back to-day. I love you, and in that there is nothing to be ashamed of; but what bitter shame to be living with *him*, practising hypocrisy. He makes me hate myself as much as I hate *him*.'

'Has he behaved brutally to you, dearest?'

'I have nothing to accuse him of, except that he persuaded me to marry him—made me think that I could love him when I didn't know what love meant. And now he wishes to get me away from all the people I know because he is jealous of every one. And how can I blame him? Hasn't he cause for jealousy? I am deceiving him—I have deceived him for a long time, pretending to be a faithful wife when I have often wished that he might die and release me. It is I who am to blame. I ought to have left him. Every woman who thinks of her husband as I do ought to go away from him. It is base and wicked to stay there—pretending—deceiving—'

Bevis came towards her and took her in his arms.

'You love me?' she panted under his hot kisses. 'You will take me away with you?'

'Yes, you shall come. We mustn't travel together, but you shall come—when I am settled there—'

'Why can't I go with you?'

'My own darling, think what it would mean if our secret were discovered—'

'Discovered? But how can we think of that? How can I go back there, with your kisses on my lips? Oh, I must live somewhere in secret until you go, and then—I have put aside the few things that I want to take. I could never have continued to live with him even if you hadn't said you love me. I was obliged to pretend that I agreed to everything, but I will beg and starve rather than bear that misery any longer. Don't you love me enough to face whatever may happen?'

'I love you with all my soul, Monica! Sit down again, dearest; let us talk about it, and see what we can do.'

He half led, half carried, her to a couch, and there, holding her embraced, gave way to such amorous frenzy that again Monica broke from him.

'If you love me,' she said in tones of bitter distress, 'you will respect me as much as before I came to you. Help me—I am suffering so dreadfully. Say at once that I shall go away with you, even if we travel as strangers. If you are afraid of it becoming known I will do everything to prevent it. I will go back and live there until Tuesday, and come away only at the last hour, so that no one will ever suspect where—I don't care how humbly I live when we are abroad. I can have lodgings somewhere in the same town, or near, and you will come—'

His hair disordered, his eyes wild, quivering throughout with excitement, he stood as if pondering possibilities.

'Shall I be a burden to you?' she asked in a faint voice. 'Is the expense more than you—'

'No, no, no! How can you think of such a thing? But it would be so much better if you could wait here until I—Oh, what a wretched thing to have to seem so cowardly to you! But the difficulties are so great, darling. I shall be a perfect stranger in Bordeaux. I don't even speak the language at all well. When I reach there I shall be met at the station by one of our people, and—just think, how could we manage? You know, if it were discovered that I had run away with you, it would damage my position terribly. I can't say what might happen. My darling, we shall have to be very careful. In a few weeks it might all be managed very easily. I would write to you to some address, and as soon as ever I had made arrangements—'

Monica broke down. The unmanliness of his tone was so dreadful a disillusion. She had expected something so entirely different—swift, virile passion, eagerness even to anticipate her desire of flight, a strength, a courage to which she could abandon herself, body and soul. She broke down utterly, and wept with her hands upon her face.

Bevis, in sympathetic distraction, threw himself on his knees before, clutching at her waist.

'Don't, don't!' he wailed. 'I can't bear that! I will do as you wish, Monica. Tell me some place where I can write to you. Don't cry, darling—don't—'

She went to the couch again, and rested her face against the back, sobbing. For a time they exchanged mere incoherences. Then passion seized upon both, and they clung together, mute, motionless.

'To-morrow I shall leave him,' whispered Monica, when at length their eyes met. 'He will be away in the morning, and I can take what I need. Tell me where I shall go to, dear—to wait until you are ready. No one will ever suspect that we have gone together. He knows I am miserable with him; he will believe that I have found some way of supporting myself in London. Where shall I live till Tuesday?'

Bevis scarcely listened to her words. The temptation of the natural man, basely selfish, was strengthening its hold upon him.

'Do you love me? Do you really love me?' he replied to her, with thick, agitated utterance.

'Why should you ask that? How can you doubt it?'

'If you really love me—-'

His face and tones frightened her.

'Don't make me doubt *your* love! If I have not perfect trust in you what will become of me?'

Yet once more she drew resolutely away from him. He pursued, and held her arms with violence.

'Oh, I am mistaken in you!' Monica cried in fear and bitterness. 'You don't know what love means, as *I* feel it. You won't speak, you won't think, of our future life together—'

'I have promised—'

'Leave loose of me! It's because I have come here. You think me a worthless woman, without sense of honour, with no self-respect—'

He protested vehemently. The anguished look in her eyes had its effect upon his senses; by degrees it subjugated him, and made him ashamed of his ignoble impulse.

'Shall I find a lodging for you till Tuesday?' he asked, after moving away arid returning.

'Will you?'

'You are sure you can leave home to-morrow—without being suspected?'

'Yes, I am sure I can. He is going to the City in the morning. Appoint some place where I can meet you. I will come in a cab, and then you can take me on to the—'

'But you are forgetting the risks. If you take a cab from Herne Hill, with your luggage, he will be able to find out the driver afterwards, and learn where you went.'

'Then I will drive only as far as the station, and come to Victoria, and you shall meet me there.'

The necessity of these paltry arrangements filled her soul with shame. On the details of her escape she had hardly reflected. All such considerations were, she deemed, naturally the care of her lover, who would act with promptitude, and so as to spare her a moment's perplexity. She had imagined everything in readiness within a few hours; on *her* no responsibility save that of breaking the hated bond. Inevitably she turned to the wretched thought that Bevis regarded her as a burden. Yes, he had already his mother and his sisters to support; she ought to have remembered that.

'What time would it be?' he was asking.

Unable to reply, she pursued her reflections. She had money, but how to obtain possession of it? Afterwards, when her flight was accomplished, secrecy, it appeared, would be no less needful than now. That necessity had never occurred to her; declaration of the love that had freed her seemed inevitable—nay, desirable. Her self-respect demanded it; only thus could she justify herself before his sisters and other people who knew her. *They*, perhaps, would not see it in the light of justification, but that mattered little; her own conscience would approve what she had done. But to steal away, and live henceforth in hiding, like a woman dishonoured even in her own eyes—from that she shrank with repugnance. Rather than that, would it not be preferable to break with her husband, and openly live apart from him, alone?

'Be honest with me,' she suddenly exclaimed. 'Had you rather I didn't come?'

'No, no! I can't live without you—'

'But, if that is true, why haven't you the courage to let every one know it? In your heart you must think that we are acting wrongly.'

'I don't! I believe, as you do, that love is the only true marriage. Very well!' He made a desperate gesture. 'Let us defy all consequences. For your sake—'

His exaggerated vehemence could not deceive Monica.

'What is it,' she asked, 'that you most fear?'

He began to babble protestations, but she would not listen to them.

'Tell me—I have every right to ask—what you most fear?'

'I fear nothing if *you* are with me. Let my relatives say and think what they like. I have made great sacrifices for them; to give up *you* would be too much.'

Yet his distress was evident. It strained the corners of his mouth, wrinkled his forehead.

'The disgrace would be more than you could bear. You would never see your mother and your sisters again.'

'If they are so prejudiced, so unreasonable, I can't help it. They must—'

He was interrupted by a loud rat-tat at the outer door. Blanched herself, Monica saw that her lover's face turned to ghastly pallor.

'Who can that be?' he whispered hoarsely. 'I expect no one.'

'Need you answer?'

'Can it be—? Have you been followed? Does any one suspect—?'

They stared at each other, still half-paralysed, and stood waiting thus until the knock was repeated impatiently.

'I daren't open,' Bevis whispered, coming close to her, as if on the impulse of seeking protection—for to offer it was assuredly not in his mind. 'It might be—'

'No! That's impossible.'

'I daren't go to the door. The risk is too frightful. He will go away, whoever it is, if no one answers.'

Both were shaking in the second stage of terror. Bevis put his arm about Monica, and felt her heart give great throbs against his own. Their passion for the moment was effectually quenched.

'Listen! That's the clink of the letter-box. A card or something has been put in. Then it's all right. I'll wait a moment.'

He stepped to the door of the room, opened it without sound, and at once heard footsteps descending the stairs. In the look which he cast back at her, a grin rather than a smile, Monica saw something that gave her a pang of shame on his behalf. On going to the letter-box he found a card, with a few words scribbled upon it.

'Only one of our partners!' he exclaimed gleefully. 'Wants to see me to-night. Of course he took it for granted I was out.'

Monica was looking at her watch. Past five o'clock.

'I think I must go,' she said timidly.

'But what are our arrangements? Do you still intend—'

'Intend? Isn't it for you to decide?'

There was a coldness in the words of both, partly the result of the great shock they had undergone, in part due to their impatience with each other.

'Darling—do what I proposed at first. Stay for a few days, until I am settled at Bordeaux.'

'Stay with my—my husband?'

She used the word purposely, significantly, to see how it would affect him. The bitterness of her growing disillusion allowed her to think and speak as if no ardent feeling were concerned.

'For both our sakes, dearest, dearest love! A few days longer, until I have written to you, and told you exactly what to do. The journey won't be very difficult for you; and think how much better, dear Monica, if we can escape discovery, and live for each other without any shame or fear to disturb us. You will be my own dear true wife. I will love and guard you as long as I live.'

He embraced her with placid tenderness, laying his cheek against hers, kissing her hands.

'We must see each other again,' he continued. 'Come on Sunday, will you? And in the meantime find out some place where I could address letters to you. You can always find a stationer's shop where they will receive letters. Be guided by me, dear little girl. Only a week or two—to save the happiness of our whole lives.'

Monica listened, but with half-attention, her look fixed on the floor. Encouraged by her silence, the lover went on in a strain of heightening enthusiasm, depicting the raptures of their retirement from the world in some suburb of Bordeaux. How this retreat was to escape the notice of his business companions, through whom the scandal might get wind, he did not suggest. The truth was, Bevis found himself in an extremely awkward position, with issues he had not contemplated, and all he cared for was to avert the immediate peril of public discovery. The easy-going, kindly fellow had never considered all the responsibility involved in making mild love—timorously selfish from the first—to a married woman who took his advances with desperate seriousness. He had not in him the stuff of vigorous rascality, still less the only other quality which can support a man in such a situation as this—heroism of moral revolt. So he cut a very poor figure, and was dolefully aware of it. He talked, talked; trying to disguise his feebleness in tinsel phrases; and Monica still kept her eyes cast down.

When another half-hour had passed, she sighed deeply and rose from her seat. She would write to him, she said, and let him know where a reply would reach her. No, she must not come here again; all he had to tell her would be communicated by letter. The subdued tone, the simple sadness of her words, distressed Bevis, and yet he secretly congratulated himself. He had done nothing for which this woman could justly reproach him; marvellous—so he considered—had been his self-restraint; absolutely, he had behaved 'like a gentleman.' To be sure, he was miserably in love, and, if circumstances by any means allowed of it, would send for Monica to join him in France. Should the thing prove impossible, he had nothing whatever on his conscience.

He held out his arms to her. Monica shook her head and looked away.

'Say once more that you love me, darling,' he pleaded. 'I shall not rest for an hour until I am able to write and say, "Come to me."'

She permitted him to hold her once more in his soft embrace.

'Kiss me, Monica!'

She put her lips to his cheek, and withdrew them, still shunning his look.

'Oh, not that kind of kiss. Like you kissed me before.'

'I can't,' she replied, with choking voice, the tears again starting forth.

'But what have I done that you should love me less, dearest?'

He kissed the falling drops, murmuring assurances, encouragements.

'You shan't leave me until I have heard you say that your love is unchanged. Whisper it to me, sweetest!'

'When we meet again—not now.'

'You frighten me. Monica, we are not saying good-bye for ever?'

'If you send for me I *will* come.'

'You promise faithfully? You will come?'

'If you send for me I will come.'

That was her last word. He opened the door for her, and listened as she departed.

## CHAPTER XXIII - IN AMBUSH

Hitherto, Widdowson had entertained no grave mistrust of his wife. The principles she had avowed, directly traceable as it seemed to her friendship with the militant women in Chelsea, he disliked and feared; but her conduct he fully believed to be above reproach. His jealously of Barfoot did not glance at Monica's attitude towards the man; merely at the man himself, whom he credited with native scoundreldom. Barfoot represented to his mind a type of licentious bachelor; why, he could not have made perfectly clear to his own understanding. Possibly the ease of Everard's bearing, the something aristocratic in his countenance and his speech, the polish of his manner, especially in formal converse with women, from the first grave offence to Widdowson's essentially middle-class sensibilities. If Monica were in danger at all, it was, he felt convinced, from that quarter. The subject of his wife's intimate dialogue with Barfoot at the Academy still remained a mystery to him. He put faith in her rebellious declaration that every word might have been safely repeated in his hearing, but, be the matter what it might, the manner of Barfoot's talk meant evil. Of that conviction he could not get rid.

He had read somewhere that a persistently jealous husband may not improbably end by irritating an innocent wife into affording real ground for jealousy. A man with small knowledge of the world is much impressed by dicta such as there; they get into the crannies of his mind, and thence direct the course of his thinking. Widdowson, before his marriage, had never suspected the difficulty of understanding a woman; had he spoken his serious belief on that subject, it would have been found to represent the most primitive male conception of the feminine being. Women were very like children; it was rather a task to amuse them and to keep them out of mischief. Therefore the blessedness of household toil, in especial the blessedness of child-bearing and all that followed. Intimacy with Monica had greatly affected his views, yet chiefly by disturbing them; no firmer ground offered itself to his threading when he perforce admitted that his former standpoint was every day assailed by some incontestable piece of evidence. Woman had individual characters; that discovery, though not a very profound one, impressed him with the force of something arrived at by independent observation. Monica often puzzled him gravely; he could not find the key to her satisfactions and discontents. To regard her simply as a human being was beyond the reach of his intelligence. He cast the blame of his difficulties upon sex, and paid more attention to the hints on such afforded him by his reading. He would endeavour to keep his jealousy out of sight, lest the mysterious tendency of the female nature might prompt Monica to deliberate wrongdoing.

To-day for the first time there flashed across him the thought that already he might have been deceived. It originated in a peculiarity of Monica's behaviour at luncheon. She ate scarcely anything; she seemed hurried, frequently glancing at the clock; and she lost herself in reverie. Discovering that his eye was upon her, she betrayed uneasiness, and began to talk without considering what she meant to say. All this might mean nothing more than her barely-concealed regret at being obliged to leave London; but Widdowson remarked it with a vivacity of feeling perhaps due to the excitement in which he had lived for the past week. Perhaps the activity, the resolution to which he had urged himself, caused a sharpening of his perceptions. And the very thought, never out of his mind, that only a few days had to elapse before he carried off his wife from the scene of peril, tended to make him more vividly conscious of that peril. Certain it was that a moment's clairvoyance assailed his peace, and left behind it all manner of ugly conjectures. Woman—so said the books—are adepts at dissimulation. Was it conceivable that Monica had taken advantage of the liberty he had of late allowed her? If a woman could not endure a direct, searching gaze, must it not imply some enormous wickedness?—seeing that nature has armed them for this very trial.

In her setting forth for the railway station hurry was again evident, and disinclination to exchange parting words. If the eagerness were simple and honest, would she not have accepted his suggestion and have gone in the morning?

For five minutes after her departure he stood in the hall, staring before him. A new jealousy, a horrible constriction of the heart, had begun to torture him. He went and walked about in the library, but could not dispel his suffering. Vain to keep repeating that Monica was incapable of baseness. Of that he was persuaded, but none the less a hideous image returned upon his mental vision—a horror—a pollution of thought.

# CHAPTER XXIII - IN AMBUSH

One thing he could do to restore his sanity. He would walk over to Lavender Hill, and accompany his wife on her return home. Indeed, the mere difficulty of getting through the afternoon advised this project. He could not employ himself, and knew that his imagination, once inflamed, would leave him not a moment's rest. Yes, he would walk to Lavender Hill, and ramble about that region until Monica had had reasonable time for talk with her sister.

About three o'clock there fell a heavy shower of rain. Strangely against his habits, Widdowson turned into a quiet public-house, and sat for a quarter of an hour at the bar, drinking a glass of whisky. During the past week he had taken considerably more wine than usual at meals; he seemed to need the support. Whilst sipping at his glass of spirits, he oddly enough fell into talk with the barmaid, a young woman of some charms, and what appeared to be unaffected modesty. Not for twenty years had Widdowson conversed with a member of this sisterhood. Their dialogue was made up of the most trifling of trivialities—weather, a railway accident, the desirability of holidays at this season. And when at length he rose and put an end to the chat it was with appreciable reluctance.

'A good, nice sort of girl,' he went away saying to himself. 'Pity she should be serving at a bar—hearing doubtful talk, and seeing very often vile sights. A nice, soft-spoken little girl.'

And he mused upon her remembered face with a complacency which soothed his feelings.

Of a sudden he was checked by the conversion of his sentiment into thought. Would he not have been a much happier man if he had married a girl distinctly his inferior in mind and station? Provided she were sweet, lovable, docile—such a wife would have spared him all the misery he had known with Monica. From the first he had understood that Monica was no representative shopgirl, and on that very account he had striven so eagerly to win her. But it was a mistake. He had loved her, still loved her, with all the emotion of which he was capable. How many hours' genuine happiness of soul had that love afforded him? The minutest fraction of the twelve months for which she had been his wife. And of suffering, often amounting to frantic misery, he could count many weeks. Could such a marriage as this be judged a marriage at all, in any true sense of the word?

'Let me ask myself a question. If Monica were absolutely free to choose between continuing to live with me and resuming her perfect liberty, can I persuade myself that she would remain my wife? She would not. Not for a day, not for an hour. Of that I am morally convinced. And I acknowledge the grounds of her dissatisfaction. We are unsuited to each other. We do not understand each other. Our marriage is physical and nothing more. My love—what is my love? I do not love her mind, her intellectual part. If I did, this frightful jealousy from which I suffer would be impossible. My ideal of the wife perfectly suited to me is far liker that girl at the public-house bar than Monica. Monica's independence of thought is a perpetual irritation to me. I don't know what her thoughts really are, what her intellectual life signifies. And yet I hold her to me with the sternest grasp. If she endeavoured to release herself I should feel capable of killing her. Is not this a strange, a brutal thing?'

Widdowson had never before reached this height of speculation. In the moment, by the very fact, of admitting that Monica and he ought not to be living together, he became more worthy of his wife's companionship than ever hitherto.

Well, he would exercise greater forebearance. He would endeavour to win her respect by respecting the freedom she claimed. His recent suspicions of her were monstrous. If she knew them, how her soul would revolt from him! What if she took an interest in other men, perchance more her equals than he? Why, had he not just been thinking of another woman, reflecting that she, or one like her, would have made him a more suitable wife than Monica? Yet this could not reasonably be called unfaithfulness.

They were bound together for life, and their wisdom lay in mutual toleration, the constant endeavour to understand each other aright—not in fierce restraint of each other's mental liberty. How many marriages were anything more than mutual forbearance? Perhaps there ought not to be such a thing as enforced permanence of marriage. This was daring speculation; he could not have endured to hear it from Monica's lips. But—perhaps, some day, marriage would be dissoluble at the will of either party to it. Perhaps the man who sought to hold a woman when she no longer loved him would be regarded with contempt and condemnation.

What a simple thing marriage had always seemed to him, and how far from simple he had found it! Why, it led him to musings which overset the order of the world, and flung all ideas of religion and morality into wildest confusion. It would not do to think like this. He was a man wedded to a woman very difficult to manage—there was the practical upshot of the matter. His duty was to manage her. He was responsible for her right conduct. With intentions perfectly harmless, she might run into unknown jeopardy—above all, just at this time when she was taking reluctant leave of her friends. The danger justified him in exceptional vigilance.

So, from his excursion into the realms of reason did he return to the safe sphere of the commonplace. And now he might venture to press on towards Mrs. Conisbee's house, for it was half-past four, and already Monica must have been talking with her sister for a couple of hours.

His knock at the door was answered by the landlady herself. She told of Mrs. Widdowson's arrival and departure. Ah, then Monica had no doubt gone straight home again. But, as Miss Madden had returned, he would speak with her.

'The poor lady isn't very well, sir,' said Mrs. Conisbee, fingering the hem of her apron.

'Not very well? But couldn't I see her for a moment?'

Virginia answered this question by appearing on the staircase.

'Some one for me, Mrs. Conisbee?' she called from above. 'Oh, is it *you*, Edmund? So very glad! I'm sure Mrs. Conisbee will have the kindness to let you come into her sitting-room. What a pity I was away when Monica called! I've had—business to see to in town; and I've walked and walked, until I'm really—hardly able—'

She sank upon a chair in the room, and looked fixedly at the visitor with a broad, benevolent smile, her head moving up and down. Widdowson was for a moment in perplexity. If the evidence of his eyes could be trusted, Miss Madden's indisposition pointed to a cause so strange that it seemed incredible. He turned to look for Mrs. Conisbee, but the landlady had hurriedly withdrawn, closing the door behind her.

'It is so foolish of me, Edmund,' Virginia rambled on, addressing him with a familiarity she had never yet used. 'When I am away from home I forget all about my meals—really forget—and then all at once I find that I am quite exhausted—quite exhausted—as you see. And the worst of it is I have altogether lost my appetite by the time I get back. I couldn't eat a mouthful of food—not a mouthful—I assure you I couldn't. And it does so distress good Mrs. Conisbee. She is exceedingly kind to me—exceedingly careful about my health. Oh, and in Battersea Park Road I saw such a shocking sight; a great cart ran over a poor little dog, and it was killed on the spot. It unnerved me dreadfully. I do think, Edmund, those drivers ought to be more careful. I was saying to Mrs. Conisbee only the other day—and that reminds me, I do so want to know all about your visit to Clevedon. Dear, dear Clevedon! And have you really taken a house there, Edmund? Oh, if we could all end our days at Clevedon! You know that our dear father and mother are buried in the old churchyard. You remember Tennyson's lines about the old church at Clevedon? Oh, and what did Mon-Monica decide about—about—really, what *was* I going to ask? It is so foolish of me to forget that dinner-time has come and gone. I get so exhausted, and even my memory fails me.'

He could doubt no longer. This poor woman had yielded to one of the temptations that beset a life of idleness and solitude. His pity was mingled with disgust.

'I only wished to tell you,' he said gravely, 'that we have taken a house at Clevedon—'

'You really *have*!' She clasped her hands together. 'Whereabouts?'

'Near Dial Hill.'

Virginia began a rhapsody which her brother-in-law had no inclination to hear. He rose abruptly.

'Perhaps you had better come and see us to-morrow.'

'But Monica left a message that she wouldn't be at home for the next few days, and that I wasn't to come till I heard from her.'

'Not at home—? I think there's a mistake.'

'Oh, impossible! We'll ask Mrs. Conisbee.'

She went to the door and called. From the landlady Widdowson learnt exactly what Monica had said. He reflected for a moment.

'She shall write to you then. Don't come just yet. I mustn't stay any longer now.'

And with a mere pretence of shaking hands he abruptly left the house.

Suspicions thickened about him. He would have thought it utterly impossible for Miss Madden to disgrace herself in this vulgar way, and the appalling discovery affected his view of Monica. They were sisters; they had characteristics in common, family traits, weaknesses. If the elder woman could fall into this degradation, might there not be possibilities in Monica's character such as he had refused to contemplate? Was there not terrible reason for mistrusting her? What did she mean by her message to Virginia.

Black and haggard, he went home as fast as a hansom could take him. It was half-past five when he reached the house. His wife was not here, and had not been here.

At this moment Monica was starting by train from Bayswater, after her parting with Bevis. Arrived at Victoria, she crossed to the main station, and went to the ladies' waiting-room for the purpose of bathing her face. She had red, swollen eyes, and her hair was in slight disorder.

This done, she inquired as to the next train for Herne Hill. One had just gone; another would leave in about a quarter of an hour.

A dreadful indecision was harassing her. Ought she, did she dare, to return home at all? Even if her strength sufficed for simulating a natural manner, could she consent to play so base a part?

There was but one possible alternative. She might go to Virginia's lodgings, and there remain, writing to her husband that she had left him. The true cause need not be confessed. She would merely declare that life with him had become intolerable to her, that she demanded a release. Their approaching removal to Clevedon offered the occasion. She would say that her endurance failed before that prospect of solitude, and that, feeling as she did, it was dishonourable to make longer pretence of doing her duty as a wife. Then, if Bevis wrote to her in such a way as to revive her love, if he seriously told her to come to him, all difficulties could be solved by her disappearance.

Was such revival of disheartened love a likely or a possible thing? At this moment she felt that to flee in secret, and live with Bevis as he proposed, would be no less dishonour than abiding with the man who had a legal claim upon her companionship. Her lover, as she had thought of him for the past two or three months, was only a figment of her imagination; Bevis had proved himself a complete stranger to her mind; she must reshape her knowledge of him. His face was all that she could still dwell upon with the old desire; nay, even that had suffered a change.

Insensibly the minutes went by. Whilst she sat in the waiting-room her train started; and when she had become aware of that, her irresolution grew more tormenting.

Suddenly there came upon her a feeling of illness, of nausea. Perspiration broke out on her forehead; her eyes dazzled; she had to let her head fall back. It passed, but in a minute or two the fit again seized her, and with a moan she lost consciousness.

Two or three women who were in the room rendered assistance. The remarks they exchanged, though expressing uncertainty and discreetly ambiguous, would have been significant to Monica. On her recovery, which took place in a few moments, she at once started up, and with hurried thanks to those about her, listening to nothing that was said and answering no inquiry, went out on to the platform. There was just time to catch the train now departing for Herne Hill.

She explained her fainting fit by the hours of agitation through which she had passed. There was no room for surprise. She had suffered indescribably, and still suffered. Her wish was to get back into the quietness of home, to rest and to lose herself in sleep.

On entering, she saw nothing of her husband. His hat hung on the hall-tree, and he was perhaps sitting in the library; the more genial temper would account for his not coming forth at once to meet her, as had been his custom when she returned from an absence alone.

She changed her dress, and disguised as far as was possible the traces of suffering on her features. Weakness and tremor urged her to lie down, but she could not venture to do this until she had spoken to her husband. Supporting herself by the banisters, she slowly descended, and opened the library door. Widdowson was reading a newspaper. He did not look round, but said carelessly,—

'So you are back?'

'Yes. I hope you didn't expect me sooner.'

'Oh, it's all right.' He threw a rapid glance at her over his shoulder. 'Had a long talk with Virginia, I suppose?'

'Yes. I couldn't get away before.'

Widdowson seemed to be much interested in some paragraph. He put his face closer to the paper, and was silent for two or three seconds. Then he again looked round, this time observing his wife steadily, but with a face that gave no intimation of unusual thoughts.

'Does she consent to go?'

Monica replied that it was still uncertain; she thought, however, that Virginia's objections would be overcome.

'You look very tired,' remarked the other.

'I am, very.'

And thereupon she withdrew, unable to command her countenance, scarce able to remain standing for another moment.

# CHAPTER XXIV - TRACKED

When Widdowson went up to the bedroom that night, Monica was already asleep. He discovered this on turning up the gas. The light fell upon her face, and he was drawn to the bedside to look at her. The features signified nothing but repose; her lips were just apart, her eyelids lay softly with their black fringe of exquisite pencilling, and her hair was arranged as she always prepared it for the pillow. He watched her for full five minutes, and detected not the slightest movement, so profound was her sleep. Then he turned away, muttering savagely under his breath, 'Hypocrite! Liar!'

But for a purpose in his thoughts he would not have lain down beside her. On getting into bed he kept as far away as possible, and all through the wakeful night his limbs shrank from the touch of hers.

He rose an hour earlier than usual. Monica had long been awake, but she moved so seldom that he could not be sure of this; her face was turned from him. When he came back to the room after his bath. Monica propped herself on her elbow and asked why he was moving so early.

'I want to be in the City at nine,' he replied, with a show of cheerfulness. 'There's a money affair I must see after.'

'Something that's going wrong?'

'I'm afraid so. I must lose no time in looking to it. What plans have you for to-day?'

'None whatever.'

'It's Saturday, you know. I promised to see Newdick this afternoon. Perhaps I may bring him to dinner.'

About twelve o'clock he returned from his business. At two he went away again, saying that he should not be back before seven, it might be a little later. In Monica these movements excited no special remark; they were merely a continuance of his restlessness. But no sooner had he departed, after luncheon, than she went to her dressing-room, and began to make slow, uncertain preparations for leaving home herself.

This morning she had tried to write a letter for Bevis, but vainly. She knew not what to say to him, uncertain of her own desires and of what lay before her. Yet, if she were to communicate with him henceforth at all, it was necessary, this very afternoon, to find an address where letters could be received for her, and to let him know of it. To-morrow, Sunday, was useless for the purpose, and on Monday it might be impossible for her to go out alone. Besides that, she could not be sure of the safety of a letter delivered at the flat on Monday night or Tuesday morning.

She dressed at length and went out. Her wisest course, probably, was to seek for some obliging shopkeeper near Lavender Hill. Then she could call on Virginia, transact the business she had pretended to discharge yesterday, and there pen a note to Bevis.

Her moods alternated with distracting rapidity. A hundred times she had resolved that Bevis could be nothing more to her, and again had thought of him with impulses of yearning, trying to persuade herself that he had acted well and wisely. A hundred times she determined to carry out her idea of yesterday—to quit her husband and resist all his efforts to recall her—and again had all but resigned herself to live with him, accepting degradation as so many wives perforce did. Her mind was in confusion, and physically she felt far from well. A heaviness weighed upon her limbs, making it hardship to walk however short a distance.

Arrived at Clapham Junction, she began to search wearily, indifferently, for the kind of shop that might answer her purpose. The receiving of letters which, for one reason or another, must be dispatched to a secret address, is a very ordinary complaisance on the part of small London stationers; hundreds of such letters are sent and called for every week within the metropolitan postal area. It did not take Monica long to find an obliging shopkeeper; the first to whom she applied—a decent woman behind a counter which displayed newspapers, tobacco, and fancy articles—willingly accepted the commission.

She came out of the shop with flushed cheeks. Another step in shameful descent—yet it had the result of strengthening once more her emotions favourable to Bevis. On his account she had braved this ignominy, and it drew her towards him, instead of producing the effect which would have seemed more natural. Perhaps the reason was that she felt herself more hopelessly an outcast from the world of honourable women, and therefore longed in her desolation for the support of a man's love. Did he not love her? It was *her* fault if she expected him to act with a boldness that did not lie in his nature. Perhaps his discretion, which she had so bitterly condemned as weakness, meant a wise regard for her interests as well as his own. The public scandal of divorce was a hideous thing. If it damaged his prospects and sundered him from his relatives, how could she hope that his love of her, the cause of it all, would long endure?

The need of love overcame her. She would submit to any conditions rather than lose this lover whose kisses were upon her lips, and whose arms had held her so passionately. She was too young to accept a life of resignation, too ardent. Why had she left him in despondency, in doubt whether he would ever again see her?

She turned back on her way to Virginia's lodgings, re-entered the station, and journeyed townwards. It was an odd incident, by Monica unperceived, that when she was taking her ticket there stood close by her a man, seemingly a mechanic, who had also stood within hearing when she booked at Herne Hill. This same man, though he had not travelled in the compartment with her, followed her when she alighted at Bayswater. She did not once observe him.

Instead of writing, she had resolved to see Bevis again—if it were possible. Perhaps he would not be at the flat; yet his wish might suggest the bare hope of her coming to-day. The risk of meeting Barfoot probably need not be considered, for he had told her that he was travelling to-day into Cumberland, and for so long a journey he would be sure to set forth in the morning. At worst she would suffer a disappointment. Indulgence of her fervid feelings had made her as eager to see Bevis as she was yesterday. Words of tenderness rushed to her lips for utterance. When she reached the building all but delirium possessed her.

She had hurried up to the first landing, when a footstep behind drew her attention. It was a man in mechanic's dress, coming up with head bent, doubtless for some task or other in one of the flats. Perhaps he was going to Bevis's. She went forward more slowly, and on the next landing allowed the man to pass her. Yes, more likely than not he was engaged in packing her lover's furniture. She stood still. At that moment a door closed above, and another step, lighter and quicker, that of a woman, came downstairs. As far as her ear could judge, this person might have left Bevis's flat. A conflict of emotions excited her to panic. She was afraid either to advance or to retreat, and in equal dread of standing without purpose. She stepped up to the nearest door, and gave a summons with the knocker.

This door was Barfoot's. She knew that; in the first instant of fear occasioned by the workman's approach, she had glanced at the door and reminded herself that here Mr. Barfoot dwelt, immediately beneath Bevis. But for the wild alarm due to her conscience-stricken state she could not have risked the possibility of the tenant being still at home; and yet it seemed to her that she was doing the only thing possible under the circumstances. For this woman whom she heard just above might perchance be one of Bevis's sisters, returned to London for some purpose or other, and in that case she preferred being seen at Barfoot's door to detection as she made for her lover's.

Uncertainty on this point lasted but a few seconds. Dreading to look at the woman, Monica yet did so, just as she passed, and beheld the face of a perfect stranger. A young and good-looking face, however. Her mind, sufficiently tumultuous, received a new impulse of disturbance. Had this woman come forth from Bevis's fiat or from the one opposite?—for on each floor there were two dwellings.

In the meantime no one answered her knock. Mr. Barfoot had gone; she breathed thankfully. Now she might venture to ascend to the next floor. But then sounded a knock from above. That, she felt convinced, was at Bevis's door, and if so her conjecture about the workman was correct. She stood waiting for certainty, as if still expecting a reply to her own signal at Mr. Barfoot's door. The mechanic looked down at her over the banisters, but of this she was unaware.

The knock above was repeated. Yes, this time there could be no mistake; it was on this side of the landing—that is to say, at her lover's door. But the door did not open; thus, without going up herself, she received assurance that Bevis was not at home. He might come later. She still had an hour or two to spare. So, as if disappointed in a call at Mr. Barfoot's, she descended the stairs and issued into the street.

Agitation had exhausted her, and a dazzling of her eyes threatened a recurrence of yesterday's faintness. She found a shop where refreshments were sold, and sat for half an hour over a cup of tea, trying to amuse herself with illustrated papers. The mechanic who had knocked at Bevis's door passed once or twice along the pavement, and, as long as she remained here, kept the shop within sight.

At length she asked for writing materials, and penned a few lines. If on her second attempt she failed to see Bevis, she would drop this note into his letter-box. It acquainted him with the address to which he might direct letters, assured him passionately of her love, and implored him to be true to her, to send for her as soon as circumstances made it possible.

Self-torment of every kind was natural to her position. Though the relief of escaping from several distinct dangers had put her mind comparatively at ease for a short time, she had now begun to suffer a fresh uneasiness with reference to the young and handsome woman who came downstairs. The fact that no one answered the workman's knock had seemed to her a sufficient proof that Bevis was not at home, and that the stranger must have come forth from the flat opposite his. But she recollected the incident which had so alarmingly disturbed her and her lover yesterday. Bevis did not then go to the door, and suppose—oh, it was folly! But suppose that woman had been with him; suppose he did not care to open to a visitor whose signal sounded only a minute or two after that person's departure?

Had she not anguish enough to endure without the addition of frantic jealousy? She would not give another thought to such absurd suggestions. The woman had of course come from the dwelling opposite. Yet why might she not have been in Bevis's flat when he himself was absent? Suppose her an intimate to whom he had entrusted a latch-key. If any such connection existed, might it not help to explain Bevis's half-heartedness?

To think thus was courting madness. Unable to sit still any longer, Monica left the shop, and strayed for some ten minutes about the neighbouring streets, drawing nearer and nearer to her goal. Finally she entered the building and went upstairs. On this occasion no one met her, and no one entered in her rear. She knocked at her lover's door, and stood longing, praying, that it might open. But it did not. Tears started to her eyes; she uttered a moan of bitterest disappointment, and slipped the envelope she was carrying into the letter-box.

The mechanic had seen her go in, and he waited outside, a few yards away. Either she would soon reappear, or her not doing so would show that she had obtained admittance somewhere. In the latter case, this workman of much curiosity and leisure had only to lurk about the staircase until she came forth again. But this trial of patience was spared him. He found that he had simply to follow the lady back to Herne Hill. Acting on very suggestive instructions, it never occurred to the worthy man that the lady's second visit was not to the same flat as in the former instance.

Monica was home again long before dinner-time. When that hour arrived her husband had not yet come; the delay, no doubt, was somehow connected with his visit to Mr. Newdick. But this went on. At nine o'clock Monica still sat alone, hungry, yet scarce conscious of hunger owing to her miseries. Widdowson had never behaved thus. Another quarter of an hour and she heard the front door open.

He came to the drawing-room, where she sat waiting.

'How late you are! Are you alone?'

'Yes, alone.'

'You haven't had dinner?'

'No.'

He seemed to be in rather a gloomy mood, but Monica noticed nothing that alarmed her. He was drawing nearer, his eyes on the ground.

'Have you had bad news—in the City?'

'Yes, I have.'

Still he came nearer, and at length, when a yard or two away, raised his look to her face.

'Have you been out this afternoon?'

She was prompted to a falsehood, but durst not utter it, so keenly was he regarding her.

'Yes, I went to see Miss Barfoot.'

'Liar!'

As the word burst from his lips, he sprang at her, clutched her dress at the throat, and flung her violently upon her knees. A short cry of terror escaped her; then she was stricken dumb, with eyes starting and mouth open. It was well that he held her by the garment and not by the neck, for his hand closed with murderous convulsion, and the desire of crushing out her life was for an instant all his consciousness.

'Liar!' again burst from him. 'Day after day you have lied to me. Liar! Adultress!'

'I am not! I am not that!'

She clung upon his arms and strove to raise herself. The bloodless lips, the choked voice, meant dread of him, but the distortion of her features was hatred and the will to resist.

'Not that? What is your word worth? The prostitute in the street is sooner to be believed. She has the honesty to say what she is, but you—Where were you yesterday when you were not at your sister's? Where were you this afternoon?'

She had nearly struggled to her feet; he thrust her down again, crushed her backwards until her head all but touched the floor.

'Where were you? Tell the truth, or you shall never speak again!'

'Oh—help! help! He will kill me!'

Her cry rang through the room.

'Call them up—let them come and look at you and hear what you are. Soon enough every one will know. Where were you this afternoon? You were watched every step of the way from here to that place where you have made yourself a base, vile, unclean creature—.'

'I am not that! Your spies have misled you.'

'Misled? Didn't you go to that man Barfoot's door and knock there? And because you were disappointed, didn't you wait about, and go there a second time?'

'What if I did? It doesn't mean what you think.'

'What? You go time after time to the private chambers of an unmarried man—a man such as that—and it means no harm?'

'I have never been there before.'

'You expect me to believe you?' Widdowson cried with savage contumely. He had just loosed his hold of her, and she was upright again before him, her eyes flashing defiance, though every muscle in her frame quivered. 'When did your lies begin? Was it when you told me you had been to hear Miss Barfoot's lecture, and never went there at all?'

He aimed the charge at a venture, and her face told him that his suspicion had been grounded.

'For how many weeks, for how many months, have you been dishonouring me and yourself?'

'I am not guilty of what you believe, but I shan't try to defend myself. Thank Heaven, this is the end of everything between us! Charge me with what you like. I am going away from you, and I hope we may never meet again.'

'Yes, you are going—no doubt of that. But not before you have answered my questions. Whether with lies or not doesn't matter much. You shall give your own account of what you have been doing.'

Both panting as if after some supreme effort of their physical force, they stood and looked at each other. Each to the other's eyes was incredibly transformed. Monica could not have imagined such brutal ferocity in her husband's face, and she herself had a wild recklessness in her eyes, a scorn and abhorrence in all the lines of her countenance, which made Widdowson feel as if a stranger were before him.

'I shall answer no question whatever,' Monica replied. 'All I want is to leave your house, and never see you again.'

He regretted what he had done. The result of the first day's espionage being a piece of evidence so incomplete, he had hoped to command himself until more solid proof of his wife's guilt were forthcoming. But jealousy was too strong for such prudence, and the sight of Monica as she uttered her falsehood made a mere madman of him. Predisposed to believe a story of this kind, he could not reason as he might have done if fear of Barfoot had never entered his thoughts. The whole course of dishonour seemed so clear; he traced it from Monica's earliest meetings with Barfoot at Chelsea. Wavering between the impulse to cast off his wife with every circumstance of public shame, and the piteous desire to arrest her on her path of destruction, he rushed into a middle course, compatible with neither of these intentions. If at this stage he chose to tell Monica what had come to his knowledge, it should have been done with the sternest calm, with dignity capable of shaming her guilt. As it was, he had spoilt his chances in every direction. Perhaps Monica understood this; he had begun to esteem her a mistress in craft and intrigue.

'You say you were never at that man's rooms before to-day?' he asked in a lower voice.

'What I have said you must take the trouble to recollect. I shall answer no question.'

Again the impulse assailed him to wring confession from her by terror. He took a step forward, the demon in his face. Monica in that moment leapt past him, and reached the door of the room before he could stop her.

'Stay where you are!' she cried, 'If your hands touch me again I shall call for help until someone comes up. I won't endure your touch!'

'Do you pretend you are innocent of any crime against me?'

'I am not what you called me. Explain everything as you like. I will explain nothing. I want only to be free from you.'

She opened the door, rapidly crossed the landing, and went upstairs. Feeling it was useless to follow, Widdowson allowed the door to remain wide, and waited. Five minutes passed and Monica came down again, dressed for leaving the house.

'Where are you going?' he asked, stepping out of the room to intercept her.

'It is nothing to you. I am going away.'

They subdued their voices, which might else have been audible to the servants below.

'No, that you shall not!'

He stepped forward to block the head of the stairs, but again Monica was too quick for him. She fled down, and across the hall, and to the house-door. Only there, as she was arrested by the difficulty of drawing back the two latches, did Widdowson overtake her.

'Make what scandal you like, you don't leave this house.'

His tones were violent rather than resolute. What could he do? If Monica persisted, what means had he of confining her to the house—short of carrying her by main force to an upper room and there locking her in? He knew that his courage would not sustain him through such a task as this.

'For scandal I care nothing,' was her reply. 'One way or another I will leave the house.'

'Where are you going?'

'To my sister's.'

His hand on the door, Widdowson stood as if determined in opposition. But her will was stronger than his. Only by homicide can a man maintain his dignity in a situation of this kind; Widdowson could not kill his wife, and every moment that he stood there made him more ridiculous, more contemptible.

He turned back into the hall and reached his hat. Whilst he was doing so Monica opened the door. Heavy rain was falling, but she paid no heed to it. In a moment Widdowson hastened after her, careless, he too, of the descending floods. Her way was towards the railway station, but the driver of a cab chancing to attract her notice, she accepted the man's offer, and bade him drive to Lavender Hill.

On the first opportunity Widdowson took like refuge from the rain, and was driven in the same direction. He alighted not far from Mrs. Conisbee's house. That Monica had come hither he felt no doubt, but he would presently make sure of it. As it still rained he sought shelter in a public-house, where he quenched a painful thirst, and then satisfied his hunger with such primitive foods as a licensed victualler is disposed to vend. It was nearing eleven o'clock, and he had neither eaten nor drunk since luncheon.

After that he walked to Mrs. Conisbee's, and knocked at the door. The landlady came.

'Will you please to tell me,' he asked 'whether Mrs. Widdowson is here?'

The sly curiosity of the woman's face informed him at once that she saw something unusual in these circumstances.

'Yes, sir. Mrs. Widdowson is with her sister,'

'Thank you.'

Without another word he departed. But went only a short distance, and until midnight kept Mrs. Conisbee's door in view. The rain fell, the air was raw; shelterless, and often shivering with fever, Widdowson walked the pavement with a constable's regularity. He could not but remember the many nights when he thus kept watch in Walworth Road and in Rutland Street, with jealousy, then too, burning in his heart, but also with amorous ardours, never again to be revived.

A little more than twelve months ago! And he had waited, longed for marriage through half a lifetime.

# CHAPTER XXV - THE FATE OF THE IDEAL

Rhoda's week at the seashore was spoilt by uncertain weather. Only two days of abiding sunshine; for the rest, mere fitful gleams across a sky heaped with stormclouds. Over Wastdale hung a black canopy; from Scawfell came mutterings of thunder; and on the last night of the week—when Monica fled from her home in pelting rain—tempest broke upon the mountains and the sea. Wakeful until early morning, and at times watching the sky from her inland-looking window, Rhoda saw the rocky heights that frown upon Wastwater illuminated by lightning-flare of such intensity and duration that miles of distance were annihilated, and it seemed but a step to these stern crags and precipices.

Sunday began with rain, but also with promise of better things; far over the sea was a broad expanse of blue, and before long the foam of the fallen tide glistened in strong, hopeful rays. Rhoda wandered about the shore towards St. Bees Head. A broad stream flowing into the sea stopped her progress before she had gone very far; the only way of crossing it was to go up on to the line of railway, which here runs along the edge of the sands. But she had little inclination to walk farther. No house, no person within sight, she sat down to gaze at the gulls fishing by the little river-mouth, their screams the only sound that blended with that of the subdued breakers.

On the horizon lay a long, low shape that might have been mistaken for cloud, though it resembled land. It was the Isle of Man. In an hour or two the outline had grown much clearer; the heights and hollows were no longer doubtful. In the north became visible another remote and hilly tract, it was the coast of Scotland beyond Solway Firth.

These distant objects acted as incentives to Rhoda's imagination. She heard Everard Barfoot's voice as he talked of travel—of the Orient Express. That joy of freedom he had offered her. Perhaps he was now very near her, anxious to repeat his offer. If he carried out the project suggested at their last interview, she would see him to-day or to-morrow morning—then she must make her choice. To have a day's walk with him among the mountains would be practically deciding. But for what? If she rejected his proposal of a free union, was he prepared to marry her in legal form? Yes; she had enough power over him for that. But how would it affect his thought of her? Constraining him to legal marriage, would she not lower herself in his estimation, and make the endurance of his love less probable? Barfoot was not a man to accept with genuine satisfaction even the appearance of bondage, and more likely than not his love of her depended upon the belief that in her he had found a woman capable of regarding life from his own point of view—a woman who, when she once, loved, would be scornful of the formalities clung to by feeble minds. He would yield to her if she demanded forms, but afterwards—when passion had subsided—.

A week had been none too long to ponder these considerations by themselves; but they were complicated with doubts of a more disturbing nature. Her mind could not free itself from the thought of Monica. That Mrs. Widdowson was not always truthful with her husband she had absolute proof; whether that supported her fear of an intimacy between Monica and Everard she was unable to determine. The grounds of suspicion seemed to her very grave; so grave, that during her first day or two in Cumberland she had all but renounced the hopes long secretly fostered. She knew herself well enough to understand how jealousy might wreck her life—even if it were only retrospective. If she married Barfoot (forms or none—that question in no way touched this other), she would demand of him a flawless faith. Her pride revolted against the thought of possessing only a share in his devotion; the moment that any faithlessness came to her knowledge she would leave him, perforce, inevitably—and what miseries were then before her!

Was flawless faith possible to Everard Barfoot? His cousin would ridicule the hope of any such thing—or so Rhoda believed. A conventional woman would of course see the completest evidence of his untrustworthiness in his dislike of legal marriage; but Rhoda knew the idleness of this argument. If love did not hold him, assuredly the forms of marriage could be no restraint upon Everard; married ten times over, he would still deem himself absolutely free from any obligation save that of love. Yet how did he think of that obligation? He might hold it perfectly compatible with the indulgence of casual impulse. And this (which she suspected to be the view of every man) Rhoda had no power of tolerating. It must be all or nothing, whole faith or none whatever.

## CHAPTER XXV - THE FATE OF THE IDEAL

In the afternoon she suffered from impatient expectancy. If Barfoot came to-day—she imagined him somewhere in the neighbourhood, approaching Seascale as the time of his appointment drew near—would he call at her lodgings? The address she had not given him, but doubtless he had obtained it from his cousin. Perhaps he would prefer to meet her unexpectedly—not a difficult thing in this little place, with its handful of residents and visitors. Certain it was she desired his arrival. Her heart leapt with joy in the thought that this very evening might bring him. She wished to study him under new conditions, and—possibly—to talk with him even more frankly than ever yet, for there would be opportunity enough.

About six o'clock a train coming from the south stopped at the station, which was visible from Rhoda's sitting-room window. She had been waiting for this moment. She could not go to the station, and did not venture even to wait anywhere in sight of the exit. Whether any passenger had alighted must remain uncertain. If Everard had arrived by this train, doubtless he would go to the hotel, which stood only a few yards from the line. He would take a meal and presently come forth.

Having allowed half an hour to elapse, she dressed and walked shoreward. Seascale has no street, no shops; only two or three short rows of houses irregularly placed on the rising ground above the beach. To cross the intervening railway, Rhoda could either pass through the little station, in which case she would also pass the hotel and be observable from its chief windows, or descend by a longer road which led under a bridge, and in this way avoid the hotel altogether. She took the former route. On the sands were a few scattered people, and some children subdued to Sunday decorum. The tide was rising. She went down to the nearest tract of hard sand, and stood there for a long time, a soft western breeze playing upon her face.

If Barfoot were here he would now be coming out to look for her. From a distance he might not recognize her figure, clad as she was in a costume such as he had never seen her wearing. She might venture now to walk up towards the dry, white sandheaps, where the little convolvulus grew in abundance, and other flowers of which she neither knew nor cared to learn the names. Scarcely had she turned when she saw Everard approaching, still far off, but unmistakable. He signalled by taking off his hat, and quickly was beside her.

'Did you know me before I happened to look round?' she asked laughingly.

'Of course I did. Up there by the station I caught sight of you. Who else bears herself as you do—with splendid disdain of common mortals?'

'Please don't make me think that my movements are ridiculous.'

'They are superb. The sea has already touched your cheeks. But I am afraid you have had abominable weather.'

'Yes, rather bad; but there's hope to-day. Where do you come from?'

'By train, only from Carnforth. I left London yesterday morning, and stopped at Morecambe—some people I know are there. As trains were awkward to-day, I drove from Morecambe to Carnforth. Did you expect me?'

'I thought you might come, as you spoke of it.'

'How I have got through the week I couldn't tell you. I should have been here days ago, but I was afraid. Let us go nearer to the sea. I was afraid of making you angry.'

'It's better to keep one's word.'

'Of course it is. And I am all the more delighted to be with you for the miserable week of waiting. Have you bathed?'

'Once or twice.'

'I had a swim this morning before breakfast, in pouring rain. Now *you* can't swim.'

'No. I can't. But why were you sure about it?'

'Only because it's so rare for any girl to learn swimming. A man who can't swim is only half the man he might be, and to a woman I should think it must be of even more benefit. As in everything else, women are trammelled by their clothes; to be able to get rid of them, and to move about with free and brave exertion of all the body, must tend to every kind of health, physical, mental, and mortal.'

'Yes, I quite believe that,' said Rhoda, gazing at the sea.

'I spoke rather exultantly, didn't I? I like to feel myself superior to you in some things. You have so often pointed out to me what a paltry, ineffectual creature I am.'

'I don't remember ever using those words, or implying them.'

'How does the day stand with you?' asked Everard in the tone of perfect comradeship. 'Have you still to dine?'

'My dining is a very simple matter; it happens at one o'clock. About nine I shall have supper.'

'Let us walk a little then. And may I smoke?'

'Why not?'

Everard lit a cigar, and, as the tide drove them back, they moved eventually to the higher ground, whence there was a fine view of the mountains, rich in evening colours.

'To-morrow you leave here?'

'Yes,' Rhoda answered. 'I shall go by railway to Coniston, and walk from there towards Helvellyn, as you suggested.'

'I have something else to propose. A man I talked to in the train told me of a fine walk in this neighbourhood. From Ravenglass, just below here, there's a little line runs up Eskdale to a terminus at the foot of Scawfell, a place called Boot. From Boot one can walk either over the top of Scawfell or by a lower track to Wastdale Head. It's very grand, wild country, especially the last part, the going down to Wastwater, and not many miles in all. Suppose we have that walk to-morrow? From Wastdale we could drive back to Seascale in the evening, and then the next day—just as you like.'

'Are you quite sure about the distances?'

'Quite. I have the Ordnance map in my pocket. Let me show you.'

He spread the map on the top of a wall, and they stood side by side inspecting it.

'We must take something to eat; I'll provide for that. And at the Wastdale Head hotel we can have dinner—about three or four, probably. It would be enjoyable, wouldn't it?'

'If it doesn't rain.'

'We'll hope it won't. As we go back we can look out the trains at the station. No doubt there's one soon after breakfast.'

Their rambling, with talk in a strain of easy friendliness, brought them back to Seascale half an hour after sunset, which was of a kind that seemed to promise well for the morrow.

'Won't you come out again after supper?' Barfoot asked.

'Not again to-night.'

'For a quarter of an hour,' he urged. 'Just down to the sea and back.'

'I have been walking all day. I shall be glad to rest and read.'

'Very well. To-morrow morning.'

Having discovered the train which would take them to Ravenglass, and connect with one on the Eskdale line, they agreed to meet at the station. Barfoot was to bring with him such refreshment as would be necessary.

Their hopes for the weather had complete fulfilment. The only fear was lest the sun's heat might be oppressive, but this anxiety could be cheerfully borne. Slung over his shoulders Barfoot had a small forage-bag, which gave him matter for talk on the railway journey; it had been his companion in many parts of the world, and had held strange kinds of food.

The journey up Eskdale, from Ravenglass to Boot, is by a miniature railway, with the oddest little engine and a carriage or two of primitive simplicity. At each station on the upward winding track—stations represented only by a wooden shed like a tool-house—the guard jumps down and acts as booking-clerk, if passengers there be desirous of booking. In a few miles the scenery changes from beauty to grandeur, and at the terminus no further steaming would be possible, for the great flank of Scawfell bars the way.

Everard and his companion began their climb through the pretty straggling village of Boot. A mountain torrent roared by the wayside, and the course they had marked upon the map showed that they must follow this stream for some miles up to the tarn where it originated. Houses, human beings, and even trodden paths they soon left behind, coming out on to a vast moorland, with hill summits near and far. Scawfell they could not hope to ascend; with the walk that lay before them it was enough to make a way over one of his huge shoulders.

'If your strength fails,' said Everard merrily, when for an hour they had been plodding through grey solitudes, 'there is no human help. I should have to choose between carrying you back to Boot or on to Wastdale.'

'My strength is not likely to fail sooner than yours,' was the laughing reply.

'I have chicken sandwiches, and wine that maketh glad the heart of man. Tell me when hunger overcomes you. I should think we had better make our halt at Burmoor Tarn.'

That, indeed, proved to be the convenient resting-place. A wild spot, a hollow amid the rolling expanse of moorland, its little lake of black water glistening under the midday sun. And here stood a shepherd's cottage, the only habitation they had seen since leaving Boot. Somewhat uncertain about the course to be henceforth followed, they made inquiry at this cottage, and a woman who appeared to be quite alone gave them the needful direction. Thus at ease in mind they crossed the bridge at the foot of the tarn, and just beyond it found a spot suitable for repose. Everard brought forth his sandwiches and his flask of wine, moreover a wine-glass, which was for Rhoda's use. They ate and drank festively.

'Now this is just what I have enjoyed in imagination for a year or more,' said Barfoot, when the luncheon was over, and he lay propped upon his elbow, gazing at Rhoda's fine eyes and her sun-warmed cheeks. 'An ideal realized, for once in one's life. A perfect moment.'

'Don't you like the scent of burning peat from that cottage?'

'Yes. I like everything about us, in heaven and earth, and most of all I like your companionship, Rhoda.'

She could not resent this first use of her Christian name; it was so natural, so inevitable; yet she moved her head as if with a slight annoyance.

'Is mine as agreeable to you?' he added, stroking the back of her hand with a spray of heather. 'Or do you just tolerate me out of good-nature?'

'I have liked your companionship all the way from Seascale. Don't disturb my enjoyment of it for the rest of the way.'

'That would be a misfortune indeed. The whole day shall be perfect. Not a note of discord. But I must have liberty to say what comes into my mind, and when you don't choose to answer I shall respect your silence.'

'Wouldn't you like to smoke a cigar before we start again?'

'Yes. But I like still better not to. The scent of peat is pleasanter to you than that of tobacco.'

'Oblige me by lighting the cigar.'

'If you command—' He did her bidding. 'The whole day shall be perfect. A delightful dinner at the inn, a drive to Seascale, an hour or two of rest, and then one more quiet talk by the sea at nightfall.'

'All but the last. I shall be too tired.'

'No. I must have that hour of talk by the sea. You are free to answer me or not, but your presence you must grant me. We are in an ideal world remember. We care nothing for all the sons and daughters of men. You and I will spend this one day together between cloudless heaven and silent earth—a memory for lifetime. At nightfall you will come out again, and meet me down by the sea, where you stood when I first saw you yesterday.'

Rhoda made no reply. She looked away from him at the black, deep water.

'What an opportunity,' he went on, raising his hand to point at the cottage, 'for saying the silliest of conceivable things!'

'What *might* that be, I wonder?'

'Why, that to dwell there together for the rest of our lives would be supreme felicity. You know the kind of man that would say that.'

'Not personally, thank goodness!'

'A week—a month, even—with weather such as this. Nay, with a storm for variety; clouds from the top of Scawfell falling thick about us; a fierce wind shrieking across the tarn; sheets and torrents and floods of rain beating upon our roof; and you and I by the peat-fire. With a good supply of books, old and new, I can picture it for three months, for half a year!'

'Be on your guard. Remember "that kind of man".'

'I am in no danger. There is a vast difference between six months and all one's life. When the half-year was over we would leave England.'

'By the Orient Express?'

They laughed together, Rhoda colouring, for the words that had escaped her meant too much for mere jest.

'By the Orient Express. We would have a house by the Bosphorus for the next half-year, and contrast our emotions with those we had known by Burmoor Tarn. Think what a rich year of life that would make! How much we should have learnt from nature and from each other!'

'And how dreadfully tired of each other we should be!'

Barfoot looked keenly at her. He could not with certainty read her countenance.

'You mean that?' he asked.

'You know it is true.'

'Hush! The day is to be perfect. I won't admit that we could ever tire of each other with reasonable variety of circumstance. You to me are infinitely interesting, and I believe that I might become so to you.'

He did not allow himself to vary from this tone of fanciful speculation, suited to the idle hour. Rhoda said very little; her remarks were generally a purposed interruption of Everard's theme. When the cigar was smoked Out they rose and set forward again. This latter half of their walk proved the most interesting, for they were expectant of the view down upon Wastdale. A bold summit came in sight, dark, desolate, which they judged to be Great Gabel; and when they had pressed on eagerly for another mile, the valley opened beneath them with such striking suddenness that they stopped on the instant and glanced at each other in silence. From a noble height they looked down upon Wastwater, sternest and blackest of the lakes, on the fields and copses of the valley head with its winding stream, and the rugged gorges which lie beyond in mountain shadow.

The descent was by a path which in winter becomes the bed of a torrent, steep and stony, zigzagging through a thick wood. Here, and when they had reached the level road leading into the village, their talk was in the same natural, light-hearted strain as before they rested. So at the inn where they dined, and during their drive homewards—by the dark lake with its woods and precipices, out into the country of green hills, and thence through Gosforth on the long road descending seaward. Since their early departure scarcely a cloud had passed over the sun—a perfect day.

They alighted before reaching Seascale. Barfoot discharged his debt to the driver—who went on to bait at the hotel—and walked with Rhoda for the last quarter of a mile. This was his own idea; Rhoda made no remark, but approved his discretion.

'It is six o'clock,' said Everard, after a short silence. 'You remember your arrangement. At eight, down on the shore.'

'I should be much more comfortable in the armchair with a book.'

'Oh, you have had enough of books. It's time to live.'

'It's time to rest.'

'Are you so very tired? Poor girl! The day has been rather too much for you.'

Rhoda laughed.

'I could walk back again to Wastwater if it were necessary.'

'Of course; I knew that. You are magnificent. At eight o'clock then—'

Nothing more was said on the subject. When in sight of Rhoda's lodgings they parted without hand-shaking.

Before eight Everard was straying about the beach, watching the sun go down in splendour. He smiled to himself frequently. The hour had come for his last trial of Rhoda, and he felt some confidence as to the result. If her mettle endured his test, if she declared herself willing not only to abandon her avowed ideal of life, but to defy the world's opinion by becoming his wife without forms of mutual bondage—she was the woman he had imagined, and by her side he would go cheerfully on his way as a married man. Legally married; the proposal of free union was to be a test only. Loving her as he had never thought to love, there still remained with him so much of the temper in which he first wooed her that he could be satisfied with nothing short of unconditional surrender. Delighting in her independence of mind, he still desired to see her in complete subjugation to him, to inspire her with unreflecting passion. Tame consent to matrimony was an everyday experience. Agnes Brissenden, he felt sure, would marry him whenever he chose to ask her—and would make one of the best wives conceivable. But of Rhoda Nunn he expected and demanded more than this. She must rise far above the level of ordinary intelligent women. She must manifest an absolute confidence in him—that was the true significance of his present motives. The censures and suspicions which she had not scrupled to confess in plain words must linger in no corner of her mind.

His heart throbbed with impatience for her coming. Come she would; it was not in Rhoda's nature to play tricks; if she had not meant to meet him she would have said so resolutely, as last night.

At a few minutes past the hour he looked landward, and saw her figure against the golden sky. She came down from the sandbank very slowly, with careless, loitering steps. He moved but a little way to meet her, and then stood still. He had done his part; it was now hers to forego female privileges, to obey the constraint of love. The western afterglow touched her features, heightening the beauty Everard had learnt to see in them. Still she loitered, stooping to pick up a piece of seaweed; but still he kept his place, motionless, and she came nearer.

'Did you see the light of sunset on the mountains?'

'Yes,' he replied.

'There has been no such evening since I came.'

'And you wanted to sit at home with a book. That was no close for a perfect day.'

'I found a letter from your cousin. She was with her friends the Goodalls yesterday.'

'The Goodalls—I used to know them.'

'Yes.'

The word was uttered with significance. Everard understood the allusion, but did not care to show that he did.

'How does Mary get on without you?'

'There's no difficulty.'

'Has she any one capable of taking your place?'

'Yes. Miss Vesper can do all that's necessary.'

'Even to inspiring the girls with zeal for an independent life?'

'Perhaps even that.'

They went along by the waves, in the warm-coloured twilight, until the houses of Seascale were hidden. Then Everard stopped.

'To-morrow we go to Coniston?' he said, smiling as he stood before her.

'You are going?'

'Do you think I can leave you?'

Rhoda's eyes fell. She held the long strip of seaweed with both hands and tightened it.

'Do you *wish* me to leave you?' he added.

'You mean that we are to go through the lakes together—as we have been to-day?'

'No. I don't mean that.'

Rhoda took a few steps onward, so that he remained standing behind. Another moment and his arms had folded about her, his lips were on hers. She did not resist. His embrace grew stronger, and he pressed kiss after kiss upon her mouth. With exquisite delight he saw the deep crimson flush that transfigured her countenance; saw her look for one instant into his eyes, and was conscious of the triumphant gleam she met there.

'Do you remember my saying in the letter how I hungered to taste your lips? I don't know how I have refrained so long—'

'What is your love worth?' asked Rhoda, speaking with a great effort. She had dropped the seaweed, and one of her hands rested upon his shoulder, with a slight repelling pressure.

'Worth your whole life!' he answered, with a low, glad laugh.

'That is what I doubt. Convince me of that.'

'Convince you? With more kisses? But what is *your* love worth?'

'Perhaps more than you yet understand. Perhaps more than you *can* understand.'

'I will believe that, Rhoda. I know, at all events, that it is something of inestimable price. The knowledge has grown in me for a year and more.'

'Let me stand away from you again. There is something more to be said before—No, let me be quite apart from you.'

He released her after one more kiss.

'Will you answer me a question with perfect truthfulness?'

Her voice was not quite steady, but she succeeded in looking at him with unflinching eyes.

'Yes. I will answer you *any* question.'

'That is spoken like a man. Tell me then—is there at this moment any woman living who has a claim upon you—a moral claim?'

'No such woman exists.'

'But—do we speak the same language?'

'Surely,' he answered with great earnestness. 'There is no woman to whom I am bound by any kind of obligation.'

A long wave rolled up, broke, and retreated, whilst Rhoda stood in silent uncertainty.

'I must put the question in another way. During the past month—the past three months—have you made profession of love—have you even pretended love—to any woman?'

'To no woman whatever,' he answered firmly.

'That satisfies me.'

'If I knew what is in your mind!' exclaimed Everard, laughing. 'What sort of life have you imagined for me? Is this the result of Mary's talk?'

'Not immediately.'

'Still, she planted the suspicion. Believe me, you have been altogether mistaken. I never was the kind of man Mary thought me. Some day you shall understand more about it—in the meantime my word must be enough. I have no thought of love for any woman but you. Did I frighten you with those joking confessions in my letters? I wrote them purposely—as you must have seen. The mean, paltry jealousies of women such as one meets every day are so hateful to me. They argue such a lack of brains. If I were so unfortunate as to love a woman who looked sour when I praised a beautiful face. I would snap the bond between us like a bit of thread. But you are not one of those poor creatures.'

He looked at her with some gravity.

'Should you think me a poor creature if I resented any kind of unfaithfulness?—whether love, in any noble sense, had part in it or not?'

'No. That is the reasonable understanding between man and wife. If I exact fidelity from you, and certainly I should, I must consider myself under the same obligation.'

'You say "man or wife." Do you say it with the ordinary meaning?'

'Not as it applies to us. You know what I mean when I ask you to be my wife. If we cannot trust each other without legal bonds, any union between us would be unjustified.'

Suppressing the agitation which he felt, he awaited her answer. They could still read each other's faces perfectly in a pale yellow light from across the sea. Rhoda's manifested an intense conflict.

'After all, you doubt of your love for me?' said Barfoot quietly.

That was not her doubt. She loved with passion, allowing herself to indulge the luxurious emotion as never yet. She longed once more to feel his arms about her. But even thus she could consider the vast issues of the step to which she was urged. The temptation to yield was very strong, for it seemed to her an easier and a nobler thing to proclaim her emancipation from social statutes than to announce before her friends the simple news that she was about to marry. That announcement would excite something more than surprise. Mary Barfoot could not but smile with gentle irony; other women would laugh among themselves; the girls would feel a shock, as at the fall of one who had made heroic pretences. A sure way of averting this ridicule was by furnishing occasion for much graver astonishment. If it became known that she had taken a step such as few women would have dared to take—deliberately setting an example of new liberty—her position in the eyes of all who knew her remained one of proud independence. Rhoda's character was specially exposed to the temptation of such a motive. For months this argument had been in her mind, again and again she decided that the sensational step was preferable to a commonplace renunciation of all she had so vehemently preached. And now that the moment of actual choice had come she felt able to dare everything—as far as the danger concerned herself; but she perceived more strongly than hitherto that not only her own future was involved. How would such practical heresy affect Everard's position?

She uttered this thought.

'Are you willing, for the sake of this idea, to abandon all society but that of the very few people who would approve or tolerate what you have done?'

'I look upon the thing in this way. We are not called upon to declare our principles wherever we go. If we regard each other as married, why, we *are* married. I am no Quixote, hoping to convert the world. It is between you and me—our own sense of what is reasonable and dignified.'

'But you would not make it a mere deception?'

'Mary would of course be told, and any one else you like.'

She believed him entirely serious. Another woman might have suspected that he was merely trying her courage, either to assure himself of her love or to gratify his vanity. But Rhoda's idealism enabled her to take him literally. She herself had for years maintained an exaggerated standard of duty and merit; desirous of seeing Everard in a nobler light than hitherto, she endeavoured to regard his scruple against formal wedlock as worthy of all respect.

'I can't answer you at once,' she said, half turning away.

'You must. Here and at once.'

The one word of assent would have satisfied him. This he obstinately required. He believed that it would confirm his love beyond any other satisfaction she could render him. He must be able to regard her as magnanimous, a woman who had proved herself worth living or dying for. And he must have the joy of subduing her to his will.

'No,' said Rhoda firmly. 'I can't answer you tonight. I can't decide so suddenly.'

This was disingenuous, and she felt humiliated by her subterfuge. Anything but a sudden decision was asked of her. Before leaving Chelsea she had 'foreseen this moment, and had made preparations for the possibility of never returning to Miss Barfoot's house—knowing the nature of the proposal that would be offered to her. But the practical resolve needed a greater effort than she had imagined. Above all, she feared an ignominious failure of purpose after her word was given; *that* would belittle her in Everard's eyes, and so shame her in her own that all hope of happiness in marriage must be at an end.

'You are still doubtful of me, Rhoda?'

He took her hand, and again drew her close. But she refused her lips.

'Or are you doubtful of your own love?'

'No. If I understand what love means, I love you.'

'Then give me the kiss I am waiting for. You have not kissed me yet.'

'I can't—until I am sure of myself—of my readiness—'

Her broken words betrayed the passion with which she was struggling. Everard felt her tremble against his side.

'Give me your hand,' he whispered. 'The left hand.'

Before she could guess his purpose he had slipped a ring upon her finger, a marriage ring. Rhoda started away from him, and at once drew off the perilous symbol.

'No—that proves to me I can't! What should we gain? You see, you dare not be quite consistent. It's only deceiving the people who don't know us.'

'But I have explained to you. The consistency is in ourselves, our own minds—'

'Take it back. Custom is too strong for us. We should only play at defying it. Take it back—or I shall drop it on the sand.'

Profoundly mortified, Everard restored the gold circlet to its hiding-place and stood gazing at the dim horizon. Some moments passed, then he heard his name murmured. He did not look round.

'Everard, dearest—'

Was that Rhoda's voice, so low, tender, caressing? It thrilled him, and with a silent laugh of scorn at his own folly, he turned to her, every thought burnt up in passion.

'Will you kiss me?'

For an answer she laid her hands on his shoulders and gazed at him. Barfoot understood. He smiled constrainedly, and said in a low voice,—

'You wish for that old, idle form—?'

'Not the religious form, which has no meaning for either of us, But—'

'You have been living here seven or eight days. Stay till the fifteenth, then we can get a licence from the registrar of the district. Does that please you?'

Her eyes made reply.

'Do you love me any the less, Everard?'

'Kiss me.'

She did, and consciousness was lost for them as their mouths clung together and their hearts throbbed like one.

'Isn't it better?' Rhoda asked, as they walked back in the darkness. 'Won't it make our life so much simpler and happier?'

'Perhaps.'

'You know it will.' She laughed joyously, trying to meet his look.

'Perhaps you are right.'

'I shall let no one hear of it until—. Then let us go abroad.'

'You dare not face Mary?'

'I dare, if you wish it. Of course she will laugh at me. They will all laugh at me.'

'Why, you may laugh as well.'

'But you have spoilt my life, you know. Such a grand life it might have been. Why did you come and interfere with me? And you have been so terribly obstinate.'

'Of course; that's my nature. But after all I have been weak.'

'Yielding in one point that didn't matter to you at all? It was the only way of making sure that you loved me.'

Barfoot laughed slightingly.

'And what if I needed the other proof that you loved *me*.'

# CHAPTER XXVI - THE UNIDEAL TESTED

And neither was content.

Barfoot, over his cigar and glass of whisky at the hotel, fell into a mood of chagrin. The woman he loved would be his, and there was matter enough for ardent imagination in the indulgence of that thought; but his temper disturbed him. After all, he had not triumphed. As usual the woman had her way. She played upon his senses, and made him her obedient slave. To prolong the conflict would have availed nothing; Rhoda, doubtless, was in part actuated by the desire to conquer, and she knew her power over him. So it was a mere repetition of the old story—a marriage like any other. And how would it result?

She had great qualities; but was there not much in her that he must subdue, reform, if they were really to spend their lives together? Her energy of domination perhaps excelled his. Such a woman might be unable to concede him the liberty in marriage which theoretically she granted to be just. Perhaps she would torment him with restless jealousies, suspecting on every trivial occasion an infringement of her right. From that point of view it would have been far wiser to persist in rejecting legal marriage, that her dependence upon him might be more complete. Later, if all went well, the concession could have been made—if, for instance, she became a mother. But then returned the exasperating thought that Rhoda had overcome his will. Was not that a beginning of evil augury?

To be sure, after marriage their relations would be different. He would not then be at the mercy of his senses. But how miserable to anticipate a long, perhaps bitter, struggle for predominance. After all, that could hardly come about. The commencement of any such discord would be the signal for separation. His wealth assured his freedom. He was not like the poor devils who must perforce live with an intolerable woman because they cannot support themselves and their families in different places. Need he entertain that worst of fears—the dread that his independence might fail him, subdued by his wife's will?

## CHAPTER XXVI - THE UNIDEAL TESTED

Free as he boasted himself from lover's silliness, he had magnified Rhoda's image. She was not the glorious rebel he had pictured. Like any other woman, she mistrusted her love without the sanction of society. Well, that was something relinquished, lost. Marriage would after all be a compromise. He had not found his ideal—though in these days it assuredly existed.

And Rhoda, sitting late in the little lodging-house parlour, visited her soul with questionings no less troublesome. Everard was not satisfied with her. He had yielded, perhaps more than half contemptuously, to what he thought a feminine weakness. In going with her to the registrar's office he would feel himself to be acting an ignoble part. Was it not a bad beginning to rule him against his conscience?

She had triumphed splendidly. In the world's eye this marriage of hers was far better than any she could reasonably have hoped, and her heart approved it with rapture. At a stage in life when she had sternly reconciled herself never to know a man's love, this love had sought her with passionate persistency of which even a beautiful young girl might feel proud. She had no beauty; she was loved for her mind, her very self. But must not Everard's conception of her have suffered? In winning her had he obtained the woman of his desire?

Why was she not more politic? Would it not have been possible to gratify him, and yet to gain his consent to legal marriage? By first of all complying she would have seemed to confirm all he believed of her; and then, his ardour at height, how simple to point out to him—without entreaty, without show of much concern—that by neglecting formalities they gained absolutely nothing. Artifice of that kind was perhaps demanded by the mere circumstances. Possibly he himself would have welcomed it—after the grateful sense of inspiring such complete devotion. It is the woman's part to exercise tact; she had proved herself lamentably deficient in that quality.

To-morrow she must study his manner. If she discerned any serious change, any grave indication of disappointment—

What was her life to be? At first they would travel together; but before long it might be necessary to have a settled home, and what then would be her social position, her duties and pleasures? Housekeeping, mere domesticities, could never occupy her for more than the smallest possible part of each day. Having lost one purpose in life, dignified, absorbing, likely to extend its sphere as time went on, what other could she hope to substitute for it?

Love of husband—perhaps of child. There must be more than that. Rhoda did not deceive herself as to the requirements of her nature.

Practical activity in some intellectual undertaking; a share—nay, leadership—in some "movement;" contact with the revolutionary life of her time—the impulses of her heart once satisfied, these things would again claim her. But how if Everard resisted such tendencies? Was he in truth capable of respecting her individuality? Or would his strong instinct of lordship urge him to direct his wife as a dependent, to impose upon her his own view of things? She doubted whether he had much genuine sympathy with woman's emancipation as she understood it. Yet in no particular had her convictions changed; nor would they change. She herself was no longer one of the 'odd women'; fortune had—or seemed to have—been kind to her; none the less her sense of a mission remained. No longer an example of perfect female independence, and unable therefore to use the same language as before, she might illustrate woman's claim of equality in marriage.—If her experience proved no obstacle.

Next morning, as had been agreed, they met at some distance from Seascale, and spent two or three hours together. There was little danger in observation unless by a casual peasant; for the most part their privacy could not have been more secure in a locked chamber. Lest curiosity should be excited by his making inquiries at the hotel, Barfoot proposed to walk over to Gosforth, the nearest town, this afternoon, and learn where the registrar for the locality of Seascale might be found. By neither was allusion made to their difference of last evening, but Rhoda distressed herself by imagining a diminished fervour in her companion; he seemed unusually silent and meditative, and was content to hold her hand now and then.

'Shall you stay here all the week?' she inquired.

'If you wish me to.'

'You will find it wearisome.'

'Impossible, with you here. But if I run up to London for a day or two it might be better. There are preparations. We shall go first of all to my rooms—'

'I would rather not have stayed in London.'

'I thought you might wish to make purchases.'

'Let us go to some other town, and spend a few days there before leaving England.'

'Very well. Manchester or Birmingham.'

'You speak rather impatiently,' said Rhoda, looking at him with an uneasy smile. 'Let it be London if you prefer—'

'On no account. It's all indifferent to me so long as we get safely away together. Every man is impatient of these preliminaries. Yes, in that case I must of course go up to London. To-morrow, and back on Saturday?'

A shower of rain caused them some discomfort. Through the afternoon it still rained at intervals whilst Barfoot was discharging his business at Gosforth. He was to see Rhoda again at eight o'clock, and as the time threatened to hang heavily on his hands he returned by a long detour, reaching the Seascale hotel about half-past six. No sooner had he entered than there was delivered to him a letter, brought by messenger an hour or two ago. It surprised him to recognize Rhoda's writing on the envelope, which seemed to contain at least two sheets of notepaper. What now? Some whimsey? Agitated and annoyed by the anticipation of trouble, he went apart and broke the letter open.

First appeared an enclosure—a letter in his cousin Mary's writing. He turned to the other sheet and read these lines,—

'I send you something that has come by post this afternoon. Please to bring it with you when you meet me at eight o'clock—if you still care to do so.'

His face flushed with anger. What contemptible woman's folly was this? 'If you still care to do so'—and written in a hand that shook. If this was to be his experience of matrimonial engagement—What rubbish had Mary been communicating?

> 'My DEAR RHODA,—I have just gone through a very painful scene, and I feel bound to let you know of it without delay, as it *may* concern you. This evening (Monday), when I came home from Great Portland Street, Emma told me that Mr. Widdowson had called, that he wished to see me as soon as possible, and would be here again at six o'clock. He came, and his appearance alarmed me, he was looking so dreadfully ill. Without preface, he said, "My wife has left me; she has gone to her sister, and refuses to return." This was astonishing in itself, and I wondered still more why he should come and tell *me* about it in so strange a way. The explanation followed very promptly, and you may judge how I heard it. Mr. Widdowson said that his wife had been behaving very badly of late; that he had discovered several falsehoods she had told him as to her employment during absences from home, in daytime and evening. Having cause for suspecting the worst, he last Saturday engaged a private detective to follow Mrs. Widdowson wherever she went. This man saw her go to the flats in Bayswater where Everard lives and knock at

*his* door. As no one replied, she went away for a time and returned, but again found no one at home. This being at once reported to Mr. Widdowson he asked his wife where she had been that afternoon. The answer was false; she said she had been here, with me. Thereupon he lost command of himself, and charged her with infidelity. She refused to offer any kind of explanation, but denied that she was guilty and at once left the house. Since, she has utterly refused to see him. Her sister can only report that Monica is very ill, and that she charges her husband with accusing her falsely.

'He had come to me, he said, in unspeakable anguish and helplessness, to ask me whether I had seen anything suspicious in the relations between Monica and my cousin when they met at this house or elsewhere. A nice question! Of course I could only reply that it had never even occurred to me to observe them—that to my knowledge they had met so rarely—and that I should never have dreamt of suspecting Monica. "Yet you see she *must* be guilty," he kept on repeating. I said no, that I thought her visit *might* have an innocent significance, though I couldn't suggest why she had told falsehoods. Then he inquired what I knew about Everard's present movements. I answered that I had every reason to think that he was out of town, but didn't know when he went, or when he might be expected to return. The poor man was grievously dissatisfied; he looked at me as if I were in a base plot against him. It was an immense relief when he went away, after begging me to respect his confidence.

'I write very hurriedly, as you see. That I *ought* to write is, I think, clear—though I may be doing lamentable mischief. I cannot credit this charge against Mrs. Widdowson; there must surely be some explanation. If you have already left Seascale, no doubt this letter will be forwarded.—Ever yours, dear Rhoda,

MARY BARFOOT.'

Everard laughed bitterly. The completeness of the case against him in Rhoda's eyes must be so overwhelming, and his absolute innocence made it exasperating to have to defend himself. How, indeed, was he to defend himself?

The story was strange enough. Could he be right in the interpretation which at once suggested itself to his mind—or perhaps to his vanity? He remembered the meeting with Mrs. Widdowson near his abode on Friday. He recollected, moreover, the signs of interest in himself which, as he now thought, she had shown on previous occasions. Had the poor little woman—doubtless miserable with her husband—actually let herself fall in love with him? But, even in that case, what a reckless thing to do—to come to his rooms! Why, she must have been driven by a despair that blinded her to all sense of delicacy! Perhaps, had he been at home, she would have made a pretence of wishing to speak about Rhoda Nunn. That was imprudent behaviour of his, making such a person his confidante. But he was tempted by his liking for her.

'By Jove!' he muttered, overcome by the thought. 'I'm glad I was *not* at home!'

But then—he had told her that he was going away on Saturday. How could she expect to find him? The hour of her visit was not stated; probably she hoped to catch him before he left. And was her appearance in the neighbourhood on Friday—her troubled aspect—to be explained as an abortive attempt to have a private interview with him?

The queerest affair—and maddening in its issues! Rhoda was raging with jealousy. Well, he too would rage. And without affectation. It was strange that he felt almost glad of a ground of quarrel with Rhoda. All day he had been in an irritable temper, and so far as he could understand himself it was due to resentment of his last night's defeat. He thought of Rhoda as ardently as ever, but an element that was very like brutality had intruded into his emotions; that was his reason from refraining from caresses this morning; he could not trust himself.

He would endure no absurdities. If Rhoda did not choose to accept his simple assurance—let her take the consequences. Even now, perhaps, he would bring her to her knees before him. Let her wrong him by baseless accusation! Then it would no longer be *he* who sued for favour. He would whistle her down the wind, and await her penitent reappearance. Sooner or later his pride and hers, the obstinacy in their natures, must battle it out; better that it should be now, before the irrevocable step had been taken.

He ate his dinner with savage appetite, and drank a good deal more wine than of wont. Then he smoked until the last minute of delay that his engagement allowed. Of course she had sent the letter to the hotel because he might be unable to read it in twilight. Wise precaution. And he was glad to have been able to think the matter over, to work himself into reasonable wrath. If ever man did well to be angry—!

There she was, down by the edge of the waves. She would not turn to see if he were coming; he felt sure of that. Whether she heard his footsteps he could not tell. When quite close to her, he exclaimed,—

'Well, Rhoda?' She must have known of his approach, for she gave no start.

She faced slowly to him. No trace of tears on her countenance; no, Rhoda was above that. Gravity of the sternest—that was all.

'Well,' he continued, 'what have you to say to me?'

'I? Nothing.'

'You mean that it is my business to explain what Mary has told you. I can't, so there's an end of it.'

'What do you mean by that?' she asked in clear, distant tones.

'Precisely what I say, Rhoda. And I am obliged to ask what *you* mean by this odd way of speaking to me. What has happened since we parted this morning?'

Rhoda could not suppress her astonishment; she gazed fixedly at him.

'If you can't explain this letter, who can?'

'I suppose Mrs. Widdowson would be able to account for her doings. I certainly am not able to. And it seems to me that you are strangely forgetful of something that passed between us yesterday.'

'Of what?' she asked coldly, her face, which was held proudly up, turning towards the sea.

'Evidently you accuse me of concealing something from you. Please to remember a certain plain question you asked me, and the equally plain answer I gave.'

He detected the beginning of a smile about her rigid lips.

'I remember,' she said.

'And you can still behave to me with indignation? Surely the indignation should be on my side. You are telling me that I deceived you.'

For a moment Rhoda lost her self-control.

'How can I help thinking so?' she exclaimed, with a gesture of misery. 'What can this letter mean? Why should she go to your rooms?'

'I simply don't know, Rhoda.'

He preserved the show of calmness just because he saw that it provoked her to anger.

'She has never been there before?'

'Never to my knowledge.'

Rhoda watched his face with greedy attention. She seemed to find there a confirmation of her doubts. Indeed, it was impossible for her to credit his denials after what she had observed in London, and the circumstances which, even before Mary's letter, had made her suspicious.

'When did you last see Mrs. Widdowson?'

'No, I shan't consent to be cross-examined,' replied Everard, with a disdainful smile. 'As soon as you refuse to accept my word it's folly to ask further questions. You don't believe me. Say it honestly and let us understand each other.'

'I have good reason for thinking that you could explain Mrs. Widdowson's behaviour if you chose.'

'Exactly. There's no misunderstanding *that*. And if I get angry I am an unpardonable brute. Come now, you can't be offended if I treat you as simply my equal, Rhoda. Let me test your sincerity. Suppose I had seen you talking somewhere with some man who seemed to interest you very much, and then—to-day, let us say—I heard that he had called upon you when you were alone. I turn with a savage face and accuse you of grossly deceiving me—in the worst sense. What would your answer be?'

'These are idle suppositions,' she exclaimed scornfully.

'But the case is possible, you must admit. I want you to realize what I am feeling. In such a case as that, you could only turn from me with contempt. How else can I behave to *you*—conscious of my innocence, yet in the nature of things unable to prove it?'

'Appearances are very strongly against you.'

'That's an accident—to me quite unaccountable. If I charged you with dishonour you would only have your word to offer in reply. So it is with me. And my word is bluntly rejected. You try me rather severely.'

Rhoda kept silence.

'I know what you are thinking. My character was previously none of the best. There is a prejudice against me in such a matter for your good. My record is not immaculate; nor, I believe, is any as this. Well, you shall hear some more plain speech, altogether man's. I have gone here and there, and have had my adventures like other men. One of them you have heard about—the story of that girl Amy Drake—the subject of Mrs. Goodall's righteous wrath. You shall know the truth, and if it offends your ears I can't help it. The girl simply threw herself into my arms, on a railway journey, when we met by pure chance.'

'I don't care to hear that,' said Rhoda, turning away.

'But you *shall* hear it. That story has predisposed you to believe the worst things of me. If I hold you by force, you shall hear every word of it. Mary seems to have given you mere dark hints—'

'No; she has told me the details. I know it all.'

'From their point of view. Very well; that saves me a lot of narrative. What those good people didn't understand was the girl's character. They thought her a helpless innocent; she was a—I'll spare you the word. She simply planned to get me into her power—thought I should be forced to marry her. It's the kind of thing that happens far oftener than you would suppose; that's the reason why men so often smile in what you would call a brutal way when certain stories are told to other men's discredit. You will have to take this into account, Rhoda, before you reach satisfactory results on the questions that have occupied you so much. I was not in the least responsible for Amy Drake's desertion of creditable paths. At the worst I behaved foolishly; and knowing I had done so, knowing how thankless it was to try and clear myself at her expense, I let people say what they would; it didn't matter. And you don't believe me; I can see you don't. Sexual pride won't let you believe me. In such a case the man must necessarily be the villain.'

'What you mean by saying you only behaved "foolishly," I can't understand.'

'Perhaps not, and I can't explain as I once did in telling the story to a man, a friend of mine. But however strict your moral ideas, you will admit that a girl of thoroughly bad character isn't a subject for the outcry that was raised about Miss Amy Drake. By taking a little trouble I could have brought things to light which would have given worthy Mrs. Goodall and cousin Mary a great shock. Well, that's enough. I have never pretended to sanctity; but, on the other hand, I have never behaved like a scoundrel. You charge me, deliberately, with being a scoundrel, and I defend myself as best I can. You argue that the man who would mislead an innocent girl and then cast her off is more likely than not to be guilty in a case like this of Mrs. Widdowson, when appearances are decidedly against him. There is only my word in each instance. The question is—Will you accept my word?'

For a wonder, their privacy was threatened by the approach of two men who were walking this way from Seascale. Voices in conversation caused Rhoda to look round; Barfoot had already observed the strangers.

'Let us go up on to the higher sand,' he said.

Without reply Rhoda accompanied him, and for several minutes they exchanged no word. The men, talking and laughing loudly, went by; they seemed to be tourists of a kind that do not often trouble this quiet spot on the coast; their cigars glowed in the dusk.

'After all this, what have you to say to me, Rhoda?'

'Will you please to give me your cousin's letter?' she said coldly.

'Here it is. Now you will go back to your lodgings, and sit with that letter open before you half through the night. You will make yourself unutterably wretched, and all for what?'

He felt himself once more in danger of weakness. Rhoda, in her haughty, resentful mood, was very attractive to him. He was tempted to take her in his arms, and kiss her until she softened, pleaded with him. He wished to see her shed tears. But the voice in which she now spoke to him was far enough from tearfulness.

'You must prove to me that you have been wrongly suspected.'

Ah, that was to be her line of conduct. She believed her power over him was absolute. She stood on her dignity, would bring him to supplication, would give him all the trouble she could before she professed herself satisfied.

'How am I to prove it?' he asked bluntly.

'If there was nothing wrong between you and Mrs. Widdowson, there must be some very simple explanation of her coming to your rooms and being so anxious to see you.'

'And is it my business to discover that explanation?'

'Can it be mine?'

'It must either be yours, Rhoda, or no one's. I shall take no single step in the matter.'

The battle was declared. Each stood at full height, pertinacious, resolved on victory.

'You are putting yourself wildly in the wrong,' Everard continued. 'By refusing to take my word you make it impossible for me to hope that we could live together as we imagined.'

The words fell upon her heart like a crushing weight. But she could not yield. Last night she had suffered in his opinion by urging what he thought a weak, womanly scruple; she had condescended to plead tenderly with him, and had won her cause. Now she would prevail in another way. If he were telling the truth, he should acknowledge that natural suspicion made it incumbent upon him to clear so strange a case of its difficulties. If he were guilty of deception, as she still believed, though willing to admit to herself that Monica might be most at fault, that there might have been no actual wrongdoing between them—he should confess with humblest penitence, and beseech pardon. Impossible to take any other attitude. Impossible to marry him with this doubt in her mind—equally out of the question to seek Monica, and humiliate herself by making inquiries on such a subject. Guilty or not, Monica would regard her with secret disdain, with woman's malice. Were she *able* to believe him, that indeed would be a grand consummation of their love, an ideal union of heart and soul. Listening to him, she had tried to put faith in his indignant words. But it was useless. The incredulity she could not help must either part them for ever, or be to her an occasion of new triumph.

'I don't refuse to take your word,' she said, with conscious quibbling. 'I only say that your name must be cleared from suspicion. Mr. Widdowson is sure to tell his story to other people. Why has his wife left him?'

'I neither know nor care.'

'You must prove to me that you are not the cause of it.'

'I shall not make the slightest effort to do so.'

Rhoda began to move away from him. As he kept silence, she walked on in the Seascale direction. He followed at a distance of a few yards, watching her movements. When they had gone so far that five minutes more must bring them within sight of the hotel, Everard spoke.

'Rhoda!'

She paused and awaited him.

'You remember that I was going to London to-morrow. It seems that I had better go and not trouble to return.'

'That is for you to decide.'

'For you rather.'

'I have said all that I *can* say.'

'And so have I. But surely you must be unconscious how grossly you are insulting me.'

'I want only to understand what purpose Mrs. Widdowson had in going to your rooms.'

'Then why not ask her? You are friends. She would doubtless tell you the truth.'

'If she comes to me voluntarily to make an explanation, I will hear it. But I shall not ask her.'

'Your view of the fitness of things is that I should request her to wait upon you for that purpose?'

'There are others who can act for you.'

'Very well. Then we are at a deadlock. It seems to me that we had better shake hands like sensible people, and say good-bye.'

'Much better—if it seems so to you.'

The time for emotional help was past. In very truth they had nothing more to say to each other, being now hardened in obstinacy. Each suffered from the other's coldness, each felt angry with the other's stubborn refusal to concede a point of dignity. Everard put out his hand.

'When you are ready to say that you have used me very ill, I shall remember only yesterday. Till then—good-bye, Rhoda.'

She made a show of taking his hand, but said nothing. And so they parted.

At eight o'clock next morning Barfoot was seated in the southward train. He rejoiced that his strength of will had thus far asserted itself. Of final farewell to Rhoda he had no thought whatever. Her curiosity would, of course, compel her to see Monica; one way or another she would learn that he was blameless. His part was to keep aloof from her, and to wait for her inevitable submission.

Violent rain was beating upon the carriage windows; it drove from the mountains, themselves invisible, though dense low clouds marked their position. Poor Rhoda! She would not have a very cheerful day at Seascale. Perhaps she would follow him by a later train. Certain it was that she must be suffering intensely—and that certainly rejoiced him. The keener her suffering the sooner her submission. Oh, but the submission should be perfect! He had seen her in many moods, but not yet in the anguish of broken pride. She must shed tears before him, declare her spirit worn and subjugated by torment of jealousy and fear. Then he would raise her, and seat her in the place of honour, and fall down at her feet, and fill her soul with rapture.

Many times between Seascale and London he smiled in anticipation of that hour.

## CHAPTER XXVII - THE REASCENT

Whilst the rain pelted, and it did so until afternoon, Rhoda sat in her little parlour, no whit less miserable than Barfoot imagined. She could not be sure whether Everard had gone to London; at the last moment reflection or emotion might have detained him. Early in the morning she had sent to post a letter for Miss Barfoot, written last night—a letter which made no revelation of her feelings, but merely expressed a cold curiosity to hear anything that might become known as to the course of Mr. Widdowson's domestic troubles. 'You may still write to this address; if I leave, letters shall be forwarded.'

When the sky cleared she went out. In the evening she again rambled about the shore. Evidently Barfoot had gone; if still here, he would have watched and joined her.

Her solitude now grew insufferable, yet she could not decide whither to betake herself. The temptation to return to London was very strong, but pride prevailed against it. Everard might perhaps go to see his cousin, and relate all that had happened at Seascale, justifying himself as he had here done. Whether Miss Barfoot became aware of the story or not, Rhoda could not reconcile it with her self-respect to curtail the stipulated three weeks of holiday. Rather she would strain her nerves to the last point of endurance—and if she were not suffering, then never did woman suffer.

Another cheerless day helped her to make up her mind. She cared nothing now for lake and mountain; human companionship was her supreme need. By the earliest train next day she started, not for London, but for her brother's home in Somerset, and there she remained until it was time to return to work. Miss Barfoot wrote twice in the interval, saying that she had heard nothing more of Monica. Of Everard she made no mention.

Rhoda got back again to Chelsea on the appointed Saturday afternoon. Miss Barfoot knew when she would arrive, but was not at home to meet her, and did not return till a couple of hours had passed. They met at length as if nothing remarkable had occurred during the three weeks. Mary, if she felt any solicitude, effectually concealed it; Rhoda talked as if very glad to be at home again, explaining her desertion of the lake country by the bad weather that prevailed there. It was not till after dinner that the inevitable subject came up between them.

'Have you seen Everard since you went away?' Miss Barfoot began by asking.

So he had not been here to tell his story and plead his cause—or it seemed not.

'Yes, I saw him at Seascale,' Rhoda replied, without sign of emotion.

'Before or after that news came?'

'Both before and after. I showed him your letter, and all he had to say was that he knew nothing of the affair.'

'That's all he has to say to me. I haven't seen him. A letter I sent to his address was answered, after a week, from a place I never heard of—Arromanches, in Normandy. The shortest and rudest letter I ever had from him. Practically he told me to mind my own business. And there things stand.'

Rhoda smiled a little, conscious of the extreme curiosity her friend must be feeling, and determined not to gratify it. For by this time, though her sunken cheeks were hard to reconcile with the enjoyment of a summer holiday, she had matured a resolve to betray nothing of what she had gone through. Her state of mind resembled that of the ascetic who has arrived at a morbid delight in self-torture. She regarded the world with an intense bitterness, and persuaded herself not only that the thought of Everard Barfoot was hateful to her soul, but that sexual love had become, and would ever be, to her an impure idea, a vice of blood.

'I suppose,' she said carelessly, 'Mr. Widdowson will try to divorce his wife.'

'I am in dread of that. But they may have made it up.'

'Of course you have no doubt of her guilt?'

Mary tried to understand the hard, austere face, with its touch of cynicism. Conjecture as to its meaning was not difficult, but, in the utter absence of information, certainty there could be none. Under any circumstances, it was to be expected that Rhoda would think and speak of Mrs. Widdowson no less severely than of the errant Bella Royston.

'I have *some* doubt,' was Miss Barfoot's answer. 'But I should be glad of some one else's favourable opinion to help my charity.'

'Miss Madden hasn't been here, you see. She certainly would have come if she had felt convinced that her sister was wronged.'

'Unless a day or two saw the end of the trouble—when naturally none of them would say any more about it.'

This was the possibility which occupied Rhoda's reflections as long as she lay awake that night.

Her feelings on entering the familiar bedroom were very strange. Even before starting for her holiday she had bidden it good-bye, and at Seascale, that night following upon the "perfect day," she had thought of it as a part of her past life, a place abandoned for ever, already infinitely remote. Her first sensation when she looked upon the white bed was one of disgust; she thought it would be impossible to use this room henceforth, and that she must ask Miss Barfoot to let her change to another. Tonight she did not restore any of the ornaments which were lying packed up. The scent of the room revived so many hours of conflict, of hope, that it caused her a sick faintness. In frenzy of detestation she cursed the man who had so disturbed and sullied the swift, pure stream of her life.

Arromanches, in Normandy—? On Sunday she sought the name on a map, but it was not marked, being doubtless too insignificant. Improbable that he had gone to such a place alone; he was enjoying himself with friends, careless what became of her. Having allowed all this time to go by he would never seek her again. He found that her will was the equal of his own, and, as he could not rule her, she was numbered among the women who had afforded him interesting experiences, to be thought of seriously no more.

During the next week she threw herself with energy upon her work, stifling the repugnance with which at first it affected her, and seeming at length to recover the old enthusiasm. This was the only way of salvation. Idleness and absence of purpose would soon degrade her in a sense she had never dreamt of. She made a plan of daily occupation, which by leaving not a vacant moment from early morning to late at night, should give her the sleep of utter weariness. New studies were begun in the hour or two before breakfast. She even restricted her diet, and ate only just enough to support life, rejecting wine and everything that was most agreeable to her palate.

She desired to speak privately with Mildred Vesper, and opportunity might have been made, but, as part of her scheme of self-subdual, this conversation was postponed until the second week. It took place one evening when work was over.

'I have been wanting to ask you,' Rhoda began, 'whether you have any news of Mrs. Widdowson.'

'I wrote to her not long ago, and she answered from a new address. She said she had left her husband and would never go back to him.'

Rhoda nodded gravely.

'Then what I had heard was true. You haven't seen her?'

'She asked me not to come. She is living with her sister.'

'Did she give you any reason for the separation from her husband?'

'None,' answered Mildred. 'But she said it was no secret; that every one knew. That's why I haven't spoken to you about it—as I should have done otherwise after our last conversation.'

'The fact is no secret,' said Rhoda coldly. 'But why will she offer no explanation?'

Mildred shook her head, signifying inability to make any satisfactory reply, and there the dialogue ended; for Rhoda could not proceed in it without appearing to encourage scandal. The hope of eliciting some suggestive information had failed; but whether Mildred had really disclosed all she knew seemed doubtful.

At the end of the week Miss Barfoot left home for her own holiday; she was going to Scotland, and would be away for nearly the whole of September. At this time of the year the work in Great Portland Street was very light; not much employment offered for the typewriters, and the pupils numbered only about half a dozen. Nevertheless, it pleased Rhoda to have the establishment under her sole direction; she desired authority, and by magnifying the importance of that which now fell into her hands, she endeavoured to sustain herself under the secret misery which, for all her efforts, weighed no less upon her as time went on. It was a dreary make-believe. On the first night of solitude at Chelsea she shed bitter tears; and not only wept, but agonized in mute frenzy, the passions of her flesh torturing her until she thought of death as a refuge. Now she whispered the name of her lover with every word and phrase of endearment that her heart could suggest; the next moment she cursed him with the fury of deadliest hatred. In the half-delirium of sleeplessness, she revolved wild, impossible schemes for revenging herself, or, as the mood changed, all but resolved to sacrifice everything to her love, to accuse herself of ignoble jealousy and entreat forgiveness. Of many woeful nights this was the worst she had yet suffered.

It recalled to her with much vividness a memory of girlhood, or indeed of childhood. She thought of that figure in the dim past, that rugged, harsh-featured man, who had given her the first suggestion of independence; thrice her own age, yet the inspirer of such tumultuous emotion in her ignorant heart; her friend at Clevedon—Mr. Smithson.

A question from Mary Barfoot had caused her to glance back at him across the years, but only for an instant, and with self-mockery. What she now endured was the ripe intensity of a woe that fell upon her, at fifteen, when Mr. Smithson passed from her sight and away for ever. Childish folly! but the misery of it, the tossing at night, the blank outlook! How contemptible to revive such sensations, with mature intellect, after so long and stern a discipline!

Dreading the Sunday, so terrible in its depressing effect upon the lonely and unhappy, she breakfasted as soon as possible, and left home—simply to walk, to exert herself physically, that fatigue and sleep might follow. There was a dull sky, but no immediate fear of rain; the weather brightened a little towards noon. Careless of the direction, she walked on and on until the last maddening church bell had ceased its clangour; she was far out in the western suburbs, and weariness began to check her quick pace. Then she turned back. Without intending it, she passed by Mrs. Cosgrove's house, or rather would have passed, when she saw Mrs. Cosgrove at the dining-room window making signs to her. In a moment the door opened and she went in. She was glad of this accident, for the social lady might have something to tell about Mrs. Widdowson, who often visited her.

'In mercy, come and talk to me!' exclaimed Mrs. Cosgrove. 'I am quite alone, and feel as if I could hang myself. Are you obliged to go anywhere?'

'No. I was having a walk.'

'A walk? What astonishing energy! It never occurs to me to take a walk in London. I came from the country last night and expected to find my sister here, but she won't arrive till Tuesday. I have been standing at the window for an hour, getting crazy with *ennui*.'

They went to the drawing-room. It was not long before Mrs. Cosgrove made an allusion which enabled Rhoda to speak of Mrs. Widdowson. For a month or more Mrs. Cosgrove had seen and heard nothing of her; she had been out of town all the time. Rhoda hesitated, but could not keep silence on the subject that had become a morbid preoccupation of her mind. She told as much as she knew—excepting the suspicion against Everard Barfoot.

'It doesn't in the least surprise me,' said the listener, with interest. 'I saw they wouldn't be able to live together very well. Without children the thing was impossible. Of course she has told you all about it?'

'I haven't seen her since it happened.'

'Do you know, I always have a distinct feeling of pleasure when I hear of married people parting. How horrible that would seem to some of our good friends! But it isn't a malicious pleasure; there's nothing personal in it. As I have told you before, I think, I led a very contented life with my husband. But marriage in general is *such* a humbug—you forgive the word.'

'Of course it is,' assented Rhoda, laughing with forced gaiety.

'I am glad of anything that seems to threaten it as an institution—in its present form. A scandalous divorce case is a delight to me—anything that makes it evident how much misery would be spared if we could civilize ourselves in this respect. There are women whose conduct I think personally detestable, and whom yet I can't help thanking for their assault upon social laws. We shall have to go through a stage of anarchy, you know, before reconstruction begins. Yes, in that sense I am an anarchist. Seriously, I believe if a few men and women in prominent position would contract marriage of the free kind, without priest or lawyer, open and defiantly, they would do more benefit to their kind than in any other possible way. I don't declare this opinion to every one, but only because I am a coward. Whatever one believes with heart and soul one ought to make known.'

Rhoda wore a look of anxious reflection.

'It needs a great deal of courage,' she said. 'To take that step, I mean.'

'Of course. We need martyrs. And yet I doubt whether the martyrdom would be very long, or very trying, to intellectual people. A woman of brains who boldly acted upon her conviction would have no lack of congenial society. The best people are getting more liberal than they care to confess to each other. Wait until some one puts the matter to the test and you will see.'

Rhoda became so busy with her tumultuous thoughts that she spoke only a word now and then, allowing Mrs. Cosgrove to talk at large on this engrossing theme.

'Where is Mrs. Widdowson living?' the revolutionist at length inquired.

'I don't know. But I can get you her address.'

'Pray do. I shall go and see her. We are quite friendly enough for me to do so without impertinence.'

Having lunched with her acquaintance, Rhoda went in the afternoon to Mildred Vesper's lodgings. Miss Vesper was at home, reading, in her usual placid mood. She gave Rhoda the address that was on Mrs. Widdowson's last brief note, and that evening Rhoda sent it to Mrs. Cosgrove by letter.

In two days she received a reply. Mrs. Cosgrove had called upon Mrs. Widdowson at her lodgings at Clapham. 'She is ill, wretched, and unwilling to talk. I could only stay about a quarter of an hour, and to ask questions was impossible. She mentioned your name, and appeared very anxious to hear about you; but when I asked whether she would like you to call she grew timid all at once, and said she hoped you wouldn't unless you really desired to see her. Poor thing! Of course I don't know what it all means, but I came away with maledictions on marriage in my heart—one is always safe in indulging that feeling.'

A week or so after this there arrived for Miss Barfoot a letter from Everard. The postmark was Ostend.

Never before had Rhoda been tempted to commit a break of confidence such as in any one else she would have scorned beyond measure. She had heard, of course, of people secretly opening letters with the help of steam; whether it could be done with absolute security from detection she did not feel sure, but her thoughts dwelt on the subject for several hours. It was terrible to hold this letter of Everard's writing, and yet be obliged to send it away without knowledge of the contents, which perhaps gravely concerned her. She could not ask Miss Barfoot to let her know what Everard had written. The information might perhaps be voluntarily granted; but perhaps not.

To steam the back of the envelope—would it not leave marks, a rumpling or discoloration? Even to be suspected of such dishonour would be more bitter to her than death. Could she even think of it? How she was degraded by this hateful passion, which wrought in her like a disease!

With two others which that day had arrived she put the letter into a large envelope, and so dispatched it. But no satisfaction rewarded her; her heart raged against the world, against every law of life.

When, in a few days, a letter came to her from Miss Barfoot, she tore it Open, and there—yes, there was Everard's handwriting. Mary had sent the communication for her to read.

> 'DEAR COUSIN MARY,—After all I was rather too grumpy In my last note to you. But my patience had been desperately tried. I have gone through a good deal; now at last I am recovering sanity, and can admit that you had no choice but to ask those questions. I know and care nothing about Mrs. Widdowson. By her eccentric behaviour she either did me a great injury or a great service, I'm not

quite sure which, but I incline to the latter view. Here is a conundrum—not very difficult to solve, I dare say.

'Do you know anything about Arromanches? A very quiet little spot on the Normandy coast. You get to it by an hour's coach from Bayeux. Not infested by English. I went there on an invitation from the Brissendens; who discovered the place last year. Excellent people these. I like them better the more I know of them. A great deal of quiet liberality—even extreme liberality—in the two girls. They would suit you, I am sure. Well instructed. Agnes, the younger, reads half a dozen languages, and shames me by her knowledge of all sorts of things. And yet delightfully feminine.

'As they were going to Ostend I thought I might as well follow them, and we continue to see each other pretty frequently.

'By-the-bye, I shall have to find new quarters if I come back to London. The engineer, back from Italy after a longer absence than he anticipated, wants his flat, and of course must have it. But then I may not come back at all, except to gather my traps. I shall not call on you, unless I have heard that you don't doubt the assurance I have now twice given.—Your profligate relative,

E. B.'

'I think,' wrote Mary, 'that we may safely believe him. Such a lie would be too bad; he is incapable of it. Remember, I have never charged him with falsehood. I shall write and tell him that I accept his word. Has it, or has it not, occurred to you to see Mrs. Widdowson herself? Or, if there are insuperable objections, why not see Miss Madden? We talk to each other in a sort of cypher, dear Rhoda. Well, I desire nothing but your good, as I think you know, and you must decide for yourself where that good lies.'

Everard's letter put Rhoda beside herself with wrath. In writing it he knew it would come into her hands; he hoped to sting her with jealousy. So Mrs. Widdowson had done him a service. He was free to devote himself to Agnes Brissenden, with her six languages, her extreme liberality, her feminine charm.

If she could not crush out her love for this man she would poison herself—as she had so often decided she would do if ever some hopeless malady, such as cancer, took hold upon her—

And be content to feed his vanity? To give him the lifelong reflection that, for love of him, a woman excelled by few in qualities of brain and heart had died like a rat?

She walked about the rooms, here and there, upstairs and downstairs, in a fever of unrest. After all, was he not behaving in the very way she ought to desire? Was he not helping her to hate him? He struck at her with unmanly blows, thinking, no doubt, to quell her pride, and bring her to him in prostrate humility. Never! Even if it were proved in the clearest way that she ought to have believed him she would make no submission. If he loved her he must woo once more.

But the suggestion in Mary's letter was not fruitless. When she had thought over it for a day or two she wrote to Virginia Madden, asking her as a favour to come to Queen's Road on Saturday afternoon. Virginia quickly replied with a promise to call, and punctually kept the engagement. Though she was much better dressed than in the days previous to Monica's marriage, she had lost something for which costume could not compensate: her face had no longer that unmistakable refinement which had been wont to make her attire a secondary consideration. A disagreeable redness tinged her eyelids and the lower part of her nose; her mouth was growing coarse and lax, the under-lip hanging a little; she smiled with a shrinking, apologetic shyness only seen in people who have done something to be ashamed of—smiled even when she was endeavouring to look sorrowful; and her glance was furtive. She sat down on the edge of a chair, like an anxious applicant for work or charity, and a moistness of the eyes, which obliged her to use her handkerchief frequently, strengthened this resemblance.

Rhoda could not play at smooth phrases with this poor, dispirited woman, whose change during the last few years, and especially during the last twelve months, had often occupied her thoughts in a very unpleasant way. She came almost at once to the subject of their interview.

'Why have you not been to see me before this?'

'I—really couldn't. The circumstances—everything is so very painful. You know—of course you know what has happened?'

'Of course I do.'

'How,' asked Virginia timidly, 'did the news first of all reach you?'

'Mr. Widdowson came here and told Miss Barfoot everything.'

'He came? We didn't know that. Then you have heard the accusation he makes?'

'Everything.'

'It is quite unfounded, I do assure you. Monica is not guilty. The poor child has done nothing—it was an indiscretion—nothing more than indiscretion—'

'I am very anxious to believe it. Can you give me certainty? Can you explain Monica's behaviour—not only on that one occasion, but the deceit she practised at other times? Her husband told Miss Barfoot that she had frequently told him untruths—such as saying that she called here when she certainly did not.'

'I can't explain that,' lamented Virginia. 'Monica won't tell me why she concealed her movements.'

'Then how can you ask me to believe your assurance that she isn't guilty?'

The sternness of this question caused Virginia to redden and become utterly disconcerted. She dropped her handkerchief, fumbled for it, breathed hard.

'Oh, Miss Nunn! How can you think Monica—? You know her better; I'm sure you do!'

'Any human being may commit a crime,' said the other impatiently, exasperated by what seemed to be merely new evidence against Barfoot. 'Who knows any one well enough to say that a charge *must* be unfounded?'

Miss Madden began to sob.

'I'm afraid that is true. But my sister—my dear sister—'

'I didn't want to distress you. Do command yourself, and let us talk about it calmly.'

'Yes—I will—I shall be so glad to talk about it with you. Oh, if I could persuade her to return to her husband! He is willing to receive her. I meet him very often on Clapham Common, and—We are living at his expense. When Monica had been with me in my old lodgings for about a week he took these new rooms for us, and Monica consented to remove. But she won't hear of going back to live with him. He has offered to let us have the house to ourselves, but it's no use. He writes to her, but she won't reply. Do you know that he has taken a house at Clevedon—a beautiful house? They were to go to it in a week or two, and Alice and I would have gone to share it with them—then this dreadful thing happened. And Mr. Widdowson doesn't even insist on her telling him what she keeps secret. He is willing to take her back under any circumstances. And she is so ill—'

Virginia broke off, as if there were something more that she did not venture to impart. Her cheeks coloured, and she looked distressfully about the room.

'Seriously ill, do you mean?' inquired Rhoda, with difficulty softening her voice.

'She gets up each day, but I'm often afraid that—She has had fainting fits—'

Rhoda gazed at the speaker with pitiless scrutiny.

'What can have caused this? Is it the result of her being falsely accused?'

'Partly that. But—'

Suddenly Virginia rose, stepped to Rhoda's side, and whispered a word or two. Rhoda turned pale; her eyes glared fiercely.

'And *still* you believe her innocent?'

'She has sworn to me that she is innocent. She says that she has a proof of it which I shall see some day—and her husband also. A presentiment has fixed itself in her mind that she can't live, and before the end she will tell everything.'

'Her husband knows of this, of course—of what you have told me?'

'No. She has forbidden me to say anything—and how could I, Miss Nunn? She has made me promise solemnly that he shall not be told. I haven't even told Alice. But she will know very soon. At the end of September she leaves her place, and will come to London to be with us—for a time at all events. We do so hope that we shall succeed in persuading Monica to go to the house at Clevedon. Mr. Widdowson is keeping it, and will move the furniture from Herne Hill at any moment. Couldn't you help us, dear Miss Nunn? Monica would listen to you; I am sure she would.'

'I'm afraid I can be of no use,' Rhoda answered coldly.

'She has been hoping to see you.'

'She has said so?'

'Not in so many words—but I am sure she wishes to see you. She has asked about you several times, and when your note came she was very pleased. It would be a great kindness to us—'

'Does she declare that she will never return to her husband?'

'Yes—I am sorry to say she does. But the poor child believes that she has only a short time to live. Nothing will shake her presentiment. "I shall die, and give no more trouble"—that's what she always says to me. And a conviction of that kind is so likely to fulfil itself. She never leaves the house, and of course that is very wrong; she ought to go out every day. She won't see a medical man.'

'Has Mr. Widdowson given her any cause for disliking him?' Rhoda inquired.

'He was dreadfully violent when he discovered—I'm afraid it was natural—he thought the worst of her, and he has always been so devoted to Monica. She says he seemed on the point of killing her. He is a man of very severe nature, I have always thought. He never could bear that Monica should go anywhere alone. They were very, very unhappy, I'm afraid—so ill-matched in almost every respect. Still, under the circumstances—surely she ought to return to him?'

'I can't say. I don't know.'

Rhoda's voice signified a conflict of feeling. Had she been disinterested her opinion would not have wavered for a moment; she would have declared that the wife's inclination must be the only law in such a case. As it was, she could only regard Monica with profound mistrust and repugnance. The story of decisive evidence kept back seemed to her only a weak woman's falsehood—a fiction due to shame and despair. Undoubtedly it would give some vague relief to her mind if Monica were persuaded to go to Clevedon, but she could not bring herself to think of visiting the suffering woman. Whatever the end might be, she would have no part in bringing it about. Her dignity, her pride, should remain unsullied by such hateful contact.

'I mustn't stay longer,' said Virginia, rising after a painful silence. 'I am always afraid to be away from her even for an hour; the fear of dreadful things that might happen haunts me day and night. How glad I shall be when Alice comes!'

Rhoda had no words of sympathy. Her commiseration for Virginia was only such as she might have felt for any stranger involved in sordid troubles; all the old friendliness had vanished. Nor would she have been greatly shocked or astonished had she followed Miss Madden on the way to the railway station and seen her, after a glance up and down the street, turn quickly into a public-house, and come forth again holding her handkerchief to her lips. A feeble, purposeless, hopeless woman; type of a whole class; living only to deteriorate—

Will! Purpose! Was *she* not in danger of forgetting these watchwords, which had guided her life out of youth into maturity? That poor creature's unhappiness was doubtless in great measure due to the conviction that in missing love and marriage she had missed everything. So thought the average woman, and in her darkest hours she too had fallen among those poor of spirit, the flesh prevailing. But the soul in her had not finally succumbed. Passion had a new significance; her conception of life was larger, more liberal; she made no vows to crush the natural instincts. But her conscience, her sincerity should not suffer. Wherever destiny might lead, she would still be the same proud and independent woman, responsible only to herself, fulfilling the nobler laws of her existence.

A day or two after this she had guests to dine with her—Mildred Vesper and Winifred Haven. Among the girls whom she had helped to educate, these two seemed by far the most self-reliant, the most courageous and hopeful. In minor details of character they differed widely, and intellectually Miss Haven was far in advance. Rhoda had a strong desire to observe them as they talked about the most various subjects; she knew them well, but hoped to find in them some new suggestion of womanly force which would be of help to her in her own struggle for redemption.

It was seldom that either of them ailed anything. Mildred still showed traces of her country breeding; she was the more robust, walked with a heavier step, had less polish of manner. Under strain of any kind Winifred's health would sooner give way, but her natural vivacity promised long resistance to oppressing influences. Mildred had worked harder, and amid privations of which the other girl knew nothing. She would never distinguish herself, but it was difficult indeed to imagine her repining so long as she had her strength and her congenial friends. Twenty years hence, in all probability, she would keep the same clear, steady eye, the same honest smile, and the same dry humour in her talk. Winifred was more likely to traverse a latitude of storm. For one thing, her social position brought her in the way of men who might fall in love with her, whereas Mildred lived absolutely apart from the male world; doubtless, too, her passions were stronger. She loved literature, spent as much time as possible in study, and had set her mind upon helping to establish that ideal woman's paper of which there was often talk at Miss Barfoot's.

In this company Rhoda felt her old ambitions regaining their power over her. To these girls she was an exemplar; it made her smile to think how little they could dream of what she had experienced during the last few weeks; if ever a moment of discontent assailed them, they must naturally think of her, of the brave, encouraging words she had so often spoken. For a moment she had deserted them, abandoning a course which her reason steadily approved for one that was beset with perils of indignity. It would shame her if they knew the whole truth—and yet she wished it were possible for them to learn that she had been passionately wooed. A contemptible impulse of vanity; away with it!

There was a chance, it seemed to her, that during Miss Barfoot's absence Everard might come to the house. Mary had written to him; he would know that she was away. What better opportunity, if he had not dismissed her memory from his thoughts?

Every evening she made herself ready to receive a possible visitor. She took thought for her appearance. But the weeks passed by, Miss Barfoot returned, and Everard had given no sign.

She would set a date, a limit. If before Christmas he neither came nor wrote all was at an end; after that she would not see him, whatever his plea. And having persuaded herself that this decision was irrevocable, she thought it as well to gratify Miss Barfoot's curiosity, for by now she felt able to relate what had happened in Cumberland with a certain satisfaction—the feeling she had foreseen when, in the beginning of her acquaintance with Everard, it flattered her to observe his growing interest. Her narrative, to which Mary listened with downcast eyes, presented the outlines of the story veraciously; she told of Everard's wish to dispense with the legal bond, of her own indecision, and of the issue.

'When your letter came, could I very well have acted otherwise than I did? It was not a flat refusal to believe him; all I asked was that things should be cleared up before our marriage. For his own sake he ought to have willingly agreed to that. He preferred to take my request as an insult. His unreasonable anger made me angry too. And now I don't think we shall ever meet again unless as mere acquaintances.'

'I think,' commented the listener, 'that he behaved with extraordinary impudence.'

'In the first proposal? But I myself attach no importance to the marriage ceremony.'

'Then why did you insist upon it?' asked Mary, with a smile that might have become sarcastic but that her eye met Rhoda's.

'Would you have received us?'

'In the one case as readily as in the other.'

Rhoda was silent and darkly thoughtful.

'Perhaps I never felt entire confidence in him.'

Mary smiled and sighed.

## CHAPTER XXVIII - THE BURDEN OF FUTILE SOULS

'My own dearest love, if I could but describe to you all I have suffered before sitting down to write this letter! Since our last meeting I have not known one hour of quietness. To think that I missed you when you called and left that note—for it was you yourself, was it not? The journey was horrible, and the week that I have spent here—I assure you I have not slept for more than a few minutes at a time, and I am utterly broken down by misery. My darling'—etc. 'I regard myself as a criminal; if *you* have suffered a thousandth part of what *I* have, I deserve any punishment that could be devised. For it has all been my fault. Knowing as I did that our love could never end in happiness, it was my duty to hide what I felt. I ought never to have contrived that first meeting alone—for it *was* contrived; I sent my sisters away on purpose. I ought never'—etc. 'The only reflection that can ever bring me comfort is that our love has been pure. We can always think of each other without shame. And why should this love ever have an end? We are separated, and perhaps shall never see each other again, but may not our hearts remain for ever true? May we not think'—etc. 'If I were to bid you leave your home and come to me, I should be once more acting with base selfishness. I should ruin your life, and load my own with endless self-reproach. I find that even mere outward circumstances would not allow of what for a moment we dreamt might be possible, and of that I am *glad*, since it helps me to overcome the terrible temptation. Oh, if you knew how that temptation'—etc. 'Time will be a friend to both of us, dearest Monica. Forget each other we never can, we *never* will. But our unsullied love'—etc.

Monica read it through again, the long rigmarole. Since the day that she received it—addressed to 'Mrs. Williamson' at the little stationer's by Lavender Hill—the day before she consented to accompany her sister into new lodgings—the letter had lain in its hiding-place. Alone this afternoon, for Virginia was gone to call on Miss Nunn, alone and miserable, every printed page a weariness to her sight, she took out the French-stamped envelope and tried to think that its contents interested her. But not a word had power of attraction or of repulsion. The tender phrases affected her no more than if they had been addressed to a stranger. Love was become a meaningless word. She could not understand how she had ever drifted into such relations with the writer. Fear and anger were the sole passions surviving in her memory from those days which had violently transformed her life, and it was not with Bevis, but her husband, that these emotions were connected. Bevis's image stood in that already distant past like a lay figure, the mere semblance of a man. And with such conception of him his letter corresponded; it was artificial, lifeless, as if extracted from some vapid novel.

But she must not destroy it. Its use was still to come. Letter and envelope must go back again into hiding, and await the day which would give them power over human lives.

Suffering, as always, from headache and lassitude, she sat by the window and watched the people who passed along—her daily occupation. This sitting-room was on the ground floor. In a room above some one was receiving a music lesson; every now and then the teacher's voice became audible, raised in sharp impatience, and generally accompanied by a clash upon the keys of the piano. At the area gate of the house opposite a servant was talking angrily with a tradesman's errand boy, who at length put his thumb to his nose with insulting significance and scampered off. Then, at the house next to that one, there stopped a cab, from which three busy-looking men alighted. Cabs full of people were always stopping at that door. Monica wondered what it meant, who might live there. She thought of asking the landlady.

Virginia's return aroused her. She went upstairs with her sister into the double-bedded room which they occupied.

'What have you heard?'

'He went there. He told them everything.'

'How did Miss Nunn look? How did she speak?'

'Oh, she was very, very distant,' lamented Virginia. 'I don't quite know why she sent for me. She said there would be no use in her coming to see you—and I don't think she ever will. I told her that there was no truth in—'

'But how did she look?' asked Monica impatiently.

'Not at all well, I thought. She had been away for her holiday, but it doesn't seem to have done her much good.'

'He went there and told them everything?'

'Yes—just after it happened. But he hasn't seen them since that. I could see they believed him. It was no use all that I said. She looked so stern and—'

'Did you ask anything about Mr. Barfoot?'

'My dear, I didn't venture to. It was impossible. But I feel quite sure that they must have broken off all intercourse with him. Whatever he may have said, they evidently didn't believe it. Miss Barfoot is away now.

'And what did you tell her about me?'

'Everything that you said I might, dear.'

'Nothing else—you are sure?'

Virginia coloured, but made asseveration that nothing else had passed her lips.

'It wouldn't have mattered if you had,' said Monica indifferently. 'I don't care.'

The sister, struggling with shame, was irritated by the needlessness of her falsehood.

'Then why were you so particular to forbid me, Monica?'

'It was better—but I don't care. I don't care for anything. Let them believe and say what they like—'

'Monica, if I find out at last that you have deceived me—'

'Oh, do, do, do be quiet!' cried the other wretchedly. 'I shall go somewhere and live alone—or die alone. You worry me—I'm tired of it.'

'You are not very grateful, Monica.'

'I can't be grateful! You must expect nothing from me. If you keep talking and questioning I shall go away. I don't care what becomes of me. The sooner I die the better.'

Scenes such as this had been frequent lately. The sisters were a great trial to each other's nerves. Tedium and pain drove Monica to the relief of altercation, and Virginia, through her secret vice, was losing all self-control. They wrangled, wailed, talked of parting, and only became quiet when their emotions had exhausted them. Yet no ill-feeling resulted from these disputes. Virginia had a rooted faith in her sister's innocence; when angry, she only tried to provoke Monica into a full explanation of the mystery, so insoluble by unaided conjecture. And Monica, say what she might, repaid this confidence with profound gratitude. Strangely, she had come to view herself as not only innocent of the specific charge brought against her, but as a woman in every sense maligned. So utterly void of significance, from her present point of view, was all that had passed between her and Bevis. One reason for this lay in the circumstance that, when exchanging declarations with her lover, she was ignorant of a fact which, had she known it, would have made their meetings impossible. Her husband she could never regard but as a cruel enemy; none the less, nature had set a seal upon their marriage against which the revolt of her heart was powerless. If she lived to bear a child, that child would be his. Widdowson, when he heard of her condition, would declare it the final proof of infidelity; and this injustice it was that exclusively occupied her mind. On this account she could think only of the accusation which connected her name with Barfoot's—all else was triviality. Had there been no slightest ground for imputation upon her conduct, she could not have resented more vigorously her husband's refusal to acquit her of dishonour.

On the following day, after their early dinner, Monica unexpectedly declared that she must go out.

'Come with me. We'll go into the town.'

'But you refused to go out this morning when it was fine,' complained Virginia. 'And now you can see it will rain.'

'Then I shall go alone.'

The sister at once started up.

'No, no; I'm quite ready. Where do you wish—'

'Anywhere out of this dead place. We'll go by train, and walk from Victoria—anywhere. To the Abbey, if you like.'

'You must be very careful not to catch cold. After all this time that you haven't left the house—'

Monica cut short the admonition and dressed herself with feverish impatience. As they set forth, drops of rain had begun to fall, but Monica would not hear of waiting. The journey by train made her nervous, but affected her spirits favourably. At Victoria it rained so heavily that they could not go out into the street.

'It doesn't matter. There's plenty to see here. Let us walk about and look at things. We'll buy something at the bookstall to take back.'

As they turned again towards the platform, Monica was confronted by a face which she at once recognized, though it had changed noticeably in the eighteen months since she last saw it. The person was Miss Eade, her old acquaintance at the shop. But the girl no longer dressed as in those days; cheap finery of the 'loudest' description arrayed her form, and it needed little scrutiny to perceive that her thin cheeks were artificially reddened. The surprise of the meeting was not Monica's only reason for evincing embarrassment. Seeing that Miss Eade was uncertain whether to make a sign of acquaintance, she felt it would be wiser to go by. But this was not permitted. As they were passing each other the girl bent her head and whispered—

'I want to speak to you—just a minute.'

Virginia perceived the communication, and looked in surprise at her sister.

'It's one of the girls from Walworth Road,' said Monica. 'Just walk on; I'll meet you at the bookstall.'

'But, my dear, she doesn't look respectable—'

'Go on; I won't be a minute.'

Monica motioned to Miss Eade, who followed her towards a more retired spot.

'You have left the shop?'

'Left—I should think so. Nearly a year ago. I told you I shouldn't stand it much longer. Are you married?'

'Yes.'

Monica did not understand why the girl should eye her so suspiciously.

'You are?' said Miss Eade. 'Nobody that I know, I suppose?'

'Quite a stranger to you.'

The other made an unpleasant click with her tongue, and looked vaguely about her. Then she remarked inconsequently that she was waiting the arrival of her brother by train.

'He's a traveller for a West-end shop; makes five hundred a year. I keep house for him, because of course he's a widower.'

The 'of course' puzzled Monica for a moment, but she remembered that it was an unmeaning expletive much used by people of Miss Eade's education. However, the story did not win her credence; by this time her disagreeable surmises had too much support.

'Was there anything you wished particularly to speak about?'

'You haven't seen nothing of Mr. Bullivant?'

To what a remote period of her life this name seemed to recall Monica! She glanced quickly at the speaker, and again detected suspicion in her eyes.

'I have neither seen nor heard of him since I left Walworth Road. Isn't he still there?'

'Not he. He went about the same time you did, and nobody knew where he hid himself.'

'Hid? Why should he hide?'

'I only mean he got out of sight somewheres. I thought perhaps you might have come across him.'

'No, I haven't. Now I must say good-bye. That lady is waiting for me.'

Miss Eade nodded, but immediately altered her mind and checked Monica as she was turning away.

'You wouldn't mind telling me what your married name may be?'

'That really doesn't concern you, Miss Eade,' replied the other stiffly. 'I must go—'

'If you don't tell me, I'll follow you till I find out, and chance it!'

The change from tolerable civility to coarse insolence was so sudden that Monica stood in astonishment. There was unconcealed malignity in the gaze fixed upon her.

'What do you mean? What interest have you in learning my name?'

The girl brought her face near, and snarled in the true voice of the pavement—

'Is it a name as you're ashamed to let out?'

Monica walked away to the bookstall. When she had joined her sister, she became aware that Miss Eade was keeping her in sight.

'Let us buy a book,' she said, 'and go home again. The rain won't stop.'

They selected a cheap volume, and, having their return tickets, moved towards the departure platform. Before she could reach the gates Monica heard Miss Eade's voice just behind her; it had changed again, and the appealing note reminded her of many conversations in Walworth Road.

'Do tell me! I beg your pardon for bein' rude. Don't go without telling me.'

The meaning of this importunity had already flashed upon Monica, and now she felt a slight pity for the tawdry, abandoned creature, in whom there seemed to survive that hopeless passion of old days.

'My name,' she said abruptly, 'is Mrs. Widdowson.'

'Are you telling me the truth?'

'I have told you what you wish to know. I can't talk—'

'And you don't really know nothing about *him*?'

'Nothing whatever.'

Miss Eade moved sullenly away, not more than half convinced. Long after Monica's disappearance she strayed about the platform and the approaches to the station. Her brother was slow in arriving. Once or twice she held casual colloquy with men who also stood waiting—perchance for their sisters; and ultimately one of these was kind enough to offer her refreshment, which she graciously accepted.

Rhoda Nunn would have classed her and mused about her: a not unimportant type of the odd woman.

After this Monica frequently went out, always accompanied by her sister. It happened more than once that they saw Widdowson, who walked past the house at least every other day; he didn't approach them, and had he done so Monica would have kept an obstinate silence.

For more than a fortnight he had not written to her. At length there came a letter, merely a repetition of his former appeals.

'I hear,' he wrote, 'that your elder sister is coming to London. Why should she live here in lodgings, when a comfortable house is at the disposal of you all? Let me again entreat you to go to Clevedon. The furniture shall be moved any moment you wish. I solemnly promise not to molest you in any way, not even by writing. It shall be understood that business makes it necessary for me to live in London. For your sister's sake do accept this offer. If I could see you in private, I should be able to give you a very good reason why your sister Virginia would benefit by the change; perhaps you yourself know of it. Do answer me, Monica. Never again will I refer by word or look to what has passed. I am anxious only to put an end to the wretched life that you are leading. Do go to the house at Clevedon, I implore you.'

It was not the first time he had hinted darkly at a benefit that might accrue to Virginia if she left London. Monica had no inkling of what he meant. She showed her sister this communication, and asked if she could understand the passage which concerned her.

'I haven't the least idea,' Virginia replied, her hand trembling as she held the paper. 'I can only suppose that he thinks that I am not looking well.'

The letter was burnt, as all the others had been, no answer vouchsafed. Virginia's mind seemed to waver with regard to the proposed settlement at Clevedon. Occasionally she had urged Monica, with extreme persistence, to accept what was offered; at other times, as now, for instance, she said nothing. Yet Alice had written beseeching her to use all means for Monica's persuasion. Miss Madden infinitely preferred the thought of dwelling at Clevedon—however humble the circumstances had been—to that of coming back into London lodgings whilst she sought for a new engagement. The situation she was about to quit had proved more laborious than any in her experience. At first merely a governess, she had gradually become children's nurse as well, and for the past three months had been expected to add the tendance of a chronic invalid to her other duties. Not a day's holiday since she came. She was broken down and utterly woebegone.

But Monica could not be moved. She refused to go again under her husband's roof until he had stated that his charge against her was absolutely unfounded. This concession went beyond Widdowson's power; he would forgive, but still declined to stultify himself by a statement that could have no meaning. To what extent his wife had deceived him might be uncertain, but the deception was a proved fact. Of course it never occurred to him that Monica's demand had a significance which emphasized the name of Barfoot. Had he said, 'I am convinced that your relations with Barfoot were innocent,' he would have seemed to himself to be acquitting her of all criminality; whereas Monica, from her point of view, illogically supposed that he might credit her on this one issue without overthrowing all the evidence that declared her untrustworthy. In short, she expected him to read a riddle which there was scarcely a possibility of his understanding.

Alice was in correspondence with the gloomy husband. She promised him to use every effort to gain Monica's confidence. Perhaps as the eldest sister she might succeed where Virginia had failed. Her faith in Monica's protestations had been much shaken by the item of intelligence which Virginia secretly communicated; she thought it too likely that her unhappy sister saw no refuge from disgrace but in stubborn denial of guilt. And in the undertaking that was before her she had no hope save through the influence of religion—with her a much stronger force than with either of the others.

Her arrival was expected on the last day of September. The evening before, Monica went to bed soon after eight o'clock; for a day or two she had suffered greatly, and at length had allowed a doctor to be called. Whenever her sister retired very early, Virginia also went to her own bedroom, saying that she preferred to sit there.

The room much surpassed in comfort that which she had occupied at Mrs. Conisbee's; it was spacious, and provided with a couple of very soft armchairs. Having locked her door, Virginia made certain preparations which had nothing to do with natural repose. From the cupboard she brought out a little spirit-kettle, and put water to boil. Then from a more private repository were produced a bottle of gin and a sugar-basin, which, together with a tumbler and spoon, found a place on a little table drawn up within reach of the chair where she was going to sit. On the same table lay a novel procured this afternoon from the library. Whilst the water was boiling, Virginia made a slight change of dress, conducive to bodily ease. Finally, having mixed a glass of gin and water—one-third only of the diluent—she sat down with one of her frequent sighs and began to enjoy the evening.

The last, the very last, of such enjoyment; so she assured herself. Alice's presence in the house would render impossible what she had hitherto succeeded in disguising from Monica. Her conscience welcomed the restraint, which was coming none too soon, for her will could no longer be depended upon. If she abstained from strong liquors for three or four days it was now a great triumph; yet worthless, for even in abstaining she knew that the hour of indulgence had only been postponed. A fit of unendurable depression soon drove her to the only resource which had immediate efficacy. The relief, she knew, was another downward step; but presently she would find courage to climb back again up to the sure ground. Save for her trouble on Monica's account the temptation would already have been conquered. And now Alice's arrival made courage a mere necessity.

Her bottle was all but empty; she would finish it to-night, and in the morning, as her custom was, take it back to the grocer's in her little hand-bag. How convenient that this kind of thing could be purchased at the grocer's! In the beginning she had chiefly made use of railway refreshment rooms. Only on rare occasions did she enter a public-house, and always with the bitterest sense of degradation. To sit comfortably at home, the bottle beside her, and a novel on her lap, was an avoidance of the worst shame attaching to this vice; she went to bed, and in the morning—ah, the morning brought its punishment, but she incurred no risk of being detected.

Brandy had first of all been her drink, as is generally the case with women of the educated class. There are so many plausible excuses for taking a drop of brandy. But it cost too much. Whisky she had tried, and did not like. Finally she had recourse to gin, which was palatable and very cheap. The name, debased by such foul associations, still confused her when she uttered it; as a rule, she wrote it down in a list of groceries which she handed over the counter.

To-night she drank her first glass quickly; a consuming thirst was upon her. By half-past eight the second was gently steaming at her elbow. At nine she had mixed the third; it must last a long time, for the bottle was now empty.

The novel entertained her, but she often let her thoughts stray from it; she reflected with exultation that to-night's indulgence was her very last. On the morrow she would be a new woman. Alice and she would devote themselves to their poor sister, and never rest till they had restored her to a life of dignity. This was a worthy, a noble task; success in it must need minister to her own peace. Before long they would all be living at Clevedon—a life of ideal contentment. It was no longer necessary to think of the school, but she would exert herself for the moral instruction of young women—on the principles inculcated by Rhoda Nunn.

The page before her was no longer legible; the book dropped from her lap. Why this excited her laughter she could not understand; but she laughed for a long time, until her eyes were dim with tears. It might be better to go to bed. What was the hour? She tried vainly to read her watch, and again laughed at such absurd incapacity. Then—

Surely that was a knock at her door? Yes; it was repeated, with a distinct calling of her name. She endeavoured to stand up.

'Miss Madden!' It was the landlady's voice. 'Miss Madden! Are you in bed yet?'

Virginia succeeded in reaching the door.

'What is it?'

Another voice spoke.

'It is I, Virginia. I have come this evening instead of to-morrow. Please let me come in.'

'Alice? You can't—I'll come—wait downstairs.'

She was still able to understand the situation, and able, she thought, to speak coherently, to disguise her condition. The things on the table must be put out of sight. In trying to do this, she upset her glass and knocked the empty bottle on to the floor. But in a few minutes bottle, glass, and spirit-kettle were hidden away. The sugar-basin she lost sight of; it still remained in its former place.

Then she opened the door, and with uncertain step went out into the passage.

'Alice!' she called aloud.

At once both her sisters appeared, coming out of Monica's chamber. Monica had partly dressed herself.

'Why have you come to-night?' Virginia exclaimed, in a voice which seemed to her own ears perfectly natural.

She tottered, and was obliged to support herself against the wall. The light from her room fell full upon her, and Alice, who had stepped forward to give her a kiss, not only saw, but smelt, that something very strange was the matter. The odour proceeding from the bedroom, and that of Virginia's breath, left small doubt as to the cause of delay in giving admittance.

Whilst Alice stood bewildered, Monica received an illumination which instantly made clear to her many things in Virginia's daily life.

At the same moment she understood those mysterious hints concerning her sister in Widdowson's letters.

'Come into the room,' she said abruptly. 'Come, Virgie.'

'I don't understand—why has Alice come to-night?—what's the time?'

Monica took hold of the tottering woman's arm and drew her out of the passage. The cold air had produced its natural effect upon Virginia, who now with difficulty supported herself.

'O Virgie!' cried the eldest sister, when the door was closed. 'What is the matter? What does it mean?'

Already she had been shedding tears at the meeting with Monica, and now distress overcame her; she sobbed and lamented.

'What have you been doing, Virgie?' asked Monica with severity.

'Doing? I feel a little faint—surprise—didn't expect—'

'Sit down at once. You are disgusting! Look, Alice.' She pointed to the sugar-basin on the table; then, after a rapid glance round the room, she went to the cupboard and threw the door open. 'I thought so. Look, Alice. And to think I never suspected this! It has been going on a long time—oh, a long time. She was doing it at Mrs. Conisbee's before I was married. I remember smelling spirits—'

Virginia was making efforts to rise.

'What are you talking about?' she exclaimed in a thick voice, and with a countenance which was changing from dazed astonishment to anger. 'It's only when I feel faint. Do you suppose I drink? Where's Alice? Wasn't Alice here?'

'O Virgie! What *does* it mean? How *could* you?'

'Go to bed at once, Virginia,' said Monica. 'We're ashamed of you. Go back into my room Alice, and I'll get her to bed.'

Ultimately this was done. With no slight trouble, Monica persuaded her sister to undress, and got her into a recumbent position, Virginia all the time protesting that she had perfect command of her faculties, that she needed no help whatever, and was utterly at a loss to comprehend the insults directed against her.

'Lie quiet and go to sleep,' was Monica's last word, uttered contemptuously.

She extinguished the lamp and returned to her own room, where Alice was still weeping. The unexpected arrival had already been explained to Monica. Sudden necessity for housing a visitor had led to the proposition that Miss Madden, for her last night, should occupy a servant's bedroom. Glad to get away, Alice chose the alternative of leaving the house at once. It had been arranged that she should share Virginia's room, but to-night this did not seem advisable.

'To-morrow,' said Monica, 'we must talk to her very seriously. I believe she has been drinking like that night after night. It explains the look she always has the first thing in the morning. Could you have imagined anything so disgraceful?'

But Alice had softened towards the erring woman.

'You must remember what her life has been, dear. I'm afraid loneliness is very often a cause—'

'She needn't have been lonely. She refused to come and live at Herne Hill, and now of course I understand why. Mrs. Conisbee must have known about it, and it was her duty to tell me. Mr. Widdowson had found out somehow, I feel sure.'

She explained the reason of this belief.

'You know what it all points to,' said Miss Madden, drying her sallow, pimpled cheeks. 'You must do as your husband wishes, dearest. We must go to Clevedon. There the poor girl will be out of temptation.'

'You and Virgie may go.'

'You too, Monica. My dear sister, it is your duty.'

'Don't use that word to me!' exclaimed the other angrily. 'It is *not* my duty. It can be no woman's duty to live with a man she hates-or even to make a pretence of living with him.'

'But, dearest—'

'You mustn't begin this to-night, Alice. I have been ill all day, and now my head is aching terribly. Go downstairs and eat the supper they have laid for you.'

'I couldn't touch a morsel,' sobbed Miss Madden. 'Oh, everything is too dreadful! Life is too hard!'

Monica had returned to bed, and lay there with her face half hidden against the pillow.

'If you don't want any supper,' she said in a moment, 'please go and tell them, so that they needn't sit up for you.'

Alice obeyed. When she came up again, her sister was, or pretended to be, asleep; even the noise made by bringing luggage into the room did not cause her to move. Having sat in despondency for a while, Miss Madden opened one of her boxes, and sought in it for the Bible which it was her custom to make use of every night. She read in the book for about half an hour, then covered her face with her hands and prayed silently. This was *her* refuge from the barrenness and bitterness of life.

# CHAPTER XXIX - CONFESSION AND COUNSEL

The sisters did not exchange a word until morning, but both of them lay long awake. Monica was the first to lose consciousness; she slept for about an hour, then the pains of a horrid dream disturbed her, and again she took up the burden of thought. Such waking after brief, broken sleep, when mind and body are beset by weariness, yet cannot rest, when night with its awful hush and its mysterious movements makes a strange, dread habitation for the spirit—such waking is a grim trial of human fortitude. The blood flows sluggishly, yet subject to sudden tremors that chill the veins and for an instant choke the heart. Purpose is idle, the will impure; over the past hangs a shadow of remorse, and life that must yet be lived shows lurid, a steep pathway to the hopeless grave. Of this cup Monica drank deeply.

A fear of death compassed her about. Night after night it had thus haunted her. In the daytime she could think of death with resignation, as a refuge from miseries of which she saw no other end; but this hour of silent darkness shook her with terrors. Reason availed nothing; its exercise seemed criminal. The old faiths, never abandoned, though modified by the breath of intellectual freedom that had just touched her, reasserted all their power. She saw herself as a wicked woman, in the eye of truth not less wicked than her husband declared her. A sinner stubborn in impenitence, defending herself by a paltry ambiguity that had all the evil of a direct lie. Her soul trembled in its nakedness.

What redemption could there be for her? What path of spiritual health was discoverable? She could not command herself to love the father of her child; the repugnance with which she regarded him seemed to her a sin against nature, yet how was she responsible for it? Would it profit her to make confession and be humbled before him? The confession must some day be made, if only for her child's sake; but she foresaw in it no relief of mind. Of all human beings her husband was the one least fitted to console and strengthen her. She cared nothing for his pardon; from his love she shrank. But if there were some one to whom she could utter her thoughts with the certainty of being understood—

Her sisters had not the sympathetic intelligence necessary for aiding her; Virginia was weaker than she herself, and Alice dealt only in sorrowful commonplaces, profitable perhaps to her own heart, but powerless over the trouble of another's. Among the few people she had called her friends there was one strong woman—strong of brain, and capable, it might be, of speaking the words that go from soul to soul; this woman she had deeply offended, yet owing to mere mischance. Whether or no Rhoda Nunn had lent ear to Barfoot's wooing she must be gravely offended; she had given proof of it in the interview reported by Virginia. The scandal spread abroad by Widdowson might even have been fatal to a happiness of which she had dreamt. To Rhoda Nunn some form of reparation was owing. And might not an avowal of the whole truth elicit from her counsel of gratitude—some solace, some guidance?

Amid the tremors of night Monica felt able to take this step, for the mere chance of comfort that it offered. But when day came the resolution had vanished; shame and pride again compelled her to silence.

And this morning she had new troubles to think about. Virginia was keeping her room; would admit no one; answered every whisper of appeal with brief, vague words that signified anything or nothing. The others breakfasted in gloom that harmonized only too well with the heavy, dripping sky visible from their windows. Only at midday did Alice succeed in obtaining speech with her remorseful sister. They were closeted together for more than an hour, and the elder woman came forth at last with red, tear-swollen eyes.

'We must leave her alone today,' she said to Monica. 'She won't take any meal. Oh, the wretched state she is in! If only I could have known of this before!'

'Has it been going on for very long?'

'It began soon after she went to live at Mrs. Conisbee's. She has told me all about it—poor girl, poor thing! Whether she can ever break herself of it, who knows? She says that she will take the pledge of total abstinence, and I encouraged her to do so; it may be some use, don't you think?'

'Perhaps—I don't know—'

'But I have no faith in her reforming unless she goes away from London. She thinks herself that only a new life in a new place will give her the strength. My dear, at Mrs. Conisbee's she starved herself to have money to buy spirits; she went without any food but dry bread day after day.'

'Of course that made it worse. She must have craved for support.'

'Of course. And your husband knows about it. He came once when she was in that state—when you were away—'

Monica nodded sullenly, her eyes averted.

'Her life has been so dreadfully unhealthy. She seems to have become weak-minded. All her old interests have gone; she reads nothing but novels, day after day.'

'I have noticed that.'

'How can we help her, Monica? Won't you make a sacrifice for the poor girl's sake? Cannot I persuade you, dear? Your position has a bad influence on her; I can see it has. She worries so about you, and then tries to forget the trouble—you know how.'

Not that day, nor the next, could Monica listen to these entreaties. But her sister at length prevailed. It was late in the evening; Virginia had gone to bed, and the others sat silently, without occupation. Miss Madden, after several vain efforts to speak, bent forward and said in a low, grave voice,—

'Monica—you are deceiving us all. You are guilty.'

'Why do you say that?'

'I know it. I have watched you. You betray yourself when you are thinking.'

The other sat with brows knitted, with hard, defiant lips.

'All your natural affection is dead, and only guilt could have caused that. You don't care what becomes of your sister. Only the fear, or the evil pride, that comes of guilt could make you refuse what we ask of you. You are afraid to let your husband know of your condition.'

Alice could not have spoken thus had she not believed what she said. The conviction had become irresistible to her mind. Her voice quivered with intensity of painful emotion.

'That last is true,' said her sister, when there had been silence for a minute.

'You confess it? O Monica—'

'I don't confess what you think,' went on the younger, with more calmness than she had yet commanded in these discussions.

'Of that I am *not* guilty. I am afraid of his knowing, because he will never believe me. I have a proof which would convince anyone else; but, even if I produced it, it would be no use. I don't think it is possible to persuade him-when once he knows—'

'If you were innocent you would disregard that.'

## CHAPTER XXIX - CONFESSION AND COUNSEL

'Listen to me, Alice. If I were guilty I should not be living here at his expense. I only consented to do that when I knew what my condition was. But for this thing I should have refused to accept another penny from him. I should have drawn upon my own money until I was able to earn my own living again. If you won't believe this it shows you know nothing of me. Your reading of my face is all foolishness.'

'I would to God I were sure of what you say!' moaned Miss Madden, with vehemence which seemed extraordinary in such a feeble, flabby person.

'You know that I told my husband lies,' exclaimed Monica, 'so you think I am never to be trusted. I did tell him lies; I can't deny it, and I am ashamed of it. But I am not a deceitful woman—I can say that boldly. I love the truth better than falsehood. If it weren't for that I should never have left home. A deceitful woman, in my circumstances—you don't understand them—would have cheated her husband into forgiving her—such a husband as mine. She would have calculated the most profitable course. I left my husband because it was hateful to me to be with a man for whom I had lost every trace of affection. In keeping away from him I am acting honestly. But I have told you that I am also afraid of his making a discovery. I want him to believe—when the time comes—'

She broke off.

'Then, Monica, you ought to make known to him what you have been concealing. If you are telling the truth, that confession can't be anything very dreadful.'

'Alice, I am willing to make an agreement. If my husband will promise never to come near Clevedon until I send for him I will go and live there with you and Virgie.'

'He has promised that, darling,' cried Miss Madden delightedly.

'Not to me. He has only said that he will make his home in London for a time: that means he would come whenever he wished, if it were only to speak to you and Virgie. But he must undertake never to come near until I give him permission. If he will promise this, and keep his word, I pledge myself to let him know the whole truth in less than a year. Whether I live or die, he shall be told the truth in less than a year.'

Before going to bed Alice wrote and dispatched a few lines to Widdowson, requesting an interview with him as soon as possible. She would come to his house at any hour he liked to appoint. The next afternoon brought a reply, and that same evening Miss Madden went to Herne Hill. As a result of what passed there, a day or two saw the beginning of the long-contemplated removal to Clevedon. Widdowson found a lodging in the neighbourhood of his old home; he had engaged never to cross the bounds of Somerset until he received his wife's permission.

As soon as this compact was established Monica wrote to Miss Nunn. A short submissive letter. 'I am about to leave London, and before I go I very much wish to see you. Will you allow me to call at some hour when I could speak to you in private? There is something I must make known to you, and I cannot write it.' After a day's interval came the reply, which was still briefer. Miss Nunn would be at home at half-past eight this or the next evening.

Monica's announcement that she must go out alone after nightfall alarmed her sisters. When told that her visit was to Rhoda Nunn they were somewhat relieved, but Alice begged to be permitted to accompany her.

'It will be lost trouble,' Monica declared. 'More likely than not there is a spy waiting to follow me wherever I go. Your assurance that I really went to Miss Barfoot's won't be needed.'

When the others still opposed her purpose she passed from irony into anger.

'Have you undertaken to save him the expense of private detectives? Have you promised never to let me go out of your sight?'

'Certainly I have not,' said Alice.

'Nor I, dear,' protested Virginia. 'He has never asked anything of the kind.'

'Then you may be sure that the spies are still watching me. Let them have something to do, poor creatures. I shall go alone, so you needn't say any more.'

She took train to York Road Station, and thence, as the night was fine, walked to Chelsea. This semblance of freedom, together with the sense of having taken a courageous resolve, raised her spirits. She hoped that a detective might be tracking her; the futility of such measures afforded her a contemptuous satisfaction. Not to arrive before the appointed hour she loitered on Chelsea Embankment, and it gave her pleasure to reflect that in doing this she was outraging the proprieties. Her mind was in a strange tumult of rebellious and distrustful thought. She had determined on making a confession to Rhoda; but would she benefit by it? Was Rhoda generous enough to appreciate her motives? It did not matter much. She would have discharged a duty at the expense of such shame, and this fact alone might strengthen her to face the miseries beyond.

## CHAPTER XXIX - CONFESSION AND COUNSEL

As she stood at Miss Barfoot's door he heart quailed. To the servant who opened she could only speak Miss Nunn's name; fortunately instructions had been given, and she was straightway led to the library. Here she waited for nearly five minutes. Was Rhoda doing this on purpose? Her face, when at length she entered, made it seem probable', a cold dignity, only not offensive haughtiness, appeared in her bearing. She did not offer to shake hands, and used no form of civility beyond requesting her visitor to be seated.

'I am going away,' Monica began, when silence compelled her to speak.

'Yes, so you told me.'

'I can see that you can't understand why I have come.'

'Your note only said that you wished to see me.'

Their eyes met, and Monica knew in the moment that succeeded that she was being examined from head to foot. It seemed to her that she had undertaken something beyond her strength; her impulse was to invent a subject of brief conversation and escape into the darkness. But Miss Nunn spoke again.

'Is it possible that I can be of any service to you?'

'Yes. You might be. But—I find it is very difficult to say what I—'

Rhoda waited, offering no help whatever, not even that of a look expressing interest.

'Will you tell me, Miss Nunn, why you behave so coldly to me?'

'Surely that doesn't need any explanation, Mrs. Widdowson?'

'You mean that you believe everything Mr. Widdowson has said?'

'Mr. Widdowson has said nothing to me. But I have seen your sister, and there seemed no reason to doubt what she told me.'

'She couldn't tell you the truth, because she doesn't know it.'

'I presume she at least told no untruth.'

'What did Virginia say? I think I have a right to ask that.'

Rhoda appeared to doubt it. She turned her eyes to the nearest bookcase, and for a moment reflected.

'Your affairs don't really concern me, Mrs. Widdowson,' she said at length. 'They have been forced upon my attention, and perhaps I regard them from a wrong point of view. Unless you have come to defend yourself against a false accusation, is there any profit in our talking of these things?'

'I *have* come for that.'

'Then I am not so unjust as to refuse to hear you.'

'My name has been spoken of together with Mr. Barfoot's. This is wrong. It began from a mistake.'

Monica could not shape her phrases. Hastening to utter the statement that would relieve her from Miss Nunn's personal displeasure, she used the first simple words that rose to her lips.

'When I went to Bayswater that day I had no thought of seeing Mr. Barfoot. I wished to see someone else.'

The listener manifested more attention. She could not mistake the signs of sincerity in Monica's look and speech.

'Some one,' she asked coldly, 'who was living with Mr. Barfoot?'

'No. Some one in the same building; in another flat. When I knocked at Mr. Barfoot's door, I knew—or I felt sure—no one would answer. I knew Mr. Barfoot was going away that day—going into Cumberland.'

Rhoda's look was fixed on the speaker's countenance.

'You knew he was going to Cumberland?' she asked in a slow, careful voice.

'He told me so. I met him, quite by chance, the day before.'

'Where did you meet him?'

'Near the flats,' Monica answered, colouring. 'He had just come out—I saw him come out. I had an appointment there that afternoon, and I walked a short way with him, so that he shouldn't—'

Her voice failed. She saw that Rhoda had begun to mistrust her, to think that she was elaborating falsehoods. The burdensome silence was broken by Miss Nunn's saying repellently,—

'I haven't asked for your confidence, remember.'

'No—and if you try to imagine what it means for me to be speaking like this—I am not shameless. I have suffered a great deal before I could bring myself to come here and tell you. If you were more human—if you tried to believe—'

The agitation which found utterance in these words had its effect upon Rhoda. In spite of herself she was touched by the note of womanly distress.

'Why have you come? Why do you tell me this?'

'Because it isn't only that I have been falsely accused. I felt I must tell you that Mr. Barfoot had never-that there was nothing between us. What has he said? How did he meet the charge Mr. Widdowson made against him?'

'Simply by denying it.'

'Hasn't he wished to appeal to *me*?'

'I don't know. I haven't heard of his expressing such a wish. I can't see that you are called upon to take any trouble about Mr. Barfoot. He ought to be able to protect his own reputation.'

'Has he done so?' Monica asked eagerly. 'Did you believe him when he denied—'

'But what does it matter whether I believed him or not?'

'He would think it mattered a great deal.'

'Mr. Barfoot would think so? Why?'

'He told me how much he wished to have your good opinion That is what we used to talk about. I don't know why he took me into his confidence. It happened first of all when we were going by train—the same train, by chance—after we had both been calling here. He asked me many questions about you, and at last said—that he loved you—or something that meant the same.'

Rhoda's eyes had fallen.

'After that,' pursued Monica, 'we several times spoke of you. We did so when we happened to meet near his rooms—as I have told you. He told me he was going to Cumberland with the hope of seeing you; and I understood him to mean he wished to ask you—'

The sudden and great change in Miss Nunn's expression checked the speaker. Scornful austerity had given place to a smile, stern indeed, but exultant. There was warmth upon her face; her lips moved and relaxed; she altered her position in the chair as if inclined for more intimate colloquy.

'There was never more than that between us,' pursued Monica with earnestness. 'My interest in Mr. Barfoot was only on your account. I hoped he might be successful. And I have come to you because I feared you would believe my husband—as I see you have done.'

Rhoda, though she thought it very unlikely that all this should be admirable acting, showed that the explanation had by no means fully satisfied her. Unwilling to put the crucial question, she waited, with gravity which had none of the former harshness, for what else Mrs. Widdowson might choose to say. A look of suffering appeal obliged her to break the silence.

'I am very sorry you have laid this task upon yourself—'

Still Monica looked at her, and at length murmured,—

'If only I could know that I had done any good—'

'But,' said Rhoda, with a searching glance, 'you don't wish me to repeat what you have said?'

'It was only for you. I thought—if you felt able to let Mr. Barfoot know that you had no longer any—'

A flash of stern intelligence shot from the listener's eyes.

'You have seen him then?' she asked with abrupt directness.

'Not since.'

'He has written to you?'—still in the same voice.

'Indeed he has not. Mr. Barfoot never wrote to me. I know nothing whatever about him. No one asked me to come to you—don't think that. No one knows of what I have been telling you.'

Again Rhoda was oppressed by the difficulty of determining how much credit was due to such assertions. Monica understood her look.

'As I have said so much I must tell you all. It would be dreadful after this to go away uncertain whether you believed me or not.'

Human feeling prompted the listener to declare that she had no doubts left. Yet she could not give utterance to the words. She knew they would sound forced, insincere. Shame at inflicting shame caused her to bend her head. Already she had been silent too long.

'I will tell you everything,' Monica was saying in low, tremulous tones. 'If no one else believes me, you at all events shall. I have not done what—'

'No—I can't hear this,' Rhoda broke in, the speaker's voice affecting her too powerfully. 'I will believe you without this.'

Monica broke into sobbing. The strain of this last effort had overtaxed her strength.

'We won't talk any more of it,' said Rhoda, with an endeavour to speak kindly. 'You have done all that could be asked of you. I am grateful to you for coming on my account.

The other controlled herself.

'Will you hear what I have to say, Miss Nunn? Will you hear it as a friend? I want to put myself right in your thoughts. I have told no one else; I shall be easier in mind if you will hear me. My husband will know everything before very long—but perhaps I shall not be alive—'

Something in Miss Nunn's face suggested to Monica that her meaning was understood. Perhaps, notwithstanding her denial, Virginia had told more when she was here than she had permission to make known.

'Why should you wish to tell *me*?' asked Rhoda uneasily.

'Because you are so strong. You will say something that will help me. I know you think that I have committed a sin which it is a shame to speak of. That isn't true. If it were true I should never consent to go and live in my husband's house.'

'You are returning to him?'

'I forgot that I haven't told you.'

And Monica related the agreement that had been arrived at. When she spoke of the time that must elapse before she would make a confession to her husband, it again seemed to her that Miss Nunn understood.

'There is a reason why I consent to be supported by him,' she continued. 'If it were true that I had sinned as he suspects I would rather kill myself than pretend still to be his wife. The day before he had me watched I thought I had left him forever. I thought that if I went back to the house again it would only be to get a few things that I needed. It was some one who lived in the same building as Mr. Barfoot. You have met him—'

She raised her eyes for an instant, and they encountered the listener's. Rhoda was at no loss to supply the omitted name; she saw at once how plain things were becoming.

'He has left England,' pursued Monica in a hurried but clear voice. 'I thought then that I should go away with him. But—it was impossible. I loved him—or thought I loved him; but I was guiltless of anything more than consenting to leave my husband. Will you believe me?'

'Yes, Monica, I do believe you.'

'If you have any doubt, I can show you a letter he wrote to me from abroad, which will prove—'

'I believe you absolutely.'

'But let me tell you more. I must explain how the misunderstanding—'

Rapidly she recounted the incidents of that fatal Saturday afternoon. At the conclusion her self-command was again overcome; she shed tears, and murmured broken entreaties for kindness.

'What shall I do, Miss Nunn? How can I live until—? I know it's only for a short time. My wretched life will soon be at an end—'

'Monica—there is one thing you must remember.'

The voice was so gentle, though firm—so unlike what she had expected to hear—that the sufferer looked up with grateful attention.

'Tell me—give me what help you can.'

'Life seems so bitter to you that you are in despair. Yet isn't it your duty to live as though some hope were before you?'

Monica gazed in uncertainty.

'You mean—' she faltered.

'I think you will understand. I am not speaking of your husband. Whether you have duties to him or not I can't say; that is for your own mind and heart to determine. But isn't it true that your health has a graver importance than if you yourself only were concerned?'

'Yes—you have understood me—'

'Isn't it your duty to remember at every moment that your thoughts, your actions, may affect another life—that by heedlessness, by abandoning yourself to despair, you may be the cause of suffering it was in your power to avert?'

Herself strongly moved, Rhoda had never spoken so impressively, had never given counsel of such earnest significance. She felt her power in quite a new way, without touch of vanity, without posing or any trivial self-consciousness. When she least expected it an opportunity had come for exerting the moral influence on which she prided herself, and which she hoped to make the ennobling element of her life. All the better that the case was one calling for courage, for contempt of vulgar reticences; the combative soul in her became stronger when faced by such conditions. Seeing that her words were not in vain, she came nearer to Monica and spoke yet more kindly.

'Why do you encourage that fear of your life coming to an end?'

'It's more a hope than a fear—at most times. I can see nothing before me. I don't wish to live.'

'That's morbid. It isn't yourself that speaks, but your trouble. You are young and strong, and in a year's time very much of this unhappiness will have passed.'

'I have felt it like a certainty—as if it had been foretold to me—ever since I knew—'

'I think it very likely that young wives have often the same dread. It is physical, Monica, and in your case there is so little relief from dark brooding. But again you must think of your responsibility. You will live, because the poor little life will need your care.'

Monica turned her head away and moaned.

'I shall not love my child.'

'Yes, you will. And that love, that duty, is the life to which you must look forward. You have suffered a great deal, but after such sorrow as yours there comes quietness and resignation. Nature will help you.'

'Oh, if you could give me some of *your* strength! I have never been able to look at life as you do. I should never have married him if I hadn't been tempted by the thoughts of living easily—and I feared so—that I might always be alone—My sisters are so miserable; it terrified me to think of struggling on through life as they do—'

'Your mistake was in looking only at the weak women. You had other examples before you—girls like Miss Vesper and Miss Haven, who live bravely and work hard and are proud of their place in the world. But it's idle to talk of the past, and just as foolish to speak as if you were sorrowing without hope. How old are you, Monica?'

'Two-and-twenty.'

'Well, I am two-and-thirty—and I don't call myself old. When you have reached my age I prophesy you will smile at your despair of ten years ago. At your age one talks so readily of "wrecked life" and "hopeless future," and all that kind of thing. My dear girl, you may live to be one of the most contented and most useful women in England. Your life isn't wrecked at all—nonsense! You have gone through a storm, that's true; but more likely than not you will be all the better for it. Don't talk or think about *sins*; simply make up your mind that you won't be beaten by trials and hardships. There cannot—can there?—be the least doubt as to how you ought to live through these next coming months. Your duty is perfectly clear. Strengthen yourself in body and mind. You *have* a mind, which is more than can be said of a great many women. Think bravely and nobly of yourself! Say to yourself: This and that it is in me to do, and I will do it!'

Monica bent suddenly forward and took one of her friend's hands, and clung to it.

'I knew you could say something that would help me. You have a way of speaking. But it isn't only now. I shall be so far away, and so lonely, all through the dark winter. Will you write to me?'

'Gladly. And tell you all we are doing.'

Rhoda's voice sank for a moment; her eyes wandered; but she recovered the air of confidence.

'We seemed to have lost you; but before long you will be one of us again. I mean, you will be one of the women who are fighting in woman's cause. You will prove by your life that we can be responsible human beings—trustworthy, conscious of purpose.'

'Tell me—do you think it right for me to live with my husband when I can't even regard him as a friend?'

'In that I dare not counsel you. If you *can* think of him as a friend, in time to come, surely it will be better. But here you must guide yourself. You seem to have made a very sensible arrangement, and before long you will see many things more clearly. Try to recover health—health; that is what you need. Drink in the air of the Severn Sea; it will be a cordial to you after this stifling London. Next summer I shall—I hope I shall be at Cheddar, and then I shall come over to Clevedon—and we shall laugh and talk as if we had never known a care.'

'Ah, if that time were come! But you have done me good. I shall try—'

She rose.

'I mustn't forget,' said Rhoda, without looking at her, 'that I owe you thanks. You have done what you felt was right in spite of all it cost you; and you have very greatly relieved my mind. Of course it is all a secret between us. If I make it understood that a doubt is no longer troubling me I shall never say how it was removed.'

'How I wish I had come before.'

'For your own sake, if I have really helped you, I wish you had. But as for anything else—it is much better as it is.'

And Rhoda stood with erect head, smiling her smile of liberty. Monica did not dare to ask any question. She moved up to her friend, holding out both hands timidly.

'Good-bye!'

'Till next summer.'

They embraced, and kissed each other, Monica, when she had withdrawn her hot lips, again murmuring words of gratitude. Then in silence they went together to the house-door, and in silence parted.

# CHAPTER XXX - RETREAT WITH HONOUR

Alighting, on his return to London, at the Savoy Hotel, Barfoot insensibly prolonged his stay there. For the present he had no need of a more private dwelling; he could not see more than a few days ahead; his next decisive step was as uncertain as it had been during the first few months after his coming back from the East.

Meantime, he led a sufficiently agreeable life. The Brissendens were not in town, but his growing intimacy with that family had extended his social outlook, and in a direction correspondent with the change in his own circumstances. He was making friends in the world with which he had a natural affinity; that of wealthy and cultured people who seek no prominence, who shrink from contact with the circles known as 'smart,' who possess their souls in quiet freedom. It is a small class, especially distinguished by the charm of its women. Everard had not adapted himself without difficulty to this new atmosphere; from the first he recognized its soothing and bracing quality, but his experiences had accustomed him to an air more rudely vigorous; it was only after those weeks spent abroad in frequent intercourse with the Brissendens that he came to understand the full extent of his sympathy with the social principles these men and women represented.

In the houses where his welcome was now assured he met some three of four women among whom it would have been difficult to assign the precedence for grace of manner and of mind. These persons were not in declared revolt against the order of things, religious, ethical, or social; that is to say, they did not think it worthwhile to identify themselves with any 'movement'; they were content with the unopposed right of liberal criticism. They lived placidly; refraining from much that the larger world enjoined, but never aggressive. Everard admired them with increasing fervour. With one exception they were married, and suitably married; that member of the charming group who kept her maiden freedom was Agnes Brissenden, and it seemed to Barfoot that, if preference were at all justified, Agnes should receive the palm. His view of her had greatly changed since the early days of their acquaintance; in fact, he perceived that till of late he had not known her at all. His quick assumption that Agnes was at his disposal if he chose to woo her had been mere fatuity; he misread her perfect simplicity of demeanour, the unconstraint of her intellectual sympathies. What might now be her personal attitude to him he felt altogether uncertain, and the result was a genuine humility such as he had never known. Nor was it Agnes only that subdued his masculine self-assertiveness; her sisters in grace had scarcely less dominion over him; and at times, as he sat conversing in one of these drawing-rooms, he broke off to marvel at himself, to appreciate the perfection of his own suavity, the vast advance he had been making in polished humanism.

Towards the end of November he learnt that the Brissendens were at their town house, and a week later he received an invitation to dine with them.

Over his luncheon at the hotel Everard reflected with some gravity, for, if he were not mistaken, the hour had come when he must make up his mind on a point too long in suspense. What was Rhoda Nunn doing? He had heard nothing whatever of her. His cousin Mary wrote to him, whilst he was at Ostend, in a kind and friendly tone, informing him that his simple assurance with regard to a certain disagreeable matter was all she had desired, and hoping that he would come and see her as usual when he found himself in London. But he had kept away from the house in Queen's Road, and it was probable that Mary did not even know his address. As the result of meditation he went to his sitting-room, and with an air of reluctance sat down to write a letter. It was a request that Mary would let him see her somewhere or other—not at her house. Couldn't they have a talk at the place in Great Portland Street, when no one else was there?

Miss Barfoot answered with brief assent. If he liked to come to Great Portland Street at three o'clock on Saturday she would be awaiting him.

On arriving, he inspected the rooms with curiosity.

'I have often wished to come here, Mary. Show me over the premises, will you?'

'That was your purpose—?'

'No, not altogether. But you know how your work interests me.'

Mary complied, and freely answered his various questions. Then they sat down on hard chairs by the fire, and Everard, leaning forward as if to warm his hands, lost no more time in coming to the point.

'I want to hear about Miss Nunn.'

'To hear about her? Pray, what do you wish to hear?'

'Is she well?'

'Very well indeed.'

'I'm very glad of that. Does she ever speak of me?'

'Let me see—I don't think she has referred to you lately.'

Everard looked up.

'Don't let us play a comedy, Mary. I want to talk very seriously. Shall I tell you what happened when I went to Seascale?'

'Ah, you went to Seascale, did you?'

'Didn't you know that?' he asked, unable to decide the question from his cousin's face, which was quite friendly, but inscrutable.

'You went when Miss Nunn was there?'

'Of course. You must have known I was going, when I asked you for her Seascale address.'

'And what did happen? I shall be glad to hear—if you feel at liberty to tell me.'

After a pause, Everard began the narrative. But he did not see fit to give it with all the detail which Mary had learnt from her friend. He spoke of the excursion to Wastwater, and of the subsequent meeting on the shore.

'The end of it was that Miss Nunn consented to marry me.'

'She consented?'

'That comes as a surprise?'

'Please go on.'

'Well, we arranged everything. Rhoda was to stay till the fifteen days were over, and the marriage would have been there. But then arrived your letter, and we quarrelled about it. I wasn't disposed to beg and pray for justice. I told Rhoda that her wish for evidence was an insult, that I would take no step to understand Mrs. Widdowson's behaviour. Rhoda was illogical, I think. She did not refuse to take my word, but she wouldn't marry me until the thing was cleared up. I told her that she must investigate it for herself, and so we parted in no very good temper.'

Miss Barfoot smiled and mused. Her duty, she now felt convinced, was to abstain from any sort of meddling. These two people must settle their affairs as they chose. To interfere was to incur an enormous responsibility. For what she had already done in that way Mary reproved herself.

'Now I want to ask you a plain question,' Everard resumed. 'That letter you wrote to me at Ostend—did it represent Rhoda's mind as well as your own?'

'It's quite impossible for me to say. I didn't know Rhoda's mind.'

'Well, perhaps that is a satisfactory answer. It implies, no doubt, that she was still resolved not to concede the point on which I insisted. But since then? Has she come to a decision?'

It was necessary to prevaricate. Mary knew of the interview between Miss Nunn and Mrs. Widdowson, knew its result; but she would not hint at this.

'I have no means of judging how she regards you, Everard.'

'It is possible she even thinks me a liar?'

'I understood you to say that she never refused to believe you.'

He made a movement of impatience.

'Plainly—you will tell me nothing?'

'I have nothing to tell.'

'Then I suppose I must see Rhoda. Perhaps she will refuse to admit me?'

'I can't say. But if she does her meaning would be unmistakable.'

'Cousin Mary'—he looked at her and laughed—'I think you will be very glad if she *does* refuse.'

She seemed about to reply with some pleasantry, but checked herself, and spoke in a serious voice.

'No. I have no such feeling. Whatever you both agree upon will satisfy me. So come by all means if you wish. I can have nothing to do with it. You had better write and ask her if she will see you, I should think.'

Barfoot rose from his seat, and Mary was glad to be released so quickly from a disagreeable situation. For her own part she had no need to put indiscreet questions; Everard's manner acquainted her quite sufficiently with what was going on in his thoughts. However, he had still something to say.

'You think I have behaved rather badly—let us say, harshly?'

'I am not so foolish as to form any judgment in such a case, cousin Everard.'

'Speaking as a woman, should you say that Rhoda had reason on her side—in the first instance?'

'I think,' Mary replied, with reluctance, but deliberately, 'that she was not unreasonable in wishing to postpone her marriage until she knew what was to be the result of Mrs. Widdowson's indiscreet behaviour.'

'Well, perhaps she was not,' Everard admitted thoughtfully.

'And what *has* been the result?'

'I only know that Mrs. Widdowson has left London and gone to live at a house her husband has taken somewhere in the country.'

'I'm relieved to hear that. By-the-bye, the little lady's "indiscreet behaviour" is as much a mystery to me as ever.'

'And to me,' Mary replied with an air of indifference.

'Well, then, let us take it for granted that I was rather harsh with Rhoda. But suppose she still meets me with the remark that things are just as they were—that nothing has been explained?'

'I can't discuss your relations with Miss Nunn.'

'However, you defend her original action. Be so good as to admit that I can't go to Mrs. Widdowson and request her to publish a statement that I have never—'

'I shall admit nothing,' interrupted Miss Barfoot rather tartily. 'I have advised you to see Miss Nunn—if she is willing. And there's nothing more to be said.'

'Good. I will write to her.'

He did so, in the fewest possible words, and received an answer of equal brevity. In accordance with permission granted, on the Monday evening he found himself once more in his cousin's drawing-room, sitting alone, waiting Miss Nunn's appearance. He wondered how she would present herself, in what costume. Her garb proved to be a plain dress of blue serge, certainly not calculated for effect; but his eye at once distinguished the fact that she had arranged her hair as she wore it when he first knew her, a fashion subsequently abandoned for one that he thought more becoming.

They shook hands. Externally Barfoot was the more agitated, and his embarrassment appeared in the awkward words with which he began.

'I had made up my mind never to come until you let me know that I was tried and acquitted But after all it is better to have reason on one's side.'

'Much better,' replied Rhoda, with a smile which emphasized her ambiguity.

She sat down, and he followed her example. Their relative positions called to mind many a conversation they had held in this room. Barfoot—he wore evening-dress—settled in the comfortable chair as though he were an ordinary guest.

'I suppose you would never have written to me?'

'Never,' she answered quietly.

'Because you are too proud, or because the mystery is still a mystery?'

'There is no longer any mystery.'

Everard made a movement of surprise.

'Indeed? You have discovered what it all meant?'

'Yes, I know what it all meant.'

'Can you gratify my not unnatural curiosity?'

'I can say nothing about it, except that I know how the misunderstanding arose.'

Rhoda was betraying the effort it had cost her to seem so self-possessed when she entered. Her colour had deepened, and she spoke hurriedly, unevenly.

'And it didn't occur to you that it would be a kindness, not inconsistent with your dignity, to make me in some way acquainted with this fact?'

'I feel no uneasiness on your account.'

Everard laughed.

'Splendidly frank, as of old. You really didn't care in the least how much I suffered?'

'You misunderstand me. I felt sure that you didn't suffer at all.'

'Ah, I see. You imagined me calm in the assurance that I should some day be justified.'

'I had every reason for imagining it,' rejoined Rhoda. 'Other wise, you would have given some sign.'

Of course he had deeply offended her by his persistent silence. He had intended to do so first of all; and afterwards—had thought it might be as well. Now that he had got over the difficulty of the meeting he enjoyed his sense of security. How the interview would end he know not; but on his side there would be nothing hasty, unconsidered, merely emotional. Had Rhoda any new revelation of personality within her resources?—that was the question. If so, he would be pleased to observe it. If not—why, it was only the end to which he had long ago looked forward.

'It was not for me to give any sign,' he remarked.

'Yet you have said that it is well to have reason on one's side.'

Perhaps a softer note allowed itself to be detected in these words. In any case, they were not plainly ironical.

'Admit, then, that an approach was due from me. I have made it. I am here.'

Rhoda said nothing. Yet she had not an air of expectancy. Her eye was grave, rather sad, as though for the moment she had forgotten what was at issue, and had lost herself in remoter thought. Regarding her, Everard felt a nobility in her countenance which amply justified all he had ever felt and said. But was there anything more—any new power?

'So we go back,' he pursued, 'to our day at Wastwater. The perfect day—wasn't it?'

'I shall never wish to forget it,' said Rhoda reflectively.

'And we stand as when we quitted each other that night—do we?'

She glanced at him.

'I think not.'

'Then what is the difference?'

He waited some seconds, and repeated the question before Rhoda answered.

'You are conscious of no difference?' she said.

'Months have lapsed. We are different because we are older. But you speak as if you were conscious of some greater change.'

'Yes, you are changed noticeably. I thought I knew you; perhaps I did. Now I should have to learn you all over again. It is difficult, you see, for me to keep pace with you. Your opportunities are so much wider.'

This was puzzling. Did it signify mere jealousy, or a profounder view of things? Her voice had something even of pathos, as though she uttered a simple thought, without caustic intention.

'I try not to waste my life,' he answered seriously. 'I have made new acquaintances.'

'Will you tell me about them?'

'Tell me first about yourself. You say you would never have written to me. That means, I think, that you never loved me. When you found that I had been wrongly suspected—and you suspected me yourself, say what you will—if you had loved me, you would have asked forgiveness.'

'I have a like reason for doubting *your* love. If you had loved me you could never have waited so long without trying to remove the obstacle that was between us.'

'It was you who put the obstacle there,' said Everard, smiling.

'No. An unlucky chance did that. Or a lucky one. Who knows?'

He began to think: If this woman had enjoyed the social advantages to which Agnes Brissenden and those others were doubtless indebted for so much of their charm, would she not have been their equal, or more? For the first time he compassionated Rhoda. She was brave, and circumstances had not been kind to her. At this moment, was she not contending with herself? Was not her honesty, her dignity, struggling against the impulses of her heart? Rhoda's love had been worth more than his, and it would be her one love in life. A fatuous reflection, perhaps; yet every moment's observation seemed to confirm it.

'Well, now,' he said, 'there's the question which we must decide. If you incline to think that the chance was fortunate—'

She would not speak.

'We must know each other's mind.'

'Ah, that is so difficult!' Rhoda murmured, just raising her hand and letting it fall.

'Yes, unless we give each other help. Let us imagine ourselves back at Seascale, down by the waves. (How cold and grim it must be there to-night!) I repeat what I said then: Rhoda, will you marry me?'

She looked fixedly at him.

'You didn't say that then.'

'What do the words matter?'

'That was not what you said.'

He watched the agitation of her features, until his gaze seemed to compel her to move. She stepped towards the fireplace, and moved a little screen that stood too near the fender.

'Why do you want me to repeat exactly what I said?' Everard asked, rising and following her.

'You speak of the "perfect day." Didn't the day's perfection end before there was any word of marriage?'

He looked at her with surprise. She had spoken without turning her face towards him; it was visible now only by the glow of the fire. Yes, what she said was true, but a truth which he had neither expected nor desired to hear. Had the new revelation prepared itself?

'Who first used the word, Rhoda?'

'Yes; I did.'

There was silence. Rhoda stood unmoving, the fire's glow upon her face, and Barfoot watched her.

'Perhaps,' he said at length, 'I was not quite serious when I—'

She turned sharply upon him, a flash of indignation in her eyes.

'Not quite serious? Yes, I have thought that. And were you quite serious in *anything* you said?'

'I loved you,' he answered curtly, answering her steady look.

'Yet wanted to see whether—'

She could not finish the sentence; her throat quivered.

'I loved you, that's all. And I believe I still love you.'

Rhoda turned to the fire again.

'Will you marry me?' he asked, moving a step nearer.

'I think you are "not quite serious".'

'I have asked you twice. I ask for the third time.'

'I won't marry you with the forms of marriage,' Rhoda answered in an abrupt, harsh tone.

'Now it is you who play with a serious matter.'

'You said we had both changed. I see now that our "perfect day" was marred by my weakness at the end. If you wish to go back in imagination to that summer night, restore everything, only let *me* be what I now am.'

Everard shook his head.

'Impossible. It must be then or now for both of us.'

'Legal marriage,' she said, glancing at him, 'has acquired some new sanction for you since then?'

'On the whole, perhaps it has.'

'Naturally. But I shall never marry, so we will speak no more of it.'

As if finally dismissing the subject she walked to the opposite side of the hearth, and there turned towards her companion with a cold smile.

'In other words, then, you have ceased to love me?'

'Yes, I no longer love you.'

'Yet, if I had been willing to revive that fantastic idealism—as you thought it—'

She interrupted him sternly.

'What *was* it?'

'Oh, a kind of idealism undoubtedly. I was so bent on making sure that you loved me.'

She laughed.

'After all, the perfection of our day was half make-believe. You never loved me with entire sincerity. And you will never love any woman—even as well as you loved me.'

'Upon my soul, I believe it, Rhoda. And even now—'

'And even now it is just possible for us to say goodbye with something like friendliness. But not if you talk longer. Don't let us spoil it; things are so straight—and clear—'

A threatened sob made her break off, but she recovered herself and offered him her hand.

He walked all the way back to his hotel, and the cold, clammy night restored his equanimity. A fortnight later, sending a Christmas present, with greetings, to Mr. and Mrs. Micklethwaite, he wrote thus—

'I am about to do my duty—as you put it—that is, to marry. The name of my future wife is Miss Agnes Brissenden. It will be in March,

I think. But I shall see you before then, and give you a fuller account of myself.'

# CHAPTER XXXI - A NEW BEGINNING

Widdowson tried two or three lodgings; he settled at length in a small house at Hampstead; occupying two plain rooms. Here, at long intervals, his friend Newdick came to see him, but no one else. He had brought with him a selection of solid books from his library, and over these the greater part of each day was spent. Not that he studied with any zeal; reading, and of a kind that demanded close attention, was his only resource against melancholia; he knew not how else to occupy himself. Adam Smith's classical work, perused with laborious thoroughness, gave him employment for a couple of months; subsequently he plodded through all the volumes of Hallam.

His landlady, and the neighbours who were at leisure to observe him when he went out for his two hours' walk in the afternoon, took him for an old gentleman of sixty-five or so. He no longer held himself upright, and when out of doors seldom raised his eyes from the ground; grey streaks had begun to brindle his hair; his face grew yellower and more deeply furrowed. Of his personal appearance, even of cleanliness, he became neglectful, and occasionally it happened that he lay in bed all through the morning, reading, dozing, or in a state of mental vacuity.

It was long since he had seen his relative, the sprightly widow; but he had heard from her. On the point of leaving England for her summer holiday, Mrs. Luke sent him a few lines, urging him, in the language of the world, to live more sensibly, and let his wife 'have her head' now and then; it would be better for both of them. Then followed the time of woe, and for many weeks he gave no thought to Mrs. Luke. But close upon the end of the year he received one day a certain society journal, addressed in a hand he knew to the house at Herne Hill. In it was discoverable, marked with a red pencil, the following paragraph.

'Among the English who this year elected to take their repose and recreation at Trouville there was no more brilliant figure than Mrs. Luke Widdowson. This lady is well known in the *monde* where one never *s'ennuie*; where smart people are gathered together, there is the charming widow sure to be seen. We are able to announce that, before leaving Trouville, Mrs. Widdowson had consented to a private engagement with Capt. William Horrocks—no other, indeed, than "Captain Bill," the universal favourite, so beloved by hostesses as a sure dancing man. By the lamented death of his father, this best of good fellows has now become Sir William, and we understand that his marriage will be celebrated after the proper delays. Our congratulations!'

Subsequently arrived a newspaper with an account of the marriage. Mrs. Luke was now Lady Horrocks: she had the title desired of her heart.

Another two months went by, and there came a letter—readdressed, like the other communications, at the post office—in which the baronet's wife declared herself anxious to hear of her friends. She found they had left Herne Hill; if this letter reached him, would not Edmund come and see her at her house in Wimpole Street?

Misery of solitude, desire for a woman's sympathy and counsel, impelled him to use this opportunity, little as it seemed to promise. He went to Wimpole Street and had a very long private talk with Lady Horrocks, who, in some way he could not understand, had changed from her old self. She began frivolously, but in rather a dull, make-believe way; and when she heard that Widdowson had parted from his wife, when a few vague, miserable words had suggested the domestic drama so familiar to her observation, she at once grew quiet, sober, sympathetic, as if really glad to have something serious to talk about.

'Now look here, Edmund. Tell the whole story from the first. You're the sort of man to make awful blunders in such a case as this. Just tell me all about it. I'm not a bad sort, you know, and I have troubles of my own—I don't mind telling you so much. Women make fools of themselves—well, never mind. Just tell me about the little girl, and see if we can't square things somehow.'

He had a struggle with himself, but at length narrated everything, often interrupted by shrewd questions.

'No one writes to you?' the listener finally inquired.

'I am expecting to hear from them,' was Widdowson's answer, as he sat in the usual position, head hanging forward and hands clasped between his knees.

'To hear what?'

'I think I shall be sent for.'

'Sent for? To make it up?'

'She is going to give birth to a child.'

Lady Horrocks nodded twice thoughtfully, and with a faint smile. 'How did you find this out?'

'I have known it long enough. Her sister Virginia told me before they went away. I had a suspicion all at once, and I forced her to tell me.'

'And if you are sent for shall you go?'

Widdowson seemed to mutter an affirmative, and added,—

'I shall hear what she has to tell me, as she promised.'

'Is it—is it possible—?'

The lady's question remained incomplete. Widdowson, though he understood it, vouchsafed no direct answer. Intense suffering was manifest in his face, and at length he spoke vehemently.

'Whatever she tells me—how can I believe it? When once a woman has lied how can she ever again be believed? I can't be sure of anything.'

'All that fibbing,' remarked Lady Horrocks, 'has an unpleasant look. No denying it. She got entangled somehow. But I think you had better believe that she pulled up just in time.'

'I have no love for her left,' he went on in a despairing voice. 'It all perished in those frightful days. I tried hard to think that I still loved her. I kept writing letters—but they meant nothing—or they only meant that I was driven half crazy by wretchedness. I had rather we lived on as we have been doing. It's miserable enough for me, God knows; but it would be worse to try and behave to her as if I could forget everything. I know her explanation won't satisfy me. Whatever it is I shall still suspect her. I don't know that the child is mine. It may be. Perhaps as it grows up there will be a likeness to help me to make sure. But what a life! Every paltry trifle will make me uneasy; and if I discovered any fresh deceit I should do something terrible. You don't know how near I was—'

He shuddered and hid his face.

'The Othello business won't do,' said Lady Horrocks not unkindly. 'You couldn't have gone on together, of course; you had to part for a time. Well, that's all over; take it as something that couldn't be helped. You were behaving absurdly, you know; I told you plainly; I guessed there'd be trouble. You oughtn't to have married at all, that's the fact; it would be better for most of us if we kept out of it. Some marry for a good reason, some for a bad, and mostly it all comes to the same in the end. But there, never mind. Pull yourself together, dear boy. It's all nonsense about not caring for her. Of course you're eating your heart out for want of her. And I'll tell you what I think: it's very likely Monica was pulled up just in time by discovering—you understand?—that she was more your wife than any one else's. Something tells me that's how it was. Just try to look at it in that way. If the child lives she'll be different. She has sowed her wild oats—why shouldn't a woman as well as a man? Go down to Clevedon and forgive her. You're an honest man, and it isn't every woman—never mind. I could tell you stories about people—but you wouldn't care to hear them. Just take things with a laugh—we *all* have to. Life's as you take it: all gloom or moderately shiny.'

With much more to the same solacing effect. For the time Widdowson was perchance a trifle comforted; at all events, he went away with a sense of gratitude to Lady Horrocks. And when he had left the house he remembered that not even a civil formality with regard to Sir William had fallen from his lips. But Sir William's wife, for whatever reason, had also not once mentioned the baronet's name.

Only a few days passed before Widdowson received the summons he was expecting. It came in the form of a telegram, bidding him hasten to his wife; not a word of news added. At the time of its arrival he was taking his afternoon walk; this delay made it doubtful whether he could get to Paddington by six-twenty, the last train which would enable him to reach Clevedon that night. He managed it, with only two or three minutes to spare.

Not till he was seated in the railway carriage could he fix his thoughts on the end of the journey. An inexpressible repugnance then affected him; he would have welcomed any disaster to the train, any injury which might prevent his going to Monica at such a time. Often, in anticipation, the event which was now come to pass had confused and darkened his mind; he loathed the thought of it. If the child, perhaps already born, were in truth his, it must be very long before he could regard it with a shadow of paternal interest; uncertainty, to which he was condemned, would in all likelihood make it an object of aversion to him as long as he lived.

He was at Bristol by a quarter past nine, and had to change for a slow train, which by ten o'clock brought him to Yatton, the little junction for Clevedon. It was a fine starry night, but extremely cold. For the few minutes of detention he walked restlessly about the platform. His chief emotion was now a fear lest all might not go well with Monica. Whether he could believe what she had to tell him or not, it would be worse if she were to die before he could hear her exculpation. The anguish of remorse would seize upon him.

## CHAPTER XXXI - A NEW BEGINNING

Alone in his compartment, he did not sit down, but stamped backwards and forwards on the floor, and before the train stopped he jumped out. No cab was procurable; he left his bag at the station, and hastened with all speed in the direction that he remembered. But very soon the crossways had confused him. As he met no one whom he could ask to direct him, he had to knock at a door. Streaming with perspiration, he came at length within sight of his own house. A church clock was striking eleven.

Alice and Virginia were both standing in the hall when the door was opened; they beckoned him into a room.

'Is it over?' he asked, staring from one to the other with his dazzled eyes.

'At four this afternoon,' answered Alice, scarce able to articulate. 'A little girl.'

'She had to have chloroform,' said Virginia, who looked a miserable, lifeless object, and shook like one in an ague.

'And all's well?'

'We think so—we hope so,' they stammered together.

Alice added that the doctor was to make another call to-night. They had a good nurse. The infant seemed healthy, but was a very, very little mite, and had only made its voice heard for a few minutes.

'She knows you sent for me?'

'Yes. And we have something to give you. You were to have this as soon as you arrived.'

Miss Madden handed him a sealed envelope; then both the sisters drew away, as if fearing the result of what they had done. Widdowson just glanced at the unaddressed missive and put it into his pocket.

'I must have something to eat,' he said, wiping his forehead. 'When the doctor comes I'll see him.'

This visit took place while he was engaged on his supper. On coming down from the patient the doctor gave him an assurance that things were progressing 'fairly well'; the morning, probably, would enable him to speak with yet more confidence. Widdowson had another brief conversation with the sisters, then bade them good-night, and went to the room that had been prepared for him. As he closed the door he heard a thin, faint wail, and stood listening until it ceased; it came from a room on the floor below.

Having brought himself with an effort to open the envelope he had received, he found several sheets of notepaper, one of them, remarked immediately, in a man's writing. At this he first glanced, and the beginning showed him that it was a love-letter written to Monica. He threw it aside and took up the other sheets, which contained a long communication from his wife; it was dated two months ago. In it Monica recounted to him, with scrupulous truthfulness, the whole story of her relations with Bevis.

'I only make this confession'—so she concluded—'for the sake of the poor child that will soon be born. The child is yours, and ought not to suffer because of what I did. The enclosed letter will prove this to you, if anything can. For myself I ask nothing. I don't think I shall live. If I do I will consent to anything you propose. I only ask you to behave without any pretence; if you cannot forgive me, do not make a show of it. Say what your will is, and that shall be enough'.

He did not go to bed that night. There was a fire in the room, and he kept it alight until daybreak, when he descended softly to the hall and let himself out of the house.

In a fierce wind that swept from the north-west down the foaming Channel, he walked for an hour or two, careless whither the roads directed him. All he desired was to be at a distance from that house, with its hideous silence and the faint cry that could scarcely be called a sound. The necessity of returning, of spending days there, was an Oppression which held him like a nightmare.

Monica's statement he neither believed nor disbelieved; he simply could not make up his mind about it. She had lied to him so resolutely before; was she not capable of elaborate falsehood to save her reputation and protect her child? The letter from Bevis might have been a result of conspiracy between them.

That Bevis was the man against whom his jealousy should have been directed at first astounded him. By now he had come to a full perception of his stupidity in never entertaining such a thought. The revelation was equivalent to a second offence just discovered; for he found it impossible to ignore his long-cherished suspicion of Barfoot, and he even surmised the possibility of Monica's having listened to love-making from that quarter previously to her intimacy with Bevis. He loathed the memory of his life since marriage; and as for pardoning his wife, he could as soon pardon and smile upon the author of that accursed letter from Bordeaux.

But go back to the house he must. By obeying his impulse, and straightway returning to London, he might be the cause of a fatal turn in Monica's illness. Constraint of bare humanity would keep him here until his wife was out of danger. But he could not see her, and as soon as possible he must escape from such unendurable circumstances.

## CHAPTER XXXI - A NEW BEGINNING

Re-entering at half-past eight, he was met by Alice, who seemed to have slept as little as he himself had done. They went into the dining-room.

'She has been inquiring about you,' began Miss Madden timorously.

'How is she?'

'Not worse, I believe. But so very weak. She wishes me to ask you—'

'What?'

His manner did not encourage the poor woman.

'I shall be obliged to tell her something. If I have nothing to say she will fret herself into a dangerous state. She wants to know if you have read her letter, and if—if you will see the child.'

Widdowson turned away and stood irresolute. He felt Miss Madden's hand upon his arm.

'Oh, don't refuse! Let me give her some comfort.'

'It's the child she's anxious about?'

Alice admitted it, looking into her brother-in-law's face with woeful appeal.

'Say I will see it,' he answered, 'and have it brought into some room—then say I *have* seen it.'

'Mayn't I take her a word of forgiveness?'

'Yes, say I forgive her. She doesn't wish me to go to her?'

Alice shook her head.

'Then say I forgive her.'

As he directed so it was done; and in the course of the morning Miss Madden brought word to him that her sister had experienced great relief. She was sleeping.

But the doctor thought it necessary to make two visits before nightfall, and late in the evening he came again. He explained to Widdowson that there were complications, not unlikely to be dangerous, and finally he suggested that, if the morrow brought no decided improvement, a second medical man should be called in to consult. This consultation was held. In the afternoon Virginia came weeping to her brother-in-law, and told him that Monica was delirious. That night the whole household watched. Another day was passed in the gravest anxiety, and at dusk the medical attendant no longer disguised his opinion that Mrs. Widdowson was sinking. She became unconscious soon after, and in the early morning breathed her last.

Widdowson was in the room, and at the end sat by the bedside for an hour. But he did not look upon his wife's face. When it was told him that she had ceased to breathe, he rose and went into his own chamber, death-pale, but tearless.

On the day after the funeral—Monica was buried in the cemetery, which is hard by the old church—Widdowson and the elder sister had a long conversation in private. It related first of all to the motherless baby. Widdowson's desire was that Miss Madden should undertake the care of the child. She and Virginia might live wherever they preferred; their needs would be provided for. Alice had hardly dared to hope for such a proposal—as it concerned the child, that is to say. Gladly she accepted it.

'But there's something I must tell you,' she said, with embarrassed appeal in her wet eyes. 'Poor Virginia wishes to go into an institution.'

Widdowson looked at her, not understanding; whereupon she broke into tears, and made known that her sister was such a slave to strong drink that they both despaired of reformation unless by help of the measure she had indicated. There were people, she had heard, who undertook the care of inebriates.

'You know that we are by no means penniless,' sobbed Alice. 'We can very well bear the expense. But will you assist us to find a suitable place?'

He promised to proceed at once in the matter.

'And when she is cured,' said Miss Madden, 'she shall come and live with me. And when baby is about two years old we will do what we have been purposing for a long time. We will open a school for young children, either here or at Weston. That will afford my poor sister occupation. Indeed, we shall both be better for the exertion of such an undertaking—don't you think so?'

'It would be a wise thing, I have no doubt whatever.'

The large house was to be abandoned, and as much of the furniture as seemed needful transported to a smaller dwelling in another part of Clevedon. For Alice resolved to stay here in spite of painful associations. She loved the place, and looked forward with quiet joy to the life that was prepared for her. Widdowson's books would go back to London; not to the Hampstead lodgings, however. Fearful of solitude, he proposed to his friend Newdick that they should live together, he, as a man of substance, bearing the larger share of the expense. And this plan also came into execution.

Three months went by, and on a day of summer, when the wooded hills and green lanes and rich meadows of Clevedon looked their best, when the Channel was still and blue, and the Welsh mountains loomed through a sunny haze, Rhoda Nunn came over from the Mendips to see

Miss Madden. It could not be a gladsome meeting, but Rhoda was bright and natural, and her talk as inspiriting as ever. She took the baby in her arms, and walked about with it for a long time in the garden, often murmuring, 'Poor little child! Dear little child!' There had been doubt whether it would live, but the summer seemed to be fortifying its health. Alice, it was plain, had found her vocation; she looked better than at any time since Rhoda had known her. Her complexion was losing its muddiness and spottiness; her step had become light and brisk.

'And where is your sister?' inquired Miss Nunn.

'Staying with friends at present. She will be back before long, I hope. And as soon as baby can walk we are going to think very seriously about the school. You remember?'

'The school? You will really make the attempt?'

'It will be so good for us both. Why, look,' she added laughingly, 'here is one pupil growing for us!'

'Make a brave woman of her,' said Rhoda kindly.

'We will try—ah, we will try! And is your work as successful as ever?'

'More!' replied Rhoda. 'We flourish like the green bay-tree. We shall have to take larger premises. By-the-bye, you must read the paper we are going to publish; the first number will be out in a month, though the name isn't quite decided upon yet. Miss Barfoot was never in such health and spirit—nor I myself. The world is moving!'

Whilst Miss Madden went into the house to prepare hospitalities, Rhoda, still nursing, sat down on a garden bench. She gazed intently at those diminutive features, which were quite placid and relaxing in soft drowsiness. The dark, bright eye was Monica's. And as the baby sank into sleep, Rhoda's vision grew dim; a sigh made her lips quiver, and once more she murmured, 'Poor little child!'

# EVE'S RANSOM

# CHAPTER I

On the station platform at Dudley Port, in the dusk of a February afternoon, half-a-dozen people waited for the train to Birmingham. A south-west wind had loaded the air with moisture, which dripped at moments, thinly and sluggishly, from a featureless sky. The lamps, just lighted, cast upon wet wood and metal a pale yellow shimmer; voices sounded with peculiar clearness; so did the rumble of a porter's barrow laden with luggage. From a foundry hard by came the muffled, rhythmic thunder of mighty blows; this and the long note of an engine-whistle wailing far off seemed to intensify the stillness of the air as gloomy day passed into gloomier night.

In clear daylight the high, uncovered platform would have offered an outlook over the surrounding country, but at this hour no horizon was discernible. Buildings near at hand, rude masses of grimy brick, stood out against a grey confused background; among them rose a turret which vomited crimson flame. This fierce, infernal glare seemed to lack the irradiating quality of earthly fires; with hard, though fluctuating outline, it leapt towards the kindred night, and diffused a blotchy darkness. In the opposite direction, over towards Dudley Town, appeared spots of lurid glow. But on the scarred and barren plain which extends to Birmingham there had settled so thick an obscurity, vapours from above blending with earthly reek, that all tile beacons of fiery toil were wrapped and hidden.

Of the waiting travellers, two kept apart from the rest, pacing this way and that, but independently of each other. They were men of dissimilar appearance; the one comfortably and expensively dressed, his age about fifty, his visage bearing the stamp of commerce; the other, younger by more than twenty years, habited in a way which made it; difficult to ascertain his social standing, and looking about him with eyes suggestive of anything but prudence or content. Now and then they exchanged a glance: he of the high hat and caped ulster betrayed an interest in the younger man, who, in his turn, took occasion to observe the other from a distance, with show of dubious recognition.

The trill of an electric signal, followed by a clanging bell, brought them both to a pause, and they stood only two or three yards apart. Presently a light flashed through the thickening dusk; there was roaring, grinding, creaking and a final yell of brake-tortured wheels. Making at once for the nearest third-class carriage, the man in the seedy overcoat sprang to a place, and threw himself carelessly back; a moment, and he was followed by the second passenger, who seated himself on the opposite side of the compartment. Once more they looked at each other, but without change of countenance.

Tickets were collected, for there would be no stoppage before Birmingham: then the door slammed, and the two men were alone together.

Two or three minutes after the train had started, the elder man leaned forward, moved slightly, and spoke.

"Excuse me, I think your name must be Hilliard."

"What then?" was the brusque reply.

"You don't remember me?"

"Scoundrels are common enough," returned the other, crossing his legs, "but I remember you for all that."

The insult was thrown out with a peculiarly reckless air; it astounded the hearer, who sat for an instant with staring eyes and lips apart; then the blood rushed to his cheeks.

"If I hadn't just about twice your muscle, my lad," he answered angrily, "I'd make you repent that, and be more careful with your tongue in future. Now, mind what you say! We've a quiet quarter of an hour before us, and I might alter my mind."

The young man laughed contemptuously. He was tall, but slightly built, and had delicate hands.

"So you've turned out a blackguard, have you?" pursued his companion, whose name was Dengate. "I heard something about that."

"From whom?"

"You drink, I am told. I suppose that's your condition now."

"Well, no; not just now," answered Hilliard. He spoke the language of an educated man, but with a trace of the Midland accent. Dengate's speech had less refinement.

"What do you mean by your insulting talk, then? I spoke to you civilly."

"And I answered as I thought fit."

The respectable citizen sat with his hands on his knees, and scrutinised the other's sallow features.

## CHAPTER I

"You've been drinking, I can see. I had something to say to you, but I'd better leave it for another time."

Hilliard flashed a look of scorn, and said sternly—

"I am as sober as you are."

"Then just give me civil answers to civil questions."

"Questions? What right have you to question me?"

"It's for your own advantage. You called me scoundrel. What did you mean by that?"

"That's the name I give to fellows who go bankrupt to get rid of their debts."

"Is it!" said Dengate, with a superior smile. "That only shows how little you know of the world, my lad. You got it from your father, I daresay; he had a rough way of talking."

"A disagreeable habit of telling the truth."

"I know all about it. Your father wasn't a man of business, and couldn't see things from a business point of view. Now, what I just want to say to you is this: there's all the difference in the world between commercial failure and rascality. If you go down to Liverpool, and ask men of credit for their opinion about Charles Edward Dengate, you'll have a lesson that would profit you. I can see you're one of the young chaps who think a precious deal of themselves; I'm often coming across them nowadays, and I generally give them a piece of my mind."

Hilliard smiled.

"If you gave them the whole, it would be no great generosity."

"Eh? Yes, I see you've had a glass or two, and it makes you witty. But wait a bit I was devilish near thrashing you a few minutes ago; but I sha'n't do it, say what you like. I don't like vulgar rows."

"No more do I," remarked Hilliard; "and I haven't fought since I was a boy. But for your own satisfaction, I can tell you it's a wise resolve not to interfere with me. The temptation to rid the world of one such man as you might prove too strong."

There was a force of meaning in these words, quietly as they were uttered, which impressed the listener.

"You'll come to a bad end, my lad."

"Hardly. It's unlikely that I shall ever be rich."

"Oh! you're one of that sort, are you? I've come across Socialistic fellows. But look here. I'm talking civilly, and I say again it's for your advantage. I had a respect for your father, and I liked your brother—I'm sorry to hear he's dead."

"Please keep your sorrow to yourself."

"All right, all right! I understand you're a draughtsman at Kenn and Bodditch's?"

"I daresay you are capable of understanding that."

Hilliard planted his elbow in the window of the carriage and propped his cheek on his hand.

"Yes; and a few other things," rejoined the well-dressed man. "How to make money, for instance.—Well, haven't you any insult ready?"

The other looked out at a row of flaring chimneys, which the train was rushing past: he kept silence.

"Go down to Liverpool," pursued Dengate, "and make inquiries about me. You'll find I have as good a reputation as any man living."

He laboured this point. It was evident that he seriously desired to establish his probity and importance in the young man's eyes. Nor did anything in his look or speech conflict with such claims. He had hard, but not disagreeable features, and gave proof of an easy temper.

"Paying one's debts," said Hilliard, "is fatal to reputation."

"You use words you don't understand. There's no such thing as a debt, except what's recognised by the laws."

"I shouldn't wonder if you think of going into Parliament. You are just the man to make laws."

"Well, who knows? What I want you to understand is, that if your father were alive at this moment, I shouldn't admit that he had claim upon me for one penny."

"It was because I understood it already that I called you a scoundrel."

"Now be careful, my lad," exclaimed Dengate, as again he winced under the epithet. "My temper may get the better of me, and I should be sorry for it. I got into this carriage with you (of course I had a first-class ticket) because I wanted to form an opinion of your character. I've been told you drink, and I see that you do, and I'm sorry for it. You'll be losing your place before long, and you'll go down. Now look here; you've called me foul names, and you've done your best to rile me. Now I'm going to make you ashamed of yourself."

Hilliard fixed the speaker with his scornful eyes; the last words had moved him to curiosity.

"I can excuse a good deal in a man with an empty pocket," pursued the other. "I've been there myself; I know how it makes you feel—how much do you earn, by the bye?"

"Mind you own business."

"All right. I suppose it's about two pounds a week. Would you like to know what *my* income is? Well, something like two pounds an hour, reckoning eight hours as the working day. There's a difference, isn't there? It comes of minding my business, you see. You'll never make anything like it; you find it easier to abuse people who work than to work yourself. Now if you go down to Liverpool, and ask how I got to my present position, you'll find it's the result of hard and honest work. Understand that: honest work."

"And forgetting to pay your debts," threw in the young man.

"It's eight years since I owed any man a penny. The people I *did* owe money to were sensible men of business—all except your father, and he never could see things in the right light. I went through the bankruptcy court, and I made arrangements that satisfied my creditors. I should have satisfied your father too, only he died."

"You paid tuppence ha'penny in the pound."

"No, it was five shillings, and my creditors—sensible men of business—were satisfied. Now look here. I owed your father four hundred and thirty-six pounds, but he didn't rank as an ordinary creditor, and if I had paid him after my bankruptcy it would have been just because I felt a respect for him—not because he had any legal claim. I *meant* to pay him—understand that."

Hilliard smiled. Just then a block signal caused the train to slacken speed. Darkness had fallen, and lights glimmered from some cottages by the line.

"You don't believe me," added Dengate.

"I don't."

The prosperous man bit his lower lip, and sat gazing at the lamp in the carriage. The train came to a standstill; there was no sound but the throbbing of the engine.

"Well, listen to me," Dengate resumed. "You're turning out badly, and any money you get you're pretty sure to make a bad use of. But"—he assumed an air of great solemnity—"all the same—now listen——"

"I'm listening."

"Just to show you the kind of a man I am, and to make you feel ashamed of yourself, I'm going to pay you the money."

For a few seconds there was unbroken stillness. The men gazed at each other, Dengate superbly triumphant, Hilliard incredulous but betraying excitement.

"I'm going to pay you four hundred and thirty-six pounds," Dengate repeated. "No less and no more. It isn't a legal debt, so I shall pay no interest. But go with me when we get to Birmingham, and you shall have my cheque for four hundred and thirty-six pounds."

The train began to move on. Hilliard had uncrossed his legs, and sat bending forward, his eyes on vacancy.

"Does that alter your opinion of me?" asked the other.

"I sha'n't believe it till I have cashed the cheque."

"You're one of those young fellows who think so much of themselves they've no good opinion to spare for anyone else. And what's more, I've still half a mind to give you a good thrashing before I give you the cheque. There's just about time, and I shouldn't wonder if it did you good. You want some of the conceit taken out of you, my lad."

Hilliard seemed not to hear this. Again he fixed his eyes on the other's countenance.

"Do you say you are going to pay me four hundred pounds?" he asked slowly.

"Four hundred and thirty-six. You'll go to the devil with it, but that's no business of mine."

"There's just one thing I must tell you. If this is a joke, keep out of my way after you've played it out, that's all."

"It isn't a joke. And one thing I have to tell *you*. I reserve to myself the right of thrashing you, if I feel in the humour for it."

Hilliard gave a laugh, then threw himself back into the corner, and did not speak again until the train pulled up at New Street station.

## CHAPTER II

An hour later he was at Old Square, waiting for the tram to Aston. Huge steam-driven vehicles came and went, whirling about the open space with monitory bell-clang. Amid a press of homeward-going workfolk, Hilliard clambered to a place on the top and lit his pipe. He did not look the same man who had waited gloomily at Dudley Port; his eyes gleamed with life; answering a remark addressed to him by a neighbour on the car, he spoke jovially.

No rain was falling, but the streets shone wet and muddy under lurid lamp-lights. Just above the house-tops appeared the full moon, a reddish disk, blurred athwart floating vapour. The car drove northward, speedily passing from the region of main streets and great edifices into a squalid district of factories and workshops and crowded by-ways. At Aston Church the young man alighted, and walked rapidly for five minutes, till he reached a row of small modern houses. Socially they represented a step or two upwards in the gradation which, at Birmingham, begins with the numbered court and culminates in the mansions of Edgbaston.

He knocked at a door, and was answered by a girl, who nodded recognition.

"Mrs. Hilliard in? Just tell her I'm here."

There was a natural abruptness in his voice, but it had a kindly note, and a pleasant smile accompanied it. After a brief delay he received permission to go upstairs, where the door of a sitting-room stood open. Within was a young woman, slight, pale, and pretty, who showed something of embarrassment, though her face made him welcome.

"I expected you sooner."

"Business kept me back. Well, little girl?"

The table was spread for tea, and at one end of it, on a high chair, sat a child of four years old. Hilliard kissed her, and stroked her curly hair, and talked with playful affection. This little girl was his niece, the child of his elder brother, who had died three years ago. The poorly furnished room and her own attire proved that Mrs. Hilliard had but narrow resources in her widowhood. Nor did she appear a woman of much courage; tears had thinned her cheeks, and her delicate hands had suffered noticeably from unwonted household work.

Hilliard remarked something unusual in her behaviour this evening. She was restless, and kept regarding him askance, as if in apprehension. A letter from her, in which she merely said she wished to speak to him, had summoned him hither from Dudley. As a rule, they saw each other but once a month.

"No bad news, I hope!" he remarked aside to her, as he took his place at the table.

"Oh, no. I'll tell you afterwards."

Very soon after the meal Mrs. Hilliard took the child away and put her to bed. During her absence the visitor sat brooding, a peculiar half-smile on his face. She came back, drew a chair up to the fire, but did not sit down.

"Well, what is it?" asked her brother-in-law, much as he might have spoken to the little girl.

"I have something very serious to talk about, Maurice."

"Have you? All right; go ahead."

"I—I am so very much afraid I shall offend you."

The young man laughed.

"Not very likely. I can take a good deal from you."

She stood with her hands on the back of the chair, and as he looked at her, Hilliard saw her pale cheeks grow warm.

"It'll seem very strange to you, Maurice."

"Nothing will seem strange after an adventure I've had this afternoon. You shall hear about it presently."

"Tell me your story first."

"That's like a woman. All right, I'll tell you. I met that scoundrel Dengate, and—he's paid me the money he owed my father."

"He has *paid* it? Oh! really?"

"See, here's a cheque, and I think it likely I can turn it into cash. The blackguard has been doing well at Liverpool. I'm not quite sure that I understand the reptile, but he seems to have given me this because I abused him. I hurt his vanity, and he couldn't resist the temptation to astonish me. He thinks I shall go about proclaiming him a noble fellow. Four hundred and thirty-six pounds; there it is."

He tossed the piece of paper into the air with boyish glee, and only just caught it as it was fluttering into the fire.

"Oh, be careful!" cried Mrs. Hilliard.

## CHAPTER II

"I told him he was a scoundrel, and he began by threatening to thrash me. I'm very glad he didn't try. It was in the train, and I know very well I should have strangled him. It would have been awkward, you know."

"Oh, Maurice, how *can* you——?"

"Well, here's the money; and half of it is yours."

"Mine? Oh, no! After all you have given me. Besides, I sha'n't want it."

"How's that?"

Their eyes mete Hilliard again saw the flush in her cheeks, and began to guess its explanation. He looked puzzled, interested.

"Do I know him?" was his next inquiry.

"Should you think it very wrong of me?" She moved aside from the line of his gaze. "I couldn't imagine how you would take it."

"It all depends. Who is the man?"

Still shrinking towards a position where Hilliard could not easily observe her, the young widow told her story. She had consented to marry a man of whom her brother-in-law knew little but the name, one Ezra Marr; he was turned forty, a widower without children, and belonged to a class of small employers of labour known in Birmingham as "little masters." The contrast between such a man and Maurice Hilliard's brother was sufficiently pronounced; but the widow nervously did her best to show Ezra Marr in a favourable light.

"And then," she added after a pause, while Hilliard was reflecting, "I couldn't go on being a burden on you. How very few men would have done what you have——"

"Stop a minute. Is *that* the real reason? If so——"

Hurriedly she interposed.

"That was only one of the reasons—only one."

Hilliard knew very well that her marriage had not been entirely successful; it seemed to him very probable that with a husband of the artisan class, a vigorous and go-ahead fellow, she would be better mated than in the former instance. He felt sorry for his little niece, but there again sentiment doubtless conflicted with common-sense. A few more questions, and it became clear to him that he had no ground of resistance.

"Very well. Most likely you are doing a wise thing. And half this money is yours; you'll find it useful."

The discussion of this point was interrupted by a tap at the door. Mrs. Hilliard, after leaving the room for a moment, returned with rosy countenance.

"He is here," she murmured. "I thought I should like you to meet him this evening. Do you mind?"

Mr. Marr entered; a favourable specimen of his kind; strong, comely, frank of look and speech. Hilliard marvelled somewhat at his choice of the frail and timid little widow, and hoped upon marriage would follow no repentance. A friendly conversation between the two men confirmed them in mutual good opinion. At length Mrs. Hilliard spoke of the offer of money made by her brother-in-law.

"I don't feel I've any right to it," she said, after explaining the circumstances. "You know what Maurice has done for me. I've always felt I was robbing him——"

"I wanted to say something about that," put in the bass-voiced Ezra. "I want to tell you, Mr. Hilliard, that you're a man I'm proud to know, and proud to shake hands with. And if my view goes for anything, Emily won't take a penny of what you're offering her. I should think it wrong and mean. It is about time—that's my way of thinking—that you looked after your own interests. Emily has no claim to a share in this money, and what's more, I don't wish her to take it."

"Very well," said Hilliard. "I tell you what we'll do. A couple of hundred pounds shall be put aside for the little girl. You can't make any objection to that."

The mother glanced doubtfully at her future husband, but Marr again spoke with emphasis.

"Yes, I do object. If you don't mind me saying it, I'm quite able to look after the little girl; and the fact is, I want her to grow up looking to me as her father, and getting all she has from me only. Of course, I mean nothing but what's friendly: but there it is; I'd rather Winnie didn't have the money."

This man was in the habit of speaking his mind; Hilliard understood that any insistence would only disturb the harmony of the occasion. He waved a hand, smiled good-naturedly, and said no more.

About nine o'clock he left the house and walked to Aston Church. While he stood there, waiting for the tram, a voice fell upon his ear that caused him to look round. Crouched by the entrance to the churchyard was a beggar in filthy rags, his face hideously bandaged, before him on the pavement a little heap of matchboxes; this creature kept uttering a meaningless sing-song, either idiot jabber, or calculated to excite attention and pity; it sounded something like "A-pah-pahky; pah-pahky; pah"; repeated a score of times, and resumed after a pause. Hilliard gazed and listened, then placed a copper in the wretch's extended palm, and turned away muttering, "What a cursed world!"

## CHAPTER II

He was again on the tram-car before he observed that the full moon, risen into a sky now clear of grosser vapours, gleamed brilliant silver above the mean lights of earth. And round about it, in so vast a circumference that it was only detected by the wandering eye, spread a softly radiant halo. This vision did not long occupy his thoughts, but at intervals he again looked upward, to dream for a moment on the silvery splendour and on that wide halo dim-glimmering athwart the track of stars.

## CHAPTER III

Instead of making for the railway station, to take a train back to Dudley, he crossed from the northern to the southern extremity of the town, and by ten o'clock was in one of the streets which lead out of Moseley Road. Here, at a house such as lodges young men in business, he made inquiry for "Mr. Narramore," and was forthwith admitted.

Robert Narramore, a long-stemmed pipe at his lips, sat by the fireside; on the table lay the materials of a satisfactory supper—a cold fowl, a ham, a Stilton cheese, and a bottle of wine.

"Hollo! You?" he exclaimed, without rising. "I was going to write to you; thanks for saving me the trouble. Have something to eat?"

"Yes, and to drink likewise."

"Do you mind ringing the bell? I believe there's a bottle of Burgundy left. If not, plenty of Bass."

He stretched forth a languid hand, smiling amiably. Narramore was the image of luxurious indolence; he had pleasant features, dark hair inclined to curliness, a well-built frame set off by good tailoring. His income from the commercial house in which he held a post of responsibility would have permitted him to occupy better quarters than these; but here he had lived for ten years, and he preferred a few inconveniences to the trouble of moving. Trouble of any kind was Robert's bugbear. His progress up the commercial ladder seemed due rather to the luck which favours amiable and good-looking young fellows than to any special ability or effort of his own. The very sound of his voice had a drowsiness which soothed—if it did not irritate—the listener.

"Tell them to lay out the truckle-bed," said Hilliard, when he had pulled the bell. "I shall stay here to-night."

"Good!"

Their talk was merely interjectional, until the visitor had begun to appease his hunger and had drawn the cork of a second bottle of bitter ale.

## CHAPTER III

"This is a great day," Hilliard then exclaimed. "I left Dudley this afternoon feeling ready to cut my throat. Now I'm a free man, with the world before me."

"How's that?"

"Emily's going to take a second husband—that's one thing."

"Heaven be praised! Better than one could have looked for."

Hilliard related the circumstances. Then he drew from his pocket an oblong slip of paper, and held it out.

"Dengate?" cried his friend. "How the deuce did you get hold of this?"

Explanation followed. They debated Dengate's character and motives.

"I can understand it," said Narramore. "When I was a boy of twelve I once cheated an apple-woman out of three-halfpence. At the age of sixteen I encountered the old woman again, and felt immense satisfaction in giving her a shilling. But then, you see, I had done with petty cheating; I wished to clear my conscience, and look my fellow-woman in the face."

"That's it, no doubt. He seems to have got some sort of position in Liverpool society, and he didn't like the thought that there was a poor devil at Dudley who went about calling him a scoundrel. By-the-bye, someone told him that I had taken to liquor, and was on my way to destruction generally. I don't know who it could be."

"Oh, we all have candid friends that talk about us.

"It's true I have been drunk now and then of late. There's much to be said for getting drunk."

"Much," assented Narramore, philosophically.

Hilliard went on with his supper; his friend puffed tobacco, and idly regarded the cheque he was still holding.

"And what are you going to do?" he asked at length.

There came no reply, and several minutes passed in silence. Then Hilliard rose from the table, paced the floor once or twice, selected a cigar from a box that caught his eye, and, in cutting off the end, observed quietly—

"I'm going to live."

"Wait a minute. We'll have the table cleared, and a kettle on the fire."

While the servant was busy, Hilliard stood with an elbow on the mantelpiece, thoughtfully smoking his cigar. At Narramore's request, he mixed two tumblers of whisky toddy, then took a draught from his own, and returned to his former position.

"Can't you sit down?" said Narramore.

"No, I can't."

"What a fellow you are! With nerves like yours, I should have been in my grave years ago. You're going to live, eh?"

"Going to be a machine no longer. Can I call myself a man? There's precious little difference between a fellow like me and the damned grinding mechanism that I spend my days in drawing—that roars all day in my ears and deafens me. I'll put an end to that. Here's four hundred pounds. It shall mean four hundred pounds'-worth of life. While this money lasts, I'll feel that I'm a human being."

"Something to be said for that," commented the listener, in his tone of drowsy impartiality.

"I offered Emily half of it. She didn't want to take it, and the man Marr wouldn't let her. I offered to lay it aside for the child, but Marr wouldn't have that either, It's fairly mine."

"Undoubtedly."

"Think! The first time in my life that I've had money on which no one else had a claim. When the poor old father died, Will and I had to go shares in keeping up the home. Our sister couldn't earn anything; she had her work set in attending to her mother. When mother died, and Marian married, it looked as if I had only myself to look after: then came Will's death, and half my income went to keep his wife and child from the workhouse. You know very well I've never grudged it. It's my faith that we do what we do because anything else would be less agreeable. It was more to my liking to live on a pound a week than to see Emily and the little lass suffer want. I've no right to any thanks or praise for it. But the change has come none too soon. There'd have been a paragraph in the Dudley paper some rainy morning."

"Yes, I was rather afraid of that," said Narramore musingly.

He let a minute elapse, whilst his friend paced the room; then added in the same voice:

"We're in luck at the same tune. My uncle Sol was found dead this morning."

"Do you come in for much?"

"We don't know what he's left, but I'm down for a substantial fraction in a will he made three years ago. Nobody knew it, but he's been stark mad for the last six months. He took a bed-room out Bordesley way, in a false name, and stored it with a ton or two of tinned meats and vegetables. There the landlady found him lying dead this morning; she learnt who he was from the papers in his pocket. It's come out that he had made friends with some old boozer of that neighbourhood; he told him that England was on the point of a grand financial smash, and that half the population would die of hunger. To secure himself, he began to lay in the stock of tinned provisions. One can't help laughing, poor old chap! That's the result, you see, of a life spent in sweating for money. As a young man he had hard times, and when his invention succeeded, it put him off balance a bit. I've often thought he had a crazy look in his eye. He may have thrown away a lot of his money in mad tricks: who knows?"

"That's the end the human race will come to," said Hilliard. "It'll be driven mad and killed off by machinery. Before long there'll be machines for washing and dressing people—machines for feeding them—machines for——"

His wrathful imagination led him to grotesque ideas which ended in laughter.

"Well, I have a year or two before me. I'll know what enjoyment means. And afterwards——"

"Yes; what afterwards?"

"I don't know. I may choose to come back; I may prefer to make an end. Impossible to foresee my state of mind after living humanly for a year or two. And what shall *you* do if you come in for a lot of money?"

"It's not likely to be more than a few thousands," replied Narramore. "And the chances are I shall go on in the old way. What's the good of a few thousands? I haven't the energy to go off and enjoy myself in your fashion. One of these days I may think of getting married, and marriage, you know, is devilish expensive. I should like to have three or four thousand a year; you can't start housekeeping on less, if you're not to be bored to death with worries. Perhaps I may get a partnership in our house. I began life in the brass bedstead line, and I may as well stick to brass bedsteads to the end the demand isn't likely to fall off. Please fill my glass again."

Hilliard, the while, had tossed off his second tumbler. He began to talk at random.

"I shall go to London first of all. I may go abroad. Reckon a pound a day. Three hundred and—how many days are there in a year? Three hundred and sixty-five. That doesn't allow me two years. I want two years of life. Half a sovereign a day, then. One can do a good deal with half a sovereign a day—don't you think?"

"Not very much, if you're particular about your wine."

"Wine doesn't matter. Honest ale and Scotch whisky will serve well enough. Understand me; I'm not going in for debauchery, and I'm not going to play the third-rate swell. There's no enjoyment in making a beast of oneself, and none for me in strutting about the streets like an animated figure out of a tailor's window. I want to know the taste of free life, human life. I want to forget that I ever sat at a desk, drawing to scale—drawing damned machines. I want to——"

He checked himself. Narramore looked at him with curiosity.

"It's a queer thing to me, Hilliard," he remarked, when his friend turned away, "that you've kept so clear of women. Now, anyone would think you were just the fellow to get hobbled in that way."

"I daresay," muttered the other. "Yes, it *is* a queer thing. I have been saved, I suppose, by the necessity of supporting my relatives. I've seen so much of women suffering from poverty that it has got me into the habit of thinking of them as nothing but burdens to a man."

"As they nearly always are."

"Yes, nearly always."

Narramore pondered with his amiable smile; the other, after a moment's gloom, shook himself free again, and talked with growing exhilaration of the new life that had dawned before him.

# CHAPTER IV

Hilliard's lodgings—they were represented by a single room—commanded a prospect which, to him a weariness and a disgust, would have seemed impressive enough to eyes beholding it for the first time. On the afternoon of his last day at Dudley he stood by the window and looked forth, congratulating himself, with a fierceness of emotion which defied misgiving, that he would gaze no more on this scene of his servitude.

The house was one of a row situated on a terrace, above a muddy declivity marked with footpaths. It looked over a wide expanse of waste ground, covered in places with coarse herbage, but for the most part undulating in bare tracts of slag and cinder. Opposite, some quarter of a mile away, rose a lofty dome-shaped hill, tree-clad from base to summit, and rearing above the bare branches of its topmost trees the ruined keep of Dudley Castle. Along the foot of this hill ran the highway which descends from Dudley town—hidden by rising ground on the left—to the low-lying railway-station; there, beyond, the eye traversed a great plain, its limit the blending of earth and sky in lurid cloud. A ray of yellow sunset touched the height and its crowning ruin; at the zenith shone a space of pure pale blue save for these points of relief the picture was colourless and uniformly sombre. Far and near, innumerable chimneys sent forth fumes of various density broad-flung jets of steam, coldly white against the murky distance; wan smoke from lime-kilns, wafted in long trails; reek of solid blackness from pits and forges, voluming aloft and far-floated by the sluggish wind.

Born at Birmingham, the son of a teacher of drawing, Maurice Hilliard had spent most of his life in the Midland capital; to its grammar school he owed an education just sufficiently prolonged to unfit him for the tasks of an underling, yet not thorough enough to qualify him for professional life. In boyhood he aspired to the career of an artist, but his father, himself the wreck of a would-be painter, rudely discouraged this ambition; by way of compromise between the money-earning craft and the beggarly art, he became a mechanical-draughtsman. Of late years he had developed a strong taste for the study of architecture; much of his leisure was given to this subject, and what money he could spare went in the purchase of books and prints which helped him to extend his architectural knowledge. In moods of hope, he had asked himself whether it might not be possible to escape from bondage to the gods of iron, and earn a living in an architect's office. That desire was now forgotten in his passionate resolve to enjoy liberty without regard for the future.

All his possessions, save the articles of clothing which he would carry with him, were packed in a couple of trunks, to be sent on the morrow to Birmingham, where they would lie in the care of his friend Narramore. Kinsfolk he had none whom he cared to remember, except his sister; she lived at Wolverhampton, a wife and mother, in narrow but not oppressive circumstances, and Hilliard had taken leave of her in a short visit some days ago. He would not wait for the wedding of his sister-in-law enough that she was provided for, and that his conscience would always be at ease on her account.

For he was troubled with a conscience—even with one unusually poignant. An anecdote from his twentieth year depicts this feature of the man. He and Narramore were walking one night in a very poor part of Birmingham, and for some reason they chanced to pause by a shop-window—a small window, lighted with one gas-jet, and laid out with a miserable handful of paltry wares; the shop, however, was newly opened, and showed a pathetic attempt at cleanliness and neatness. The friends asked each other how it could possibly benefit anyone to embark in such a business as that, and laughed over the display. While he was laughing, Hilliard became aware of a woman in the doorway, evidently the shopkeeper; she had heard their remarks and looked distressed. Infinitely keener was the pang which Maurice experienced; he could not forgive himself, kept exclaiming how brutally he had behaved, and sank into gloominess. Not very long after, he took Narramore to walk in the same direction; they came again to the little shop, and Hilliard surprised his companion with a triumphant shout. The window was now laid out in a much more promising way, with goods of modest value. "You remember?" said the young man. "I couldn't rest till I had sent her something. She'll wonder to the end of her life who the money came from. But she's made use of it, poor creature, and it'll bring her luck."

Only the hopeless suppression of natural desires, the conflict through years of ardent youth with sordid circumstances, could have brought him to the pass he had now reached—one of desperation centred in self. Every suggestion of native suavity and prudence was swept away in tumultuous revolt. Another twelvemonth of his slavery and he would have yielded to brutalising influences which rarely relax their hold upon a man. To-day he was prompted by the instinct of flight from peril threatening all that was worthy in him.

Just as the last glimmer of daylight vanished from his room there sounded a knock at the door.

"Your tea's ready, Mr. Hilliard," called a woman's voice.

He took his meals downstairs in the landlady's parlour. Appetite at present lie had none, but the pretence of eating was a way of passing the time; so he descended and sat down at the prepared table.

His wandering eyes fell on one of the ornaments of the room—Mrs. Brewer's album. On first coming to live in the house, two years ago, he had examined this collection of domestic portraits, and subsequently, from time to time, had taken up the album to look at one photograph which interested him. Among an assemblage of types excelling in ugliness of feature and hideousness of costume—types of toil-worn age, of ungainly middle life, and of youth lacking every grace, such as are exhibited in the albums of the poor—there was discoverable one female portrait in which, the longer he gazed at it, Hilliard found an ever-increasing suggestiveness of those qualities he desired in woman. Unclasping the volume, he opened immediately at this familiar face. A month or two had elapsed since he last regarded it, and the countenance took possession of him with the same force as ever.

It was that of a young woman probably past her twentieth year. Unlike her neighbours in the album, she had not bedizened herself before sitting to be portrayed. The abundant hair was parted simply and smoothly from her forehead and tightly plaited behind; she wore a linen collar, and, so far as could be judged from the portion included in the picture, a homely cloth gown. Her features were comely and intelligent, and exhibited a gentleness, almost a meekness of expression which was as far as possible from seeming affected. Whether she smiled or looked sad Hilliard had striven vainly to determine. Her lips appeared to smile, but in so slight a degree that perchance it was merely an effect of natural line; whereas, if the mouth were concealed, a profound melancholy at once ruled the visage.

Who she was Hilliard had no idea. More than once he had been on the point of asking his landlady, but characteristic delicacies restrained him: he feared Mrs. Brewer's mental comment, and dreaded the possible disclosure that he had admired a housemaid or someone of yet lower condition. Nor could he trust his judgment of the face: perhaps it shone only by contrast with so much ugliness on either side of it; perhaps, in the starved condition of his senses, he was ready to find perfection in any female countenance not frankly repulsive.

Yet, no; it was a beautiful face. Beautiful, at all events, in the sense of being deeply interesting, in the strength of its appeal to his emotions. Another man might pass it slightingly; to him it spoke as no other face had ever spoken. It awakened in him a consciousness of profound sympathy.

While he still sat at table his landlady came in. She was a worthy woman of her class, not given to vulgar gossip. Her purpose in entering the room at this moment was to ask Hilliard whether he had a likeness of himself which he could spare her, as a memento.

"I'm sorry I don't possess such a thing," he answered, laughing, surprised that the woman should care enough about him to make the request. "But, talking of photographs, would you tell me who this is?"

The album lay beside him, and a feeling of embarrassment, as he saw Mrs. Brewer's look rest upon it, impelled him to the decisive question.

"That? Oh! that's a friend of my daughter Martha's—Eve Madeley. I'm sure I don't wonder at you noticing her. But it doesn't do her justice; she's better looking than that. It was took better than two years ago—why, just before you came to me, Mr. Hilliard. She was going away—to London."

"Eve Madeley." He repeated the name to himself, and liked it.

"She's had a deal of trouble, poor thing," pursued the landlady. "We was sorry to lose sight of her, but glad, I'm sure, that she went away to do better for herself. She hasn't been home since then, and we don't hear of her coming, and I'm sure nobody can be surprised. But our Martha heard from her not so long ago—why, it was about Christmas-time."

"Is she"—he was about to add, "in service?" but could not voice the words. "She has an engagement in London?"

"Yes; she's a bookkeeper, and earns her pound a week. She was always clever at figures. She got on so well at the school that they wanted her to be a teacher, but she didn't like it. Then Mr. Reckitt, the ironmonger, a friend of her father's, got her to help him with his books and bills of an evening, and when she was seventeen, because his business was growing and he hadn't much of a head for figures himself, he took her regular into the shop. And glad she was to give up the school-teaching, for she could never abear it."

"You say she had a lot of trouble?"

## CHAPTER IV

"Ah, that indeed she had! And all her father's fault. But for him, foolish man, they might have been a well-to-do family. But he's had to suffer for it himself, too. He lives up here on the hill, in a poor cottage, and takes wages as a timekeeper at Robinson's when he ought to have been paying men of his own. The drink—that's what it was. When our Martha first knew them they were living at Walsall, and if it hadn't a' been for Eve they'd have had no home at all. Martha got to know her at the Sunday-school; Eve used to teach a class. That's seven or eight years ago; she was only a girl of sixteen, but she had the ways of a grown-up woman, and very lucky it was for them belonging to her. Often and often they've gone for days with nothing but a dry loaf, and the father spending all he got at the public."

"Was it a large family?" Hilliard inquired.

"Well, let me see; at that time there was Eve's two sisters and her brother. Two other children had died, and the mother was dead, too. I don't know much about *her*, but they say she was a very good sort of woman, and it's likely the eldest girl took after her. A quieter and modester girl than Eve there never was. Our Martha lived with her aunt at Walsall—that's my only sister, and she was bed-rid, poor thing, and had Martha to look after her. And when she died, and Martha came back here to us, the Madeley family came here as well, 'cause the father got some kind of work. But he couldn't keep it, and he went off I don't know where, and Eve had the children to keep and look after. We used to do what we could to help her, but it was a cruel life for a poor thing of her age—just when she ought to have been enjoying her life, as you may say."

Hilliard's interest waxed.

"Then," pursued Mrs. Brewer, "the next sister to Eve, Laura her name was, went to Birmingham, into a sweetstuff shop, and that was the last ever seen or heard of her. She wasn't a girl to be depended upon, and I never thought she'd come to good, and whether she's alive or dead there's no knowing. Eve took it to heart, that she did. And not six months after, the other girl had the 'sipelas, and she died, and just as they was carrying her coffin out of the house, who should come up but her father! He'd been away for nearly two years, just sending a little money now and then, and he didn't even know the girl had been ailing. And when he saw the coffin, it took him so that he fell down just like a dead man. You wouldn't have thought it, but there's no knowing what goes on in people's minds. Well, if you'll believe it, from that day he was so changed we didn't seem to know him. He turned quite religious, and went regular to chapel, and has done ever since; and he wouldn't touch a drop of anything, tempt him who might. It was a case of conversion, if ever there was one.

"So there remained only Eve and her brother?"

"Yes. He was a steady lad, Tom Madeley, and never gave his sister much trouble. He earns his thirty shillings a week now. Well, and soon after she saw her father going on all right, Eve left home. I don't wonder at it; it wasn't to be expected she could forgive him for all the harm and sorrows he'd caused. She went to Birmingham for a few months, and then she came back one day to tell us she'd got a place in London. And she brought that photo to give us to remember her by. But, as I said, it isn't good enough."

"Does she seem to be happier now?"

"She hasn't wrote more than once or twice, but she's doing well, and whatever happens she's not the one to complain. It's a blessing she's always had her health. No doubt she's made friends in London, but we haven't heard about them. Martha was hoping she'd have come for Christmas, but it seems she couldn't get away for long enough from business. I'd tell you her address, but I don't remember it. I've never been in London myself. Martha knows it, of course. She might look in to-night, and if she does I'll ask her."

Hilliard allowed this suggestion to pass without remark. He was not quite sure that he desired to know Miss Madeley's address.

But later in the evening, when, after walking for two or three hours about the cold, dark roads, he came in to have his supper and go to bed, Mrs. Brewer smilingly offered him a scrap of paper.

"There," she said, "that's where she's living. London's a big place, and you mayn't be anywhere near, but if you happened to walk that way, we should take it kindly if you'd just leave word that we're always glad to hear from her, and hope she's well."

With a mixture of reluctance and satisfaction the young man took the paper, glanced at it, and folded it to put in his pocket. Mrs. Brewer was regarding him, and he felt that his silence must seem ungracious.

"I will certainly call and leave your message," he said.

Up in his bed-room lie sat for a long time with the paper lying open before him. And when he slept his rest was troubled with dreams of an anxious search about the highways and byways of London for that half-sad, half-smiling face which had so wrought upon his imagination.

Long before daylight he awoke at the sound of bells, and hootings, and whistlings, which summoned the Dudley workfolk to their labour. For the first time in his life he heard these hideous noises with pleasure: they told him that the day of his escape had come. Unable to lie still, he rose at once, and went out into the chill dawn. Thoughts of Eve Madeley no longer possessed him; a glorious sense of freedom excluded every recollection of his past life, and he wandered aimlessly with a song in his heart.

At breakfast, the sight of Mrs. Brewer's album tempted him to look once more at the portrait, but he did not yield.

"Shall we ever see you again, I wonder?" asked his landlady, when the moment arrived for leave-taking.

"If I am ever again in Dudley, I shall come here," he answered kindly.

But on his way to the station he felt a joyful assurance that fate would have no power to draw him back again into this circle of fiery torments.

# CHAPTER V

Two months later, on a brilliant morning of May, Hilliard again awoke from troubled dreams, but the sounds about him had no association with bygone miseries. From the courtyard upon which his window looked there came a ringing of gay laughter followed by shrill, merry gossip in a foreign tongue. Somewhere in the neighbourhood a church bell was pealing. Presently footsteps hurried along the corridor, and an impatient voice shouted repeatedly, "Alphonse! Alphonse!"

He was in Paris; had been there for six weeks, and now awoke with a sense of loneliness, a desire to be back among his own people.

In London he had spent only a fortnight. It was not a time that he cared to reflect upon. No sooner had he found himself in the metropolis, alone and free, with a pocketful of money, than a delirium possessed him. Every resolution notwithstanding, he yielded to London's grossest lures. All he could remember, was a succession of extravagances, beneath a sunless sky, with chance companions whose faces he had forgotten five minutes after parting with them. Sovereign after sovereign melted out of his hand; the end of the second week found his capital diminished by some five-and-twenty pounds. In an hour of physical and moral nausea, he packed his travelling-bag, journeyed to Newhaven, and as a sort of penance, crossed the Channel by third-class passage. Arrived in Paris, he felt himself secure, and soon recovered sanity.

Thanks to his studious habits, he was equipped with book-French; now, both for economy's sake and for his mental advantage, he struggled with the spoken language, and so far succeeded as to lodge very cheaply in a rather disreputable hotel, and to eat at restaurants where dinner of several courses cost two francs and a half. His life was irreproachable; he studied the Paris of art and history. But perforce he remained companionless, and solitude had begun to weigh upon him.

## CHAPTER V

This morning, whilst he sat over his bowl of coffee and *petit pain*, a certain recollection haunted him persistently. Yesterday, in turning out his pockets, he had come upon a scrap of paper, whereon was written:

"93, Belmont Street, Chalk Farm Road, London, N.W."

This formula it was which now kept running through his mind, like a refrain which will not be dismissed.

He reproached himself for neglect of his promise to Mrs. Brewer. More than that, he charged himself with foolish disregard of a possibility which might have boundless significance for him. Here, it seemed, was sufficient motive for a return to London. The alternative was to wander on, and see more of foreign countries; a tempting suggestion, but marred by the prospect of loneliness. He would go back among his own people and make friends. Without comradeship, liberty had little savour.

Still travelling with as small expense as might be, he reached London in the forenoon, left his luggage at Victoria Station, and, after a meal, betook himself in the northerly direction. It was a rainy and uncomfortable day, but this did not much affect his spirits; he felt like a man new risen from illness, seemed to have cast off something that had threatened his very existence, and marvelled at the state of mind in which it had been possible for him to inhabit London without turning his steps towards the address of Eve Madeley.

He discovered Belmont Street. It consisted of humble houses, and was dreary enough to look upon. As he sought for No. 93, a sudden nervousness attacked him; he became conscious all at once of the strangeness of his position. At this hour it was unlikely that Eve would be at home an inquiry at the house and the leaving of a verbal message would discharge his obligation; but he proposed more than that. It was his resolve to see Eve herself, to behold the face which, in a picture, had grown so familiar to him. Yet till this moment he had overlooked the difficulties of the enterprise. Could he, on the strength of an acquaintance with Mrs. Brewer, claim the friendly regards of this girl who had never heard his name? If he saw her once, on what pretext could he seek for a second meeting?

Possibly he would not desire it. Eve in her own person might disenchant him.

Meanwhile he had discovered the house, and without further debate he knocked. The door was opened by a woman of ordinary type, slatternly, and with suspicious eye.

"Miss Madeley *did* live here," she said, "but she's been gone a month or more."

"Can you tell me where she is living now?"

After a searching look the woman replied that she could not. In the manner of her kind, she was anxious to dismiss the inquirer and get the door shut. Gravely disappointed, Hilliard felt unable to turn away without a further question.

"Perhaps you know where she is, or was, employed?"

But no information whatever was forthcoming. It very rarely is under such circumstances, for a London landlady, compounded in general of craft and caution, tends naturally to reticence on the score of her former lodgers. If she has parted with them on amicable terms, her instinct is to shield them against the menace presumed in every inquiry; if her mood is one of ill-will, she refuses information lest the departed should reap advantage. And then, in the great majority of cases she has really no information to give.

The door closed with that severity of exclusion in which London doors excel, and Hilliard turned despondently away. He was just consoling himself with the thought that Eve would probably, before long, communicate her new address to the friends at Dudley, and by that means he might hear of it, when a dirty-faced little girl, who had stood within earshot while he was talking, and who had followed him to the end of the street, approached him with an abrupt inquiry.

"Was you asking for Miss Madeley, Sir?"

"Yes, I was; do you know anything of her?"

"My mother did washing for her, and when she moved I had to take some things of hers to the new address."

"Then you remember it?"

"It's a goodish way from 'ere, Sir. Shall I go with you?"

Hilliard understood. Like the good Samaritan of old, he took out twopence. The face of the dirty little girl brightened wonderfully.

"Tell me the address; that will be enough."

"Do you know Gower Place, Sir?"

"Somewhere near Gower Street, I suppose?"

His supposition was confirmed, and he learnt the number of the house to which Miss Madeley had transferred herself. In that direction he at once bent his steps.

Gower Place is in the close neighbourhood of Euston Road; Hilliard remembered that he had passed the end of it on his first arrival in London, when he set forth from Euston Station to look for a lodging. It was a mere chance that he had not turned into this very street, instead of going further. Several windows displayed lodging-cards. On the whole, it looked a better locality than Belmont Street. Eve's removal hither might signify an improvement of circumstances.

The house which he sought had a clean doorstep and unusually bright windows. His knock was answered quickly, and by a young, sprightly woman, who smiled upon him.

"I believe Miss Madeley lives here?"

"Yes, she does."

"She is not at home just now?"

"No. She went out after breakfast, and I'm sure I can't say when she'll be back."

Hilliard felt a slight wonder at this uncertainty. The young woman, observing his expression, added with vivacious friendliness:

"Do you want to see her on business?"

"No; a private matter."

This occasioned a smirk.

"Well, she hasn't any regular hours at present. Sometimes she comes to dinner, sometimes she doesn't. Sometimes she comes to tea, but just as often she isn't 'ome till late. P'r'aps you'd like to leave your name?"

"I think I'll call again."

"Did you expect to find her at 'ome now?" asked the young woman, whose curiosity grew more eager as she watched Hilliard's countenance.

"Perhaps," he replied, neglecting the question, "I should find her here to-morrow morning?"

"Well, I can say as someone's going to call, you know."

"Please do so."

Therewith he turned away, anxious to escape a volley of interrogation for which the landlady's tongue was primed.

He walked into Gower Street, and pondered the awkward interview that now lay before him. On his calling to-morrow, Miss Madeley would doubtless come to speak with him at the door; even supposing she had a parlour at her disposal, she was not likely to invite a perfect stranger into the house. How could he make her acquaintance on the doorstep? To be sure, he brought a message, but this commission had been so long delayed that he felt some shame about discharging it. In any case, his delivery of the message would sound odd; there would be embarrassment on both sides.

Why was Eve so uncertain in her comings and goings? Necessity of business, perhaps. Yet he had expected quite the opposite state of things. From Mrs. Brewer's description of the girl's character, he had imagined her leading a life of clockwork regularity. The point was very trivial, but it somehow caused a disturbance of his thoughts, which tended to misgiving.

In the meantime he had to find quarters for himself. Why not seek them in Gower Place?

After ten minutes' sauntering, he retraced his steps, and walked down the side of the street opposite to that on which Eve's lodgings were situated. Nearly over against that particular house was a window with a card. Carelessly he approached the door, and carelessly asked to see the rooms that were to let. They were comfortless, but would suit his purpose for a time. He engaged a sitting-room on the ground-floor, and a bed-room above, and went to fetch his luggage from Victoria Station.

On the steamer last night he had not slept, and now that he was once more housed, an overpowering fatigue constrained him to lie down and close his eyes. Almost immediately lie fell into oblivion, and lay sleeping on the cranky sofa, until the entrance of a girl with tea-things awakened him.

From his parlour window he could very well observe the houses opposite without fear of drawing attention from any one on that side; and so it happened that, without deliberate purpose of espial, he watched the door of Eve Madeley's residence for a long time; till, in fact, he grew weary of the occupation. No one had entered; no one had come forth. At half-past seven he took his hat and left the house.

Scarcely had he closed the door behind him when he became aware that a lightly tripping and rather showily dressed girl, who was coming down the other side of the way, had turned off the pavement and was plying the knocker at the house which interested him. He gazed eagerly. Impossible that a young person of that garb and deportment should be Eve Madeley. Her face was hidden from him, and at this distance he could not have recognised the features, even presuming that his familiarity with the portrait, taken more than two years ago, would enable him to identify Eve when he saw her. The door opened; the girl was admitted. Afraid of being noticed, he walked on.

The distance to the head of the street was not more than thirty yards; there lay Gower Street, on the right hand the Metropolitan station, to the left a long perspective southwards. Delaying in doubt as to his course, Hilliard glanced back. From the house which attracted his eyes he saw come forth the girl who had recently entered, and close following her another young woman. They began to walk sharply towards where he stood.

## CHAPTER V

He did not stir, and the couple drew so near that he could observe their faces. In the second girl he recognised—or believed that he recognised—Eve Madeley.

She wore a costume in decidedly better taste than her companion's; for all that, her appearance struck him as quite unlike that he would have expected Eve Madeley to present. He had thought of her as very plainly, perhaps poorly, clad; but this attire was ornate, and looked rather expensive; it might be in the mode of the new season. In figure, she was altogether a more imposing young woman than he had pictured to himself. His pulses were sensibly quickened as he looked at her.

The examination was of necessity hurried. Walking at a sharp pace, they rapidly came close to where he stood. He drew aside to let them pass, and at that moment caught a few words of their conversation.

"I told you we should be late," exclaimed the unknown girl, in friendly remonstrance.

"What does it matter?" replied Eve—if Eve it were. "I hate standing at the doors. We shall find seats somewhere."

Her gay, careless tones astonished the listener. Involuntarily he began to follow; but at the edge of the pavement in Gower Street they stopped, and by advancing another step or two he distinctly overheard the continuation of their talk.

"The 'bus will take a long time."

"Bother the 'bus!" This was Eve Madeley again—if Eve it could really be. "We'll have a cab. Look, there's a crawler in Euston Road. I've stopped him!"

"I say, Eve, you *are* going it!"

This exclamation from the other girl was the last sentence that fell on Hilliard's ear. They both tripped off towards the cab which Eve's gesture had summoned. He saw them jump in and drive away.

"I say, Eve, you *are* going it!" Why, there his doubt was settled; the name confirmed him in his identification. But he stood motionless with astonishment.

They were going to a theatre, of course. And Eve spoke as if money were of no consequence to her. She had the look, the tones, of one bent on enjoying herself, of one who habitually pursued pleasure, and that in its most urban forms.

Her companion had a voice of thinner quality, of higher note, which proclaimed a subordinate character. It sounded, moreover, with the London accent, while Eve's struck a more familiar note to the man of the Midlands. Eve seemed to be the elder of the two; it could not be thought for a moment that her will was guided by that of the more trivial girl.

Eve Madeley—the meek, the melancholy, the long-suffering, the pious—what did it all mean?

Utterly bewildered, the young man walked on without thought of direction, and rambled dreamily about the streets for an hour or two. He could not make up his mind whether or not to fulfil the promise of calling to see Miss Madeley to-morrow morning. At one moment he regretted having taken lodgings in Gower Place; at another he determined to make use of his advantage, and play the spy upon Eve's movements without scruple. The interest she had hitherto excited in him was faint indeed compared with emotions such as this first glimpse of her had kindled and fanned. A sense of peril warned him to hold aloof; tumult of his senses rendered the warning useless.

At eleven o'clock he was sitting by his bedroom window, in darkness, watching the house across the way.

## CHAPTER VI

It was just upon midnight when Eve returned. She came at a quick walk, and alone; the light of the street-lamps showed her figure distinctly enough to leave the watcher in no doubt. A latchkey admitted her to the house. Presently there appeared a light at an upper window, and a shadow kept moving across the blind. When the light was extinguished Hilliard went to bed, but that night he slept little.

The next morning passed in restless debate with himself. He did not cross the way to call upon Eve: the thought of speaking with her on the doorstep of a lodging-house proved intolerable. All day long he kept his post of observation. Other persons he saw leave and enter the house, but Miss Madeley did not come forth. That he could have missed her seemed impossible, for even while eating his meals he remained by the window. Perchance she had left home very early in the morning, but it was unlikely.

Through the afternoon it rained: the gloomy sky intensified his fatigue and despondence. About six o'clock, exhausted in mind and body, he had allowed his attention to stray, when the sudden clang of a street organ startled him. His eyes turned in the wonted direction—and instantly he sprang up. To clutch his hat, to rush from the room and from the house, occupied but a moment. There, walking away on the other side, was Eve. Her fawn-coloured mantle, her hat with the yellow flowers, were the same as yesterday. The rain had ceased; in the western sky appeared promise of a fair evening.

Hilliard pursued her in a parallel line. At the top of the street she crossed towards him; he let her pass by and followed closely. She entered the booking-office of Gower Street station; he drew as near as possible and heard her ask for a ticket—

"Healtheries; third return."

The slang term for the Health Exhibition at Kensington was familiar to him from the English papers he had seen in Paris. As soon as Eve had passed on he obtained a like ticket and hastened down the steps in pursuit. A minute or two and he was sitting face to face with her in the railway carriage.

He could now observe her at his leisure and compare her features with those represented in the photograph. Mrs. Brewer had said truly that the portrait did not do her justice; he saw the resemblance, yet what a difference between the face he had brooded over at Dudley and that which lived before him! A difference not to be accounted for by mere lapse of time. She could not, he thought, have changed greatly in the last two or three years, for her age at the time of sitting for the photograph must have been at least one-and-twenty. She did not look older than he had expected: it was still a young face, but—and herein he found its strangeness—that of a woman who views life without embarrassment, without anxiety. She sat at her ease, casting careless glances this way and that. When her eyes fell upon him he winced, yet she paid no more heed to him than to the other passengers.

Presently she became lost in thought; her eyes fell. Ah! now the resemblance to the portrait came out more distinctly. Her lips shaped themselves to that expression which he knew so well, the half-smile telling of habitual sadness.

His fixed gaze recalled her to herself, and immediately the countenance changed beyond recognition. Her eyes wandered past him with a look of cold if not defiant reserve; the lips lost all their sweetness. He was chilled with vague distrust, and once again asked himself whether this could be the Eve Madeley whose history he had heard.

Again she fell into abstraction, and some trouble seemed to grow upon her mind. It was difficult now to identify her with the girl who had talked and laughed so gaily last evening. Towards the end of the journey a nervous restlessness began to appear in her looks and movements. Hilliard felt that he had annoyed her by the persistency of his observation, and tried to keep his eyes averted. But no; the disturbance she betrayed was due to some other cause; probably she paid not the least regard to him.

At Earl's Court she alighted hurriedly. By this time Hilliard had begun to feel shame in the ignoble part he was playing, but choice he had none—the girl drew him irresistibly to follow and watch her. Among the crowd entering the Exhibition he could easily keep her in sight without risk of his espial being detected. That Eve had come to keep an appointment with some acquaintance he felt sure, and at any cost he must discover who the person was.

## CHAPTER VI

The event justified him with unexpected suddenness. No sooner had she passed the turnstile than a man stepped forward, saluting her in form. Eve shook hands with him, and they walked on.

Uncontrollable wrath seized on Hilliard and shook him from head to foot. A meeting of this kind was precisely what he had foreseen, and he resented it violently.

Eve's acquaintance had the external attributes of a gentleman. One could not easily imagine him a clerk or a shop-assistant smartened up for the occasion. He was plain of feature, but wore a pleasant, honest look, and his demeanour to the girl showed not only good breeding but unmistakable interest of the warmest kind. His age might perhaps be thirty; he was dressed well, and in all respects conventionally.

In Eve's behaviour there appeared a very noticeable reserve; she rarely turned her face to him while he spoke, and seemed to make only the briefest remarks. Her attention was given to the objects they passed.

Totally unconscious of the scenes through which he was moving, Hilliard tracked the couple for more than an hour. He noticed that the man once took out his watch, and from this trifling incident he sought to derive a hope; perhaps Eve would be quit ere long of the detested companionship. They came at length to where a band was playing, and sat down on chairs; the pursuer succeeded in obtaining a seat behind them, but the clamour of instruments overpowered their voices, or rather the man's voice, for Eve seemed not to speak at all. One moment, when her neighbour's head approached nearer than usual to hers, she drew slightly away.

The music ceased, whereupon Eve's companion again consulted his watch.

"It's a most unfortunate thing." He was audible now. "I can't possibly stay longer."

Eve moved on her chair, as if in readiness to take leave of him, but she did not speak.

"You think it likely you will meet Miss Ringrose?"

Eve answered, but the listener could not catch her words.

"I'm so very sorry. If there had been any——"

The voice sank, and Hilliard could only gather from observance of the man's face that he was excusing himself in fervent tones for the necessity of departure. Then they both rose and walked a few yards together. Finally, with a sense of angry exultation, Hilliard saw them part.

For a little while Eve stood watching the musicians, who were making ready to play a new piece. As soon as the first note sounded she moved slowly, her eyes cast down. With fiercely throbbing heart, thinking and desiring and hoping he knew not what, Hilliard once more followed her. Night had now fallen; the grounds of the Exhibition shone with many-coloured illumination; the throng grew dense. It was both easy and necessary to keep very near to the object of his interest.

There sounded a clinking of plates, cups, and glasses. People were sitting at tables in the open air, supplied with refreshments by the waiters who hurried hither and thither. Eve, after a show of hesitation, took a seat by a little round table which stood apart; her pursuer found a place whence he could keep watch. She gave an order, and presently there was brought to her a glass of wine with a sandwich.

Hilliard called for a bottle of ale: he was consumed with thirst.

"Dare I approach her?" he asked himself. "Is it possible? And, if possible, is it any use?"

The difficulty was to explain his recognition of her. But for that, he might justify himself in addressing her.

She had finished her wine and was looking round. Her glance fell upon him, and for a moment rested. With a courage not his own, Hilliard rose, advanced, and respectfully doffed his hat.

"Miss Madeley——"

The note was half interrogative, but his voice failed before he could add another syllable. Eve drew herself up, rigid in the alarm of female instinct.

"I am a stranger to you," Hilliard managed to say. "But I come from Dudley; I know some of your friends——"

His hurried words fell into coherence. At the name "Dudley" Eve's features relaxed.

"Was it you who called at my lodgings the day before yesterday?"

"I did. Your address was given me by Mrs. Brewer, in whose house I have lived for a long time. She wished me to call and to give you a kind message—to say how glad they would be to hear from you——"

"But you *didn't* leave the message."

The smile put Hilliard at his ease, it was so gentle and friendly.

"I wasn't able to come at the time I mentioned. I should have called to-morrow."

"But how is it that you knew me? I think," she added, without waiting for a reply, "that I have seen you somewhere. But I can't remember where."

## CHAPTER VI

"Perhaps in the train this evening?"

"Yes so it was You knew me then?"

"I thought I did, for I happened to come out from my lodgings at the moment you were leaving yours, just opposite, and we walked almost together to Gower Street station. I must explain that I have taken rooms in Gower Place. I didn't like to speak to you in the street; but now that I have again chanced to see you——"

"I still don't understand," said Eve, who was speaking with the most perfect ease of manner. "I am not the only person living in that house. Why should you take it for granted that I was Miss Madeley?"

Hilliard had not ventured to seat himself; he stood before her, head respectfully bent.

"At Mrs. Brewer's I saw your portrait."

Her eyes fell.

"My portrait. You really could recognise me from that?"

"Oh, readily! Will you allow me to sit down?"

"Of course. I shall be glad to hear the news you have brought. I couldn't imagine who it was had called and wanted to see me. But there's another thing. I didn't think Mrs. Brewer knew my address. I have moved since I wrote to her daughter."

"No; it was the old address she gave me. I ought to have mentioned that: it escaped my mind. First of all I went to Belmont Street."

"Mysteries still!" exclaimed Eve. "The people *there* couldn't know where I had gone to."

"A child who had carried some parcel for you to Gower Place volunteered information."

Outwardly amused, and bearing herself as though no incident could easily disconcert her, Eve did not succeed in suppressing every sign of nervousness. Constrained by his wonder to study her with critical attention, the young man began to feel assured that she was consciously acting a part. That she should be able to carry it off so well, therein lay the marvel. Of course, London had done much for her. Possessing no common gifts, she must have developed remarkably under changed conditions, and must, indeed, have become a very different person from the country girl who toiled to support her drunken father's family. Hilliard remembered the mention of her sister who had gone to Birmingham disappeared; it suggested a characteristic of the Madeley blood, which possibly must be borne in mind if he would interpret Eve.

She rested her arms on the little round table.

"So Mrs. Brewer asked you to come and find me?"

"It was only a suggestion, and I may as well tell you how it came about. I used to have my meals in Mrs. Brewer's parlour, and to amuse myself I looked over her album. There I found your portrait, and—well, it interested me, and I asked the name of the original."

Hilliard was now in command of himself; he spoke with simple directness, as his desires dictated.

"And Mrs. Brewer," said Eve, with averted eyes, "told you about me?"

"She spoke of you as her daughter's friend," was the evasive answer. Eve seemed to accept it as sufficient, and there was a long silence.

"My name is Hilliard," the young man resumed. "I am taking the first holiday, worth speaking of, that I have known for a good many years. At Dudley my business was to make mechanical drawings, and I can't say that I enjoyed the occupation."

"Are you going back to it?"

"Not just yet. I have been in France, and I may go abroad again before long."

"For your pleasure?" Eve asked, with interest.

"To answer 'Yes' wouldn't quite express what I mean. I am learning to live."

She hastily searched his face for the interpretation of these words, then looked away, with grave, thoughtful countenance.

"By good fortune," Hilliard pursued. "I have become possessed of money enough to live upon for a year or two. At the end of it I may find myself in the old position, and have to be a living machine once more. But I shall be able to remember that I was once a man."

Eve regarded him strangely, with wide, in tent eyes, as though his speech had made a peculiar impression upon her.

"Can you see any sense in that?" he asked, smiling.

"Yes. I think I understand you."

She spoke slowly, and Hilliard, watching her, saw in her face more of the expression of her portrait than he had yet discovered. Her soft tone was much more like what he had expected to hear than her utterances hitherto.

"Have you always lived at Dudley?" she asked.

He sketched rapidly the course of his life, without reference to domestic circumstances. Before he had ceased speaking he saw that Eve's look was directed towards something at a distance behind him; she smiled, and at length nodded, in recognition of some person who approached. Then a voice caused him to look round.

## CHAPTER VI

"Oh, there you are! I have been hunting for you ever so long."

As soon as Hilliard saw the speaker, he had no difficulty in remembering her. It was Eve's companion of the day before yesterday, with whom she had started for the theatre. The girl evidently felt some surprise at discovering her friend in conversation with a man she did not know; but Eve was equal to the situation, and spoke calmly.

"This gentleman is from my part of the world—from Dudley. Mr. Hilliard—Miss Ringrose."

Hilliard stood up. Miss Ringrose, after attempting a bow of formal dignity, jerked out her hand, gave a shy little laugh, and said with amusing abruptness—

"Do you really come from Dudley?"

"I do really, Miss Ringrose. Why does it sound strange to you?"

"Oh, I don't mean that it sounds strange." She spoke in a high but not unmusical note, very quickly, and with timid glances to either side of her collocutor. "But Eve—Miss Madeley—gave me the idea that Dudley people must be great, rough, sooty men. Don't laugh at me, please. You know very well, Eve, that you always talk in that way. Of course, I knew that there must be people of a different kind, but—there now, you're making me confused, and I don't know what I meant to say."

She was a thin-faced, but rather pretty girl, with auburn hair. Belonging to a class which, especially in its women, has little intelligence to boast of, she yet redeemed herself from the charge of commonness by a certain vivacity of feature and an agreeable suggestion of good feeling in her would-be frank but nervous manner. Hilliard laughed merrily at the vision in her mind of "great, rough, sooty men."

"I'm sorry to disappoint you, Miss Ringrose."

"No, but really—what sort of a place is Dudley? Is it true that they call it the Black Country?"

"Let us walk about," interposed Eve. "Mr. Hilliard will tell you all he can about the Black Country."

She moved on, and they rambled aimlessly; among cigar-smoking clerks and shopmen, each with the female of his kind in wondrous hat and drapery; among domestic groups from the middle-class suburbs, and from regions of the artisan; among the frankly rowdy and the solemnly superior; here and there a man in evening dress, generally conscious of his white tie and starched shirt, and a sprinkling of unattached young women with roving eyes. Hilliard, excited by the success of his advances, and by companionship after long solitude, became very unlike himself, talking and jesting freely. Most of the conversation passed between him and Miss Ringrose; Eve had fallen into an absent mood, answered carelessly when addressed, laughed without genuine amusement, and sometimes wore the look of trouble which Hilliard had observed whilst in the train.

Before long she declared that it was time to go home.

"What's the hurry?" said her friend. "It's nothing like ten o'clock yet—is it, Mr. Hilliard?"

"I don't wish to stay any longer. Of course you needn't go unless you like, Patty."

Hilliard had counted on travelling back with her; to his great disappointment, Eve answered his request to be allowed to do so with a coldly civil refusal which there was no misunderstanding.

"But I hope you will let me see you again?"

"As you live so near me," she answered, "we are pretty sure to meet. Are you coming or not, Patty?"

"Oh, of course I shall go if you do."

The young man shook hands with them; rather formally with Eve, with Patty Ringrose as cordially as if they were old friends. And then he lost sight of them amid the throng.

# CHAPTER VII

How did Eve Madeley contrive to lead this life of leisure and amusement? The question occupied Hilliard well on into the small hours; he could hit upon no explanation which had the least plausibility.

Was she engaged to be married to the man who met her at the Exhibition? Her behaviour in his company by no means supported such a surmise; yet there must be something more than ordinary acquaintance between the two.

Might not Patty Ringrose be able and willing to solve for him the riddle of Eve's existence? But he had no idea where Patty lived. He recalled her words in Gower Street: "You *are* going it, Eve!" and they stirred miserable doubts; yet something more than mere hope inclined him to believe that the girl's life was innocent. Her look, her talk reassured him; so did her friendship with such a person as the ingenuous Patty. On learning that he dwelt close by her she gave no sign of an uneasy conscience.

In any case, the contrast between her actual life and that suggested by Mrs. Brewer's talk about her was singular enough. It supplied him with a problem of which the interest would not easily be exhausted. But he must pursue the study with due regard to honour and delicacy; he would act the spy no more. As Eve had said, they were pretty sure to meet before long; if his patience failed it was always possible for him to write a letter.

Four days went by and he saw nothing of her. On the fifth, as he was walking homeward in the afternoon, he came face to face with Miss Madeley in Gower Street. She stopped at once, and offered a friendly hand.

"Will you let me walk a little way with you?" he asked.

"Certainly. I'm just going to change a book at Mudie's." She carried a little handbag. "I suppose you have been going about London a great deal? Don't the streets look beautiful at this time of the year?"

"Beautiful? I'm not sure that I see much beauty."

"Oh, don't you? I delight in London. I had dreamt of it all my life before I came here. I always said to myself I should some day live in London."

Her voice to-day had a vibrant quality which seemed to result from some agreeable emotion. Hilliard remarked a gleam in her eyes and a colour in her cheeks which gave her an appearance of better health than a few days ago.

"You never go into the country?" he said, feeling unable to join in her praise of London, though it was intelligible enough to him.

"I go now and then as far as Hampstead Heath," Eve answered with a smile. "If it's fine I shall be there next Sunday with Patty Ringrose."

Hilliard grasped the opportunity. Would she permit him to meet her and Miss Ringrose at Hampstead? Without shadow of constraint or affectation, Eve replied that such a meeting would give her pleasure: she mentioned place and time at which they might conveniently encounter.

He walked with her all the way to the library, and attended her back to Gower Place. The result of this conversation was merely to intensify the conflict of feelings which Eve had excited in him. Her friendliness gave him no genuine satisfaction; her animated mood, in spite of the charm to which he submitted, disturbed him with mistrust. Nothing she said sounded quite sincere, yet it was more difficult than ever to imagine that she played a part quite alien to her disposition.

No word had fallen from her which threw light upon her present circumstances, and he feared to ask any direct question. It had surprised him to learn that she subscribed to Mudie's. The book she brought away with her was a newly published novel, and in the few words they exchanged on the subject while standing at the library counter she seemed to him to exhibit a surprising acquaintance with the literature of the day. Of his own shortcomings in this respect he was but too sensible, and he began to feel himself an intellectual inferior, where every probability had prepared him for the reverse.

The next morning he went to Mudie's on his own account, and came away with volumes chosen from those which lay on the counter. He was tired of wandering about the town, and might as well pass his time in reading.

When Sunday came, he sought the appointed spot at Hampstead, and there, after an hour's waiting, met the two friends. Eve was no longer in her vivacious mood; brilliant sunshine, and the breeze upon the heath, had no power to inspirit her; spoke in monosyllables, and behaved with unaccountable reserve. Hilliard had no choice but to converse with Patty, who was as gay and entertaining as ever. In the course of their gossip he learnt that Miss Ringrose was employed at a music-shop, kept by her uncle, where she sold the latest songs and dances, and "tried over" on a piano any unfamiliar piece which a customer might think of purchasing. It was not easy to understand how these two girls came to be so intimate, for they seemed to have very little in common. Compared with Eve Madeley, Patty was an insignificant little person; but of her moral uprightness Hilliard felt only the more assured the longer he talked with her, and this still had a favourable effect upon his estimate of Eve.

Again there passed a few days without event. But about nine o'clock on Wednesday evening, as he sat at home over a book, his landlady entered the room with a surprising announcement.

"There's a young lady wishes to see you, Sir. Miss Ringrose is the name."

Hilliard sprang up.

"Please ask her to come in."

The woman eyed him in a manner he was too excited to understand.

"She would like to speak to you at the door, Sir, if you wouldn't mind going out."

He hastened thither. The front door stood open, and a light from the passage shone on Patty's face. In the girl's look he saw at once that something was wrong.

"Oh, Mr. Hilliard—I didn't know your number—I've been to a lot of houses asking for you——"

"What is it?" he inquired, going out on to the doorstep.

"I called to see Eve, and—I don't know what it meant, but she's gone away. The landlady says she left this morning with her luggage—went away for good. And it's so strange that she hasn't let me know anything. I can't understand it. I wanted to ask if you know——"

Hilliard stared at the house opposite.

"I? I know nothing whatever about it. Come in and tell me——"

"If you wouldn't mind coming out——"

"Yes, yes. One moment; I'll get my hat."

He rejoined the girl, and they turned in the direction of Euston Square, where people were few.

"I couldn't help coming to see you, Mr. Hilliard," said Patty, whose manner indicated the gravest concern. "It has put me in such a fright. I haven't seen her since Sunday. I came to-night, as soon as I could get away from the shop, because I didn't feel easy in my mind about her."

"Why did you feel anxious? What has been going on?"

He search her face. Patty turned away, kept silence for a moment, al at length, with one of her wonted outbursts of confidence, said nervously:

"It's something I can't explain. But as you were a friend of hers——"

A man came by, and Patty broke off.

## CHAPTER VIII

Hilliard waited for her to continue, but Patty kept her eyes down and said no more.

"Did you think," he asked, "that I was likely to be in Miss Madeley's confidence?"

"You've known her a long time, haven't you?"

This proof of reticence, or perhaps of deliberate misleading, on Eve's part astonished Hilliard. He replied evasively that he had very little acquaintance with Miss Madeley's affairs, and added:

"May she not simply have changed her lodgings?"

"Why should she go so suddenly, and without letting me know?"

"What had the landlady to say?"

"She heard her tell the cab to drive to Mudie's—the library, you know."

"Why," said Hilliard; "that meant, perhaps, that she wanted to return a book before leaving London. Is there any chance that she has gone home—to Dudley? Perhaps her father is ill, and she was sent for."

Patty admitted this possibility, but with every sign of doubt.

"The landlady said she had a letter this morning."

"Did she? Then it may have been from Dudley. But you know her so much better than I do. Of course, you mustn't tell me anything you don't feel it right to speak of; still, did it occur to you that I could be of any use?"

"No, I didn't think; I only came because I was so upset when I found her gone. I knew you lived in Gower Place somewhere, and I thought you might have seen her since Sunday."

"I have not. But surely you will hear from her very soon. You may even get a letter tonight, or to-morrow morning."

Patty gave a little spring of hopefulness.

"Yes; a letter might come by the last post to-night. I'll go home at once."

"And I will come with you," said Hilliard. "Then you can tell me whether you have any news."

They turned and walked towards the foot of Hampstead Road, whence they could go by tram-car to Patty's abode in High Street, Camden Town. Supported by the hope of finding a letter when she arrived, Miss Ringrose grew more like herself.

"You must have wondered what *ever* I meant by calling to see you, Mr. Hilliard. I went to five or six houses before I hit on the right one. I do wish now that I'd waited a little, but I'm always doing things in that way and being sorry for them directly after. Eve is my best friend, you know, and that makes me so anxious about her."

"How long have you known her?"

"Oh, ever so long—about a year."

The temptation to make another inquiry was too strong for Hilliard.

"Where has she been employed of late?"

Patty looked up at him with surprise.

"Oh, don't you know? She isn't doing anything now. The people where she was went bankrupt, and she's been out of a place for more than a month."

"Can't find another engagement?"

"She hasn't tried yet. She's taking a holiday. It isn't very nice work, adding up money all day. I'm sure it would drive me out of my senses very soon. I think she might find something better than that."

Miss Ringrose continued to talk of her friend all the way to Camden Town, but the information he gathered did not serve to advance Hilliard in his understanding of Eve's character. That she was keeping back something of grave import the girl had already confessed, and in her chatter she frequently checked herself on the verge of an indiscretion. Hilliard took for granted that the mystery had to do with the man he had seen at Earl's Court. If Eve actually disappeared, he would not scruple to extract from Patty all that she knew; but he must see first whether Eve would communicate with her friend.

In High Street Patty entered a small shop which was on the point of being closed for the night.

Hilliard waited for her a few yards away; on her return he saw at once that she was disappointed.

"There's nothing!"

"It may come in the morning. I should like to know whether you hear or not."

## CHAPTER VIII

"Would this be out of your way?" asked Patty. "I'm generally alone in the shop from half-past one to half-past two. There's very seldom any business going on then."

"Then I will come to-morrow at that time."

"Do, please? If I haven't heard anything I shall be that nervous."

They talked to no purpose for a few minutes, and bade each other good-night.

Next day, at the hour Patty had appointed, Hilliard was again in High Street. As he approached the shop he heard from within the jingle of a piano. A survey through the closed glass door showed him Miss Ringrose playing for her own amusement. He entered, and Patty jumped up with a smile of welcome.

"It's all right! I had a letter this morning. She *has* gone to Dudley."

"Ah! I am glad to hear it. Any reason given?"

"Nothing particular," answered the girl, striking a note on the piano with her forefinger. "She thought she might as well go home for a week or two before taking another place. She has heard of something in Holborn."

"So your alarm was groundless."

"Oh—I didn't really feel alarmed, Mr. Hilliard. You mustn't think that. I often do silly things."

Patty's look and tone were far from reassuring. Evidently she had been relieved from her suspense, but no less plainly did she seek to avoid an explanation of it. Hilliard began to glance about the shop.

"My uncle," resumed Patty, turning with her wonted sprightliness to another subject, "always goes out for an hour or two in the middle of the day to play billiards. I can tell by his face when he comes back whether he's lost or won; he does so take it to heart, silly man! Do *you* play billiards?"

The other shook his head.

"I thought not. You have a serious look."

Hilliard did not relish this compliment. He imagined he had cast away his gloom; he desired to look like the men who take life with easy courage. As he gazed through the glass door into the street, a figure suddenly blocked his prospect, and a face looked in. Then the door opened, and there entered a young man of clerkly appearance, who glanced from Miss Ringrose to her companion with an air of severity. Patty had reddened a little.

"What are *you* doing here at this time of day?" she asked familiarly.

"Oh—business—had to look up a man over here. Thought I'd speak a word as I passed."

Hilliard drew aside.

"Who has opened this new shop opposite?" added the young man, beckoning from the doorway.

A more transparent pretext for drawing Patty away could not have been conceived; but she readily lent herself to it, and followed. The door closed behind them. In a few minutes Patty returned alone, with rosy cheeks and mutinous lips.

"I'm very sorry to have been in the way," said Hilliard, smiling.

"Oh, not you. It's all right. Someone I know. He can be sensible enough when he likes, but sometimes he's such a silly there's no putting up with him. Have you heard the new waltz—the Ballroom Queen?"

She sat down and rattled over this exhilarating masterpiece.

"Thank you," said Hilliard. "You play very cleverly."

"Oh, so can anybody—that's nothing."

"Does Miss Madeley play at all?"

"No. She's always saying she wishes she could but I tell her, what does it matter? She knows no end of things that I don't, and I'd a good deal rather have that."

"She reads a good deal, I suppose?"

"Oh, I should think she does, just! And she can speak French."

"Indeed? How did she learn?"

"At the place where she was bookkeeper there was a young lady from Paris, and they shared lodgings, and Eve learnt it from her. Then her friend went to Paris again, and Eve wanted very much to go with her, but she didn't see how to manage it. Eve," she added, with a laugh, "is always wanting to do something that's impossible."

A week later, Hilliard again called at the music-shop, and talked for half an hour with Miss Ringrose, who had no fresh news from Eve. His visits were repeated at intervals of a few days, and at length, towards the end of June, he learnt that Miss Madeley was about to return to London; she had obtained a new engagement, at the establishment in Holborn of which Patty had spoken.

"And will she come back to her old lodgings?" he inquired.

Patty shook her head.

"She'll stay with me. I wanted her to come here before, but she didn't care about it. Now she's altered her mind, and I'm very glad."

Hilliard hesitated in putting the next question.

"Do you still feel anxious about her?"

The girl met his eyes for an instant.

"No. It's all right now."

## CHAPTER VIII

"There's one thing I should like you to tell me—if you can."

"About Miss Madeley?"

"I don't think there can be any harm in your saying yes or no. Is she engaged to be married?"

Patty replied with a certain eagerness.

"No! Indeed she isn't. And she never has been."

"Thank you." Hilliard gave a sigh of relief. "I'm very glad to know that."

"Of course you are," Patty answered, with a laugh.

As usual, after one of her frank remarks, she turned away and struck chords on the piano. Hilliard meditated the while, until his companion spoke again.

"You'll see her before long, I dare say?"

"Perhaps. I don't know."

"At all events, you'll *want* to see her."

"Most likely."

"Will you promise me something?"

"If it's in my power to keep the promise."

"It's only—I should be so glad if you wouldn't mention anything about my coming to see you that night in Gower Place."

"I won't speak of it."

"Quite sure?"

"You may depend upon me. Would you rather she didn't know that I have seen you at all?"

"Oh, there's no harm in that. I should be sure to let it out. I shall say we met by chance somewhere."

"Very well. I feel tempted to ask a promise iii return."

Patty stood with her hands behind her, eyes wide and lips slightly apart.

"It is this," he continued, lowering his voice. "If ever you should begin to feel anxious again about her will you let me know?"

Her reply was delayed; it came at length in the form of an embarrassed nod. Thereupon Hilliard pressed her hand and departed.

He knew the day on which Eve would arrive in London; from morning to night a feverish unrest drove him about the streets. On the morrow he was scarcely more at ease, and for several days he lived totally without occupation, save in his harassing thoughts. He paced and repaced the length of Holborn, wondering where it was that Eve had found employment; but from Camden Town he held aloof.

One morning there arrived for him a postcard on which was scribbled: "We are going to the Savoy on Saturday night. Gallery." No signature, no address; but of course the writer must be Patty Ringrose. Mentally, he thanked her with much fervour. And on the stated evening, nearly an hour before the opening of the doors, he climbed the stone steps leading to the gallery entrance of the Savoy Theatre. At the summit two or three persons were already waiting—strangers to him. He leaned against the wall, and read an evening paper. At every sound of approaching feet his eyes watched with covert eagerness. Presently he heard a laugh, echoing from below, and recognised Patty's voice; then Miss Ringrose appeared round the winding in the staircase, and was followed by Eve Madeley. Patty glanced up, and smiled consciously as she discovered the face she had expected to see; but Eve remained for some minutes unaware of her acquaintance's proximity. Scrutinising her appearance, as he could at his ease, Hilliard thought she looked far from well: she had a tired, dispirited expression, and paid no heed to the people about her. Her dress was much plainer than that she wore a month ago.

He saw Patty whispering to her companion, and, as a result, Eve's eyes turned in his direction. He met her look, and had no difficulty in making his way down two or three steps, to join her. The reception she gave him was one of civil indifference. Hilliard made no remark on what seemed the chance of their encounter, nor did he speak of her absence from London; they talked, as far as talk was possible under the circumstances, of theatrical and kindred subjects. He could not perceive that the girl was either glad or sorry to have met him again; but by degrees her mood brightened a little, and she exclaimed with pleasure when the opening of the door caused an upward movement.

"You have been away," he said, when they were in their places, he at one side of Eve, Patty on the other.

"Yes. At Dudley."

"Did you see Mrs. Brewer?"

"Several times. She hasn't got another lodger yet, and wishes you would go back again. A most excellent character she gave you."

This sounded satirical.

"I deserved the best she could say of me," Hilliard answered.

Eve glanced at him, smiled doubtfully, and turned to talk with Patty Ringrose. Through the evening there was no further mention of Dudley. Eve could with difficulty be induced to converse at all, and when the entertainment was over she pointedly took leave of him within the theatre. But while shaking hands with Patty, he saw something in that young lady's face which caused him to nod and smile.

# CHAPTER IX

There came an afternoon early in July when Hilliard, tired with a long ramble in search of old City churches—his architectural interests never failed—sought rest and coolness in a Fleet Street tavern of time-honoured name. It was long since he had yielded to any extravagance; to-day his palate demanded wine, and with wine he solaced it. When he went forth again into the roaring highway things glowed before him in a mellow light: the sounds of Fleet Street made music to his ears; he looked with joyous benignity into the faces of men and women, and nowhere discovered a countenance inharmonious with his gallant mood.

No longer weary, he strolled westward, content with the satisfactions of each passing moment. "This," he said to himself, "is the joy of life. Past and future are alike powerless over me; I live in the glorious sunlight of this summer day, under the benediction of a greathearted wine. Noble wine! Friend of the friendless, companion of the solitary, lifter-up of hearts that are oppressed, inspirer of brave thoughts in them that fail beneath the burden of being. Thanks to thee, O priceless wine!"

A bookseller's window arrested him. There, open to the gaze of every pedestrian, stood a volume of which the sight made him thrill with rapture; a finely illustrated folio, a treatise on the Cathedrals of France. Five guineas was the price it bore. A moment's lingering, restrained by some ignoble spirit of thrift which the wine had not utterly overcome, and he entered the shop. He purchased the volume. It would have pleased him to carry it away, but in mere good-nature he allowed the shopman's suggestion to prevail, and gave his address that the great tome might be sent to him.

How cheap it was—five guineas for so much instant delight and such boundless joy of anticipation!

On one of the benches in Trafalgar Square he sat for a long time watching the fountains, and ever and anon letting them lead his eyes upwards to the great snowy clouds that gleamed upon the profound blue. Some ragged children were at play near him; he searched his pocket, collected coppers and small silver, and with a friendly cry of "Holloa, you ragamuffins!" scattered amazement and delight.

St. Martin's Church told him that the hour was turned of six. Then a purpose that had hung vaguely in his mind like a golden mist took form and substance. He set off to walk northward, came out into Holborn, and loitered in the neighbourhood of a certain place of business, which of late he had many times observed. It was not long that he had to wait. Presently there came forth someone whom he knew, and with quick steps he gained her side.

Eve Madeley perceived him without surprise.

"Yes," he said, "I am here again. If it's disagreeable to you, tell me, and I will go my own way at once."

"I have no wish to send you away," she answered, with a smile of self-possession. "But all the same, I think it would be wiser if you did go."

"Ah, then, if you leave me to judge for myself——! You look tired this evening. I have something to say to you; let us turn for a moment up this byway."

"No, let us walk straight on."

"I beg of you!—Now you are kind. I am going to dine at a restaurant. Usually, I eat my dinner at home—a bad dinner and a cheerless room. On such an evening as this I can't go back and appease hunger in that animal way. But when I sit down in the restaurant I shall be alone. It's miserable to see the groups of people enjoying themselves all round and to sit lonely. I can't tell you how long it is since I had a meal in company. Will you come and dine with me?"

"I can't do that."

"Where's the impossibility?"

"I shouldn't like to do it."

"But would it be so very disagreeable to sit and talk? Or, I won't ask you to talk; only to let me talk to you. Give me an hour or two of your time—that's what I ask. It means so much to me, and to you, what does it matter?"

Eve walked on in silence; his entreaties kept pace with her. At length she stopped.

"It's all the same to me—if you wish it——"

"Thank you a thousand times!"

They walked back into Holborn, and Hilliard, talking merely of trifles, led the way to a great hall, where some scores of people were already dining. He selected a nook which gave assurance of privacy, sketched to the waiter a modest but carefully chosen repast, and from his seat on the opposite side of the table laughed silently at Eve as she leaned back on the plush cushions. In no way disconcerted by the show of luxury about her, Eve seemed to be reflecting, not without enjoyment.

"You would rather be here than going home in the Camden Town 'bus?"

"Of course."

"That's what I like in you. You have courage to tell the truth. When you said that you couldn't come, it was what you really thought Now that you have learnt your mistake, you confess it."

"I couldn't have done it if I hadn't made up my mind that it was all the same, whether I came or refused."

"All the same to you. Yes; I'm quite willing that you should think it so. It puts me at my ease. I have nothing to reproach myself with. Ah, but how good it is to sit here and talk!"

"Don't you know anyone else who would come with you? Haven't you made any friends?"

"Not one. You and Miss Ringrose are the only persons I know in London."

"I can't understand why you live in that way."

"How should I make friends—among men? Why, it's harder than making money—which I have never done yet, and never shall, I'm afraid."

Eve averted her eyes, and again seemed to meditate.

"I'll tell you," pursued the young man "how the money came to me that I am living on now. It'll fill up the few moments while we are waiting."

He made of it an entertaining narrative, which he concluded just as the soup was laid before them. Eve listened with frank curiosity, with an amused smile. Then came a lull in the conversation. Hilliard began his dinner with appetite and gusto; the girl, after a few sips, neglected her soup and glanced about the neighboring tables.

"In my position," said Hilliard at length, "what would you have done?"

"It's a difficult thing to put myself in your position."

"Is it, really? Why, then, I will tell you something more of myself. You say that Mrs. Brewer gave me an excellent character?"

"I certainly shouldn't have known you from her description."

Hilliard laughed.

"I seem to you so disreputable?"

"Not exactly that," replied Eve thoughtfully. "But you seem altogether a different person from what you seemed to her."

"Yes, I can understand that. And it gives me an opportunity for saying that you, Miss Madeley, are as different as possible from the idea I formed of you when I heard Mrs. Brewer's description."

"She described me? I should so like to hear what she said."

The changing of plates imposed a brief silence. Hilliard drank a glass of wine and saw that Eve just touched hers with her lips.

"You shall hear that—but not now. I want to enable you to judge me, and if I let you know the facts while dinner goes on it won't be so tiresome as if I began solemnly to tell you my life, as people do in novels."

He erred, if anything, on the side of brevity, but in the succeeding quarter of an hour Eve was able to gather from his careless talk, which sedulously avoided the pathetic note, a fair notion of what his existence had been from boyhood upward. It supplemented the account of himself she had received from him when they met for the first time. As he proceeded she grew more attentive, and occasionally allowed her eyes to encounter his.

"There's only one other person who has heard all this from me," he said at length. "That's a friend of mine at Birmingham—a man called Narramore. When I got Dengate's money I went to Narramore, and I told him what use I was going to make of it."

"That's what you haven't told me," remarked the listener.

"I will, now that you can understand me. I resolved to go right away from all the sights and sounds that I hated, and to live a man's life, for just as long as the money would last."

"What do you mean by a man's life?"

"Why, a life of enjoyment, instead of a life not worthy to be called life at all. This is part of it, this evening. I have had enjoyable hours since I left Dudley, but never yet one like this. And because I owe it to you, I shall remember you with gratitude as long as I remember anything at all."

"That's a mistake," said Eve. "You owe the enjoyment, whatever it is, to your money, not to me."

"You prefer to look at it in that way. Be it so. I had a delightful month in Paris, but I was driven back to England by loneliness. Now, if *you* had been there! If I could have seen you each evening for an hour or two, had dinner with you at the restaurant, talked with you about what I had seen in the day—but that would have been perfection, and I have never hoped for more than moderate, average pleasure—such as ordinary well-to-do men take as their right."

"What did you do in Paris?"

"Saw things I have longed to see any time the last fifteen years or so. Learned to talk a little French. Got to feel a better educated man than I was before."

"Didn't Dudley seem a long way off when you were there?" asked Eve half absently.

"In another planet.—You thought once of going to Paris; Miss Ringrose told me."

Eve knitted her brows, and made no answer.

## CHAPTER X

When fruit had been set before them—and as he was peeling a banana:

"What a vast difference," said Hilliard, "between the life of people who dine, and of those who don't! It isn't the mere pleasure of eating, the quality of the food—though that must have a great influence on mind and character. But to sit for an hour or two each evening in quiet, orderly enjoyment, with graceful things about one, talking of whatever is pleasant—how it civilises! Until three months ago I never dined in my life, and I know well what a change it has made in me."

"I never dined till this evening," said Eve.

"Never? This is the first time you have been at a restaurant?"

"For dinner—yes."

Hilliard heard the avowal with surprise and delight. After all, there could not have been much intimacy between her and the man she met at the Exhibition.

"When I go back to slavery," he continued, "I shall bear it more philosophically. It was making me a brute, but I think there'll be no more danger of that. The memory of civilisation will abide with me. I shall remind myself that I was once a free man, and that will support me."

Eve regarded him with curiosity.

"Is there no choice?" she asked. "While you have money, couldn't you find some better way of earning a living?"

"I have given it a thought now and then, but it's very doubtful. There's only one thing at which I might have done well, and that's architecture. From studying it just for my own pleasure, I believe I know more about architecture than most men who are not in the profession; but it would take a long time before I could earn money by it. I could prepare myself to be an architectural draughtsman, no doubt, and might do as well that way as drawing machinery. But——"

"Then why don't you go to work! It would save you from living in hideous places."

## CHAPTER X

"After all, does it matter much? If I had anything else to gain. Suppose I had any hope of marriage, for instance——"

He said it playfully. Eve turned her eyes away, but gave no other sign of self-consciousness.

"I have no such hope. I have seen too much of marriage in poverty."

"So have I," said his companion, with quiet emphasis.

"And when a man's absolutely sure that he will never have an income of more than a hundred and fifty pounds——"

"It's a crime if he asks a woman to share it," Eve added coldly.

"I agree with you. It's well to understand each other on that point.—Talking of architecture, I bought a grand book this afternoon."

He described the purchase, and mentioned what it cost.

"But at that rate," said Eve, "your days of slavery will come again very soon."

"Oh! it's so rarely that I spend a large sum. On most days I satisfy myself with the feeling of freedom, and live as poorly as ever I did. Still, don't suppose that I am bent on making my money last a very long time. I can imagine myself spending it all in a week or two, and feeling I had its worth. The only question is, how can I get most enjoyment? The very best of a lifetime may come within a single day. Indeed, I believe it very often does."

"I doubt that—at least, I know that it couldn't be so with me."

"Well, what do you aim at?" Hilliard asked disinterestedly.

"Safety," was the prompt reply.

"Safety? From what?"

"From years of struggle to keep myself alive, and a miserable old age."

"Then you might have said—a safety-match."

The jest, and its unexpectedness, struck sudden laughter from Eve. Hilliard joined in her mirth.

After that she suggested, "Hadn't we better go?"

"Yes. Let us walk quietly on. The streets are pleasant after sunset."

On rising, after he had paid the bill, Hilliard chanced to see himself in a mirror. He had flushed cheeks, and his hair was somewhat disorderly. In contrast with Eve's colourless composure, his appearance was decidedly bacchanalian; but the thought merely amused him.

They crossed Holborn, and took their way up Southampton Row, neither speaking until they were within sight of Russell Square.

"I like this part of London," said Hilliard at length, pointing before him. "I often walk about the squares late at night. It's quiet, and the trees make the air taste fresh."

"I did the same, sometimes, when I lived in Gower Place."

"Doesn't it strike you that we are rather like each other in some things?"

"Oh, yes!" Eve replied frankly. "I have noticed that."

"You have? Even in the lives we have led there's a sort of resemblance, isn't there?"

"Yes, I see now that there is."

In Russell Square they turned from the pavement, and walked along the edge of the enclosure.

"I wish Patty had been with us," said Eve all at once. "She would have enjoyed it so thoroughly."

"To be sure she would. Well, we can dine again, and have Patty with us. But, after all, dining in London can't be quite what it is in Paris. I wish you hadn't gone back to work again. Do you know what I should have proposed?"

She glanced inquiringly at him.

"Why shouldn't we all have gone to Paris for a holiday? You and Patty could have lived together, and I should have seen you every day."

Eve laughed.

"Why not? Patty and I have both so much more money than we know what to do with," she answered.

"Money? Oh, what of that! I have money."

She laughed again.

Hilliard was startled.

"You are talking rather wildly. Leaving myself out of the question, what would Mr. Dally say to such a proposal?"

"Who's Mr. Dally?"

"Don't you know? Hasn't Patty told you that she is engaged?"

"Ah! No; she hasn't spoken of it. But I think I must have seen him at the music-shop one day. Is she likely to marry him?"

"It isn't the wisest thing she could do, but that may be the end of it. He's in an auctioneer's office, and may have a pretty good income some day."

A long silence followed. They passed out of Russell into Woburn Square. Night was now darkening the latest tints of the sky, and the lamps shone golden against dusty green. At one of the houses in the narrow square festivities were toward; carriages drew up before the entrance, from which a red carpet was laid down across the pavement; within sounded music.

"Does this kind of thing excite any ambition in you?" Hilliard asked, coming to a pause a few yards away from the carriage which was discharging its occupants.

"Yes, I suppose it does. At all events, it makes me feel discontented."

"I have settled all that with myself. I am content to look on as if it were a play. Those people have an idea of life quite different from mine. I shouldn't enjoy myself among them. You, perhaps, would."

"I might," Eve replied absently. And she turned away to the other side of the square.

"By-the-bye, you *have* a friend in Paris. Do you ever hear from her?"

"She wrote once or twice after she went back; but it has come to an end."

"Still, you might find her again, if you were there."

Eve delayed her reply a little, then spoke impatiently.

"What is the use of setting my thoughts upon such things? Day after day I try to forget what I most wish for. Talk about yourself, and I will listen with pleasure; but never talk about me."

"It's very hard to lay that rule upon me. I want to hear you speak of yourself. As yet, I hardly know you, and I never shall unless you——"

"Why should you know me?" she interrupted, in a voice of irritation.

"Only because I wish it more than anything else, I have wished it from the day when I first saw your portrait."

"Oh! that wretched portrait! I should be sorry if I thought it was at all like me."

"It is both like and unlike," said Hilliard. "What I see of it in your face is the part of you that most pleases me."

"And that isn't my real self at all."

"Perhaps not. And yet, perhaps, you are mistaken. That is what I want to learn. From the portrait, I formed an idea of you. When I met you, it seemed to me that I was hopelessly astray; yet now I don't feel sure of it."

"You would like to know what has changed me from the kind of girl I was at Dudley?"

"*Are* you changed?"

"In some ways, no doubt. You, at all events, seem to think so."

"I can wait. You will tell me all about it some day."

"You mustn't take that for granted. We have made friends in a sort of way just because we happened to come from the same place, and know the same people. But——"

He waited.

"Well, I was going to say that there's no use in our thinking much about each other."

"I don't ask you to think of me. But I shall think a great deal about you for long enough to come."

"That's what I want to prevent."

"Why?"

"Because, in the end, it might be troublesome to me."

Hilliard kept silence awhile, then laughed. When he spoke again, it was of things indifferent natures.

# CHAPTER XI

Laziest of men and worst of correspondents, Robert Narramore had as yet sent no reply to the letters in which Hilliard acquainted him with his adventures in London and abroad; but at the end of July he vouchsafed a perfunctory scrawl. "Too bad not to write before, but I've been floored every evening after business in this furious heat. You may like to hear that my uncle's property didn't make a bad show. I have come in for a round five thousand, and am putting it into brass bedsteads. Sha'n't be able to get away until the end of August. May see you then." Hilliard mused enviously on the brass bedstead business.

On looking in at the Camden Town music-shop about this time he found Patty Ringrose flurried and vexed by an event which disturbed her prospects. Her uncle the shopkeeper, a widower of about fifty, had announced his intention of marrying again, and, worse still, of giving up his business.

"It's the landlady of the public-house where he goes to play billiards," said Patty with scornful mirth; "a great fat woman! Oh! And he's going to turn publican. And my aunt and me will have to look out for ourselves."

This aunt was the shopkeeper's maiden sister who had hitherto kept house for him. "She had been promised an allowance," said Patty, "but a very mean one."

"I don't care much for myself," the girl went on; "there's plenty of shops where I can get an engagement, but of course it won't be the same as here, which has been home for me ever since I was a child. There! the things that men will do! I've told him plain to his face that he ought to be ashamed of himself, and so has aunt. And he *is* ashamed, what's more. Don't you call it disgusting, such a marriage as that?"

Hilliard avoided the delicate question.

"I shouldn't wonder if it hastens another marriage," he said with a smile.

"I know what you mean, but the chances are that marriage won't come off at all. I'm getting tired of men; they're so selfish and unreasonable. Of course I don't mean you, Mr. Hilliard, but—oh! you know what I mean."

"Mr. Dally has fallen under your displeasure?"

"Please don't talk about him. If he thinks he's going to lay down the law to me he'll find his mistake; and it's better he should find it out before it's too late."

They were interrupted by the entrance of Patty's amorous uncle, who returned from his billiards earlier than usual to-day. He scowled at the stranger, but passed into the house without speaking. Hilliard spoke a hurried word or two about Eve and went his way.

Something less than a week after this he chanced to be away from home throughout the whole day, and on returning he was surprised to see a telegram upon his table. It came from Patty Ringrose, and asked him to call at the shop without fail between one and two that day. The hour was now nearly ten; the despatch had arrived at eleven in the morning.

Without a minute's delay he ran out in search of a cab, and was driven to High Street. Here, of course, he found the shop closed, but it was much too early for the household to have retired to rest; risking an indiscretion, he was about to ring the house bell when the door opened, and Patty showed herself.

"Oh, is it *you*, Mr. Hilliard!" she exclaimed, in a flurried voice. "I heard the cab stop, and I thought it might be——You'd better come in—quick!"

He followed her along the passage and into the shop, where one gas-jet was burning low.

"Listen!" she resumed, whispering hurriedly. "If Eve comes—she'll let herself in with the latchkey—you must stand quiet here. I shall turn out the gas, and I'll let you out after she's gone upstairs? Couldn't you come before?"

Hilliard explained, and begged her to tell him what was the matter. But Patty kept him in suspense.

"Uncle won't be in till after twelve, so there's no fear. Aunt has gone to bed—she's upset with quarrelling about this marriage. Mind! You won't stir if Eve comes in. Don't talk loud; I must keep listening for the door."

"But what is it? Where is Eve?"

# CHAPTER XI

"I don't know. She didn't come home till very late last night, and I don't know where she was. You remember what you asked me to promise?"

"To let me know if you were anxious about her."

"Yes, and I am. She's in danger I only hope——"

"What?"

"I don't like to tell you all I know. It doesn't seem right. But I'm so afraid for Eve."

"I can only imagine one kind of danger——"

"Yes—of course, it's that—you know what I mean. But there's more than you could fancy."

"Tell me, then, what has alarmed you?"

"When did you see her last?" Patty inquired.

"More than a week ago. Two or three days before I came here."

"Had you noticed anything?"

"Nothing unusual."

"No more did I, till last Monday night. Then I saw that something was wrong. Hush!"

She gripped his arm, and they listened. But no sound could be heard.

"And since then," Patty pursued, with tremulous eagerness, "she's been very queer. I know she doesn't sleep at night, and she's getting ill, and she's had letters from—someone she oughtn't to have anything to do with."

"Having told so much, you had better tell me all," said Hilliard impatiently. There was a cold sweat on his forehead, and his heart beat painfully.

"No. I can't. I can only give you a warning."

"But what's the use of that? What can I do? How can I interfere?"

"I don't know," replied the girl, with a helpless sigh. "She's in danger, that's all I call tell you."

"Patty, don't be a fool! Out with it! Who is the man? Is it some one you know?"

"I don't exactly know him I've seen him."

"Is he—a sort of gentleman?"

"Oh, yes, he's a gentleman. And you'd never think to look at him that he could do anything that wasn't right."

"Very well. What reason have you for supposing that he's doing wrong?"

Patty kept silence. A band of rowdy fellows just then came shouting along the street, and one of them crashed up against the shop door, making Patty jump and scream. Oaths and foul language followed; and then the uproar passed away.

"Look here," said Hilliard. "You'll drive me out of my senses. Eve is in love with this man, is she?"

"I'm afraid so. She was."

"Before she went away, you mean. And, of course, her going away had something to do with it?"

"Yes, it had."

Hilliard laid his hands on the girl's shoulders.

"You've got to tell me the plain truth, and be quick about it. I suppose you haven't any idea of the torments I'm suffering. I shall begin to think you're making a fool of me, and that there's nothing but—though that's bad enough for me."

"Very well, I'll tell you. She went away because it came out that the man was married."

"Oh, that's it?" He spoke from a dry throat. "She told you herself?"

"Yes, not long after she came back. She said, of course, she could have no more to do with him. She used to meet him pretty often——"

"Stay, how did she get to know him first?"

"Just by chance—somewhere."

"I understand," said Hilliard grimly. "Go on."

"And his wife got someone to spy on him, and they found out he was meeting Eve, and she jumped out on them when they were walking somewhere together, and told Eve everything. He wasn't living with his wife, and hasn't been for a long time."

"What's his position?"

"He's in business, and seems to have lots of money; but I don't exactly know what it is he does."

"You are afraid, then, that Eve is being drawn back to him?"

"I feel sure she is—and it's dreadful."

"What I should like to know," said Hilliard, harshly, "is whether she really cares for him, or only for his money."

"Oh! How horrid you are! I never thought you could say such a thing!"

"Perhaps you didn't. All the same, it's a question. I don't pretend to understand Eve Madeley, and I'm afraid you are just as far from knowing her."

"I don't know her? Why, what are you talking about, Mr. Hilliard?"

"What do you think of her, then? Is she a good-hearted girl or——"

"Or what? Of course she's good-hearted. The things that men do say! They seem to be all alike."

## CHAPTER XI

"Women are so far from being all alike that one may think she understands another, and be utterly deceived. Eve has shown her best side to you, no doubt. With me, she hasn't taken any trouble to do so. And if——"

"Hush!"

This time the alarm was justified. A latchkey rattled at the house-door, the door opened, and in the same moment Patty turned out the light.

"It's my uncle," she whispered, terror-stricken. "Don't stir."

## CHAPTER XII

A heavy footstep sounded in the passage, and Hilliard, to whose emotions was now added a sense of ludicrous indignity, heard talk between Patty and her uncle.

"You mustn't lock up yet," said the girl, "Eve is out."

"What's she doing?"

"I don't know. At the theatre with friends, I dare say."

"If we'd been staying on here, that young woman would have had to look out for another lodging. There's something I don't like about her, and if you take my advice, Patty, you'll shake her off. She'll do you no good, my girl."

They passed together into the room behind the shop, and though their voices were still audible, Hilliard could no longer follow the conversation. He stood motionless, just where Patty had left him, with a hand resting on the top of the piano, and it seemed to him that at least half an hour went by. Then a sound close by made him start; it was the snapping of a violin string; the note reverberated through the silent shop. But by this time the murmur of conversation had ceased, and Hilliard hoped that Patty's uncle had gone upstairs to bed.

As proved to be the case. Presently the door opened, and a voice called to him in a whisper. He obeyed the summons, and, not without stumbling, followed Patty into the open air.

"She hasn't come yet."

"What's the time?"

"Half-past eleven. I shall sit up for her. Did you hear what my uncle said? You mustn't think anything of that; he's always finding fault with people."

"Do you think she will come at all?" asked Hilliard.

"Oh, of course she will!"

"I shall wait about. Don't stand here. Good-night."

"You won't let her know what I've told you?" said Patty, retaining his hand.

## CHAPTER XII

"No, I won't. If she doesn't come back at all, I'll see you to-morrow."

He moved away, and the door closed.

Many people were still passing along the street. In his uncertainty as to the direction by which Eve would return—if return she did—Hilliard ventured only a few yards away. He had waited for about a quarter of an hour, when his eye distinguished a well-known figure quickly approaching. He hurried forward, and Eve stopped before he had quite come up to her.

"Where have you been to-night?" were his first words, sounding more roughly than he intended.

"I wanted to see you, I passed your lodgings and saw there was no light in the windows, else I should have asked for you."

She spoke in so strange a voice, with such show of agitation, that Hilliard stood gazing at her till she again broke silence,

"Have you been waiting here for me?"

"Yes. Patty told me you weren't back."

"Why did you come?"

"Why do I ever come to meet you?"

"We can't talk here," said Eve, turning away. "Come into a quieter place."

They walked in silence to the foot of High Street, and there turned aside into the shadowed solitude of Mornington Crescent. Eve checked her steps and said abruptly—

"I want to ask you for something."

"What is it?"

"Now that it comes to saying it, I—I'm afraid. And yet if I had asked you that evening when we were at the restaurant——"

"What is it?" Hilliard repeated gruffly.

"That isn't your usual way of speaking to me."

"Will you tell me where you have been tonight?"

"Nowhere—walking about——"

"Do you often walk about the streets till midnight?"

"Indeed I don't."

The reply surprised him by its humility. Her voice all but broke on the words. As well as the dim light would allow, he searched her face, and it seemed to him that her eyes had a redness, as if from shedding tears.

"You haven't been alone?"

"No—I've been with a friend."

"Well, I have no claim upon you. It's nothing to me what friends you go about with. What were you going to ask of me?"

"You have changed so all at once. I thought you would never talk in this way."

"I didn't mean to," said Hilliard. "I have lost control of myself, that's all. But you can say whatever you meant to say—just as you would have done at the restaurant. I'm the same man I was then."

Eve moved a few steps, but he did not follow her, and she returned. A policeman passing threw a glance at them.

"It's no use asking what I meant to ask," she said, with her eyes on the ground. "You won't grant it me."

"How can I say till I know what it is? There are not many things in my power that I wouldn't do for you."

"I was going to ask for money."

"Money? Why, it depends what you are going to do with it. If it will do you any good, all the money I have is yours, as you know well enough. But I must understand why you want it."

"I can't tell you that. I don't want you to give me money—only to lend it. You shall have it back again, though I can't promise the exact time. If you hadn't changed so, I should have found it easy enough to ask. Hut I don't know you to-night; it's like talking to a stranger. What has happened to make you so different?"

"I have been waiting a long time for you, that's all," Hilliard replied, endeavouring to use the tone of frank friendliness in which he had been wont to address her. "I got nervous and irritable. I felt uneasy about you. It's all right now: Let us walk on a little. You want money. Well, I have three hundred pounds and more. Call it mine, call it yours. But I must know that you're not going to do anything foolish. Of course, you don't tell me everything; I have no right to expect it. You haven't misled me; I knew from the first that—well, a girl of your age, and with your face, doesn't live alone in London without adventures. I shouldn't think of telling you all mine, and I don't ask to know yours—unless I begin to have a part in them. There's something wrong: of course, I can see that. I think you've been crying, and you don't shed tears for a trifle. Now you come and ask me for money. If it will do you good, take all you want. But I've an uncomfortable suspicion that harm may come of it."

"Why not treat me just like a man-friend? I'm old enough to take care of myself."

"You think so, but I know better. Wait a moment. How much money do you want?"

## CHAPTER XII

"Thirty-five pounds."

"Exactly thirty-five? And it isn't for your own use?"

"I can't tell you any more. I am in very great need of the money, and if you will lend it me I shall feel very grateful."

"I want no gratitude, I want nothing from you, Eve, except what you can't give me. I can imagine a man in my position giving you money in the hope that it might be your ruin just to see you brought down, humiliated. There's so much of the brute in us all. But I don't feel that desire."

"Why should you?" she asked, with a change to coldness. "What harm have I done you?"

"No harm at all, and perhaps a great deal of good. I say that I wish you nothing but well. Suppose a gift of all the money I have would smooth your whole life before you, and make you the happy wife of some other man. I would give it you gladly. That kind of thing has often been said, when it meant nothing: it isn't so with me. It has always been more pleasure to me to give than to receive. No merit of mine; I have it from my father. Make clear to me that you are to benefit by this money, and you shall have the cheque as soon as you please."

"I shall benefit by it, because it will relieve me from a dreadful anxiety."

"Or, in other words, will relieve someone else?"

"I can speak only of myself. The kindness will be done to me."

"I must know more than that. Come now, we assume that there's someone in the background. A friend of yours, let us say. I can't Imagine why this friend of yours wants money, but so it is. You don't contradict me?"

Eve remained mute, her head bent.

"What about your friend and you in the future? Are you bound to this friend in any irredeemable way?"

"No—I am not," she answered, with emotion.

"There's nothing between you but—let us call it mere friendship."

"Nothing—nothing!"

"So far, so good." He looked keenly into her face. "But how about the future?"

"There will never be anything more—there can't be."

"Let us say that you think so at present. Perhaps I don't feel quite so sure of it. I say again, it's nothing to me, unless I get drawn into it by you yourself. I am not your guardian. If I tell you to be careful, it's an impertinence. But the money; that's another affair. I won't help you to misery."

"You will be helping me *out* of misery!" Eve exclaimed.

"Yes, for the present. I will make a bargain with you."

She looked at him with startled eyes.

"You shall have your thirty-five pounds on condition that you go to live, for as long as I choose, in Paris. You are to leave London in a day or two. Patty shall go with you; her uncle doesn't want her, and she seems to have quarrelled with the man she was engaged to. The expenses are my affair. I shall go to Paris myself, and be there while you are, but you need see no more of me than you like. Those are the terms."

"I can't think you are serious," said Eve.

"Then I'll explain why I wish you to do this. I've thought about you a great deal; in fact, since we first met, my chief occupation has been thinking about you. And I have come to the conclusion that you are suffering from an illness, the result of years of hardship and misery. We have agreed, you remember, that there are a good many points of resemblance between your life and mine, and perhaps between your character and mine. Now I myself, when I escaped from Dudley, was thoroughly ill—body and soul. The only hope for me was a complete change of circumstances—to throw off the weight of my past life, and learn the meaning of repose, satisfaction, enjoyment. I prescribe the same for you. I am your physician; I undertake your cure. If you refuse to let me, there's an end of everything between us; I shall say good-bye to you tonight, and to-morrow set off for some foreign country."

"How can I leave my work at a moment's notice?"

"The devil take your work—for he alone is the originator of such accursed toil!"

"How can I live at your expense?"

"That's a paltry obstacle. Oh, if you are too proud, say so, and there's an end of it. You know me well enough to feel the absolute truth of what I say, when I assure you that you will remain just as independent of me as you ever were. I shall be spending my money in a way that gives me pleasure; the matter will never appear to me in any other light. Why, call it an additional loan, if it will give any satisfaction to you. You are to pay me back some time. Here in London you perish; across the Channel there, health of body and mind is awaiting you; and are we to talk about money? I shall begin to swear like a trooper; the thing is too preposterous."

Eve said nothing: she stood half turned from him.

"Of course," he pursued, "you may object to leave London. Perhaps the sacrifice is too great. In that case, I should only do right if I carried you off by main force; but I'm afraid it can't be; I must leave you to perish."

"I am quite willing to go away," said Eve in a low voice. "But the shame of it—to be supported by you."

"Why, you don't hate me?"

"You know I do not."

"You even have a certain liking for me. I amuse you; you think me an odd sort of fellow, perhaps with more good than bad in me. At all events, you can trust me?"

"I can trust you perfectly."

"And it ain't as if I wished you to go alone. Patty will be off her head with delight when the thing is proposed to her."

"But how can I explain to her?"

"Don't attempt to. Leave her curiosity a good hard nut to crack. Simply say you are off to Paris, and that if she'll go with you, you will bear all her expenses."

"It's so difficult to believe that you are in earnest."

"You must somehow bring yourself to believe it. There will be a cheque ready for you to-morrow morning, to take or refuse. If you take it, you are bound in honour to leave England not later than—we'll say Thursday. That you are to be trusted, I believe, just as firmly as you believe it of me."

"I can't decide to-night."

"I can give you only till to-morrow morning. If I don't hear from you by midday, I am gone."

"You shall hear from me—one way or the other."

"Then don't wait here any longer. It's after midnight, and Patty will be alarmed about you. No, we won't shake hands; not that till we strike a bargain."

Eve seemed about to walk away, but she hesitated and turned again.

"I will do as you wish—I will go."

"Excellent! Then speak of it to Patty as soon as possible, and tell me what she says when we meet to-morrow—where and when you like."

"In this same place, at nine o'clock."

"So be it. I will bring the cheque."

"But I must be able to cash it at once."

"So you can. It will be on a London bank. I'll get the cash myself if you like."

Then they shook hands and went in opposite directions.

## CHAPTER XIII

On the evening of the next day, just after he had lit his lamp, Hilliard's attention was drawn by a sound as of someone tapping at the window. He stood to listen, and the sound was repeated—an unmistakable tap of fingers on the glass. In a moment he was out in the street, where he discovered Patty Ringrose.

"Why didn't you come to see me?" she asked excitedly.

"I was afraid *she* might be there. Did she go to business, as usual?"

"Yes. At least I suppose so. She only got home at the usual time. I've left her there: I was bound to see you. Do you know what she told me last night when she came in?"

"I dare say I could guess."

Hilliard began to walk down the street. Patty, keeping close at his side, regarded him with glances of wonder.

"Is it true that we're going to Paris? I couldn't make out whether she meant it, and this morning I couldn't get a word from her."

"Are you willing to go with her?"

"And have all my expenses paid?"

"Of course."

"I should think I am! But I daren't let my uncle and aunt know; there'd be no end of bother. I shall have to make up some sort of tale to satisfy my aunt, and get my things sent to the station while uncle's playing billiards. How long is it for?"

"Impossible to say. Three months—half a year—I don't know. What about Mr. Daily?"

"Oh, I've done with *him*!"

"And you are perfectly sure that you can get employment whenever you need it?"

"Quite sure: no need to trouble about that. I'm very good friends with aunt, and she'll take me in for as long as I want when I come back. But it's easy enough for anybody like me to get a place. I've had two or three offers the last half-year, from good shops where they were losing their young ladies. We're always getting married, in our business, and places have to be filled up."

"That settles it, then."

"But I want to know—I can't make it out—Eve won't tell me how she's managing to go. Are *you* going to pay for her?"

"We won't talk of that, Patty. She's going; that's enough."

"You persuaded her, last night?"

"Yes, I persuaded her. And I am to hear by the first post in the morning whether she will go to-morrow or Thursday. She'll arrange things with you to-night, I should think."

"It didn't look like it. She's shut herself in her room."

"I can understand that. She is ill. That's why I'm getting her away from London. Wait till we've been in Paris a few weeks, and you'll see how she changes. At present she is downright ill—ill enough to go to bed and be nursed, if that would do any good. It's your part to look after her. I don't want you to be her servant."

"Oh, I don't mind doing anything for her."

"No, because you are a very good sort of girl. You 'Ii live at a hotel, and what you have to do is to make her enjoy herself. I shouldn't wonder if you find it difficult at first, but we shall get her round before long."

"I never thought there was anything the' matter with her."

"Perhaps not, but I understand her better. Of course you won't say a word of this to her. You take it as a holiday—as good fun. No doubt I shall be able to have a few words in private with you now and then. But at other times we must talk as if nothing special had passed between us."

Patty mused. The lightness of her step told in what a spirit of gaiety she looked forward to the expedition.

"Do you think," she asked presently, "that it'll all come to an end—what I told you of?"

"Yes, I think so."

"You didn't let her know that I'd been talking——"

"Of course not. And, as I don't want her to know that you've seen me to-night, you had better stay no longer. She's sure to have something to tell you to-night or to-morrow morning. Get your packing done, and be ready at any moment. When I hear from Eve in the morning, I shall send her a telegram. Most likely we sha'n't see each other again until we meet at Charing Cross. I hope it may be tomorrow; but Thursday is the latest."

So Patty took her departure, tripping briskly homeward. As for Hilliard, he returned to his sitting-room, and was busy for some time with the pencilling of computations in English and French money. Towards midnight, he walked as far as High Street, and looked at the windows above the music-shop. All was dark.

He rose very early next morning, and as post-time drew near he walked about the street in agonies of suspense. He watched the letter-carrier from house to house, followed him up, and saw him pass the number at which he felt assured that he would deliver a letter. In frenzy of disappointment a fierce oath burst from his lips.

"That's what comes of trusting a woman!—she is going to cheat me. She has gained her end, and will put me off with excuses."

But perhaps a telegram would come. He made a pretence of breakfasting, and paced his room for an hour like a caged animal. When the monotony of circulating movement had all but stupefied him, he was awakened by a double postman's knock at the front door, the signal that announces a telegram.

Again from Patty, and again a request that he would come to the shop at mid-day.

"Just as I foresaw—excuses—postponement. What woman ever had the sense of honour!"

To get through the morning he drank—an occupation suggested by the heat of the day, which blazed cloudless. The liquor did not cheer him, but inspired a sullen courage, a reckless resolve. And in this frame of mind he presented himself before Patty Ringrose.

"She can't go to-day," said Patty, with an air of concern. "You were quite right—she is really ill."

"Has she gone out?"

"No, she's upstairs, lying on the bed. She says she has a dreadful headache, and if you saw her you'd believe it. She looks shocking. It's the second night she hasn't closed her eyes."

A savage jealousy was burning Hilliard's vitals. He had tried to make light of the connection between Eve and that unknown man, even after her extraordinary request for money, which all but confessedly she wanted on his account. He had blurred the significance of such a situation, persuading himself that neither was Eve capable of a great passion, nor the man he had seen able to inspire one. Now he rushed to the conviction that Eve had fooled him with a falsehood.

"Tell her this." He glared at Patty with eyes which made the girl shrink in alarm. "If she isn't at Charing Cross Station by a quarter to eleven to-morrow, there's an end of it. I shall be there, and shall go on without her. It's her only chance."

"But if she really *can't*——"

"Then it's her misfortune—she must suffer for it. She goes to-morrow or not at all. Can you make her understand that?"

"I'll tell her."

"Listen, Patty. If you bring her safe to the station to-morrow you shall have a ten-pound note, to buy what you like in Paris."

The girl reddened, half in delight, half in shame.

"I don't want it—she shall come——"

"Very well; good-bye till to-morrow, or for good."

"No, no; she shall come."

He was drenched in perspiration, yet walked for a mile or two at his topmost speed. Then a consuming thirst drove him into the nearest place where drink was sold. At six o'clock he remembered that he had not eaten since breakfast; he dined extravagantly, and afterwards fell asleep in the smoking-room of the restaurant. A waiter with difficulty aroused him, and persuaded him to try the effect of the evening air. An hour later he sank in exhaustion on one of the benches near the river, and there slept profoundly until stirred by a policeman.

"What's the time?" was his inquiry, as he looked up at the starry sky.

He felt for his watch, but no watch was discoverable. Together with the gold chain it had disappeared.

"Damnation! someone has robbed me."

The policeman was sympathetic, but reproachful.

"Why do you go to sleep on the Embankment at this time of night? Lost any money?"

Yes, his money too had flown; luckily, only a small sum. It was for the loss of his watch and chain that he grieved; they had been worn for years by his father, and on that account had a far higher value for him than was represented by their mere cost.

As a matter of form, he supplied the police with information concerning the theft. Of recovery there could be little hope.

Thoroughly awakened and sober, he walked across London to Gower Place arriving in the light of dawn. Too spiritless to take off his clothing, he lay upon the bed, and through the open window watched a great cloud that grew rosy above the opposite houses.

Would Eve be at the place of meeting today? It seemed to him totally indifferent whether she came or not; nay, he all but hoped that she would not. He had been guilty of prodigious folly. The girl belonged to another man; and even had it not been so, what was the use of flinging away his money at this rate? Did he look for any reward correspondent to the sacrifice? She would never love him, and it was not in his power to complete the work he had begun, by freeing her completely from harsh circumstances, setting her in a path of secure and pleasant life.

But she would not come, and so much the better. With only himself to provide for he had still money enough to travel far. He would see something of the great world, and leave his future to destiny.

He dozed for an hour or two.

Whilst he was at breakfast a letter arrived for him. He did not know the handwriting on the envelope, but it must be Eve's. Yes. She wrote a couple of lines: "I will be at the station to-morrow at a quarter to eleven.—E. M."

## CHAPTER XIV

One travelling bag was all he carried. Some purchases that he had made in London—especially the great work on French cathedrals—were already despatched to Birmingham, to lie in the care of Robert Narramore.

He reached Charing Cross half an hour before train-time, and waited at the entrance. Several cabs that drove up stirred his expectation only to disappoint him. He was again in an anguish of fear lest Eve should not come. A cab arrived, with two boxes of modest appearance. He stepped forward and saw the girls' faces.

Between him and Eve not a word passed. They avoided each other's look. Patty, excited and confused, shook hands with him.

"Go on to the platform," he said. "I'll see after everything. This is all the luggage?"

"Yes. One box is mine, and one Eve's. I had to face it out with the people at home," she added, between laughing and crying. "They think I'm going to the seaside, to stay with Eve till she gets better. I never told so many fibs in my life. Uncle stormed at me, but I don't care."

"All right; go on to the platform."

Eve was already walking in that direction. Undeniably she looked ill; her step was languid; she did not raise her eyes. Hilliard, when he had taken tickets and booked the luggage through to Paris, approached his travelling companions. Seeing him, Eve turned away.

"I shall go in a smoking compartment," he said to Patty. "You had better take your tickets."

"But when shall we see you again?"

"Oh, at Dover, of course."

"Will it be rough, do you think? I do wish Eve would talk. I can't get a word out of her. It makes it all so miserable, when we might be enjoying ourselves."

"Don't trouble: leave her to herself. I'll get you some papers."

On returning from the bookstall, he slipped loose silver into Patty's hands.

"Use that if you want anything on the journey. And—I haven't forgot my promise."

"Nonsense!"

"Go and take your places now: there's only ten minutes to wait."

He watched them as they passed the harrier. Neither of the girls was dressed very suitably for travelling; but Eve's costume resembled that of a lady, while Patty's might suggest that she was a lady's-maid. As if to confirm this distinction, Patty had burdened herself with several small articles, whereas her friend carried only a sunshade. They disappeared among people upon the platform. In a few minutes Hilliard followed, glanced along the carriages till he saw where the girls were seated, and took his own place. He wore a suit which had been new on his first arrival in London, good enough in quality and cut to give his features the full value of their intelligence; a brown felt hat, a russet necktie, a white flannel shirt. Finding himself with a talkative neighbour in the carriage, he chatted freely. As soon as the train had started, he lit his pipe and tasted the tobacco with more relish than for a long time.

On board the steamer Eve kept below from first to last. Patty walked the deck with Hilliard, and vastly to her astonishment, achieved the voyage without serious discomfort. Hilliard himself, with the sea wind in his nostrils, recovered that temper of buoyant satisfaction which had accompanied his first escape from London. He despised the weak misgivings and sordid calculations of yesterday. Here he was, on a Channel steamer, bearing away from disgrace and wretchedness the woman whom his heart desired. Wild as the project had seemed to him when first he conceived it, he had put it into execution. The moment was worth living for. Whatever the future might keep in store for him of dreary, toilsome, colourless existence, the retrospect would always show him this patch of purple—a memory precious beyond all the possible results of prudence and narrow self-regard.

The little she-Cockney by his side entertained him with the flow of her chatter; it had the advantage of making him feel a travelled man.

"I didn't cross this way when I came before," he explained to her. "From Newhaven it's a much longer voyage."

"You like the sea, then?"

"I chose it because it was cheaper—that's all."

"Yet you're so extravagant now," remarked Patty, with eyes that confessed admiration of this quality.

## CHAPTER XIV

"Oh, because I am rich," he answered gaily. "Money is nothing to me."

"Are you really rich? Eve said you weren't."

"Did she?"

"I don't mean she said it in a disagreeable way. It was last night. She thought you were wasting your money upon us."

"If I choose to waste it, why not? Isn't there a pleasure in doing as you like?"

"Oh, of course there is," Patty assented. "I only wish I had the chance. But it's awfully jolly, this! Who'd have thought, a week ago, that I should be going to Paris? I have a feeling all the time that I shall wake up and find I've been dreaming."

"Suppose you go down and see whether Eve wants anything? You needn't say I sent you."

From Calais to Paris he again travelled apart from the girls. Fatigue overcame him, and for the last hour or two he slept, with the result that, on alighting at the Gare du Nord, he experienced a decided failure of spirits. Happily, there was nothing before him but to carry out a plan already elaborated. With the aid of his guide-book he had selected an hotel which seemed suitable for the girls, one where English was spoken, and thither he drove with them from the station. The choice of their rooms, and the settlement of details took only a few minutes; then, for almost the first time since leaving Charing Cross, he spoke to Eve.

"Patty will do everything she can for you," he said; "I shall be not very far away, and you can always send me a message if you wish. To-morrow morning I shall come at about ten to ask how you are—nothing more than that—unless you care to go anywhere."

The only reply was "Thank you," in a weary tone. And so, having taken his leave he set forth to discover a considerably less expensive lodging for himself. In this, after his earlier acquaintance with Paris, he had no difficulty; by half-past eight his business was done, and he sat down to dinner at a cheap restaurant. A headache spoilt his enjoyment of the meal. After a brief ramble about the streets, he went home and got into a bed which was rather too short for him, but otherwise promised sufficient comfort.

The first thing that came into his mind when he awoke next morning was that he no longer possessed a watch; the loss cast a gloom upon him. But he had slept well, and a flood of sunshine that streamed over his scantily carpeted floor, together with gladly remembered sounds from the street, soon put him into an excellent humour. He sprang tip, partly dressed himself, and unhasped the window. The smell of Paris had become associated in his mind with thoughts of liberty; a grotesque dance about the bed-room expressed his joy.

As he anticipated, Patty alone received him when he called upon the girls. She reported that Eve felt unable to rise.

"What do you think about her?" he asked. "Nothing serious, is it?"

"She can't get rid of her headache."

"Let her rest as long as she likes. Are you comfortable here?"

Patty was in ecstasies with everything, and chattered on breathlessly. She wished to go out; Eve had no need of her—indeed had told her that above all she wished to be left alone.

"Get ready, then," said Hilliard, "and we'll have an hour or two."

They walked to the Madeleine and rode thence on the top of a tram-car to the Bastille. By this time Patty had come to regard her strange companion in a sort of brotherly light; no restraint whatever appeared in her conversation with him. Eve, she told him, had talked French with the chambermaid.

"And I fancy it was something she didn't want *me* to understand."

"Why should you think so?"

"Oh, something in the way the girl looked at me."

"No, no; you were mistaken. She only wanted to show that she knew some French."

But Hilliard wondered whether Patty could be right. Was it not possible that Eve had gratified her vanity by representing her friend as a servant—a lady's-maid? Yet why should he attribute such a fault to her? It was an odd thing that he constantly regarded Eve in the least favourable light, giving weight to all the ill he conjectured in her, and minimising those features of her character which, at the beginning, he had been prepared to observe with sympathy and admiration. For a man in love his reflections followed a very unwonted course. And, indeed, he had never regarded his love as of very high or pure quality; it was something that possessed him and constrained him—by no means a source of elevating emotion.

"Do you like Eve?" he asked abruptly, disregarding some trivial question Patty had put to him.

"Like her? Of course I do."

"And *why* do you like her?"

"Why?—ah—I don't know. Because I do."

And she laughed foolishly.

"Does Eve like *you*?" Hilliard continued.

"I think she does. Else I don't see why she kept up with me."

## CHAPTER XIV

"Has she ever done you any kindness?"

"I'm sure I don't know. Nothing particular. She never gave anything, if you mean that. But she has paid for me at theatres and so on."

Hilliard quitted the subject.

"If you like to go out alone," he told her before they parted, "there's no reason why you shouldn't—just as you do in London. Remember the way back, that's all, and don't be out late. And you'll want some French money."

"But I don't understand it, and how can I buy anything when I can't speak a word?"

"All the same, take that and keep it till you are able to make use of it. It's what I promised you."

Patty drew back her hand, but her objections were not difficult to overcome.

"I dare say," Hilliard continued, "Eve doesn't understand the money much better than you do. But she'll soon be well enough to talk, and then I shall explain everything to her. On this piece of paper is my address; please let Eve have it. I shall call to-morrow morning again."

He did so, and this time found Eve, as well as her companion, ready to go out. No remark or inquiry concerning her health passed his lips; he saw that she was recovering from the crisis she had passed through, whatever its real nature. Eve shook hands with him, and smiled, though as if discharging an obligation.

"Can you spare time to show us something of Paris?" she asked.

"I am your official guide. Make use of me whenever it pleases you."

"I don't feel able to go very far. Isn't there some place where we could sit down in the open air?"

A carriage was summoned, and they drove to the Fields Elysian. Eve benefited by the morning thus spent. She left to Patty most of the conversation, but occasionally made inquiries, and began to regard things with a healthy interest. The next day they all visited the Louvre, for a light rain was falling, and here Hilliard found an opportunity of private talk with Eve; they sat together whilst Patty, who cared little for pictures, looked out of a window at the Seine.

"Do you like the hotel I chose?" he began.

"Everything is very nice."

"And you are not sorry to be here?"

"Not in one way. In another I can't understand how I come to be here at all."

"Your physician has ordered it."

"Yes—so I suppose it's all right."

"There's one thing I'm obliged to speak of. Do you understand French money?"

Eve averted her face, and spoke after a slight delay.

"I can easily learn."

"Yes. You shall take this Paris guide home with you. You'll find all information of that sort in it. And I shall give you an envelope containing money—just for your private use. You have nothing to do with the charges at the hotel."

"I've brought it on myself; but I feel more ashamed than I can tell you."

"If you tried to tell me I shouldn't listen. What you have to do now is to get well. Very soon you and Patty will be able to find your way about together; then I shall only come with you when you choose to invite me. You have my address."

He rose and broke off the dialogue.

For a week or more Eve's behaviour in his company underwent little change. In health she decidedly improved, but Hilliard always found her reserved, coldly amicable, with an occasional suggestion of forced humility which he much disliked. From Patty he learnt that she went about a good deal and seemed to enjoy herself.

"We don't always go together," said the girl. "Yesterday and the day before Eve was away by herself all the afternoon. Of course she can get on all right with her French. She takes to Paris as if she'd lived here for years."

On the day after, Hilliard received a postcard in which Eve asked him to be in a certain room of the Louvre at twelve o'clock. He kept the appointment, and found Eve awaiting him alone.

"I wanted to ask whether you would mind if we left the hotel and went to live at another place?"

He heard her with surprise.

"You are not comfortable?"

"Quite. But I have been to see my friend Mdlle. Roche—you remember. And she has shown me how we can live very comfortably at a quarter of what it costs now, in the same house where she has a room. I should like to change, if you'll let me."

"Pooh! You're not to think of the cost——"

"Whether I am to or not, I do, and can't help myself. I know the hotel is fearfully expensive, and I shall like the other place much better. Miss Roche is a very nice girl, and she was glad to see me; and if I'm near her, I shall get all sorts of advantages—in French, and so on."

## CHAPTER XIV

Hilliard wondered what accounts of herself Eve had rendered to the Parisienne, but he did not venture to ask.

"Will Patty like it as well?"

"Just as well. Miss Roche speaks English, you know, and they'll get on very well together."

"Where is the place?"

"Rather far off—towards the Jardin des Plantes. But I don't think that would matter, would it?"

"I leave it entirely to you."

"Thank you," she answered, with that intonation he did not like. "Of course, if you would like to meet Miss Roche, you can."

"We'll think about it. It's enough that she's an old friend of yours."

# CHAPTER XV

When this change had been made Eve seemed to throw off a burden. She met Hilliard with something like the ease of manner, the frank friendliness, which marked her best moods in their earlier intercourse. At a restaurant dinner, to which he persuaded her in company with Patty, she was ready in cheerful talk, and an expedition to Versailles, some days after, showed her radiant with the joy of sunshine and movement. Hilliard could not but wonder at the success of his prescription.

He did not visit the girls in their new abode, and nothing more was said of his making the acquaintance of Mdlle. Roche. Meetings were appointed by post-card—always in Patty's hand if the initiative were female; they took place three or four times a week. As it was now necessary for Eve to make payments on her own account, Hilliard despatched to her by post a remittance in paper money, and of this no word passed between them. Three weeks later he again posted the same sum. On the morrow they went by river to St. Cloud—it was always a trio, Hilliard never making any other proposal—and the steamboat afforded Eve an opportunity of speaking with her generous friend apart.

"I don't want this money," she said, giving him an envelope. "What you sent before isn't anything like finished. There's enough for a month more."

"Keep it all the same. I won't have any pinching."

"There's nothing of the kind. If I don't have my way in this I shall go back to London."

He put the envelope in his pocket, and stood silent, with eyes fixed on the river bank.

"How long do you intend us to stay?" asked Eve.

"As long as you find pleasure here."

"And—what am I to do afterwards?"

He glanced at her.

## CHAPTER XV

"A holiday must come to an end," she added, trying, but without success, to meet his look.

"I haven't given any thought to that," said Hilliard, carelessly; "there's plenty of time. It will be fine weather for many weeks yet."

"But I have been thinking about it. I should be crazy if I didn't."

"Tell me your thoughts, then."

"Should you be satisfied if I got a place at Birmingham?"

There again Was the note of self-abasement. It irritated the listener.

"Why do you put it in that way? There's no question of what satisfies me, but of what is good for you."

"Then I think it had better be Birmingham."

"Very well. It's understood that when we leave Paris we go there."

A silence. Then Eve asked abruptly:

"You will go as well?"

"Yes, I shall go back."

"And what becomes of your determination to enjoy life as long as you can?"

"I'm carrying it out. I shall go back satisfied, at all events."

"And return to your old work?"

"I don't know. It depends on all sorts of things. We won't talk of it just yet."

Patty approached, and Hilliard turned to her with a bright, jesting face.

Midway in August, on his return home one afternoon, the concierge let him know that two English gentlemen had been inquiring for him; one of them had left a card. With surprise and pleasure Hilliard read the name of Robert Narramore, and beneath it, written in pencil, an invitation to dine that evening at a certain hotel in the Rue de Provence. As usual, Narramore had neglected the duties of a correspondent; this was the first announcement of his intention to be in Paris. Who the second man might be Hilliard could not conjecture.

He arrived at the hotel, and found Narramore in company with a man of about the same age, his name Birching, to Hilliard a stranger. They had reached Paris this morning, and would remain only for a day or two, as their purpose was towards the Alps.

"I couldn't stand this heat," remarked Narramore, who, in the very lightest of tourist garbs, sprawled upon a divan, and drank something iced out of a tall tumbler. "We shouldn't have stopped here at all if it hadn't been for you. The idea is that you should go on with us."

"Can't—impossible——"

"Why, what are you doing here—besides roasting?"

"Eating and drinking just what suits my digestion."

"You look pretty fit—a jolly sight better than when we met last. All the same, you will go on with us. We won't argue it now; it's dinner-time. Wait till afterwards."

At table, Narramore mentioned that his friend Birching was an architect.

"Just what this fellow ought to have been," he said, indicating Hilliard. "Architecture is his hobby. I believe he could sit down and draw to scale a front elevation of any great cathedral in Europe—couldn't you, Hilliard?"

Laughing the joke aside, Hilliard looked with interest at Mr. Birching, and began to talk with him. The three young men consumed a good deal of wine, and after dinner strolled about the streets, until Narramore's fatigue and thirst brought them to a pause at a cafe on the Boulevard des Italiens. Birching presently moved apart, to reach a newspaper, and remained out of earshot while Narramore talked with his other friend.

"What's going on?" he began. "What are you doing here? Seriously, I want you to go along with us. Birching is a very good sort of chap, but just a trifle heavy—takes things rather solemnly for such hot weather. Is it the expense? Hang it! You and I know each other well enough, and, thanks to my old uncle——"

"Never mind that, old boy," interposed Hilliard. "How long are you going for?"

"I can't very well be away for more than three weeks. The brass bedsteads, you know——"

Hilliard agreed to join in the tour.

"That's right: I've been looking forward to it," said his friend heartily. "And now, haven't you anything to tell me? Are you alone here? Then, what the deuce do you do with yourself?"

"Chiefly meditate."

"You're the rummest fellow I ever knew. I've wanted to write to you, but—hang it!—what with hot weather and brass bedsteads, and this and that——Now, what *are* you going to do? Your money won't last for ever. Haven't you any projects? It was no good talking about it before you left Dudley. I saw that. You were all but fit for a lunatic asylum, and no wonder. But you've pulled round, I see. Never saw you looking in such condition. What is to be the next move?"

"I have no idea."

"Well, now, *I* have. This fellow Birching is partner with his brother, in Brum, and they're tolerably flourishing. I've thought of you ever since I came to know him; I think it was chiefly on your account that I got thick with him—though there was another reason I'll tell you about that some time. Now, why shouldn't you go into their office? Could you manage to pay a small premium? I believe I could square it with them. I haven't said anything. I never hurry—like things to ripen naturally. Suppose you saw your way, in a year or two, to make only as much in an architect's office as you did in that——machine-shop, wouldn't it be worth while?"

Hilliard mused. Already he had a flush on his cheek, but his eyes sensibly brightened.

"Yes," he said at length with deliberation. "It would be worth while."

"So I should think. Well, wait till you've got to be a bit chummy with Birching. I think you'll suit each other. Let him see that you do really know something about architecture—there'll be plenty of chances."

Hilliard, still musing, repeated with mechanical emphasis:

"Yes, it would be worth while."

Then Narramore called to Birching, and the talk became general again.

The next morning they drove about Paris, all together. Narramore, though it was his first visit to the city, declined to see anything which demanded exertion, and the necessity for quenching his thirst recurred with great frequency. Early in the afternoon he proposed that they should leave Paris that very evening.

"I want to see a mountain with snow on it. We're bound to travel by night, and another day of this would settle me. Any objection, Birching?"

The architect agreed, and time-tables were consulted. Hilliard drove home to pack. When this was finished, he sat down and wrote a letter:

> "DEAR MISS MADELEY,—My friend Narramore is here, and has persuaded me to go to Switzerland with him. I shall be away for a week or two, and will let you hear from me in the meantime. Narramore says I am looking vastly better, and it is you I have to thank for this. Without you, my attempts at 'enjoying life' would have been a poor business. We start in an hour or two,—Yours ever,
>
> "MAURICE HILLIARD."

## CHAPTER XVI

He was absent for full three weeks, and arrived with his friends at the Gare de Lyon early one morning of September. Narramore and the architect delayed only for a meal, and pursued their journey homeward; Hilliard returned to his old quarters despatched a post-card asking Eve and Patty to dine with him that evening, and thereupon went to bed, where for some eight hours he slept the sleep of healthy fatigue.

The place he had appointed for meeting with the girls was at the foot of the Boulevard St. Michel. Eve came alone.

"And where's Patty?" he asked, grasping her hand heartily in return for the smile of unfeigned pleasure with which she welcomed him.

"Ah, where indeed? Getting near to Charing Cross by now, I think."

"She has gone back?"

"Went this very morning, before I had your card—let us get out of the way of people. She has been dreadfully home-sick. About a fortnight ago a mysterious letter came for her she hid it away from me. A few days after another came, and she shut herself up for a long time, and when she came out again I saw she had been crying. Then we talked it over. She had written to Mr. Dally and got an answer that made her miserable; that was the *first* letter. She wrote again, and had a reply that made her still more wretched; and that was the *second*. Two or three more came, and yesterday she could bear it no longer."

"Then she has gone home to make it up with him?"

"Of course. He declared that she has utterly lost her character and that no honest man could have anything more to say to her! I shouldn't wonder if they are married in a few weeks' time."

Hilliard laughed light-heartedly.

"I was to beg you on my knees to forgive her," pursued Eve. "But I can't very well do that in the middle of the street, can I? Really, she thinks she has behaved disgracefully to you. She wouldn't write a letter—she was ashamed. 'Tell him to forget all about me!' she kept saying."

"Good little girl! And what sort of a husband will this fellow Dally make her?"

"No worse than husbands in general, I dare say—but how well you look! How you must have been enjoying yourself!"

"I can say exactly the same about you!"

"Oh, but you are sunburnt, and look quite a different man!"

"And you have an exquisite colour in your cheeks, and eyes twice as bright as they used to be; and one would think you had never known a care."

"I feel almost like that," said Eve, laughing.

He tried to meet her eyes; she eluded him.

"I have an Alpine hunger; where shall we dine?"

The point called for no long discussion, and presently they were seated in the cool restaurant. Whilst he nibbled an olive, Hilliard ran over the story of his Swiss tour.

"If only *you* had been there! It was the one thing lacking."

"You wouldn't have enjoyed yourself half so much. You amused me by your description of Mr. Narramore, in the letter from Geneva."

"The laziest rascal born! But the best-tempered, the easiest to live with. A thoroughly good fellow; I like him better than ever. Of course he is improved by coming in for money—who wouldn't be, that has any good in him at all? But it amazes me that he can be content to go back to Birmingham and his brass bedsteads. Sheer lack of energy, I suppose. He'll grow dreadfully fat, I fear, and by when he becomes really a rich man—it's awful to think of."

Eve asked many questions about Narramore; his image gave mirthful occupation to her fancy. The dinner went merrily on, and when the black coffee was set before them:

"Why not have it outside?" said Eve. "You would like to smoke, I know."

Hilliard assented, and they seated themselves under the awning. The boulevard glowed in a golden light of sunset; the sound of its traffic was subdued to a lulling rhythm.

"There's a month yet before the leaves will begin to fall," murmured the young man, when he had smoked awhile in silence.

"Yes," was the answer. "I shall be glad to have a little summer still in Birmingham."

"Do you wish to go?"

"I shall go to-morrow, or the day after," Eve replied quietly.

Then again there came silence.

"Something has been proposed to me," said Hilliard, at length, leaning forward with his elbows upon the table. "I mentioned that our friend Birching is an architect. He's in partnership with his brother, a much older man. Well, they have offered to take me into their office if I pay a premium of fifty guineas. As soon as I can qualify myself to be of use to them, they'll give me a salary. And I shall have the chance of eventually doing much better than I ever could at the old grind, where, in fact, I had no prospect whatever."

"That's very good news," Eve remarked, gazing across the street.

"You think I ought to accept?"

"I suppose you can pay the fifty guineas, and still leave yourself enough to live upon?"

"Enough till I earn something," Hilliard answered with a smile.

"Then I should think there's no doubt."

"The question is this—are you perfectly willing to go back to Birmingham?"

"I'm *anxious* to go."

"You feel quite restored to health?"

"I was never so well in my life."

Hilliard looked into her face, and could easily believe that she spoke the truth. His memory would no longer recall the photograph in Mrs. Brewer's album; the living Eve, with her progressive changes of countenance, had obliterated that pale image of her bygone self. He saw her now as a beautiful woman, mysterious to him still in many respects, yet familiar as though they had been friends for years.

"Then, whatever life is before me," he said. "I shall have done *one* thing that is worth doing."

"Perhaps—if everyone's life is worth saving," Eve answered in a voice just audible.

"Everyone's is not; but yours was."

Two men who had been sitting not far from them rose and walked away. As if more at her ease for this secession, Eve looked at her companion, and said in a tone of intimacy:

"How I must have puzzled you when you first saw me in London!"

He answered softly:

"To be sure you did. And the thought of it puzzles me still."

"Oh, but can't you understand? No; of course you can't—I have told you so little. Just give me an idea of what sort of person you expected to find."

## CHAPTER XVI

"Yes, I will. Judging from your portrait, and from what I was told of you, I looked for a sad, solitary, hard-working girl—rather poorly dressed—taking no pleasure—going much to chapel—shrinking from the ordinary world."

"And you felt disappointed?"

"At first, yes; or, rather, bewildered—utterly unable to understand you."

"You are disappointed still?" she asked.

"I wouldn't have you anything but what you are."

"Still, that other girl was the one you *wished* to meet."

"Yes, before I had seen you. It was the sort of resemblance between her life and my own. I thought of sympathy between us. And the face of the portrait—but I see better things in the face that is looking at me now."

"Don't be quite sure of that—yes, perhaps. It's better to be healthy, and enjoy life, than broken-spirited and hopeless. The strange thing is that you were right—you fancied me just the kind of a girl I was: sad and solitary, and shrinking from people—true enough. And I went to chapel, and got comfort from it—as I hope to do again. Don't think that I have no religion. But I was so unhealthy, and suffered so in every way. Work and anxiety without cease, from when I was twelve years old. You know all about my father? If I hadn't been clever at figures, what would have become of me? I should have drudged at some wretched occupation until the work and the misery of everything killed me."

Hilliard listened intently, his eyes never stirring from her face.

"The change in me began when father came back to us, and I began to feel my freedom. Then I wanted to get away, and to live by myself. I thought of London—I've told you how much I always thought of London—but I hadn't the courage to go there. In Birmingham I began to change my old habits; but more in what I thought than what I did. I wished to enjoy myself like other girls, but I couldn't. For one thing, I thought it wicked; and then I was so afraid of spending a penny—I had so often known what it was to be in want of a copper to buy food. So I lived quite alone; sat in my room every evening and read books. You could hardly believe what a number of books I read in that year. Sometimes I didn't go to bed till two or three o'clock."

"What sort of books?"

"I got them from the Free Library—books of all kinds; not only novels. I've never been particularly fond of novels; they always made me feel my own lot all the harder. I never could understand what people mean when they say that reading novels takes them 'out of themselves.' It was never so with me. I liked travels and lives of people, and books about the stars. Why do you laugh?"

"You escaped from yourself *there*, at all events."

"At last I saw an advertisement in a newspaper—a London paper in the reading-room—which I was tempted to answer; and I got an engagement in London. When the time came for starting I was so afraid and low-spirited that I all but gave it up. I should have done, if I could have known what was before me. The first year in London was all loneliness and ill-health. I didn't make a friend, and I starved myself, all to save money. Out of my pound a week I saved several shillings—just because it was the habit of my whole life to pinch and pare and deny myself. I was obliged to dress decently, and that came out of my food. It's certain I must have a very good constitution to have gone through all that and be as well as I am to-day."

"It will never come again," said Hilliard.

"How can I be sure of that? I told you once before that I'm often in dread of the future. It would be ever so much worse, after knowing what it means to enjoy one's life. How do people feel who are quite sure they can never want as long as they live? I have tried to imagine it, but I can't; it would be too wonderful."

"You may know it some day."

Eve reflected.

"It was Patty Ringrose," she continued, "who taught me to take life more easily. I was astonished to find how much enjoyment she could get out of an hour or two of liberty, with sixpence to spend. She did me good by laughing at me, and in the end I astonished *her*. Wasn't it natural that I should be reckless as soon as I got the chance?"

"I begin to understand."

"The chance came in this way. One Sunday morning I went by myself to Hampstead, and as I was wandering about on the Heath I kicked against something. It was a cash-box, which I saw couldn't have been lying there very long. I found it had been broken open, and inside it were a lot of letters—old letters in envelopes; nothing else. The addresses on the envelopes were all the same—to a gentleman living at Hampstead. I thought the best I could do was to go and inquire for this address; and I found it, and rang the door-bell. When I told the servant what I wanted—it was a large house—she asked me to come in, and after I had waited a little she took me into a library, where a gentleman was sitting. I had to answer a good many questions, and the man talked rather gruffly to me. When he had made a note of my name and where

I lived, he said that I should hear from him, and so I went away. Of course I hoped to have a reward, but for two or three days I heard nothing; then, when I was at business, someone asked to see me—a man I didn't know. He said he had come from Mr. So and So, the gentleman at Hampstead, and had brought something for me—four five-pound notes. The cash-box had been stolen by someone, with other things, the night before I found it, and the letters in it, which disappointed the thief, had a great value for their owner. All sorts of inquiries had been made about me and no doubt I very nearly got into the hands of the police, but it was all right, and I had twenty pounds reward. Think! twenty pounds!"

Hilliard nodded.

"I told no one about it—not even Patty. And I put the money into the Post Office savings bank. I meant it to stay there till I might be in need; but I thought of it day and night. And only a fortnight after, my employers shut up their place of business, and I had nothing to do. All one night I lay awake, and when I got up in the morning I felt as if I was no longer my old self. I saw everything in a different way—felt altogether changed. I had made up my mind not to look for a new place, but to take my money out of the Post Office—I had more than twenty-five pounds there altogether—and spend it for my pleasure. It was just as if something had enraged me, and I was bent on avenging myself. All that day I walked about the town, looking at shops, and thinking what I should like to buy: but I only spent a shilling or two, for meals. The next day I bought some new clothing. The day after that I took Patty to the theatre, and astonished her by my extravagance; but I gave her no explanation, and to this day she doesn't understand how I got my money. In a sort of way, I *did* enjoy myself. For one thing, I took a subscription at Mudie's, and began to read once more. You can't think how it pleased me to get my books—new books—where rich people do. I changed a volume about every other day—I had so many hours I didn't know what to do with. Patty was the only friend I had made, so I took her about with me whenever she could get away in the evening."

"Yet never once dined at a restaurant," remarked Hilliard, laughing. "There's the difference between man and woman."

"My ideas of extravagance were very modest, after all."

Hilliard, fingering his coffee-cup, said in a lower voice:

"Yet you haven't told me everything."

Eve looked away, and kept silence.

"By the time I met you"—he spoke in his ordinary tone—"you had begun to grow tired of it."

"Yes—and——" She rose. "We won't sit here any longer."

When they had walked for a few minutes:

"How long shall you stay in Paris?" she asked.

"Won't you let me travel with you?"

"I do whatever you wish," Eve answered simply.

# CHAPTER XVII

Her accent of submission did not affect Hilliard as formerly; with a nervous thrill, he felt that she spoke as her heart dictated. In his absence Eve had come to regard him, if not with the feeling he desired, with something that resembled it; he read the change in her eyes. As they walked slowly away she kept nearer to him than of wont; now and then her arm touched his, and the contact gave him a delicious sensation. Askance he observed her figure, its graceful, rather languid, movement; to-night she had a new power over him, and excited with a passion which made his earlier desires seem spiritless.

"One day more of Paris?" he asked softly.

"Wouldn't it be better——?" she hesitated in the objection.

"Do you wish to break the journey in London?"

"No; let us go straight on."

"To-morrow, then?"

"I don't think we ought to put it off. The holiday is over."

Hilliard nodded with satisfaction. An incident of the street occupied them for a few minutes, and their serious conversation was only resumed when they had crossed to the south side of the river, where they turned eastwards and went along the quays.

"Till I can find something to do," Eve said at length, "I shall live at Dudley. Father will be very glad to have me there. He wished me to stay longer."

"I am wondering whether it is really necessary for you to go back to your drudgery."

"Oh, of course it is," she answered quickly. "I mustn't be idle. That's the very worst thing for me. And how am I to live?"

"I have still plenty of money," said Hilliard, regarding her.

"No more than you will need."

"But think—how little more it costs for two than for one——"

He spoke in spite of himself, having purposed no such suggestion. Eve quickened her step.

"No, no, no! You have a struggle before you; you don't know what——"

"And if it would make it easier for me?—there's no real doubt about my getting on well enough——"

"Everything is doubtful." She spoke in a voice of agitation. "We can't see a day before us. We have arranged everything very well——"

Hilliard was looking across the river. He walked more and more slowly, and turned at length to stand by the parapet. His companion remained apart from him, waiting. But he did not turn towards her again, and she moved to his side.

"I know how ungrateful I must seem." She spoke without looking at him. "I have no right to refuse anything after all you——"

"Don't say that," he interrupted impatiently. "That's the one thing I shall never like to think of."

"I shall think of it always, and be glad to remember it——"

"Come nearer—give me your hand——"

Holding it, he drew her against his side, and they stood in silence looking upon the Seine, now dark beneath the clouding night.

"I can't feel sure of you," fell at length from Hilliard.

"I promise——"

"Yes; here, now, in Paris. But when you are back in that hell——"

"What difference can it make in me? It can't change what I feel now. You have altered all my life, my thoughts about everything. When I look back, I don't know myself. You were right; I must have been suffering from an illness that affected my mind. It seems impossible that I could ever have done such things. I ought to tell you. Do you wish me to tell you everything?"

Hilliard spoke no answer, but he pressed her hand more tightly in his own.

"You knew it from Patty, didn't you?"

"She told me as much as she knew that night when I waited for you in High Street. She said you were in danger, and I compelled her to tell all she could."

"I *was* in danger, though I can't understand now how it went so far as that. It was he who came to me with the money, from the gentleman at Hampstead. That was how I first met him. The next day he waited for me when I came away from business."

"It was the first time that anything of that kind had happened?"

"The first time. And you know what the state of my mind was then. But to the end I never felt any—I never really loved him. We met and went to places together. After my loneliness—you can understand. But I distrusted him. Did Patty tell you why I left London so suddenly?"

"Yes."

"When that happened I knew my instinct had been right from the first. It gave me very little pain, but I was ashamed and disgusted. He hadn't tried to deceive me in words; he never spoke of marriage; and from what I found out then, I saw that he was very much to be pitied."

"You seem to contradict yourself," said Hilliard. "Why were you ashamed and disgusted?"

"At finding myself in the power of such a woman. He married her when she was very young, and I could imagine the life he had led with her until he freed himself. A hateful woman!"

"Hateful to you, I see," muttered the listener, with something tight at his heart.

"Not because I felt anything like jealousy. You must believe me. I should never have spoken if I hadn't meant to tell you the simple truth."

Again he pressed her hand. The warmth of her body had raised his blood to fever-heat.

"When we met again, after I came back, it was by chance. I refused to speak to him, but he followed me all along the street, and I didn't know it till I was nearly home. Then he came up again, and implored me to hear what he had to say. I knew he would wait for me again in High Street, so I had no choice but to listen, and then tell him that there couldn't be anything more between us. And, for all that, he followed me another day. And again I had to listen to him."

Hilliard fancied that he could feel her heart beat against his arm.

"Be quick!" he said. "Tell all, and have done with it."

"He told me, at last, that he was ruined. His wife had brought him into money difficulties; she ran up bills that he was obliged to pay, and left him scarcely enough to live upon. And he had used money that was not his own—he would have to give an account of it in a day or two. He was trying to borrow, but no one would lend him half what he needed——"

"That's enough," Hilliard broke in, as her voice became inaudible.

"No, you ought to know more than I have told you. Of course he didn't ask me for money; he had no idea that I could lend him even a pound. But what I wish you to know is that he hadn't spoken to me again in the old way. He said he had done wrong, when he first came to know me; he begged me to forgive him that, and only wanted me to be his friend."

"Of course."

"Oh, don't be ungenerous: that's so unlike you."

"I didn't mean it ungenerously. In his position I should have done exactly as he did."

"Say you believe me. There was not a word of love between us. He told me all about the miseries of his life—that was all; and I pitied him so. I felt he was so sincere."

"I believe it perfectly."

"There was no excuse for what I did. How I had the courage—the shamelessness—is more than I can understand now."

Hilliard stirred himself, and tried to laugh.

"As it turned out, you couldn't have done better. Well, there's an end of it. Come."

He walked on, and Eve kept closely beside him, looking up into his face.

"I am sure he will pay the money back," she said presently.

"Hang the money!"

Then he stood still.

"How is he to pay it back? I mean, how is he to communicate with you?"

"I gave him my address at Dudley."

Again Hilliard moved on.

"Why should it annoy you?" Eve asked. "If ever he writes to me, I shall let you know at once: you shall see the letter. It is quite certain that he *will* pay his debt; and I shall be very glad when he does."

"What explanation did you give him?"

"The true one. I said I had borrowed from a friend. He was in despair, and couldn't refuse what I offered."

"We'll talk no more of it. It was right to tell me. I'm glad now it's all over. Look at the moon rising—harvest moon, isn't it?"

Eve turned aside again, and leaned on the parapet. He, lingering apart for a moment, at length drew nearer. Of her own accord she put her hands in his.

"In future," she said, "you shall know everything I do. You can trust me: there will be no more secrets."

"Yet you are afraid——"

"It's for your sake. You must be free for the next year or two. I shall be glad to get to work again. I am well and strong and cheerful."

Her eyes drew him with the temptation he had ever yet resisted. Eve did not refuse her lips.

## CHAPTER XVII

"You must write to Patty," she said, when they were at the place of parting. "I shall have her new address in a day or two."

"Yes, I will write to her."

# CHAPTER XVIII

By the end of November Hilliard was well at work in the office of Messrs. Birching, encouraged by his progress and looking forward as hopefully as a not very sanguine temperament would allow. He lived penuriously, and toiled at professional study night as well as day. Now and then he passed an evening with Robert Narramore, who had moved to cozy bachelor quarters a little distance out of town, in the Halesowen direction. Once a week, generally on Saturday, he saw Eve. Other society he had none, nor greatly desired any.

But Eve had as yet found no employment. Good fortune in this respect seemed to have deserted her, and at her meetings with Hilliard she grew fretful over repeated disappointments. Of her day-to-day life she made no complaint, but Hilliard saw too clearly that her spirits were failing beneath a burden of monotonous dulness. That the healthy glow she had brought back in her cheeks should give way to pallor was no more than he had expected, but he watched with anxiety the return of mental symptoms which he had tried to cheat himself into believing would not reappear. Eve did not fail in pleasant smiles, in hopeful words; but they cost her an effort which she lacked the art to conceal. He felt a coldness in her, divined a struggle between conscience and inclination. However, for this also he was prepared; all the more need for vigour and animation on his own part.

Hilliard had read of the woman who, in the strength of her love and loyalty, heartens a man through all the labours he must front he believed in her existence, but had never encountered her—as indeed very few men have. From Eve he looked for nothing of the kind. If she would permit herself to rest upon his sinews, that was all he desired. The mood of their last night in Paris might perchance return, but only with like conditions. Of his workaday passion she knew nothing; habit of familiarity and sense of obligation must supply its place with her until a brightening future once more set her emotions to the gladsome tune.

## CHAPTER XVIII

Now that the days of sun and warmth were past, it was difficult to arrange for a meeting under circumstances that allowed of free comfortable colloquy. Eve declared that her father's house offered no sort of convenience; it was only a poor cottage, and Hilliard would be altogether out of place there. To his lodgings she could not come. Of necessity they had recourse to public places in Birmingham, where an hour or two of talk under shelter might make Eve's journey hither worth while. As Hilliard lived at the north end of the town, he suggested Aston Hall as a possible rendezvous, and here they met, early one Saturday afternoon in December.

From the eminence which late years have encompassed with a proletarian suburb, its once noble domain narrowed to the bare acres of a stinted breathing ground, Aston Hall looks forth upon joyless streets and fuming chimneys, a wide welter of squalid strife. Its walls, which bear the dints of Roundhead cannonade, are blackened with ever-driving smoke; its crumbling gateway, opening aforetime upon a stately avenue of chestnuts, shakes as the steam-tram rushes by. Hilliard's imagination was both attracted and repelled by this relic of what he deemed a better age. He enjoyed the antique chambers, the winding staircases, the lordly gallery, with its dark old portraits and vast fireplaces, the dim-lighted nooks where one could hide alone and dream away the present; but in the end, reality threw scorn upon such pleasure. Aston Hall was a mere architectural relic, incongruous and meaningless amid its surroundings; the pathos of its desecrated dignity made him wish that it might be destroyed, and its place fittingly occupied by some People's Palace, brand new, aglare with electric light, ringing to the latest melodies of the street. When he had long gazed at its gloomy front, the old champion of royalism seemed to shrink together, humiliated by Time's insults.

It was raining when he met Eve at the entrance.

"This won't do," were his first words. "You can't come over in such weather as this. If it hadn't seemed to be clearing tip an hour or two ago, I should have telegraphed to stop you."

"Oh, the weather is nothing to me," Eve answered, with resolute gaiety. "I'm only too glad of the change. Besides, it won't go on much longer. I shall get a place."

Hilliard never questioned her about her attempts to obtain an engagement; the subject was too disagreeable to him.

"Nothing yet," she continued, as they walked up the muddy roadway to the Hall. "But I know you don't like to talk about it."

"I have something to propose. How if I take a couple of cheap rooms in some building let out for offices, and put in a few sticks of furniture? Would you come to see me there?"

He watched her face as she listened to the suggestion, and his timidity seemed justified by her expression.

"You would be so uncomfortable in such a place. Don't trouble. We shall manage to meet somehow. I am certain to be living here before long."

"Even when you are," he persisted, "we shall only be able to see each other in places like this. I can't talk—can't say half the things I wish to——"

"We'll think about it. Ah, it's warm in here!"

This afternoon the guardians of the Hall were likely to be troubled with few visitors. Eve at once led the way upstairs to a certain suite of rooms, hung with uninteresting pictures, where she and Hilliard had before this spent an hour safe from disturbance. She placed herself in the recess of a window: her companion took a few steps backward and forward.

"Let me do what I wish," he urged. "There's a whole long winter before us. I am sure I could find a couple of rooms at a very low rent, and some old woman would come in to do all that's necessary."

"If you like."

"I may? You would come there?" he asked eagerly.

"Of course I would come. But I sha'n't like to see you in a bare, comfortless place."

"It needn't be that. A few pounds will make a decent sort of sitting-room."

"Anything to tell me?" Eve asked, abruptly quitting the subject.

She seemed to be in better spirits than of late, notwithstanding the evil sky; and Hilliard smiled with pleasure as he regarded her.

"Nothing unusual. Oh, yes; I'm forgetting. I had a letter from Emily, and went to see her."

Hilliard had scarcely seen his quondam sister-in-law since she became Mrs. Marr. On the one occasion of his paying a call, after his return from Paris, it struck him that her husband offered no very genial welcome. He had expected this, and willingly kept aloof.

"Read the letter."

Eve did so. It began, "My dear Maurice," and ended, "Ever affectionately and gratefully yours." The rest of its contents ran thus:

"I am in great trouble—dreadfully unhappy. It would be such a kindness if you would let me see you. I can't put in a letter what I want to say, and I do hope you won't refuse to come. Friday afternoon, at three, would do, if you can get away from business for once. How I look back on the days when you used to come over from Dudley and have tea with us in the dear little room. Do come!"

"Of course," said Hilliard, laughing as he met Eve's surprised look. "I knew what *that* meant. I would much rather have got out of it, but it would have seemed brutal. So I went. The poor simpleton has begun to find that marriage with one man isn't necessarily the same thing as marriage with another. In Ezra Marr she has caught a Tartar."

"Surely he doesn't ill-use her?"

"Not a bit of it. He is simply a man with a will, and finds it necessary to teach his wife her duties. Emily knows no more about the duties of life than her little five-year-old girl. She thought she could play with a second husband as she did with the first, and she was gravely mistaken. She complained to me of a thousand acts of tyranny—every one of them, I could see, merely a piece of rude commonsense. The man must be calling himself an idiot for marrying her. I could only listen with a long face. Argument with Emily is out of the question. And I shall take good care not to go there again."

Eve asked many questions, and approved his resolve.

"You are not the person to console and instruct her. But she must look upon you as the best and wisest of men. I can understand that."

"You can understand poor, foolish Emily thinking so——"

"Put all the meaning you like into my words," said Eve, with her pleasantest smile. "Well, I too have had a letter. From Patty. She isn't going to be married, after all."

"Why, I thought it was over by now."

"She broke it off less than a week before the day. I wish I could show you her letter, but, of course, I mustn't. It's very amusing. They had quarrelled about every conceivable thing—all but one, and this came up at last. They were talking about meals, and Mr. Dally said that he liked a bloater for breakfast every morning. 'A bloater!' cried Patty. 'Then I hope you won't ask me to cook it for you. I can't bear them.' 'Oh, very well: if you can't cook a bloater, you're not the wife for me.' And there they broke off, for good and all."

"Which means for a month or two, I suppose."

"Impossible to say. But I have advised her as strongly as I could not to marry until she knows her own mind better. It is too bad of her to have gone so far. The poor man had taken rooms, and all but furnished them. Patty's a silly girl, I'm afraid."

"Wants a strong man to take her in hand—like a good many other girls."

Eve paid no attention to the smile.

"Paris spoilt her for such a man as Mr. Dally. She got all sorts of new ideas, and can't settle down to the things that satisfied her before. It isn't nice to think that perhaps we did her a great deal of harm."

"Nonsense! Nobody was ever harmed by healthy enjoyment."

"Was it healthy—for *her*? That's the question."

Hilliard mused, and felt disinclined to discuss the matter.

"That isn't the only news I have for you," said Eve presently. "I've had another letter."

Her voice arrested Hilliard's step as he paced near her.

"I had rather not have told you anything about it, but I promised. And I have to give you something."

She held out to him a ten-pound note.

"What's this?"

"He has sent it. He says he shall be able to pay something every three months until he has paid the whole debt. Please to take it."

After a short struggle with himself, Hilliard recovered a manly bearing.

"It's quite right he should return the money, Eve, but you mustn't ask me to have anything to do with it. Use it for your own expenses. I gave it to you, and I can't take it back."

She hesitated, her eyes cast down,

"He has written a long letter. There's not a word in it I should be afraid to show you. Will you read it—just to satisfy me? Do read it!"

Hilliard steadily refused, with perfect self-command.

"I trust you—that's enough. I have absolute faith in you. Answer his letter in the way you think best, and never speak to me of the money again. It's yours; make what use of it you like."

"Then I shall use it," said Eve, after a pause, "to pay for a lodging in Birmingham. I couldn't live much longer at home. If I'm here, I can get books out of the library, and time won't drag so. And I shall be near you."

"Do so, by all means."

As if more completely to dismiss the unpleasant subject, they walked into another room. Hilliard began to speak again of his scheme for providing a place where they could meet and talk at their ease. Eve now entered into it with frank satisfaction.

"Have you said anything yet to Mr. Narramore?" she asked at length.

## CHAPTER XVIII

"No. I have never felt inclined to tell him. Of course I shall some day. But it isn't natural to me to talk of this kind of thing, even with so intimate a friend. Some men couldn't keep it to themselves: for me the difficulty is to speak."

"I asked again, because I have been thinking—mightn't Mr. Narramore be able to help me to get work?"

Hilliard repelled the suggestion with strong distaste. On no account would he seek his friend's help in such a matter. And Eve said no more of it.

On her return journey to Dudley, between eight and nine o'clock, she looked cold and spiritless. Her eyelids dropped wearily as she sat in the corner of the carriage with some papers on her lap, which Hilliard had given her. Rain had ceased, and the weather seemed turning to frost. From Dudley station she had a walk of nearly half an hour, to the top of Kate's Hill.

Kate's Hill is covered with an irregular assemblage of old red-tiled cottages, grimy without, but sometimes, as could be seen through an open door admitting into the chief room, clean and homely-looking within. The steep, narrow alleys leading upward were scarce lighted; here and there glimmered a pale corner-lamp, but on a black night such as this the oil-lit windows of a little shop, and the occasional gleam from doors, proved very serviceable as a help in picking one's path. Towards the top of the hill there was no paving, and mud lay thick. Indescribable the confusion of this toilers' settlement—houses and workshops tumbled together as if by chance, the ways climbing and winding into all manner of pitch-dark recesses, where eats prowled stealthily. In one spot silence and not a hint of life; in another, children noisily at play amid piles of old metal or miscellaneous rubbish. From the labyrinth which was so familiar to her, Eve issued of a sudden on to a sort of terrace, where the air blew shrewdly: beneath lay cottage roofs, and in front a limitless gloom, which by daylight would have been an extensive northward view, comprising the towns of Bilston and Wolverhampton. It was now a black gulf, without form and void, sputtering fire. Flames that leapt out of nothing, and as suddenly disappeared; tongues of yellow or of crimson, quivering, lambent, seeming to snatch and devour and then fall back in satiety. When a cluster of these fires shot forth together, the sky above became illumined with a broad glare, which throbbed and pulsed in the manner of sheet-lightning, though more lurid, and in a few seconds was gone.

She paused here for a moment, rather to rest after her climb than to look at what she had seen so often, then directed her steps to one of the houses within sight. She pushed the door, and entered a little parlour, where a fire and a lamp made cheery welcome. By the hearth, in a round-backed wooden chair, sat a grizzle-headed man, whose hard features proclaimed his relation to Eve, otherwise seeming so improbable. He looked up from the volume open on his knee—a Bible—and said in a rough, kind voice:

"I was thinkin' it 'ud be about toime for you. You look starved, my lass."

"Yes; it has turned very cold."

"I've got a bit o' supper ready for you. I don't want none myself; there's food enough for me *here*." He laid his hand on the book. "D'you call to mind the eighteenth of Ezekiel, lass?—'But if the wicked will turn from all his sins that he hath committed——'"

Eve stood motionless till he had read the verse, then nodded and began to take off her out-of-door garments. She was unable to talk, and her eyes wandered absently.

# CHAPTER XIX

After a week's inquiry, Hilliard discovered the lodging that would suit his purpose. It was Camp Hill; two small rooms at the top of a house, the ground-floor of which was occupied as a corn-dealer's shop, and the story above that tenanted by a working optician with a blind wife. On condition of papering the rooms and doing a few repairs necessary to make them habitable, he secured them at the low rent of four shillings a week.

Eve paid her first visit to this delectable abode on a Sunday afternoon; she saw only the sitting-room, which would bear inspection; the appearance of the bed-room was happily left to her surmise. Less than a five-pound note had paid for the whole furnishing. Notwithstanding the reckless invitation to Eve to share his fortunes straightway, Hilliard, after paving his premium of fifty guineas to the Birching Brothers, found but a very small remnant in hand of the money with which he had set forth from Dudley some nine months ago. Yet not for a moment did he repine; he had the value of his outlay; his mind was stored with memories and his heart strengthened with hope.

At her second coming—she herself now occupied a poor little lodging not very far away—Eve beheld sundry improvements. By the fireside stood a great leather chair, deep, high-backed, wondrously self-assertive over against the creaky cane seat which before had dominated the room. Against the wall was a high bookcase, where Hilliard's volumes, previously piled on the floor, stood in loose array; and above the mantelpiece hung a framed engraving of the Parthenon.

"This is dreadful extravagance!" she exclaimed, pausing at the threshold, and eying her welcomer with mock reproof.

"It is, but not on my part. The things came a day or two ago, simply addressed to me from shops."

"Who was the giver, then?"

"Must be Narramore, of course. He was here not long ago, and growled a good deal because I hadn't a decent chair for his lazy bones."

"I am much obliged to him," said Eve, as she sank back in the seat of luxurious repose. "You ought to hang his portrait in the room. Haven't you a photograph?" she added carelessly.

"Such a thing doesn't exist. Like myself, he hasn't had a portrait taken since he was a child. A curious thing, by-the-bye, that you should have had yours taken just when you did. Of course it was because you were going far away for the first time; but it marked a point in your life, and put on record the Eve Madeley whom no one would see again If I can't get that photograph in any other way I shall go and buy, beg, or steal it from Mrs. Brewer."

"Oh, you shall have one if you insist upon it."

"Why did you refuse it before?"

"I hardly know—a fancy—I thought you would keep looking at it, and regretting that I had changed so."

As on her previous visit, she soon ceased to talk, and, in listening to Hilliard, showed unconsciously a tired, despondent face.

"Nothing yet," fell from her lips, when he had watched her silently.

"Never mind; I hate the mention of it."

"By-the-bye," he resumed, "Narramore astounded me by hinting at marriage. It's Miss Birching, the sister of my man. It hasn't come to an engagement yet, and if it ever does I shall give Miss Birching the credit for it. It would have amused you to hear him talking about her, with a pipe in his mouth and half asleep. I understand now why he took young Birching with him to Switzerland. He'll never carry it through; unless, as I said, Miss Birching takes the decisive step."

"Is she the kind of girl to do that?" asked Eve, waking to curiosity.

"I know nothing about her, except from Narramore's sleepy talk. Rather an arrogant beauty, according to him. He told me a story of how, when he was calling upon her, she begged him to ring the bell for something or other, and he was so slow in getting up that she went and rang it herself. 'Her own fault,' he said; 'she asked me to sit on a chair with a seat some six inches above the ground, and how can a man hurry up from a thing of that sort?'"

"He must be a strange man. Of course he doesn't care anything about Miss Birching."

"But I think he does, in his way."

"How did he ever get on at all in business?"

"Oh, he's one of the lucky men." Hilliard replied, with a touch of good-natured bitterness. "He never exerted himself; good things fell into his mouth. People got to like him—that's one explanation, no doubt."

## CHAPTER XIX

"Don't you think he may have more energy than you imagine?"

"It's possible. I have sometimes wondered."

"What sort of life does he lead? Has he many friends I mean?"

"Very few. I should doubt whether there's anyone he talks with as he does with me. He'll never get much good out of his money; but if he fell into real poverty—poverty like mine—it would kill him. I know he looks at me as an astonishing creature, and marvels that I don't buy a good dose of chloral and have done with it."

Eve did not join in his laugh.

"I can't bear to hear you speak of your poverty," she said in an undertone. "You remind me that I am the cause of it."

"Good Heavens! As if I should mention it if I were capable of such a thought!"

"But it's the fact," she persisted, with something like irritation. "But for me, you would have gone into the architect's office with enough to live upon comfortably for a time."

"That's altogether unlikely," Hilliard declared. "But for you, it's improbable that I should have gone to Birching's at all. At this moment I should be spending my money in idleness, and, in the end, should have gone back to what I did before. You have given me a start in a new life."

This, and much more of the same tenor, failed to bring a light upon Eve's countenance. At length she asked suddenly, with a defiant bluntness——

"Have you ever thought what sort of a wife I am likely to make?"

Hilliard tried to laugh, but was disagreeably impressed by her words and the look that accompanied them.

"I have thought about it, to be sure," he answered carelessly

"And don't you feel a need of courage?"

"Of course. And not only the need but the courage itself."

"Tell me the real, honest truth." She bent forward, and gazed at him with eyes one might have thought hostile. "I demand the truth of you: I have a right to know it. Don't you often wish you had never seen me?"

"You 're in a strange mood."

"Don't put me off. Answer!"

"To ask such a question," he replied quietly, "is to charge me with a great deal of hypocrisy. I did *once* all but wish I had never seen you. If I lost you now I should lose what seems to me the strongest desire of my life. Do you suppose I sit down and meditate on your capacity as cook or housemaid? It would be very prudent and laudable, but I have other thoughts—that give me trouble enough."

"What thoughts?"

"Such as one doesn't talk about—if you insist on frankness."

Her eyes wandered.

"It's only right to tell you," she said, after silence, "that I dread poverty as much as ever I did. And I think poverty in marriage a thousand times worse than when one is alone."

"Well, we agree in that. But why do you insist upon it just now? Are *you* beginning to be sorry that we ever met?"

"Not a day passes but I feel sorry for it."

"I suppose you are harping on the old scruple. Why will you plague me about it?"

"I mean," said Eve, with eyes down, "that you are the worse off for having met me, but I mean something else as well. Do you think it possible that anyone can owe too much gratitude, even to a person one likes?"

He regarded her attentively.

"You feel the burden?"

She delayed her answer, glancing at him with a new expression—a deprecating tenderness.

"It's better to tell you. I *do* feel it, and have always felt it."

"Confound this infernal atmosphere!" Hilliard broke out wrathfully. "It's making you morbid again. Come here to me! Eve—come!"

As she sat motionless, he caught her hands and drew her forward, and sat down again with her passive body resting upon his knees. She was pale, and looked frightened.

"Your gratitude be hanged! Pay me back with your lips—so—and so! Can't you understand that when my lips touch yours, I have a delight that would be well purchased with years of semi-starvation? What is it to me how I won you? You are mine for good and all—that's enough."

She drew herself half away, and stood brightly flushed, touching her hair to set it in order again. Hilliard, with difficulty controlling himself, said in a husky voice—

"Is the mood gone?"

Eve nodded, and sighed.

# CHAPTER XX

At the time appointed for their next meeting, Hilliard waited in vain. An hour passed, and Eve, who had the uncommon virtue of punctuality, still did not come. The weather was miserable—rain, fog, and slush—but this had heretofore proved no obstacle, for her lodgings were situated less than half a mile away. Afraid of missing her if he went out, he fretted through another hour, and was at length relieved by the arrival of a letter of explanation. Eve wrote that she had been summoned to Dudley; her father was stricken with alarming illness, and her brother had telegraphed.

For two days he heard nothing; then came a few lines which told him that Mr. Madeley could not live many more hours. On the morrow Eve wrote that her father was dead.

To the letter which he thereupon despatched Hilliard had no reply for nearly a week. When Eve wrote, it was from a new address at Dudley. After thanking him for the kind words with which he had sought to comfort her, she continued—

"I have at last found something to do, and it was quite time, for I have been very miserable, and work is the best thing for me. Mr. Welland, my first employer, when I was twelve years old, has asked me to come and keep his books for him, and I am to live in his house. My brother has gone into lodgings, and we see no more of the cottage on Kate's Hill. It's a pity I have to be so far from you again, but there seems to be no hope of getting anything to do in Birmingham, and here I shall be comfortable enough, as far as mere living goes. On Sunday I shall be quite free, and will come over as often as possible; but I have caught a bad cold, and must be content to keep in the house until this dreadful weather changes. Be more careful of yourself than you generally are, and let me hear often. In a few months' time we shall be able to spend pleasant hours on the Castle Hill. I have heard from Patty, and want to tell you about her letter, but this cold makes me feel too stupid Will write again soon."

It happened that Hilliard himself was just now blind and voiceless with a catarrh. The news from Dudley by no means solaced him. He crouched over his fire through the long, black day, tormented with many miseries, and at eventide drank half a bottle of whisky, piping hot, which at least assured him of a night's sleep.

Just to see what would be the result of his silence, he wrote no reply to this letter. A fortnight elapsed; he strengthened himself in stubbornness, aided by the catarrh, which many bottles of whisky would not overcome. When his solitary confinement grew at length insufferable, he sent for Narramore, and had not long to wait before his friend appeared. Narramore was rosy as ever: satisfaction with life beamed from his countenance.

"I've ordered you in some wine," he exclaimed genially, sinking into the easy-chair which Hilliard had vacated for him—an instance of selfishness in small things which did not affect his generosity in greater. "It isn't easy to get good port nowadays, but they tell me that this is not injurious. Hasn't young Birching been to see you? No, I suppose he would think it *infra dig.* to come to this neighbourhood. There's a damnable self-conceit in that family: you must have noticed it, eh? It comes out very strongly in the girl. By-the-bye I've done with her—haven't been there for three weeks, and don't think I shall go again, unless it's for the pleasure of saying or doing something that'll irritate her royal highness."

"Did you quarrel?"

"Quarrel? I never quarrel with anyone; it's bad for one's nerves."

"Did you get as far as proposing?"

"Oh, I left *her* to do that. Women are making such a row about their rights nowadays, that it's as well to show you grant them perfect equality. I gave her every chance of saying something definite. I maintain that she trifled with my affections. She asked me what my views in life were. Ah, thought I, now it's coming; and I answered modestly that everything depended on circumstances. I might have said it depended on the demand for brass bedsteads; but perhaps that would have verged on indelicacy—you know that I am delicacy personified. 'I thought,' said Miss Birching, 'that a man of any energy made his own circumstances?' 'Energy!' I shouted. 'Do you look for energy in *me*? It's the greatest compliment anyone ever paid me.' At that she seemed desperately annoyed, and wouldn't pursue the subject. That's how it always was, just when the conversation grew interesting."

"I'm sorry to see you so cut up about it," remarked Hilliard.

# CHAPTER XX

"None of your irony, old fellow. Well, the truth is, I've seen someone I like better."

"Not surprised."

"It's a queer story; I'll tell it you some day, if it comes to anything. I'm not at all sure that it will, as there seems to be a sort of lurking danger that I may make a damned fool of myself."

"Improbable?" commented the listener. "Your blood is too temperate."

"So I thought; but one never knows. Unexpected feelings crop up in a fellow. We won't talk about it just now. How have things been going in the architectural line?"

"Not amiss. Steadily, I think."

Narramore lay back at full length, his face turned to the ceiling.

"Since I've been living out yonder, I've got a taste for the country. I have a notion that, if brass bedsteads keep firm, I shall some day build a little house of my own; an inexpensive little house, with a tree or two about it. Just make me a few sketches, will you? When you've nothing better to do, you know."

He played with the idea, till it took strong hold of him, and he began to talk with most unwonted animation.

"Five or six thousand pounds—I ought to be able to sink that in a few years. Not enough, eh? But I don't want a mansion. I'm quite serious about this, Hilliard. When you're feeling ready to start on your own account, you shall have the job."

Hilliard laughed grimly at the supposition that he would ever attain professional independence, but his friend talked on, and overleaped difficulties with a buoyancy of spirit which ultimately had its effect upon the listener. When he was alone again, Hilliard felt better, both in body and mind, and that evening, over the first bottle of Narramore's port, he amused himself with sketching ideal cottages.

"The fellow's in love, at last. When a man thinks of pleasant little country houses, 'with a tree or two' about them——"

He sighed, and ground his teeth, and sketched on.

Before bedtime, a sudden and profound shame possessed him. Was he not behaving outrageously in neglecting to answer Eve's letter? For all he knew the cold of which she complained might have caused her more suffering than he himself had gone through from the like cause, and that was bad enough. He seized paper and wrote to her as he had never written before, borne on the very high flood of passionate longing. Without regard to prudence he left the house at midnight and posted his letter.

"It never occurred to me to blame you for not writing," Eve quickly replied; "I'm afraid you are more sensitive than I am, and, to tell the truth, I believe men generally *are* more sensitive than women in things of this kind. It pleased me very much to hear of the visit you had had from Mr. Narramore, and that he had cheered you. I do so wish I could have come, but I have really been quite ill, and I must not think of risking a journey till the weather improves. Don't trouble about it; I will write often."

"I told you about a letter I had had from poor Patty, and I want to ask you to do something. Will you write to her? Just a nice, friendly little letter. She would be so delighted, she would indeed. There's no harm in copying a line or two from what she sent me. 'Has Mr. Hilliard forgotten all about me?' she says. 'I would write to him, but I feel afraid. Not afraid of *you*, dear Eve, but he might feel I was impertinent. What do you think? We had such delicious times together, he and you and I, and I really don't want him to forget me altogether?' Now I have told her that there is no fear whatever of your forgetting her, and that we often speak of her. I begin to think that I have been unjust to Patty in calling her silly, and making fun of her. She was anything but foolish in breaking off with that absurd Mr. Dally, and I can see now that she will never give a thought to him again. What I fear is that the poor girl will never find any one good enough for her. The men she meets are very vulgar, and vulgar Patty is *not*—as you once said to me, you remember. So, if you can spare a minute, write her a few lines, to show that you still think of her. Her address is——, etc."

To Hilliard all this seemed merely a pleasant proof of Eve's amiability, of her freedom from that acrid monopolism which characterises the ignoble female in her love relations. Straightway he did as he was requested, and penned to Miss Ringrose a chatty epistle, with which she could not but be satisfied. A day or two brought him an answer. Patty's handwriting lacked distinction, and in the matter of orthography she was not beyond reproach, but her letter chirped with a prettily expressed gratitude. "I am living with my aunt, and am likely to for a long time. And I get on very well at my new shop, which I have no wish to leave." This was her only allusion to the shattered matrimonial project: "I wish there was any chance of you and Eve coming to live in London, but I suppose that's too good to hope for. We don't get many things as we wish them in this world. And yet I oughtn't to say that either, for if it hadn't been for you I should never have seen Paris, which was so awfully jolly! But you'll be coming for a holiday, won't you? I should so like just to see you, if ever you do. It isn't like it was at the old shop. There's a great deal of business done here, and very little time to talk to anyone in the shop. But many girls have worse things to put up with than I have, and I won't make you think I'm a grumbler."

The whole of January went by before Hilliard and Eve again saw each other. The lover wrote at length that he could bear it no longer, that he was coming to Dudley, if only for the mere sight of Eve's face; she must meet him in the waiting-room at the railway station. She answered by return of post, "I will come over next Sunday, and be with you at twelve o'clock, but I must leave very early, as I am afraid to be out after nightfall." And this engagement was kept.

The dress of mourning became her well; it heightened her always noticeable air of refinement, and would have constrained to a reverential tenderness even had not Hilliard naturally checked himself from any bolder demonstration of joy. She spoke in a low, soft voice, seldom raised her eyes, and manifested a new gentleness very touching to Hilliard, though at the same time, and he knew not how or why, it did not answer to his desire. A midday meal was in readiness for her; she pretended to eat, but in reality scarce touched the food.

"You must taste old Narramore's port wine," said her entertainer. "The fellow actually sent a couple of dozen."

She was not to be persuaded; her refusal puzzled and annoyed Hilliard, and there followed a long silence. Indeed, it surprised him to find how little they could say to each other to-day. An unknown restraint had come between them.

"Well," he exclaimed at length, "I wrote to Patty, and she answered."

"May I see the letter?"

"Of course. Here it is."

Eve read it, and smiled with pleasure.

"Doesn't she write nicely! Poor girl!"

"Why have you taken so to commiserating her all at once?" Hilliard asked. "She's no worse off than she ever was. Rather better, I think."

"Life isn't the same for her since she was in Paris," said Eve, with peculiar softness.

"Well, perhaps it improved her."

"Oh, it certainly did! But it gave her a feeling of discontent for the old life and the people about her."

"A good many of us have to suffer that. She's nothing like as badly off as you are, my dear girl."

Eve coloured, and kept silence.

"We shall hear of her getting married before long," resumed the other. "She told me herself that marriage was the scourge of music-shops—it carries off their young women at such a rate."

"She told you that? It was in one of your long talks together in London? Patty and you got on capitally together. It was very natural she shouldn't care much for men like Mr. Dally afterwards."

Hilliard puzzled over this remark, and was on the point of making some impatient reply, but discretion restrained him. He turned to Eve's own affairs, questioned her closely about her life in the tradesman's house, and so their conversation followed a smoother course. Presently, half in jest, Hilliard mentioned Narramore's building projects.

"But who knows? It *might* come to something of importance for me. In two or three years, if all goes well, such a thing might possibly give me a start."

A singular solemnity had settled upon Eve's countenance. She spoke not a word, and seemed unaccountably ill at ease.

"Do you think I am in the clouds?" said Hilliard.

"Oh, no! Why shouldn't you get on—as other men do?"

But she would not dwell upon the hope, and Hilliard, not a little vexed, again became silent.

Her next visit was after a lapse of three weeks. She had again been suffering from a slight illness, and her pallor alarmed Hilliard. Again she began with talk of Patty Ringrose.

"Do you know, there's really a chance that we may see her before long! She'll have a holiday at Easter, from the Thursday night to Monday night, and I have all but got her to promise that she'll come over here. Wouldn't it be fun to let her see the Black Country? You remember her talk about it. I could get her a room, and if it's at all bearable weather, we would all have a day somewhere. Wouldn't you like that?"

"Yes; but I should greatly prefer a day with you alone."

"Oh, of course, the time is coming for that, Would you let us come here one day?"

With a persistence not to be mistaken Eve avoided all intimate topics; at the same time her manner grew more cordial. Through February and March, she decidedly improved in health. Hilliard saw her seldom, but she wrote frequent letters, and their note was as that of her conversation, lively, all but sportive. Once again she had become a mystery to her lover; he pondered over her very much as in the days when they were newly acquainted. Of one thing he felt but too well assured. She did not love him as he desired to be loved. Constant she might be, but it was the constancy of a woman unaffected with ardent emotion. If she granted him her lips they had no fervour respondent to his own; she made a sport of it, forgot it as soon as possible. Upon Hilliard's vehement nature this acted provocatively; at times he was all but frenzied with the violence of his sensual impulses. Yet Eve's control of him grew more assured the less she granted of herself; a look, a motion of her lips, and he drew apart, quivering but subdued. At one such moment he exclaimed:

"You had better not come here at all. I love you too insanely."

Eve looked at him, and silently began to shed tears. He implored her pardon, prostrated himself, behaved in a manner that justified his warning. But Eve stifled the serious drama of the situation, and forced him to laugh with her.

In these days architectural study made little way.

Patty Ringrose was coming for the Easter holidays. She would arrive on Good Friday. "As the weather is so very bad still," wrote Eve to Hilliard, "will you let us come to see you on Saturday? Sunday may be better for an excursion of some sort."

And thus it was arranged. Hilliard made ready his room to receive the fair visitors, who would come at about eleven in the morning. As usual nowadays, he felt discontented, but, after all, Patty's influence might be a help to him, as it had been in worse straits.

# CHAPTER XXI

To-day he had the house to himself. The corn-dealers shop was closed, as on a Sunday; the optician and his blind wife had locked up their rooms and were spending Easter-tide, it might be hoped, amid more cheerful surroundings. Hilliard sat with his door open, that he might easily hear the knock which announced his guests at the entrance below.

It sounded, at length, but timidly. Had he not been listening, he would not have perceived it. Eve's handling of the knocker was firmer than that, and in a different rhythm. Apprehensive of disappointment, he hurried downstairs and opened the door to Patty Ringrose—Patty alone.

With a shy but pleased laugh, her cheeks warm and her eyes bright, she jerked out her hand to him as in the old days.

"I know you won't be glad to see me. I'm so sorry. I said I had better not come."

"Of course I am glad to see you. But where's Eve?"

"It's so unfortunate—she has such a bad headache!" panted the girl. "She couldn't possibly come, and I wanted to stay with her, I said. I should only disappoint you."

"It's a pity, of course; but I'm glad you came, for all that." Hilliard stifled his dissatisfaction and misgivings. "You'll think this a queer sort of place. I'm quite alone here to-day. But after you have rested a little we can go somewhere else."

"Yes. Eve told me you would be so kind as to take me to see things. I'm not tired. I won't come in, if you'd rather——"

"Oh, you may as well see what sort of a den I've made for myself."

He led the way upstairs. When she reached the top, Patty was again breathless, the result of excitement more than exertion. She exclaimed at sight of the sitting-room. How cosy it was! What a scent from the flowers! Did he always buy flowers for his room? No doubt it was to please Eve. What a comfortable chair! Of course Eve always sat in this chair?

## CHAPTER XXI

Then her babbling ceased, and she looked up at Hilliard, who stood over against her, with nervous delight. He could perceive no change whatever in her, except that she was better dressed than formerly. Not a day seemed to have been added to her age; her voice had precisely the intonations that he remembered. After all, it was little more than half a year since they were together in Paris; but to Hilliard the winter had seemed of interminable length, and he expected to find Miss Ringrose a much altered person.

"When did this headache begin?" he inquired, trying to speak without over-much concern.

"She had a little yesterday, when she met me at the station. I didn't think she was looking at all well."

"I'm surprised to hear that. She looked particularly well when I saw her last. Had you any trouble in making your way here?"

"Oh, not a bit. I found the tram, just as Eve told me. But I'm so sorry! And a fine day too! You don't often have fine days here, do you, Mr. Hilliard?"

"Now and then. So you've seen Dudley at last. What do you think of it?"

"Oh, I like it! I shouldn't mind living there a bit. But of course I like Birmingham better."

"Almost as fine as Paris, isn't it?"

"You don't mean that, of course. But I've only seen a few of the streets, and most of the shops are shut up to-day. Isn't it a pity Eve has to live so far off? Though, of course, it isn't really very far—and I suppose you see each other often?"

Hilliard took a seat, crossed his legs, and grasped his knee. The girl appeared to wait for an answer to her last words, but he said nothing, and stared at the floor.

"If it's fine to-morrow," Patty continued, after observing him furtively, "are you coming to Dudley?"

"Yes, I shall come over. Did she send any message?"

"No—nothing particular——"

Patty looked confused, stroked her dress, and gave a little cough.

"But if it rains—as it very likely will—there's no use in my coming."

"No, she said not."

"Or if her headache is still troubling her——"

"Let's hope it will be better. But—in any case, she'll be able to come with me to Birmingham on Monday, when I go back I must be home again on Monday night."

"Don't you think," said Hilliard carelessly, "that Eve would rather have you to herself, just for the short time you are here?"

Patty made vigorous objection.

"I don't think that at all. It's quite settled that you are to come over to-morrow, if it's fine. Oh, and I *do* hope it will be! It would be so dreadful to be shut up in the house all day at Dudley. How very awkward that there's no place where she can have you there! If it rains, hadn't we better come here? I'm sure it would be better for Eve. She seems to get into such low spirits—just like she was sometimes in London."

"That's quite news to me," said the listener gravely.

"Doesn't she let you know? Then I'm so sorry I mentioned it. You won't tell her I said anything?"

"Wait a moment. Does she say that she is often in low spirits?"

Patty faltered, stroking her dress with the movement of increasing nervousness.

"It's better I should know," Hilliard added, "I'm afraid she keeps all this from me. For several weeks I have thought her in particularly good health."

"But she tells me just the opposite. She says——"

"Says what?"

"Perhaps it's only the place that doesn't agree with her. I don't think Dudley is *very* healthy, do you?"

"I never heard of doctors sending convalescents there. But Eve must be suffering from some other cause, I think. Does it strike you that she is at all like what she used to be when—when you felt so anxious about her?"

He met the girl's eyes, and saw them expand in alarm.

"I didn't think—I didn't mean——" she stammered.

"No, but I have a reason for asking. Is it so or not?"

"Don't frighten me, Mr. Hilliard! I do so wish I hadn't said anything. She isn't in good health, that's all. How can you think——? That was all over long ago. And she would never—I'm *sure* she wouldn't, after all you've done for her."

Hilliard ground the carpet with his foot, and all but uttered a violent ejaculation.

"I know she is all gratitude," were the words that became audible.

"She is indeed!" urged Patty. "She says that—even if she wished—she could never break off with you; as I am *sure* she would never wish!"

## CHAPTER XXI

"Ah! that's what she says," murmured the other. And abruptly he rose. "There's no use in talking about this. You are here for a holiday, and not to be bored with other people's troubles. The sun is trying to shine. Let us go and see the town, and then—yes, I'll go back with you to Dudley, just to hear whether Eve is feeling any better. You could see her, and then come out and tell me."

"Mr. Hilliard, I'm quite sure you are worrying without any cause—you are, indeed!"

"I know I am. It's all nonsense. Come along, and let us enjoy the sunshine."

They spent three or four hours together, Hilliard resolute in his discharge of hospitable duties, and Miss Ringrose, after a brief spell of unnatural gravity, allowing no reflection to interfere with her holiday mood. Hilliard had never felt quite sure as to the limits of Patty's intelligence; he could not take her seriously, and yet felt unable to treat her altogether as a child or an imbecile. To-day, because of his preoccupied thoughts, and the effort it cost him to be jocose, he talked for the most part in a vein of irony which impressed, but did not much enlighten, his hearer.

"This," said he, when they had reached the centre of things, "is the Acropolis of Birmingham. Here are our great buildings, of which we boast to the world. They signify the triumph of Democracy—and of money. In front of you stands the Town Hall. Here, to the left, is the Midland Institute, where a great deal of lecturing goes on, and the big free library, where you can either read or go to sleep. I have done both in my time. Behind yonder you catch a glimpse of the fountain that plays to the glory of Joseph Chamberlain—did you ever hear of him? And further back still is Mason College, where young men are taught a variety of things, including discontent with a small income. To the right there, that's the Council Hall—splendid, isn't it! We bring our little boys to look at it, and tell them if they make money enough they may some day go in and out as if it were their own house. Behind it you see the Art Gallery. We don't really care for pictures; a great big machine is our genuine delight; but it wouldn't be nice to tell everybody that."

"What a lot I have learnt from you!" exclaimed the girl ingenuously, when at length they turned their steps towards the railway station. "I shall always remember Birmingham. You like it much better than London, don't you?"

"I glory in the place!"

Hilliard was tired out. He repented of his proposal to make the journey to Dudley and back, but his companion did not suspect this.

"I'm sure Eve will come out and have a little walk with us," she said comfortingly. "And she'll think it so kind of you."

At Dudley station there were crowds of people; Patty asked leave to hold by her companion's arm as they made their way to the exit. Just outside Hilliard heard himself hailed in a familiar voice; he turned and saw Narramore.

"I beg your pardon," said his friend, coming near. "I didn't notice—I thought you were alone, or, of course I shouldn't have shouted. Shall you be at home to-morrow afternoon?"

"If it rains."

"It's sure to rain. I shall look in about four."

## CHAPTER XXII

With a glance at Miss Ringrose, he raised his hat and passed on. Hilliard, confused by the rapid rencontre, half annoyed at having been seen with Patty, and half wishing he had not granted the appointment for tomorrow, as it might interfere with a visit from the girls, walked forward in silence.

"So we really sha'n't see you if it's wet tomorrow," said Patty.

"Better not. Eve would be afraid to come, she catches cold so easily."

"It may be fine, like to-day. I do hope——"

She broke off and added:

"Why, isn't that Eve in front?"

Eve it certainly was, walking slowly away from the station, a few yards in advance of them. They quickened their pace, and Patty caught her friend by the arm. Eve, startled out of abstraction, stared at her with eyes of dismay and bloodless cheeks.

"Did I frighten you? Mr. Hilliard has come back with me to ask how you are. Is your head better?"

"I've just been down to the station—for something to do," said Eve, her look fixed on Hilliard with what seemed to him a very strange intensity. "The afternoon was so fine."

"We've had a splendid time," cried Patty. "Mr. Hilliard has shown me everything."

"I'm so glad. I should only have spoilt it if I had been with you. It's wretched going about with a headache, and I can't make believe to enjoy Birmingham."

Eve spoke hurriedly, still regarding Hilliard, who looked upon the ground.

"Have you been alone all day?" he asked, taking the outer place at her side, as they walked on.

"Of course—except for the people in the house," was her offhand reply.

"I met Narramore down at the station; he must have passed you. What has brought him here to-day, I wonder?"

Appearing not to heed the remark, Eve glanced across at Patty, and said with a laugh:

"It's like Paris again, isn't it—we three? You ought to come and live here, Patty. Don't you think you could get a place in Birmingham? Mr. Hilliard would get a piano for his room, and you could let him have some music. I'm too old to learn."

"I'm sure he wouldn't want *me* jingling there."

"Wouldn't he? He's very fond of music indeed."

Hilliard stopped.

"Well, I don't think I'll go any further," he said mechanically. "You're quite well again, Eve, and that's all I wanted to know."

"What about to-morrow?" Eve asked.

The sun had set, and in the westward sky rose a mountain of menacing cloud. Hilliard gave a glance in that direction before replying.

"Don't count upon me. Patty and you will enjoy the day together, in any case. Yes, I had rather have it so. Narramore said just now he might look in to see me in the after' noon. But come over on Monday. When does Patty's train go from New Street?"

Eve was mute, gazing at the speaker as if she did not catch what he had said. Patty answered for herself.

"Then you can either come to my place," he continued, "or I'll meet you at the station."

Patty's desire was evident in her face; she looked at Eve.

"We'll come to you early in the afternoon," said the latter, speaking like one aroused from reverie. "Yes, we'll come whatever the weather is."

The young man shook hands with them, raised his hat, and walked away without further speech. It occurred to him that he might overtake Narramore at the station, and in that hope he hastened; but Narramore must have left by a London and North-Western train which had just started; he was nowhere discoverable. Hilliard travelled back by the Great Western, after waiting about an hour; he had for companions half-a-dozen beer-muddled lads, who roared hymns and costers' catches impartially.

His mind was haunted with deadly suspicions: he felt sick at heart.

Eve's headache, undoubtedly, was a mere pretence for not accompanying Patty to-day. She had desired to be alone, and—this he discovered no less clearly—she wished the friendship between him and Patty to be fostered. With what foolish hope? Was she so shallow-natured as to imagine that he might transfer his affections to Patty Ringrose? it proved how strong her desire had grown to be free from him.

The innocent Patty (*was* she so innocent?) seemed not to suspect the meaning of her friend's talk. Yet Eve must have all but told her in so many words that she was weary of her lover. That hateful harping on "gratitude"! Well, one cannot purchase a woman's love. He had missed the right, the generous, line of conduct. That would have been to rescue Eve from manifest peril, and then to ask nothing of her. Could he but have held his passions in leash, something like friendship—rarest of all relations between man and woman—might have come about between him and Eve. She, too, certainly had never got beyond the stage of liking him as a companion; her senses had never answered to his appeal He looked back upon the evening when they had dined together at the restaurant in Holborn. Could he but have stopped at *that* point! There would have been no harm in such avowals as then escaped him, for he recognised without bitterness that the warmth of feeling was all on one side, and Eve, in the manner of her sex, could like him better for his love without a dream of returning it. His error was to have taken advantage—perhaps a mean advantage—of the strange events that followed. If he restrained himself before, how much more he should have done so when the girl had put herself at his mercy, when to demand her love was the obvious, commonplace, vulgar outcome of the situation? Of course she harped on "gratitude." What but a sense of obligation had constrained her?

Something had taken place to-day; he felt it as a miserable certainty. The man from London had been with her. She expected him, and had elaborately planned for a day of freedom. Perhaps her invitation of Patty had no other motive.

That Patty was a conspirator against him he could not believe. No! She was merely an instrument of Eve's subtlety. And his suspicion had not gone beyond the truth. Eve entertained the hope that Patty might take her place. Perchance the silly, good-natured girl would feel no objection; though it was not very likely that she foresaw or schemed for such an issue.

At Snow Hill station it cost him an effort to rise and leave the carriage. His mood was sluggish; he wished to sit still and think idly over the course of events.

He went by way of St. Philip's Church, which stands amid a wide graveyard, enclosed with iron railings, and crossed by paved walks. The locality was all but forsaken; the church rose black against the grey sky, and the lofty places of business round about were darkly silent. A man's footstep sounded in front of him, and a figure approached along the narrow path between the high bars. Hilliard would have passed without attention, but the man stopped his way.

"Hollo! Here we are again!"

He stared at the speaker, and recognised Mr. Dengate.

"So you've come back?"

"Where from?" said Hilliard. "What do you know of me?"

"As much as I care to," replied the other with a laugh. "So you haven't quite gone to the devil yet? I gave you six months. I've been watching the police news in the London papers."

In a maddening access of rage, Hilliard clenched his fist and struck fiercely at the man. But he did no harm, for his aim was wild, and Dengate easily warded off the blows.

"Hold on! You're drunk, of course. Stop it, my lad, or I'll have you locked up till Monday morning. Very obliging of you to offer me the pleasure I was expecting, but you *will* have it, eh?"

A second blow was repaid in kind, and Hilliard staggered back against the railings. Before he could recover himself, Dengate, whose high hat rolled between their feet, pinned his arms.

"There's someone coming along. It's a pity. I should enjoy thrashing you and then running you in. But a man of my position doesn't care to get mixed up in a street row. It wouldn't sound well at Liverpool. Stand quiet, will you!"

A man and a woman drew near, and lingered for a moment in curiosity. Hilliard already amazed at what he had done, became passive, and stood with bent head.

"I must have a word or two With you," said Dengate, when he had picked up his hat. "Can you walk straight? I didn't notice you were drunk before I spoke to you. Come along this way."

To escape the lookers-on, Hilliard moved forward.

"I've always regretted," resumed his companion, "that I didn't give you a sound thrashing that night in the train. It would have done you good. It might have been the making of you. I didn't hurt you, eh?"

"You've bruised my lips—that's all. And I deserved it for being such a damned fool as to lose my temper."

"You look rather more decent than I should have expected. What have you been doing in London?"

"How do you know I have been in London?"

"I took that for granted when I knew you'd left your work at Dudley."

"Who told you I had left it?"

"What does it matter?"

"I should like to know," said Hilliard, whose excitement had passed and left him cold. "And I should like to know who told you before that I was in the habit of getting drunk?"

"Are you drunk now, or not?"

"Not in the way you mean. Do you happen to know a man called Narramore?"

"Never heard the name."

Hilliard felt ashamed of his ignoble suspicion. He became silent.

"There's no reason why you shouldn't be told," added Dengate; "it was a friend of yours at Dudley that I came across when I was making inquiries about you: Mullen his name was."

A clerk at the ironworks, with whom Hilliard had been on terms of slight intimacy.

"Oh, that fellow," he uttered carelessly. "I'm glad to know it was no one else. Why did you go inquiring about me?"

"I told you. If I'd heard a better account I should have done a good deal more for you than pay that money. I gave you a chance, too. If you'd shown any kind of decent behaviour when I spoke to you in the train—but it's no good talking about that now. This is the second time you've let me see what a natural blackguard you are. It's queer, too, you didn't get that from your father. I could have put you in the way of something good at Liverpool. Now, I'd see you damned first, Well, have you run through the money?"

"Every penny of it gone in drink."

"And what are you doing?"

"Walking with a man I should be glad to be rid of."

"All right. Here's my card. When you get into the gutter, and nobody'll give you a hand out, let me know."

With a nod, Dengate walked off. Hilliard saw him smooth his silk hat as he went; then, without glancing at the card, he threw it away.

The next morning was cold and wet. He lay in bed till eleven o'clock, when the charwoman came to put his rooms in order. At midday he left home, had dinner at the nearest place he knew where a meal could be obtained on Sunday, and afterwards walked the streets for an hour under his umbrella. The exercise did him good; on returning he felt able to sit down by the fire, and turn over the plates of his great book on French Cathedrals. This, at all events, remained to him out of the wreck, and was a joy that could be counted upon in days to come.

He hoped Narramore would keep his promise, and was not disappointed. On the verge of dusk his friend knocked and entered.

"The blind woman was at the door below," he explained, "looking for somebody."

"It isn't as absurd as it sounds. She does look for people—with her ears. She knows a footstep that no one else can hear. What were *you* doing at Dudley yesterday?"

Narramore took his pipe out of its case and smiled over it.

"Colours well, doesn't it?" he remarked. "You don't care about the colouring of a pipe? I get a lot of satisfaction out of such little things! Lazy fellows always do; and they have the best of life in the end. By-the-bye, what were *you* doing at Dudley?"

"Had to go over with a girl."

"Rather a pretty girl, too. Old acquaintance?"

"Someone I got to know in London. No, no, not at all what you suppose."

"Well, I know you wouldn't talk about it. It isn't my way, either, to say much about such things. But I half-promised, not long ago, to let you know of something that was going on—if it came to anything. And it rather looks as if it might. What do you think! Birching has been at me, wanting to know why I don't call. I wonder whether the girl put him up to it?"

"You went rather far, didn't you?"

"Oh, I drew back in time. Besides, those ideas are old-fashioned. It'll have to be understood that marriageable girls have nothing specially sacred about them. They must associate with men on equal terms. The day has gone by for a hulking brother to come asking a man about his 'intentions.' As a rule, it's the girl that has intentions. The man is just looking round, anxious to be amiable without making a fool of himself. We're at a great disadvantage. A girl who isn't an idiot can very soon know all about the men who interest her; but it's devilish difficult to get much insight into *them*—until you've hopelessly committed yourself—won't you smoke? I've something to tell you, and I can't talk to a man who isn't smoking, when my own pipe's lit."

Hilliard obeyed, and for a few moments they puffed in silence, twilight thickening about them.

"Three or four months ago," resumed Narramore, "I was told one day—at business—that a lady wished to see me. I happened to have the room to myself, and told them to show the lady in. I didn't in the least know who it could be, and I was surprised to see rather a good-looking girl—not exactly a lady—tallish, and with fine dark eyes—what did you say?"

"Nothing."

"A twinge of gout?"

"Go on."

Narramore scrutinised his friend, who spoke in an unusual tone.

"She sat down, and began to tell me that she was out of work—wanted a place as a bookkeeper, or something of the kind. Could I help her? I asked her why she came to *me*. She said she had heard of me from someone who used to be employed at our place. That was flattering. I showed my sense of it. Then I asked her name, and she said it was Miss Madeley."

A gust threw rain against the windows. Narramore paused, looking into the fire, and smiling thoughtfully.

## CHAPTER XXIII

"You foresee the course of the narrative?"

"Better tell it in detail," muttered Hilliard.

"Why this severe tone? Do you anticipate something that will shock your moral sense? I didn't think you were so straitlaced."

"Do you mean to say——"

Hilliard was sitting upright; his voice began on a harsh tremor, and suddenly failed. The other gazed at him in humorous astonishment.

"What the devil do you mean? Even suppose—who made you a judge and a ruler? This is the most comical start I've known for a long time. I was going to tell you that I have made up my mind to marry the girl."

"I see—it's all right——"

"But do you really mean," said Narramore, "that anything else would have aroused your moral indignation?"

Hilliard burst into a violent fit of laughter. His pipe fell to the floor, and broke; whereupon he interrupted his strange merriment with a savage oath.

"It was a joke, then?" remarked his friend.

"Your monstrous dulness shows the state of your mind. This is what comes of getting entangled with women. You need to have a sense of humour."

"I'm afraid there's some truth in what you say, old boy. I've been conscious of queer symptoms lately—a disposition to take things with absurd seriousness, and an unwholesome bodily activity now and then."

"Go on with your tragic story. The girl asked you to find her a place——"

"I promised to think about it, but I couldn't hear of anything suitable. She had left her address with me, so at length I wrote her a line just saying I hadn't forgotten her. I got an answer on black-edged paper. Miss Madeley wrote to tell me that her father had recently died, and that she had found employment at Dudley; with thanks for my kindness—and so on. It was rather a nicely written letter, and after a day or two I wrote again. I heard nothing—hardly expected to; so in a fortnight's time I wrote once more. Significant, wasn't it? I'm not fond of writing letters, as you know. But I've written a good many since then. At last it came to another meeting. I went over to Dudley on purpose, and saw Miss Madeley on the Castle Hill. I had liked the look of her from the first, and I liked it still better now. By dint of persuasion, I made her tell me all about herself."

"Did she tell you the truth?"

"Why should you suppose she didn't?" replied Narramore with some emphasis. "You must look at this affair in a different light, Hilliard. A joke is a joke, but I've told you that the joking time has gone by. I can make allowance for you: you think I have been making a fool of myself, after all."

"The beginning was ominous."

"The beginning of our acquaintance? Yes, I know how it strikes you. But she came in that way because she had been trying for months——"

"Who was it that told her of you?"

"Oh, one of our girls, no doubt. I haven't asked her—never thought again about it."

"And what's her record?"

"Nothing dramatic in it, I'm glad to say. At one time she had an engagement in London for a year or two. Her people, 'poor but honest'—as the stories put it. Father was a timekeeper at Dudley; brother, a mechanic there. I was over to see her yesterday; we had only just said good-bye when I met you. She's remarkably well educated, all things considered: very fond of reading; knows as much of books as I do—more, I daresay. First-rate intelligence; I guessed that from the first. I can see the drawbacks, of course. As I said, she isn't what *you* would call a lady; but there's nothing much to find fault with even in her manners. And the long and the short of it is, I'm in love with her."

"And she has promised to marry you?"

"Well, not in so many words. She seems to have scruples—difference of position, and that kind of thing."

"Very reasonable scruples, no doubt."

"Quite right that she should think of it in that way, at all events. But I believe it was practically settled yesterday. She isn't in very brilliant health, poor girl! I want to get her away from that beastly place as soon as possible. I shall give myself a longish holiday, and take her on to the Continent. A thorough change of that kind would set her up wonderfully.

"She has never been on to the Continent?"

"What a preposterous question! You're going to sleep, sitting here in the dark. Oh, don't trouble to light up for me; I can't stay much longer."

Hilliard had risen, but instead of lighting the lamp he turned to the window and stood there drumming with his fingers on a pane.

"Are you seriously concerned for me?" said his friend. "Does it seem a piece of madness?"

"You must judge for yourself, Narramore."

"When you have seen her I think you'll take my views. Of course it's the very last thing I ever imagined myself doing; but I begin to see that the talk about fate isn't altogether humbug. I want this girl for my wife, and I never met any one else whom I really *did* want. She suits me exactly. It isn't as if I thought of marrying an ordinary, ignorant, low-class girl. Eve—that's her name—is very much out of the common, look at her how you may. She's rather melancholy, but that's a natural result of her life."

"No doubt, as you say, she wants a thorough change," remarked Hilliard, smiling in the gloom.

"That's it. Her nerves are out of order. Well, I thought I should like to tell you this, old chap. You'll get over the shock in time. I more than half believe, still, that your moral indignation was genuine. And why not? I ought to respect you for it."

"Are you going?"

"I must be in Bristol Road by five—promised to drink a cup of Mrs. Stocker's tea this afternoon. I'm glad now that I have kept up a few homely acquaintances; they may be useful, Of course I shall throw over the Birchings and that lot. You see now why my thoughts have been running on a country house!"

He went off laughing, and his friend sat down again by the fireside.

Half an hour passed. The fire had burnt low, and the room was quite dark. At length, Hilliard bestirred himself. He lit the lamp, drew down the blind, and seated himself at the table to write. With great rapidity he covered four sides of note-paper, and addressed an envelope. But he had no postage-stamp. It could be obtained at a tobacconist's.

So he went out, and turned towards a little shop hard by. But when he had stamped the letter he felt undecided about posting it. Eve had promised to come to-morrow with Patty. If she again failed him it would be time enough to write. If she kept her promise the presence of a third person would be an intolerable restraint upon him. Yet why? Patty might as well know all, and act as judge between them. There needed little sagacity to arbitrate in a matter such as this.

To sit at home was impossible. He walked for the sake of walking, straight on, without object. Down the long gas-lit perspective of Bradford Street, with its closed, silent workshops, across the miserable little river Rea—canal rather than river, sewer rather than canal—up the steep ascent to St. Martin's and the Bull Ring, and the bronze Nelson, dripping with dirty moisture; between the big buildings of New Street, and so to the centre of the town. At the corner by the Post Office he stood in idle contemplation. Rain was still falling, but lightly. The great open space gleamed with shafts of yellow radiance reflected on wet asphalt from the numerous lamps. There was little traffic. An omnibus clattered by, and a tottery cab, both looking rain-soaked. Near the statue of Peel stood a hansom, the forlorn horse crooking his knees and hanging his hopeless head. The Town Hall colonnade sheltered a crowd of people, who were waiting for the rain to stop, that they might spend their Sunday evening, as usual, in rambling about the streets. Within the building, which showed light through all its long windows, a religious meeting was in progress, and hundreds of voices peeled forth a rousing hymn, fortified with deeper organ-note.

Hilliard noticed that as rain-drops fell on the heated globes of the street-lamps they were thrown off again in little jets and puffs of steam. This phenomenon amused him for several minutes. He wondered that he had never observed it before.

Easter Sunday. The day had its importance for a Christian mind. Did Eve think about that? Perhaps her association with him, careless as he was in all such matters, had helped to blunt her religious feeling. Yet what hope was there, in such a world as this, that she would retain the pieties of her girlhood?

Easter Sunday. As he walked on, he pondered the Christian story, and tried to make something out of it. Had it any significance for *him*? Perhaps, for he had never consciously discarded the old faith; he had simply let it fall out of his mind. But a woman ought to have religious convictions. Yes; he saw the necessity of that. Better for him if Eve were in the Town Hall yonder, joining her voice with those that sang.

Better for *him*. A selfish point of view. But the advantage would be hers also. Did he not desire her happiness? He tried to think so, but after all was ashamed to play the sophist with himself. The letter he carried in his pocket told the truth. He had but to think of her as married to Robert Narramore and the jealous fury of natural man drove him headlong.

Monday was again a holiday. When would the cursed people get back to their toil, and let the world resume its wonted grind and clang? They seemed to have been making holiday for a month past.

He walked up and down on the pavement near his door, until at the street corner there appeared a figure he knew. It was Patty Ringrose, again unaccompanied.

# CHAPTER XXIV

They shook hands without a word, their eyes meeting for an instant only. Hilliard led the way upstairs; and Patty, still keeping an embarrassed silence, sat down on the easy-chair. Her complexion was as noticeably fresh as Hilliard's was wan and fatigued. Where Patty's skin showed a dimple, his bore a gash, the result of an accident in shaving this morning.

With hands behind he stood in front of the girl.

"She chose not to come, then?"

"Yes. She asked me to come and see you alone."

"No pretence of headache this time."

"I don't think it was a pretence," faltered Patty, who looked very ill at ease, for all the bloom on her cheeks and the clear, childish light in her eyes.

"Well, then, why hasn't she come to-day?"

"She has sent a letter for you, Mr. Hilliard."

Patty handed the missive, and Hilliard laid it upon the table.

"Am I to read it now?"

"I think it's a long letter."

"Feels like it. I'll study it at my leisure. You know what it contains?"

Patty nodded, her face turned away.

"And why has she chosen to-day to write to me?" Patty kept silence. "Anything to do with the call I had yesterday from my friend Narramore?"

"Yes—that's the reason. But she has meant to let you know for some time."

Hilliard drew a long breath. He fixed his eyes on the letter.

"She has told me everything," the girl continued, speaking hurriedly. "Did you know about it before yesterday?"

"I'm not so good an actor as all that. Eve has the advantage of me in that respect. She really thought it possible that Narramore had spoken before?"

"She couldn't be sure."

"H'm! Then she didn't know for certain that Narramore was going to talk to me about her yesterday?"

"She knew it *must* come."

"Patty, our friend Miss Madeley is a very sensible person—don't you think so?"

"You mustn't think she made a plan to deceive you. She tells you all about it in the letter, and I'm quite sure it's all true, Mr. Hilliard. I was astonished when I heard of it, and I can't tell you how sorry I feel——"

"I'm not at all sure that there's any cause for sorrow," Hilliard interrupted, drawing up a chair and throwing himself upon it. "Unless you mean that you are sorry for Eve."

"I meant that as well."

"Let us understand each other. How much has she told you?"

"Everything, from beginning to end. I had no idea of what happened in London before we went to Paris. And she does so repent of it! She doesn't know how she could do it. She wishes you had refused her."

"So do I."

"But you saved her—she can never forget that. You mustn't think that she only pretends to be grateful. She will be grateful to you as long as she lives. I know she will."

"On condition that I—what?"

Patty gave him a bewildered look.

"What does she ask of me now?"

"She's ashamed to ask anything. She fears you will never speak to her again."

Hilliard meditated, then glanced at the letter.

"I had better read this now, I think, if you will let me."

"Yes—please do——"

He tore open the envelope, and disclosed two sheets of note-paper, covered with writing. For several minutes there was silence; Patty now and then gave a furtive glance at her companion's face as he was reading. At length he put the letter down again, softly.

"There's something more here than I expected. Can you tell me whether she heard from Narramore this morning?"

"She has had no letter."

"I see. And what does she suppose passed between Narramore and me yesterday?"

"She is wondering what you told him."

## CHAPTER XXIV

"She takes it for granted, in this letter, that I have put an end to everything between them. Well, hadn't I a right to do so?"

"Of course you had," Patty replied, with emphasis. "And she knew it must come. She never really thought that she could marry Mr. Narramore. She gave him no promise."

"Only corresponded with him, and made appointments with him, and allowed him to feel sure that she would be his wife."

"Eve has behaved very strangely. I can't understand her. She ought to have told you that she had been to see him, and that he wrote to her. It's always best to be straightforward. See what trouble she has got herself into!"

Hilliard took up the letter again, and again there was a long silence.

"Have you said good-bye to her?" were his next words.

"She's going to meet me at the station to see me off."

"Did she come from Dudley with you?"

"No."

"It's all very well to make use of you for this disagreeable business——"

"Oh, I didn't mind it!" broke in Patty, with irrelevant cheerfulness.

"A woman 'who does such things as this should have the courage to go through with it. She ought to have come herself, and have told me that. She was aiming at much better things than *I* could have promised her. There would have been something to admire in that. The worst of it is she is making me feel ashamed of her. I'd rather have to do with a woman who didn't care a rap for my feelings than with a weak one, who tried to spare me to advantage herself at the same time. There's nothing like courage, whether in good or evil. What do you think? Does she like Narramore?"

"I think she does," faltered Patty, nervously striking her dress.

"Is she in love with him?"

"I—I really don't know!"

"Do you think she ever was in love with anyone, or ever will be?"

Patty sat mute.

"Just tell me what you think."

"I'm afraid she never—Oh, I don't like to say it, Mr. Hilliard!"

"That she never was in love with *me*? I know it."

His tone caused Patty to look up at him, and what she saw in his face made her say quickly:

"I am so sorry; I am indeed! You deserve——"

"Never mind what I deserve," Hilliard interrupted with a grim smile. "Something less than hanging, I hope. That fellow in London; she was fond of *him*?"

The girl whispered an assent.

"A pity I interfered."

"Ah! But think what——"

"We won't discuss it, Patty. It's a horrible thing to be mad about a girl who cares no more for you than for an old glove; but it's a fool's part to try to win her by the way of gratitude. When we came back from Paris I ought to have gone my way, and left her to go hers. Perhaps just possible—if I had seemed to think no more of her——"

Patty waited, but he did not finish his speech.

"What are you going to do, Mr. Hilliard?"

"Yes, that's the question. Shall I hold her to her promise? She says here that she will keep her word if I demand it."

"She says that!" Patty exclaimed, with startled eyes.

"Didn't you know?"

"She told me it was impossible. But perhaps she didn't mean it. Who can tell *what* she means?"

For the first time there sounded a petulance in the girl's voice. Her lips closed tightly, and she tapped with her foot on the floor.

"Did she say that the other thing was also impossible—to marry Narramore?"

"She thinks it is, after what you've told him."

"Well, now, as a matter of fact I told him nothing."

Patty stared, a new light in her eyes.

"You told him—nothing?"

"I just let him suppose that I had never heard the girl's name before."

"Oh, how kind of you! How——"

"Please to remember that it wasn't very easy to tell the truth. What sort of figure should I have made?"

"It's too bad of Eve! It's cruel! I can never like her as I did before."

"Oh, she's very interesting. She gives one such a lot to talk about."

"I don't like her, and I shall tell her so before I leave Birmingham. What right has she to make people so miserable?"

"Only one, after all."

"Do you mean that you will let her marry Mr. Narramore?" Patty asked with interest.

"We shall have to talk about that."

"If I were you I should never see her again!"

## CHAPTER XXIV

"The probability is that we shall see each other many a time."

"Then *you* haven't much courage, Mr. Hilliard!" exclaimed the girl, with a flush on her cheeks.

"More than you think, perhaps," he answered between his teeth.

"Men are very strange," Patty commented in a low voice of scorn, mitigated by timidity.

"Yes, we play queer pranks when a woman has made a slave of us. I suppose you think I should have too much pride to care any more for her. The truth is that for years to come I shall tremble all through whenever she is near me. Such love as I have felt for Eve won't be trampled out like a spark. It's the best and the worst part of my life. No woman can ever be to me what Eve is."

Abashed by the grave force of this utterance, Patty shrank back into the chair, and held her peace.

"You will very soon know what conies of it all," Hilliard continued with a sudden change of voice. "It has to be decided pretty quickly, one way or another."

"May I tell Eve what you have said to me?" the girl asked with diffidence.

"Yes, anything that I have said."

Patty lingered a little, then, as her companion said no more, she rose.

"I must say good-bye, Mr. Hilliard."

"I am afraid your holiday hasn't been as pleasant as you expected."

"Oh, I have enjoyed myself very much. And I hope"—her voice wavered—"I do hope it'll be all right. I'm sure you'll do what seems best."

"I shall do what I find myself obliged to, Patty. Good-bye. I won't offer to go with you, for I should be poor company."

He conducted her to the foot of the stairs, again shook hands with her, put all his goodwill into a smile, and watched her trip away with a step not so light as usual. Then he returned to Eve's letter. It gave him a detailed account of her relations with Narramore. "I went to him because I couldn't bear to live idle any longer; I had no other thought in my mind. If he had been the means of my finding work, I should have confessed it to you at once. But I was tempted into answering his letters.... I knew I was behaving wrongly; I can't defend myself.... I have never concealed my faults from you—the greatest of them is my fear of poverty. I believe it is this that has prevented me from returning your love as I wished to do. For a long time I have been playing a deceitful part, and the strange thing is that I *knew* my exposure might come at any moment. I seem to have been led on by a sort of despair. Now I am tired of it; whether you were prepared for this or not, I must tell you.... I don't ask you to release me. I have been wronging you and acting against my conscience, and if you can forgive me I will try to make up for the ill I have done...."

How much of this could he believe? Gladly he would have fooled himself into believing it all, but the rational soul in him cast out credulity. Every phrase of the letter was calculated for its impression. And the very risk she had run, was not that too a matter of deliberate speculation? She *might* succeed in her design upon Narramore; if she failed, the 'poorer man was still to be counted upon, for she knew the extent of her power over him. It was worth the endeavour. Perhaps, in her insolent self-confidence, she did not fear the effect on Narramore of the disclosure that might be made to him. And who could say that her boldness was not likely to be justified?

He burned with wrath against her, the wrath of a hopelessly infatuated man. Thoughts of revenge, no matter how ignoble, harassed his mind. She counted on his slavish spirit, and even in saying that she did not ask him to release her, she saw herself already released. At each reperusal of her letter he felt more resolved to disappoint the hope that inspired it. When she learnt from Patty that Narramore was still ignorant of her history how would she exult! But that joy should be brief. In the name of common honesty he would protect his friend. If Narramore chose to take her with his eyes open——

Jealous frenzy kept him pacing the room for an hour or two. Then he went forth and haunted the neighbourhood of New Street station until within five minutes of the time of departure of Patty's train. If Eve kept her promise to see the girl off he might surprise her upon the platform.

From the bridge crossing the lines he surveyed the crowd of people that waited by the London train, a bank-holiday train taking back a freight of excursionists. There-amid he discovered Eve, noted her position, descended to the platform, and got as near to her as possible. The train moved off. As Eve turned away among the dispersing people, he stepped to meet her.

## CHAPTER XXV

She gave no sign of surprise. Hilliard read in her face that she had prepared herself for this encounter.

"Come away where we can talk," he said abruptly.

She walked by him to a part of the station where only a porter passed occasionally. The echoings beneath the vaulted roof allowed them to speak without constraint, for their voices were inaudible a yard or two off. Hilliard would not look into her face, lest he should be softened to foolish clemency.

"It's very kind of you," he began, with no clear purpose save the desire of harsh speech, "to ask me to overlook this trifle, and let things be as before."

"I have said all I *can* say in the letter. I deserve all your anger."

That was the note he dreaded, the too well remembered note of pathetic submission. It reminded him with intolerable force that he had never held her by any bond save that of her gratitude.

"Do you really imagine," he exclaimed, "that I could go on with make-believe—that I could bring myself to put faith in you again for a moment?"

"I don't ask you to," Eve replied, in firmer accents. "I have lost what little respect you could ever feel for me. I might have repaid you with honesty—I didn't do even that. Say the worst you can of me, and I shall think still worse of myself."

The voice overcame him with a conviction of her sincerity, and he gazed at her, marvelling.

"Are you honest *now*? Anyone would think so; yet how am I to believe it?"

Eve met his eyes steadily.

"I will never again say one word to you that isn't pure truth. I am at your mercy, and you may punish me as you like."

"There's only one way in which I can punish you. For the loss of *my* respect, or of my love, you care nothing. If I bring myself to tell Narramore disagreeable things about you, you will suffer a disappointment, and that's all. The cost to me will be much greater, and you know it. You pity yourself. You regard me as holding you ungenerously by an advantage you once gave me. It isn't so at all. It is I who have been held by bonds I couldn't break, and from the day when you pretended a love you never felt, all the blame lay with you."

"What could I do?"

"Be truthful—that was all."

"You were not content with the truth. You forced me to think that I could love you, Only remember what passed between us."

"Honesty was still possible, when you came to know yourself better. You should have said to me in so many words: 'I can't look forward to our future with any courage; if I marry it must be a man who has more to offer.' Do you think I couldn't have endured to hear that? You have never understood me. I should have said: 'Then let us shake hands, and I am your friend to help you all I can.'"

"You say that *now*——"

"I should have said it at any time."

"But I am not so mean as you think me. If I loved a man I could face poverty with him, much as I hate and dread it. It was because I only liked you, and could not feel more——"

"Your love happens to fall upon a man who has solid possessions."

"It's easy to speak so scornfully. I have not pretended to love the man you mean."

"Yet you have brought him to think that you are willing to marry him."

"Without any word of love from me. If I had been free I would have married him—just because I am sick of the life I lead, and long for the kind of life he offered me."

"When it's too late you are frank enough."

"Despise me as much as you like. You want the truth, and you shall hear nothing else from me."

"Well, we get near to understanding each other. But it astonishes me that you spoilt your excellent chance. How could you hope to carry through this——"

Eve broke in impatiently.

"I told you in the letter that I had no hope of it. It's your mistake to think me a crafty, plotting, selfish woman. I'm only a very miserable one—it went on from this to that, and I meant nothing. I didn't scheme; I was only tempted into foolishness. I felt myself getting into difficulties that would be my ruin, but I hadn't strength to draw back."

## CHAPTER XXV

"You do yourself injustice," said Hilliard, coldly. "For the past month you have acted a part before me, and acted it well. You seemed to be reconciling yourself to my prospects, indifferent as they were. You encouraged me—talked with unusual cheerfulness—showed a bright face. If this wasn't deliberate acting what did it mean?"

"Yes, it was put on," Eve admitted, after a pause. "But I couldn't help that. I was obliged to keep seeing you, and if I had looked as miserable as I felt——" She broke off. "I tried to behave just like a friend. You can't charge me with pretending—anything else. I *could* be your friend: that was honest feeling."

"It's no use to me. I must have more, or nothing."

The flood of passion surged in him again. Some trick of her voice, or some indescribable movement of her head—the trifles which are all-powerful over a man in love—beat down his contending reason.

"You say," he continued, "that you will make amends for your unfair dealing. If you mean it, take the only course that shows itself. Confess to Narramore what you have done; you owe it to him as much as to me."

"I can't do that," said Eve, drawing away. "It's for you to tell him—if you like."

"No. I had my opportunity, and let it pass. I don't mean that you are to inform him of all there has been between us; that's needless. We have agreed to forget everything that suggests the word I hate. But that you and I have been lovers and looked—I, at all events—to be something more, this you must let him know."

"I can never do that."

"Without it, how are you to disentangle yourself?"

"I promise you he shall see no more of me."

"Such a promise is idle, and you know it. Remember, too, that Narramore and I are friends. He will speak to me of you, and I can't play a farce with him. It would be intolerable discomfort to me, and grossly unfair to him. Do, for once, the simple, honourable thing, and make a new beginning. After that, be guided by your own interests. Assuredly I shall not stand in your way."

Eve had turned her eyes in the direction of crowd and bustle. When she faced Hilliard again, he saw that she had come to a resolve.

"There's only one way out of it for me," she said impulsively. "I can't talk any longer. I'll write to you."

She moved from him; Hilliard followed. At a distance of half-a-dozen yards, just as he was about to address her again, she stopped and spoke—

"You hate to hear me talk of 'gratitude.' I have always meant by it less than you thought. I was grateful for the money, not for anything else. When you took me away, perhaps it was the unkindest thing you could have done."

An unwonted vehemence shook her voice. Her muscles were tense; she stood in an attitude of rebellious pride.

"If I had been true to myself then——But it isn't too late. If I am to act honestly, I know very well what I must do. I will take your advice."

Hilliard could not doubt of her meaning. He remembered his last talk with Patty. This was a declaration he had not foreseen, and it affected him otherwise than he could have anticipated.

"My advice had nothing to do with *that*," was his answer, as he read her face. "But I shall say not a word against it. I could respect you, at all events."

"Yes, and I had rather have your respect than your love."

With that, she left him. He wished to pursue, but a physical languor held him motionless. And when at length he sauntered from the place, it was with a sense of satisfaction at what had happened. Let her carry out that purpose: he faced it, preferred it. Let her be lost to him in that way rather than any other. It cut the knot, and left him with a memory of Eve that would not efface her dishonouring weakness.

Late at night, he walked about the streets near his home, debating with himself whether she would act as she spoke, or had only sought to frighten him with a threat. And still he hoped that her resolve was sincere. He could bear that conclusion of their story better than any other—unless it were her death. Better a thousand times than her marriage with Narramore.

In the morning, fatigue gave voice to conscience. He had bidden her go, when, perchance, a word would have checked her. Should he write, or even go to her straightway and retract what he had said? His will prevailed, and he did nothing.

The night that followed plagued him with other misgivings. It seemed more probable now that she had threatened what she would never have the courage to perform. She meant it at the moment—it declared a truth but an hour after she would listen to commonplace morality or prudence. Narramore would write to her; she might, perhaps, see him again. She would cling to the baser hope.

Might but the morrow bring him a letter from London!

It brought nothing; and day after day disappointed him. More than a week passed: he was ill with suspense, but could take no step for setting his mind at rest. Then, as he sat one morning at his work in the architect's office, there arrived a telegram addressed to him—

"I must see you as soon as possible. Be here before six.—Narramore."

## CHAPTER XXVI

"What the devil does this mean, Hilliard?"

If never before, the indolent man was now thoroughly aroused. He had an open letter in his hand. Hilliard, standing before him in a little office that smelt of ledgers and gum, and many other commercial things, knew that the letter must be from Eve, and savagely hoped that it was dated London.

"This is from Miss Madeley, and it's all about you. Why couldn't you speak the other day?"

"What does she say about me?"

"That she has known you for a long time; that you saw a great deal of each other in London; that she has led you on with a hope of marrying her, though she never really meant it; in short, that she has used you very ill, and feels obliged now to make a clean breast of it."

The listener fixed his eye upon a copying-press, but without seeing it. A grim smile began to contort his lips.

"Where does she write from?"

"From her ordinary address—why not? I think this is rather too bad of you. Why didn't you speak, instead of writhing about and sputtering? That kind of thing is all very well—sense of honour and all that—but it meant that I was being taken in. Between friends—hang it! Of course I have done with her. I shall write at once. It's amazing; it took away my breath. No doubt, though she doesn't say it, it was from you that she came to know of me. She began with a lie. And who the devil could have thought it! Her face—her way of talking! This will cut me up awfully. Of course, I'm sorry for you, too, but it was your plain duty to let me know what sort of a woman I had got hold of. Nay, it's she that has got hold of me, confound her! I don't feel myself! I'm thoroughly knocked over!"

Hilliard began humming an air. He crossed the room and sat down.

"Have you seen her since that Saturday?"

"No; she has made excuses, and I guessed something was wrong. What has been going on? *You* have seen her?"

"Of course."

Narramore glared.

"It's devilish underhand behaviour! Look here, old fellow, we're not going to quarrel. No woman is worth a quarrel between two old friends. But just speak out—can't you? What did you mean by keeping it from me?"

"It meant that I had nothing to say," Hilliard replied, through his moustache.

"You kept silence out of spite, then? You said to yourself, 'Let him marry her and find out afterwards what she really is!'"

"Nothing of the kind." He looked up frankly. "I saw no reason for speaking. She accuses herself without a shadow of reason; it's mere hysterical conscientiousness. We have known each other for half a year or so, and I have made love to her, but I never had the least encouragement. I knew all along she didn't care for me. How is she to blame? A girl is under no obligation to speak of all the men who have wanted to marry her, provided she has done nothing to be ashamed of. There's just one bit of insincerity. It's true she knew of you from me. But she looked you up because she despaired of finding employment; she was at an end of her money, didn't know what to do. I have heard this since I saw you last. It wasn't quite straightforward, but one can forgive it in a girl hard driven by necessity."

Narramore was listening with eagerness, his lips parted, and a growing hope in his eyes.

"There never was anything serious between you?"

"On her side, never for a moment. I pursued and pestered her, that was all."

"Do you mind telling me who the girl was that I saw you with at Dudley?"

"A friend of Miss Madeley's, over here from London on a holiday. I have tried to make use of her—to get her influence on my side——"

Narramore sprang from the corner of the table on which he had been sitting.

"Why couldn't she hold her tongue! That's just like a woman, to keep a thing quiet when she ought to speak of it, and bring it out when she had far better say nothing. I feel as if I had treated you badly, Hilliard. And the way you take it—I'd rather you eased your mind by swearing at me."

"I could swear hard enough. I could grip you by the throat and jump on you——"

"No, I'm hanged if you could!" He forced a laugh. "And I shouldn't advise you to try. Here, give me your hand instead." He seized it. "We're going to talk this over like two reasonable beings. Does this girl know her own mind? It seems to me from this letter that she wants to get rid of me."

"You must find out whether she does or not."

"Do you *think* she does?"

"I refuse to think about it at all."

"You mean she isn't worth troubling about? Tell the truth, and be hanged to you! Is she the kind of a girl a man may marry?"

"For all I know."

"Do you suspect her?" Narramore urged fiercely.

"She'll marry a rich man rather than a poor one—that's the worst I think of her."

"What woman won't?"

When question and answer had revolved about this point for another quarter of an hour, Hilliard brought the dialogue to an end. He was clay-colour, and perspiration stood on his forehead.

"You must make her out without any more help from me. I tell you the letter is all nonsense, and I can say no more."

He moved towards the exit.

"One thing I must know, Hilliard—Are you going to see her again?"

"Never—if I can help it."

"Can we be friends still?"

"If you never mention her name to me."

Again they shook hands, eyes crossing in a smile of shamed hostility. And the parting was for more than a twelvemonth.

Late in August, when Hilliard was thinking of a week's rest in the country, after a spell of harder and more successful work than he had ever previously known, he received a letter from Patty Ringrose.

"Dear Mr. Hilliard," wrote the girl, "I have just heard from Eve that she is to be married to Mr. Narramore in a week's time. She says you don't know about it; but I think you *ought* to know. I haven't been able to make anything of her two last letters, but she has written plainly at last. Perhaps she means me to tell you. Will you let me have a line? I should like to know whether you care much, and I do so hope you don't! I felt sure it would come to this, and if you'll believe me, it's just as well. I haven't answered her letter, and I don't know whether I shall. I might say disagreeable things. Everything is the same with me and always will be, I suppose." In conclusion, she was his sincerely. A postscript remarked: "They tell me I play better. I've been practising a great deal, just to kill the time."

"Dear Miss Ringrose," he responded, "I am very glad to know that Eve is to be comfortably settled for life. By all means answer her letter, and by all means keep from saying disagreeable things. It is never wise to quarrel with prosperous friends, and why should you? With every good wish——" he remained sincerely hers.

## CHAPTER XXVII

When Hilliard and his friend again shook hands it was the autumn of another year. Not even by chance had they encountered in the interval and no written message had passed between them. Their meeting was at a house newly acquired by the younger of the Birching brothers, who, being about to marry, summoned his bachelor familiars to smoke their pipes in the suburban abode while yet his rule there was undisputed. With Narramore he had of late resumed the friendship interrupted by Miss Birching's displeasure, for that somewhat imperious young lady, now the wife of an elderly ironmaster, moved in other circles; and Hilliard's professional value, which was beginning to be recognised by the Birchings otherwise than in the way of compliment, had overcome the restraints at first imposed by his dubious social standing.

They met genially, without a hint of estrangement.

"Your wife well?" Hilliard took an opportunity of asking apart.

"Thanks, she's getting all right again. At Llandudno just now. Glad to see that you're looking so uncommonly fit."

Hilliard had undoubtedly improved in personal appearance. He grew a beard, which added to his seeming age, but suited with his features; his carriage was more upright than of old.

A week or two after this, Narramore sent a friendly note—

"Shall I see you at Birching's on Sunday? My wife will be there, to meet Miss Marks and some other people. Come if you can, old fellow. I should take it as a great kindness."

And Hilliard went. In the hall he was confronted by Narramore, who shook hands with him rather effusively, and said a few words in an undertone.

"She's out in the garden. Will be delighted to see you. Awfully good of you, old boy! Had to come sooner or later, you know."

Not quite assured of this necessity, and something less than composed, Hilliard presently passed through the house into the large walled garden behind it. Here he was confusedly aware of a group of ladies, not one of whom, on drawing nearer, did he recognise. A succession of formalities discharged, he heard his friend's voice saying—

"Hilliard, let me introduce you to my wife."

There before him stood Eve. He had only just persuaded himself of her identity; his eyes searched her countenance with wonder which barely allowed him to assume a becoming attitude. But Mrs. Narramore was perfect in society's drill. She smiled very sweetly, gave her hand, said what the occasion demanded. Among the women present—all well bred—she suffered no obscurement. Her voice was tuned to the appropriate harmony; her talk invited to an avoidance of the hackneyed.

Hilliard revived his memories of Gower Place—of the streets of Paris. Nothing preternatural had come about; nothing that he had not forecasted in his hours of hope. But there were incidents in the past which this moment blurred away into the region of dreamland, and which he shrank from the effort of reinvesting with credibility.

"This is a pleasant garden."

Eve had approached him as he stood musing, after a conversation with other ladies.

"Rather new, of course; but a year will do wonders. Have you seen the chrysanthemums?"

She led him apart, as they stood regarding the flowers, Hilliard was surprised by words that fell from her.

"Your contempt for me is beyond expression, isn't it?"

"It is the last feeling I should associate with you," he answered.

"Oh, but be sincere. We have both learnt to speak another language—you no less than I. Let me hear a word such as you used to speak. I know you despise me unutterably."

"You are quite mistaken. I admire you very much."

"What—my skill? Or my dress?"

"Everything. You have become precisely what you were meant to be."

"Oh, the scorn of that!"

"I beg you not to think it for a moment. There was a time when I might have found a foolish pleasure in speaking to you with sarcasm. But that has long gone by."

"What am I, then?"

"An English lady—with rather more intellect than most."

Eve flushed with satisfaction.

"It's more than kind of you to say that. But you always had a generous spirit. I never thanked you. Not one poor word. I was cowardly—afraid to write. And you didn't care for my thanks."

"I do now."

"Then I thank you. With all my heart, again and again!"

Her voice trembled under fulness of meaning.

"You find life pleasant?"

"You do, I hope?" she answered, as they paced on.

"Not unpleasant, at all events. I am no longer slaving under the iron gods. I like my work, and it promises to reward me."

Eve made a remark about a flower-bed. Then her voice subdued again.

"How do you look back on your great venture—your attempt to make the most that could be made of a year in your life?"

"Quite contentedly. It was worth doing, and is worth remembering."

"Remember, if you care to," Eve resumed, "that all I am and have I owe to you. I was all but lost—all but a miserable captive for the rest of my life. You came and ransomed me. A less generous man would have spoilt his work at the last moment. But you were large minded enough to support my weakness till I was safe."

Hilliard smiled for answer.

"You and Robert are friends again?"

"Perfectly."

She turned, and they rejoined the company.

A week later Hilliard went down into the country, to a quiet spot where he now and then refreshed his mind after toil in Birmingham. He slept at a cottage, and on the Sunday morning walked idly about the lanes.

A white frost had suddenly hastened the slow decay of mellow autumn. Low on the landscape lay a soft mist, dense enough to conceal everything at twenty yards away, but suffused with golden sunlight; overhead shone the clear blue sky. Roadside trees and hedges, their rich tints softened by the medium through which they were discerned, threw shadows of exquisite faintness. A perfect quiet possessed the air, but from every branch, as though shaken by some invisible hand, dead foliage dropped to earth in a continuous shower; softly pattering from beech to maple, or with the heavier fall of ash-leaves, while at long intervals sounded the thud of apples tumbling from a crab-tree. Thick-clustered berries arrayed the hawthorns, the briar was rich in scarlet fruit; everywhere the frost had left the adornment of its subtle artistry.

Each leaf upon the hedge shone silver-outlined; spiders' webs, woven from stein to stem, glistened in the morning radiance; the grasses by the way side stood stark in gleaming mail.

And Maurice Hilliard, a free man in his own conceit, sang to himself a song of the joy of life.

## THE END.

# THE PAYING GUEST

# CHAPTER I

It was Mumford who saw the advertisement and made the suggestion. His wife gave him a startled look.

'But—you don't mean that it's necessary? Have we been extrav—'

'No, no! Nothing of the kind. It just occurred to me that some such arrangement might be pleasant for you. You must feel lonely, now and then, during the day, and as we have plenty of room—'

Emmeline took the matter seriously, but, being a young woman of some discretion, did not voice all her thoughts. The rent was heavy: so was the cost of Clarence's season-ticket. Against this they had set the advantage of the fine air of Sutton, so good for the child and for the mother, both vastly better in health since they quitted London. Moreover, the remoteness of their friends favoured economy; they could easily decline invitations, and need not often issue them. They had a valid excuse for avoiding public entertainments—an expense so often imposed by mere fashion. The house was roomy, the garden delightful. Clarence, good fellow, might be sincere in his wish for her to have companionship; at the same time, this advertisement had probably appealed to him in another way.

'A YOUNG LADY desires to find a home with respectable, well-connected family, in a suburb of London, or not more than 15 miles from Charing Cross. Can give excellent references. Terms not so much a consideration as comfort and pleasant society. No boarding-house.—Address: Louise, Messrs. Higgins & Co., Fenchurch St., E.C.'

She read it again and again.

'It wouldn't be nice if people said that we were taking lodgers.'

'No fear of that. This is evidently some well-to-do person. It's a very common arrangement nowadays, you know; they are called "paying guests." Of course I shouldn't dream of having anyone you didn't thoroughly like the look of.'

'Do you think,' asked Emmeline doubtfully, 'that we should quite *do*? "Well-connected family"—'

'My dear girl! Surely we have nothing to be ashamed of?'

'Of course not, Clarence. But—and "pleasant society." What about that?'

'Your society is pleasant enough, I hope,' answered Mumford, gracefully. 'And the Fentimans—'

This was the only family with whom they were intimate at Sutton. Nice people; a trifle sober, perhaps, and not in conspicuously flourishing circumstances; but perfectly presentable.

'I'm afraid—' murmured Emmeline, and stopped short. 'As you say,' she added presently, 'this is someone very well off. "Terms not so much a consideration"—'

'Well, I tell you what—there can be no harm in dropping a note. The kind of note that commits one to nothing, you know. Shall I write it, or will you?'

They concocted it together, and the rough draft was copied by Emmeline. She wrote a very pretty hand, and had no difficulty whatever about punctuation. A careful letter, calculated for the eye of refinement; it supplied only the indispensable details of the writer's position, and left terms for future adjustment.

'It's so easy to explain to people,' said Mumford, with an air of satisfaction, when he came back from the post, 'that you wanted a companion. As I'm quite sure you do. A friend coming to stay with you for a time—that's how I should put it.'

A week passed, and there came no reply. Mumford pretended not to care much, but Emmeline imagined a new anxiety in his look.

'Do be frank with me, dear,' she urged one evening. 'Are we living too—'

He answered her with entire truthfulness. Ground for serious uneasiness there was none whatever; he could more than make ends meet, and had every reason to hope it would always be so; but it would relieve his mind if the end of the year saw a rather larger surplus. He was now five-and-thirty—getting on in life. A man ought to make provision beyond the mere life-assurance—and so on.

'Shall I look out for other advertisements?' asked Emmeline.

'Oh, dear, no! It was just that particular one that caught my eye.'

Next morning arrived a letter, signed 'Louise E. Derrick.' The writer said she had been waiting to compare and think over some two hundred answers to her advertisement. 'It's really too absurd. How can I remember them all? But I liked yours as soon as I read it, and I am writing to you first of all. Will you let me come and see you? I can tell you about myself much better than writing. Would tomorrow do, in the afternoon? Please telegraph yes or no to Coburg Lodge, Emilia Road, Tulse Hill.'

To think over this letter Mumford missed his ordinary train. It was not exactly the kind of letter he had expected, and Emmeline shared his doubts. The handwriting seemed just passable; there was no orthographic error; but—refinement? This young person wrote, too, with such singular nonchalance. And she said absolutely nothing about her domestic circumstances. Coburg Lodge, Tulse Hill. A decent enough locality, doubtless; but—

'There's no harm in seeing her,' said Emmeline at length. 'Send a telegram, Clarence. Do you know, I think she *may* be the right kind of girl. I was thinking of someone awfully grand, and it's rather a relief. After all, you see, you—you are in business—'

'To be sure. And this girl seems to belong to a business family. I only wish she wrote in a more ladylike way.'

Emmeline set her house in order, filled the drawing-room with flowers, made the spare bedroom as inviting as possible, and, after luncheon, spent a good deal of time in adorning her person. She was a slight, pretty woman of something less than thirty; with a good, but pale, complexion, hair tending to auburn, sincere eyes. Her little vanities had no roots of ill-nature; she could admire without envy, and loved an orderly domestic life. Her husband's desire to increase his income had rather unsettled her; she exaggerated the importance of today's interview, and resolved with nervous energy to bring it to a successful issue, if Miss Derrick should prove a possible companion.

About four o'clock sounded the visitor's ring. From her bedroom window Emmeline had seen Miss Derrick's approach. As the distance from the station was only five minutes' walk, the stranger naturally came on foot. A dark girl, and of tolerably good features; rather dressy; with a carriage corresponding to the tone of her letter—an easy swing; head well up and shoulders squared. 'Oh, how I *hope* she isn't vulgar!' said Emmeline to herself. 'I don't like the hat—I don't. And that sunshade with the immense handle.' From the top of the stairs she heard a clear, unaffected voice: 'Mrs. Mumford at home?' Yes, the aspirate *was* sounded—thank goodness!

It surprised her, on entering the room, to find that Miss Derrick looked no less nervous than she was herself. The girl's cheeks were flushed, and she half choked over her 'How do you do?'

'I hope you had no difficulty in finding the house. I would have met you at the station if you had mentioned the train. Oh, but—how silly!—I shouldn't have known you.'

Miss Derrick laughed, and seemed of a sudden much more at ease.

'Oh, I like you for that!' she exclaimed mirthfully. 'It's just the kind of thing I say myself sometimes. And I'm so glad to see that you are—you mustn't be offended—I mean you're not the kind of person to be afraid of.'

They laughed together. Emmeline could not subdue her delight when she found that the girl really might be accepted as a lady. There were faults of costume undeniably; money had been misspent in several directions; but no glaring vulgarity hurt the eye. And her speech, though not strictly speaking refined, was free from the faults that betray low origin. Then, she seemed good-natured though there was something about her mouth not altogether charming.

'Do you know Sutton at all?' Emmeline inquired.

'Never was here before. But I like the look of it. I like this house, too. I suppose you know a lot of people here, Mrs. Mumford?'

'Well—no. There's only one family we know at all well. Our friends live in London. Of course they often come out here. I don't know whether you are acquainted with any of them. The Kirby Simpsons, of West Kensington; and Mrs. Hollings, of Highgate—'

Miss Derrick cast down her eyes and seemed to reflect. Then she spoke abruptly.

'I don't know any people to speak of. I ought to tell you that my mother has come down with me. She's waiting at the station till I go back; then she'll come and see you. You're surprised? Well, I had better tell you that I'm leaving home because I can't get on with my people. Mother and I have always quarrelled, but it has been worse than ever lately. I must explain that she has married a second time, and Mr. Higgins—I'm glad to say that isn't *my* name—has a daughter of his own by a first marriage; and we can't bear each other—Miss Higgins, I mean. Some day, if I come to live here, I daresay I shall tell you more. Mr. Higgins is rich, and I can't say he's unkind to me; he'll give me as much as I want; but I'm sure he'll be very glad to get me out of the house. I have no money of my own—worse luck! Well, we thought it best for me to come alone, first, and see—just to see, you know—whether we were likely to suit each other. Then mother will come and tell you all she has to say about me. Of course I know what it'll be. They all say I've a horrible temper. I don't think so myself; and I'm sure I don't think I should quarrel with *you*, you look so nice. But I can't get on at home, and it's better for all that we should part. I'm just two-and-twenty—do I look older? I haven't learnt to do anything, and I suppose I shall never need to.'

## CHAPTER I

'Do you wish to see *much* society?' inquired Mrs. Mumford, who was thinking rapidly, 'or should you prefer a few really nice people? I'm afraid I don't quite understand yet whether you want society of the pleasure-seeking kind, or—'

She left the alternative vague. Miss Derrick again reflected for a moment before abruptly declaring herself.

'I feel sure that your friends are the kind I want to know. At all events, I should like to try. The great thing is to get away from home and see how things look.'

They laughed together. Emmeline, after a little more talk, offered to take her visitor over the house, and Miss Derrick had loud praise for everything she saw.

'What I like about you,' she exclaimed of a sudden, as they stood looking from a bedroom window on to the garden, 'is that you don't put on any—you know what I mean. People seem to me to be generally either low and ignorant, or so high and mighty there's no getting on with them at all. You're just what I wanted to find. Now I must go and send mother to see you.'

Emmeline protested against this awkward proceeding. Why should not both come together and have a cup of tea? If it were desired, Miss Derrick could step into the garden whilst her mother said whatever she wished to say. The girl assented, and in excellent spirits betook herself to the railway station. Emmeline waited something less than a quarter of an hour; then a hansom drove up, and Mrs. Higgins, after a deliberate surveyal of the house front, followed her daughter up the pathway.

The first sight of the portly lady made the situation clearer to Mrs. Mumford. Louise Derrick represented a certain stage of civilisation, a degree of conscious striving for better things; Mrs. Higgins was prosperous and self-satisfied vulgarity. Of a complexion much lighter than the girl's, she still possessed a coarse comeliness, which pointed back to the dairymaid type of damsel. Her features revealed at the same time a kindly nature and an irascible tendency. Monstrously overdressed, and weighted with costly gewgaws, she came forward panting and perspiring, and, before paying any heed to her hostess, closely surveyed the room.

'Mrs. Mumford,' said the girl, 'this is my mother. Mother, this is Mrs. Mumford. And now, please, let me go somewhere while you have your talk.'

'Yes, that'll be best, that'll be best,' exclaimed Mrs. Higgins. 'Dear, 'ow 'ot it is! Run out into the garden, Louise. Nice little 'ouse, Mrs. Mumford. And Louise seems quite taken with you. She doesn't take to people very easy, either. Of course, you can give satisfactory references? I like to do things in a business-like way. I understand your 'usband is in the City; shouldn't wonder if he knows some of Mr. 'Iggins's friends. Yes, I will take a cup, if you please. I've just had one at the station, but it's such thirsty weather. And what do you think of Louise? Because I'd very much rather you said plainly if you don't think you could get on.'

'But, indeed, I fancy we could, Mrs. Higgins.'

'Well, I'm sure I'm very glad *of* it. It isn't everybody can get on with Louise. I dessay she's told you a good deal about me and her stepfather. I don't think she's any reason to complain of the treatment—'

'She said you were both very kind to her,' interposed the hostess.

'I'm sure we *try* to be, and Mr. 'Iggins, he doesn't mind what he gives her. A five-pound note, if you'll believe me, is no more than a sixpence to him when he gives her presents. You see, Mrs. Rumford—no, Mumford, isn't it?—I was first married very young—scarcely eighteen, I was; and Mr. Derrick died on our wedding-day, two years after. Then came Mr. 'Iggins. Of course I waited a proper time. And one thing I can say, that no woman was ever 'appier with two 'usbands than I've been. I've two sons growing up, hearty boys as ever you saw. If it wasn't for this trouble with Louise—' She stopped to wipe her face. 'I dessay she's told you that Mr. 'Iggins, who was a widower when I met him, has a daughter of his first marriage—her poor mother died at the birth, and she's older than Louise. I don't mind telling *you*, Mrs. Mumford, she's close upon six-and-twenty, and nothing like so good-looking as Louise, neither. Mr. 'Iggins, he's kindness itself; but when it comes to differences between his daughter and *my* daughter, well, it isn't in nature he shouldn't favour his own. There's more be'ind, but I dessay you can guess, and I won't trouble you with things that don't concern you. And that's how it stands, you see.'

By a rapid calculation Emmeline discovered; with surprise, that Mrs. Higgins could not be much more than forty years of age. It must have been a life of gross self-indulgence that had made the woman look at least ten years older. This very undesirable parentage naturally affected Emmeline's opinion of Louise, whose faults began to show in a more pronounced light. One thing was clear: but for the fact that Louise aimed at a separation from her relatives, it would be barely possible to think of receiving her. If Mrs. Higgins thought of coming down to Sutton at unexpected moments—no, that was too dreadful.

'Should you wish, Mrs. Higgins, to entrust your daughter to me entirely?'

## CHAPTER I

'My dear Mrs. Rumford, it's very little that *my* wishes has to do with it! She's made up her mind to leave 'ome, and all I can do is to see she gets with respectable people, which I feel sure you are; and of course I shall have your references.'

Emmeline turned pale at the suggestion. She all but decided that the matter must go no further.

'And what might your terms be—inclusive?' Mrs. Higgins proceeded to inquire.

At this moment a servant entered with tea, and Emmeline, sorely flurried, talked rapidly of the advantages of Sutton as a residence. She did not allow her visitor to put in a word till the door closed again. Then, with an air of decision, she announced her terms; they would be three guineas a week. It was half a guinea more than she and Clarence had decided to ask. She expected, she hoped, Mrs. Higgins would look grave. But nothing of the kind; Louise's mother seemed to think the suggestion very reasonable. Thereupon Emmeline added that, of course, the young lady would discharge her own laundress's bill. To this also Mrs. Higgins readily assented.

'A hundred and sixty pounds per annum!' Emmeline kept repeating to herself. And, alas! it looked as if she might have asked much more. The reference difficulty might be minimised by naming her own married sister, who lived at Blackheath, and Clarence's most intimate friend, Mr. Tarling, who held a good position in a City house, and had a most respectable address at West Kensington. But her heart misgave her. She dreaded her husband's return home.

The conversation was prolonged for half-an-hour. Emmeline gave her references, and in return requested the like from Mrs. Higgins. This astonished the good woman. Why, her husband was Messrs. 'Iggins of Fenchurch Street! Oh, a mere formality, Emmeline hastened to add—for Mr. Mumford's satisfaction. So Mrs. Higgins very pompously named two City firms, and negotiations, for the present, were at an end.

Louise, summoned to the drawing-room, looked rather tired of waiting.

'When can you have me, Mrs. Mumford?' she asked. 'I've quite made up my mind to come.'

'I'm afraid a day or two must pass, Miss Derrick—'

'The references, my dear,' began Mrs. Higgins.

'Oh, nonsense! It's all right; anyone can see.'

'There you go! Always cutting short the words in my mouth. I can't endure such behaviour, and I wonder what Mrs. Rumford thinks of it. I've given Mrs. Rumford fair warning—'

They wrangled for a few minutes, Emmeline feeling too depressed and anxious to interpose with polite commonplaces. When at length they took their leave, she saw the last of them with a sigh of thanksgiving. It had happened most fortunately that no one called this afternoon.

'Clarence, it's *quite* out of the question.' Thus she greeted her husband. 'The girl herself I could endure, but oh, her odious mother!—Three guineas a week! I could cry over the thought.'

By the first post in the morning came a letter from Louise. She wrote appealingly, touchingly. 'I know you couldn't stand my mother, but do please have me. I like Sutton, and I like your house, and I like you. I promise faithfully nobody from home shall ever come to see me, so don't be afraid. Of course if you won't have me, somebody else will; I've got two hundred to choose from, but I'd rather come to you. Do write and say I may come. I'm so sorry I quarrelled with mother before you. I promise never to quarrel with you. I'm very good-tempered when I get what I want.' With much more to the same effect.

'We *will* have her,' declared Mumford. 'Why not, if the old people keep away?—You are quite sure she sounds her *h's*?'

'Oh, quite. She has been to pretty good schools, I think. And I dare say I could persuade her to get other dresses and hats.'

'Of course you could. Really, it seems almost a duty to take her—doesn't it?'

So the matter was settled, and Mumford ran off gaily to catch his train.

Three days later Miss Derrick arrived, bringing with her something like half-a-ton of luggage. She bounded up the doorsteps, and, meeting Mrs. Mumford in the hall, kissed her fervently.

'I've got such heaps to tell you Mr. Higgins has given me twenty pounds to go on with—for myself; I mean; of course he'll pay everything else. How delighted I am to be here! Please pay the cabman I've got no change.'

A few hours before this there had come a letter from Mrs. Higgins; better written and spelt than would have seemed likely.

'Dear Mrs. Mumford,' it ran, 'L. is coming to-morrow morning, and I hope you won't repent. There's just one thing I meant to have said to you but forgot, so I'll say it now. If it should happen that any gentleman of your acquaintance takes a fancy to L., and if it should come to anything, I'm sure both Mr. H. and me would be *most thankful*, and

Mr. H. would behave handsome to her. And what's more, I'm sure he would be only too glad to show *in a handsome way* the thanks he would owe to you and Mr. M.—Very truly yours, Susan H. Higgins.'

## CHAPTER II

'Runnymede' (so the Mumfords' house was named) stood on its own little plot of ground in one of the tree-shadowed roads which persuade the inhabitants of Sutton that they live in the country. It was of red brick, and double-fronted, with a porch of wood and stucco; bay windows on one side of the entrance, and flat on the other, made a contrast pleasing to the suburban eye. The little front garden had a close fence of unpainted lath, a characteristic of the neighbourhood. At the back of the house lay a long, narrow lawn, bordered with flowerbeds, and shaded at the far end by a fine horse-chestnut.

Emmeline talked much of the delightful proximity of the Downs; one would have imagined her taking long walks over the breezy uplands to Banstead or Epsom, or yet further afield The fact was, she saw no more of the country than if she had lived at Brixton. Her windows looked only upon the surrounding houses and their garden foliage. Occasionally she walked along the asphalt pavement of the Brighton Road—a nursemaids' promenade—as far as the stone which marks twelve miles from Westminster Bridge. Here, indeed, she breathed the air of the hills, but villas on either hand obstructed the view, and brought London much nearer than the measured distance. Like her friends and neighbours, Emmeline enjoyed Sutton because it was a most respectable little portion of the great town, set in a purer atmosphere. The country would have depressed her.

In this respect Miss Derrick proved a congenial companion. Louise made no pretence of rural inclinations, but had a great liking for tree-shadowed asphalt, for the results of elaborate horticulture, for the repose and the quiet of villadom.

'I should like to have a house just like this,' she declared, on her first evening at "Runnymede," talking with her host and hostess out in the garden. 'It's quite big enough, unless, of course, you have a very large family, which must be rather a bore.' She laughed ingenuously. 'And one gets to town so easily. What do you pay for your season-ticket, Mr. Mumford? Oh, well! that isn't much. I almost think I shall get one.'

'Do you wish to go up very often, then?' asked Emmeline, reflecting on her new responsibilities.

'Oh! not every day, of course. But a season-ticket saves the bother each time, and you have a sort of feeling, you know, that you can be in town whenever you like.'

It had not hitherto been the Mumfords' wont to dress for dinner, but this evening they did so, and obviously to Miss Derrick's gratification. She herself appeared in a dress which altogether outshone that of her hostess. Afterwards, in private, she drew Emmeline's attention to this garb, and frankly asked her opinion of it.

'Very nice indeed,' murmured the married lady, with a good-natured smile. 'Perhaps a little—'

'There, I know what you're going to say. You think it's too showy. Now I want you to tell me just what you think about everything—everything. I shan't be offended. I'm not so silly. You know I've come here to learn all sorts of things. To-morrow you shall go over all my dresses with me, and those you don't like I'll get rid of. I've never had anyone to tell me what's nice and what isn't. I want to be—oh, well, you know what I mean.'

'But, my dear,' said Emmeline, 'there's something I don't quite understand. You say I'm to speak plainly, and so I will. How is it that you haven't made friends long ago with the sort of people you wish to know? It isn't as if you were in poor circumstances.'

'How *could* I make friends with nice people when I was ashamed to have them at home? The best I know are quite poor—girls I went to school with. They're much better educated than I am, but they make their own living, and so I can't see very much of them, and I'm not sure they want to see much of *me*. I wish I knew what people think of me; they call me vulgar, I believe—the kind I'm speaking of. Now, do tell me, Mrs. Mumford, *am* I vulgar?'

'My dear Miss Derrick—' Emmeline began in protest, but was at once interrupted.

'Oh! that isn't what I want. You must call me Louise, or Lou, if you like, and just say what you really think. Yes, I see, I *am* rather vulgar, and what can you expect? Look at mother; and if you saw Mr. Higgins, oh! The mistake I made was to leave school so soon. I got sick of it, and left at sixteen, and of course the idiots at home—I mean the foolish people—let me have my own way. I'm not clever, you know, and I didn't get on well at school. They used to say I could do much better if I liked, and perhaps it was more laziness than stupidity, though I don't care for books—I wish I did. I've had lots of friends, but I never keep them for very long. I don't know whether it's their fault or mine. My oldest friends are Amy Barker and Muriel Featherstone; they were both at the school at Clapham, and now Amy does type-writing in the City, and Muriel is at a photographer's. They're awfully nice girls, and I like them so much; but then, you see, they haven't enough money to live in what *I* call a nice way, and, you know, I should never think of asking them to advise me about my dresses, or anything of that kind. A friend of mine once began to say something and I didn't like it; after that we had nothing to do with each other.'

Emmeline could not hide her amusement.

'Well, that's just it,' went on the other frankly. 'I *have* rather a sharp temper, and I suppose I don't get on well with most people. I used to quarrel dreadfully with some of the girls at school—the uppish sort. And yet all the time I wanted to be friends with them. But, of course, I could never have taken them home.'

Mrs. Mumford began to read the girl's character, and to understand how its complexity had shaped her life. She was still uneasy as to the impression this guest would make upon their friends, but on the whole it seemed probable that Louise would conscientiously submit herself to instruction, and do her very best to be "nice." Clarence's opinion was still favourable; he pronounced Miss Derrick "very amusing," and less of a savage than his wife's description had led him to expect.

Having the assistance of two servants and a nurse-girl, Emmeline was not overburdened with domestic work. She soon found it fortunate that her child, a girl of two years old, needed no great share of her attention; for Miss Derrick, though at first she affected an extravagant interest in the baby, very soon had enough of that plaything, and showed a decided preference for Emmeline's society out of sight and hearing of nursery affairs. On the afternoon of the second day they went together to call upon Mrs. Fentiman, who lived at a distance of a quarter of an hour's walk, in a house called "Hazeldene"; a semi-detached house, considerably smaller than "Runnymede," and neither without nor within so pleasant to look upon. Mrs. Fentiman, a tall, hard-featured, but amiable lady, had two young children who occupied most of her time; at present one of them was ailing, and the mother could talk of nothing else but this distressing circumstance. The call lasted only for ten minutes, and Emmeline felt that her companion was disappointed.

## CHAPTER II

'Children are a great trouble,' Louise remarked, when they had left the house. 'People ought never to marry unless they can keep a lot of servants. Not long ago I was rather fond of somebody, but I wouldn't have him because he had no money. Don't you think I was quite right?'

'I have no doubt you were.'

'And now,' pursued the girl, poking the ground with her sunshade as she walked, 'there's somebody else. And that's one of the things I want to tell you about. He has about three hundred a year. It isn't much, of course; but I suppose Mr. Higgins would give me something. And yet I'm sure it won't come to anything. Let's go home and have a good talk, shall we?'

Mrs. Higgins's letter had caused Emmeline and her husband no little amusement; but at the same time it led them to reflect. Certainly they numbered among their acquaintances one or two marriageable young men who might perchance be attracted by Miss Derrick, especially if they learnt that Mr. Higgins was disposed to 'behave handsomely' to his stepdaughter; but the Mumfords had no desire to see Louise speedily married. To the bribe with which the letter ended they could give no serious thought. Having secured their "paying guest," they hoped she would remain with them for a year or two at least. But already Louise had dropped hints such as Emmeline could not fail to understand, and her avowal of serious interest in a lover came rather as an annoyance than a surprise to Mrs. Mumford.

It was a hot afternoon, and they had tea brought out into the garden, under the rustling leaves of the chestnut.

'You don't know anyone else at Sutton except Mrs. Fentiman?' said Louise, as she leaned back in the wicker chair.

'Not intimately. But some of our friends from London will be coming on Sunday. I've asked four people to lunch.'

'How jolly! Of course you'll tell me all about them before then. But I want to talk about Mr. Cobb. Please, *two* lumps of sugar. I've known him for about a year and a half. We seem quite old friends, and he writes to me; I don't answer the letters, unless there's something to say. To tell the truth, I don't like him.'

'How can that be if you seem old friends?'

'Well, he likes *me*; and there's no harm in that, so long as he understands. I'm sure *you* wouldn't like him. He's a rough, coarse sort of man, and has a dreadful temper.'

'Good gracious! What is his position?'

'Oh, he's connected with the what-d'ye-call-it Electric Lighting Company. He travels about a good deal. I shouldn't mind that; it must be rather nice not to have one's husband always at home. Just now I believe he's in Ireland. I shall be having a letter from him very soon, no doubt. He doesn't know I've left home, and it'll make him wild. Yes, that's the kind of man he is. Fearfully jealous, and such a temper! If I married him, I'm quite sure he would beat me some day.'

'Oh!' Emmeline exclaimed. 'How can you have anything to do with such a man?'

'He's very nice sometimes,' answered Louise, thoughtfully.

'But do you really mean that he is "rough and coarse"?'

'Yes, I do. You couldn't call him a gentleman. I've never seen his people; they live somewhere a long way off; and I shouldn't wonder if they are a horrid lot. His last letter was quite insulting. He said—let me see, what was it? Yes—"You have neither heart nor brains, and I shall do my best not to waste another thought on you?" What do you think of that?'

'It seems very extraordinary, my dear. How can he write to you in that way if you never gave him any encouragement?'

'Well, but I suppose I have done. We've met on the Common now and then, and—and that kind of thing. I'm afraid you're shocked, Mrs. Mumford. I know it isn't the way that nice people behave, and I'm going to give it up.'

'Does your mother know him?'

'Oh, yes! there's no secret about it. Mother rather likes him. Of course he behaves himself when he's at the house. I've a good mind to ask him to call here so that you could see him. Yes, I should like you to see him. You wouldn't mind?'

'Not if you really wish it, Louise. But—I can't help thinking you exaggerate his faults.'

'Not a bit. He's a regular brute when he gets angry.'

'My dear,' Emmeline interposed softly, 'that isn't quite a ladylike expression.'

'No, it isn't. Thank you, Mrs. Mumford. I meant to say he is horrid—very disagreeable. Then there's something else I want to tell you about. Cissy Higgins—that's Mr. Higgins's daughter, you know—is half engaged to a man called Bowling—an awful idiot—'

'I don't think I would use that word, dear.'

'Thank you, Mrs. Mumford. I mean to say he's a regular silly. But he's in a very good position—a partner in Jannaway Brothers of Woolwich, though he isn't thirty yet. Well, now, what do you think? Mr. Bowling doesn't seem to know his own mind, and just lately he's been paying so much attention to *me* that Cissy has got quite frantic about it. This was really and truly the reason why I left home.'

'I see,' murmured the listener, with a look of genuine interest.

'Yes. They wanted to get me out of the way. There wasn't the slightest fear that I should try to cut Cissy Higgins out; but it was getting very awkward for her, I admit. Now that's the kind of thing that doesn't go on among nice people, isn't it?'

'But what do you mean, Louise, when you say that Miss Higgins and Mr.—Mr. Bowling are *half* engaged?'

'Oh, I mean she has refused him once, just for form's sake; but he knows very well she means to have him. People of your kind don't do that sort of thing, do they?'

'I hardly know,' Emmeline replied, colouring a little at certain private reminiscences. 'And am I to understand that you wouldn't on any account listen to Mr. Bowling?'

Louise laughed.

'Oh, there's no knowing what I might do to spite Cissy. We hate each other, of course. But I can't fancy myself marrying him, He has a long nose, and talks through it. And he says "think you" for "thank you," and he sings—oh, to hear him sing! I can't bear the man.'

The matter of this conversation Emmeline reported to her husband at night, and they agreed in the hope that neither Mr. Cobb nor Mr. Bowling would make an appearance at "Runnymede." Mumford opined that these individuals were "cads." Small wonder, he said, that the girl wished to enter a new social sphere. His wife, on the other hand, had a suspicion that Miss Derrick would not be content to see the last of Mr. Cobb. He, the electrical engineer, or whatever he was, could hardly be such a ruffian as the girl depicted. His words, 'You have neither heart nor brains,' seemed to indicate anything but a coarse mind.

'But what a bad-tempered lot they are!' Mumford observed. 'I suppose people of that sort quarrel and abuse each other merely to pass the time. They seem to be just one degree above the roughs who come to blows and get into the police court. You must really do your best to get the girl out of it; I'm sure she is worthy of better things.'

'She is—in one way,' answered his wife judicially. 'But her education stopped too soon. I doubt if it's possible to change her very much. And—I really should like, after all, to see Mr. Cobb.'

Mumford broke into a laugh.

'There you go! The eternal feminine. You'll have her married in six months.'

'Don't be vulgar, Clarence. And we've talked enough of Louise for the present.'

Miss Derrick's presentiment that a letter from Mr. Cobb would soon reach her was justified the next day; it arrived in the afternoon, readdressed from Tulse Hill. Emmeline observed the eagerness with which this epistle was pounced upon and carried off for private perusal. She saw, too, that in half-an-hour's time Louise left the house—doubtless to post a reply. But, to her surprise, not a word of the matter escaped Miss Derrick during the whole evening.

In her school-days, Louise had learned to "play the piano," but, caring little or nothing for music, she had hardly touched a key for several years. Now the idea possessed her that she must resume her practising, and to-day she had spent hours at the piano, with painful effect upon Mrs. Mumford's nerves. After dinner she offered to play to Mumford, and he, good-natured fellow, stood by her to turn over the leaves. Emmeline, with fancy work in her hands, watched the two. She was not one of the most foolish of her sex, but it relieved her when Clarence moved away.

The next morning Louise was an hour late for breakfast. She came down when Mumford had left the house, and Emmeline saw with surprise that she was dressed for going out.

'Just a cup of coffee, please. I've no appetite this morning, and I want to catch a train for Victoria as soon as possible.'

'When will you be back?'

'Oh, I don't quite know. To tea, I think.'

The girl had all at once grown reticent, and her lips showed the less amiable possibilities of their contour.

## CHAPTER III

At dinner-time she had not returned. It being Saturday, Mumford was back early in the afternoon, and Miss Derrick's absence caused no grief. Emmeline could play with baby in the garden, whilst her husband smoked his pipe and looked on in the old comfortable way. They already felt that domestic life was not quite the same with a stranger to share it. Doubtless they would get used to the new restraints; but Miss Derrick must not expect them to disorganise their mealtimes on her account. Promptly at half-past seven they sat down to dine, and had just risen from the table, when Louise appeared.

She was in excellent spirits, without a trace of the morning's ill-humour. No apologies! If she didn't feel quite free to come and go, without putting people out, there would be no comfort in life. A slice of the joint, that was all she wanted, and she would have done in a few minutes.

'I've taken tickets for Toole's Theatre on Monday night. You must both come. You can, can't you?'

Mumford and his wife glanced at each other. Yes, they could go; it was very kind of Miss Derrick; but—

'That's all right, it'll be jolly. The idea struck me in the train, as I was going up; so I took a cab from Victoria and booked the places first thing. Third row from the front, dress circle; the best I could do. Please let me have my dinner alone. Mrs. Mumford, I want to tell you something afterwards.'

Clarence went round to see his friend Fentiman, with whom he usually had a chat on Saturday evening. Emmeline was soon joined by the guest in the drawing-room.

'There, you may read that,' said Louise, holding out a letter. 'It's from Mr. Cobb; came yesterday, but I didn't care to talk about it then. Yes, please read it; I want you to.'

Reluctantly, but with curiosity, Emmeline glanced over the sheet. Mr. Cobb wrote in ignorance of Miss Derrick's having left home. It was a plain, formal letter, giving a brief account of his doings in Ireland, and making a request that Louise would meet him, if possible, on Streatham Common, at three o'clock on Saturday afternoon. And he signed himself—'Very sincerely yours.'

'I made up my mind at once,' said the girl, 'that I wouldn't meet him. That kind of thing will have to stop. I'm not going to think any more of him, and it's better to make him understand it at once—isn't it?'

Emmeline heartily concurred.

'Still,' pursued the other, with an air of great satisfaction, 'I thought I had better go home for this afternoon. Because when he didn't see me on the Common he was pretty sure to call at the house, and I didn't want mother or Cissy to be talking about me to him before he had heard my own explanation.'

'Didn't you answer the letter?' asked Emmeline.

'No. I just sent a line to mother, to let her know I was coming over to-day, so that she might stay at home. Well, and it happened just as I thought. Mr. Cobb came to the house at half-past three. But before that I'd had a terrible row with Cissy. That isn't a nice expression, I know, but it really was one of our worst quarrels. Mr. Bowling hasn't been near since I left, and Cissy is furious. She said such things that I had to tell her very plainly what I thought of her; and she positively foamed at the mouth! "Now look here," she said, "if I find out that he goes to Sutton, you'll see what will happen." "*What* will happen?" I asked. "Father will stop your allowance, and you'll have to get on as best you can." "Oh, very well," I said, "in that case I shall marry Mr. Bowling." You should have seen her rage! "You said you wouldn't marry him if he had ten thousand a year!" she screamed. "I dare say I did; but if I've nothing to live upon—" "You can marry your Mr. Cobb, can't you?" And she almost cried; and I should have felt sorry for her if she hadn't made me so angry. "No," I said, "I can't marry Mr. Cobb. And I never dreamt of marrying Mr. Cobb. And—"'

Emmeline interposed.

'Really, Louise, that kind of talk isn't at all ladylike. What a pity you went home.'

'Yes, I was sorry for it afterwards. I shan't go again for a long time; I promise you I won't. However, Mr. Cobb came, and I saw him alone. He was astonished when he heard what had been going on; he was astonished at *me*, too—I mean, the way I spoke. I wanted him to understand at once that there was nothing between us; I talked in rather a—you know the sort of way.' She raised her chin slightly, and looked down from under her eyelids. 'Oh, I assure you I behaved quite nicely.

But he got into a rage, as he always does, and began to call me names, and I wouldn't stand it. "Mr. Cobb," I said, very severely, "either you will conduct yourself properly, or you will leave the house." Then he tried another tone, and said very different things—the kind of thing one likes to hear, you know; but I pretended that I didn't care for it a bit. "It's all over between us then?" he shouted at last; yes, really shouted, and I'm sure people must have heard. "All over?" I said. "But there never *was* anything—nothing serious." "Oh, all right. Good-bye, then." And off he rushed. And I dare say I've seen the last of him—for a time.'

'Now do try to live quietly, my dear,' said Emmeline. 'Go on with your music, and read a little each day—'

'Yes, that's just what I'm going to do, dear Mrs. Mumford. And your friends will be here to-morrow; it'll be so quiet and nice. And on Monday we shall go to the theatre, just for a change. And I'm not going to think of those people. It's all settled. I shall live very quietly indeed.'

She banged on the piano till nearly eleven o'clock, and went off to bed with a smile of virtuous contentment.

The guests who arrived on Sunday morning were Mr. and Mrs. Grove, Mr. Bilton, and Mr. Dunnill. Mrs. Grove was Emmeline's elder sister, a merry, talkative, kindly woman. Aware of the circumstances, she at once made friends with Miss Derrick, and greatly pleased that young lady by a skilful blending of "superior" talk with easy homeliness. Mr. Bilton, a stockbroker's clerk, represented the better kind of City young man—athletic, yet intelligent, spirited without vulgarity a breezy, good-humoured, wholesome fellow. He came down on his bicycle, and would return in the same way. Louise at once made a resolve to learn cycling.

'I wish you lived at Sutton, Mr. Bilton. I should ask you to teach me.'

'I'm really very sorry that I don't,' replied the young man discreetly.

'Oh, never mind. I'll find somebody.'

The fourth arrival, Mr. Dunnill, was older and less affable. He talked chiefly with Mr. Grove, a very quiet, somewhat careworn man; neither of them seemed able to shake off business, but they did not obtrude it on the company in general. The day passed pleasantly, but in Miss Derrick's opinion, rather soberly. Doing her best to fascinate Mr. Bilton, she felt a slight disappointment at her inability to engross his attention, and at the civil friendliness which he thought a sufficient reply to her gay sallies. For so good-looking and well-dressed a man he struck her as singularly reserved. But perhaps he was "engaged"; yes, that must be the explanation. When the guests had left, she put a plain question to Mrs. Mumford.

'I don't *think* he is engaged,' answered Emmeline, who on the whole was satisfied with Miss Derrick's demeanour throughout the day.

'Oh! But, of course, he *may* be, without you knowing it. Or is it always made known?'

'There's no rule about it, my dear.'

'Well, they're very nice people,' said Louise, with a little sigh. 'And I like your sister so much. I'm glad she asked me to go and see her. Is Mr. Bilton often at her house?—Don't misunderstand me, Mrs. Mumford. It's only that I *do* like men's society; there's no harm, is there? And people like Mr. Bilton are very different from those I've known; and I want to see more of them, you know.'

'There's no harm in saying that to *me*, Louise,' replied Mrs. Mumford. 'But pray be careful not to seem "forward." People think—and say—such disagreeable things.'

Miss Derrick was grateful, and again gave an assurance that repose and modesty should be the rule of her life.

At the theatre on Monday evening she exhibited a childlike enjoyment which her companions could not but envy. The freshness of her sensibilities was indeed remarkable, and Emmeline observed with pleasure that her mind seemed to have a very wholesome tone. Louise might commit follies, and be guilty of bad taste to any extent, but nothing in her savoured of depravity.

Tuesday she spent at home, pretending to read a little, and obviously thinking a great deal. On Wednesday morning she proposed of a sudden that Emmeline should go up to town with her on a shopping expedition. They had already turned over her wardrobe, numerous articles whereof were condemned by Mrs. Mumford's taste, and by Louise cheerfully sacrificed; she could not rest till new purchases had been made. So, after early luncheon, they took train to Victoria, Louise insisting that all the expenses should be hers. By five o'clock she had laid out some fifteen pounds, vastly to her satisfaction. They took tea at a restaurant, and reached Sutton not long before Mumford's return.

On Friday they went to London again, to call upon Mrs. Grove. Louise promised that this should be her last "outing" for a whole week. She admitted a feeling of restlessness, but after to-day she would overcome it. And that night she apologised formally to Mumford for taking his wife so much from home.

## CHAPTER III

'Please don't think I shall always be running about like this. I feel that I'm settling down. We are going to be very comfortable and quiet.'

And, to the surprise of her friends, more than a week went by before she declared that a day in town was absolutely necessary. Mr. Higgins had sent her a fresh supply of money, as there were still a few things she needed to purchase. But this time Emmeline begged her to go alone, and Louise seemed quite satisfied with the arrangement.

Early in the afternoon, as Mrs. Mumford was making ready to go out, the servant announced to her that a gentleman had called to see Miss Derrick; on learning that Miss Derrick was away, he had asked sundry questions, and ended by requesting an interview with Mrs. Mumford. His name was Cobb.

'Show him into the drawing-room,' said Emmeline, a trifle agitated. 'I will be down in a few moments.'

Beset by anxious anticipations, she entered the room, and saw before her a figure not wholly unlike what she had imagined: a wiry, resolute-looking man, with knitted brows, lips close-set, and heavy feet firmly planted on the carpet. He was respectably dressed, but nothing more, and in his large bare hands held a brown hat marked with a grease spot. One would have judged him a skilled mechanic. When he began to speak, his blunt but civil phrases were in keeping with this impression. He had not the tone of an educated man, yet committed no vulgar errors.

'My name is Cobb. I must beg your pardon for troubling you. Perhaps you have heard of me from Miss Derrick?'

'Yes, Mr. Cobb, your name has been mentioned,' Emmeline replied nervously. 'Will you sit down?'

'Thank you, I will.'

He twisted his hat about, and seemed to prepare with difficulty the next remark, which at length burst, rather than fell, from his lips.

'I wanted to see Miss Derrick. I suppose she is still living with you? They told me so.'

A terrible man, thought Emmeline, when roused to anger; his words must descend like sledge-hammers. And it would not take much to anger him. For all that, he had by no means a truculent countenance. He was trying to smile, and his features softened agreeably enough. The more closely she observed him, the less grew Emmeline's wonder that Louise felt an interest in the man.

'Miss Derrick is likely to stay with us for some time, I believe. She has only gone to town, to do some shopping.'

'I see. When I met her last she talked a good deal about you, Mrs. Mumford, and that's why I thought I would ask to see you. You have a good deal of influence over her.'

'Do you think so?' returned Emmeline, not displeased. 'I hope I may use it for her good.'

'So do I. But—well, it comes to this, Mrs. Mumford. She seemed to hint—though she didn't exactly say so—that you were advising her to have nothing more to do with me. Of course you don't know me, and I've no doubt you do what you think the best for her. I should feel it a kindness if you would just tell me whether you are really persuading her to think no more about me.'

It was an alarming challenge. Emmeline's fears returned; she half expected an outbreak of violence. The man was growing very nervous, and his muscles showed the working of strong emotion.

'I have given her no such advice, Mr. Cobb,' she answered, with an attempt at calm dignity. 'Miss Derrick's private affairs don't at all concern me. In such matters as this she is really quite old enough to judge for herself.'

'That's what *I* should have said,' remarked Mr. Cobb sturdily. 'I hope you'll excuse me; I don't wish to make myself offensive. After what she said to me when we met last, I suppose most men would just let her go her own way. But—but somehow I can't do that. The thing is, I can't trust what she says; I don't believe she knows her own mind. And so long as you tell me that you're not interfering—I mean, that you don't think it right to set her against me—'

'I assure you, nothing of the kind.'

There was a brief silence, then Cobb's voice again sounded with blunt emphasis.

'We're neither of us very good-tempered. We've known each other about a year, and we must have quarrelled about fifty times.'

'Do you think, then,' ventured the hostess, 'that it would ever be possible for you to live peacefully together?'

'Yes, I do,' was the robust answer. 'It would be a fight for the upper hand, but I know who'd get it, and after that things would be all right.'

Emmeline could not restrain a laugh, and her visitor joined in it with a heartiness which spoke in his favour.

'I promise you, Mr. Cobb, that I will do nothing whatever against your interests.'

'That's very kind of you, and it's all I wanted to know.'

He stood up. Emmeline, still doubtful how to behave, asked him if he would call on another day, when Miss Derrick might be at home.

## CHAPTER III

'It's only by chance I was able to get here this afternoon,' he replied. 'I haven't much time to go running about after her, and that's where I'm at a disadvantage. I don't know whether there's anyone else, and I'm not asking you to tell me, if you know. Of course I have to take my chance; but so long as you don't speak against me—and she thinks a great deal of your advice—'

'I'm very glad to be assured of that. All I shall do, Mr. Cobb, is to keep before her mind the duty of behaving straightforwardly.'

'That's the thing! Nobody can ask more than that.'

Emmeline hesitated, but could not dismiss him without shaking hands. That he did not offer to do so until invited, though he betrayed no sense of social inferiority, seemed another point in his favour.

## CHAPTER IV

Not half an hour after Cobb's departure Louise returned. Emmeline was surprised to see her back so soon; they met near the railway station as Mrs. Mumford was on her way to a shop in High Street.

'Isn't it good of me! If I had stayed longer I should have gone home to quarrel with Cissy; but I struggled against the temptation. Going to the grocer's? Oh, do let me go with you, and see how you do that kind of thing. I never gave an order at the grocer's in my life—no, indeed I never did. Mother and Cissy have always looked after that. And I want to learn about housekeeping; you promised to teach me.'

Emmeline made no mention of Mr. Cobb's call until they reached the house.

'He came here!' Louise exclaimed, reddening. 'What impudence! I shall at once write and tell him that his behaviour is outrageous. Am I to be hunted like this?'

Her wrath seemed genuine enough; but she was vehemently eager to learn all that had passed. Emmeline made a truthful report.

'You're quite sure that was all? Oh, his impertinence! Well, and now that you've seen him, don't you understand how—how impossible it is?'

'I shall say nothing more about it, Louise. It isn't my business to—'

The girl's face threatened a tempest. As Emmeline was moving away, she rudely obstructed her.

'I insist on you telling me what you think. It was abominable of him to come when I wasn't at home; and I don't think you ought to have seen him. You've no right to keep your thoughts to yourself!'

Mrs. Mumford was offended, and showed it.

'I have a perfect right, and I shall do so. Please don't let us quarrel. You may be fond of it, but I am not.'

Louise went from the room and remained invisible till just before dinner, when she came down with a grave and rather haughty countenance. To Mumford's remarks she replied with curt formality; he, prepared for this state of things, began conversing cheerfully with his wife, and Miss Derrick kept silence. After dinner, she passed out into the garden.

'It won't do,' said Mumford. 'The house is upset. I'm afraid we shall have to get rid of her.'

'If she can't behave herself, I'm afraid we must. It's my fault. I ought to have known that it would never do.'

At half-past ten, Louise was still sitting out of doors in the dark. Emmeline, wishing to lock up for the night, went to summon her troublesome guest.

'Hadn't you better come in?'

'Yes. But I think you are very unkind, Mrs. Mumford.'

'Miss Derrick, I really can't do anything but leave you alone when you are in such an unpleasant humour.'

'But that's just what you *oughtn't* to do. When I'm left alone I sulk, and that's bad for all of us. If you would just get angry and give me what I deserve, it would be all over very soon.'

'You are always talking about "nice" people. Nice people don't have scenes of that kind.'

'No, I suppose not. And I'm very sorry, and if you'll let me beg your pardon—. There, and we might have made it up hours ago. I won't ask you to tell me what you think of Mr. Cobb. I've written him the kind of letter his impudence deserves.'

'Very well. We won't talk of it any more. And if you *could* be a little quieter in your manners, Louise—'

'I will, I promise I will! Let me say good-night to Mr. Mumford.'

For a day or two there was halcyon weather. On Saturday afternoon Louise hired a carriage and took her friends for a drive into the country; at her special request the child accompanied them. Nothing could have been more delightful. She had quite made up her mind to have a house, some day, at Sutton. She hoped the Mumfords would "always" live there, that they might perpetually enjoy each other's society. What were the rents? she inquired. Well, to begin with, she would be content with one of the smaller houses; a modest, semidetached little place, like those at the far end of Cedar Road. They were perfectly respectable—were they not? How this change in her station was to come about Louise offered no hint, and did not seem to think of the matter.

Then restlessness again came upon her. One day she all but declared her disappointment that the Mumfords saw so few people. Emmeline, repeating this to her husband, avowed a certain compunction.

'I almost feel that I deliberately misled her. You know, Clarence, in our first conversation I mentioned the Kirby Simpsons and Mrs. Hollings, and I feel sure she remembers. It wouldn't be nice to be taking her money on false pretences, would it?'

'Oh, don't trouble. It's quite certain she has someone in mind whom she means to marry before long.'

'I can't help thinking that. But I don't know who it can be. She had a letter this morning in a man's writing, and didn't speak of it. It wasn't Mr. Cobb.'

Louise, next day, put a point-blank question.

'Didn't you say that you knew some people at West Kensington?'

'Oh, yes,' answered Emmeline, carelessly. 'The Kirby Simpsons. They're away from home.'

'I'm sorry for that. Isn't there anyone else we could go and see, or ask over here?'

'I think it very likely Mr. Bilton will come down in a few days.'

Louise received Mr. Bilton's name with moderate interest. But she dropped the subject, and seemed to reconcile herself to domestic pleasures.

It was on the evening of this day that Emmeline received a letter which gave her much annoyance. Her sister, Mrs. Grove, wrote thus:

'How news does get about! And what ridiculous forms it takes! Here is Mrs. Powell writing to me from Birmingham, and she says she has heard that you have taken in the daughter of some wealthy *parvenu*, for a consideration, to train her in the ways of decent society! Just the kind of thing Mrs. Powell would delight in talking about—she is so very malicious. Where she got her information I can't imagine. She doesn't give the slightest hint. "They tell me"—I copy her words—"that the girl is all but a savage, and does and says the most awful things. I quite admire Mrs. Mumford's courage. I've heard of people doing this kind of thing, and I always wondered how they got on with their friends." Of course I have written to contradict this rubbish. But it's very annoying, I'm sure.'

Mumford was angry. The source of these fables must be either Bilton or Dunnill, yet he had not thought either of them the kind of men to make mischief. Who else knew anything of the affair? Searching her memory, Emmeline recalled a person unknown to her, a married lady, who had dropped in at Mrs. Grove's when she and Louise were there.

'I didn't like her—a supercilious sort of person. And she talked a great deal of her acquaintance with important people. It's far more likely to have come from her than from either of those men. I shall write and tell Molly so.'

They began to feel uncomfortable, and seriously thought of getting rid of the burden so imprudently undertaken. Louise, the next day, wanted to take Emmeline to town, and showed dissatisfaction when she had to go unaccompanied. She stayed till late in the evening, and came back with a gay account of her calls upon two or three old friends—the girls of whom she had spoken to Mrs. Mumford. One of them, Miss Featherstone, she had taken to dine with her at a restaurant, and afterwards they had spent an hour or two at Miss Featherstone's lodgings.

'I didn't go near Tulse Hill, and if you knew how I am wondering what is going on there! Not a line from anyone. I shall write to mother to-morrow.'

Emmeline produced a letter which had arrived for Miss Derrick.

'Why didn't you give it me before?' Louise exclaimed, impatiently.

'My dear, you had so much to tell me. I waited for the first pause.'

'That isn't from home,' said the girl, after a glance at the envelope. 'It's nothing.'

After saying good-night, she called to Emmeline from her bedroom door. Entering the room, Mrs. Mumford saw the open letter in Louise's hand, and read in her face a desire of confession.

'I want to tell you something. Don't be in a hurry; just a few minutes. This letter is from Mr. Bowling. Yes, and I've had one from him before, and I was obliged to answer it.'

'Do you mean they are love-letters?'

'Yes, I'm afraid they are. And it's so stupid, and I'm so vexed. I don't want to have anything to do with him, as I told you long ago.' Louise often used expressions which to a stranger would have implied that her intimacy with Mrs. Mumford was of years' standing. 'He wrote for the first time last week. Such a silly letter! I wish you would read it. Well, he said that it was all over between him and Cissy, and that he cared only for me, and always had, and always would—you know how men write. He said he considered himself quite free. Cissy had refused him, and wasn't that enough? Now that I was away from home, he could write to me, and wouldn't I let him see me? Of course I wrote that I didn't *want* to see him, and I thought he was behaving very badly—though I don't really think so, because it's all that idiot Cissy's fault. Didn't I do quite right?'

'I think so.'

'Very well. And now he's writing again, you see; oh, such a lot of rubbish! I can hear him saying it all through his nose. Do tell me what I ought to do next.'

'You must either pay no attention to the letter, or reply so that he can't possibly misunderstand you.'

'Call him names, you mean?'

'My dear Louise!'

'But that's the only way with such men. I suppose you never were bothered with them. I think I'd better not write at all.'

Emmeline approved this course, and soon left Miss Derrick to her reflections.

The next day Louise carried out her resolve to write for information regarding the progress of things at Coburg Lodge. She had not long to wait for a reply, and it was of so startling a nature that she ran at once to Mrs. Mumford, whom she found in the nursery.

'Do please come down. Here's something I must tell you about. What do you think mother says? I've to go back home again at once.'

'What's the reason?' Emmeline inquired, knowing not whether to be glad or sorry.

'I'll read it to you:—"Dear Lou," she says, "you've made a great deal of trouble, and I hope you're satisfied. Things are all upside down, and I've never seen dada"—that's Mr. Higgins, of course—"I've never seen dada in such a bad temper, not since first I knew him. Mr. B."—that's Mr. Bowling, you know—"has told him plain that he doesn't think any more of Cissy, and that nothing mustn't be expected of him."—Oh what sweet letters mother does write!—"That was when dada went and asked him about his intentions, as he couldn't help doing, because Cissy is fretting so. It's all over, and of course you're the cause of it; and, though I can't blame you as much as the others do, I think you *are* to blame. And Cissy said she must go to the seaside to get over it, and she went off yesterday to Margate to your Aunt Annie's boarding-house, and there she says she shall stay as long as she doesn't feel quite well, and dada has to pay two guineas a week for her. So he says at once, 'Now Loo 'll have to come back. I'm not going to pay for the both of them boarding out,' he says. And he means it. He has told me to write to you at once, and you're to come as soon as you can, and he won't be responsible to Mrs. Mumford for more than another week's payment."—There! But I shan't go, for all that. The idea! I left home just to please them, and now I'm to go back just when it suits their convenience. Certainly not.'

## CHAPTER IV

'But what will you do, Louise,' asked Mrs. Mumford, 'if Mr. Higgins is quite determined?'

'Do? Oh! I shall settle it easy enough. I shall write at once to the old man and tell him I'm getting on so nicely in every way that I couldn't dream of leaving you. It's all nonsense, you'll see.'

Emmeline and her husband held a council that night, and resolved that, whatever the issue of Louise's appeal to her stepfather, this was a very good opportunity for getting rid of their guest. They would wait till Louise made known the upshot of her negotiations. It seemed probable that Mr. Higgins would spare them the unpleasantness of telling Miss Derrick she must leave. If not, that disagreeable necessity must be faced.

'I had rather cut down expenses all round,' said Emmeline, 'than have our home upset in this way. It isn't like home at all. Louise is a whirlwind, and the longer she stays, the worse it'll be.'

'Yes, it won't do at all,' Mumford assented. 'By the bye, I met Bilton to-day, and he asked after Miss Derrick. I didn't like his look or his tone at all. I feel quite sure there's a joke going round at our expense. Confound it!'

'Never mind. It'll be over in a day or two, and it'll be a lesson to you, Clarence, won't it?'

'I quite admit that the idea was mine,' her husband replied, rather irritably. 'But it wasn't I who accepted the girl as a suitable person.'

'And certainly it wasn't *me*!' rejoined Emmeline. 'You will please to remember that I said again and again—'

'Oh, hang it, Emmy! We made a blunder, both of us, and don't let us make it worse by wrangling about it. There you are; people of that class bring infection into the house. If she stayed here a twelvemonth, we should have got to throwing things at each other.'

The answer to Louise's letter of remonstrance came in the form of Mrs. Higgins herself. Shortly before luncheon that lady drove up to "Runnymede" in a cab, and her daughter, who had just returned from a walk, was startled to hear of the arrival.

'You've got to come home with me, Lou,' Mrs. Higgins began, as she wiped her perspiring face. 'I've promised to have you back by this afternoon. Dada's right down angry; you wouldn't know him. He blames everything on to you, and you'd better just come home quiet.'

'I shall do nothing of the kind,' answered Louise, her temper rising.

Mrs. Higgins glared at her and began to rail; the voice was painfully audible to Emmeline, who just then passed through the hall. Miss Derrick gave as good as she received; a battle raged for some minutes, differing from many a former conflict only in the moderation of pitch and vocabulary due to their being in a stranger's house.

'Then you won't come?' cried the mother at length. 'I've had my journey for nothing, have I? Then just go and fetch Mrs. What's-her-name. She must hear what I've got to say.'

'Mrs. Mumford isn't at home,' answered Louise, with bold mendacity. 'And a very good thing too. I should be sorry for her to see you in the state you're in.'

'I'm in no more of a state than you are, Louise! And just you listen to this. Not one farthing more will you have from 'ome—not one farthing! And you may think yourself lucky if you still *'ave* a 'ome. For all I know, you'll have to earn your own living, and I'd like to hear how you mean to do it. As soon as I get back I shall write to Mrs. What's-her-name and tell her that nothing will be paid for you after the week that's due and the week that's for notice. Now just take heed of what you're doing, Lou. It may have more serious results than you think for.'

'I've thought all I'm going to think,' replied the girl. 'I shall stay here as long as I like, and be indebted neither to you nor to stepfather.'

Mrs. Mumford breathed a sigh of thankfulness that she was not called upon to take part in this scene. It was bad enough that the servant engaged in laying lunch could hear distinctly Mrs. Higgins's coarse and violent onslaught. When the front door at length closed she rejoiced, but with trembling; for the words that fell upon her ear from the hall announced too plainly that Louise was determined to stay.

# CHAPTER V

Miss Derrick had gone back into the drawing-room, and, to Emmeline's surprise, remained there. This retirement was ominous; the girl must be taking some resolve. Emmeline, on her part, braced her courage for the step on which she had decided. Luncheon awaited them, but it would be much better to arrive at an understanding before they sat down to the meal. She entered the room and found Louise leaning on the back of a chair.

'I dare say you heard the row,' Miss Derrick remarked coldly. 'I'm very sorry, but nothing of that kind shall happen again.'

Her countenance was disturbed, she seemed to be putting a restraint upon herself, and only with great effort to subdue her voice.

'What are you going to do?' asked Emmeline, in a friendly tone, but, as it were, from a distance.

'I am going to ask you to do me a great kindness, Mrs. Mumford.'

There was no reply. The girl paused a moment, then resumed impulsively.

'Mr. Higgins says that if I don't come home, he won't let me have any more money. They're going to write and tell you that they won't be responsible after this for my board and lodging. Of course I shall not go home; I shouldn't dream of it; I'd rather earn my living as—as a scullery maid. I want to ask you, Mrs. Mumford, whether you will let me stay on, and trust me to pay what I owe you. It won't be for very long, and I promise you I *will* pay, every penny.'

The natural impulse of Emmeline's disposition was to reply with hospitable kindliness; she found it very difficult to maintain her purpose; it shamed her to behave like the ordinary landlady, to appear actuated by mean motives. But the domestic strain was growing intolerable, and she felt sure that Clarence would be exasperated if her weakness prolonged it.

'Now do let me advise you, Louise,' she answered gently. 'Are you acting wisely? Wouldn't it be very much better to go home?',

Louise lost all her self-control. Flushed with anger, her eyes glaring, she broke into vehement exclamations.

'You want to get rid of me! Very well, I'll go this moment. I was going to tell you something; but you don't care what becomes of me. I'll send for my luggage; you shan't be troubled with it long. And you'll be paid all that's owing. I didn't think you were one of that kind. I'll go this minute.'

'Just as you please,' said Emmeline, 'Your temper is really so very—'

'Oh, I know. It's always my temper, and nobody else is ever to blame. I wouldn't stay another night in the house, if I had to sleep on the Downs!'

She flung out of the room and flew upstairs. Emmeline, angered by this unwarrantable treatment, determined to hold aloof, and let the girl do as she would. Miss Derrick was of full age, and quite capable of taking care of herself, or at all events ought to be. Perhaps this was the only possible issue of the difficulties in which they had all become involved; neither Louise nor her parents could be dealt with in the rational, peaceful way preferred by well-conditioned people. To get her out of the house was the main point; if she chose to depart in a whirlwind, that was her own affair. All but certainly she would go home, tomorrow if not to-day.

In less than a quarter of an hour her step sounded on the stairs—would she turn into the dining-room, where Emmeline now sat at table? No; straight through the hall, and out at the front door, which closed, however, quite softly behind her. That she did not slam it seemed wonderful to Emmeline. The girl was not wholly a savage.

Presently Mrs. Mumford went up to inspect the forsaken chamber. Louise had packed all her things: of course she must have tumbled them recklessly into the trunks. Drawers were left open, as if to exhibit their emptiness, but in other respects the room looked tidy enough. Neatness and order came by no means naturally to Miss Derrick, and Emmeline did not know what pains the girl had taken, ever since her arrival, to live in conformity with the habits of a 'nice' household.

Louise, meanwhile, had gone to the railway station, intending to take a ticket for Victoria. But half an hour must elapse before the arrival of a train, and she walked about in an irresolute mood. For one thing, she felt hungry; at Sutton her appetite had been keen, and mealtimes were always welcome. She entered the refreshment room, and with inward murmurs made a repast which reminded her of the excellent luncheon she might now have been enjoying. All the time, she pondered her situation. Ultimately, instead of booking for Victoria, she procured a ticket for Epsom Downs, and had not long to wait for the train.

It was a hot day at the end of June. Wafts of breezy coolness passed now and then over the high open country, but did not suffice to combat the sun's steady glare. After walking half a mile or so, absorbed in thought, Louise suffered so much that she looked about for shadow. Before her was the towering ugliness of the Grand Stand; this she had seen and admired when driving past it with her friends; it did not now attract her. In another direction the Downs were edged with trees, and that way she turned. All but overcome with heat and weariness, she at length found a shaded spot where her solitude seemed secure. And, after seating herself, the first thing she did was to have a good cry.

Then for an hour she sat thinking, and as she thought her face gradually emerged from gloom—the better, truer face which so often allowed itself to be disguised at the prompting of an evil spirit; her softening lips all but smiled, as if at an amusing suggestion, and her eyes, in their reverie, seemed to behold a pleasant promise. Unconsciously she plucked and tasted the sweet stems of grass that grew about her. At length, the sun's movements having robbed her of shadow, she rose, looked at her watch, and glanced around for another retreat. Hard by was a little wood, delightfully grassy and cool, fenced about with railings she could easily have climbed; but a notice-board, severely admonishing trespassers, forbade the attempt. With a petulant remark to herself on the selfishness of "those people," she sauntered past.

Along this edge of the Downs stands a picturesque row of pine-trees, stunted, bittered, and twisted through many a winter by the upland gales. Louise noticed them, only to think for a moment what ugly trees they were. Before her, east, west, and north, lay the wooded landscape, soft of hue beneath the summer sky, spreading its tranquil beauty far away to the mists of the horizon. In vivacious company she would have called it, and perhaps have thought it, a charming view; alone, she had no eye for such things—an indifference characteristic of her mind, and not at all dependent upon its mood. Presently another patch of shade invited her to repose again, and again she meditated for an hour or more.

The sun had grown less ardent, and a breeze, no longer fitful, made walking pleasant. The sight of holiday-making school-children, who, in their ribboned hats and white pinafores, were having tea not far away, suggested to Louise that she also would like such refreshment.

Doubtless it might be procured at the inn yonder, near the racecourse, and thither she began to move. Her thoughts were more at rest; she had made her plan for the evening; all that had to be done was to kill time for another hour or so. Walking lightly over the turf, she noticed the chalk marks significant of golf, and wondered how the game was played. Without difficulty she obtained her cup of tea, loitered over it as long as possible, strayed yet awhile about the Downs, and towards half-past six made for the railway station.

She travelled no further than Sutton, and there lingered in the waiting room till the arrival of a certain train from London Bridge. As the train came in she took up a position near the exit. Among the people who had alighted, her eye soon perceived Clarence Mumford. She stepped up to him and drew his attention.

'Oh! have you come by the same train?' he asked, shaking hands with her.

'No. I've been waiting here because I wanted to see you, Mr. Mumford. Will you spare me a minute or two?'

'Here? In the station?'

'Please—if you don't mind.'

Astonished, Mumford drew aside with her to a quiet part of the long platform. Louise, keeping a very grave countenance, told him rapidly all that had befallen since his departure from home in the morning.

'I behaved horridly, and I was sorry for it as soon as I had left the house. After all Mrs. Mumford's kindness to me, and yours, I don't know how I could be so horrid. But the quarrel with mother had upset me so, and I felt so miserable when Mrs. Mumford seemed to want to get rid of me. I feel sure she didn't really want to send me away: she was only advising me, as she thought, for my good. But I can't, and won't, go home. And I've been waiting all the afternoon to see you. No; not here. I went to Epsom Downs and walked about, and then came back just in time. And—do you think I might go back? I don't mean now, at once, but this evening, after you've had dinner. I really don't know where to go for the night, and it's such a stupid position to be in, isn't it?'

With perfect naivete, or with perfect simulation of it, she looked him in the face, and it was Mumford who had to avert his eyes. The young man felt very uncomfortable.

'Oh! I'm quite sure Emmy will be glad to let you come for the night, Miss Derrick—'

## CHAPTER V

'Yes, but—Mr. Mumford, I want to stay longer—a few weeks longer. Do you think Mrs. Mumford would forgive me? I have made up my mind what to do, and I ought to have told her. I should have, if I hadn't lost my temper.'

'Well,' replied the other, in grave embarrassment, but feeling that he had no alternative, 'let us go to the house—'

'Oh! I couldn't. I shouldn't like anyone to know that I spoke to you about it. It wouldn't be nice, would it? I thought if I came later, after dinner. And perhaps you could talk to Mrs. Mumford, and—and prepare her. I mean, perhaps you wouldn't mind saying you were sorry I had gone so suddenly. And then perhaps Mrs. Mumford—she's so kind—would say that she was sorry too. And then I might come into the garden and find you both sitting there—'

Mumford, despite his most uneasy frame of mind, betrayed a passing amusement. He looked into the girl's face and saw its prettiness flush with pretty confusion, and this did not tend to restore his tranquillity.

'What shall you do in the meantime?'

'Oh! go into the town and have something to eat, and then walk about.'

'You must be dreadfully tired already.'

'Just a little; but I don't mind. It serves me right. I shall be so grateful to you, Mr. Mumford. If you won't let me come, I suppose I must go to London and ask one of my friends to take me in.'

'I will arrange it. Come about half-past eight. We shall be in the garden by then.'

Avoiding her look, he moved away and ran up the stairs. But from the exit of the station he walked slowly, in part to calm himself, to assume his ordinary appearance, and in part to think over the comedy he was going to play.

Emmeline met him at the door, herself too much flurried to notice anything peculiar in her husband's aspect. She repeated the story with which he was already acquainted.

'And really, after all, I am so glad!' was her conclusion. 'I didn't think she had really gone; all the afternoon I've been expecting to see her back again. But she won't come now, and it is a good thing to have done with the wretched business. I only hope she will tell the truth to her people. She might say that we turned her out of the house. But I don't think so; in spite of all her faults, she never seemed deceitful or malicious.'

Mumford was strongly tempted to reveal what had happened at the station, but he saw danger alike in disclosure and in reticence.

When there enters the slightest possibility of jealousy, a man can never be sure that his wife will act as a rational being. He feared to tell the simple truth lest Emmeline should not believe his innocence of previous plotting with Miss Derrick, or at all events should be irritated by the circumstances into refusing Louise a lodging for the night. And with no less apprehension he decided at length to keep the secret, which might so easily become known hereafter, and would then have such disagreeable consequences.

'Well, let us have dinner, Emmy; I'm hungry. Yes, it's a good thing she has gone; but I wish it hadn't happened in that way. What a spitfire she is!'

'I never, never saw the like. And if you had heard Mrs. Higgins! Oh, what dreadful people! Clarence, hear me register a vow—'

'It was my fault, dear. I'm awfully sorry I got you in for such horrors. It was wholly and entirely my fault.'

By due insistence on this, Mumford of course put his wife into an excellent humour, and, after they had dined, she returned to her regret that the girl should have gone so suddenly. Clarence, declaring that he would allow himself a cigar, instead of the usual pipe, to celebrate the restoration of domestic peace, soon led Emmeline into the garden.

'Heavens! how hot it has been. Eighty-five in our office at noon—eighty-five! Fellows are discarding waistcoats and wearing what they call a cummerbund—silk sash round the waist. I think I must follow the fashion. How should I look, do you think?'

'You don't really mind that we lose the money?' Emmeline asked presently.

'Pooh! We shall do well enough.—Who's that?'

Someone was entering the garden by the side path. And in a moment there remained no doubt who the person was. Louise came forward, her head bent, her features eloquent of fatigue and distress.

'Mrs. Mumford—I couldn't—without asking you to forgive me—'

Her voice broke with a sob. She stood in a humble attitude, and Emmeline, though pierced with vexation, had no choice but to hold out a welcoming hand.

'Have you come all the way back from London just to say this?'

'I haven't been to London. I've walked about—all day—and oh, I'm so tired and miserable! Will you let me stay, just for to-night? I shall be so grateful.'

## CHAPTER V

'Of course you may stay, Miss Derrick. It was very far from my wish to see you go off at a moment's notice. But I really couldn't stop you.'

Mumford had stepped aside, out of hearing. He forgot his private embarrassment in speculation as to the young woman's character. That she was acting distress and penitence he could hardly believe; indeed, there was no necessity to accuse her of dishonest behaviour. The trivial concealment between him and her amounted to nothing, did not alter the facts of the situation. But what could be at the root of her seemingly so foolish existence? Emmeline held to the view that she was in love with the man Cobb, though perhaps unwilling to admit it, even in her own silly mind. It might be so, and, *if* so, it made her more interesting; for one was tempted to think that Louise had not the power of loving at all. Yet, for his own part, he couldn't help liking her; the eyes that had looked into his at the station haunted him a little, and would not let him think of her contemptuously. But what a woman to make ones wife! Unless—unless—

Louise had gone into the house. Emmeline approached her husband.

'There! I foresaw it. Isn't vexing?'

'Never mind, dear. She'll go tomorrow, or the day after.'

'I wish I could be sure of that.'

## CHAPTER VI

Louise did not appear again that evening. Thoroughly tired, she unpacked her trunks, sat awhile by the open window, listening to a piano in a neighbouring house, and then jumped into bed. From ten o'clock to eight next morning she slept soundly.

At breakfast her behaviour was marked with excessive decorum. To the ordinary civilities of her host and hostess she replied softly, modestly, in the manner of a very young and timid girl; save when addressed, she kept silence, and sat with head inclined; a virginal freshness breathed about her; she ate very little, and that without her usual gusto, but rather as if performing a dainty ceremony. Her eyes never moved in Mumford's direction.

The threatened letter from Mrs. Higgins had arrived; Emmeline and her husband read it before their guest came down. If Louise continued to reside with them, they entertained her with a full knowledge that no payment must be expected from Coburg Lodge. Emmeline awaited the disclosure of her guest's project, which had more than once been alluded to yesterday; she could not dream of permitting Louise to stay for more than a day or two, whatever the suggestion offered. This morning she had again heard from her sister, Mrs. Grove, who was strongly of opinion that Miss Derrick should be sent back to her native sphere.

'I shall always feel,' she said to her husband, 'that we have behaved badly. I was guilty of false pretences. Fortunately, we have the excuse of her unbearable temper. But for that, I should feel dreadfully ashamed of myself.'

Very soon after Mumford's departure, Louise begged for a few minutes' private talk.

'Every time I come into this drawing-room, Mrs. Mumford, I think how pretty it is. What pains you must have taken in furnishing it! I never saw such nice curtains anywhere else. And that little screen—I *am* so fond of that screen!'

## CHAPTER VI

'It was a wedding present from an old friend,' Emmeline replied, complacently regarding the object, which shone with embroidery of many colours.

'Will you help me when *I* furnish *my* drawing-room?' Louise asked sweetly. And she added, with a direct look, 'I don't think it will be very long.'

'Indeed?'

'I am going to marry Mr. Bowling.'

Emmeline could no longer feel astonishment at anything her guest said or did. The tone, the air, with which Louise made this declaration affected her with a sense of something quite unforeseen; but, at the same time, she asked herself why she had not foreseen it. Was not this the obvious answer to the riddle? All along, Louise had wished to marry Mr. Bowling. She might or might not have consciously helped to bring about the rupture between Mr. Bowling and Miss Higgins; she might, or might not, have felt genuinely reluctant to take advantage of her half-sister's defeat. But a struggle had been going on in the girl's conscience, at all events. Yes, this explained everything. And, on the whole, it seemed to speak in Louise's favour. Her ridicule of Mr. Bowling's person and character became, in this new light, a proof of desire to resist her inclinations. She had only yielded when it was certain that Miss Higgins's former lover had quite thrown off his old allegiance, and when no good could be done by self-sacrifice.

'When did you make up your mind to this, Louise?'

'Yesterday, after our horrid quarrel. No, *you* didn't quarrel; it was all my abominable temper. This morning I'm going to answer Mr. Bowling's last letter, and I shall tell him—what I've told you. He'll be delighted!'

'Then you have really wished for this from the first?'

Louise plucked at the fringe on the arm of her chair, and replied at length with maidenly frankness.

'I always thought it would be a good marriage for me. But I never—do believe me—I never tried to cut Cissy out. The truth is I thought a good deal of the other—of Mr. Cobb. But I knew that I *couldn't* marry him. It would be dreadful; we should quarrel frightfully, and he would kill me—I feel sure he would, he's so violent in his temper. But Mr. Bowling is very nice; he couldn't get angry if he tried. And he has a much better position than Mr. Cobb.'

Emmeline began to waver in her conviction and to feel a natural annoyance.

'And you think,' she said coldly, 'that your marriage will take place soon?'

'That's what I want to speak about, dear Mrs. Mumford. Did you hear from my mother this morning? Then you see what my position is. I am homeless. If I leave you, I don't know where I shall go. When Mr. Higgins knows I'm going to marry Mr. Bowling he won't have me in the house, even if I wanted to go back. Cissy will be furious: she'll come back from Margate just to keep up her father's anger against me. If you could let me stay here just a short time, Mrs. Mumford; just a few weeks I should *so* like to be married from your house.'

The listener trembled with irritation, and before she could command her voice Louise added eagerly:

'Of course, when we're married, Mr. Bowling will pay all my debts.'

"You are quite mistaken,' said Emmeline distantly, 'if you think that the money matter has anything to do with—with my unreadiness to agree—'

'Oh, I didn't think it—not for a moment. I'm a trouble to you; I know I am. But I'll be so quiet, dear Mrs. Mumford. You shall hardly know I'm in the house. If once it's all settled I shall *never* be out of temper. Do, please, let me stay! I like you so much, and how wretched it would be if I had to be married from a lodging-house.'

'I'm afraid, Louise—I'm really afraid—'

'Of my temper?' the girl interrupted. 'If ever I say an angry word you shall turn me out that very moment. Dear Mrs. Mumford! Oh! *what* shall I do if you won't be kind to me? What will become of me? I have no home, and everybody hates me.'

'Tears streamed down her face; she lay back, overcome with misery. Emmeline was distracted. She felt herself powerless to act as common-sense dictated, yet desired more than ever to rid herself of every shadow of responsibility for the girl's proceedings. The idea of this marriage taking place at "Runnymede" made her blood run cold. No, no; *that* was absolutely out of the question. But equally impossible did it seem to speak with brutal decision. Once more she must temporise, and hope for courage on another day.

'I can't—I really can't give you a definite answer till I have spoken with Mr. Mumford.'

'Oh! I am sure he will do me this kindness,' sobbed Louise.

A slight emphasis on the "he" touched Mrs. Mumford unpleasantly. She rose, and began to pick out some overblown flowers from a vase on the table near her. Presently Louise became silent. Before either of them spoke again a postman's knock sounded at the house-door, and Emmeline went to see what letter had been delivered. It was for Miss Derrick; the handwriting, as Emmeline knew, that of Mr. Cobb.

'Oh, bother!' Louise murmured, as she took the letter from Mrs. Mumford's hand. 'Well, I'm a trouble to everybody, and I don't know how it'll all end. I daresay I shan't live very long.'

'Don't talk nonsense, Louise.'

'Should you like me to go at once, Mrs. Mumford?' the girl asked, with a submissive sigh.

'No, no. Let us think over it for a day or two. Perhaps you haven't quite made up your mind, after all.'

To this, oddly enough, Louise gave no reply. She lingered by the window, nervously bending and rolling her letter, which she did not seem to think of opening. After a glance or two of discreet curiosity, Mrs. Mumford left the room. Daily duties called for attention, and she was not at all inclined to talk further with Louise. The girl, as soon as she found herself alone, broke Mr. Cobb's envelope, which contained four sides of bold handwriting—not a long letter, but, as usual, vigorously worded. 'Dear Miss Derrick,' he wrote, 'I haven't been in a hurry to reply to your last, as it seemed to me that you were in one of your touchy moods when you sent it. It wasn't my fault that I called at the house when you were away. I happened to have business at Croydon unexpectedly, and ran over to Sutton just on the chance of seeing you. And I have no objection to tell you all I said to your friend there. I am not in the habit of saying things behind people's backs that I don't wish them to hear. All I did was to ask out plainly whether Mrs. M. was trying to persuade you to have nothing to do with me. She said she wasn't, and that she didn't wish to interfere one way or another. I told her that I could ask no more than that. She seemed to me a sensible sort of woman, and I don't suppose you'll get much harm from her, though I daresay she thinks more about dress and amusements, and so on, than is good for her or anyone else. You say at the end of your letter that I'm to let you know when I think of coming again, and if you mean by that that you would be glad to see me, I can only say, thank you. I don't mean to give you up yet, and I don't believe you want me to say what you will. I don't spy after you; you're mistaken in that. But I'm pretty much always thinking about you, and I wish you were nearer to me. I may have to go to Bristol in a week or two, and perhaps I shall be there for a month or more, so I must see you before then. Will you tell me what day would suit you, after seven? If you don't want me to come to the house, then meet me where you like. And there's only one more thing I have to say—you must deal honestly with me. I can wait, but I won't be deceived.'

Louise pondered for a long time, turning now to this part of the letter, now to that. And the lines of her face, though they made no approach to smiling, indicated agreeable thoughts. Tears had left just sufficient trace to give her meditations a semblance of unwonted seriousness.

About midday she went up to her room and wrote letters. The first was to Miss Cissy Higgins:—'Dear Ciss,—I dare say you would like to know that Mr. B. has proposed to me. If you have any objection, please let me know it by return.—Affectionately yours, L. E. DERRICK.' This she addressed to Margate, and stamped with a little thump of the fist. Her next sheet of paper was devoted to Mr. Bowling, and the letter, though brief, cost her some thought. 'Dear Mr. Bowling,—Your last is so very nice and kind that I feel I ought to answer it without delay, but I cannot answer in the way you wish. I must have a long, long time to think over such a very important question. I don't blame you in the least for your behaviour to someone we know of; and I think, after all that happened, you were quite free. It is quite true that she did not behave straightforwardly, and I am very sorry to have to say it. I shall not be going home again: I have quite made up my mind about that. I am afraid I must not let you come here to call upon me. I have a particular reason for it. To tell you the truth, my friend Mrs. Mumford is *very* particular, and rather fussy, and has a rather trying temper. So please do not come just yet. I am quite well, and enjoying myself in a *very* quiet way.—I remain, sincerely yours, LOUISE E. DERRICK.' Finally she penned a reply to Mr. Cobb, and this, after a glance at a railway time-table, gave her no trouble at all. 'Dear Mr. Cobb,' she scribbled, 'if you really *must* see me before you go away to Bristol, or wherever it is, you had better meet me on Saturday at Streatham Station, which is about halfway between me and you. I shall come by the train from Sutton, which reaches Streatham at 8.6.—Yours truly, L. E. D.'

To-day was Thursday. When Saturday came the state of things at "Runnymede" had undergone no change whatever; Emmeline still waited for a moment of courage, and Mumford, though he did not relish the prospect, began to think it more than probable that Miss Derrick would hold her ground until her actual marriage with Mr. Bowling. Whether that unknown person would discharge the debt his betrothed was incurring seemed an altogether uncertain matter. Louise, in the meantime, kept quiet as a mouse—so strangely quiet, indeed, that Emmeline's prophetic soul dreaded some impending disturbance, worse than any they had yet suffered.

At luncheon, Louise made known that she would have to leave in the middle of dinner to catch a train. No explanation was offered or asked, but Emmeline, it being Saturday, said she would put the dinner-hour earlier, to suit her friend's convenience. Louise smiled pleasantly, and said how very kind it was of Mrs. Mumford.

She had no difficulty in reaching Streatham by the time appointed. Unfortunately, it was a cloudy evening, and a spattering of rain fell from time to time.

'I suppose you'll be afraid to walk to the Common,' said Mr. Cobb, who stood waiting at the exit from the station, and showed more satisfaction in his countenance when Louise appeared than he evinced in words.

'Oh, I don't care,' she answered. 'It won't rain much, and I've brought my umbrella, and I've nothing on that will take any harm.'

She had, indeed, dressed herself in her least demonstrative costume. Cobb wore the usual garb of his leisure hours, which was better than that in which he had called the other day at "Runnymede." For some minutes they walked towards Streatham Common without interchange of a word, and with no glance at each other. Then the man coughed, and said bluntly that he was glad Louise had come.

'Well, I wanted to see you,' was her answer.

'What about?'

'I don't think I shall be able to stay with the Mumfords. They're very nice people, but they're not exactly my sort, and we don't get on very well. Where had I better go?'

'Go? Why home, of course. The best place for you.'

Cobb was prepared for a hot retort, but it did not come. After a moment's reflection, Louise said quietly:

'I can't go home. I've quarrelled with them too badly. You haven't seen mother lately? Then I must tell you how things are.'

She did so, with no concealment save of the correspondence with Mr. Bowling, and the not unimportant statements concerning him which she had made to Mrs. Mumford. In talking with Cobb, Louise seemed to drop a degree or so in social status; her language was much less careful than when she conversed with the Mumfords, and even her voice struck a note of less refinement. Decidedly she was more herself, if that could be said of one who very rarely made conscious disguise of her characteristics.

'Better stay where you are, then, for the present,' said Cobb, when he had listened attentively. 'I dare say you can get along well enough with the people, if you try.'

'That's all very well; but what about paying them? I shall owe three guineas for every week I stop.'

'It's a great deal, and they ought to feed you very well for it,' replied the other, smiling rather sourly.

'Don't be vulgar. I suppose you think I ought to live on a few shillings a week.'

'Lots of people have to. But there's no reason why *you* should. But look here: why should you be quarrelling with your people now about that fellow Bowling? You don't see him anywhere, do you?'

He flashed a glance at her, and Louise answered with a defiant motion of the head.

'No, I don't. But they put the blame on me, all the same. I shouldn't wonder if they think I'm trying to get him.'

She opened her umbrella, for heavy drops had begun to fall; they pattered on Cobb's hard felt hat, and Louise tried to shelter him as well as herself.

'Never mind me,' he said. 'And here, let me hold that thing over you. If you just put your arm in mine, it'll be easier. That's the way. Take two steps to my one; that's it.'

Again they were silent for a few moments. They had reached the Common, and Cobb struck along a path most likely to be unfrequented. No wind was blowing; the rain fell in steady spots that could all but be counted, and the air grew dark.

'Well, I can only propose one thing,' sounded the masculine voice. 'You can get out of it by marrying me.'

Louise gave a little laugh, rather timid than scornful.

'Yes, I suppose I can. But it's an awkward way. It would be rather like using a sledge-hammer to crack a nut.'

'It'll come sooner or later,' asserted Cobb, with genial confidence.

'That's what I don't like about you.' Louise withdrew her arm petulantly. 'You always speak as if I couldn't help myself. Don't you suppose I have any choice?'

'Plenty, no doubt,' was the grim answer.

'Whenever we begin to quarrel it's your fault,' pursued Miss Derrick, with unaccustomed moderation of tone. 'I never knew a man who behaved like you do. You seem to think the way to make anyone like you is to bully them. We should have got on very much better if you had tried to be pleasant.'

## CHAPTER VI

'I don't think we've got along badly, all things considered,' Cobb replied, as if after weighing a doubt. 'We'd a good deal rather be together than apart, it seems to me; or else, why do we keep meeting? And I don't want to bully anybody—least of all, you. It's a way I have of talking, I suppose. You must judge a man by his actions and his meaning, not by the tone of his voice. You know very well what a great deal I think of you. Of course I don't like it when you begin to speak as if you were only playing with me; nobody would.'

'I'm serious enough,' said Louise, trying to hold the umbrella over her companion, and only succeeding in directing moisture down the back of his neck. 'And it's partly through you that I've got into such difficulties.'

'How do you make that out?'

'If it wasn't for you, I should very likely marry Mr. Bowling.'

'Oh, he's asked you, has he?' cried Cobb, staring at her. 'Why didn't you tell me that before?—Don't let me stand in your way. I dare say he's just the kind of man for you. At all events, he's like you in not knowing his own mind.'

'Go on! Go on!' Louise exclaimed carelessly. 'There's plenty of time. Say all you've got to say.'

From the gloom of the eastward sky came a rattling of thunder, like quick pistol-shots. Cobb checked his steps.

'We mustn't go any further. You're getting wet, and the rain isn't likely to stop.'

'I shall not go back,' Louise answered, 'until something has been settled.' And she stood before him, her eyes cast down, whilst Cobb looked at the darkening sky. 'I want to know what's going to become of me. The Mumfords won't keep me much longer, and I don't wish to stay where I'm not wanted.'

'Let us walk down the hill.'

A flash of lightning made Louise start, and the thunder rattled again. But only light drops were falling. The girl stood her ground.

'I want to know what I am to do. If you can't help me, say so, and let me go my own way.'

'Of course I can help you. That is, if you'll be honest with me. I want to know, first of all, whether you've been encouraging that man Bowling.'

'No, I haven't.'

'Very well, I believe you. And now I'll make you a fair offer. Marry me as soon as I can make the arrangements, and I'll pay all you owe, and see that you are in comfortable lodgings until I've time to get a house. It could be done before I go to Bristol, and then, of course, you could go with me.'

'You speak,' said Louise, after a short silence, 'just as if you were making an agreement with a servant.'

'That's all nonsense, and you know it. I've told you how I think, often enough, in letters, and I'm not good at saying it. Look here, I don't think it's very wise to stand out in the middle of the Common in a thunderstorm. Let us walk on, and I think I would put down your umbrella.'

'It wouldn't trouble you much if I were struck with lightning.'

'All right, take it so. I shan't trouble to contradict.'

Louise followed his advice, and they began to walk quickly down the slope towards Streatham. Neither spoke until they were in the high road again. A strong wind was driving the rain-clouds to other regions and the thunder had ceased; there came a grey twilight; rows of lamps made a shimmering upon the wet ways.

'What sort of a house would you take?' Louise asked suddenly.

'Oh, a decent enough house. What kind do you want?'

'Something like the Mumfords'. It needn't be quite so large,' she added quickly; 'but a house with a garden, in a nice road, and in a respectable part.'

'That would suit me well enough,' answered Cobb cheerfully. 'You seem to think I want to drag you down, but you're very much mistaken. I'm doing pretty well, and likely, as far as I can see, to do better. I don't grudge you money; far from it. All I want to know is, that you'll marry me for my own sake.'

He dropped his voice, not to express tenderness, but because other people were near. Upon Louise, however, it had a pleasing effect, and she smiled.

'Very well,' she made answer, in the same subdued tone. 'Then let us settle it in that way.'

They talked amicably for the rest of the time that they spent together. It was nearly an hour, and never before had they succeeded in conversing so long without a quarrel. Louise became light-hearted and mirthful; her companion, though less abandoned to the mood of the moment, wore a hopeful countenance. Through all his roughness, Cobb was distinguished by a personal delicacy which no doubt had impressed Louise, say what she might of pretended fears. At parting, he merely shook hands with her, as always.

# CHAPTER VII

Glad of a free evening, Emmeline, after dinner, walked round to Mrs. Fentiman's. Louise had put a restraint upon the wonted friendly intercourse between the Mumfords and their only familiar acquaintances at Sutton. Mrs. Fentiman liked to talk of purely domestic matters, and in a stranger's presence she was never at ease. Coming alone, and when the children were all safe in bed, Emmeline had a warm welcome. For the first time she spoke of her troublesome guest without reserve. This chat would have been restful and enjoyable but for a most unfortunate remark that fell from the elder lady, a perfectly innocent mention of something her husband had told her, but, secretly, so disturbing Mrs. Mumford that, after hearing it, she got away as soon as possible, and walked quickly home with dark countenance.

It was ten o'clock; Louise had not yet returned, but might do so any moment. Wishing to be sure of privacy in a conversation with her husband, Emmeline summoned him from his book to the bedroom.

'Well, what has happened now?' exclaimed Mumford. 'If this kind of thing goes on much longer I shall feel inclined to take a lodging in town.'

'I have heard something very strange. I can hardly believe it; there must have been a mistake.'

'What is it? Really, one's nerves—'

'Is it true that, on Thursday evening, you and Miss Derrick were seen talking together at the station? Thursday: the day she went off and came back again after dinner.'

Mumford would gladly have got out of this scrape at any expense of mendacity, but he saw at once how useless such an attempt would prove. Exasperated by the result of his indiscretion, and resenting, as all men do, the undignified necessity of defending himself, he flew into a rage. Yes, it *was* true, and what next? The girl had waylaid him, begged him to intercede for her with his wife. Of course it would have been better to come home and reveal the matter; he didn't do so because it seemed to put him in a silly position. For Heaven's sake, let the whole absurd business be forgotten and done with!

Emmeline, though not sufficiently enlightened to be above small jealousies, would have been ashamed to declare her feeling with the energy of unsophisticated female nature. She replied coldly and loftily that the matter, of course, *was* done with; that it interested her no more; but that she could not help regretting an instance of secretiveness such as she had never before discovered in her husband. Surely he had put himself in a much sillier position, as things turned out, than if he had followed the dictates of honour.

'The upshot of it is this,' cried Mumford: 'Miss Derrick has to leave the house, and, if necessary, I shall tell her so myself.'

Again Emmeline was cold and lofty. There was no necessity whatever for any further communication between Clarence and Miss Derrick. Let the affair be left entirely in her hands. Indeed, she must very specially request that Clarence would have nothing more to do with Miss Derrick's business. Whereupon Mumford took offence. Did Emmeline wish to imply that there had been anything improper in his behaviour beyond the paltry indiscretion to which he had confessed? No; Emmeline was thankful to say that she did not harbour base suspicions. Then, rejoined Mumford, let this be the last word of a difference as hateful to him as to her. And he left the room.

His wife did not linger more than a minute behind him, and she sat in the drawing-room to await Miss Derrick's return; Mumford kept apart in what was called the library. To her credit, Emmeline tried hard to believe that she had learnt the whole truth; her mind, as she had justly declared, was not prone to ignoble imaginings; but acquitting her husband by no means involved an equal charity towards Louise. Hitherto uncertain in her judgment, she had now the relief of an assurance that Miss Derrick was not at all a proper person to entertain as a guest, on whatever terms. The incident of the railway station proved her to be utterly lacking in self-respect, in feminine modesty, even if her behaviour merited no darker description. Emmeline could now face with confidence the scene from which she had shrunk; not only was it a duty to insist upon Miss Derrick's departure, it would be a positive pleasure.

Louise very soon entered; she came into the room with her brightest look, and cried gaily:

'Oh, I hope I haven't kept you waiting for me. Are you alone?'

'No. I have been out.'

## CHAPTER VII

'Had you the storm here? I'm not going to keep you talking; you look tired.'

'I am rather,' said Emmeline, with reserve. She had no intention of allowing Louise to suspect the real cause of what she was about to say—that would have seemed to her undignified; but she could not speak quite naturally. 'Still, I should be glad if you would sit down for a minute.'

The girl took a chair and began to draw off her gloves. She understood what was coming; it appeared in Emmeline's face.

'Something to say to me, Mrs. Mumford?'

'I hope you won't think me unkind. I feel obliged to ask you when you will be able to make new arrangements.'

'You would like me to go soon?' said Louise, inspecting her finger-nails, and speaking without irritation.

'I am sorry to say that I think it better you should leave us. Forgive this plain speaking, Miss Derrick. It's always best to be perfectly straightforward, isn't it?'

Whether she felt the force of this innuendo or not, Louise took it in good part. As if the idea had only just struck her, she looked up cheerfully.

'You're quite right, Mrs. Mumford. I'm sure you've been very kind to me, and I've had a very pleasant time here, but it wouldn't do for me to stay longer. May I wait over to-morrow, just till Wednesday morning, to have an answer to a letter?'

'Certainly, if it is quite understood that there will be no delay beyond that. There are circumstances—private matters—I don't feel quite able to explain. But I must be sure that you will have left us by Wednesday afternoon.'

'You may be sure of it. I will write a line and post it to-night, for it to go as soon as possible.'

Therewith Louise stood up and, smiling, withdrew. Emmeline was both relieved and surprised; she had not thought it possible for the girl to conduct herself at such a juncture with such perfect propriety. An outbreak of ill-temper, perhaps of insolence, had seemed more than likely; at best she looked for tears and entreaties. Well, it was over, and by Wednesday the house would be restored to its ancient calm. Ancient, indeed! One could not believe that so short a time had passed since Miss Derrick first entered the portals. Only one more day.

'Oh, blindness to the future, kindly given, That each may fill the circle marked by Heaven.' At school, Emmeline had learnt and recited these lines; but it was long since they had recurred to her memory.

In ten minutes Louise had written her letter. She went out, returned, and looked in at the drawing-room, with a pleasant smile. 'Good-night, Mrs. Mumford.' 'Good-night, Miss Derrick.' For the grace of the thing, Emmeline would have liked to say 'Louise,' but could not bring her lips to utter the name.

About a year ago there had been a little misunderstanding between Mr. and Mrs. Mumford, which lasted for some twenty-four hours, during which they had nothing to say to each other. To-night they found themselves in a similar situation, and remembered that last difference, and wondered, both of them, at the harmony of their married life. It was in truth wonderful enough; twelve months without a shadow of ill-feeling between them. The reflection compelled Mumford to speak when his head was on the pillow.

'Emmy, we're making fools of ourselves. Just tell me what you have done.'

'I can't see how *I* am guilty of foolishness,' was the clear-cut reply.

'Then why are you angry with me?'

'I don't like deceit.'

'Hanged if I don't dislike it just as much. When is that girl going?'

Emmeline made known the understanding at which she had arrived, and her husband breathed an exclamation of profound thankfulness. But peace was not perfectly restored.

In another room, Louise lay communing with her thoughts, which were not at all disagreeable. She had written to Cobb, telling him what had happened, and asking him to let her know by Wednesday morning what she was to do. She could not go home; he must not bid her do so; but she would take a lodging wherever he liked. The position seemed romantic and enjoyable. Not till after her actual marriage should the people at home know what had become of her. She was marrying with utter disregard of all her dearest ambitions all the same, she had rather be the wife of Cobb than of anyone else. Her stepfather might recover his old kindness and generosity as soon as he knew she no longer stood in Cissy's way, and that she had never seriously thought of marrying Mr. Bowling. Had she not thought of it? The question did not enter her own mind, and she would have been quite incapable of passing a satisfactory cross-examination on the subject.

Mrs. Mumford, foreseeing the difficulty of spending the next day at home, told her husband in the morning that she would have early luncheon and go to see Mrs. Grove.

'And I should like you to fetch me from there, after business, please.'

# CHAPTER VII

'I will,' answered Clarence readily. He mentally added a hope that his wife did not mean to supervise him henceforth and for ever. If so, their troubles were only beginning.

At breakfast, Louise continued to be discretion itself. She talked of her departure on the morrow as though it had long been a settled thing, and was quite unconnected with disagreeable circumstances. Only midway in the morning did Mrs. Mumford, who had been busy with her child, speak of the early luncheon and her journey to town. She hoped Miss Derrick would not mind being left alone.

'Oh, don't speak of it,' answered Louise. 'I've lots to do. You'll give my kind regards to Mrs. Grove?'

So they ate together at midday, rather silently, but with faces composed. And Emmeline, after a last look into the nursery, hastened away to catch her train. She had no misgivings; during her absence, all would be well as ever.

Louise passed the time without difficulty, and at seven o'clock made an excellent dinner. This evening no reply could be expected from Cobb, as he was not likely to have received her letter of last night till his return home from business. Still, there might be something from someone; she always looked eagerly for the postman.

The weather was gloomy. Not long after eight the housemaid brought in a lighted lamp, and set it, as usual, upon the little black four-legged table in the drawing-room. And in the same moment the knocker of the front door sounded a vigorous rat-tat-tat, a visitor's summons.

## CHAPTER VIII

'It may be someone calling upon me,' said Louise to the servant. 'Let me know the name before you show anyone in.'

'Of course, miss,' replied the domestic, with pert familiarity, and took her time in arranging the shade of the lamp. When she returned from the door it was to announce, smilingly, that Mr. Cobb wished to see Miss Derrick.

'Please to show him in.'

Louise stood in an attitude of joyous excitement, her eyes sparkling. But at the first glance she perceived that her lover's mood was by no means correspondingly gay. Cobb stalked forward and kept a stern gaze upon her, but said nothing.

'Well? You got my letter, I suppose?'

'What letter?'

He had not been home since breakfast-time, so Louise's appeal to him for advice lay waiting his arrival. Impatiently, she described the course of events. As soon as she had finished, Cobb threw his hat aside and addressed her harshly.

'I want to know what you mean by writing to your sister that you are going to marry Bowling. I saw your mother this morning, and that's what she told me. It must have been only a day or two ago that you said that. Just explain, if you please. I'm about sick of this kind of thing, and I'll have the truth out of you.'

His anger had never taken such a form as this; for the first time Louise did in truth feel afraid of him. She shrank away, her heart throbbed, and her tongue refused its office.

'Say what you mean by it!' Cobb repeated, in a voice that was all the more alarming because he kept it low.

'Did you write that to your sister?'

'Yes—but I never meant it—it was just to make her angry—'

'You expect me to believe that? And, if it's true, doesn't it make you out a nice sort of girl? But I don't believe it You've been thinking of him in that way all along; and you've been writing to him, or meeting him, since you came here. What sort of behaviour do you call this?'

Louise was recovering self-possession; the irritability of her own temper began to support her courage.

'What if I have? I'd never given *you* any promise till last night, had I? I was free to marry anyone I liked, wasn't I? What do *you* mean by coming here and going on like this? I've told you the truth about that letter, and I've always told you the truth about everything. If you don't like it, say so and go.'

Cobb was impressed by the energy of her defence. He looked her straight in the eyes, and paused a moment; then spoke less violently.

'You haven't told me the *whole* truth. I want to know when you saw Bowling last.'

'I haven't seen him since I left home.'

'When did you write to him last?'

'The same day I wrote to Cissy. And I shall answer no more questions.'

'Of course not. But that's quite enough. You've been playing a double game; if you haven't told lies, you've acted them. What sort of a wife would you make? How could I ever believe a word you said? I shall have no more to do with you.'

He turned away, and, in the violence of the movement, knocked over a little toy chair, one of those perfectly useless, and no less ugly, impediments which stand about the floor of a well-furnished drawing-room. Too angry to stoop and set the object on its legs again, he strode towards the door. Louise followed him.

'You are going?' she asked, in a struggling voice.

Cobb paid no attention, and all but reached the door. She laid a hand upon him.

'You are going?'

The touch and the voice checked him. Again he turned abruptly and seized the hand that rested upon his arm.

'Why are you stopping me? What do you want with me? I'm to help you out of the fix you've got into, is that it? I'm to find you a lodging, and take no end of trouble, and then in a week's time get a letter to say that you want nothing more to do with me.'

Louise was pale with anger and fear, and as many other emotions as her little heart and brain could well hold. She did not look her best—far from it but the man saw something in her eyes which threw a fresh spell upon him. Still grasping her one hand, he caught her by the other arm, held her as far off as he could, and glared passionately as he spoke.

'What do you want?'

'You know—I've told you the truth—'

His grasp hurt her; she tried to release herself, and moved backwards. For a moment Cobb left her free; she moved backward again, her eyes drawing him on. She felt her power, and could not be content with thus much exercise of it.

'You may go if you like. But you understand, if you do—'

Cobb, inflamed with desire and jealousy, made an effort to recapture her. Louise sprang away from him; but immediately behind her lay the foolish little chair which he had kicked over, and just beyond *that* stood the scarcely less foolish little table which supported the heavy lamp, with its bowl of coloured glass and its spreading yellow shade. She tottered back, fell with all her weight against the table, and brought the lamp crashing to the floor. A shriek of terror from Louise, from her lover a shout of alarm, blended with the sound of breaking glass. In an instant a great flame shot up half way to the ceiling. The lamp-shade was ablaze; the much-embroidered screen, Mrs. Mumford's wedding present, forthwith caught fire from a burning tongue that ran along the carpet; and Louise's dress, well sprinkled with paraffin, aided the conflagration. Cobb, of course, saw only the danger to the girl. He seized the woollen hearthrug and tried to wrap it about her; but with screams of pain and frantic struggles, Louise did her best to thwart his purpose.

The window was open, and now a servant, rushing in to see what the uproar meant, gave the blaze every benefit of draught.

'Bring water!' roared Cobb, who had just succeeded in extinguishing Louise's dress, and was carrying her, still despite her struggles, out of the room. 'Here, one of you take Miss Derrick to the next house. Bring water, you!'

All three servants were scampering and screeching about the hall. Cobb caught hold of one of them and all but twisted her arm out of its socket. At his fierce command, the woman supported Louise into the garden, and thence, after a minute or two of faintness on the sufferer's part, led her to the gate of the neighbouring house. The people who lived there chanced to be taking the air on their front lawn. Without delay, Louise was conveyed beneath the roof, and her host, a man of energy, sped towards the fire to be of what assistance he could.

The lamp-shade, the screen, the little table and the diminutive chair blazed gallantly, and with such a volleying of poisonous fumes that

## CHAPTER VIII

Cobb could scarce hold his ground to do battle. Louise out of the way, he at once became cool and resourceful. Before a flame could reach the window he had rent down the flimsy curtains and flung them outside. Bellowing for the water which was so long in coming, he used the hearthrug to some purpose on the outskirts of the bonfire, but had to keep falling back for fresh air. Then appeared a pail and a can, which he emptied effectively, and next moment sounded the voice of the gentleman from next door.

'Have you a garden hose? Set it on to the tap, and bring it in here.'

The hose was brought into play, and in no great time the last flame had flickered out amid a deluge. When all danger was at an end, one of the servants, the nurse-girl, uttered a sudden shriek; it merely signified that she had now thought for the first time of the little child asleep upstairs. Aided by the housemaid, she rushed to the nursery, snatched her charge from bed, and carried the unhappy youngster into the breezes of the night, where he screamed at the top of his gamut.

Cobb, when he no longer feared that the house would be burnt down, hurried to inquire after Louise. She lay on a couch, wrapped in a dressing-gown; for the side and one sleeve of her dress had been burnt away. Her moaning never ceased; there was a fire-mark on the lower part of her face, and she stared with eyes of terror and anguish at whoever approached her. Already a doctor had been sent for, and Cobb, reporting that all was safe at 'Runnymede,' wished to remove her at once to her own bed room, and the strangers were eager to assist.

'What will the Mumfords say?' Louise asked of a sudden, trying to raise herself.

'Leave all that to me,' Cobb replied reassuringly. 'I'll make it all right; don't trouble yourself.'

The nervous shock had made her powerless; they carried her in a chair back to 'Runnymede,' and upstairs to her bedroom. Scarcely was this done when Mr. and Mrs. Mumford, after a leisurely walk from the station, approached their garden gate. The sight of a little crowd of people in the quiet road, the smell of burning, loud voices of excited servants, caused them to run forward in alarm. Emmeline, frenzied by the certainty that her own house was on fire, began to cry aloud for her child, and Mumford rushed like a madman through the garden.

'It's all right,' said a man who stood in the doorway. 'You Mr. Mumford? It's all right. There's been a fire, but we've got it out.'

Emmeline learnt at the same moment that her child had suffered no harm, but she would not pause until she saw the little one and held him in her embrace. Meanwhile, Cobb and Mumford talked in the devastated drawing-room, which was illumined with candles.

'It's a bad job, Mr. Mumford. My name is Cobb: I daresay you've heard of me. I came to see Miss Derrick, and I was clumsy enough to knock the lamp over.'

'Knock the lamp over! How could you do that? Were you drunk?'

'No, but you may well ask the question. I stumbled over something—a little chair, I think—and fell against the table with the lamp on it.'

'Where's Miss Derrick?'

'Upstairs. She got rather badly burnt, I'm afraid. We've sent for a doctor.'

'And here I am,' spoke a voice behind them. 'Sorry to see this, Mr. Mumford.'

The two went upstairs together, and on the first landing encountered Emmeline, sobbing and wailing hysterically with the child in her arms. Her husband spoke soothingly.

'Don't, don't, Emmy. Here's Dr. Billings come to see Miss Derrick. She's the only one that has been hurt. Go down, there's a good girl, and send somebody to help in Miss Derrick's room; you can't be any use yourself just now.'

'But how did it happen? Oh, *how* did it happen?'

'I'll come and tell you all about it. Better put the boy to bed again, hadn't you?'

When she had recovered her senses Emmeline took this advice, and, leaving the nurse by the child's cot, went down to survey the ruin of her property. It was a sorry sight. Where she had left a reception-room such as any suburban lady in moderate circumstances might be proud of; she now beheld a mere mass of unrecognisable furniture, heaped on what had once been a carpet, amid dripping walls and under a grimed ceiling.

'Oh! Oh!' She all but sank before the horror of the spectacle. Then, in a voice of fierce conviction, 'She did it! *She* did it! It was because I told her to leave. I *know* she did it on purpose!'

Mumford closed the door of the room, shutting out Cobb and the cook and the housemaid. He repeated the story Cobb had told him, and quietly urged the improbability of his wife's explanation. Miss Derrick, he pointed out, was lying prostrate from severe burns; the fire must have been accidental, but the accident, to be sure, was extraordinary enough. Thereupon Mrs. Mumford's wrath turned against Cobb. What business had such a man—a low-class savage—in *her* drawing-room? He must have come knowing that she and her husband were away for the evening.

'You can question him, if you like,' said Mumford. 'He's out there.'

Emmeline opened the door, and at once heard a cry of pain from upstairs. Mumford, also hearing it, and seeing Cobb's misery-stricken face by the light of the hall lamp, whispered to his wife:

'Hadn't you better go up, dear? Dr. Billings may think it strange.'

It was much wiser to urge this consideration than to make a direct plea for mercy. Emmeline did not care to have it reported that selfish distress made her indifferent to the sufferings of a friend staying in her house. But she could not pass Cobb without addressing him severely.

'So *you* are the cause of this!'

'I am, Mrs. Mumford, and I can only say that I'll do my best to make good the damage to your house.'

'Make good I fancy you have strange ideas of the value of the property destroyed.'

Insolence was no characteristic of Mrs. Mumford. But calamity had put her beside herself; she spoke, not in her own person, but as a woman whose carpets, curtains and bric-a-brac have ignominiously perished.

'I'll make it good,' Cobb repeated humbly, 'however long it takes me. And don't be angry with that poor girl, Mrs. Mumford. It wasn't her fault, not in any way. She didn't know I was coming; she hadn't asked me to come. I'm entirely to blame.'

'You mean to say you knocked over the table by accident?'

'I did indeed. And I wish I'd been burnt myself instead of her.'

He had suffered, by the way, no inconsiderable scorching, to which his hands would testify for many a week; but of this he was still hardly aware. Emmeline, with a glance of uttermost scorn, left him, and ascended to the room where the doctor was busy. Free to behave as he thought fit, Mumford beckoned Cobb to follow him into the front garden, where they conversed with masculine calm.

'I shall put up at Sutton for the night,' said Cobb, 'and perhaps you'll let me call the first thing in the morning to ask how she gets on.'

'Of course. We'll see the doctor when he comes down. But I wish I could understand how you managed to throw the lamp down.'

'The truth is,' Cobb replied, 'we were quarrelling. I'd heard something about her that made me wild, and I came and behaved like a fool. I feel just now as if I could go and cut my throat, that's the fact. If anything happens to her, I believe I shall. I might as well, in any case; she'll never look at me again.'

'Oh, don't take such a dark view of it.'

The doctor came out, on his way to fetch certain requirements, and the two men walked with him to his house in the next road. They learned that Louise was not dangerously injured; her recovery would be merely a matter of time and care. Cobb gave a description of the fire, and his hearers marvelled that the results were no worse.

'You must have some burns too?' said the doctor, whose curiosity was piqued by everything he saw and heard of the strange occurrence. 'I thought so; those hands must be attended to.'

Meanwhile, Emmeline sat by the bedside and listened to the hysterical lamentation in which Louise gave her own—the true—account of the catastrophe. It was all her fault, and upon her let all the blame fall. She would humble herself to Mr. Higgins and get him to pay for the furniture destroyed. If Mrs. Mumford would but forgive her! And so on, as her poor body agonised, and the blood grew feverish in her veins.

## CHAPTER IX

'Accept it? Certainly. Why should we bear the loss if he's able to make it good? He seems to be very well off for an unmarried man.'

'Yes,' replied Mumford, 'but he's just going to marry, and it seems—Well, after all, you know, he didn't really cause the damage. I should have felt much less scruple if Higgins had offered to pay—'

'He *did* cause the damage,' asseverated Emmeline. 'It was his gross or violent behaviour. If we had been insured it wouldn't matter so much. And pray let this be a warning, and insure at once. However you look at it, he ought to pay.'

Emmeline's temper had suffered much since she made the acquaintance of Miss Derrick. Aforetime, she could discuss difference of opinion; now a hint of diversity drove her at once to the female weapon—angry and iterative assertion. Her native delicacy, also, seemed to have degenerated. Mumford could only hold his tongue and trust that this would be but a temporary obscurement of his wife's amiable virtues.

Cobb had written from Bristol, a week after the accident, formally requesting a statement of the pecuniary loss which the Mumfords had suffered; he was resolved to repay them, and would do so, if possible, as soon as he knew the sum. Mumford felt a trifle ashamed to make the necessary declaration; at the outside, even with expenses of painting and papering, their actual damage could not be estimated at more than fifty pounds, and even Emmeline did not wish to save appearances by making an excessive demand. The one costly object in the room—the piano—was practically uninjured, and sundry other pieces of furniture could easily be restored; for Cobb and his companion, as amateur firemen, had by no means gone recklessly to work. By candlelight, when the floor was still a swamp, things looked more desperate than they proved to be on subsequent investigation; and it is wonderful at how little outlay, in our glistening times, a villa drawing-room may be fashionably equipped. So Mumford wrote to his correspondent that only a few 'articles' had absolutely perished; that it was not his wish to make any demand at all; but that, if Mr. Cobb insisted on offering restitution, why, a matter of fifty pounds, etc. etc. And in a few days this sum arrived, in the form of a draft upon respectable bankers.

Of course the house was in grievous disorder. Upholsterers' workmen would have been bad enough, but much worse was the establishment of Mrs. Higgins by her daughter's bedside, which naturally involved her presence as a guest at table, and the endurance of her conversation whenever she chose to come downstairs. Mumford urged his wife to take her summer holiday—to go away with the child until all was put right again—a phrase which included the removal of Miss Derrick to her own home; but of this Emmeline would not hear. How could she enjoy an hour of mental quietude when, for all she knew, Mrs. Higgins and the patient might be throwing lamps at each other? And her jealousy was still active, though she did not allow it to betray itself in words. Clarence seemed to her quite needlessly anxious in his inquiries concerning Miss Derrick's condition. Until that young lady had disappeared from 'Runnymede' for ever, Emmeline would keep matronly watch and ward.

Mrs. Higgins declared at least a score of times every day that she could *not* understand how this dreadful affair had come to pass. The most complete explanation from her daughter availed nothing; she deemed the event an insoluble mystery, and, in familiar talk with Mrs. Mumford, breathed singular charges against Louise's lover. 'She's shielding him, my dear. I've no doubt of it. I never had a very good opinion of him, but now she shall never marry him with *my* consent.' To this kind of remark Emmeline at length deigned no reply. She grew to detest Mrs. Higgins, and escaped her society by every possible manoeuvre.

'Oh, how pleasant it is,' she explained bitterly to her husband, 'to think that everybody in the road is talking about us with contempt! Of course the servants have spread nice stories. And the Wilkinsons'—these were the people next door—'look upon us as hardly respectable. Even Mrs. Fentiman said yesterday that she really could not conceive how I came to take that girl into the house. I acknowledged that I must have been crazy.'

'Whilst we're thoroughly upset,' replied Mumford, with irritation at this purposeless talk, 'hadn't we better leave the house and go to live as far away as possible?'

'Indeed, I very much wish we could. I don't think I shall ever be happy again at Sutton.'

## CHAPTER IX

And Clarence went off muttering to himself about the absurdity and the selfishness of women.

For a week or ten days Louise lay very ill; then her vigorous constitution began to assert itself. It helped her greatly towards convalescence when she found that the scorches on her face would not leave a permanent blemish. Mrs. Mumford came into the room once a day and sat for a few minutes, neither of them desiring longer communion, but they managed to exchange inquiries and remarks with a show of friendliness. When the fifty pounds came from Cobb, Emmeline made no mention of it. Louise said with an air of satisfaction,

'So he has paid the money! I'm very glad of that.'

'Mr. Cobb insisted on paying,' Mrs. Mumford answered with reserve. 'We could not hurt his feelings by refusing.'

'Well, that's all right, isn't it? You won't think so badly of us now? Of course you wish you'd never set eyes on me, Mrs. Mumford; but that's only natural: in your place I'm sure I should feel the same. Still, now the money's paid, you won't always think unkindly of me, will you?'

The girl lay propped on pillows; her pale face, with its healing scars, bore witness to what she had undergone, and one of her arms was completely swathed in bandages. Emmeline did not soften towards her, but the frank speech, the rather pathetic little smile, in decency demanded a suave response.

'I shall wish you every happiness, Louise.'

'Thank you. We shall be married as soon as ever I'm well, but I'm sure I don't know where. Mother hates his very name, and does her best to set me against him; but I just let her talk. We're beginning to quarrel a little—did you hear us this morning? I try to keep down my voice, and I shan't be here much longer, you know. I shall go home at first my stepfather has written a kind letter, and of course he's glad to know I shall marry Mr. Cobb. But I don't think the wedding will be there. It wouldn't be nice to go to church in a rage, as I'm sure I should with mother and Cissy looking on.'

This might, or might not, signify a revival of the wish to be married from 'Runnymede.' Emmeline quickly passed to another subject.

Mrs. Higgins was paying a visit to Coburg Lodge, where, during the days of confusion, the master of the house had been left at his servants' mercy. On her return, late in the evening, she entered flurried and perspiring, and asked the servant who admitted her where Mrs. Mumford was.

'With master, in the library, 'm.'

'Tell her I wish to speak to her at once.'

Emmeline came forth, and a lamp was lighted in the dining-room, for the drawing-room had not yet been restored to a habitable condition. Silent, and wondering in gloomy resignation what new annoyance was prepared for her, Emmeline sat with eyes averted, whilst the stout woman mopped her face and talked disconnectedly of the hardships of travelling in such weather as this; when at length she reached her point, Mrs. Higgins became lucid and emphatic.

'I've heard things as have made me that angry I can hardly bear myself. Would you believe that people are trying to take away my daughter's character? It's Cissy 'Iggins's doing: I'm sure of it, though I haven't brought it 'ome to her yet. I dropped in to see some friends of ours—I shouldn't wonder if you know the name; it's Mrs. Jolliffe, a niece of Mr. Baxter—Baxter, Lukin and Co., you know. And she told me in confidence what people are saying—as how Louise was to marry Mr. Bowling, but he broke it off when he found *the sort of people she was living with*, here at Sutton—and a great many more things as I shouldn't like to tell you. Now what *do* you think of—'

Emmeline, her eyes flashing, broke in angrily:

'I think nothing at all about it, Mrs. Higgins, and I had very much rather not hear the talk of such people.'

'I don't wonder it aggravates you, Mrs. Mumford. Did anyone ever hear such a scandal! I'm sure nobody that knows you could say a word against your respectability, and, as I told Mrs. Jolliffe, she's quite at liberty to call here to-morrow or the next day—'

'Not to see *me*, I hope,' said Emmeline. 'I must refuse—'

'Now just let me tell you what I've thought,' pursued the stout lady, hardly aware of this interruption. 'This'll have to be set right, both for Lou's sake and for yours, and to satisfy us all. They're making a mystery, d'you see, of Lou leaving 'ome and going off to live with strangers; and Cissy's been doing her best to make people think there's something wrong—the spiteful creature! And there's only one way of setting it right. As soon as Lou can be dressed and got down, and when the drawing-room's finished, I want her to ask all our friends here to five o'clock tea, just to let them see with their own eyes—'

'Mrs. Higgins!'

'Of course there'll be no expense for *you*, Mrs. Mumford—not a farthing. I'll provide everything, and all I ask of you is just to sit in your own drawing-room—'

'Mrs. Higgins, be so kind as to listen to me. This is quite impossible. I can't dream of allowing any such thing.'

## CHAPTER IX

The other glared in astonishment, which tended to wrath.

'But can't you see, Mrs. Mumford, that it's for your *own* good as well as ours? Do you want people to be using your name—'

'What can it matter to me how *such* people think or speak of me?' cried Emmeline, trembling with exasperation.

'Such people! I don't think you know who you're talking about, Mrs. Mumford. You'll let me tell you that my friends are as respectable as yours—'

'I shall not argue about it,' said Emmeline, standing up. 'You will please to remember that already I've had a great deal of trouble and annoyance, and what you propose would be quite intolerable. Once for all, I can't dream of such a thing.'

'Then all I can say is, Mrs. Mumford'—the speaker rose with heavy dignity—'that you're not behaving in a very ladylike way. I'm not a quarrelsome person, as you well know, and I don't say nasty things if I can help it. But there's one thing I *must* say and *will* say, and that is, that when we first came here you gave a very different account of yourself to what it's turned out. You told me and my daughter distinctly that you had a great deal of the very best society, and that was what Lou came here *for*, and you knew it, and you can't deny that you did. And I should like to know how much society she's seen all the time she's been here—that's the question I *ask* you. I don't believe she's seen more than three or four people altogether. They may have been respectable enough, and I'm not the one to say they weren't, but I *do* say it isn't what we was led to expect, and that you can't deny, Mrs. Mumford.'

She paused for breath. Emmeline had moved towards the door, and stood struggling with the feminine rage which impelled her to undignified altercation. To withdraw in silence would be like a shamed confession of the charge brought against her, and she suffered not a little from her consciousness of the modicum of truth therein.

'It was a most unfortunate thing, Mrs. Higgins,' burst from her lips, 'that I ever consented to receive your daughter, knowing as I did that she wasn't our social equal.'

'Wasn't *what*?' exclaimed the other, as though the suggestion startled her by its novelty. 'You think yourself superior to us? You did us a favour—'

Whilst Mrs. Higgins was uttering these words the door opened, and there entered a figure which startled her into silence. It was that of Louise, in a dressing-gown and slippers, with a shawl wrapped about the upper part of her body.

'I heard you quarrelling,' she began. (Her bedroom was immediately above, and at this silent hour the voices of the angry ladies had been quite audible to her as she lay in bed.) 'What *is* it all about? It's too bad of you, mother—'

'The idea, Louise, of coming down like that!' cried her parent indignantly. 'How did you know Mr. Mumford wasn't here? For shame! Go up again this moment.'

'I don't see any harm if Mr. Mumford had been here,' replied the girl calmly.

'I'm sure it's most unwise of you to leave your bed,' began Emmeline, with anxious thought for Louise's health, due probably to her dread of having the girl in the house for an indefinite period.

'Oh, I've wrapped up. I feel shaky, that's all, and I shall have to sit down.' She did so, on the nearest chair, with a little laugh at her strange feebleness.

'Now please *don't* quarrel, you two. Mrs. Mumford, don't mind anything that mother says.'

Thereupon Louise's mother burst into a vehement exposition of the reasons of discord, beginning with the calumnious stories she had heard at Mrs. Jolliffe's, and ending with the outrageous arrogance of Mrs. Mumford's latest remark. Louise listened with a smile.

'Now look here, mother,' she said, when silence came for a moment, 'you can't expect Mrs. Mumford to have a lot of strangers coming to the house just on my account. She's sick and tired of us all, and wants to see our backs as soon as ever she can. I don't say it to offend you, Mrs. Mumford, but you know it's true. And I tell you what it is: To-morrow morning I'm going back home. Yes, I am. You can't stay here, mother, after this, and I'm not going to have anyone new to wait on me. I shall go home in a cab, straight from this house to the other, and I'm quite sure I shan't take any harm.'

'You won't do it till the doctor's given you leave,' said Mrs. Higgins with concern.

'He'll be here at ten in the morning, and I know he will give me leave. So there's an end of it. And you can go to bed and sleep in peace, Mrs. Mumford.'

It was not at all unamiably said. But for Mrs. Higgins's presence, Emmeline would have responded with a certain kindness. Still smarting under the stout lady's accusations, which continued to sound in sniffs and snorts, she answered as austerely as possible.

'I must leave you to judge, Miss Derrick, how soon you feel able to go. I don't wish you to do anything imprudent. But it will be much better if Mrs. Higgins regards me as a stranger during the rest of her stay here. Any communication she wishes to make to me must be made through a servant.'

Having thus delivered herself; Emmeline quitted the room. From the library, of which the door was left ajar, she heard Louise and her mother pass upstairs, both silent. Mumford, too well aware that yet another disturbance had come upon his unhappy household, affected to read, and it was only when the door of Louise's room had closed that Emmeline spoke to him.

'Mrs. Higgins will breakfast by herself to-morrow,' she said severely. 'She may perhaps go before lunch; but in any case we shall not sit down at table with her again.'

'All right,' Mumford replied, studiously refraining from any hint of curiosity.

So, next morning, their breakfast was served in the library. Mrs. Higgins came down at the usual hour, found the dining-room at her disposal, and ate with customary appetite, alone. Had Emmeline's experience lain among the more vigorously vulgar of her sex she would have marvelled at Mrs. Higgins's silence and general self-restraint during these last hours. Louise's mother might, without transgressing the probabilities of the situation, have made this a memorable morning indeed. She confined herself to a rather frequent ringing of the bedroom bell. Her requests of the servants became orders, such as she would have given in a hotel or lodging-house, but no distinctly offensive word escaped her. And this was almost entirely due to Louise's influence for the girl impressed upon her mother that 'to make a row' would be the sure and certain way of proving that Mrs. Mumford was justified in claiming social superiority over her guests.

The doctor, easily perceiving how matters stood, made no difficulty about the patient's removal in a closed carriage, and, with exercise of all obvious precautions, she might travel as soon as she liked. Anticipating this, Mrs. Higgins had already packed all the luggage, and Louise, as well as it could be managed, had been clad for the journey.

'I suppose you'll go and order the cab yourself?' she said to her mother, when they were alone again.

'Yes, I must, on account of making a bargain about the charge. A nice expense you've been to us, Louise. That man ought to pay every penny.'

'I'll tell him you say so, and no doubt he will.'

They wrangled about this whilst Mrs. Higgins was dressing to go out. As soon as her mother had left the house Louise stole downstairs and to the door of the drawing-room, which was half open. Emmeline, her back turned, stood before the fireplace, as if considering some new plan of decoration; she did not hear the girl's light step. Whitewashers and paperhangers had done their work; a new carpet was laid down; but pictures had still to be restored to their places, and the furniture stood all together in the middle of the room. Not till Louise had entered did her hostess look round.

'Mrs. Mumford, I want to say good-bye.'

'Oh, yes,' Emmeline answered civilly, but without a smile. 'Good-bye, Miss Derrick.'

And she stepped forward to shake hands.

'Don't be afraid,' said the girl, looking into her face good-humouredly. 'You shall never see me again unless you wish to.'

'I'm sure I wish you all happiness,' was the embarrassed reply. 'And—I shall be glad to hear of your marriage.'

'I'll write to you about it. But you won't talk—unkindly about me when I've gone—you and Mr. Mumford?'

'No, no; indeed we shall not.'

Louise tried to say something else, but without success. She pressed Emmeline's hand, turned quickly, and disappeared. In half-an-hour's time arrived the vehicle Mrs. Higgins had engaged; without delay mother and daughter left the house, and were driven off. Mrs. Mumford kept a strict retirement. When the two had gone she learnt from the housemaid that their luggage would be removed later in the day.

A fortnight passed, and the Mumfords once more lived in enjoyment of tranquillity, though Emmeline could not quite recover her old self. They never spoke of the dread experiences through which they had gone. Mumford's holiday time approached, and they were making arrangements for a visit to the seaside, when one morning a carrier's cart delivered a large package, unexpected and of unknown contents. Emmeline stripped off the matting, and found—a drawing-room screen, not unlike that which she had lost in the fire. Of course it came from Louise, and, though she professed herself very much annoyed, Mrs. Mumford had no choice but to acknowledge it in a civil little note addressed to Coburg Lodge.

They were away from home for three weeks. On returning, Emmeline found a letter which had arrived for her the day before; it was from Louise, and announced her marriage. 'Dear Mrs. Mumford,—I know you'll be glad to hear it's all over. It was to have been at the end of October, when our house was ready for us. We have taken a very nice one at Holloway. But of course something happened, and mother and Cissy and I quarrelled so dreadfully that I went off and took a lodging. And then Tom said that we must be married at once; and so we were, without any fuss at all, and I think it was ever so much better, though some girls would not care to go in their plain dress and without friends or anything. After it was over, Tom and I had just a little disagreement about something, but of course he gave way, and I don't think we shall get on together at all badly. My stepfather has been very nice, and is paying for all the furniture, and has promised me a lot of things. Of course he is delighted to see me out of the house, just as you were. You see that I write from Broadstairs, where we are spending our honeymoon. Please remember me to Mr. Mumford, and believe me, very sincerely yours, Louise L. Cobb.'

Enclosed was a wedding-card.

'Mr. and Mrs. Thomas Cobb,' in gilt lettering, occupied the middle, and across the right-hand upper corner ran 'Louise E. Derrick,' an arrow transfixing the maiden surname.

# WILL WARBURTON

# CHAPTER 1

The sea-wind in his hair, his eyes agleam with the fresh memory of Alpine snows, Will Warburton sprang out of the cab, paid the driver a double fare, flung on to his shoulder a heavy bag and ran up, two steps at a stride, to a flat on the fourth floor of the many-tenanted building hard by Chelsea Bridge. His rat-tat-tat brought to the door a thin yellow face, cautious in espial, through the narrow opening.

"Is it you, sir?"

"All right, Mrs. Hopper! How are you?—how are you?"

He threw his bag into the passage, and cordially grasped the woman's hands.

"Dinner ready? Savagely hungry. Give me three minutes, and serve."

For about that length of time there sounded in the bedroom a splashing and a blowing; then Warburton came forth with red cheeks. He seized upon a little pile of letters and packets which lay on his writing-table, broke envelopes, rent wrappers, and read with now an ejaculation of pleasure, now a grunt of disgust, and again a mirthful half roar. Then, dinner—the feeding of a famished man of robust appetite and digestion, a man three or four years on the green side of thirty. It was a speedy business, in not much more than a quarter of an hour there disappeared a noble steak and its appurtenances, a golden-crusted apple tart, a substantial slice of ripe Cheddar, two bottles of creamy Bass.

"Now I can talk!" cried Will to his servant, as he threw himself into a deep chair, and began lighting his pipe. "What's the news? I seem to have been away three months rather than three weeks."

"Mr. Franks called yesterday, sir, late in the afternoon, when I was here cleaning. He was very glad to hear you'd be back to-day, and said he might look in to-night."

"Good! What else?"

"My brother-in-law wishes to see you, sir. He's in trouble again—lost his place at Boxon's a few days ago. I don't exac'ly know how it happened, but he'll explain everything. He's very unfortunate, sir, is Allchin."

"Tell him to come before nine to-morrow morning, if he can."

"Yes, sir. I'm sure it's very kind of you, sir."

"What else?"

"Nothing as I can think of just now, sir."

Warburton knew from the woman's way of speaking that she had something still in her mind; but his pipe being well lit, and a pleasant lassitude creeping over him, he merely nodded. Mrs. Hopper cleared the table, and withdrew.

The window looked across the gardens of Chelsea Hospital (old-time Ranelagh) to the westward reach of the river, beyond which lay Battersea Park, with its lawns and foliage. A beam of the July sunset struck suddenly through the room. Warburton was aware of it with half-closed eyes; he wished to stir himself, and look forth, but languor held his limbs, and wreathing tobacco-smoke kept his thoughts among the mountains. He might have quite dozed off had not a sudden noise from within aroused him—the unmistakable crash of falling crockery. It made him laugh, a laugh of humorous expostulation. A minute or two passed, then came a timid tap at his door, and Mrs. Hopper showed her face.

"Another accident, sir, I'm sorry to say," were her faltering words.

"Extensive?"

"A dish and two plates, I'm sorry to say, sir."

"Oh, that's nothing."

"Of course I shall make them good, sir."

"Pooh! Aren't there plates enough?"

"Oh, quite enough—just yet, sir."

Warburton subdued a chuckle, and looked with friendly smile at his domestic, who stood squeezing herself between the edge of the door and the jamb—her habit when embarrassed. Mrs. Hopper had served him for three years; he knew all her weaknesses, but thought more of her virtues, chief of which were honest intention and a moderate aptitude for plain cooking. A glance about this room would have proved to any visitor that Mrs. Hopper's ideas of cleanliness were by no means rigid, her master had made himself to a certain extent responsible for this defect; he paid little attention to dust, provided that things were in their wonted order. Mrs. Hopper was not a resident domestic; she came at stated hours. Obviously a widow, she had a poor, loose-hung, trailing little body, which no nourishment could plump or fortify. Her visage was habitually doleful, but contracted itself at moments into a grin of quaint drollery, which betrayed her for something of a humorist.

"My fingers is all gone silly to-day, sir," she pursued. "I daresay it's because I haven't had much sleep these last few nights."

"How's that?"

"It's my poor sister, sir—my sister Liza, I mean—she's had one of her worst headaches—the extra special, we call 'em. This time it's lasted more than three days, and not one minute of rest has the poor thing got."

Warburton was all sympathy; he inquired about the case as though it were that of an intimate friend. Change of air and repose were obvious remedies; no less obviously, these things were out of the question for a working woman who lived on a few shillings a week.

"Do you know of any place she could go to?" asked Warburton, adding carelessly, "if the means were provided."

Mrs. Hopper squeezed herself more tightly than ever between door and jamb. Her head was bent in an abashed way, and when she spoke it was in a thick, gurgling tone, only just intelligible.

"There's a little lodging 'ouse at Southend, sir, where we used to go when my 'usband could afford it."

"Well, look here. Get a doctor's opinion whether Southend would do; if not, which place would. And just send her away. Don't worry about the money."

Experience enabled Mrs. Hopper to interpret this advice. She stammered gratitude.

"How's your other sister—Mrs. Allchin?" Warburton inquired kindly.

"Why, sir, she's doing pretty well in her 'ealth, sir, but her baby died yesterday week. I hope you'll excuse me, sir, for all this bad news just when you come back from your holiday, and when it's natural as you don't feel in very good spirits."

Will had much ado not to laugh. On his return from a holiday, Mrs. Hopper always presumed him to be despondent in view of the resumption of daily work. He was beginning to talk of Mrs. Allchin's troubles, when at the outer door sounded a long nervous knock.

"Ha! That's Mr. Franks."

Mrs. Hopper ran to admit the visitor.

## CHAPTER 2

"Warburton!" cried a high-pitched voice from the passage. "Have you seen *The Art World*?"

And there rushed into the room a tall, auburn-headed young man of five-and-twenty, his comely face glowing in excitement. With one hand he grasped his friend's, in the other he held out a magazine.

"You haven't seen it! Look here! What d'you think of that, confound you!"

He had opened the magazine so as to display an illustration, entitled "Sanctuary," and stated to be after a painting by Norbert Franks.

"Isn't it good? Doesn't it come out well?—deuce take you, why don't you speak?"

"Not bad—for a photogravure," said Warburton, who had the air of a grave elder in the presence of this ebullient youth.

"Be hanged! We know all about that. The thing is that it's *there*. Don't you feel any surprise? Haven't you got anything to say? Don't you see what this means, you old ragamuffin?"

"Shouldn't wonder if it meant coin of the realm—for your shrewd dealer."

"For me too, my boy, for me too! Not out of this thing, of course. But I've arrived, I'm *lance*, the way is clear! Why, you don't seem to know what it means getting into *The Art World*."

"I seem to remember," said Warburton, smiling, "that a month or two ago, you hadn't language contemptuous enough for this magazine and all connected with it."

"Don't be an ass!" shrilled the other, who was all this time circling about the little room with much gesticulation. "Of course one talks like that when one hasn't enough to eat and can't sell a picture. I don't pretend to have altered my opinion about photogravures, and all that. But come now, the thing itself? Be honest, Warburton. Is it bad, now? Can you look at that picture, and say that it's worthless?"

"I never said anything of the kind."

## CHAPTER 2

"No, no! You're too deucedly good-natured. But I always detected what you were thinking, and I saw it didn't surprise you at all when the Academy muffs refused it."

"There you're wrong," cried Warburton. "I was really surprised."

"Confound your impudence! Well, you may think what you like. I maintain that the thing isn't half bad. It grows upon me. I see its merits more and more."

Franks was holding up the picture, eyeing it intently. "Sanctuary" represented the interior of an old village church. On the ground against a pillar, crouched a young and beautiful woman, her dress and general aspect indicating the last degree of vagrant wretchedness; worn out, she had fallen asleep in a most graceful attitude, and the rays of a winter sunset smote upon her pallid countenance. Before her stood the village clergyman, who had evidently just entered, and found her here; his white head was bent in the wonted attitude of clerical benevolence; in his face blended a gentle wonder and a compassionate tenderness.

"If that had been hung at Burlington House, Warburton, it would have been the picture of the year."

"I think it very likely."

"Yes, I know what you mean, you sarcastic old ruffian. But there's another point of view. Is the drawing good or not? Is the colour good or not? Of course you know nothing about it, but I tell you, for your information, I think it's a confoundedly clever bit of work. There remains the subject, and where's the harm in it? The incident's quite possible. And why shouldn't the girl be good-looking?"

"Angelic!"

"Well why not? There *are* girls with angelic faces. Don't I know one?"

Warburton, who had been sitting with a leg over the arm of his chair suddenly changed his position.

"That reminds me," he said. "I came across the Pomfrets in Switzerland."

"Where? When?"

"At Trient ten days ago. I spent three or four days with them. Hasn't Miss Elvan mentioned it?"

"I haven't heard from her for a long time," replied Franks. "Well, for more than a week. Did you meet them by chance?"

"Quite. I had a vague idea that the Pomfrets and their niece were somewhere in Switzerland."

"Vague idea!" cried the artist "Why, I told you all about it, and growled for five or six hours one evening here because I couldn't go with them."

"So you did," said Warburton, "but I'm afraid I was thinking of something else, and when I started for the Alps, I had really forgotten all about it. I made up my mind suddenly, you know. We're having a troublesome time in Ailie Street, and it was holiday now or never. By the bye, we shall have to wind up. Sugar spells ruin. We must get out of it whilst we can do so with a whole skin."

"Ah, really?" muttered Franks. "Tell me about that presently; I want to hear of Rosamund. You saw a good deal of her, of course?"

"I walked from Chamonix over the Col de Balme—grand view of Mont Blanc there! Then down to Trient, in the valley below. And there, as I went in to dinner at the hotel, I found the three. Good old Pomfret would have me stay awhile, and I was glad of the chance of long talks with him. Queer old bird, Ralph Pomfret."

"Yes, yes, so he is," muttered the artist, absently. "But Rosamund—was she enjoying herself?"

"Very much, I think. She certainly looked very well."

"Have much talk with her?" asked Franks, as if carelessly.

"We discussed you, of course. I forget whether our conclusion was favourable or not."

The artist laughed, and strode about the room with his hands in his pockets.

"You know what?" he exclaimed, seeming to look closely at a print on the wall. "I'm going to be married before the end of the year. On that point I've made up my mind. I went yesterday to see a house at Fulham—Mrs. Cross's, by the bye, it's to let at Michaelmas, rent forty-five. All but settled that I shall take it. Risk be hanged. I'm going to make money. What an ass I was to take that fellow's first offer for 'Sanctuary'! It was low water with me, and I felt bilious. Fifty guineas! Your fault, a good deal, you know; you made me think worse of it than it deserved. You'll see; Blackstaffe'll make a small fortune out of it; of course he has all the rights—idiot that I was! Well, it's too late to talk about that.—And I say, old man, don't take my growl too literally. I don't really mean that you were to blame. I should be an ungrateful cur if I thought such a thing."

"How's 'The Slummer' getting on?" asked Warburton good-humouredly.

"Well, I was going to say that I shall have it finished in a few weeks. If Blackstaffe wants 'The Slummer' he'll have to pay for it. Of course it must go to the Academy, and of course I shall keep all the rights—unless Blackstaffe makes a really handsome offer. Why, it ought to be worth five or six hundred to me at least. And that would start us. But I don't care even if I only get half that, I shall be married all the same. Rosamund has plenty of pluck. I couldn't ask her to start life on a pound a week—about my average for the last two years; but with two or three hundred in hand, and a decent little house, like that of Mrs. Cross's, at a reasonable rent—well, we shall risk it. I'm sick of waiting. And it isn't fair to a girl—that's my view. Two years now; an engagement that lasts more than two years isn't likely to come to much good. You'll think my behaviour pretty cool, on one point. I don't forget, you old usurer, that I owe you something more than a hundred pounds—"

"Pooh!"

"Be poohed yourself! But for you, I should have gone without dinner many a day; but for you, I should most likely have had to chuck painting altogether, and turn clerk or dock-labourer. But let me stay in your debt a little longer, old man. I can't put off my marriage any longer, and just at first I shall want all the money I can lay my hands on."

At this moment Mrs. Hopper entered with a lamp. There was a pause in the conversation. Franks lit a cigarette, and tried to sit still, but was very soon pacing the floor again. A tumbler of whisky and soda reanimated his flagging talk.

"No!" he exclaimed. "I'm not going to admit that 'Sanctuary' is cheap and sentimental, and all the rest of it. The more I think about it, the more convinced I am that it's nothing to be ashamed of. People have got hold of the idea that if a thing is popular it must be bad art. That's all rot. I'm going in for popularity. Look here! Suppose that's what I was meant for? What if it's the best I have in me to do? Shouldn't I be a jackass if I scorned to make money by what, for me, was good work, and preferred to starve whilst I turned out pretentious stuff that was worth nothing from my point of view?"

"I shouldn't wonder if you're right," said Warburton reflectively. "In any case, I know as much about art as I do about the differential calculus. To make money is a good and joyful thing as long as one doesn't bleed the poor. So go ahead, my son, and luck be with you!"

"I can't find my model yet for the Slummer's head. It mustn't be too like the 'Sanctuary' girl, but at the same time it must be a popular type of beauty. I've been haunting refreshment bars and florists' shops; lots of good material, but never *quite* the thing. There's a damsel at the Crystal Palace—but this doesn't interest you, you old misogynist."

"Old what?" exclaimed Warburton, with an air of genuine surprise.

"Have I got the word wrong? I'm not much of a classic—"

"The word's all right. But that's your idea of me, is it?"

The artist stood and gazed at his friend with an odd expression, as if a joke had been arrested on his lips by graver thought.

"Isn't it true?"

"Perhaps it is; yes, yes, I daresay."

And he turned at once to another subject.

# CHAPTER 3

The year was 1886.

When at business, Warburton sat in a high, bare room, which looked upon little Ailie Street, in Whitechapel; the air he breathed had a taste and odour strongly saccharine. If his eye strayed to one of the walls, he saw a map of the West Indies; if to another, it fell upon a map of St. Kitts; if to the third, there was before him a plan of a sugar estate on that little island. Here he sat for certain hours of the solid day, issuing orders to clerks, receiving commercial callers, studying trade journals in sundry languages—often reading some book which had no obvious reference to the sugar-refining industry. It was not Will's ideal of life, but hither he had suffered himself to be led by circumstance, and his musings suggested no practicable issue into a more congenial world.

The death of his father when he was sixteen had left him with a certain liberty for shaping a career. What he saw definitely before him was a small share in the St. Kitts property of Messrs. Sherwood Brothers, a small share in the London business of the same firm, and a small sum of ready money—these things to be his when he attained his majority. His mother and sister, who lived in a little country house down in Huntingdonshire, were modestly but securely provided for, and Will might have gone quietly on with his studies till he could resolve upon a course in life. But no sooner was he freed from paternal restraint than the lad grew restive; nothing would please him but an adventure in foreign lands; and when it became clear that he was only wasting his time at school, Mrs. Warburton let him go to the West Indies, where a place was found for him in the house of Sherwood Brothers. At St. Kitts, Will remained till he was one-and-twenty. Long before that, he had grown heartily tired of his work disgusted with the climate, and oppressed with home sickness, but pride forbade him to return until he could do so as a free man.

One thing this apprenticeship to life had taught him—that he was not made for subordination. "I don't care how poor I am," thus he wrote to his mother, "but I will be my own master. To be at other people's orders brings out all the bad in me; it makes me sullen and bearish, and all sorts of ugly things, which I certainly am not when my true self has play. So, you see, I must find some independent way of life. If I had to live by carrying round a Punch and Judy show, I should vastly prefer it to making a large income as somebody's servant."

Meanwhile, unfortunately for a young man of this temperament, his prospects had become less assured. There was perturbation in the sugar world; income from St. Kitts and from Whitechapel had sensibly diminished, and it seemed but too likely, would continue to do so. For some half-year Will lived in London, "looking about him," then he announced that Godfrey Sherwood, at present sole representative of Sherwood Brothers, had offered him an active partnership in Little Ailie Street, and that he had accepted it. He entered upon this position without zeal, but six months' investigation had taught him that to earn money without surrendering his independence was no very easy thing; he probably might wait a long time before an opening would present itself more attractive than this at the sugar-refinery.

Godfrey Sherwood was a schoolfellow of his, but some two or three years older; much good feeling existed between them, their tastes and tempers having just that difference in similarity which is the surest bond of friendship. Judged by his talk, Sherwood was all vigour, energy, fire; his personal habits, on the other hand, inclined to tranquillity and ease—a great reader, he loved the literature of romance and adventure, knew by heart authors such as Malory and Froissart, had on his shelves all the books of travel and adventure he could procure. As a boy he seemed destined to any life save that of humdrum commerce, of which he spoke with contempt and abhorrence; and there was no reason why he should not have gratified his desire of seeing the world, of leading what he called "the life of a man." Yet here he was, sitting each day in a counting-house in Whitechapel, with nothing behind him but a few rambles on the continent, and certainly with no immediate intention of going far afield. His father's death left him in sole command of the business, and his reasonable course would have been to retire from it as soon as possible, for foreign competition was making itself felt in the English trade, and many firms more solidly established than that in Little Ailie Street had either come to grief or withdrawn from the struggle. But Godfrey's inertia kept him in the familiar routine, with day-to-day postponement of practical decision. When Warburton came back from St. Kitts, and their friendship was renewed, Godfrey's talk gave full play to his imaginative energies. Yes,

yes, the refining business was at a bad pass just now, but this was only temporary; those firms that could weather the storm for a year or two longer would enter upon a time of brilliant prosperity. Was it to be supposed that the Government would allow a great industry to perish out of mere regard for the fetish of Free Trade? City men with first-hand information declared that "measures" were being prepared; in one way or another, the English trade would be rescued and made triumphant over those bounty-fed foreigners.

"Hold on?" cried Sherwood. "Of course I mean to hold on. There's pleasure and honour in the thing. I enjoy the fight. I've had thoughts of getting into Parliament, to speak for sugar. One might do worse, you know. There'll be a dissolution next year, certain. First-rate fun, fighting a constituency. But in that case I must have a partner here—why that's an idea. How would it suit you? Why not join me?"

And so the thing came about. The terms which Godfrey offered were so generous that Will had to reduce them before he accepted: even thus, he found his income, at a stroke, all but doubled. Sherwood, to be sure, did not stand for Parliament, nor was anything definite heard about that sugar-protecting budget which he still believed in. In Little Ailie Street business steadily declined.

"It's a disgrace to England!" cried Godfrey. "Monstrous that not a finger should be lifted to save one of our most important industries. You, of course, are free to retire at any moment, Will. For my own part, here I stand, come what may. If it's ruin, ruin let it be. I'll fight to the last. A man owes me ten thousand pounds. When I recover it, and I may any day—I shall put every penny into the business."

"Ten thousand pounds!" exclaimed Warburton in astonishment. "A trade debt, do you mean?"

"No, no. A friend of mine, son of a millionaire, who got into difficulties some time ago, and borrowed of me to clear himself. Good interest, and principal safe as Consols. In a year at most I shall have the money back, and every penny shall go into the business."

Will had his private view of the matter, and not seldom suffered a good deal of uneasiness as he saw the inevitable doom approach. But already it was too late to withdraw his share from the concern; that would have been merely to take advantage of Sherwood's generosity, and Will was himself not less chivalrous. In Godfrey's phrase, they continued "to fight the ship," and perhaps would have held out to the moment of sinking, had not the accession of the Liberals to power in the spring of this present year caused Sherwood so deep a disgust that he turned despondent and began to talk of surrender to hopeless circumstance.

"It's all up with us, Will. This Government spells ruin, and will count it one of its chief glories if we come to grief. But, by Heaven, they shan't have that joy. We'll square up, quietly, comfortably, with dignity. We'll come out of this fight with arms and baggage. It's still possible, you know. We'll sell the St. Kitts estate to the Germans. We'll find some one to buy us up here—the place would suit a brewer. And then—by Jove! we'll make jam."

"Jam?"

"Isn't it an idea? Cheap sugar has done for the refiners, but it's a fortune for the jam trade. Why not put all we can realize into a jam factory? We'll go down into the country; find some delightful place where land is cheap; start a fruit farm; run up a building. Doesn't it take you, Will? Think of going to business every day through lanes overhung with fruit-tree blossoms! Better that than the filth and stench and gloom and uproar of Whitechapel—what? We might found a village for our workpeople—the ideal village, perfectly healthy, every cottage beautiful. Eh? What? How does it strike you, Will?"

"Pleasant. But the money?"

"We shall have enough to start; I think we shall. If not, we'll find a moneyed man to join us."

"What about that ten thousand pounds?" suggested Warburton.

Sherwood shook his head.

"Can't get it just yet. To tell you the truth, it depends on the death of the man's father. No, but if necessary, some one will easily be found. Isn't the idea magnificent? How it would rile the Government if they heard of it! Ho, ho!"

One could never be sure how far Godfrey was serious when he talked like this; the humorous impulse so blended with the excitability of his imagination, that people who knew him little and heard him talking at large thought him something of a crack-brain. The odd thing was that, with all his peculiarities, he had many of the characteristics of a sound man of business; indeed, had it been otherwise, the balance-sheets of the refinery must long ago have shown a disastrous deficit. As Warburton knew, things had been managed with no little prudence and sagacity; what he did not so clearly understand was that Sherwood had simply adhered to the traditions of the firm, following very exactly the path marked out for him by his father and his uncle, both notable traders. Concerning Godfrey's private resources, Warburton knew little or nothing; it seemed probable that the elder Sherwood had left a considerable fortune, which his only son must have inherited. No doubt, said Will to himself, this large reserve was the explanation of his partner's courage.

So the St. Kitts estate was sold, and, with all the deliberate dignity demanded by the fact that the Government's eye was upon them, Sherwood Brothers proceeded to terminate their affairs in Whitechapel. In July, Warburton took his three weeks' holiday, there being nothing better for him to do. And among the letters he found on his table when he returned, was one from Sherwood, which contained only these words:

"Great opportunity in view. Our fortunes are made!"

# CHAPTER 4

When Franks was gone, Warburton took up *The Art World*, which his friend had left, and glanced again at the photogravure of "Sanctuary." He knew, as he had declared, nothing about art, and judged pictures as he judged books, emotionally. His bent was to what is called the realistic point of view, and "Sanctuary" made him smile. But very good-naturedly; for he liked Norbert Franks, and believed he would do better things than this. Unless—?

The thought broke off with an uneasy interrogative.

He turned to the few lines of text devoted to the painter. Norbert Franks, he read, was still a very young man; "Sanctuary," now on exhibition at Birmingham, was his first important picture; hitherto he had been chiefly occupied with work in black and white. There followed a few critical comments, and prophecy of achievements to come.

Yes. But again the uneasy interrogative.

Their acquaintance dated from the year after Warburton's return from St. Kitts. Will had just established himself in his flat near Chelsea Bridge, delighted to be a Londoner, and was spending most of his leisure in exploration of London's vastness. He looked upon all his earlier years as wasted, because they had not been passed in the city on the Thames. The history of London, the multitudinous life of London as it lay about him, with marvels and mysteries in every highway and byway, occupied his mind, and wrought upon his imagination. Being a stout walker, and caring little for any other form of exercise, in his free hours he covered many a league of pavement. A fine summer morning would see him set forth, long before milk-carts had begun to rattle along the streets, and on one such expedition, as he stepped briskly through a poor district south of the river, he was surprised to see an artist at work, painting seriously, his easel in the dry gutter. He slackened his pace to have a glimpse of the canvas, and the painter, a young, pleasant-looking fellow, turned round and asked if he had a match. Able to supply this demand, Warburton talked whilst the other relit his pipe. It rejoiced him, he said, to see a painter engaged upon such a subject as this—a bit of squalid London's infinite picturesqueness.

The next morning Warburton took the same walk, and again found the painter at work. They talked freely; they exchanged invitations; and that same evening Norbert Franks climbed the staircase to Will's flat, and smoked his first pipe and drank his first whisky-and-soda in the pleasant room overlooking Ranelagh. His own quarters were in Queen's Road, Battersea, at no great distance. The two young men were soon seeing a great deal of each other. When their friendship had ripened through a twelvemonth, Franks, always impecunious, cheerily borrowed a five-pound note; not long after, he mirthfully doubled his debt; and this grew to a habit with him.

"You're a capitalist, Warburton," he remarked one day, "and a generous fellow, too. Of course I shall pay what I owe you when I sell a big picture. Meanwhile, you have the gratification of supporting a man of genius, without the least inconvenience to yourself. Excellent idea of yours to strike up a friendship, wasn't it?"

The benefit was reciprocal. Warburton did not readily form intimacies; indeed Godfrey Sherwood had till now been almost the only man he called friend, and the peculiarity of his temper exposed him to the risk of being too much alone. Though neither arrogant nor envious, Will found little pleasure in the society of people who, from any point of view, were notably his superiors; even as he could not subordinate himself in money-earning relations, so did he become ill-at-ease, lose all spontaneity, in company above his social or intellectual level. Such a man's danger was obvious; he might, in default of congenial associates, decline upon inferiors; all the more that a softness of heart, a fineness of humanity, ever disposed him to feel and show special kindness for the poor, the distressed, the unfortunate. Sherwood's acquaintances had little attraction for him; they were mostly people who lived in a luxurious way, went in for sports, talked about the money market—all of which things fascinated Godfrey, though in truth he was far from belonging by nature to that particular world. With Franks, Will could be wholly himself, enjoying the slight advantage of his larger means, extending his knowledge without undue obligation, and getting all the good that comes to a man from the exercise of his kindliest feelings.

With less of geniality, because more occupied with himself, Norbert Franks resembled his new friend in a distaste for ordinary social pleasures and an enjoyment of the intimacies of life. He stood very much alone in the world, and from the age of eighteen he had in one way or another supported himself, chiefly by work on illustrated papers. His father, who belonged to what is called a good family, began life in easy circumstances, and gained some reputation as a connoisseur of art; imprudence and misfortune having obliged him to sell his collection, Mr. Franks took to buying pictures and bric-a-brac for profit, and during the last ten years of his life was associated in that capacity with a London firm. Norbert, motherless from infancy and an only child, received his early education at expensive schools, but, showing little aptitude for study and much for use of the pencil, was taken by his father at twelve years old to Paris, and there set to work under a good art-teacher. At sixteen he went to Italy, where he remained for a couple of years. Then, on a journey in the East, the elder Franks died. Norbert returned to England, learnt that a matter of fifty pounds was all his heritage, and pluckily turned to the task of keeping himself alive. Herein his foreign sketch-books proved serviceable, but the struggle was long and hard before he could house himself decently, and get to serious work as a painter. Later on, he was wont to say that this poverty had been the best possible thing for him, its enforced abstinences having come just at the time when he had begun to "wallow"—his word for any sort of excess; and "wallowing" was undoubtedly a peril to which Norbert's temper particularly exposed him. Short commons made him, as they have made many another youth, sober and chaste, at all events in practice; and when he began to lift up his head, a little; when, at the age of three-and-twenty, he earned what seemed to him at first the luxurious income of a pound or so a week; when, in short, the inclination to "wallow" might again have taken hold upon him, it was his chance to fall in love so seriously and hopefully that all the better features of his character were drawn out, emphasized, and, as it seemed, for good and all established in predominance.

Not long after his first meeting with Warburton, he one day received, through the publishers of a book he had illustrated, a letter signed "Ralph Pomfret," the writer of which asked whether "Norbert Franks" was the son of an old friend of whom he had lost sight for many years. By way of answer, Franks called upon his correspondent, who lived in a pleasant little house at Ashtead, in Surrey; he found a man of something less than sixty, with a touch of eccentricity in his thoughts and ways, by whom he was hospitably received, and invited to return whenever it pleased him. It was not very long before Franks asked permission to make the Pomfrets acquainted with his friend Warburton, a step which proved entirely justifiable. Together or separately, the two young men were often to be seen at Ashtead, whither they were attracted not only by the kindly and amusing talk of Ralph Pomfret, but at least as much by the grace and sweetness and sympathetic intelligence of the mistress of the house, for whom both entertained respect and admiration.

One Sunday afternoon, Warburton, tempted as usual by the thought of tea and talk in that delightful little garden, went out to Ashtead, and, as he pushed open the gate, was confused and vexed at the sight of strangers; there, before the house, stood a middle-aged gentleman and a young girl, chatting with Mrs. Pomfret. He would have turned away and taken himself off in disappointment, but that the clank of the gate had attracted attention, and he had no choice but to move forward. The strangers proved to be Mrs. Pomfret's brother and his daughter; they had been spending half a year in the south of France, and were here for a day or two before returning to their home at Bath. When he had recovered his equanimity, Warburton became aware that the young lady was fair to look upon. Her age seemed about two-and-twenty; not very tall, she bore herself with perhaps a touch of conscious dignity and impressiveness; perfect health, a warm complexion, magnificent hair, eyes that shone with gaiety and good-nature, made of Rosamund Elvan a living picture such as Will Warburton had not often seen; he was shy in her presence, and by no means did himself justice that afternoon. His downcast eyes presently noticed that she wore shoes of a peculiar kind—white canvas with soles of plaited cord; in the course of conversation he learnt that these were a memento of the Basque country, about which Miss Elvan talked with a very pretty enthusiasm. Will went away, after all, in a dissatisfied mood. Girls were to him merely a source of disquiet. "If she be not fair for me—" was his ordinary thought; and he had never yet succeeded in persuading himself that any girl, fair or not, was at all likely to conceive the idea of devoting herself to his happiness. In this matter, an excessive modesty subdued him. It had something to do with his holding so much apart from general society.

On the evening of the next day, there was a thunderous knock at Warburton's flat, and in rushed Franks.

"You were at Ashtead yesterday," he cried.

"I was. What of that?"

"And you didn't come to tell me about the Elvans!"

"About Miss Elvan, I suppose you mean?" said Will.

"Well, yes, I do. I went there by chance this afternoon. The two men were away somewhere,—I found Mrs. Pomfret and that girl alone together. Never had such a delightful time in my life! But I say, Warburton, we must understand each other. Are you—do you—I mean, did she strike you particularly?"

Will threw back his head and laughed.

"You mean that?" shouted the other, joyously. "You really don't care—it's nothing to you?"

"Why, is it anything to *you*?"

"Anything? Rosamund Elvan is the most beautiful girl I ever saw, and the sweetest, and the brightest, and the altogether flooringest! And, by heaven and earth, I'm resolved to marry her!"

# CHAPTER 5

As he sat musing, *The Art World* still in his hand, Warburton could hear his friend's voice ring out that audacious vow. He could remember, too, the odd little pang with which he heard it, a half spasm of altogether absurd jealousy. Of course the feeling did not last. There was no recurrence of it when he heard that Franks had again seen Miss Elvan before she left Ashtead; nor when he learnt that the artist had been spending a day or two at Bath. Less than a month after their first meeting, Franks won Rosamund's consent. He was frantic with exultation. Arriving with the news at ten o'clock one night, he shouted and maddened about Warburton's room until finally turned out at two in the morning. His circumstances being what they were, he could not hope for marriage yet awhile; he must work and wait. Never mind; see what work he would produce! Yet it appeared to his friend that all through the next twelvemonth he merely wasted time, such work as he did finish being of very slight value. He talked and talked, now of Rosamund, now of what he was *going* to do, until Warburton, losing patience, would cut him short with "Oh, go to Bath!"—an old cant phrase revived for its special appropriateness in this connection. Franks went to Bath far oftener than he could afford, money for his journey being generally borrowed from his long-enduring friend.

Rosamund herself had nothing, and but the smallest expectations should her father die. Two years before this, it had occurred to her that she should like to study art, and might possibly find in it a means of self-support. She was allowed to attend classes at South Kensington, but little came of this except a close friendship with a girl of her own age, by name Bertha Cross, who was following the art course with more serious purpose. When she had been betrothed for about a year, Rosamund chanced to spend a week in London at her friend's house, and this led to acquaintance between Franks and the Crosses. For a time, Warburton saw and heard less of the artist, who made confidantes of Mrs. Cross and her daughter, and spent many an evening with them talking, talking, talking about Rosamund; but this intimacy did not endure very long, Mrs. Cross being a person of marked peculiarities, which in the end overtried Norbert's temper. Only on the fourth story flat by Chelsea Bridge could the lover find that sort of sympathy which he really needed, solacing yet tonic. But for Warburton he would have worked even less. To Will it seemed an odd result of fortunate love that the artist, though in every other respect a better man than before, should have become, to all appearances, less zealous, less efficient, in his art. Had Rosamund Elvan the right influence on her lover; in spite of Norbert's lyric eulogy, had she served merely to confuse his aims, perhaps to bring him down to a lower level of thought?

There was his picture, "Sanctuary." Before he knew Rosamund, Franks would have scoffed at such a subject, would have howled at such treatment of it. There was notable distance between this and what Norbert was painting in that summer sunrise four years ago, with his portable easel in the gutter. And Miss Elvan admired "Sanctuary"—at least, Franks said she did. True, she also admired the picture of the pawnshop and the public-house; Will had himself heard her speak of it with high praise, and with impatient wonder that no purchaser could be found for it. Most likely she approved of everything Norbert did, and had no more serious criterion. Unless, indeed, her private test of artistic value were the financial result.

Warburton could not altogether believe that. Annoyance with the artist now and then inclined him to slighting thought of Rosamund; yet, on the whole, his view of her was not depreciatory. The disadvantage to his mind was her remarkable comeliness. He could not but fear that so much beauty must be inconsistent with the sterling qualities which make a good wife.

Will's eye fell on Sherwood's note, and he went to bed wondering what the project might be which was to make their fortune.

# CHAPTER 6

He had breakfasted, and was smoking his pipe as he wrote a letter, when Mrs. Hopper announced the visit, by appointment, of her brother-in-law, Allchin. There entered a short, sturdy, red-headed young fellow, in a Sunday suit of respectable antiquity; his features were rude, his aspect dogged; but a certain intelligence showed in his countenance, and a not unamiable smile responded to the bluff heartiness of Warburton's greeting. By original calling, Allchin was a grocer's assistant, but a troublesome temper had more than once set him adrift, the outcast of grocerdom, to earn a living as best he could by his vigorous thews, and it was in one of these intervals that, having need of a porter at the works, Warburton had engaged him, on Mrs. Hopper's petition. After a month or so of irreproachable service, Allchin fought with a foreman, and took his discharge. The same week, Mrs. Allchin presented him with their first child; the family fell into want; Mrs. Hopper (squeezed between door and jamb) drew her master's attention to the lamentable case, and help was of course forthcoming. Then, by good luck, Allchin was enabled to resume his vocation; he got a place at a grocer's in Fulham Road, and in a few weeks presented himself before his benefactor, bringing half-a-crown as a first instalment toward the discharge of his debt; for only on this condition had he accepted the money. Half a year elapsed without troublesome incident; the man made regular repayment in small sums; then came the disaster which Mrs. Hopper had yesterday announced.

"Well, Allchin," cried Warburton, "what's the latest?"

Before speaking, the other pressed his lips tightly together and puffed out his cheeks, as if it cost him an effort to bring words to the surface. His reply came forth with explosive abruptness.

"Lost my place at Boxon's, sir."

"And how's that?"

"It happened last Saturday, sir. I don't want to make out as I wasn't at all to blame. I know as well as anybody that I've got a will of my own. But we're open late, as perhaps you know, sir, on Saturday night, and Mr. Boxon—well, it's only the truth—he's never quite himself after ten o'clock. I'd worked from eight in the morning to something past midnight—of course I don't think nothing of that, 'cause it's reg'lar in the trade. But—well, in come a customer, sir, a woman as didn't rightly know what she wanted; and she went out without buying, and Mr. Boxon he see it, and he come up to me and calls me the foulest name he could turn his tongue to. And so—well, sir, there was unpleasantness, as they say—"

He hesitated, Warburton eyeing him with a twinkle of subdued amusement.

"A quarrel, in fact, eh?"

"It did about come to that, sir!"

"You lost your temper, of course."

"That's about the truth, sir."

"And Boxon turned you out?"

Allchin looked hurt.

"Well, sir, I've no doubt he'd have liked to, but I was a bit beforehand with him. When I see him last, he was settin' on the pavement, sir, rubbin' his 'ead."

In spite of his inclination to laugh, Will kept a grave countenance.

"I'm afraid that kind of thing won't do, Allchin. You'll be in serious trouble one of these days."

"That's what my wife says, sir. I know well enough as it's hard on her, just after we've lost the baby—as perhaps Mrs. Hopper'll have told you, sir."

"I was very sorry to hear it, Allchin."

"Thank you, sir. You've always something kind to say. And I'm that vexed, because I was getting on well with paying my debts. But Mr. Boxon, sir, he's many a time made me that mad that I've gone out into the back yard and kicked the wall till my toes were sore, just to ease my feelings, like. To tell the truth, sir, I don't think he's ever rightly sober, and I've heard others say the same. And his business is fallin' off, something shockin'. Customers don't like to be insulted; that's only natural. He's always going down to Kempton Park, or Epsom, or some such place. They do say as he lost 'undreds of pounds at Kempton Park last week. It's my opinion the shop can't go on much longer. Well, sir, I thought I just ought to come and tell you the truth of things, and I won't disturb you no longer. I shall do my best to find another place."

Warburton's impulse was to offer temporary work in Little Ailie Street, but he remembered that the business was not in a position to increase expenses, and that the refinery might any day be closed.

"All right," he answered cheerily, "let me know how you get on."

When Allchin's heavy footsteps had echoed away down the stairs, Mrs. Hopper answered her master's call.

"I suppose they have a little money to go on with?" Warburton inquired. "I mean, enough for a week or so."

"Yes, I think they have that, sir. But I see how it'll be. My poor sister'll end in the work'us. Allchin'll never keep a place. Not that I can blame him, sir, for givin' it to that Boxon, 'cause every one says he's a brute."

"Well, just let me know if they begin to be in want. But of course Allchin can always get work as a porter. He must learn to keep his fists down, if he doesn't want to be perpetually out of employment."

"That's what I tell him, sir. And my poor sister, sir, she's never stopped talkin' to him, day or night you may say, ever since it happened—"

"Merciful Heavens!" groaned Warburton to himself.

# CHAPTER 7

At half-past nine he reached Little Ailie Street.

"Mr. Sherwood not here yet, I suppose?" asked Will.

"Oh yes, he is, sir," replied the manager; "been here for half an hour."

Warburton went on to the senior partner's room. There sat Godfrey Sherwood bent over a book which, to judge from the smile upon his face, could have nothing to do with the sugar-refining question.

"How do, Will?" he exclaimed, with even more than his usual cheerfulness. "Did you ever read 'The Adventures of a Younger Son'? Oh, you must. Listen here. He's describing how he thrashed an assistant master at school; thrashed him, he says, till 'the sweat dropped from his brows like rain-drops from the eaves of a pig-sty!' Ho-ho-ho! What do you think of that for a comparison? Isn't it strong? By Jove! a bracing book! Trelawny, you know; the friend of Byron. As breezy a book as I know. It does one good."

Godfrey Sherwood was, as regards his visage, what is called a plain young man, but his smile told of infinite good-nature, and his voice, notwithstanding its frequent note of energy or zeal, had a natural softness of intonation which suggested other qualities than the practical and vigorous.

"Enjoyed your holiday?" he went on, rising, stretching himself, and offering a box of cigarettes. "You look well. Done any summits? When we get our affairs in order, I must be off somewhere myself. Northward, I think. I want a little bracing cold. I should like to see Iceland. You know the Icelandic sagas? Magnificent! There's the saga of Grettir the Strong—by Jove! But come, this isn't business. I have news for you, real, substantial, hopeful news."

They seated themselves in roundbacked chairs, and Will lighted a cigarette.

"You know my thoughts were running on jam; jam is our salvation; of that I have long been convinced. I looked about, made a few inquiries, and by good luck, not long after you went off for your holiday, met just the man I wanted. You've heard of Applegarth's jams?"

Will said he had seen them advertised.

"Well, I came across Applegarth himself. I was talking to Linklater—and jams came up. 'You ought to see my friend Applegarth,' said he; and he arranged for us to meet. Applegarth happened to be in town, but he lives down in Somerset, and his factory is at Bristol. We all dined together at the Junior Carlton, and Applegarth and I got on so well that he asked me down to his place. Oxford man, clever, a fine musician, and an astronomer; has built himself a little observatory—magnificent telescope. By Jove! you should hear him handle the violin. Astonishing fellow! Not much of a talker; rather dry in his manner; but no end of energy, bubbling over with vital force. He began as a barrister, but couldn't get on, and saw his capital melting. 'Hang it!' said he, 'I must make some use of what money I have'; and he thought of jam. Brilliant idea! He began in a very modest way, down at Bristol, only aiming at local trade. But his jams were good; the demand grew; he built a factory; profits became considerable. And now, he wants to withdraw from active business, keeping an interest. Wants to find some one who would run and extend the concern—put in a fair capital, and leave him to draw his income quietly. You see?"

"Seems a good opportunity," said Warburton.

"Good? It's simply superb. He took me over the works—a really beautiful sight, everything so admirably arranged. Then we had more private talk. Of course I spoke of you, said I could do nothing till we had consulted together. I didn't seem too eager—not good policy. But we've had some correspondence, and you shall see the letters."

He handed them to his partner. Warburton saw that there was a question of a good many thousand pounds.

"Of course," he remarked, "I could only stand for a very small part in this."

"Well, we must talk about that. To tell you the truth, Will," Sherwood continued, crossing his legs and clasping his hands behind his head, "I don't see my way to find the whole capital, and yet I don't want to bring in a stranger. Applegarth could sell to a company any moment, but that isn't his idea; he wants to keep the concern in as few hands as possible. He has a first-rate manager; the mere jam-making wouldn't worry us at all; and the office work is largely a matter of routine. Will you take time to think about it?"

The figures which Warburton had before him were decidedly stimulating; they made a very pleasant contrast to the balance-sheets with which he had recently had to deal. He knew roughly what sum was at his disposal for investment; the winding-up of the business here could be completed at any moment, and involved no risk of surprises. But a thought had occurred to him which kept him silently reflecting for some minutes.

"I suppose," he said presently, "this affair has about as little risk as anything one could put money in?"

"I should say," Godfrey answered, with his man-of-business air, "that the element of risk is non-existent. What can be more solid than jam? There's competition to be sure; but Applegarth is already a good name throughout England, and in the West they swear by it. At Bristol, Exeter, Dorchester—all over there—Applegarth holds the field. Very seriously speaking, I see in this proposal nothing but sure and increasing gain."

"You know as well as I do," Will resumed, "how I stand. I have no resources of my own beyond what you are aware of. But I've been thinking—"

He broke off, stared at the window, drummed on the arm of his chair, Sherwood waiting with a patient smile.

"It's my mother and sister I have in mind," Will resumed. "That property of theirs; it brings them about a hundred and fifty pounds a year in cash, and three times that in worry. At any moment they might sell. A man at St. Neots offers four thousand pounds; I suspect more might be got if Turnbull, their lawyer, took the matter in hand. Suppose I advise them to sell and put the money in Applegarth?"

"By Jove!" cried Sherwood. "How could they do better? Splendid idea!"

"Yes—if all goes well. Bear in mind, on the other hand, that if they lost this money, they would have nothing to live upon, or as good as nothing. They draw some fifty pounds a year from another source, and they have their own house—that's all. Ought I to take this responsibility?"

"I don't hesitate to guarantee," said Sherwood, with glowing gravity, "that in two years' time their four thousand pounds shall produce three times what it does now. Only think, my dear fellow! Jam—think what it means!"

For ten minutes Godfrey rhapsodised on the theme. Warburton was moved by his eloquence.

"I shall run down to St. Neots," said Will at length.

"Do. And then we'll both of us go down to Bristol. I'm sure you'll like Applegarth. By the bye, you never went in for astronomy, did you? I felt ashamed of my ignorance. Why, it's one of the most interesting subjects a man can study. I shall take it up. One might have a little observatory of one's own. Do you know Bristol at all? A beastly place, the town, but perfectly delightful country quite near at hand. Applegarth lives in an ideal spot—you'll see."

There was a knock at the door and the manager entered. Other business claimed their attention.

# CHAPTER 8

Warburton often returned from Whitechapel to Chelsea on foot, enjoying the long walk after his day in the office. This evening, a heavily clouded sky and sobbing wind told that rain was not far off; nevertheless, wishing to think hard, which he could never do so well as when walking at a brisk pace, he set off in the familiar direction—a straight cut across South London.

In Lower Kennington Lane he stopped, as his habit was, at a little stationer's shop, over which was the name Potts. During his last year in the West Indies, he had befriended an English lad whose health was suffering from the climate, and eventually had paid his passage to the United States, whither the young adventurer wished to go in pursuit of his fortune. Not long after he received a letter of thanks from the lad's father, and, on coming to London, he sought out Mr. Potts, whose gratitude and its quaint expression had pleased him. The acquaintance continued; whenever Warburton passed the shop he stepped in and made purchases—generally of things he did not in the least want. Potts had all the characteristics which were wont to interest Will, and touch his sympathies; he was poor, weak of body, humble-spirited, and of an honest, simple mind. Nothing more natural and cordial than Will's bearing as he entered and held out his hand to the shopkeeper. How was business? Any news lately from Jack? Jack, it seemed, was doing pretty well at Pittsburgh; would Mr. Warburton care to read a long letter that had arrived from him a week ago? To his satisfaction, Will found that the letter had enclosed a small sum of money, for a present on the father's birthday. Having, as usual, laden himself with newspapers, periodicals and notepaper, he went his way.

At grimy Vauxhall he crossed the river, and pursued his course along Grosvenor Road. Rain had begun to fall, and the driving of the wind obliged him to walk with the umbrella before his face. Happening to glance ahead, when not far from home, he saw, at a distance of twenty yards, a man whom he took for Norbert Franks. The artist was coming toward him, but suddenly he turned round about, and walked rapidly away, disappearing in a moment down a side street. Franks it certainly was; impossible to mistake his figure, his gait; and Warburton felt sure that the abrupt change of direction was caused by his friend's desire to avoid him. At the end of the byway he looked, and there was the familiar figure, marching with quick step into the rainy distance. Odd! but perhaps it simply meant that Franks had not seen him.

He reached home, wrote some letters, made preparations for leaving town by an early train next morning, and dined with his customary appetite. Whilst smoking his after-dinner pipe, he thought again of that queer little incident in Grosvenor Road, and resolved of a sudden to go and see Franks. It still rained, so he took advantage of a passing hansom, and drove in a few minutes to the artist's lodging on the south side of Battersea Park. The door was opened to him by the landlady, who smiled recognition.

"No, sir, Mr. Franks isn't at home, and hasn't been since after breakfast this morning. And I don't understand it; because he told me last night that he'd be working all day, and I was to get meals for him as usual. And at ten o'clock the model came—that rough man he's putting into the new picture, you know, sir; and I had to send him away, when he'd waited more than an hour."

Warburton was puzzled.

"I'll take my turn at waiting," he said. "Will you please light the gas for me in the studio?"

The studio was merely, in lodging-house language, the first floor front; a two-windowed room, with the advantage of north light. On the walls hung a few framed paintings, several unframed and unfinished, water-colour sketches, studies in crayon, photographs, and so on. In the midst stood the easel, supporting a large canvas, the artist's work on which showed already in a state of hopeful advancement. "The Slummer" was his provisional name for this picture; he had not yet hit upon that more decorous title which might suit the Academy catalogue. A glance discovered the subject. In a typical London slum, between small and vile houses, which lowered upon the narrow way, stood a tall, graceful, prettily-clad young woman, obviously a visitant from other spheres; her one hand carried a book, and the other was held by a ragged, cripple child, who gazed up at her with a look of innocent adoration. Hard by stood a miserable creature with an infant at her breast, she too adoring the representative of health, wealth, and charity. Behind, a costermonger, out of work, sprawled on the curbstone, viewing the invader; he, with resentful eye, his lip suggestive of words unreportable. Where the face of the central figure should have shone, the canvas still remained blank.

"I'm afraid he's worried about *her*," said the landlady, when she had lit the gas, and stood with Warburton surveying the picture. "He can't find a model good-looking enough. I say to Mr. Franks why not make it the portrait of his own young lady? I'm sure *she's* good-looking enough for anything and—"

Whilst speaking, the woman had turned to look at a picture on the wall. Words died upon her lips; consternation appeared in her face; she stood with finger extended. Warburton, glancing where he was accustomed to see the portrait of Rosamund Elvan, also felt a shock. For, instead of the face which should have smiled upon him, he saw an ugly hole in the picture, the canvas having been violently cut, or rent with a blow.

"Hallo! What the deuce has he been doing?"

"Well, I never!" exclaimed the landlady. "It must be himself that's done it! What does *that* mean now, I wonder?"

Warburton was very uneasy. He no longer doubted that Franks had purposely avoided him this afternoon.

"I daresay," he added, with a pretence of carelessness, "the portrait had begun to vex him. He's often spoken of it discontentedly, and talked of painting another. It wasn't very good."

Accepting, or seeming to accept this explanation, the landlady withdrew, and Will paced thoughtfully about the floor. He was back in Switzerland, in the valley which rises to the glacier of Trient. Before him rambled Ralph Pomfret and his wife; at his side was Rosamund Elvan, who listened with a flattering air of interest to all he said, but herself spoke seldom, and seemed, for the most part, preoccupied with some anxiety. He spoke of Norbert Franks; Miss Elvan replied mechanically, and at once made a remark about the landscape. At the time, he had thought little of this; now it revived in his memory, and disturbed him.

An hour passed. His patience was nearly at an end. He waited another ten minutes, then left the room, called to the landlady that he was going, and let himself out.

Scarcely had he walked half a dozen yards, when he stood face to face with Franks.

"Ah! Here you are! I waited as long as I could—"

"I'll walk with you," said the artist, turning on his heels.

He had shaken hands but limply. His look avoided Warburton's. His speech was flat, wearied.

## CHAPTER 8

"What's wrong, Franks?"

"As you've been in the studio, I daresay you know."

"I saw something that surprised me."

"*Did* it surprise you?" asked Norbert, in a half-sullen undertone.

"What do you mean by that?" said Will with subdued resentment.

The rain had ceased; a high wind buffeted them as they went along the almost deserted street. The necessity of clutching at his hat might have explained Norbert's silence for a moment; but he strode on without speaking.

"Of course, if you don't care to talk about it," said Will, stopping short.

"I've been walking about all day," Franks replied; "and I've got hell inside me; I'd rather not have met you to-night, that's the truth. But I can't let you go without asking a plain question. *Did* it surprise you to see that portrait smashed?"

"Very much. What do you hint at?"

"I had a letter this morning from Rosamund, saying she couldn't marry me, and that all must be over between us. Does *that* surprise you?"

"Yes, it does. Such a possibility had never entered my mind."

Franks checked his step, just where the wind roared at an unprotected corner.

"I've no choice but to believe you," he said, irritably. "And no doubt I'm making a fool of myself. That's why I shot out of your way this afternoon—I wanted to wait till I got calmer. Let's say good-night."

"You're tired out," said Warburton. "Don't go any farther this way, but let me walk back with you—I won't go in. I can't leave you in this state of mind. Of course I begin to see what you mean, and a wilder idea never got into any man's head. Whatever the explanation of what has happened, *I* have nothing to do with it."

"You say so, and I believe you."

"Which means, that you don't. I shan't cut up rough; you're not yourself, and I can make all allowances. Think over what I've said, and come and have another talk. Not to-morrow; I have to go down to St. Neots. But the day after, in the evening."

"Very well. Good-night."

This time they did not shake hands. Franks turned abruptly, with a wave of the arm, and walked off unsteadily, like a man in liquor. Observing this, Warburton said to himself that not improbably the artist had been trying to drown his misery, which might account for his strange delusion. Yet this explanation did not put Will's mind at ease. Gloomily he made his way homeward through the roaring night.

# CHAPTER 9

Ten o'clock next morning saw him alighting from the train at St. Neots. A conveyance for which he had telegraphed awaited him at the station; its driver, a young man of his own age (they had known each other from boyhood), grinned his broadest as he ran toward Will on the platform, and relieved him of his bag.

"Well, Sam, how goes it? Everybody flourishing?—Drive first to Mr. Turnbull's office."

Mr. Turnbull was a grey-headed man of threescore, much troubled with lumbago, which made him stoop as he walked. He had a visage of extraordinary solemnity, and seemed to regard every one, no matter how prosperous or cheerful, with anxious commiseration. At the sight of Will, he endeavoured to smile, and his handshake, though the flabbiest possible, was meant for a cordial response to the young man's heartiness.

"I'm on my way to The Haws, Mr. Turnbull, and wanted to ask if you could come up and see us this evening?"

"Oh, with pleasure," answered the lawyer, his tone that of one invited to a funeral. "You may count on me."

"We're winding up at Sherwood's. I don't mean in bankruptcy; but that wouldn't be far off if we kept going."

"Ah! I can well understand that," said Mr. Turnbull, with a gleam of satisfaction. Though a thoroughly kind man, it always brightened him to hear of misfortune, especially when he had himself foretold it; and he had always taken the darkest view of Will's prospects in Little Ailie Street.

"I have a project I should like to talk over with you—"

"Ah?" said the lawyer anxiously.

"As it concerns my mother and Jane—"

"Ah?" said Mr. Turnbull, with profound despondency.

"Then we shall expect you.—Will it rain, do you think?"

"I fear so. The glass is very low indeed. It wouldn't surprise me if we had rain through the whole month of August."

"Good Heavens! I hope not," replied Will laughing.

He drove out of the town again, in a different direction, for about a mile. On rising ground, overlooking the green valley of the Ouse, stood a small, plain, solidly-built house, sheltered on the cold side by a row of fine hawthorns, nearly as high as the top of its chimneys. In front, bordered along the road by hollies as impenetrable as a stone wall, lay a bright little flower garden. The Haws, originally built for the bailiff of an estate, long since broken up, was nearly a century old. Here Will's father was born, and here, after many wanderings, he had spent the greater part of his married life.

"Sam," said Will, as they drew up at the gate, "I don't think I shall pay for this drive. You're much richer than I am."

"Very good, sir," was the chuckling reply, for Sam knew he always had to expect a joke of this kind from young Mr. Warburton. "As you please, sir."

"You couldn't lend me half-a-crown, Sam?"

"I daresay I could, sir, if you really wanted it."

"Do then."

Will pocketed the half-crown, jumped off the trap, and took his bag.

"After all, Sam, perhaps I'd better pay. Your wife might grumble. Here you are."

He handed two shillings and sixpence in small change, which Sam took and examined with a grin of puzzlement.

"Well, what's the matter? Don't you say thank you, nowadays?"

"Yes, sir—thank you, sir—it's all right, Mr. Will."

"I should think it is indeed. Be here to-morrow morning, to catch the 6.30 up train, Sam."

As Will entered the garden, there came forward a girl of something and twenty, rather short, square shouldered, firmly planted on her feet, but withal brisk of movement; her face was remarkable for nothing but a grave good-humour. She wore a broad-brimmed straw hat, and her gardening gloves showed how she was occupied. Something of shyness appeared in the mutual greeting of brother and sister.

"Of course, you got my letter this morning?" said Will.

"Yes."

"Mr. Turnbull is coming up to-night."

"I'm glad of that," said Jane thoughtfully, rubbing her gloves together to shake off moist earth.

"Of course he'll prophesy disaster, and plunge you both into the depths of discouragement. But I don't mind that. I feel so confident myself that I want some one to speak on the other side. He'll have to make inquiries, of course.—Where's mother?"

The question was answered by Mrs. Warburton herself, who at that moment came forth from the house; a tall, graceful woman, prematurely white-headed, and enfeebled by ill-health. Between her and Jane there was little resemblance of feature; Will, on the other hand, had inherited her oval face, arched brows and sensitive mouth. Emotion had touched her cheek with the faintest glow, but ordinarily it was pale as her hand. Nothing, however, of the invalid declared itself in her tone or language; the voice, soft and musical, might have been that of a young woman, and its vivacity was only less than that which marked the speech of her son.

"Come and look at the orange lilies," were her first words, after the greeting. "They've never been so fine."

"But notice Pompey first," said Jane. "He'll be offended in a minute."

A St. Bernard, who had already made such advances as his dignity permitted, stood close by Will, with eyes fixed upon him in grave and surprised reproach. The dog's name indicated a historical preference of Jane in her childhood; she had always championed Pompey against Caesar, following therein her brother's guidance.

"Hallo, old Magnus!" cried the visitor, cordially repairing his omission. "Come along with us and see the lilies."

It was only when all the sights of the little garden had been visited, Mrs. Warburton forgetting her weakness as she drew Will hither and thither, that the business for which they had met came under discussion. Discussion, indeed, it could hardly be called, for the mother and sister were quite content to listen whilst Will talked, and accept his view of things. Small as their income was, they never thought of themselves as poor; with one maid-servant and the occasional help of a gardener, they had all the comfort they wished for, and were able to bestow of their superfluity in vegetables and flowers upon less fortunate acquaintances. Until a year or two ago, Mrs. Warburton had led a life of ceaseless activity, indoors and out; such was the habit of her daughter, who enjoyed vigorous health, and cared little for sedentary pursuits and amusements. Their property, land and cottages hard by, had of late given them a good deal of trouble, and the proposal to sell had more than once been considered, but Mr. Turnbull, most cautious of counsellors, urged delay. Now, at length, the hoped-for opportunity of a good investment seemed to have presented itself; Will's sanguine report of what he had learnt from Sherwood was gladly accepted.

"It'll be a good thing for you as well," said Jane. "Yes, it comes just in time. Sherwood knew what he was doing; now and then I've thought he was risking too much, but he's a clear-headed fellow. The way he has kept things going so long in Ailie Street is really remarkable."

"I daresay you had your share in that, Will," said Mrs. Warburton.

"A very small one; my work has never been more than routine. I don't pretend to be a man of business. If it had depended upon me, the concern would have fallen to pieces years ago, like so many others. House after house has gone down; our turn must have come very soon. As it is, we shall clear out with credit, and start afresh gloriously. By the bye, don't get any but Applegarth's jams in future."

"That depends," said Jane laughing, "if we like them."

In their simple and wholesome way of living, the Warburtons of course dined at midday, and Will, who rarely ate without appetite, surpassed himself as trencherman; nowhere had food such a savour for him as under this roof. The homemade bread and home-grown vegetables he was never tired of praising; such fragrant and toothsome loaves, he loudly protested, were to be eaten nowhere else in England. He began to talk of his holiday abroad, when all at once his countenance fell, his lips closed; in the pleasure of being "at home," he had forgotten all about Norbert Franks, and very unwelcome were the thoughts which attached themselves to this recollection of his days at Trient.

"What's the matter?" asked Jane, noticing his change of look.

"Oh, nothing—a stupid affair. I wrote to you about the Pomfrets and their niece. I'm afraid that girl is an idiot. She used the opportunity of her absence, I find, to break with Franks. No excuse whatever; simply sent him about his business."

"Oh!" exclaimed both the ladies, who had been interested in the artist's love story, as narrated to them, rather badly, by Will on former occasions.

"Of course, I don't know much about it. But it looks bad. Perhaps it's the best thing that could have happened to Franks, for it may mean that he hasn't made money fast enough to please her."

"But you gave us quite another idea of Miss Elvan," said his mother.

"Yes, I daresay I did. Who knows? I don't pretend to understand such things."

A little before sunset came Mr. Turnbull, who took supper at The Haws, and was fetched away by his coachman at ten o'clock. With this old friend, who in Will's eyes looked no older now than when he first knew him in early childhood, they talked freely of the Applegarth business, and Mr. Turnbull promised to make inquiries at once. Of course, he took a despondent view of jam. Jam, he inclined to think, was being overdone; after all, the country could consume only a certain quantity of even the most wholesome preserves, and a glut of jam already threatened the market. Applegarth? By the bye, did he not remember proceedings in bankruptcy connected with that unusual name? He must look into the matter. And, talking about bankruptcy—oh! how bad his lumbago was to-night!—poor Thomas Hart, of Three Ash Farm, was going to be sold up. Dear, dear! On every side, look where one would, nothing but decline and calamity. What was England coming to? Day by day he had expected to see the failure of Sherwood Brothers; how had they escaped the common doom of sugar refiners? Free trade, free trade; all very fine in theory, but look at its results on corn and sugar. For his own part he favoured a policy of moderate protection.

All this was not more than Will had foreseen. It would be annoying if Mr. Turnbull ultimately took an adverse view of his proposal; in that case, though his mother was quite free to manage her property as she chose, Will felt that he should hot venture to urge his scheme against the lawyer's advice, and money must be sought elsewhere. A few days would decide the matter. As he went upstairs to bed, he dismissed worries from his mind.

The old quiet, the old comfort of home. Not a sound but that of pattering rain in the still night. As always, the room smelt of lavender, blended with that indescribable fragrance which comes of extreme cleanliness in an old country house. But for changed wall paper and carpet, everything was as Will remembered it ever since he could remember anything at all; the same simple furniture, the same white curtains, the same pictures, the same little hanging shelf, with books given to him in childhood. He thought of the elder brother who had died at school, and lay in the little churchyard far away. His only dark memory, that of the poor boy's death after a very short illness, before that other blow which made him fatherless.

The earlier retrospect was one of happiness unbroken; for all childish sorrows lost themselves in the very present sense of peace and love enveloping those far-away years. His parents' life, as he saw it then, as in reflection he saw it now, remained an ideal; he did not care to hope for himself, or to imagine, any other form of domestic contentment. As a child, he would have held nothing less conceivable than a moment's discord between father and mother, and manhood's meditation did but confirm him in the same view.

The mutual loyalty of kindred hearts and minds—that was the best life had to give. And Will's thoughts turned once more to Norbert Franks; he, poor fellow, doubtless now raging against the faithlessness which had blackened all his sky. In this moment of softened feeling, of lucid calm, Warburton saw Rosamund's behaviour in a new light. Perhaps she was not blameworthy at all, but rather deserving of all praise; for, if she had come to know, beyond doubt, that she did not love Norbert Franks as she had thought, then to break the engagement was her simple duty, and the courage with which she had taken this step must be set to her credit. Naturally, it would be some time before Franks himself took that view. A third person, whose vanity was not concerned, might moralise thus—

Will checked himself on an unpleasant thought. Was *his* vanity, in truth, unconcerned in this story? Why, then, had he been conscious of a sub-emotion, quite unavowable, which contradicted his indignant sympathy during that talk last night in the street? If the lover's jealousy were as ridiculous as he pretended, why did he feel what now he could confess to himself was an unworthy titillation, when Franks seemed to accuse him of some part in the girl's disloyalty? Vanity, that, sure enough; vanity of a very weak and futile kind. He would stamp the last traces of it out of his being. Happily it was but vanity, and no deeper feeling. Of this he was assured by the reposeful sigh with which he turned his head upon the pillow, drowsing to oblivion.

One unbroken sleep brought him to sunrise; a golden glimmer upon the blind in his return to consciousness told him that the rain was over, and tempted him to look forth. What he saw was decisive; with such a sky as that gleaming over the summer world, who could lie in bed? Will always dressed as if in a fury; seconds sufficed him for details of the toilet, which, had he spent minutes over them, would have fretted his nerves intolerably. His bath was one wild welter—not even the ceiling being safe from splashes; he clad himself in a brief series of plunges; his shaving might have earned the applause of an assembly gathered to behold feats of swift dexterity. Quietly he descended the stairs, and found the house-door already open; this might only mean that the servant was already up, but he suspected that the early riser was Jane. So it proved; he walked toward the kitchen garden, and there stood his sister, the sun making her face rosy.

"Come and help to pick scarlet runners," was her greeting, as he approached. "Aren't they magnificent?"

## CHAPTER 9

Her eyes sparkled with pleasure as she pointed to the heavy clusters of dark-green pods, hanging amid leaves and scarlet bloom.

"Splendid crop!" exclaimed Will, with answering enthusiasm.

"Doesn't the scent do one good?" went on his sister. "When I come into the garden on a morning like this, I have a feeling—oh, I can't describe it to you—perhaps you wouldn't understand—"

"I know," said Will, nodding.

"It's as if nature were calling out to me, like a friend, to come and admire and enjoy what she has done. I feel grateful for the things that earth offers me."

Not often did Jane speak like this; as a rule she was anything but effusive or poetical. But a peculiar animation shone in her looks this morning, and sounded in her voice. Very soon the reason was manifest; she began to speak of the Applegarth business, and declared her great satisfaction with it.

"There'll be an end of mother's worry," she said, "and I can't tell you how glad I shall be. It seems to me that women oughtn't to have to think about money, and mother hates the name of it; she always has done. Oh, what a blessing when it's all off our hands! We shouldn't care, even if the new arrangement brought us less."

"And it is certain to bring you more," remarked Will, "perhaps considerably more."

"Well, I shan't object to that; there are lots of uses for money; but it doesn't matter."

Jane's sincerity was evident. She dismissed the matter, and her basket being full of beans, seized a fork to dig potatoes.

"Here, let me do that," cried Will, interposing.

"You? Well then, as a very great favour."

"Of course I mean that. It's grand to turn up potatoes. What sort are these?"

"Pink-eyed flukes," replied Jane, watching him with keen interest. "We haven't touched them yet."

"Mealy, eh?"

"Balls of flour!"

Their voices joined in a cry of exultation, as the fork threw out even a finer root than they had expected. When enough had been dug, they strolled about, looking at other vegetables. Jane pointed to some Savoy seedlings, which she was going to plant out to-day. Then there sounded a joyous bark, and Pompey came bounding toward them.

"That means the milk-boy is here," said Jane. "Pompey always goes to meet him in the morning. Come and drink a glass—warm."

# CHAPTER 10

Back at Chelsea, Will sent a note to Norbert Franks, a line or two without express reference to what had happened, asking him to come and have a talk. Three days passed, and there was no reply. Will grew uneasy; for, though the artist's silence perhaps meant only sullenness, danger might lurk in such a man's thwarted passion. On the fourth evening, just as he had made up his mind to walk over to Queen's Road, the familiar knock sounded. Mrs. Hopper had left; Will went to the door, and greeted his visitor in the usual way. But Franks entered without speaking. The lamplight showed a pitiful change in him; he was yellow and fishy-eyed, unshaven, disorderly in dress indeed, so well did he look the part of the despairing lover that Warburton suspected a touch of theatric consciousness.

"If you hadn't come to-night," said Will, "I should have looked you up."

Franks lay limply in the armchair, staring blankly.

"I ought to have come before," he replied in low, toneless voice. "That night when I met you, I made a fool of myself. For one thing, I was drunk, and I've been drunk ever since."

"Ha! That accounts for your dirty collar," remarked Will, in his note of dry drollery.

"Is it dirty?" said the other, passing a finger round his neck. "What does it matter? A little dirt more or less, in a world so full of it—"

Warburton could not contain himself; he laughed, and laughed again. And his mirth was contagious; Franks chuckled, unwillingly, dolefully.

"You are not extravagant in sympathy," said the artist, moving with fretful nervousness.

"If I were, would it do you any good, old fellow? Look here, are we to talk of this affair or not? Just as you like. For my part, I'd rather talk about 'The Slummer.' I had a look at it the other day. Uncommonly good, the blackguard on the curbstone, you've got him."

# CHAPTER 10

"You think so?" Franks sat a little straighter, but still with vacant eye. "Yes, not bad, I think. But who knows whether I shall finish the thing."

"If you don't," replied his friend, in a matter-of-fact tone, "you'll do something better. But I should finish it, if I were you. If you had the courage to paint in the right sort of face—the girl, you know."

"What sort of face, then?"

"Sharp-nosed, thin-lipped, rather anaemic, with a universe of self-conceit in the eye."

"They wouldn't hang it, and nobody would buy it. Besides, Warburton, you're wrong if you think the slummers are always that sort. Still, I'm not sure I shan't do it, out of spite. There's another reason, too—I hate beautiful women; I don't think I shall ever be able to paint another."

He sprang up, and paced, as of old, about the room. Will purposely kept silence.

"I've confessed," Franks began again, with effort, "that I made a fool of myself the other night. But I wish you'd tell me something about your time at Trient. Didn't you notice anything? Didn't anything make you suspect what she was going to do?"

"I never for a moment foresaw it," replied Will, with unemphasised sincerity.

"Yet she must have made up her mind whilst you were there. Her astounding hypocrisy! I had a letter a few days before, the same as usual—"

"Quite the same?"

"Absolutely!—Well, there was no difference that struck me. Then all at once she declares that for months she had felt her position false and painful. What a monstrous thing! Why did she go on pretending, playing a farce? I could have sworn that no girl lived who was more thoroughly honest in word and deed and thought. It's awful to think how one can be deceived. I understand now the novels about unfaithful wives, and all that kind of thing. I always said to myself—'Pooh, as if a fellow wouldn't know if his wife were deceiving him'! By Jove this has made me afraid of the thought of marriage. I shall never again trust a woman."

Warburton sat in meditation, only half smiling.

"Of course, she's ashamed to face me. For fear I should run after her, she wrote that they were just leaving Trient for another place, not mentioned. If I wrote, I was to address to Bath, and the letter would be forwarded. I wrote—of course a fool's letter; I only wish I'd never sent it. Sometimes I think I'll never try to see her again; sometimes I think I'll make her see me, and tell her the truth about herself. The only thing is—I'm half afraid—I've gone through torture enough; I don't want to begin again. Yet if I saw her—"

He took another turn across the room, then checked himself before Warburton.

"Tell me honestly what you think about it. I want advice. What's your opinion of her?"

"I have no opinion at all. I don't pretend to know her well enough."

"Well, but," persisted Franks, "your impression—your feeling. How does the thing strike you?"

"Why, disagreeably enough; that's a matter of course."

"You don't excuse her?" asked Norbert, his eyes fixed on the other.

"I can imagine excuses—"

"What? What excuse can there be for deliberate hypocrisy, treachery?"

"If it *was* deliberate," replied Warburton, "there's nothing to be said. In your position—since you ask advice—I should try to think that it wasn't, but that the girl had simply changed her mind, and went on and on, struggling with herself till she could stand it no longer. I've no taste for melodrama quiet comedy is much more in my line—comedy ending with mutual tolerance and forgiveness. To be sure, if you feel you can't live without her, if you're determined to fight for her—"

"Fight with whom?" cried Franks.

"With *her*; then read Browning, and blaze away. It may be the best; who can tell? Only—on this point I am clear—no self-deception! Don't go in for heroics just because they seem fine. Settle with yourself whether she is indispensable to you or not.— Indispensable? why, no woman is that to any man; sooner or later, it's a matter of indifference. And if you feel, talking plainly with yourself, that the worst is over already, that it doesn't after all matter as much as you thought; why, get back to your painting. If you can paint only ugly women, so much the better, I've no doubt."

Franks stood reflecting. Then he nodded.

"All that is sensible enough. But, if I give her up, I shall marry some one else straight away."

Then he abruptly said good-night, leaving Warburton not unhopeful about him, and much consoled by the disappearance of the shadow which had threatened their good understanding.

# CHAPTER 11

The Crosses, mother and daughter, lived at Walham Green. The house was less pleasant than another which Mrs. Cross owned at Putney, but it also represented a lower rental, and poverty obliged them to take this into account. When the second house stood tenantless, as had now been the case for half a year, Mrs. Cross' habitually querulous comment on life rose to a note of acrimony very afflictive to her daughter Bertha. The two bore as little resemblance to each other, physical or mental, as mother and child well could. Bertha Cross was a sensible, thoughtful girl, full of kindly feeling, and blest with a humorous turn that enabled her to see the amusing rather than the carking side of her pinched life. These virtues she had from her father. Poor Cross, who supplemented a small income from office routine by occasional comic journalism, and even wrote a farce (which brought money to a theatrical manager), made on his deathbed a characteristic joke. He had just signed his will, and was left alone with his wife. "I'm sure I've, always wished to make your life happy," piped the afflicted woman. "And I yours," he faintly answered; adding, with a sad, kind smile, as he pointed to the testamentary document, "Take the will for the deed."

The two sons had emigrated to British Columbia, and Bertha would not have been sorry to join her brothers there, for domestic labour on a farm, in peace and health, seemed to her considerably better than the quasi-genteel life she painfully supported. She had never dreamt of being an artist, but, showing some facility with the pencil, was sent by her father to South Kensington, where she met and made friends with Rosamund Elvan. Her necessity and her application being greater than Rosamund's, Bertha before long succeeded in earning a little money; without this help, life at home would scarcely have been possible for her. They might, to be sure, have taken a lodger, having spare rooms, but Mrs. Cross could only face that possibility if the person received into the house were "respectable" enough to be called a paying guest, and no such person offered. So they lived, as no end of "respectable" families do, a life of penury and seclusion, sometimes going without a meal that they might have decent clothing to wear abroad, never able to buy a book, to hear a concert, and only by painful sacrifice able to entertain a friend. When, on a certain occasion, Miss Elvan passed a week at their house (Mrs. Cross approved of this friendship, and hoped it might be a means of discovering the paying guest), it meant for them a near approach to starvation during the month that ensued.

Time would have weighed heavily on Mrs. Cross but for her one recreation, which was perennial, ever fresh, constantly full of surprises and excitement. Poor as she was, she contrived to hire a domestic servant; to say that she "kept" one would come near to a verbal impropriety, seeing that no servant ever remained in the house for more than a few months, whilst it occasionally happened that the space of half a year would see a succession of some half dozen "generals." Underpaid and underfed, these persons (they varied in age from fourteen to forty) were of course incompetent, careless, rebellious, and Mrs. Cross found the sole genuine pleasure of her life in the war she waged with them. Having no reasonable way of spending her hours, she was thus supplied with occupation; being of acrid temper, she was thus supplied with a subject upon whom she could fearlessly exercise it; being remarkably mean of disposition, she saw in the paring-down of her servant's rations to a working minimum, at once profit and sport; lastly, being fond of the most trivial gossip, she had a never-failing topic of discussion with such ladies as could endure her society.

Bertha, having been accustomed to this domestic turbulence all her life long, for the most part paid no heed to it. She knew that if the management of the house were in her hands, instead of her mother's, things would go much more smoothly, but the mere suggestion of such a change (ventured once at a moment of acute crisis) had so amazed and exasperated Mrs. Cross, that Bertha never again looked in that direction. Yet from time to time a revolt of common sense forced her to speak, and as the only possible way, if quarrel were to be avoided, she began her remonstrance on the humorous note. Then when her mother had been wearying her for half an hour with complaints and lamentations over the misdoings of one Emma, Bertha as the alternative to throwing up her hands and rushing out of the house, began laughing to herself, whereat Mrs. Cross indignantly begged to be informed what there was so very amusing in a state of affairs which would assuredly bring her to her grave.

"If only you could see the comical side of it, mother," replied Bertha. "It really has one, you know. Emma, if only you would be patient with her, is a well-meaning creature, and she says the funniest things. I asked her this morning if she didn't think she could find some way of remembering to put the salt on the table. And she looked at me very solemnly, and said, 'Indeed, I will, miss. I'll put it into my prayers, just after 'our daily bread.'"

Mrs. Cross saw nothing in this but profanity. She turned the attack on Bertha, who, by her soft way of speaking, simply encouraged the servants, she declared, in negligence and insolence.

"Look at it in this way, mother," replied the girl, as soon as she was suffered to speak. "To be badly served is bad enough, in itself; why make it worse by ceaseless talking about it, so leaving ourselves not a moment of peace and quiet? I'm sure I'd rather put the salt on the table myself at every meal, and think no more about it, than worry, worry, worry over the missing salt-cellars from one meal to the next. Don't you feel, dear mother, that it's shocking waste of life?"

"What nonsense you talk, child! Are we to live in dirt and disorder? Am I *never* to correct a servant, or teach her her duties? But of course everything *I* do is wrong. Of course *you* could do everything so very much better. That's what children are nowadays."

Whilst Mrs. Cross piped on, Bertha regarded her with eyes of humorous sadness. The girl often felt it a dreary thing not to be able to respect—nay, not to be able to feel much love for—her mother. At such times, her thought turned to the other parent, with whom, had he and she been left alone, she could have lived so happily, in so much mutual intelligence and affection. She sighed and moved away.

The unlet house was a very serious matter, and when one day Norbert Franks came to talk about it, saying that he would want a house very soon, and thought this of Mrs. Cross's might suit him, Bertha rejoiced no less than her mother. In consequence of the artist's announcement, she wrote to her friend Rosamund, saying how glad she was to hear that her marriage approached. The reply to this letter surprised her. Rosamund had been remiss in correspondence for the last few months; her few and brief letters, though they were as affectionate as ever, making no mention of what had formerly been an inexhaustible topic—the genius, goodness, and brilliant hopes of Franks. Now she wrote as if in utter despondency, a letter so confused in style and vague in expression, that Bertha could gather from it little or nothing except a grave doubt whether Franks' marriage was as near as he supposed. A week or two passed, and Rosamund again wrote—from Switzerland; again the letter was an unintelligible maze of dreary words, and a mere moaning and sighing, which puzzled Bertha as much as it distressed her. Rosamund's epistolary style, when she wrote to this bosom friend, was always pitched in a key of lyrical emotion, which now and then would have been trying to Bertha's sense of humour but for the sincerity manifest in every word; hitherto, however, she had expressed herself with perfect lucidity, and this sudden change seemed ominous of alarming things. Just when Bertha was anxiously wondering what could have happened,—of course inclined to attribute blame, if blame there were, to the artist rather than to his betrothed—a stranger came to inquire about the house to let. It was necessary to ascertain at once whether Mr. Franks intended to become their tenant or not. Mrs. Cross wrote to him, and received the briefest possible reply, to the effect that his plans were changed.

"How vexatious!" exclaimed Mrs. Cross. "I had very much rather have let to people we know I suppose he's seen a house that suits him better."

"I think there's another reason," said Bertha, after gazing for a minute or two at the scribbled, careless note. "The marriage is put off."

"And you knew that," cried her mother, "all the time, and never told me! And I might have missed twenty chances of letting. Really, Bertha, I never did see anything like you. There's that house standing empty month after month, and we hardly know where to turn for money, and you knew that Mr. Franks wouldn't take it, and yet you say not a word! How can you behave in such an extraordinary way? I think you really find pleasure in worrying me. Any one would fancy you wished to see me in my grave. To think that you knew all the time!"

## CHAPTER 12

There passed a fortnight. Bertha heard nothing more of Miss Elvan, till a letter arrived one morning in an envelope, showing on the back an address at Teddington. Rosamund wrote that she had just returned from Switzerland, and was staying for a few days with friends; would it be possible for Bertha to come to Teddington the same afternoon, for an hour or two's talk? The writer had so much to say that could not be conveyed in a letter, and longed above all things to see Bertha, the only being in whom, at a very grave juncture in her life, she could absolutely confide. "We shall be quite alone—Mr. and Mrs. Capron are going to town immediately after lunch. This is a lovely place, and we shall have it to ourselves all the afternoon. So don't be frightened—I know how you hate strangers—but come, come, come!"

Bertha took train early in the afternoon. By an avenue of elms she passed into a large and beautiful garden, and so came to the imposing front door. Led into the drawing-room, she had time to take breath, and to gaze at splendours such as she had never seen before; then with soundless footfall, entered a slim, prettily-dressed girl who ran towards her, and caught her hands, and kissed her with graceful tenderness.

"My dear, dear old Bertha! What a happiness to see you again! How good of you to come! Isn't it a lovely place? And the nicest people. You've heard me speak of Miss Anderton, of Bath. She is Mrs. Capron—married half a year ago. And they're just going to Egypt for a year, and—what do you think?—I'm going with them."

Rosamund's voice sunk and faltered. She stood holding Bertha's hands, and gazing into her face with eyes which grew large as if in a distressful appeal.

"To Egypt?"

"Yes. It was decided whilst I was in Switzerland. Mrs. Capron wants a friend to be with her; one who can help her in water-colours. She thought, of course, that I couldn't go; wrote to me just wishing it were possible. And I caught at the chance! Oh, caught at it!"

"That's what I don't understand," said Bertha.

"I want to explain it all. Come into this cosy corner. Nobody will disturb us except when they bring tea.—Do you know that picture of Leader's? Isn't it exquisite!—Are you tired, Bertha? You look so, a little. I'm afraid you walked from the station, and it's such a hot day. But oh, the loveliness of the trees about here! Do you remember our first walk together? You were shy, stiff; didn't feel quite sure whether you liked me or not. And I thought you—just a little critical. But before we got back again, I think we had begun to understand each other. And I wonder whether you'll understand me now. It would be dreadful if I felt you disapproved of me. Of course if you do, I'd much rather you said so. You will—won't you?"

She again fixed her eyes upon Bertha with the wide, appealing look.

"Whether I say it or not," replied the other, "you'll see what I think. I never could help that."

"That's what I love in you! And that's what I've been thinking of, all these weeks of misery—your perfect sincerity. I've asked myself whether it would be possible for you to find yourself in such a position as mine; and how you would act, how you would speak. You're my ideal of truth and rightness, Bertha; I've often enough told you that."

Bertha moved uncomfortably, her eyes averted.

"Suppose you just tell me what has happened," she added quietly.

"Yes, I will. I hope you haven't been thinking it was some fault of *his*?"

"I couldn't help thinking that."

"Oh! Put that out of your mind at once. The fault is altogether mine. He has done nothing whatever—he is good and true, and all that a man should be. It's I who am behaving badly; so badly that I feel hot with shame now that I come to tell you. I have broken it off. I've said I couldn't marry him."

Their eyes met for an instant. Bertha looked rather grave, but with her wonted kindliness of expression; Rosamund's brows were wrinkled in distress, and her lips trembled.

"I've seen it coming since last Christmas," she continued, in a hurried, tremulous undertone. "You know he came down to Bath; that was our last meeting; and I felt that something was wrong. Ah, so hard to know oneself! I wanted to talk to you about it; but then I said to myself—what can Bertha do but tell me to know my own mind? And that's just what I couldn't come to,—to understand my own feelings. I was changing, I knew that. I dreaded to look into my own thoughts, from day to day. Above all, I dreaded to sit down and write to him.

Oh, the hateful falsity of those letters—Yet what could I do, what could I do? I had no right to give such a blow, unless I felt that anything else was utterly, utterly impossible."

"And at last you did feel it?"

"In Switzerland—yes. It came like a flash of lightning. I was walking up that splendid valley—you remember my description—up toward the glacier. That morning I had had a letter, naming the very day for our marriage, and speaking of the house—your house at Putney—he meant to take. I had said to myself—'It must be; I can do nothing. I haven't the courage.' Then, as I was walking, a sort of horror fell upon me, and made me tremble; and when it passed I saw that, so far from not having the courage to break, I should never dare to go through with it. And I went back to the hotel, and sat down and wrote, without another moment's thought or hesitation."

"What else could you have done?" said Bertha, with a sigh of relief. "When it comes to horror and tremblings!"

There was a light in her eye which seemed the precursor of a smile; but her voice was not unsympathetic, and Rosamund knew that one of Bertha Cross smiles was worth more in the way of friendship than another's tragic emotion.

"Have patience with me," she continued, "whilst I try to explain it all. The worst of my position is, that so many people will know what I have done, and so few of them, hardly any one, will understand why. One can't talk to people about such things. Even Winnie and father—I'm sure they don't really understand—though I'm afraid they're both rather glad. What a wretched thing it is to be misjudged. I feel sure, Bertha, that it's just this kind of thing that makes a woman sit down and write a novel—where she can speak freely in disguise, and do herself justice. Don't you think so?"

"I shouldn't wonder," replied the listener, thoughtfully. "But does it really matter? If you know you're only doing what you must do?"

"But that's only how it seems to me. Another, in my place, would very likely see the must on the other side. Of course it's a terribly complicated thing—a situation like this. I haven't the slightest idea how one ought to be guided. One could argue and reason all day long about it—as I have done with myself for weeks past."

"Try just to tell me the reason which seems to you the strongest," said Bertha.

"That's very simple. I thought I loved him, and I find I don't."

"Exactly. But I hardly see how the change came about."

"I will try to tell you," replied Rosamund. "It was that picture, 'Sanctuary,' that began it. When I first saw it, it gave me a shock. You know how I have always thought of him—an artist living for his own idea of art, painting just as he liked, what pleased him, without caring for the public taste. I got enthusiastic; and when I saw that he seemed to care for my opinion and my praise—of course all the rest followed. He told me about his life as an art student—Paris, Rome, all that; and it was my ideal of romance. He was very poor, sometimes so poor that he hardly had enough to eat, and this made me proud of him, for I felt sure he could have got money if he would have condescended to do inferior work. Of course, as I too was poor, we could not think of marrying before his position improved. At last he painted 'Sanctuary.' He told me nothing about it. I came and saw it on the easel, nearly finished. And—this is the shocking thing—I pretended to admire it. I was astonished, pained—yet I had the worldliness to smile and praise. There's the fault of my character. At that moment, truth and courage were wanted, and I had neither. The dreadful thing is to think that he degraded himself on my account. If I had said at once what I thought, he would have confessed—would have told me that impatience had made him untrue to himself. And from that day; oh, this is the worst of all, Bertha—he has adapted himself to what he thinks my lower mind and lower aims; he has consciously debased himself, out of thought for me. Horrible! Of course he believes in his heart that I was a hypocrite before. The astonishing thing is that this didn't cause him to turn cold to me. He must have felt that, but somehow he overcame it. All the worse! The very fact that he still cared for me shows how bad my influence has been. I feel that I have wrecked his life, Bertha—and yet I cannot give him my own, to make some poor sort of amends."

Bertha was listening with a face that changed from puzzled interest to wondering confusion.

"Good gracious!" she exclaimed when the speaker ceased. "Is it possible to get into such entanglements of reasoning about what one thinks and feels? It's beyond me. Oh they're bringing the tea. Perhaps a cup of tea will clear my wits."

Rosamund at once began to speak of the landscape by Leader, which hung near them, and continued to do so even after the servant had withdrawn. Her companion was silent, smiling now and then in an absent way. They sipped tea.

"The tea is doing me so much good," Bertha said, "I begin to feel equal to the most complicated reflections. And so you really believe that Mr. Franks is on the way to perdition, and that you are the cause of it?"

Rosamund did not reply. She had half averted her look; her brows were knit in an expression of trouble; she bit her lower lip. A moment passed, and—

"Suppose we go into the garden," she said, rising. "Don't you feel it a little close here?"

They strolled about the paths. Her companion, seeming to have dismissed from mind their subject of conversation, began to talk of Egypt, and the delight she promised herself there.

Presently Bertha reverted to the unfinished story.

"Oh, it doesn't interest you."

"Doesn't it indeed! Please go on. You had just explained all about 'Sanctuary'—which isn't really a bad picture at all."

"Oh, Bertha!" cried the other in pained protest. "That's your good nature. You never can speak severely of anybody's work. The picture is shameful, shameful! And its successor, I am too sure, will be worse still, from what I have heard of it. Oh, I can't bear to think of what it all means—Now that it's too late, I see what I ought to have done. In spite of everything and everybody I ought to have married him in the first year, when I had courage and hope enough to face any hardships. We spoke of it, but he was too generous. What a splendid thing to have starved with him—to have worked for him whilst he was working for art and fame, to have gone through and that together, and have come out triumphant! That was a life worth living. But to begin marriage at one's ease on the profits of pictures such as 'Sanctuary'—oh, the shame of it! Do you think I could face the friends who would come to see me?"

"How many friends," asked Bertha, "would be aware of your infamy? I credit myself with a little imagination. But I should never have suspected the black baseness which had poisoned your soul."

Again Rosamund bit her lip, and kept a short silence.

"It only shows," she said with some abruptness, "that I shall do better not to speak of it at all, and let people think what they like of me. If even *you* can't understand."

Bertha stood still, and spoke in a changed voice.

"I understand very well—or think I do. I'm perfectly sure that you could never have broken your engagement unless for the gravest reason—and for me it is quite enough to know that. Many a girl ought to do this, who never has the courage. Try not to worry about explanations, the thing is done, and there's an end of it. I'm very glad indeed you're going quite away; it's the best thing possible. When do you start?" she added.

"In three days.—Listen, Bertha, I have something very serious to ask of you. It is possible—isn't it?—that he may come to see you some day. If he does, or if by chance you see him alone, and if he speaks of me, I want you to make him think—you easily can—that what has happened is all for his good. Remind him how often artists have been spoilt by marriage, and hint—you surely could—that I am rather too fond of luxury, and that kind of thing."

Bertha wore an odd smile.

"Trust me," she replied, "I will blacken you most effectually."

"You promise? But, at the same time, you will urge him to be true to himself, to endure poverty—"

"I don't know about that. Why shouldn't poor Mr. Franks have enough to eat it he can get it?"

"Well—but you promise to help him in the other way? You needn't say very bad things; just a smile, a hint—"

"I quite understand," said Bertha, nodding.

# CHAPTER 13

Warburton had never seen Godfrey Sherwood so restless and excitable as during these weeks when the business in Little Ailie Street was being brought to an end, and the details of the transfer to Bristol were being settled. Had it not been inconsistent with all the hopeful facts of the situation, as well as with the man's temper, one would have thought that Godfrey suffered from extreme nervousness; that he lived under some oppressive anxiety, which it was his constant endeavour to combat with resolute high spirits. It seemed an odd thing that a man who had gone through the very real cares and perils of the last few years without a sign of perturbation, nay, with the cheeriest equanimity, should let himself be thrown into disorder by the mere change to a more promising state of things. Now and then Warburton asked himself whether his partner could be concealing some troublesome fact with regard to Applegarth's concern; but he dismissed the idea as too improbable; Sherwood was far too good a fellow, far too conscientious a man of business, to involve his friend in obvious risk—especially since it had been decided that Mrs. Warburton's and her money should go into the affair. The inquiries made by Mr. Turnbull had results so satisfactory that even the resolute pessimist could not but grudgingly admit his inability to discover storm-signals. Though a sense of responsibility made a new element in his life, which would not let him sleep quite so soundly as hitherto, Will persuaded himself that he had but to get to work, and all would be right.

The impression made upon him by Applegarth himself was very favourable. The fact that the jam manufacturer was a university man, an astronomer, and a musician, had touched Warburton's weak point, and he went down to Bristol the first time with an undeniable prejudice at the back of his mind; but this did not survive a day or two's intercourse. Applegarth recommended himself by an easy and humorous geniality of bearing which Warburton would have been the last man to resist; he talked of his affairs with the utmost frankness.

"The astonishing thing to me is," he said, "that I've made this business pay. I went into it on abstract principle. I knew nothing of business. At school, I rather think, I learnt something about 'single and double entry,' but I had forgotten it all—just as I find myself forgetting how to multiply and divide, now that I am accustomed to the higher mathematics. However, I had to earn a little money, somehow, and I thought I'd try jam. And it went by itself, I really don't understand it, mere good luck, I suppose. I hear of fellows who have tried business, and come shocking croppers. Perhaps they were classical men nothing so hopeless as your classic. I beg your pardon; before saying that, I ought to have found out whether either of you is a classic."

The listeners both shook their heads, and laughed.

"So much the better. An astronomer, it is plain, may manufacture jam; a fellow brought up on Greek and Latin verses couldn't possibly."

They were together at Bristol for a week, then Sherwood received a telegram, and told Warburton that he must return to London immediately.

"Something that bothers you?" said Will, noting a peculiar tremor on his friend's countenance.

"No, no; a private affair; nothing to do with us. You stay on till Saturday? I might be back in twenty-four hours."

"Good. Yes; I want to have some more talk with Applegarth about that advertising proposal. I don't like to start with quite such a heavy outlay."

"Nor I either," replied Godfrey, his eyes wandering. He paused, bit the end of his moustache, and added. "By the bye, the St. Neots money will be paid on Saturday, you said?"

"I believe so. Or early next week."

"That's right. I want to get done. Queer how these details fidget me. Nerves! I ought to have had a holiday this summer. You were wiser."

The next day Warburton went out with Applegarth to his house some ten miles south of Bristol, and dined there, and stayed overnight. It had not yet been settled where he and Sherwood should have their permanent abode; there was a suggestion that they should share a house which was to let not far from Applegarth's, but Will felt uneasy at the thought of a joint tenancy, doubting whether he could live in comfort with any man. He was vexed at having to leave his flat in Chelsea, which so thoroughly suited his habits and his tastes.

Warburton and his host talked much of Sherwood.

"When I first met him," said the jam-manufacturer, "he struck me as the queerest man of business—except myself—that I had ever seen.

He talked about Norse sagas, witchcraft, and so on, and when he began about business, I felt uneasy. Of course I know him better now."

"There are not many steadier and shrewder men than Sherwood," remarked Will.

"I feel sure of that," replied the other. And he added, as if to fortify himself in the opinion: "Yes, I feel sure of it."

"In spite of all his energy, never rash."

"No, no; I can see that. Yet," added Applegarth, again as if for self-confirmation, "he has energy of an uncommon kind."

"That will soon show itself," replied Warburton, smiling. "He's surveying the field like a general before battle."

"Yes. No end of bright ideas. Some of them—perhaps—not immediately practicable."

"Oh, Sherwood looks far ahead."

Applegarth nodded, and for a minute or two each was occupied with his own reflections.

# CHAPTER 14

Godfrey having telegraphed that he must remain in town, Warburton soon joined him. His partner was more cheerful and sanguine than ever; he had cleared off numberless odds and ends of business; there remained little to be done before the day, a week hence, appointed for the signature of the new deed, for which purpose Applegarth would come to London. Mr. Turnbull, acting with his wonted caution, had at length concluded the sale of Mrs. Warburton's property, and on the day after his return, Will received from St. Neots a letter containing a cheque for four thousand pounds! All his own available capital was already in the hands of Sherwood; a sum not much greater in amount than that invested by his mother and sister. Sherwood, for his part, put in sixteen thousand, with regrets that it was all he had at command just now; before long, he might see his way greatly to increase their capital, but they had enough for moderate enterprise in the meanwhile.

Not half an hour after the post which brought him the cheque, Warburton was surprised by a visit from his friend.

"I thought you wouldn't have left home yet," said Godfrey, with a nervous laugh. "I had a letter from Applegarth last night, which I wanted you to see at once."

He handed it, and Will, glancing over the sheet, found only an unimportant discussion of a small detail.

"Well, that's all right," he said, "but I don't see that it need have brought you from Wimbledon to Chelsea before nine o'clock in the morning. Aren't you getting a little overstrung, old man?"

Godfrey looked it. His face was noticeably thinner than a month ago, and his eyes had a troubled fixity such as comes of intense preoccupation.

"Daresay I am," he admitted with a show of careless good-humour. "Can't get much sleep lately."

"But why? What the deuce is there to fuss about? Sit down and smoke a cigar. I suppose you've had breakfast?"

"No—yes, I mean, yes, of course, long ago."

Will did not believe the corrected statement. He gazed at his friend curiously and with some anxiety.

"It's an unaccountable thing that you should fret your gizzard out about this new affair, which seems all so smooth, when you took the Ailie Street worries without turning a hair."

"Stupid—nerves out of order," muttered Godfrey, as he crossed, uncrossed, recrossed his legs, and bit at a cigar, as if he meant to breakfast on it. "I must get away for a week or two as soon as we've signed."

"Yes, but look here." Warburton stood before him, hands on hips, regarding him gravely, and speaking with decision. "I don't quite understand you. You're not like yourself. Is there anything you're keeping from me?"

"Nothing—nothing whatever, I assure you, Warburton."

But Will was only half satisfied.

"You have no doubts of Applegarth?"

"Doubts!" cried the other. "Not a shadow of doubt of any sort, I declare and protest. No, no; it's entirely my own idiotic excitability. I can't account for it. Just don't notice it, there's a good fellow."

"There was a pause. Will glanced again at Applegarth's note, whilst Sherwood went, as usual, to stand before the bookcase, and run his eye along the shelves.

"Anything new in my way?" he asked. "I want a good long quiet read. —Palgrave's *Arabia*! Where did you pick up that? One of the most glorious books I know. That and Layard's *Early Travels* sent me to heaven for a month, once upon a time. You don't know Layard? I must give it to you. The essence of romance! As good in its way as the *Arabian Nights*."

Thus he talked on for a quarter of an hour, and it seemed to relieve him. Returning to matters of the day, he asked, half abruptly:

"Have you the St. Neots cheque yet?"

"Came this morning."

"Payable to Sherwood Brothers, I suppose?" said Godfrey. "Right. It's most convenient so."

Will handed him the cheque, and he gazed at it as if with peculiar satisfaction. He sat smiling, cheque in one hand, cigar in the other, until Warburton asked what he was thinking over.

"Nothing—nothing. Well, I suppose I'd better take it with me; I'm on my way to the bank."

As Will watched the little slip of paper disappear into his friend's pocket-book, he had an unaccountable feeling of disquiet. Nothing could be more unworthy than distrust of Godfrey Sherwood; nothing less consonant with all his experience of the man; and, had the money been his, he would have handed it over as confidently as when, in fact, dealing with his own capital the other day. But the sense of responsibility to others was a new thing to which he could not yet accustom himself. It occurred to him for the first time that there was no necessity for accumulating these funds in the hands of Sherwood; he might just as well have retained his own money and this cheque until the day of the signing of the new deed. To be sure, he had only to reflect a moment to see the foolishness of his misgiving; yet, had he thought of it before—

He, too, was perhaps a little overstrung in the nerves. Not for the first time, he mentally threw a malediction at business, and all its sordid appurtenances.

A change came over Sherwood. His smile grew more natural; his eye lost its fixity; he puffed at his cigar with enjoyment.

"What news of Franks?" were his next words.

"Nothing very good," answered Will, frowning. "He seems to be still playing the fool. I've seen him only once in the last fortnight, and then it was evident he'd been drinking. I couldn't help saying a plain word or two, and he turned sullen. I called at his place last night, but he wasn't there; his landlady tells me he's been out of town several times lately, and he's done no work."

"Has the girl gone?"

"A week ago. I have a letter from Ralph Pomfret. The good old chap worries about this affair; so does Mrs. Pomfret. He doesn't say it plainly, but I suspect Franks has been behaving theatrically down at Ashstead; it's possible he went there in the same state in which I saw him last. Pomfret would have done well to punch his head, but I've no doubt they've stroked and patted and poor-fellow'd him—the very worst thing for Franks."

"Or for any man," remarked Sherwood.

"Worse for him than for most. I wish I had more of the gift of brutality; I see a way in which I might do him good; but it goes against the grain with me."

"That I can believe," said Godfrey, with his pleasantest look and nod.

"I was afraid he might somehow scrape together money enough to pursue her to Egypt. Perhaps he's trying for that. The Pomfrets want me to go down to Ashstead and have a talk with them about him. Whether he managed to see the girl before she left England, I don't know."

"After all, he *has* been badly treated," said Sherwood sympathetically.

"Well, yes, he has. But a fellow must have common sense, most of all with regard to women. I'm rather afraid Franks might think it a fine thing to go to the devil because he's been jilted. It isn't fashionable nowadays; there might seem to be a sort of originality about it."

They talked for a few minutes of business matters, and Sherwood briskly went his way.

Four days passed. Warburton paid a visit to the Pomfrets, and had from them a confirmation of all he suspected regarding Norbert Franks. The artist's behaviour at Ashstead had been very theatrical indeed; he talked much of suicide, preferably by the way of drink, and, when dissuaded from this, with a burst of tears—veritable tears—begged Ralph Pomfret to lend him money enough to go to Cairo; on which point, also, he met with kindliest opposition. Thereupon, he had raged for half an hour against some treacherous friend, unnamed. Who this could be, the Pomfrets had no idea. Warburton, though he affected equal ignorance, could not doubt but that it was himself, and he grew inwardly angry. Franks had been to Bath, and had obtained a private interview with Winifred Elvan, in which (Winifred wrote to her aunt) he had demeaned himself very humbly and pathetically, first of all imploring the sister's help with Rosamund, and, when she declared she could do nothing, entreating to be told whether or not he was ousted by a rival. Rather impatient with the artist's follies than troubled about his sufferings, Will came home again. He wrote a brief, not unfriendly letter to Franks, urging him to return to his better mind—the half-disdainful, half-philosophical resignation which he seemed to have attained a month ago. The answer to this was a couple of lines; "Thanks. Your advice, no doubt, is well meant, but I had rather not have it just now. Don't let us meet for the present." Will shrugged his shoulders, and tried to forget all about the affair.

He did not see Sherwood, but had a note from him written in high spirits. Applegarth would be in town two days hence, and all three were to dine at his hotel. Having no occupation, Warburton spent most of his time in walking about London; but these rambles did not give him the wonted pleasure, and though at night he was very tired, he did not sleep well. An inexplicable nervousness interfered with all his habits of mind and body He was on the point of running down to St.

Neots, to get through the last day of intolerable idleness, when the morning post again brought a letter from Sherwood.

"Confound the fellow!" he muttered, as he tore open the envelope. "What else can he have to say? No infernal postponement, I hope—"

He read the first line and drew himself up like a man pierced with pain.

> "My dear Warburton"—thus wrote his partner, in a hand less legible than of wont—"I have such bad news for you that I hardly know how to tell it. If I dared, I would come to you at once, but I simply have not the courage to face you until you know the worst, and have had time to get accustomed to it. It is seven o'clock; an hour ago I learnt that all our money is lost—all yours, all that from St. Neots, all mine—every penny I have. I have been guilty of unpardonable folly—how explain my behaviour? The truth is, after the settlement in Little Ailie Street; I found myself much worse off than I had expected. I went into the money market, and made a successful deal. Counting on being able to repeat this, I guaranteed the sixteen thousand for Bristol; but the second time I lost. So it has gone on; all these last weeks I have been speculating, winning and losing. Last Tuesday, when I came to see you, I had about twelve thousand, and hoped somehow to make up the deficiency. As the devil would have it, that same morning I met a City acquaintance, who spoke of a great *coup* to be made by any one who had some fifteen thousand at command. It meant an immediate profit of 25 per cent. Like a fool, I was persuaded—as you will see when I go into details, the thing looked horribly tempting. I put it all—every penny that lay at our bank in the name of Sherwood Bros. And now I learn that the house I trusted has smashed. It's in the papers this evening—Biggles, Thorpe and Biggles—you'll see it. I dare not ask you to forgive me. Of course I shall at once take steps to raise the money owing to you, and hope to be able to do that soon, but it's all over with the Bristol affair. I shall come to see you at twelve tomorrow.
>
> "Yours,
>
> "G. F. SHERWOOD."

## CHAPTER 15

"After all, there's something in presentiment."

This was the first thought that took shape in Will's whirling mind. The second was, that he might rationally have foreseen disaster. All the points of strangeness which had struck him in Sherwood's behaviour came back now with such glaring significance that he accused himself of inconceivable limpness in having allowed things to go their way—above all in trusting Godfrey with the St. Neots cheque. On this moment of painful lucidity followed blind rage. Why, what a grovelling imbecile was this fellow! To plunge into wild speculation, on the word of some City shark, with money not his own! But could one credit the story? Was it not more likely that Sherwood had got involved in some cunning thievery which he durst not avow? Perhaps he was a mere liar and hypocrite. That story of the ten thousand pounds he had lent to somebody—how improbable it sounded; why might he not have invented it, to strengthen confidence at a critical moment? The incredible baseness of the man! He, who knew well all that depended upon the safe investment of the St. Neots money—to risk it in this furiously reckless way. In all the records of City scoundrelism, was there a blacker case?

Raging thus, Warburton became aware that Mrs. Hopper spoke to him. She had just laid breakfast, and, as usual when she wished to begin a conversation, had drawn back to the door, where she paused.

"That Boxon, the grocer, has had a bad accident, sir."

"Boxon?—grocer?"

"In the Fulham Road, sir; him as Allchin was with."

"Ah!"

Heedless of her master's gloomy abstraction, Mrs. Hopper continued. She related that Boxon had been at certain races where he had lost money and got drunk; driving away in a trap, he had run into something, and been thrown out, with serious injuries, which might prove fatal.

"So much the worse for him," muttered Warburton. "I've no pity to spare for fools and blackguards."

"I should think not, indeed sir. I just mentioned it, sir, because Allchin was telling us about it last night. He and his wife looked in to see my sister, Liza, and they both said they never see such a change in anybody. And they said how grateful we ought to be to you, sir, and that I'm sure we are, for Liza'd never have been able to go away without your kindness."

Listening as if this talk sounded from a vague distance, Warburton was suddenly reminded of what had befallen himself; for as yet he had thought only of his mother and sister. He was ruined. Some two or three hundred pounds, his private bank account, represented all he had in the world, and all prospect of making money had been taken away from him. Henceforth, small must be his charities. If he gained his own living, he must count himself lucky; nothing more difficult than for a man of his age and position, unexpectedly cut adrift, to find work and payment. By good fortune, his lease of this flat came to an end at Michaelmas, and already he had given notice that he did not mean to renew. Mrs. Hopper knew that he was on the point of leaving London, and mot a little lamented it, for to her the loss would be serious indeed. Warburton's habitual generosity led her to hope for some signal benefaction ere his departure; perhaps on that account she was specially emphatic in gratitude for her sister's restoration to health.

"We was wondering, sir," she added, now having wedged herself between door and jamb, "whether you'd be so kind as to let my sister Liza see you just for a minute or two, to thank you herself as I'm sure she ought? She could come any time as wouldn't be ill-convenient to you."

"I'm extremely busy, Mrs. Hopper," Will replied. "Please tell your sister I'm delighted to hear she's done so well at Southend, and I hope to see her some day; but not just now. By the bye, I'm not going out this morning, so don't wait, when you've finished."

By force of habit he ate and drank. Sherwood's letter lay open before him; he read it through again and again. But he could not fix his thoughts upon it. He found himself occupied with the story of Boxon, wondering whether Boxon would live or die. Boxon, the grocer—why, what an ass a man must be, a man with a good grocery business, to come to grief over drink and betting! Shopkeeping—what a sound and safe life it was; independent, as far as any money-earning life can be so. There must be a pleasure in counting the contents of one's till every night. Boxon! Of course, a mere brute. There came into Will's memory the picture of Boxon landed on the pavement one night, by Allchin's fist or toe—and of a sudden he laughed. When he had half-smoked his pipe, comparative calmness fell upon him. Sherwood spoke of at once raising the money he owed, and, if he succeeded in doing so, much of the mischief would be undone. The four thousand pounds might be safely invested somewhere, and life at The Haws would go on as usual. But was it certain that Sherwood could "raise" such sums, being himself, as he declared, penniless? This disclosure showed him in an unpleasantly new light, as anything but the cautious man of business, the loyal friend, he had seemed to be. Who could put faith in a money-market gambler? Why, there was no difference to speak of between him and Boxon. And if his promise proved futile—what was to be done?

For a couple of hours, Will stared at this question. When the clock on his mantelpiece struck eleven, he happened to notice it, and was surprised to find how quickly time had passed. By the bye, he had never thought of looking at his newspaper, though Sherwood referred him to that source of information on the subject of Biggles, Thorpe and Biggles. Yes, here it was. A firm of brokers; unfortunate speculations; failure of another house—all the old story. As likely as not, the financial trick of a cluster of thieves. Will threw the paper aside. He had always scorned that cunning of the Stock Exchange, now he thought of it with fiery hatred.

Another hour passed in feverish waiting; then, just at mid-day, a knock sounded at the outer door. Anything but a loud knock; anything but the confident summons of a friend. Will went to open. There stood Godfrey Sherwood, shrunk together like a man suffering from cold; he scarcely raised his eyes.

Will's purpose, on finding Sherwood at his door, was to admit him without a word, or any form of greeting; but the sight of that changed face and pitiful attitude overcame him; he offered a hand, and felt it warmly pressed.

They were together in the room; neither had spoken. Will pointed to a chair, but did not himself sit down.

"I suppose it's all true, Warburton," began the other in a low voice, "but I can't believe it yet. I seem to be walking in a nightmare; and when you gave me your hand at the door, I thought for a second that I'd just woke up."

"Sit down," said Will, "and let's have it out. Give me the details."

"That's exactly what I wish to do. Of course I haven't been to bed, and I've spent the night in writing out a statement of all my dealings for the past fifteen months. Here it is—and here are my pass-books."

Will took the paper, a half-sheet of foolscap, one side almost covered with figures. At a glance he saw that the statement was perfectly intelligible. The perusal of a few lines caused him to look up in astonishment.

"You mean to say that between last September and the end of the year you lost twenty-five thousand pounds?"

"I did."

"And you mean to say that you still went on with your gambling?"

"Things were getting bad in Ailie Street, you know."

"And you did your best to make them desperate." Sherwood's head seemed trying to bury itself between his shoulders; his feet hid themselves under the chair, he held his hat in a way suggestive of the man who comes to beg.

"The devil of the City got hold of me," he replied, with a miserable attempt to look Warburton in the face.

"Yes," said Will, "that's clear. Then, a month ago, you really possessed only nine thousand pounds?"

"That was all I had left, out of nearly forty thousand."

"What astonishes me is, that you won from time to time."

"I did!" exclaimed Godfrey, with sudden animation. "Look at the fifth of February—that was a great day! It's that kind of thing that tempts a man on. Afterwards I lost steadily but I might have won any day. And I had to make a good deal, if we were to come to terms with Applegarth. I nearly did it. I was as cautious as a man could be—content with small things. If only I hadn't been pressed for time! It was only the want of time that made me use your money. Of course, it was criminal. Don't think I wish to excuse myself for one moment. Absolutely criminal. I knew what was at stake. But I thought the thing was sure. It promised at the least twenty-five per cent. We should have started brilliantly at Bristol—several thousands for advertisement, beyond our estimate. I don't think the Biggles people were dishonest—"

"You don't *think* so!" interrupted Will, contemptuously. "If there's any doubt we know on which side it weighs. Just tell me the facts. What was the security?"

Sherwood replied with a brief, clear, and obviously honest account of the speculation into which he had been drawn. To the listener it seemed astounding that any responsible man should be lured by such gambler's chance; he could hardly find patience to point out the manifest risks so desperately incurred. And Sherwood admitted the full extent of his folly; he could only repeat that he had acted on an irresistible impulse, to be explained, though not defended, by the embarrassment in which he found himself.

"Thank Heaven, this is over!" he exclaimed at last, passing his handkerchief over a moist forehead. "I don't know how I got through last night. More than once, I thought it would be easier to kill myself than to come and face you. But there was the certainty that I could make good your loss. I may be able to do so very soon. I've written to—"

He checked himself on the point of uttering a name; then with eyes down, reflected for a moment.

"No; I haven't the right to tell you, though I should like to, to give you confidence. It's the story of the ten thousand pounds, you remember? When I lent that money, I promised never to let any one know. Even if I can't realise your capital at once, I can pay you good interest until the money's forthcoming. That would be the same thing to you?"

Warburton gave him a keen look, and said gravely—

"Let's understand each other, Sherwood. Have you any income at all?"

"None whatever now, except the interest on the ten thousand; and that—well, I'm sorry to say it hasn't been paid very regularly. But in future it must be—it *shall* be. Between two and three thousand are owing to me for arrears."

"It's a queer story."

"I know it is," admitted Godfrey. "But I hope you don't doubt my word?"

"No, I don't—What's to be done about Applegarth?"

"I must see him," replied Sherwood with a groan. "Of course you have no part in the miserable business. I must write at once, and then go and face him."

"Of course I shall go with you."

"You will? That's kind of you. Luckily he's a civilised man, not one of the City brutes one might have had to deal with."

"We must hope he'll live up to his reputation," said Warburton, with the first smile, and that no cheery one, which had risen to his lips during this interview.

From that point the talk became easier. All the aspects of their position were considered, without stress of feeling, for Will had recovered his self-control; and Sherwood, soothed by the sense of having discharged an appalling task, tended once more to sanguine thoughts. To be sure, neither of them could see any immediate way out of the gulf in which they found themselves; all hope of resuming business was at an end; the only practical question was, how to earn a living; but both were young men, and neither had ever known privation; it was difficult for them to believe all at once that they were really face to face with that grim necessity which they had thought of as conquering others, but never them. Certain unpleasant steps, however, had at once to be taken. Sherwood must give up his house at Wimbledon; Warburton must look about for a cheap lodging into which to remove at Michaelmas. Worse still, and more urgent, was the duty of making known to Mrs. Warburton what had happened.

"I suppose I must go down at once," said Will gloomily.

"I see no hurry," urged the other. "As a matter of fact, your mother and sister will lose nothing. You undertook to pay them a minimum of three per cent. on their money, and that you can do; I guarantee you that, in any case."

Will mused. If indeed it were possible to avoid the disclosure—? But that would involve much lying, a thing, even in a good cause, little to his taste. Still, when he thought of his mother's weak health, and how she might be affected by the news of this catastrophe, he began seriously to ponder the practicability of well-meaning deception. That, of course, must depend upon their difficulties with Applegarth remaining strictly private; and even so, could Mr. Turnbull's scent for disaster be successfully reckoned with?

"Don't do anything hastily, Warburton, I beg of you," continued the other. "Things are never so bad as they look at first sight. Wait till I have seen—you know who. I might even be able to—but it's better not to promise. Wait a day or two, at all events."

And this Warburton resolved to do; for, if the worst came to the worst, he had some three hundred pounds of his own still in the bank, and so could assure, for two years at all events, the income of which his mother and Jane had absolute need. For himself, he should find some way of earning bread and cheese; he could no longer stand on his dignity, and talk of independence, that was plain.

When at length his calamitous partner had gone, he made an indifferent lunch on the cold meat he found in Mrs. Hopper's precincts, and then decided that he had better take a walk; to sit still and brood was the worst possible way of facing such a crisis. There was no friend with whom he could discuss the situation; none whose companionship would just now do him any particular good. Better to walk twenty miles, and tire himself out, and see how things looked after a good night's sleep, So he put on his soft hat, and took his walking-stick, and slammed the door behind him. Some one was coming up the stairs; sunk in his own thoughts he paid no heed, even when the other man stood in front of him. Then a familiar voice claimed his attention.

"Do you want to cut me, Warburton?"

# CHAPTER 16

Warburton stopped, and looked into the speaker's face, as if he hardly recognised him.

"You're going out," added Franks, turning round. "I won't keep you."

And he seemed about to descend the stairs quickly. But Will at length found voice.

"Come in. I was thinking of something, and didn't see you."

They entered, and passed as usual into the sitting-room, but not with the wonted exchange of friendly words. The interval since their last meeting seemed to have alienated them more than the events which preceded it. Warburton was trying to smile, but each glance he took at the other's face made his lips less inclined to relax from a certain severity rarely seen in them; and Franks succeeded but ill in his attempt to lounge familiarly, with careless casting of the eye this way and that. It was he who broke silence.

"I've found a new drink—gin and laudanum. First rate for the nerves."

"Ah!" replied Warburton gravely. "My latest tipple is oil of vitriol with a dash of strychnine. Splendid pick-me-up."

Franks laughed loudly, but unmirthfully.

"No, but I'm quite serious," he continued. "It's the only thing that keeps me going. If I hadn't found the use of laudanum in small doses, I should have tried a very large one before now."

His language had a note of bravado, and his attitude betrayed the self-conscious actor, but there was that in his countenance which could only have come of real misery. The thin cheeks, heavy-lidded and bloodshot eyes, ill-coloured lips, made a picture anything but agreeable to look upon; and quite in keeping with it was the shabbiness of his garb. After an intent and stern gaze at him, Will asked bluntly:

"When did you last have a bath?"

"Bath? Good God—how do I know?"

And again Franks laughed in the key of stage recklessness.

# CHAPTER 16

"I should advise a Turkish," said Will, "followed by rhubarb of the same country. You'd feel vastly better next day."

"The remedies," answered Franks, smiling disdainfully, "of one who has never been through moral suffering."

"Yet efficacious, even morally, I can assure you. And, by the bye, I want to know when you're going to finish 'The Slummer.'"

"Finish it? Why, never! I could as soon turn to and build a bridge over the Thames."

"What do you mean? I suppose you have to earn your living?"

"I see no necessity for it. What do I care, whether I live or not?"

"Well, then, I am obliged to ask whether you feel it incumbent upon you—to pay your debts?"

The last words came out with a jerk, after a little pause which proved what it cost Warburton to speak them. To save his countenance, he assumed an unnatural grimness of feature, staring Franks resolutely in the face. And the result was the artist's utter subjugation; he shuffled, dropped his head, made confused efforts to reply.

"Of course I shall do so—somehow," he muttered at length.

"Have you any other way—honest way—except by working?"

"Very well, then, I'll find work. Real work. Not that cursed daubing, which it turns my stomach to think of."

Warburton paused a moment, then said kindly:

"That's the talk of a very sore and dazed man. Before long, you'll be yourself again, and you'll go back to your painting with an appetite And the sooner you try the better. I don't particularly like dunning people for money, as I think you know, but, when you can pay that debt of yours, I shall be glad. I've had a bit of bad luck since last we saw each other."

Franks gazed in heavy-eyed wonder, uncertain whether to take this as a joke or not.

"Bad luck? What sort of bad luck?"

"Why, neither on the turf nor at Monte Carlo. But a speculation has gone wrong, and I'm adrift. I shall have to leave this flat. How I'm going to keep myself alive, I don't know yet. The Bristol affair is of course off. I'm as good as penniless, and a hundred pounds or so will come very conveniently, whenever you can manage it."

"Are you serious, Warburton?"

"Perfectly."

"You've really lost everything? You've got to leave this flat because you can't afford it?"

"That, my boy, is the state of the case."

"By Jove! No wonder you didn't see me as I came upstairs. What the deuce! You in Queer Street! I never dreamt of such a thing as a possibility. I've always thought of you as a flourishing capitalist—sound as the Mansion House. Why didn't you begin by telling me this? I'm about as miserable as a fellow can be, but I should never have bothered you with my miseries.—Warburton in want of money? Why, the idea is grotesque; I can't get hold of it. I came to you as men go to a bank. Of course, I meant to pay it all, some day, but you were so generous and so rich, I never thought there would be any hurry. I'm astounded—I'm floored!"

With infinite satisfaction, Warburton saw the better man rising again in his friend, noted the change of countenance, of bearing, of tone.

"You see," he said, with a nod and a smile, "that you've no choice but to finish 'The Slummer!'"

Franks looked about him uneasily, fretfully.

"Either that—or something else," he muttered.

"No—*that*! It'll bring you two or three hundred pounds without much delay."

"I daresay it would. But if you knew how I loathe and curse the very sight of the thing—Why I haven't burnt it I don't know."

"Probably," said Will, "because in summer weather you take your gin and laudanum cold."

This time the artist's laugh was more genuine.

"The hideous time I have been going through!" he continued. "It's no use trying to give you an idea of it. Of course you'd say it was all damned foolery. Well, I shan't go through it again, that's one satisfaction. I've done with women. One reason why I loathe the thought of going on with that picture is because I still have the girl's head to put in. But I'll do it. I'll go back and get to work at once. If I can't find a model, I'll fake the head—get it out of some woman's paper where the fashions are illustrated; that'll do very well. I'll go and see how the beastly thing looks. It's turned against the wall, and I wonder I haven't put my boot through it."

# CHAPTER 17

Warburton waited for a quarter of an hour after the artist had gone, then set out for his walk. The result of this unexpected conversation with Franks was excellent; the foolish fellow seemed to have recovered his common sense. But Will felt ashamed of himself. Of course he had acted solely with a view to the other's good, seeing no hope but this of rescuing Franks from the slough in which he wallowed; nevertheless, he was stung with shame. For the first time in his life he had asked repayment of money lent to a friend. And he had done the thing blunderingly, without tact. For the purpose in view, it would have been enough to speak of his own calamity; just the same effect would have been produced on Franks. He saw this now, and writhed under the sense of his grossness. The only excuse he could urge for himself was that Franks' behaviour provoked and merited rough handling. Still, he might have had perspicacity enough to understand that the artist was not so sunk in squalor as he pretended.

"Just like me," he growled to himself, with a nervous twitching of the face. "I've no presence of mind. I see the right thing when it's too late, and when I've made myself appear a bounder. How many thousand times have I blundered in this way! A man like me ought to live alone—as I've a very fair chance of doing in future."

His walk did him no good, and on his return he passed a black evening. With Mrs. Hopper, who came as usual to get dinner for him, he held little conversation; in a few days he would have to tell her what had befallen him, or invent some lie to account for the change in his arrangements, and this again tortured Will's nerves. In one sense of the word, no man was less pretentious; but his liberality of thought and behaviour consisted with a personal pride which was very much at the mercy of circumstance. Even as he could not endure subjection, so did he shrink from the thought of losing dignity in the eyes of his social inferiors. Mere poverty and lack of ease did not frighten him at all; he had hardly given a thought as yet to that aspect of misfortune. What most of all distressed his imagination (putting aside thought of his mother and sister) was the sudden fall from a position of genial authority, of beneficent command, with all the respect and gratitude and consideration attaching thereto. He could do without personal comforts, if need were, but it pained him horribly to think of being no longer a patron and a master. With a good deal more philosophy than the average man, and vastly more benevolence, he could not attain to the humility which would have seen in this change of fortune a mere surrender of privileges perhaps quite unjustifiable. Social grades were an inseparable part of his view of life; he recognised the existence of his superiors—though resolved to have as little to do with them as possible, and took it as a matter of course that multitudes of men should stand below his level. To imagine himself an object of pity for Mrs. Hopper and Allchin and the rest of them wrought upon his bile, disordered his digestion.

He who had regarded so impatiently the trials of Norbert Franks now had to go through an evil time, with worse results upon his temper, his health, and whole being, than he would have thought conceivable. For a whole fortnight he lived in a state of suspense and forced idleness, which helped him to understand the artist's recourse to gin and laudanum. The weather was magnificent, but for him no sun rose in the sky. If he walked about London, he saw only ugliness and wretchedness, his eyes seeming to have lost the power of perceiving other things. Every two or three days he heard from Sherwood, who wrote that he was doing his utmost, and continued to hold out hope that he would soon have money: but these letters were not reassuring. The disagreeable interview with Applegarth had passed off better than might have been expected. Though greatly astonished, and obviously in some doubt as to the facts of the matter, Applegarth behaved as a gentleman, resigned all claims upon the defaulters, and brought the affair to a decent close as quickly as possible. But Warburton came away with a face so yellow that he seemed on the point of an attack of jaundice. For him to be the object of another man's generous forbearance was something new and intolerable. Before parting with Sherwood, he spoke to him bitterly, all but savagely. A few hours later, of course, repentance came upon him, and he wrote to ask pardon. An evil time.

At length Sherwood came to Chelsea, having written to ask for a meeting. Will's forebodings were but too well justified. The disastrous man came only to say that all his efforts had failed. His debtor for ten thousand pounds was himself in such straits that he could only live by desperate expedients, and probably would not be able to pay a penny of interest this year.

"Happily," said Sherwood, "his father's health is breaking. One is obliged to talk in this brutal way, you know. At the father's death it will be all right; I shall then have my legal remedy, if there's need of it. To take any step of that sort now would be ruinous; my friend would be cut off with a shilling, if the affair came to his father's ears."

"So this is how we stand," said Warburton, grimly. "It's all over."

Sherwood laid on the table a number of bank-notes, saying simply:

"There's two hundred and sixty pounds—the result of the sale of my furniture and things. Will you use that and trust me a little longer?"

Warburton writhed in his chair.

"What have you to live upon?" he asked with eyes downcast.

"Oh, I shall get on all right. I've one or two ideas."

"But this is all the money you have?"

"I've kept about fifty pounds," answered the other, "out of which I can pay my debts—they're small—and the rent of my house for this quarter."

Warburton pushed back the notes.

"I can't take it—you know I can't."

"You must."

"How the devil are you going to live?" cried Will, in exasperation.

"I shall find a way," replied Sherwood with an echo of his old confident tone. "I need a little time to look about me, that's all, There's a relative of mine, an old fellow who lives comfortably in North Wales, and who invites me down every two or three years. The best thing will be for me to go and spend a short time with him, and get my nerves into order—I'm shaky, there's no disguising it. I haven't exhausted all the possibilities of raising money; there's hope still in one or two directions; if I get a little quietness and rest I shall be able to think things out more clearly Don't you think this justifiable?"

As to the money he remained inflexible. Very reluctantly Warburton consented to keep this sum, giving a receipt in form.

"You haven't said anything to Mrs. Warburton yet?" asked Sherwood nervously.

"Not yet," muttered Will.

"I wish you could postpone it a little longer. Could you—do you think—without too much strain of conscience? Doesn't it seem a pity—when any day may enable me to put things right?"

Will muttered again that he would think of it; that assuredly he preferred not to disclose the matter if it could decently be kept secret. And on this Sherwood took his leave, going away with a brighter face than he had brought to the interview; whilst Will remained brooding gloomily, his eyes fixed on the bank-notes, in an unconscious stare.

Little of a man of business as he was, Warburton knew very well that things at the office were passing in a flagrantly irregular way: he knew that any one else in his position would have put this serious affair into legal hands, if only out of justice to Sherwood himself. More than once he had thought of communicating with Mr. Turnbull, but shame withheld him. It seemed improbable, too, that the solicitor would connive at keeping his friends at The Haws ignorant of what had befallen them, and with every day that passed Will felt more disposed to hide that catastrophe, if by any means that were possible. Already he had half committed himself to this deception, having written to his mother (without mention of any other detail) that he might, after all, continue to live in London, where Applegarth's were about to establish a warehouse. The question was how; if he put aside all the money he had for payment of pretended dividend to his mother and sister, how, in that case, was he himself to live? At the thought of going about applying for clerk's work, or anything of that kind, cold water flowed down his back; rather than that, he would follow Allchin's example, and turn porter—an independent position compared with bent-backed slavery on an office-stool. Some means of earning money he must find without delay. To live on what he had, one day longer than could be helped, would be sheer dishonesty. Sherwood might succeed in bringing him a few hundreds—of the ten thousand Will thought not at all, so fantastic did the whole story sound—but that would be merely another small instalment of the sum due to the unsuspecting victims at St. Neots. Strictly speaking, he owned not a penny; his very meals to-day were at the expense of his mother and Jane. This thought goaded him. His sleep became a mere nightmare; his waking, a dry-throated misery.

In spite of loathing and dread, he began to read the thick-serried columns of newspaper advertisement, Wanted! Wanted! Wanted! Wants by the thousand; but many more those of the would-be employed than those of the would-be employers, and under the second heading not one in a hundred that offered him the slightest hint or hope. Wanted! Wanted. To glance over these columns is like listening to the clamour of a hunger-driven multitude; the ears sing, the head turns giddy. After a quarter of an hour of such search, Will flung the paper aside, and stamped like a madman about his room. A horror of life seized him; he understood, with fearful sympathy, the impulse of those who, rather than be any longer hustled in this howling mob dash themselves to destruction.

He thought over the list of his friends. Friends—what man has more than two or three? At this moment he knew of no one who wished him well who could be of the slightest service. His acquaintances were of course more numerous. There lay on his table two invitations just received—the kind of invitation received by every man who does not live the life of a hermit. But what human significance had they? Not a name rose in his mind which symbolised helpfulness. True, that might be to some extent his own fault; the people of whom he saw most were such as needed, not such as could offer, aid. He thought of Ralph Pomfret. There, certainly, a kindly will would not be lacking, but how could he worry with his foolish affairs a man on whom he had no shadow of claim? No: he stood alone. It was a lesson in social science such as reading could never have afforded him. His insight into the order of a man's world had all at once been marvellously quickened, the scope of his reflections incredibly extended. Some vague consciousness of this now and then arrested him in his long purposeless walks; he began to be aware of seeing common things with new eyes. But the perception was akin to fear; he started and looked nervously about, as if suddenly aware of some peril.

One afternoon he was on his way home from a westward trudge, plodding along the remoter part of Fulham Road, when words spoken by a woman whom he passed caught his ears.

"See 'ere! The shutters is up. Boxon must be dead."

Boxon? How did he come to know that name? He slackened his pace, reflecting. Why, Boxon was the name of the betting and drinking grocer, with whom Allchin used to be. He stopped, and saw a group of three or four women staring at the closed shop. Didn't Mrs. Hopper say that Boxon had been nearly killed in a carriage accident? Doubtless he was dead.

He walked on, but before he had gone a dozen yards, stopped abruptly, turned, crossed to the other side of the road, and went back till he stood opposite the closed shop. The name of the tradesman in great gilt letters proved that there was no mistake. He examined the building; there were two storeys above the shop; the first seemed to be used for storage; white blinds at the windows of the second showed it to be inhabited. For some five minutes Will stood gazing and reflecting; then, with head bent as before, he pursued his way.

When he reached home, Mrs. Hopper regarded him compassionately; the good woman was much disturbed by the strangeness of his demeanour lately, and feared he was going to be ill.

"You look dre'ful tired, sir," she said. "I'll make you a cup of tea at once. It'll do you good."

"Yes, get me some tea," answered Warburton, absently. Then, as she was leaving the room, he asked, "Is it true that the grocer Boxon is dead?"

"I was going to speak of it this morning, sir," replied Mrs. Hopper, "but you seemed so busy. Yes, sir, he's died—died the day before yesterday, they say, and it'd be surprising to hear as anybody's sorry."

"Who'll take his business?" asked Warburton.

"We was talking about that last night, sir, me and my sister Liza, and the Allchins. It's fallen off a great deal lately, what else could you expect? since Boxon got into his bad ways. But anybody as had a little money might do well there. Allchin was saying he wished he had a few 'undreds."

"A few hundred would be enough?" interrupted the listener, without noticing the look of peculiar eagerness on Mrs. Hopper's face.

"Allchin thinks the goodwill can be had for about a 'undred, sir; and the rent, it's only eighty pounds—"

"Shop and house?"

"Yes, sir; so Allchin says. It isn't much of a 'ouse, of course."

"What profits could be made, do you suppose, by an energetic man?"

"When Boxon began, sir," replied Mrs. Hopper, with growing animation, "he used to make—so Allchin says—a good five or six 'undred a year. There's a good deal of profit in the grocery business, and Boxon's situation is good; there's no other grocer near him. But of course—as Allchin says—you want to lay out a good deal at starting—"

"Yes, yes, of course, you must have stock." said Will carelessly. "Bring me some tea at once, Mrs. Hopper."

It had suddenly occurred to him that Allchin might think of trying to borrow the capital wherewith to start this business, and that Mrs. Hopper might advise her brother-in-law to apply to him for the loan.

But this was not at all the idea which had prompted Will's inquiries.

# CHAPTER 18

Another week went by. Warburton was still living in the same restless way, but did not wear quite so gloomy a countenance; now and then he looked almost cheerful. That was the case when one morning he received a letter from Sherwood. Godfrey wrote that, no sooner had he arrived at his relative's in North Wales than he was seized with a violent liver-attack, which for some days prostrated him; he was now recovering, and better news still, had succeeded in borrowing a couple of hundred pounds. Half of this sum he sent to Warburton; the other half he begged to be allowed to retain, as he had what might prove a very fruitful idea for the use of the money—details presently. To this letter Will immediately replied at some length. The cheque he paid into his account, which thus reached a total of more than six hundred pounds.

A few days later, after breakfast as usual, he let his servant clear the table, then said with a peculiar smile.

"I want to have a little talk with you, Mrs. Hopper. Please sit down."

To seat herself in her master's presence went against all Mrs. Hopper's ideas of propriety. Seeing her hesitate, Will pointed steadily to a chair, and the good woman, much flurried, placed herself on the edge of it.

"You have noticed," Warburton resumed, "that I haven't been quite myself lately. There was a good reason for it. I've had a misfortune in business; all my plans are changed; I shall have to begin quite a new life—a different life altogether from that I have led till now."

Mrs. Hopper seemed to have a sudden pain in the side. She groaned under her breath, staring at the speaker pitifully.

"There's no need to talk about it, you know," Will went on with a friendly nod. "I tell you, because I'm thinking of going into a business in which your brother-in-law could help me, if he cares to."

He paused. Mrs. Hopper kept her wide eyes on him.

"Allchin'll be very glad to hear of that, sir. What am I saying? Of course I don't mean he'll be glad you've had misfortune, sir, and I'm that sorry to hear it, I can't tell you. But it does just happen as he's out of work, through that nasty temper of his. Not," she corrected herself hastily, "as I ought to call him nasty-tempered. With a good employer, I'm sure he'd never get into no trouble at all."

"Does he still wish to get back into the grocery business?"

"He'd be only too glad, sir, But, of course, any place as *you* offered him—"

"Well, it happens," said Warburton, "that it is the grocery business I'm thinking about."

"You, sir?" gasped Mrs. Hopper.

"I think I shall take Boxon's shop."

"*You*, sir? Take a grocer's shop?—You mean, you'd put Allchin in to manage it?"

"No, I don't, Mrs. Hopper," replied Will, smiling mechanically. "I have more than my own living to earn; other people are dependent upon me, so I must make as much money as possible. I can't afford to pay a manager. I shall go behind the counter myself, and Allchin, if he cares for the place, shall be my assistant."

The good woman could find no words to express her astonishment.

"Suppose you have a word with Allchin, and send him to see me this evening? I say again, there's no need to talk about the thing to anybody else. We'll just keep it quiet between us."

"You can depend upon me, sir," declared Mrs. Hopper. "But did you *hever*! It's come upon me so sudden like. And what'll Allchin say! Why, he'll think I'm having a game with him."

To this point had Will Warburton brought himself, urged by conscience and fear. Little by little, since the afternoon when he gazed at Boxon's closed shop, had this purpose grown in his mind, until he saw it as a possibility—a desirability—a fact. By shopkeeping, he might hope to earn sufficient for supply of the guaranteed income to his mother and sister, and at the same time be no man's servant. His acquaintance with Allchin enabled him to disregard his lack of grocery experience; with Allchin for an assistant, he would soon overcome initial difficulties. Only to Godfrey Sherwood had he communicated his project. "What difference is there," he wrote, "between selling sugar from an office in Whitechapel, and selling it from behind a counter in Fulham Road?" And Sherwood—who was still reposing in North Wales—wrote a long, affectionate, admiring reply. "You are splendid! What energy! What courage! I could almost say that I don't regret my criminal recklessness, seeing that it has given the occasion for such a magnificent display of character." He added, "Of course it will be only for a short time. Even if the plans I am now working out—details shortly—come to nothing (a very unlikely thing), I am sure to recover my ten thousand pounds in a year or so."—"Of course," he wrote in a postscript, "I breathe no word of it to any mortal."

This letter—so are we made—did Warburton good. It strengthened him in carrying through the deception of his relatives and of Mr. Turnbull, for he saw himself as *splendide mendax*. In Sherwood's plans and assurances he had no shadow of faith, but Sherwood's admiration was worth having, and it threw a gilding upon the name of grocer. Should he impart the secret to Norbert Franks? That question he could not decide just yet. In any case, he should tell no one else; all other acquaintances must be content—if they cared to inquire—with vague references to an "agency," or something of the sort. Neither his mother nor Jane ever came to London for them, his change of address to a poorer district would have no significance. In short, London, being London, it seemed perfectly feasible to pass his life in a grocer's shop without the fact becoming known to any one from whom he wished to conceal it.

The rent of the shop and house was eighty-five pounds—an increase upon that paid by Boxon. "Plant" was estimated at a hundred and twenty-five; the stock at one hundred and fifty, and the goodwill at a round hundred. This made a total of four hundred and sixty pounds, leaving Warburton some couple of hundred for all the expenses of his start. The landlord had consented to do certain repairs, including a repainting of the shop, and this work had already begun. Not a day must be lost. Will knew that the first half-year would decide his fate as a tradesman. Did he come out at the end of six months with sufficient profit to pay a bare three per cent. on the St. Neots money, all would be safe and well. If the balance went against him, why then the whole battle of life was lost, and he might go hide his head in some corner even more obscure.

Of course he counted largely on the help of Allchin. Allchin, though pig-headed and pugnacious, had a fair knowledge of the business, to which he had been bred, and of business matters in general always talked shrewdly. Unable, whatever his own straits, to deal penuriously with my one, Will had thought out a liberal arrangement, whereby all the dwelling part of the house should be given over, rent free, to Allchin and his wife, with permission to take one lodger; the assistant to be paid a small salary, and a percentage on shop takings when they reached a certain sum per month. This proposal, then, he set before the muscular man on his presenting himself this afternoon. Allchin's astonishment at the story he had heard from Mrs. Hopper was not less than that of the woman herself. With difficulty persuaded to sit down, he showed a countenance in which the gloom he thought decorous struggled against jubilation on his own account: and Warburton had not talked long before his listener's features irresistibly expanded in a happy grin.

"How would something of this kind suit you?" asked Will.

"Me, sir?" Allchin slapped his leg. "You ask how it suits *me*?"

His feelings were too much for him. He grew very red, and could say no more.

"Then suppose we settle it so. I've written out the terms of your engagement. Read and sign."

Allchin pretended to read the paper, but obviously paid no attention to it. He seemed to be struggling with some mental obstacle.

"Something you want to alter?" asked Warburton.

"Why, sir, you've altogether forgot as I'm in your debt. It stands to reason as you must take that money out before you begin to pay me anything."

"Oh, we won't say anything more about that trifle. We're making a new beginning. But look here, Allchin, I don't want you to quarrel with me, as you do with every one else—"

"With *you*, sir? Ho, ho!"

Allchin guffawed, and at once looked ashamed of himself.

"I quarrel," he added, "with people as are insulting, or as try to best me. It goes against my nature, sir, to be insulted and to be bested."

They talked about the details of the business, and presently Allchin asked what name was to be put up over the shop.

"I've thought of that," answered Will. "What do you say to—*Jollyman*?"

The assistant was delighted; he repeated the name a dozen times, snorting and choking with appreciation of the joke. Next morning, they met again, and went together to look at the shop. Here Allchin made great play with his valuable qualities. He pointed out the errors and negligencies of the late Boxon, declared it a scandal that a business such as this should have been allowed to fall off, and was full of ingenious ideas for a brilliant opening. Among other forms of inexpensive advertisement, he suggested that, for the first day, a band should be engaged to play in the front room over the shop, with the windows open; and he undertook to find amateur bandsmen who would undertake the job on very moderate terms.

Not many days elapsed before the old name had disappeared from the house front, giving place to that of Jollyman. Whilst this was being painted up, Allchin stood on the opposite side of the way, watching delightedly.

"When I think as the name used to be Boxon," he exclaimed to his employer, "why, I can't believe as any money was ever made here. Boxon! Why, it was enough to drive customers away! If you ever heard a worse name, sir, for a shopkeeper, I should be glad to be told of it. But *Jollyman*! Why, it'll bring people from Putney, from Battersea, from who knows how far. Jollyman's Teas, Jollyman's sugar—can't you *hear* 'em saying it, already? It's a fortune in itself, that name. Why, sir, if a grocer called Boxon came at this moment, and offered to take me into partnership on half profits, I wouldn't listen to him—there!"

Naturally, all this did not pass without many a pang in Warburton's sensitive spots. He had set his face like brass, or tried to do so; but in the night season he could all but have shed tears of humiliation, as he tossed on his comfortless pillow. The day was spent in visits to wholesale grocery establishments, in study of trade journals, in calculating innumerable petty questions of profit and loss. When nausea threatened him: when an all but horror of what lay before him assailed his mind; he thought fixedly of The Haws, and made a picture to himself of that peaceful little home devastated by his own fault. And to think that all this sweat and misery arose from the need of gaining less than a couple of hundred pounds a year! Life at The Haws, a life of refinement and goodness and tranquillity such as can seldom be found, demanded only that—a sum which the wealthy vulgar throw away upon the foolish amusement of an hour. Warburton had a tumultuous mind in reflecting on these things; but the disturbance was salutary, bearing him through trials of nerve and patience and self-respect which he could not otherwise have endured.

Warburton had now to find cheap lodgings for himself, unfurnished rooms in some poor quarter not too far from the shop.

At length, in a new little street of very red brick, not far from Fulham Palace Road at the Hammersmith end, he came upon a small house which exhibited in its parlour window a card inscribed: "Two unfurnished rooms to be let to single gentlemen only." The precision of this notice made him hopeful, and a certain cleanliness of aspect in the woman who opened to him was an added encouragement; but he found negotiations not altogether easy. The landlady, a middle-aged widow, seemed to regard him with some peculiar suspicion; before even admitting him to the house, she questioned him closely as to his business, his present place of abode, and so on, and Warburton was all but turning away in impatience, when at last she drew aside, and cautiously invited him to enter. Further acquaintance with Mrs. Wick led him to understand that the cold, misgiving in her eye, the sour rigidity of her lips, and her generally repellant manner, were characteristics which meant nothing in particular—save as they resulted from a more or less hard life amid London's crowd; at present, the woman annoyed him, and only the clean freshness of her vacant rooms induced him to take the trouble of coming to terms with her.

"There's one thing I must say to you quite plain, to begin with," remarked Mrs. Wick, whose language, though not disrespectful, had a certain bluntness. "I can't admit female visitors—not on any excuse."

Speaking thus, she set her face at its rigidest and sourest, and stared past Warburton at the wall. He, unable to repress a smile, declared his perfect readiness to accept this condition of tenancy.

"Another thing," pursued the landlady, "is that I don't like late hours." And she eyed him as one might a person caught in flagrant crapulence at one o'clock a.m.

"Why, neither do I," Will replied. "But for all that, I may be obliged to come home late now and then."

"From the theatre, I suppose?"

"I very seldom go to the theatre." (Mrs. Wick looked sanguine for an instant, but at once relapsed into darker suspicion than ever.) "But as to my hour of returning home, I must have entire liberty."

The woman meditated, profound gloom on her brows.

"You haven't told me," she resumed, shooting a glance of keen distrust, "exactly what your business may be."

"I am in the sugar line," responded Will.

"Sugar? You wouldn't mind giving me the name of your employers?"

The word so rasped on Warburton's sensitive temper that he seemed about to speak angrily. This the woman observed, and added at once:

"I don't doubt but that you're quite respectable, sir, but you can understand as I have to be careful who I take into my house."

"I understand that, but I must ask you to be satisfied with a reference to my present landlord. That, and a month's payment in advance, ought to suffice."

## CHAPTER 18

Evidently it did, for Mrs. Wick, after shooting one or two more of her sharpest looks, declared herself willing to enter into discussion of details. He required attendance, did he? Well it all depended upon what sort of attendance he expected; if he wanted cooking at late hours.—Warburton cut short these anticipatory objections, and made known that his wants were few and simple: plain breakfast at eight o'clock, cold supper on the table when he came home, a mid-day meal on Sundays, and the keeping of his rooms in order; that was all. After morose reflection, Mrs. Wick put her demand for rooms and service at a pound a week, but to this Warburton demurred. It cost him agonies to debate such a matter; but, as he knew very well, the price was excessive for unfurnished lodgings, and need constrained him. He offered fifteen shillings, and said he would call for Mrs. Wick's decision on the morrow. The landlady allowed him to go to the foot of the stairs, then stopped him.

"I wouldn't mind taking fifteen shillings," she said, "if I knew it was for a permanency."

"I can't bind myself more than by the month."

"Would you be willing to leave a deposit?"

So the matter was settled, and Warburton arranged to enter into possession that day week.

Without delay the shop repairs were finished, inside and out; orders for stock were completed; in two days—as a great bill on the shutters announced—"Jollyman's Grocery Stores" would be open to the public. Allchin pleaded strongly for the engagement of the brass band; it wouldn't cost much, and the effect would be immense. Warburton shrugged, hesitated, gave way, and the band was engaged.

# CHAPTER 19

Rosamund Elvan was what ladies call a good correspondent. She wrote often, she wrote at length, and was satisfied with few or brief letters in reply. Scarcely had she been a week at Cairo, when some half dozen sheets of thin paper, covered with her small swift writing, were dispatched to Bertha Cross, and, thence onwards, about once a fortnight such a letter arrived at Walham Green. Sitting by a fire kept, for economical reasons, as low as possible, with her mother's voice sounding querulously somewhere in the house, and too often a clammy fog at the window, Bertha read of Egyptian delights and wonders, set glowingly before her in Rosamund's fluent style. She was glad of the letters, for they manifested a true affection, and were in every way more interesting than any others that she received; but at times they made the cheerless little house seem more cheerless still, and the pang of contrast between her life and Rosamund's called at such moments for all Bertha's sense of humour to make it endurable.

Not that Miss Elvan represented herself as happy. In her very first letter she besought Bertha not to suppose that her appreciation of strange and beautiful things meant forgetfulness of what must be a lifelong sorrow. "I am often worse than depressed. I sleep very badly, and in the night I often shed wretched tears. Though I did only what conscience compelled me to do, I suffer all the miseries of remorse. And how can I wish that it should be otherwise? It is better, surely, to be capable of such suffering, than to go one's way in light-hearted egoism. I'm not sure that I don't sometimes *encourage* despondency. You can understand that? I know you can, dear Bertha, for many a time I have detected the deep feeling which lies beneath your joking way." Passages such as this Bertha was careful to omit when reading from the letters to her mother. Mrs. Cross took very little interest in her daughter's friend, and regarded the broken engagement with no less disapproval than surprise; but it would have gravely offended her if Bertha had kept this correspondence altogether to herself.

# CHAPTER 19

"I suppose," she remarked, on one such occasion, "we shall never again see Mr. Franks."

"He would find it rather awkward to call, no doubt," replied Bertha.

"I shall *never* understand it!" Mrs. Cross exclaimed, in a vexed tone, after thinking awhile. "No doubt there's something you keep from me."

"About Rosamund? Nothing whatever, I assure you, mother."

"Then you yourself don't know all, that's *quite* certain."

Mrs. Cross had made the remark many times, and always with the same satisfaction. Her daughter was content that the discussion should remain at this point; for the feeling that she had said something at once unpleasant and unanswerable made Mrs. Cross almost good humoured for at least an hour.

Few were the distressful lady's sources of comfort, but one sure way of soothing her mind and temper, was to suggest some method of saving money, no matter how little. One day in the winter, Bertha passing along the further part of Fulham Road, noticed a new-looking grocer's, the window full of price tickets, some of them very attractive to a housekeeper's eye; on returning home she spoke of this, mentioning figures which moved her mother to a sour effervescence of delight. The shop was rather too far away for convenience, but that same evening Mrs. Cross went to inspect it, and came back quite flurried with what she had seen.

"I shall most certainly deal at Jollyman's," she exclaimed. "What a pity we didn't know of him before! Such a gentlemanly man—indeed, *quite* a gentleman. I never saw a shopkeeper who behaved so nicely. So different from Billings—a man I have always thoroughly disliked, and his coffee has been getting worse and worse. Mr. Jollyman is quite willing to send even the smallest orders. Isn't that nice of him—such a distance! Billings was quite insolent to me the day before yesterday, when I asked him to send; yet it was nearly a two-shilling order. Never go into that shop again, Bertha. It's really quite a pleasure to buy of Mr. Jollyman; he knows how to behave; I really almost felt as if I was talking to some one of our own class. Without his apron, he must be a thorough gentleman."

Bertha could not restrain a laugh.

"How thoughtless of him to wear an apron at all!" she exclaimed merrily. "Couldn't one suggest to him discreetly, that *but* for the apron—"

"Don't be ridiculous, Bertha!" interrupted her mother. "You always make nonsense of what one says. Mr. Jollyman is a shopkeeper, and it's just because he doesn't forget that, after all, that his behaviour is so good. Do you remember that horrid Stokes, in King's Road? There was a man who thought himself too good for his business, and in reality was nothing but an underbred, impertinent creature. I can hear his 'Yes, Mrs. Cross—no, Mrs. Cross—thank you, Mrs. Cross'—and once, when I protested against an overcharge, he cried out, 'Oh, my *dear* Mrs. Cross!' The insolence of that man! Now, Mr. Jollyman—"

It was not long before Bertha had an opportunity of seeing this remarkable shopkeeper, and for once she was able to agree with her mother. Mr. Jollyman bore very little resemblance to the typical grocer, and each visit to his shop strengthened Bertha's suspicion that he had not grown up in this way of life. It cost her some constraint to make a very small purchase of him, paying a few coppers, and still more when she asked him if he had nothing cheaper than this or that; all the more so that Mr. Jollyman seemed to share her embarrassment, lowering his voice as if involuntarily, and being careful not to meet her eye. One thing Bertha noticed was that, though the grocer invariable addressed her mother as "madam," in speaking to *her* he never used the grocerly "miss" and when, by chance, she heard him bestow this objectionable title upon a servant girl who was making purchases at the same time, Bertha not only felt grateful for the distinction, but saw in it a fresh proof of Mr. Jollyman's good breeding.

The winter passed, and with the spring came events in which Bertha was interested. Mr. Elvan, who for his health's sake spent the winter in the south-west of France, fell so ill early in the year that Rosamund was summoned from Egypt. With all speed she travelled to St. Jean de Luz. When she arrived, her father was no longer in danger; but there seemed no hope of his being able to return to England for some months, so Rosamund remained with him and her sister, and was soon writing to her friend at Walham Green in a strain of revived enthusiasm for the country of the Basques. A postscript to one of these letters, written in the middle of May, ran as follows: "I hear that N. F. has a picture in the Academy called 'A Ministering Angel,' and that it promises to be one of the most popular of the year. Have you seen it?" To this, Rosamund's correspondent was able to reply that she had seen "N.F's" picture, and that it certainly was a good deal talked about; she added no opinion as to the merits of the painting, and, in her next letter, Miss Elvan left the subject untouched. Bertha was glad of this. "A Ministering Angel" seemed to her by no means a very remarkable production, and she liked much better to say nothing about it than to depreciate the painter; for to do this would have been like seeking to confirm Rosamund in her attitude towards Norbert Franks, which was not at all Bertha's wish.

A few weeks later, Rosamund returned to the topic. "N. F's picture," she wrote, "is evidently a great success—and you can imagine how I feel about it. I saw it, you remember, at an early stage, when he called it 'The Slummer,' and you remember too, the effect it had upon me. Oh, Bertha, this is nothing less than a soul's tragedy! When I think what he used to be, what I hoped of him, what he hoped for himself! Is it not dreadful that he should have fallen so low, and in so short a time! A popular success! Oh, the shame of it, the bitter shame!"

At this point, the reader's smile threatened laughter. But, feeling sure that her friend, if guilty of affectation, was quite unconscious of it, she composed her face to read gravely on.

"A soul's tragedy, Bertha, and *I* the cause of it One can see now, but too well, what is before him. All his hardships are over, and all his struggles. He will become a popular painter—one of those whose name is familiar to the crowd, like—" instances were cited. "I can say, with all earnestness, that I had rather have seen him starved to death. Poor, poor N. F.! Something whispers to me that perhaps I was always under an illusion about him. *Could* he so rapidly sink to this, if he were indeed the man I thought him? Would he not rather have—oh, have done *anything*?—Yet this may be only a temptation of my lower self, a way of giving ease to my conscience. Despair may account for his degradation. And when I remember that a word, one word, from me, the right moment, would have checked him on the dangerous path! When I saw 'Sanctuary,' why had I not the courage to tell him what I thought? No, I became the accomplice of his suicide, and I, alone, am the cause of this wretched disaster.—Before long he will be rich. Can you imagine N. F. *rich*? I shudder at the thought."

The paper rustled in Bertha's hand; her shoulders shook; she could no longer restrain the merry laugh. When she sat down to answer Rosamund, a roguish smile played about her lips.

"I grieve with you"—thus she began—"over the shocking prospect of N. F.'s becoming *rich*. Alas! I fear the thing is past praying for; I can all but see the poor young man in a shiny silk hat and an overcoat trimmed with the most expensive fur. His Academy picture is everywhere produced; a large photogravure will soon be published; all day long a crowd stands before it at Burlington House, and his name—shall we ever again dare to speak it?—is on the lips of casual people in train and 'bus and tram. How shall I write on such a painful subject? You see that my hand is unsteady. Don't blame yourself too much. The man capable of becoming rich *will* become so, whatever the noble influences which endeavour to restrain him. I suspect—I feel all but convinced—that N. F. could not help himself; the misfortune is that his fatal turn for moneymaking did not show itself earlier, and so warn you away. I don't know whether I dare send you a paragraph I have cut from yesterday's *Echo*. Yet I will—it will serve to show you that—as you used to write from Egypt—all this is Kismet."

The newspaper cutting showed an item of news interesting alike to the fashionable and the artistic world. Mr. Norbert Franks, the young painter whose Academy picture had been so much discussed, was about to paint the portrait of Lady Rockett, recently espoused wife of Sir Samuel Rockett, the Australian millionaire. As every one knew, Lady Rockett had made a brilliant figure in the now closing Season, and her image had been in all the society journals. Mr. Franks might be congratulated on this excellent opportunity for the display of his admirable talent as an exponent of female beauty.— "Exponent" was the word.

# CHAPTER 20

In these summer days, whilst Norbert Franks was achieving popularity, success in humbler guise came to the humorous and much-enduring artist at Walham Green. For a year or two, Bertha Cross had spent what time she could spare upon the illustration of a quaint old story-book, a book which had amused her own childhood, and still held its place in her affection. The work was now finished; she showed it to a publisher of her acquaintance, who at once offered to purchase it on what seemed to Bertha excellent terms. Of her own abilities she thought very modestly in deed, and had always been surprised when any one consented to pay—oftener in shillings than in pounds—for work which had cost her an infinity of conscientious trouble; now, however, she suspected that she had done something not altogether bad, and she spoke of it in a letter to Rosamund Elvan, still in the country of the Basques.

"As you know," Rosamund replied, "I have never doubted that you would make a success one day, for you are wonderfully clever, and only need a little more self-confidence in making yourself known. I wish I could feel anything like so sure of earning money. For I shall have to, that is now certain. Poor father, who gets weaker and weaker, talked to us the other day about what we could expect after his death; and it will be only just a little sum for each of us, nothing like enough to invest and live upon. I am working at my water-colours, and I have been trying pastel—there's no end of good material here. When the end comes—and it can't be long—I must go to London, and see whether my things have any market value. I don't like the prospect of life in a garret on bread and water—by myself, that is. You know how joyfully, gladly, proudly, I would have accepted it, under *other* circumstances. If I had real talent myself—but I feel more than doubtful about that. I pray that I may not fall too low. Can I trust you to overwhelm me with scorn, if I seem in danger of doing vulgar work?"

Bertha yielded to the temptations of a later summer rich in warmth and hue, and made little excursions by herself into the country, leaving home before her mother was up in the morning, and coming back after sunset. Her sketching materials and a packet of sandwiches were but a light burden; she was a good walker; and the shilling or two spent on the railway, which formerly she could not have spared, no longer frightened her.

In this way, one morning of September, she went by early train as far as Epsom, walked through the streets, and came into that high-banked lane which leads up to the downs. Blackberries shone thick upon the brambles, and above, even to the very tops of the hedge-row trees, climbed the hoary clematis. Glad in this leafy solitude, Bertha rambled slowly on. She made no unpleasing figure against the rural background, for she was straight and slim, graceful in her movements, and had a face from which no one would have turned indifferently, so bright was it with youthful enjoyment and with older thought.

Whilst thus she lingered, a footstep approached, that of a man who was walking in the same direction. When close to her, this pedestrian stopped, and his voice startled Bertha with unexpected greeting. The speaker was Norbert Franks.

"How glad I am to see you!" he exclaimed, in a tone and with a look which vouched for his sincerity. "I ought to have been to Walham Green long ago. Again and again I meant to come. But this is jolly; I like chance meetings. Are you often down here in Surrey?"

With amusement Bertha remarked the evidence of prosperity in Franks' dress and bearing; he had changed notably since the days when he used to come to their little house to talk of Rosamund, and was glad of an indifferent cup of tea. He seemed to be in very fair health, his countenance giving no hint of sentimental sorrows.

Franks noticed a bunch of tinted leafage which she was carrying, and spoke of its beauty.

"Going to make use of them, no doubt. What are you working at just now?"

Bertha told of her recent success with the illustrated story-book, and Franks declared himself delighted. Clearly, he was in the mood to be delighted with everything. Between his remarks, which were uttered in the sprightliest tone, he hummed phrases of melody.

"Your Academy picture was a great success," said Bertha, discreetly watching him as she spoke.

"Yes, I suppose it was," he answered, with a light-hearted laugh. "Did you see it?—And what did you think of it?—No, seriously; I should like your real opinion. I know you *have* opinions."

"You meant it to be successful," was Bertha's reply.

"Well, yes, I did. At the same time I think some of the critics—the high and mighty ones, you know—were altogether wrong about it. Perhaps, on the whole, you take their view?"

"Oh no, I don't," answered his companion, cheerfully. "I thought the picture very clever, and very true."

"I'm delighted! I've always maintained that it was perfectly true. A friend of mine—why, you remember me speaking of Warburton—Warburton wanted me to make the Slummer ugly. But why? It's just the prettiest girls—of that kind—who go slumming nowadays. Still, you are quite right. I did mean it to be 'successful.' I *had* to make a success, that's the fact of the matter. You know what bad times I was having. I got sick of it, that's the truth. Then, I owed money, and money that had to be paid back, one way or another. Now I'm out of debt, and see my way to live and work in decent comfort. And I maintain that I've done nothing to be ashamed of."

Bertha smiled approvingly.

"I've just finished a portrait—a millionaire's wife, Lady Rockett," went on Franks. "Of course it was my Slummer that got me the job. Women have been raving about that girl's head; and it isn't bad, though I say it. I had to take a studio at a couple of days' notice—couldn't ask Lady Rockett to come and sit at that place of mine in Battersea; a shabby hole. She isn't really anything out of the way, as a pretty woman; but I've made her—well, you'll see it at some exhibition this winter, if you care to. Pleased? Isn't she pleased! And her husband, the podgy old millionaire baronet, used to come every day and stare in delight. To tell you the truth, I think it's rather a remarkable bit of painting. I didn't quite know I could turn out anything so *chic*. I shouldn't be surprised if I make a specialty of women's portraits. How many men can flatter, and still keep a good likeness? That's what I've done. But wait till you see the thing."

Bertha was bubbling over with amusement; for, whilst the artist talked, she thought of Rosamund's farewell entreaty, that she would do her best, if occasion offered, to strengthen Norbert Franks under his affliction, even by depreciatory comment on the faithless girl; there came into her mind, too, those many passages of Rosamund's letters where Franks was spoken of in terms of profoundest compassion mingled with dark remorse. Perhaps her smile, which quivered on the verge of laughter, betrayed the nature of her thought. Of a sudden, Franks ceased to talk; his countenance changed, overcast with melancholy; and when, after some moments' silence, Bertha again spoke of the landscape, he gave only a dull assent to her words.

"And it all comes too late," fell from him, presently. "Too late."

"Your success?"

"What's the good of it to me?" He smote his leg with the rattan he was swinging. "A couple of years ago, money would have meant everything. Now—what do I care about it!"

Bertha's surprise obliged her to keep an unnaturally solemn visage.

"Don't you think it'll grow upon you," she said, "if you give it time?"

"Grow upon me? Why, I'm only afraid it may. That's just the danger. To pursue success—vulgar success—when all the better part has gone out of life—"

He ended on a sigh and again whacked his leg with the stick.

"But" urged his companion, as though gravely, "isn't it easy *not* to pursue success? I mean if it really makes you uncomfortable. There are so many kinds of work in art which would protect you against the perils of riches."

Franks was watching her as she spoke.

"Miss Cross" he said, "I suspect you are satirical. I remember you used to have a turn that way. Well, well, never mind; I don't expect you to understand me."

They had passed out of Ashtead Park and were now ascending by the lane which leads up to Epsom Common.

"I suppose we are both going the same way," said Franks, who had recovered all his cheerfulness. "There's a train at something after five, if we can catch it. Splendid idea of yours to have a whole day's walking. I don't walk enough. Are you likely to be going again before long?"

Bertha replied that she never made plans beforehand. Her mood and the weather decided an excursion.

"Of course. That's the only way. Well, if you'll let me, I must come to Walham Green, one of these days. How's Mrs. Cross? I ought to have asked before, but I never do the right thing.—Have you any particular day for being at home?—All right. If you had had, I should have asked you to let me come on some other. I don't care much, you know, for general society; and ten to one, when I do come I shall be rather gloomy. Old memories, you know.—Really very jolly, this meeting with you. I should have done the walk to Epsom just as a constitutional, without enjoying it a bit. As it is—"

# CHAPTER 21

It was a week or two after the day in Surrey, that Bertha Cross, needing a small wooden box in which to pack a present for her brothers in British Columbia, bethought herself of Mr. Jollyman. The amiable grocer could probably supply her want, and she went off to the shop. There the assistant and an errand boy were unloading goods just arrived by cart, and behind the counter, reading a newspaper—for it was early in the morning stood Mr. Jollyman himself. Seeing the young lady enter, he smiled and bowed; not at all with tradesmanlike emphasis, but rather, it seemed to Bertha, like a man tired and absent-minded, performing a civility in the well-bred way. The newspaper thrown aside, he stood with head bent and eyes cast down, listening to her request.

"I think I have something that will do very well," he replied. "Excuse me for a moment."

From regions behind the shop, he produced a serviceable box just of the right dimensions.

"It will do? Then you shall have it in about half an hour."

"I'm ashamed to trouble you," said Bertha "I could carry it—"

"On no account. The boy will be free in a few minutes."

"And I owe you—?" asked Bertha, purse in hand.

"The box has no value," replied Mr. Jollyman, with that smile, suggestive of latent humour, which always caused her to smile responsively. "And at the same time," he continued, a peculiar twinkle in his eyes, "I will ask you to accept one of these packets of chocolate. I am giving one to-day to every customer—to celebrate the anniversary of my opening shop."

"Thank you very much," said Bertha. And, on an impulse, she added: "I will put it with what I am sending in the box—a present for two brothers of mine who are a long way off in Canada."

His hands upon the counter, his body bent forward, Mr. Jollyman looked her for a moment in the face. A crease appeared on his forehead, as he said slowly and dreamily:

"Canada? Do they like their life out there?"

"They seem to enjoy it, on the whole. But it evidently isn't an easy life."

"Not many kinds of life are." rejoined the grocer. "But the open air—the liberty—"

"Oh yes, that must be the good side of it," assented Bertha.

"On a morning like this—"

Mr. Jollyman's eyes wandered to a gleam of sunny sky visible through the shop window. The girl's glance passed quickly over his features, and she was on the point of saying something; but discretion interposed. Instead of the too personal remark, she repeated her thanks, bent her head with perhaps a little more than the wonted graciousness, and left the shop. The grocer stood looking toward the doorway. His countenance had fallen. Something of bitterness showed in the hardness of his lips.

# CHAPTER 22

Just a year since the day when Allchin's band played at the first floor windows above Jollyman's new grocery stores.

From the very beginning, business promised well. He and his assistant had plenty of work; there was little time for meditation; when not serving customers, he was busy with practical details of grocerdom, often such as he had not foreseen, matters which called for all his energy and ingenuity. A gratifying aspect of the life was that, day by day, he handled his returns in solid cash. Jollyman's gave no credit; all goods had to be paid for on purchase or delivery; and to turn out the till when the shop had closed—to make piles of silver and mountains of copper, with a few pieces of gold beside them—put a cheering end to the day's labour. Warburton found himself clinking handfuls of coin, pleased with the sound. Only at the end of the first three months, the close of the year, did he perceive that much less than he had hoped of the cash taken could be reckoned as clear profit. He had much to learn in the cunning of retail trade, and it was a kind of study that went sorely against the grain with him. Happily, at Christmas time came Norbert Franks (whom Will had decided *not* to take into his confidence) and paid his debt of a hundred and twenty pounds. This set things right for the moment. Will was able to pay a three-and-a-half per cent. dividend to his mother and sister, and to fare ahead hopefully.

He would rather not have gone down to The Haws that Christmastide, but feared that his failure to do so might seem strange. The needful prevarication cost him so many pangs that he came very near to confessing the truth; he probably would have done so, had not his mother been ailing, and, it seemed to him, little able to bear the shock of such a disclosure. So the honest deception went on. Will was supposed to be managing a London branch of the Applegarth business. Great expenditure on advertising had to account for the smallness of the dividend at first. No one less likely than the ladies at The Haws to make trouble in such a matter. They had what sufficed to them, and were content with it. Thinking over this in shame-faced solitude, Warburton felt a glow of proud thankfulness that his mother and sister were so unlike the vulgar average of mankind—that rapacious multitude, whom nothing animates but a chance of gain, with whom nothing weighs but a commercial argument. A new tenderness stirred within him, and resolutely he stamped underfoot the impulses of self-esteem, of self-indulgence, which made his life hard to bear.

It was with a hard satisfaction that he returned to the shop, and found all going on in the usual way, Allchin grinning a hearty welcome as he weighed out sugar. Will's sister talked of the scents of her garden, how they refreshed and inspirited her to him, the odour of the shop—new-roasted coffee predominated to-day—had its invigorating effect; it meant money, and money meant life, the peaceful, fruitful life of those dear to him. He scarcely gave himself time to eat dinner, laid for him, as usual, by Mrs. Allchin, in the sitting-room behind the shop; so eager was he to get on his apron, and return to profitable labour.

At first, he had endured a good deal of physical fatigue. Standing for so many hours a day wearied him much more than walking would have done, and with bodily exhaustion came at times a lowness of spirits such as he had never felt. His resource against this misery was conversation with Allchin. In Allchin he had a henchman whose sturdy optimism and gross common sense were of the utmost value. The brawny assistant, having speedily found a lodger according to the agreement, saw himself in clover, and determined that, if *he* could help it, his fortunes should never again suffer eclipse. He and his wife felt a reasonable gratitude to the founder of their prosperity—whom, by the bye, they invariably spoke of as "Mr. Jollyman"—and did their best to smooth for him the unfamiliar path he was treading.

The success with which Warburton kept his secret, merely proved how solitary most men are amid the crowds of London, and how easy it is for a Londoner to disappear from among his acquaintances whilst continuing to live openly amid the city's roar. No one of those who cared enough about him to learn that he had fallen on ill-luck harboured the slightest suspicion of what he was doing; he simply dropped out of sight, except for the two or three who, in a real sense of the word, could be called his friends. The Pomfrets, whom he went to see at very long intervals, supposed him to have some sort of office employment, and saw nothing in his demeanour to make them anxious about him. As for Norbert Franks, why, he was very busy, and came not oftener than once a month to his friend's obscure lodgings; he asked no intrusive questions, and, like the Pomfrets, could only suppose that Warburton had found a clerkship somewhere. They were not quite on the old terms, for each had gone through a crisis of life, and was not altogether the same as before; but their mutual liking subsisted. Obliged to retrench his hospitality, Warburton never seemed altogether at his ease when Franks was in his room; nor could he overcome what seemed to him the shame of having asked payment of a debt from a needy friend, notwithstanding the fact, loudly declared by Franks himself, that nothing could have been more beneficial to the debtor's moral health. So Will listened rather than talked, and was sometimes too obviously in no mood for any sort of converse.

Sherwood he had not seen since the disastrous optimist's flight into Wales; nor had there come any remittance from him since the cheque for a hundred pounds. Two or three times, however, Godfrey had written—thoroughly characteristic letters—warm, sanguine, self-reproachful. From Wales he had crossed over to Ireland, where he was working at a scheme for making a fortune out of Irish eggs and poultry. In what the "work" consisted, was not clear, for he had no money, beyond a small loan from his relative which enabled him to live; but he sent a sheet of foolscap covered with computations whereby his project was proved to be thoroughly practical and vastly lucrative.

Meanwhile, he had made one new acquaintance, which was at first merely a source of amusement to him, but little by little became something more. In the winter days, when his business was new, there one day came into the shop a rather sour-lipped and querulous-voiced lady, who after much discussion of prices, made a modest purchase and asked that the goods might be sent for her. On hearing her name—Mrs. Cross—the grocer smiled, for he remembered that the Crosses of whom he knew from Norbert Franks, lived at Walham Green, and the artist's description of Mrs. Cross tallied very well with the aspect and manner of this customer. Once or twice the lady returned; then, on a day of very bad weather, there came in her place a much younger and decidedly more pleasing person, whom Will took to be Mrs. Cross's daughter. Facial resemblance there was none discoverable; in bearing, in look, in tone, the two were different as women could be; but at the younger lady's second visit, his surmise was confirmed, for she begged him to change a five-pound note, and, as the custom is in London shops, endorsed it with her name—"Bertha Cross." Franks had never spoken much of Miss Cross; "rather a nice sort of girl," was as far as his appreciation went. And with this judgment Will at once agreed; before long, he would have inclined to be more express in his good opinion. Before summer came, he found himself looking forward to the girl's appearance in the shop, with a sense of disappointment when—as generally happened—Mrs. Cross came in person. The charm of the young face lay for him in its ever-present suggestion of a roguishly winsome smile, which made it difficult not to watch too intently the play of her eyes and lips. Then, her way of speaking, which was altogether her own. It infused with a humorous possibility the driest, most matter-of-fact remarks, and Will had to guard himself against the temptation to reply in a corresponding note.

"I suppose you see no more of those people—what's their name—the Crosses?" he let fall, as if casually, one evening when Franks had come to see him.

"Lost sight of them altogether," was the reply. "Why do you ask?"

"I happened to think of them," said Will; and turned to another subject.

## CHAPTER 23

Was he to be a grocer for the rest of his life?—This question, which at first scarcely occurred to him, absorbed as he was in the problem of money-earning for immediate needs, at length began to press and worry. Of course he had meant nothing of the kind; his imagination had seen in the shop a temporary expedient; he had not troubled to pursue the ultimate probabilities of the life that lay before him, but contented himself with the vague assurance of his hopeful temper. Yet where was the way out? To save money, to accumulate sufficient capital for his release, was an impossibility, at all events within any reasonable time. And for what windfall could he look? Sherwood's ten thousand pounds hovered in his memory, but no more substantial than any fairy-tale. No man living, it seemed to him, had less chance of being signally favoured by fortune. He had donned his apron and aproned he must remain.

Suppose, then, he so far succeeded in his business as to make a little more than the household at St. Neots required; suppose it became practicable to—well, say, to think of marriage, of course on the most modest basis; could he quite see himself offering to the girl he chose the hand and heart of a grocer? He laughed. It was well to laugh; merriment is the great digestive, and an unspeakable boon to the man capable of it in all but every situation; but what if *she* also laughed, and not in the sympathetic way? Worse still, what if she could *not* laugh, but looked wretchedly embarrassed, confused, shamed? That would be a crisis it needed some philosophy to contemplate.

For the present, common sense made it rigorously plain to him that the less he thought of these things, the better. He had not a penny to spare. Only by exercising an economy which in the old days would have appalled him, could he send his mother and sister an annual sum just sufficient to their needs. He who scorned and loathed all kinds of parsimony had learnt to cut down his expenditure at every possible point. He still smoked his pipe; he bought newspapers; he granted himself an excursion, of the cheapest, on fine Sundays; but these surely were necessities of life. In food and clothing and the common expenses of a civilised man, he pinched remorselessly; there was no choice. His lodgings cost him very little; but Mrs. Wick, whose profound suspiciousness was allied with unperfect honesty, now and then made paltry overcharges in her bill, and he was angry with himself for his want of courage to resist them. It meant only a shilling or two, but retail trade had taught him the importance of shillings. He had to remind himself that, if he was poor, his landlady was poorer still, and that in cheating him she did but follow the traditions of her class. To debate an excess of sixpence for paraffin, of ninepence for bacon, would have made him flush and grind his teeth for hours afterwards; but he noticed the effect upon himself of the new habit of niggardliness—how it disposed him to acerbity of temper. No matter how pure the motive, a man cannot devote his days to squeezing out pecuniary profits without some moral detriment. Formerly this woman, Mrs. Wick, with her gimlet eyes, and her leech lips, with her spyings and eavesdroppings, with her sour civility, her stinted discharge of obligations, her pilferings and mendacities, would have rather amused than annoyed him. "Poor creature, isn't it a miserable as well as a sordid life. Let her have her pickings, however illegitimate, and much good may they do her." Now he too often found himself regarding her with something like animosity, whereby, to be sure, he brought himself to the woman's level. Was it not a struggle between him and her for a share of life's poorest comforts? When he looked at it in that light, his cheeks were hot.

A tradesman must harden himself. Why, in the early months, it cost him a wrench somewhere to take coppers at the counter from very poor folk who perhaps made up the odd halfpenny in farthings, and looked at the coins reluctantly as they laid them down. More than once, he said, "Oh never mind the ha'penny," and was met with a look—not of gratitude but of blank amazement. Allchin happened to be a witness of one such incident, and, in the first moment of privacy, ventured a respectful yet a most energetic, protest. "It's the kindness of your 'eart, sir, and if anybody knows how much of that you have, I'm sure it's me, and I ought to be the last to find fault with it. But that'll never do behind the counter, sir, never! Why, just think. The profit on what that woman bought was just three farthings." He detailed the computation. "And there you've been and given her a whole ha'penny, so that you've only one blessed farthing over on the whole transaction! That ain't business, sir; that's charity; and Jollyman's ain't a charitable institution. You really must not, sir. It's unjust to yourself." And Will, with an uneasy shrug, admitted his folly. But he was ashamed to the core. Only in the second half-year did he really accustom himself to disregard a customer's poverty. He had thought the thing out, faced all its most sordid aspects. Yes, he was fighting with these people for daily bread; he and his could live only if his three farthings of profit were plucked out of that toil worn hand of charwoman or sempstress. Accept the necessity, and think no more of it. He was a man behind the counter; he saw face to face the people who supported him. With this exception had not things been just the same when he sat in the counting-house at the sugar refinery? It was an unpleasant truth, which appearances had formerly veiled from him.

With the beginning of his second winter came a new anxiety, a new source of bitter and degrading reflections. At not more than five minutes' walk away, another grocer started business; happily no great capitalist, but to all appearances a man of enterprise who knew what he was about. Morning and evening, Warburton passed the new shop and felt his very soul turn sour in the thought that he must do what in him lay to prevent that man from gaining custom; if he could make his business a failure, destroy all his hopes, so much the better. With Allchin, he held long and eager conferences. The robust assistant was of course troubled by no scruples; he warmed to the combat, chuckled over each good idea for the enemy's defeat; every nerve must be strained for the great Christmas engagement; as much money as possible must be spent in making a brave show. And it was only by pausing every now and then to remember *why* he stood here, in what cause he was so debasing the manner of his life, that Warburton could find strength to go through such a trial of body and of spirit. When, the Christmas fight well over, with manifest triumph on his side he went down for a couple of days to St. Neots, once more he had his reward. But the struggle was telling upon his health; it showed in his face, in his bearing. Mother and sister spoke uneasily of a change they noticed; surely he was working too hard; what did he mean by taking no summer holiday? Will laughed.

"Business, business! A good deal to do at first, you know. Things'll be smoother next year."

And the comfort, the quiet, the simple contentment of that little house by the Ouse, sent him back to Fulham Road, once more resigned, courageous.

Naturally, he sometimes contrasted his own sordid existence with the unforeseen success which had made such changes in the life of Norbert Franks. It was more than three months since he and Franks had met, when, one day early in January, he received a note from the artist. "What has become of you? I haven't had a chance of getting your way—work and social foolery. Could you come and lunch with me here, on Sunday, alone, like the old days? I have a portrait to show you." So on Sunday, Warburton went to his friend's new studio, which was in the Holland Park region. Formerly it was always he who played the host, and he did not like this change of positions; but Franks, however sensible of his good luck, and inclined at times to take himself rather seriously, had no touch of the snob in his temper; when with him, Will generally lost sight of unpleasant things in good-natured amusement. To-day, however, grocerdom lay heavily on his soul. On the return journey from St. Neots he had caught a cold, and a week of sore throat behind the counter—a week too, of quarrel with a wholesale house which had been cheating him—left his nerves in a bad state. For reply to the artist's cordial greeting he could only growl inarticulately.

"Out of sorts?" asked the other, as they entered the large well-warmed studio "You look rather bad."

"Leave me alone," muttered Warburton.

"All right. Sit down here and thaw yourself."

But Will's eye had fallen on a great canvas, showing the portrait of a brilliant lady who reclined at ease and caressed the head of a great deer-hound. He went and stood before it.

"Who's that?"

"Lady Caroline—I told you about her—don't you think it's rather good?"

"Yes. And for that very reason I'm afraid it's bad."

The artist laughed.

"That's good satire on the critics. When anything strikes them as good—by a new man, that is—they're ashamed to say so, just because they never dare trust their own judgment.—But it *is* good, Warburton; uncommonly good. If there's a weak point, it's doggy; I can't come the Landseer. Still, you can see it's meant for a doggy, eh?"

"I guessed it," replied Will, warming his hands.

"Lady Caroline is superb," went on Franks, standing before the canvas, head aside and hands in his pocket. "This is my specialty, old boy—lovely woman made yet lovelier, without loss of likeness. She'll be the fury of the next Academy.—See that something in the eyes, Warburton? Don't know how to call it. My enemies call it claptrap. But they can't do the trick, my boy, they can't do it. They'd give the end of their noses if they could."

## CHAPTER 23

He laughed gaily, boyishly. How well he was looking! Warburton, having glanced at him, smiled with a surly kindness.

"All your doing, you know," pursued Franks, who had caught the look and the smile. "You've made me. But for you I should have gone to the devil. I was saying so yesterday to the Crosses."

"The Crosses?"

Will had sharply turned his head, with a curious surprise.

"Don't you remember the Crosses?" said Franks, smiling with a certain embarrassment, "Rosamund's friends at Walham Green. I met them by chance not long ago, and they wanted me to go and see them. The old lady's a bore, but she can be agreeable when she likes; the girl's rather clever—does pictures for children's books, you know. She seems to be getting on better lately. But they are wretchedly poor. I was saying to them—oh, but that reminds me of something else. You haven't seen the Pomfrets lately?"

"No."

"Then you don't know that Mr. Elvan's dead?"

"No."

"He died a month ago, over there in the South of France. Rosamund has gone back to Egypt, to stay with that friend of hers at Cairo. Mrs. Pomfret hints to me that the girls will have to find a way of earning their living; Elvan has left practically nothing. I wonder whether—"

He smiled and broke off.

"Whether what?" asked the listener.

"Oh, nothing. What's the time?"

"Whether *what*?" repeated Warburton, savagely.

"Well—whether Rosamund doesn't a little regret?"

"Do *you*?" asked Will, without looking round.

"I? Not for a moment, my dear boy! She did me the greatest possible kindness—only *you* even did me a greater. At this moment I should have been cursing and smoking cheap tobacco in Battersea—unless I had got sick of it all and done the *hic jacet* business, a strong probability. Never did a girl behave more sensibly. Some day I hope to tell her so; of course when she has married somebody else. Then I'll paint her portrait, and make her the envy of a season—by Jove, I will! Splendid subject, she'd be. . . . When I think of that beastly so-called portrait that I put my foot through, the day I was in hell! Queer how one develops all at a jump. Two years ago I could no more paint a woman's portrait than I could build a cathedral. I caught the trick in the Slummer, but didn't see all it meant till Blackstaffe asked me to paint Lady Rockett.—Rosamund ought to have given me the sack when she saw that daub, meant for her. Good little girl; she held as long as she could. Oh, I'll paint her divinely, one of these days."

The soft humming of a gong summoned them to another room, where lunch was ready. Never had Warburton showed such lack of genial humour at his friend's table. He ate mechanically, and spoke hardly at all. Little by little, Franks felt the depressing effect of this companionship. When they returned to the studio, to smoke by the fireside, only a casual word broke the cheerless silence.

"I oughtn't to have come to-day," said Will, at length, half apologetically. "I feel like a bear with a sore head. I think I'm going."

"Shall I come and see you some evening?" asked the other in his friendliest tone.

"No—I mean not just yet.—I'll write and ask you."

And Will went out into the frosty gloom.

## CHAPTER 24

By way of Allchin, who knew all the gossip of the neighbourhood, Warburton learnt that his new competitor in trade was a man with five children and a wife given to drink; he had been in business in another part of London, and was suspected to have removed with the hope that new surroundings might help his wife to overcome her disastrous failing. A very respectable man, people said; kind husband, good father, honest dealer. But Allchin reported, with a twinkle of the eye, that all his capital had gone in the new start, and it was already clear that his business did not thrive.

"We shall starve him out!" cried the assistant, snapping his thumb and finger.

"And what'll become of him then?" asked Will.

"Oh, that's for him to think about," replied Allchin. "Wouldn't he starve us, if he could, sir?"

And Warburton, brooding on this matter, stood appalled at the ferocity of the struggle amid which he lived, in which he had his part. Gone was all his old enjoyment of the streets of London. In looking back upon his mood of that earlier day, he saw himself as an incredibly ignorant and careless man; marvelled at the lightness of heart which had enabled him to find amusement in rambling over this vast slaughter-strewn field of battle. Picturesque, forsooth! Where was its picturesqueness for that struggling, soon-to-be-defeated tradesman, with his tipsy wife, and band of children who looked to him for bread? "And I myself am crushing the man—as surely as if I had my hand on his gullet and my knee on his chest! Crush him I must; otherwise, what becomes of that little home down at St. Neots—dear to me as his children are to him. There's no room for both of us; he has come too near; he must pay the penalty of his miscalculation. Is there not the workhouse for such people?" And Will went about repeating to himself. "There's the workhouse—don't I pay poor-rates?—the workhouse is an admirable institution."

He lay awake many an hour of these winter nights, seeing in vision his own life and the life of man. He remembered the office in Little Ailie Street; saw himself and Godfrey Sherwood sitting together, talking, laughing, making a jest of their effort to support a doomed house. Godfrey used to repeat legends, sagas, stories of travel, as though existence had not a care, or the possibility of one; and he, in turn, talked about some bit of London he had been exploring, showed an old map he had picked up, an old volume of London topography. The while, world-wide forces, the hunger-struggle of nations, were shaking the roof above their heads. Theoretically they knew it. But they could escape in time; they had a cosy little corner preserved for themselves, safe from these pestilent worries. Fate has a grudge against the foolishly secure. If he laughed now, it was in self-mockery.

The night of London, always rife with mysterious sounds, spoke dreadfully to his straining ear. He heard voices near and far, cries of pain or of misery, shouts savage or bestial; over and through all, that low, far-off rumble or roar, which never for a moment ceases, the groan, as it seemed, of suffering multitudes. There tripped before his dreaming eyes a procession from the world of wealth and pleasure, and the amazement with which he viewed it changed of a sudden to fiery wrath; he tossed upon the bed, uttered his rage in a loud exclamation, felt his heart pierced with misery which brought him all but to tears. Close upon astonishment and indignation followed dread. Given health and strength, he might perhaps continue to hold his own in this merciless conflict; perhaps, only; but what if some accident, such as befalls this man or that in every moment of time, threw him among the weaklings? He saw his mother, in her age and ill-health, reduced to the pittance of the poorest; his sister going forth to earn her living; himself, a helpless burden upon both.—Nay, was there not rat-poison to be purchased?

How—he cried within himself—how, in the name of sense and mercy, is mankind content to live on in such a world as this? By what devil are they hunted, that, not only do they neglect the means of solace suggested to every humane and rational mind, but, the vast majority of them spend all their strength and ingenuity in embittering the common lot? Overwhelmed by the hateful unreason of it all, he felt as though his brain reeled on the verge of madness.

Every day, and all the day long, the shop, the counter. Had he chosen, he might have taken a half-holiday, now and then; on certain days Allchin was quite able, and abundantly willing, to manage alone; but what was the use? To go to a distance was merely to see with more distinctness the squalor of his position. Never for a moment was he tempted to abandon this work; he saw no hope whatever of earning money in any other way, and money he must needs earn, as long as he lived. But the life weighed upon him with a burden such as he had never imagined. Never had he understood before what was meant by the sickening weariness of routine; his fretfulness as a youth in the West Indies seemed to him now inconceivable. His own master? Why, he was the slave of every kitchen wench who came into the shop to spend a penny; he trembled at the thought of failing to please her, and so losing her custom. The grocery odours, once pleasant to him, had grown nauseating. And the ever repeated tasks, the weighing, parcel making, string cutting; the parrot phrases a thousand times repeated; the idiot bowing and smiling—how these things gnawed at his nerves, till he quivered like a beaten horse. He tried to console himself by thinking that things were now at the worst; that he was subduing himself, and would soon reach a happy, dull indifference; but in truth it was with fear that he looked forward—fear of unknown possibilities in himself; fear that he might sink yet more wretchedly in his own esteem.

For the worst part of his suffering was self-scorn. When he embarked upon this strange enterprise, he knew, or thought he knew, all the trials to which he would be exposed, and not slight would have been his indignation had any one ventured to hint that his character might prove unequal to the test. Sherwood's letter had pleased him so much, precisely because it praised his resolve as courageous, manly. On manliness of spirit, Will had always piqued himself; it was his pride that he carried a heart equal to any lot imposed upon him by duty. Yet little more than a twelvemonth of shopkeeping had so undermined his pluck, enfeebled his temper, that he could not regard himself in the glass without shame. He tried to explain it by failure of health. Assuredly his physical state had for months been declining and the bad cold from which he had recently suffered seemed to complete his moral downfall. In this piercing and gloom-wrapped month of February, coward thoughts continually beset him. In his cold lodgings, in the cold streets, in the draughts of the shop, he felt soul and body shrink together, till he became as the meanest of starveling hucksters.

Then something happened, which rescued him for awhile from this haunting self. One night, just at closing time—a night of wild wind and driven rain—Mrs. Hopper came rushing into the shop, her face a tale of woe. Warburton learnt that her sister "Liza," the ailing girl whom he had befriended in his comfortable days, had been seized with lung hemorrhage, and lay in a lamentable state; the help of Mrs. Allchin was called for, and any other that might be forthcoming. Two years ago Will would have responded to such an appeal as this with lavish generosity; now, though the impulse of compassion blinded him for a moment to his changed circumstances, he soon remembered that his charity must be that of a poor man, of a debtor. He paid for a cab, that the two women might speed to their sister through the stormy night as quickly as possible, and he promised to think of what could be done for the invalid—with the result that he lost a night's sleep in calculating what sum he might spare. On the morrow came the news he had expected; the doctor suggested Brompton Hospital, if admission could be obtained; home treatment at this time of the year, and in the patient's circumstances, was not likely to be of any good. Warburton took the matter in hand, went about making inquiries, found that there must necessarily be delay. Right or wrong, he put his hand in his pocket, and Mrs. Hopper was enabled to nurse her sister in a way otherwise impossible. He visited the sick-room, and for half an hour managed to talk as of old, in the note of gallant sympathy and encouragement. Let there be no stint of fire, of food, of anything the doctor might advise. Meanwhile, he would ask about other hospitals—do everything in his power. As indeed he did, with the result that in a fortnight's time, the sufferer was admitted to an institution to which, for the nonce, Warburton had become a subscriber.

He saw her doctor. "Not much chance, I'm afraid. Of course, if she were able to change climate—that kind of thing. But, under the circumstances—"

And through a whole Sunday morning Will paced about his little sitting-room, not caring to go forth, nor caring to read, caring for nothing at all in a world so full of needless misery. "Of course, if she were able to change climate—" Yes, the accident of possessing money; a life to depend upon that! In another station—though, as likely as not, with no moral superiority to justify the privilege—the sick woman would be guarded, soothed, fortified by every expedient of science, every resource of humanity. Chance to be poor, and not only must you die when you need not, but must die with the minimum of comfort, the extreme of bodily and mental distress. This commonplace struck so forcibly upon Will's imagination, that it was as a new discovery to him. He stood amazed, bewildered—as men of any thinking power are wont to do when experience makes real to them the truisms of life. A few coins, or pieces of printed paper to signify all that! An explosion of angry laughter broke the mood.

## CHAPTER 24

Pacing, pacing, back and fro in the little room, for hour after hour, till his head whirled, and his legs ached. Out of doors there was fitfully glinting sunshine upon the wet roofs; a pale blue now and then revealed amid the grey rack. Two years ago he would have walked twenty miles on a day like this, with eyes for nothing but the beauty and joy of earth. Was he not—he suddenly asked himself—a wiser man now than then? Did he not see into the truth of things; whereas, formerly, he had seen only the deceptive surface? There should be some solace in this reflection, if he took it well to heart.

Then his mind wandered away to Norbert Franks, who at this moment was somewhere enjoying himself. This afternoon he might be calling upon the Crosses. Why should that thought be disagreeable? It was, as he perceived, not for the first time. If he pictured the artist chatting side by side with Bertha Cross, something turned cold within him. By the bye, it was rather a long time since he had seen Miss Cross; her mother had been doing the shopping lately. She might come, perhaps, one day this week; the chance gave him something to look forward to.

How often had he called himself a fool for paying heed to Bertha Cross's visits?

## CHAPTER 25

Again came springtime, and, as he stood behind the counter, Warburton thought of all that was going on in the world he had forsaken. Amusements for which he had never much cared haunted his fancy; feeling himself shut out from the life of grace and intellect, he suffered a sense of dishonour, as though his position resulted from some personal baseness, some crime. He numbered the acquaintances he had dropped, and pictured them as mentioning his name—if ever they did so—with cold disapproval. Godfrey Sherwood had ceased to write; it was six months since his last letter, in which he hinted a fear that the Irish enterprise would have to be abandoned for lack of capital. Even Franks, good fellow as he was, seemed to grow lukewarm in friendship. The painter had an appointment for a Sunday in May at Will's lodgings, to smoke and talk, but on the evening before he sent a telegram excusing himself. Vexed, humiliated, Warburton wasted the Sunday morning, and only after his midday meal yielded to the temptation of a brilliant sky, which called him forth. Walking westward, with little heed to distance or direction, he presently found himself at Kew; on the bridge he lingered awhile, idly gazing at boats, and; as he thus leaned over the parapet, the sound of a voice behind him fell startlingly upon his ear. He turned, just in time to catch a glimpse of the features which that voice had brought before his mind's eye, Bertha Cross was passing, with her mother. Probably they had not seen him. And even if they had, if they had recognised him—did he flatter himself that the Crosses would give any sign in public of knowing their grocer?

With his eyes on the graceful figure of Bertha, he slowly followed. The ladies were crossing Kew Green; doubtless they would enter the Gardens to spend the afternoon there. Would it not be pleasant to join them, to walk by Bertha's side, to talk freely with her, forgetting the counter, which always restrained their conversation? Bertha was nicely dressed, though one saw that her clothes cost nothing. In the old days, if he had noticed her at all she would have seemed to him rather a pretty girl of the lower middle class, perhaps a little less insignificant than her like; now she shone for him against a background of "customers," the one in whom he saw a human being of his own kind, and who, within the imposed limits, had given proof of admitting his humanity. He saw her turn to look at her mother, and smile; a smile of infinite kindness and good-humour. Involuntarily his own lips responded; he walked on smiling—smiling.

They passed through the gates; he, at a distance of a dozen yards, still followed. There was no risk of detection; indeed he was doing no harm; even a grocer might observe, from afar off, a girl walking with her mother. But, after strolling for a quarter of an hour, they paused beside a bench, and there seated themselves. Mrs. Cross seemed to be complaining of something; Bertha seemed to soothe her. When he was near enough to be aware of this Will saw that he was too near. He turned abruptly on his heels, and—stood face to face with Norbert Franks.

"Hallo!" exclaimed the painter, with an air of embarrassment. "I thought that was your back!"

"Your engagement was here?" asked Will bluntly, referring to the other's telegram of excuse.

"Yes. I was obliged to—"

He broke off, his eyes fixed on the figures of Bertha and her mother.

"You were obliged—?"

"You see the ladies there," said Franks in a lower voice, "there, on the seat? It's Mrs. Cross and her daughter—you remember the Crosses? I called to see them yesterday, and only Mrs. Cross was at home, and—the fact is, I as good as promised to meet them here, if it was fine."

"Very well," replied Warburton carelessly, "I won't keep you."

"Go, but—"

Franks was in great confusion. He looked this way and that, as if seeking for an escape. As Will began to move away, he kept at his side.

"Look here, Warburton, let me introduce you to them. They're very nice people; I'm sure you'd like them; do let me—"

"Thank you, no. I don't want any new acquaintances."

"Why? Come along old man," urged the other. "You're getting too grumpy; you live too much alone. Just to please me—"

"No!" answered Will, resolutely, walking on.

"Very well—just as you like. But, I say, should I find you at home this evening? Say, nine o'clock. I particularly want to have a talk."

"Good. I'll be there," replied Will, and so, with knitted brows strode away.

Very punctually did the visitor arrive that evening. He entered the room with that same look of embarrassment which he had worn during the brief colloquy at Kew; he shook hands awkwardly, and, as he seated himself, talked about the fall of temperature since sunset, which made a fire agreeable. Warburton, ashamed of the sullenness he could not overcome, rolled this way and that in his chair, holding the poker and making lunges with it at a piece of coal which would not break.

"That was a lucky chance," began Franks at length, "our meeting this afternoon."

"Lucky? Why?"

"Because it has given me the courage to speak to you about something. Queerest chance I ever knew that you should be there close by the Crosses."

"Did they ask who I was?" inquired Warburton after a violent lunge with the poker, which sent pieces of coal flying into the room.

"They didn't happen to see me whilst I was talking with you. But, in any case," added Franks, "they wouldn't have asked. They're well-bred people, you know—really ladies. I suspect you've had a different idea of them. Wasn't that why you wouldn't let me introduce you?"

"Not at all," answered Will, with a forced laugh. "I've no doubt of their ladyhood."

"The fact of the matter is," continued the other, crossing and uncrossing, and re-crossing his legs in nervous restlessness, "that I've been seeing them now and then since I told you I was going to call there. You guess why? It isn't Mrs. Cross, depend upon it."

"Mrs. Cross's tea, perhaps?" said Will, with a hard grin.

"Not exactly. It's the worst tea I ever tasted. I must advise her to change her grocer."

Warburton exploded in a roar of laughter, and cried, as Franks stared wonderingly at him:

"You'll never make a better joke in your life than that."

"Shows what I can do when I try," answered the artist. "However, the tea is shockingly bad."

"What can you expect for one and sevenpence halfpenny per pound?" cried Will.

"How do *you* know what she pays?"

Warburton's answer was another peal of merriment.

## CHAPTER 25

"Well, I shouldn't wonder," Franks went on. "The fact is, you know, they're very poor. It's a miserable sort of a life for a girl like Bertha Cross. She's clever, in her way; did you ever see any of her work? Children's book-illustrating? It's more than passable, I assure you. But of course she's wretchedly paid. Apart from that, a really nice girl."

"So this is what you had to tell me?" said Warburton, in a subdued voice, when the speaker hesitated.

"I wanted to talk about it, old man, that's the truth."

Franks accompanied these words with a shy smiling look of such friendly appeal that Will felt his hard and surly humour begin to soften, and something of the old geniality stirring under the dull weight that had so long oppressed him.

"I suppose it's settled," he asked, staring at the fire.

"Settled? How?"

"When it comes to meetings at Kew Gardens—"

"Oh don't misunderstand," exclaimed Franks nervously, "I told you that it was with the mother I made the appointment—not with Bertha herself. I'm quite sure Bertha never heard a word of it."

"Well, it comes to the same thing."

"Not at all! I half wish it did."

"Half?" asked Warburton, with a quick glance.

"Can't you see that I haven't really made up my mind," said Franks, fidgeting in his chair. "I'm not sure of myself—and I'm still less sure of her. It's all in the air. I've been there perhaps half a dozen times—but only like any other acquaintance. And, you know, she isn't the kind of girl to meet one half way. I'm sorry you don't know her. You'd be able to understand better.—Then, you see, there's something a little awkward in her position and mine. She's the intimate friend of—of the other one, you know; at least, I suppose she still is; of course we haven't said anything about that. It makes misunderstandings very possible. Suppose she thought I made friends with her in the hope of getting round to the other again? You see how difficult it is to judge her behaviour—to come to any conclusion."

"Yes, I see," Warburton let fall, musingly.

"And, even if I were sure of understanding *her*—there's myself. Look at the position, now. I suppose I may call myself a successful man; well on the way to success, at all events. Unless fortune plays me a dirty trick, I ought soon to be making my three or four thousand a year; and there's the possibility of double that. Think what that means, in the way of opportunity. Once or twice, when I was going to see the

Crosses, I've pulled myself up and asked what the deuce I was doing—but I went all the same. The truth is, there's something about Bertha—I wish you knew her, Warburton; I really wish you did. She's the kind of girl any man might marry. Nothing brilliant about her—but—well, I can't describe it. As different as could be from—the other. In fact, it isn't easy to see how they became such close friends. Of course, she knows all about me—what I'm doing, and so on. In the case of an ordinary girl in her position, it would be irresistible; but I'm not at all sure that *she* looks at it in that way. She behaves to one—well, in the most natural way possible. Now and then I rather think she makes fun of me."

Warburton allowed a low chuckle to escape him.

"Why do you laugh?—I don't mean that she does it disagreeably. It's her way to look at things on the humorous side—and I rather like that. Don't you think it a good sign in a girl?"

"That depends," muttered Will.

"Well, that's how things are. I wanted to tell you. There's nobody else I should think of talking to about it."

Silence hung between them for a minute or two.

"You'll have to make up your mind pretty soon, I suppose," said Warburton at length, in a not unpleasant voice.

"That's the worst of it. I don't want to be in a hurry—it's just what I don't want."

"Doesn't it occur to you," asked Will, as if a sudden idea had struck him, "that perhaps she's no more in a hurry than you are?"

"It's possible. I shouldn't wonder. But if I seem to be playing the fool—?"

"That depends on yourself.—But," Will added, with a twinkle in his eye, "there's just one piece of advice I should like to offer you."

"Let me have it," replied the other eagerly. "Very good of you, old man, not to be bored."

"Don't," said Warburton, in an impressive undertone, "don't persuade Mrs. Cross to change her grocer."

# CHAPTER 26

This conversation brought Warburton a short relief. Laughter, even though it come from the throat rather than the midriff, tends to dispel morbid humours, and when he woke next morning, after unusually sound sleep, Will had a pleasure in the sunlight such as he had not known for a long time. He thought of Norbert Franks, and chuckled; of Bertha Cross, and smiled. For a day or two the toil of the shop was less irksome. Then came sordid troubles which again overcast the sky. Acting against his trusty henchman's advice, Will had made a considerable purchase of goods from a bankrupt stock; and what seemed to be a great bargain was beginning to prove a serious loss. Customers grumbled about the quality of articles supplied to them out of this unlucky venture, and among the dissatisfied was Mrs. Cross, who came and talked for twenty minutes about some tapioca that had been sent to her, obliging Mr. Jollyman to make repeated apologies and promises that such a thing should never occur again. When the querulous-voiced lady at length withdrew, Will was boiling over with rage.

"Idiot!" he exclaimed, regardless of the fact that Allchin overheard him.

"You see, sir," remarked the assistant. "It's just as I said; but I couldn't persuade you."

Will held his lips tight and stared before him.

"There'll be a net loss of ten pounds on that transaction," pursued Allchin. "It's a principle of honest business, never buy a bankrupt stock. But you wouldn't listen to me, sir—"

"That'll do, Allchin, that'll do!" broke in the master, quivering with the restraint he imposed upon himself. "Can't you see I'm not in a mood for that sort of thing?"

This same day, there was a leakage of gas on the premises, due to bad workmanship in some new fittings which had cost Will more than he liked. Then the shop awning gave way, and fell upon the head of a passer-by, who came into the shop swearing at large and demanding compensation for his damaged hat. Sundry other things went wrong in the course of the week, and by closing-time on Saturday night Warburton's nerves were in a state of tension which threatened catastrophe. He went to bed at one o'clock; at six in the morning, not having closed his eyes for a moment, he tumbled out again, dressed with fury, and rushed out of the house.

It was a morning of sunny showers; one moment the stones were covered with shining moisture, and the next were steaming themselves dry under unclouded rays. Heedless whither he went, so he did but move quickly enough, Will crossed the river, and struck southward, till he found himself by Clapham Junction. The sun had now triumphed; the day would be brilliant. Feeling already better for his exercise, he stood awhile reflecting, and decided at length to go by rail into the country. He might perhaps call on the Pomfrets at Ashtead; that would depend upon his mood. At all events he would journey in that direction.

It was some three months since he had seen the Pomfrets. He had a standing invitation to the pleasant little house, where he was always received with simple, cordial hospitality. About eleven o'clock, after a ramble about Ashtead Common, he pushed open the garden wicket, and knocked at the door under the leafy porch. So quiet was the house, that he half feared he would find nobody at home; but the servant at once led him in, and announced him at the door of her master's sanctum.

"Warburton?" cried a high, hearty voice, before he had entered. "Good fellow. Every day this week I've been wanting to ask you to come; but I was afraid; it's so long since we saw you, I fancied you must have been bored the last time you were here."

A small, thin, dry-featured man, with bald occiput and grizzled beard, Ralph Pomfret sat deep in an easy chair, his legs resting on another. Humour and kindliness twinkled in his grey eye. The room, which was full of books, had a fair view of meadows, and hill. Garden perfumes floated in at the open window.

"Kind fellow, to come like this," he went on. "You see that the old enemy has a grip on me. He pinches, he pinches. He'll get at my vitals one of these days, no doubt. And I've not even the satisfaction of having got my gout in an honourable way. If it had come to me from a fine old three-bottle ancestor! But I, who never had a grandfather, and hardly tasted wine till I was thirty years old—why, I feel ashamed to call myself gouty. Sit down, my wife's at church. Strange thing that people still go to church—but they do, you know. Force of habit, force of habit. Rosamund's with her."

## CHAPTER 26

"Miss Elvan?" asked Warburton, with surprise.

"Ah, yes I forgot you didn't know she was here. Came back with those friends of hers from Egypt a week ago. She has no home in England now; don't know where she will decide to live."

"Have you seen Norbert lately?" continued Mr. Pomfret, all in one breath. "He's too busy to come out to Ashtead, perhaps too prosperous. But no, I won't say that; I won't really think it. A good lad, Norbert—better, I suspect, than his work. There's a strange thing now; a painter without enthusiasm for art. He used to have a little; more than a little; but it's all gone. Or so it seems to me."

"He's very honest about it," said Warburton. "Makes no pretences—calls his painting a trick, and really feels surprised, I'm sure, that he's so successful."

"Poor Norbert! A good lad, a good lad. I wonder—do you think if I wrote a line, mentioning, by the way, that Rosamund's here, do you think he'd come?"

The speaker accompanied his words with an intimate glance. Will averted his eyes, and gazed for a moment at the sunny landscape.

"How long will Miss Elvan stay?" he asked.

"Oh, as long as she likes. We are very glad to have her."

Their looks met for an instant.

"A pity, a pity!" said Ralph, shaking his head and smiling. "Don't *you* think so?"

"Why, yes. I've always thought so."

Will knew that this was not strictly the truth. But in this moment he refused to see anything but the dimly suggested possibility that Franks might meet again with Rosamund Elvan, and again succumb to her charm.

"Heaven forbid!" resumed Ralph, "that one should interfere where lives are at stake! Nothing of that, nothing of that. You are as little disposed for it as I am. But simply to acquaint him with the fact—?"

"I see no harm. If I met him—?"

"Ah! To be sure. It would be natural to say—"

"I owe him a visit," remarked Will.

They talked of other things. All at once Warburton had become aware that he was hungry; he had not broken his fast to-day. Happily, the clock on the mantelpiece pointed towards noon. And at this moment there sounded voices within the house, followed by a tap at the study door which opened, admitting Mrs. Pomfret. The lady advanced with hospitable greeting; homely of look and speech, she had caught her husband's smile, and something of his manner—testimony to the happiness of a long wedded life. Behind her came the figure of youth and grace which Warburton's eyes expected; very little changed since he last saw it, in the Valley of Trient, Warburton was conscious of an impression that the young lady saw him again with pleasure. In a minute or two, Mrs. Pomfret and her niece had left the room, but Warburton still saw those pure, pale features, the emotional eyes and lips, the slight droop of the head to one side. Far indeed—so he said within himself—from his ideal; but, he easily understood, strong in seductiveness for such a man as Franks, whom the old passion had evidently left lukewarm in his thought of other women.

The bell gave a welcome summons to lunch—or dinner, as it was called in this household of simple traditions. Helped by his friend's arm, Ralph managed to hobble to table; he ate little, and talked throughout the meal in his wonted vein of cheerful reflection. Will enjoyed everything that was set before him; the good, wholesome food, which did credit to Mrs. Pomfret's housekeeping, had a rare savour after months of dining in the little parlour behind his shop, varied only by Mrs. Wick's cooking on Sundays. One thing, however, interfered with his ease; seated opposite to Rosamund Elvan, he called to mind the fact that his toilet this morning had been of the most summary description; he was unshaven, and his clothing was precisely what he had worn all yesterday at the counter. The girl's eyes passed observantly over him now and then; she was critical of appearances, no doubt. That his aspect and demeanour might be in keeping, he bore himself somewhat bluffly, threw out brief, blunt phrases, and met Miss Elvan's glance with a confident smile. No resentment of this behaviour appeared in her look or speech; as the meal went on, she talked more freely, and something of frank curiosity began to reveal itself in her countenance as she listened to him.

Ralph Pomfret having hobbled back to his study chair, to doze, if might be, for an hour or two, the others presently strolled out into the garden, where rustic chairs awaited them on the shadowy side.

"You have your pipe, I hope?" said the hostess, as Warburton stretched himself out with a sigh of content.

"I have."

"And matches?"

"Yes—No! The box is empty."

"I'll send you some. I have one or two things to see to indoors."

So Will and Rosamund sat alone, gazing idly at the summer sky, hearing the twitter of a bird, the hum of insects, whilst the scents of flower and leaf lulled them to a restful intimacy. Without a word of ceremony, Will used the matches that were brought him, and puffed a cloud into the warm air. They were talking of the beauties of this neighbourhood, of the delightful position of the house.

"You often come out to see my uncle, I suppose," said Rosamund.

"Not often, I'm seldom free, and not always in the humour."

"Not in the humour for *this*?"

"It sounds strange, doesn't it?" said Will, meeting her eyes. "When I'm here, I want to be here always; winter or summer, there's nothing more enjoyable—in the way of enjoyment that does only good. Do you regret Egypt?"

"No, indeed. I shall never care to go there again."

"Or the Pyrenees?"

"Have you seen them yet?" asked Rosamund.

Will shook his head.

"I remember your saying," she remarked, "you would go for your next holiday to the Basque country."

"Did I? Yes—when you had been talking much about it. But since then I've had no holiday."

"No holiday—all this time?"

Rosamund's brows betrayed her sympathy.

"How long is it since we were together in Switzerland?" asked Will, dreamily, between puffs. "This is the second summer, isn't it? One loses count of time, there in London. I was saying to Franks the other day—"

He stopped, but not abruptly; the words seemed to murmur away as his thoughts wandered. Rosamund's eyes were for a moment cast down. But for a moment only; then she fixed them upon him in a steady, untroubled gaze.

"You were saying to Mr. Franks—?"

The quiet sincerity of her voice drew Warburton's look. She was sitting straight in the cane chair, her hands upon her lap, with an air of pleasant interest.

"I was saying—oh, I forget—it's gone."

"Do you often see him?" Rosamund inquired in the same calmly interested tone.

"Now and then. He's a busy man, with a great many friends—like most men who succeed."

"But you don't mean, I hope, that he cares less for his friends of the old time, before he succeeded?"

"Not at all," exclaimed Will, rolling upon his chair, and gazing at the distance. "He's the same as ever. It's my fault that we don't meet oftener. I was always a good deal of a solitary, you know, and my temper hasn't been improved by ill-luck."

"Ill-luck?"

Again there was sympathy in Rosamund's knitted brow; her voice touched a note of melodious surprise and pain.

"That's neither here nor there. We were talking of Franks. If anything, he's improved, I should say. I can't imagine any one bearing success better—just the same bright, good-natured, sincere fellow. Of course, he enjoys his good fortune—he's been through hard times."

"Which would have been harder still, but for a friend of his," said Rosamund, with eyes thoughtfully drooped.

Warburton watched her as she spoke. Her look and her voice carried him back to the Valley of Trient; he heard the foaming torrent; saw the dark fir-woods, felt a cool breath from the glacier. Thus had Rosamund been wont to talk; then, as now, touching his elementary emotions, but moving his reflective self to a smile.

"Have you seen Miss Cross since you came back?" he asked, as if casually.

"Oh, yes. If I stay in England, I hope to live somewhere near her. Perhaps I shall take rooms in London, and work at water-colours and black-and-white. Unless I go to the Basque country, where my sister is. Don't you think, Mr. Warburton, one might make a lot of drawings in the Pyrenees, and then have an exhibition of them in London? I have to earn my living, and I must do something of that kind."

Whilst Will was shaping his answer Mrs. Pomfret came toward them from the house, and the current of the conversation was turned. Presently Ralph summoned his guest to the book-room, where they talked till the kindly hour of tea. But before setting out for his homeward journey, Warburton had another opportunity of exchanging words with Miss Elvan in the garden.

"Well, I shall hear what you decide to do," he said, bluffly. "If you go to the Pyrenees—but I don't think you will."

"No, perhaps not. London rather tempts me," was the girl's dreamy reply.

"I'm glad to hear it."

"I must get Bertha's advice—Miss Cross'."

Will nodded. He was about to say something, but altered his mind; and so the colloquy ended.

# CHAPTER 27

Toward ten o'clock that evening, Warburton alighted from a train at Notting Hill Gate, and walked through heavy rain to the abode of Norbert Franks. With satisfaction, he saw the light at the great window of his studio, and learnt from the servant who admitted him that Franks had no company. His friend received him with surprise, so long was it since Warburton had looked in unexpectedly.

"Nothing amiss?" said Franks, examining the hard-set face, with its heavy eyes, and cheeks sunken.

"All right. Came to ask for news, that's all."

"News? Ah, I understand. There's no news."

"Still reflecting?"

"Yes. Keeping away, just to see how I like it. Sensible that, don't you think?"

Warburton nodded. The conversation did not promise much vivacity, for Franks looked tired, and the visitor seemed much occupied with his own thoughts. After a few words about a canvas which stood on the easel—another woman the artist was boldly transforming into loveliness—Will remarked carelessly that he had spent the day at Ashtead.

"By Jove, I ought to go and see those people," said Franks.

"Better wait a little, perhaps," returned the other with a smile. "Miss Elvan is with them."

"Ah! Lucky you told me—not that it matters much," added Franks, after a moment's reflection, "at all events as far as I'm concerned. But it might be a little awkward for her. How long is she staying?"

Will told all he knew of Miss Elvan's projects. He went on to say that she seemed to him more thoughtful, more serious, than in the old time; to be sure, she had but recently lost her father, and the subduing influence of that event might have done her good.

"You had a lot of talk?" said Franks.

"Oh, we gossiped in the garden. Poor old Pomfret has his gout, and couldn't come out with us. What do you think, by the bye, of her chance of living by art? She says she'll have to."

"By that, or something else, no doubt," Franks replied disinterestedly. "I know her father had nothing to leave, nothing to make an income."

"Are her water-colours worth anything?"

"Not much, I'm afraid, I can't quite see her living by anything of that sort. She's the amateur, pure and simple. Now, Bertha Cross—there's the kind of girl who does work and gets paid for it. In her modest line, Bertha is a real artist. I do wish you knew her, Warburton."

"So you have said a good many times," remarked Will. "But I don't see how it would help you. I know Miss Elvan, and—"

He paused, as if musing on a thought.

"And what?" asked Franks impatiently.

"Nothing—except that I like her better than I used to."

As he spoke, he stood up.

"Well, I can't stay. It's raining like the devil. I wanted to know whether you'd done anything decisive, that's all."

"I'll let you know when I do," answered Franks, suppressing a yawn. "Good-night, old man."

For a fortnight, Warburton led his wonted life, shut off as usual from the outer world. About this time, Allchin began to observe with anxiety the change in his master's aspect and general behaviour.

"I'm afraid you're not feeling quite yourself, sir," he said at closing time one night. "I've noticed lately you don't seem quite well."

"Have you? Well, perhaps you are right. But it doesn't matter."

"If you'll excuse *me*, sir," returned the assistant, "I'm afraid it does matter. I hope, sir, you won't think I speak disrespectful, but I've been noticing that you didn't seem to care about waiting on customers lately."

"You've noticed that?"

"I have, sir, if the truth must be told. And I kept saying to myself as it wasn't like you. What I'm afraid of, sir, if you don't mind me saying it, is that the customers themselves are beginning to notice it. Mrs. Gilpin said to me yesterday—'What's come to Mr. Jollyman?' she says. 'He hasn't a civil word for me!' she says. Of course, I made out as you'd been suffering from a bad 'eadache, and I shouldn't wonder if that's the truth, sir."

Warburton set his teeth and said nothing.

## CHAPTER 27

"You wouldn't like to take just a little 'oliday, sir?" returned Allchin. "This next week, I could manage well enough. It might do you good, sir, to have a mouthful of sea air—"

"I'll think about it," broke in the other abruptly.

He was going away without another word, but, in crossing the shop, he caught his henchman's eye fixed on him with a troublous gaze. Self-reproach checked his steps.

"You're quite right, Allchin," he said in a confidential tone. "I'm not quite up to the mark, and perhaps I should do well to take a holiday. Thank you for speaking about it."

He walked home, and there, on his table, he found a letter from Franks, which he eagerly tore open. "I have as good as decided," wrote the artist. "Yesterday, I went to Ashtead, and saw R. We met like old friends—just as I wished. Talked as naturally as you and I. I suspect—only suspect of course—that she knows of my visits to Walham Green, and smiles at them! Yes, as you say, I think she has improved—decidedly. The upshot of it all is that I shall call on the Crosses again, and, when an opportunity offers, try my chance. I think I am acting sensibly, don't you?"

After reading this, Will paced about his room for an hour or two. Then he flung himself into bed, but got no sleep until past dawn. Rising at the usual hour, he told himself that this would not do; to live on in this way was mere moral suicide; he resolved to run down to St. Neots, whence, if his mother were capable of the journey, she and Jane might go for a week or two to the seaside. So, having packed his travelling bag, he walked to the shop, and arranged with Allchin for a week's absence, greatly to the assistant's satisfaction. Before noon he was at The Haws. But the idea of a family expedition to the seaside could not be carried out: Mrs. Warburton was not strong enough to leave home, and Jane had just invited a friend to come and spend a week with them. Disguising as best he could his miserable state of mind and body, Will stayed for a couple of days. The necessity for detailed lying about his affairs in London—lying which would long ago have been detected, but for the absolute confidence of his mother and sister, and the retired habits of their life—added another cause of unrest to those already tormenting him, and he was glad to escape into solitude. Though with little faith in the remedy, he betook himself to a quiet spot on the coast of Norfolk, associated with memories of holiday in childhood, and there for the rest of the time he had allowed himself did what a man could do to get benefit from sea and sky.

And in these endless hours of solitude there grew upon him a perception of the veritable cause of his illness. Not loss of station, not overwork, not love; but simply the lie to which he was committed. There was the root of the matter. Slowly, dimly, he groped toward the fact that what rendered his life intolerable was its radical dishonesty. Lived openly, avowedly, it would have involved hardships indeed, but nothing of this dull wretchedness which made the world a desert. He began to see how much better, how much easier, it would have been to tell the truth two years ago. His mother was not so weak-minded a woman as to be stricken down by loss of money; and as for Sherwood, his folly merited more than the unpleasantness that might have resulted to him from disclosure. Grocerdom with a clear conscience would have been a totally different thing from grocerdom surreptitiously embraced. Instead of slinking into a corner for the performance of an honourable act, he should have declared it, frankly, unaffectedly, to all who had any claim upon him. At once, the enterprise became amusing, interesting. If it disgraced him with any of his acquaintances, so much the worse for them; all whose friendship was worth having would have shown only the more his friends; as things stood, he was ashamed, degraded, not by circumstances, but by himself.

To undo it all—? To proclaim the truth—? Was it not easy enough? He had proved now that his business would yield income sufficient for his mother and sister, as well as for his own needs; the crisis was surmounted; why not cast off this load of mean falsehood, which was crushing him to the ground? By Heaven! he would do so.

Not immediately. Better wait till he had heard from Jane that their mother was a little stronger, which would probably be the case in a week or two. But (he declared ill his mind) the resolve was taken. At the first favourable moment he would undo his folly. Before taking this step, he must of course announce it to Godfrey Sherwood; an unpleasant necessity; but no matter.

He walked about the beach in a piping wind, waved his arms, talked to himself, now and then raised a great shout. And that night he slept soundly.

# CHAPTER 28

He got back to Fulham Road in time for the press of Saturday night. Allchin declared that he looked much better, and customers were once more gratified by Mr. Jollyman's studious civility. On Sunday morning he wrote a long letter to Sherwood, which, for lack of other address, he sent to the care of Godfrey's relative in Wales. This was something done. In the afternoon he took a long walk, which led him through the Holland Park region. He called to see Franks, but the artist was not at home; so he left a card asking for news. And the next day brought Franks' telegraphic reply. "Nothing definite yet. Shall come to see you late one of these evenings. I have not been to Walham Green." Though he had all but persuaded himself that he cared not at all, one way or the other, this message did Warburton good. Midway in the week, business being slack, he granted himself a half holiday, and went to Ashtead, merely in friendliness to Ralph Pomfret—so he said to himself.

From Ashtead station to the Pomfrets' house was a good twenty minutes' walk. As he strode along, eyes upon the ground, Will all at once saw the path darkened by a shadow; he then became conscious of a female figure just in front of him, and heedlessly glancing at the face, was arrested by a familiar smile.

"You were coming to see us?" asked Miss Elvan, offering her hand. "What a pity that I have to go to town! Only just time to catch the train."

"Then I'll walk back to the station with you—may I?"

"I shall be delighted, if you don't mind the trouble. I have an appointment with Miss Cross. She has found rooms which she thinks will suit me, and we're going to look at them together."

"So you have decided for London?"

"I think so. The rooms are at Chelsea, in Oakley Crescent. I know how fond you are of London, and how well you know it. And I know so little; only a street or two here and there. I mean to remedy my ignorance. If ever you have an afternoon to spare, Mr. Warburton, I should be so glad if you would let me go with you to see interesting places."

For an instant, Will was surprised, confused, but Rosamund's entire simplicity and directness of manner rebuked this sensation. He replied in a corresponding tone that nothing would please him more. They were now at the railway station, and the train approached. Rosamund having sprung into a carriage, gave her hand through the window, saying:

"I may be settled in a day or two. You will hear—"

With the sentence unfinished, she drew back, and the train rolled away. For a minute or two, Warburton stood on the platform, his lips mechanically prolonging the smile which had answered Miss Elvan's, and his thoughts echoing her last words. When he turned, he at first walked slowly; then his pace quickened, and he arrived at the Pomfrets' house, as though on urgent business. In the garden he caught sight of Ralph, recovered from his attack of gout, sitting at his ease, pipe in mouth. Will told of his meeting with Miss Elvan.

"Yes, yes; she's off to London town—wants to live there, like all the rest of the young people. In thirty years' time she'll have had enough of it, and be glad to creep into a quiet corner like this. My wife's in the house, teaching our new maid to make tea-cakes—you shall have some at five o'clock. I wonder whether any girl could be found nowadays who knows how to make tea-cakes? There's Rosamund—she knows no more about that kind of thing than of shipbuilding. Do you know any young lady who could make a toothsome tea-cake?"

"I'm not quite sure," answered Will reflectively, "but I have one in mind who perhaps does—it wouldn't surprise me."

"That's to your credit. By the bye, you know that Norbert has been here."

"Yes, I heard of it. He wrote to tell me."

"Aye, but he's been twice—did you know that? He was here yesterday."

"Indeed?"

Ralph looked at the other with an odd smile.

"One might have expected a little awkwardness between them," he continued. "Not a bit of it. There again—your girl of to-day; she has a way of her own with all this kind of thing. Why they just shook hands as if they'd never been anything but pleasant friends. All the same, as I tell you, Norbert has been a second time."

"I'm glad to hear it," said Warburton.

# CHAPTER 28

Will had purposed getting back to the shop about seven o'clock. He was, indeed, back in London at that hour, but his state of mind tempted him to shirk squalid duty; instead of turning toward Fulham Road, he took his way into the Strand, and there loitered in the evening sunshine, self-reproachful, yet enjoying the unwonted liberty. It was dinner-time; restaurants exhaled their pungent odours, and Will felt sharpening appetite. For the first time since his catastrophe, he granted himself the dinner of a well-to-do man, and, as would naturally befall in such a case, made his indulgence large.

Several days passed and brought no letter from any one. But at midnight on Saturday, there lay awaiting him a letter addressed in Sherwood's well-known hand. Godfrey began by excusing himself for his delay in replying; he had had rather a nasty attack of illness, and was only now able to hold his pen. But it was lucky he had not written before; this very morning there had reached him the very best news. "The father of the man who owes me ten thousand pounds is dying. Off and on he has been ill for a long time, but I hear at length that there can be no doubt whatever that the end is near. I can't pretend to any human feeling in this matter; the man's death means life for us—so the world goes. Any day now, you may have a telegram from me announcing the event. Of the prompt payment of the debt as soon as my friend inherits, there is no shadow of doubt. I therefore urge you very strongly not to make a disclosure. It will be needless. Wait till we see each other. I am still in Ireland—for a reason which I will explain when we meet."

Will drew a long breath. If ever news came opportunely, it was this. He threw up the window of his stuffy little sitting-room, and looked out into the summer night. The murmur of London once more made music to his ears.

# CHAPTER 29

Rosamund took the Chelsea lodgings proposed to her by Bertha Cross, and in a few days went to live there. The luggage which she brought from Ashtead enabled her to add a personal touch to the characterless rooms: in the place of the landlady's ornaments, which were not things of beauty, she scattered her own *bibelots*, and about the walls she hung a number of her own drawings, framed for the purpose, as well as several which bore the signature, "Norbert Franks." Something less than a year ago, when her father went abroad, their house at Bath had been given up, and the furniture warehoused; for the present, Rosamund and her sister were content to leave things thus. The inheritance of each amounted only to a few hundred pounds.

"It's enough to save one from worry for a year or two," said Rosamund to her friend Bertha. "I'm not extravagant; I can live here very comfortably. And there's a pleasure in the thought that one's work not only *may* succeed but *must*."

"I'm sure I hope so," replied Bertha, "but where's the *must*?"

"What am I to do if it doesn't?" asked Miss Elvan, with her sweet smile, and in a tone of irresistible argument.

"True," conceded her humorous friend. "There's no other way out of the difficulty."

This was on the day of Rosamund's coming to Chelsea. A week later, Bertha found the sitting-room brightened with the hanging watercolours, with curtains of some delicate fabric at the windows, with a new rug before the fire place.

"These things have cost so little," said Rosamund, half apologetically. "And—yes, I was obliged to buy this little tea service; I really couldn't use Mrs. Darby's; it spoilt the taste of the tea. Trifles, but they really have their importance; they help to keep one in the right mind. Oh, I must show you an amusing letter I've had from Winnie. Winifred is prudence itself. She wouldn't spend a sixpence unnecessarily. 'Suppose one fell ill,' she writes, 'what a blessing it would be to feel that one wasn't helpless and dependent. Oh, do be careful with your money, and consider very, very seriously what is the best course to take in your position.' Poor, dear old Winnie! I know she frets and worries about me, and pictures me throwing gold away by the handful. Yet, as you know, that isn't my character at all. If I lay out a few sovereigns to make myself comfortable here, I know what I'm doing; it'll all come back again in work. As you know, Bertha, I'm not afraid of poverty—not a bit! I had very much rather be shockingly poor, living in a garret and half starved, than just keep myself tidily going in lodgings such as these were before I made the little changes. Winnie has a terror of finding herself destitute. She jumped for joy when she was offered that work, and I'm sure she'd be content to live there in the same way for years. She feels safe as long as she needn't touch her money."

Winifred Elvan, since her father's death, had found an engagement as governess in an English family at St. Jean de Luz. This, in the younger sister's eyes, involved a social decline, more disagreeable to her than she chose to confess.

"The one thing," pursued Rosamund, "that I really dread, is the commonplace. If I were utterly, wretchedly, grindingly poor, there'd be at all events a savour of the uncommon about it. I can't imagine myself marrying a prosperous shopkeeper; but if I cared for a clerk who had nothing but a pound a week, I would marry him to-morrow."

"The result," said Bertha, "might be lamentably commonplace."

"Not if it was the right sort of man.—Tell me what you think of that bit." She pointed to a framed drawing. "It's in the valley of Bidassoa."

They talked art for a little, then Rosamund fell into musing, and presently said:

"Don't you think Norbert has behaved very well."

"How well?"

"I mean, it would have been excusable, perhaps, if he had betrayed a little unkind feeling toward me. But nothing of the kind, absolutely nothing. I'm afraid I didn't give him credit for so much manliness. When he came to Ashtead the second time, of course I understood his motive at once. He wished to show me that his behaviour at the first meeting wasn't mere bravado and to assure me that I needn't be afraid of him. There's a great deal of delicacy in that; it really pleased me."

Bertha Cross was gazing at her friend with a puzzled smile.

"You're a queer girl," she remarked.

"Queer? Why?"

"Do you mean that you were really and truly surprised that Mr. Franks behaved like a gentleman?"

"Oh, Bertha!" protested the other. "What a word!"

"Well, like a man, then."

"Perhaps I oughtn't to have felt that," admitted Rosamund thoughtfully. "But I did, and it meant a good deal. It shows how very right I was when I freed myself."

"Are you quite sure of that?" asked Bertha, raising her eyebrows and speaking more seriously than usual.

"I never was more sure of anything."

"Do you know, I can't help thinking it an argument on the other side."

Rosamund looked her friend in the eyes.

"Suppose it means that you were altogether mistaken about Mr. Franks?" went on Bertha, in the same pleasant tone between jest and earnest.

"I wasn't mistaken in my own feeling," said Rosamund in her melodious undertone.

"No; but your feeling, you have always said, was due to a judgment you formed of Mr. Franks' character and motives. And now you confess that it looks very much as if you had judged him wrongly."

Rosamund smiled and shook her head.

"Do you know," asked Bertha, after a pause, "that he has been coming to our house lately?"

"You never mentioned it. But why shouldn't he go to your house?"

"Rather, why should he?" asked Bertha, with a laugh. "Don't trouble to guess. The reason was plain enough. He came to talk about you."

"Oh!" exclaimed the listener with amused deprecation.

"There's no doubt of it; no—shadow—of—doubt. In fact, we've had very pleasant little chats about you. Of course I said all the disagreeable things I could; I knew that was what you would wish."

"Certainly," fell from Rosamund.

"I didn't positively calumniate you, but just the unpleasant little hints that a friend is so well able to throw out; the sort of thing likely to chill any one. I hope you quite approve?"

"Quite."

"Well, the odd thing was that they didn't quite have the effect I aimed at. He talked of you more and more, instead of less and less. Wasn't it provoking, Rosamund?"

Again their eyes encountered.

"I wish," continued Miss Elvan, "I knew how much of this is truth, and how much Bertha's peculiar humour."

# CHAPTER 29

"It's substantial truth. That there may be humour in it, I don't deny, but it isn't of my importing."

"When did he last come to see you?" Rosamund inquired.

"Let me see. Just before he went to see you."

"It doesn't occur to you," said Rosamund, slowly meditative, "that he had some other reason—not the apparent one—for coming to your house?"

"It doesn't occur to me, and never will occur to me," was Bertha's amused answer.

When it was time for Bertha to walk home wards, Rosamund put her hat on, and they went out together. Turning to the west, they passed along Cheyne Walk, and paused awhile by old Chelsea Church. The associations of the neighbourhood moved Miss Elvan to a characteristic display of enthusiasm. Delightful to live here! A joy to work amid such memories, of ancient and of latter time!

"I must get Mr. Warburton to come and walk about Chelsea with me," she added.

"Mr. Warburton?"

"He's a great authority on London antiquities. Bertha, if you happen to see Norbert these days, do ask him for Mr. Warburton's address."

"Why not ask your people at Ashtead?" said Bertha.

"I shan't be going there for two or three weeks. Promise to ask Norbert—will you? For me, of course."

Bertha had turned to look at the river. Her face wore a puzzled gravity.

"I'll try to think of it," she replied, walking slowly on.

"He's a great mystery," were Rosamund's next words. "My uncle has no idea what he does, and Norbert, they tell me, is just as ignorant, or at all events, professes to be. Isn't it a queer thing? He came to grief in business two years ago, and since then he has lived out of sight. Uncle Ralph supposes he had to take a clerk's place somewhere, and that he doesn't care to talk about it."

"Is he such a snob?" asked Bertha, disinterestedly.

"No one would think so who knows him. I'm convinced there's some other explanation."

"Perhaps the truth is yet more awful," said Bertha solemnly. "He may have got a place *in a shop*."

"Hush! hush!" exclaimed the other, with a pained look. "Don't say such things! A poor clerk is suggestive—it's possible to see him in a romantic light—but a shopman! If you knew him,' you would laugh at the idea. Mystery suits him very well indeed; to tell the truth, he's much more interesting now than when one knew him as a partner in a manufactory of some kind. You see he's unhappy—there are lines in his face—"

"Perhaps," suggested Bertha, "he has married a rich widow and daren't confess it."

# CHAPTER 30

It was on Saturday night that Godfrey Sherwood came at length to Warburton's lodgings. Reaching home between twelve and one o'clock Will saw a man who paced the pavement near Mrs. Wick's door; the man, at sight of him, hastened forward; there were exclamations of surprise and of pleasure.

"I came first of all at nine o'clock," said Sherwood. "The landlady said you wouldn't be back before midnight, so I came again. Been to the theatre, I suppose?"

"Yes," answered Will, "taking part in a play called 'The Grocer's Saturday Night.'

"I'd forgotten. Poor old fellow! You won't have much more of *that* thank Heaven!—Are you too tired to talk to-night?"

"No, no; come in."

The house was silent and dark. Will struck a match to light the candle placed for him at the foot of the stairs, and led the way up to his sitting-room on the first floor. Here he lit a lamp, and the two friends looked at each other. Each saw a change. If Warburton was thin and heavy-eyed, Sherwood's visage showed an even more noticeable falling-off in health.

"What's been the matter with you?" asked Will. "Your letter said you had had an illness, and you look as if you hadn't got over it yet."

"Oh, I'm all right now," cried the other. "Liver got out of order—or the spleen, or something—I forget. The best medicine was the news I got about old Strangwyn.—There, by Jove! I've let the name out. The wonder is I never did it before, when we were talking. It doesn't matter now. Yes, it's Strangwyn, the whisky man. He'll die worth a million or two, and Ted is his only son. I was a fool to lend that money to Ted, but we saw a great deal of each other at one time, and when he came asking for ten thousand—a mere nothing for a fellow of his expectations—nobody thought his father could live a year, but the old man has held out all this time, and Ted, the rascal, kept swearing he couldn't pay the interest on his debt. Of course I could have made him; but he knew I shouldn't dare to risk the thing coming to his father's ears. I've had altogether about three hundred pounds, instead of the four hundred a year he owed me—it was at four per cent. Now, of course, I shall get all the arrears—but that won't pay for all the mischief that's been done."

"Is it certain," asked Will, "that Strangwyn will pay?"

"Certain? If he doesn't I sue him. The case is plain as daylight."

"There's no doubt that he'll have his father's money?"

"None whatever. For more than a year now, he's been on good terms with the old man. Ted is a very decent fellow, of his sort. I don't say that I care as much for him now as I used to; we've both of us altered; but his worst fault is extravagance. The old man, it must be confessed, isn't very good form; he smells rather of the distillery; but Ted Strangwyn might come of the best family in the land. Oh, you needn't have the least anxiety. Strangwyn will pay, principal and interest, as soon as the old man has retired; and that may happen any day, any hour.—How glad I am to see you again, Will! I've known one or two plucky men, but no one like you. I couldn't have gone through it; I should have turned coward after a month of that. Well, it's over, and it'll be something to look back upon. Some day, perhaps, you'll amuse your sister by telling her the story. To tell you the truth, I couldn't bear to come and see you; I should have been too miserably ashamed of myself.—And not a soul has found you out, all this time?"

"No one that I know of."

"You must have suffered horribly from loneliness.—But I have things to tell you, important things." He waved his arm. "Not to-night; it's too late, and you look tired to death."

"Tell on," said Warburton. "If I went to bed I shouldn't sleep—where are you staying?"

"Morley's Hotel. Not at my own expense," Sherwood added hastily. "I'm acting as secretary to a man—a man I got to know in Ireland. A fine fellow! You'll know him very soon. It's about him that I want to tell you. But first of all, that idea of mine about Irish eggs. The trouble was I couldn't get capital enough. My cousin Hackett risked a couple of hundred pounds; it was all lost before the thing could really be set going. I had a bad time after that, Will, a bad time, I tell you. Yet good results came of it. For two or three months I lived on next to nothing—a few pence a day, all told. Of course, if I had let Strangwyn know how badly off I was, he'd have sent a cheque; but I didn't feel I had any right to his money, it was yours, not mine. Besides, I said to myself that, if I suffered, it was only what I deserved; I took it as a sort of expiation of the harm I'd done. All that time I was in Dublin, I tried to get employment but nobody had any use for me—until at last, when I was all but dying of hunger, somebody spoke to me of a certain Milligan, a young and very rich man living in Dublin. I resolved to go and see him, and a lucky day it was. You remember Conolly—Bates's traveller? Well, Milligan is just that man, in appearance; a thorough Irishman, and one of the best hearted fellows that ever lived. Though he's rich I found him living in a very plain way, in a room which looked like a museum, full of fossils, stuffed birds and animals, queer old pictures, no end of such things. Well, I told him plainly who I was, and where I was; and almost without thinking, he cried out—'What could be simpler? Come and be my secretary.'—'You want a secretary?'—'I hadn't thought of it,' said Milligan, 'but now it strikes me it's just what I *do* want. I knew there was something. Yes, yes, come and be my secretary; you're just the man.' He went on to tell me he had a lot of correspondence with sellers of curiosities, and it bored him to write the letters. Would I come for a couple of hours a day? He'd pay me twenty pounds a month. You may suppose I wasn't long in accepting. We began the next day, and in a week's time we were good friends. Milligan told me that he'd always had weak health, and he was convinced his life had been saved by vegetarianism. I myself wasn't feeling at all fit just then; he persuaded me to drop meat, and taught me all about the vegetarian way of living. I hadn't tried it for a month before I found the most wonderful results. Never in my life had I such a clear mind, and such good spirits. It remade me."

"So you've come to London to hunt for curios?" interposed Will.

"No, no; let me go on. When I got to know Milligan well, I found that he had a large estate somewhere in Connaught. And, as we talked, an idea came to me." Again he sprang up from his chair. "'If I were a landowner on that scale,' I said, 'do you know what I should do—I should make a vegetarian colony; a self-supporting settlement of people who ate no meat, drank no alcohol, smoked no tobacco; a community which, as years went on, might prove to the world that there was the true ideal of civilised life—health of mind and of body, true culture, true humanity!'" The eyes glowed in his fleshless, colourless face; he spoke with arm raised, head thrown back—the attitude of an enthusiastic preacher. "Milligan caught at the idea—caught at it eagerly. 'There's something fine in that!' he said. 'Why shouldn't it be done?' 'You're the man that could do it,' I told him. 'You'd be a benefactor to the human race. Isolated examples are all very well, but what we want is an experiment on a large scale, going on through more than one generation. Let children be born of vegetarian parents, brought up as vegetarians, and this in conditions of life every way simple, natural, healthy. This is the way to convert the world.' So that's what we're working at now, Milligan and I. Of course there are endless difficulties; the thing can't be begun in a hurry; we have to see no end of people, and correspond with the leaders of vegetarianism everywhere. But isn't it a grand idea? Isn't it worth working for?"

Warburton mused, smiling.

"I want you to join us," said Sherwood abruptly.

"Ho, ho! That's another matter."

"I shall bring you books to read."

"I've no time. I'm a grocer."

"Pooh!" exclaimed Sherwood. "In a few days you'll be an independent man.—Yes, yes, I know that you'll have only a small capital, when things are settled; but it's just people with a small capital that we want to enlist; the very poor and the well-to-do will be no use to us. It's too late to-night to go into details. We have time to talk, plenty of time. That you will join us, I feel sure. Wait till you've had time to think about it. For my own part, I've found the work of my life, and I'm the happiest man living!"

He walked round and round the table, waving his arms, and Warburton, after regarding him curiously, mused again, but without a smile.

# CHAPTER 31

Behind his counter next morning, Will thought over Sherwood's story, and laughed to himself wonderingly. Not that any freak of his old partner's—of the man whom he had once regarded as, above all, practical and energetic—could now surprise him; but it seemed astonishing that Godfrey should have persuaded a man of solid means, even a Celt, to pledge himself to such an enterprise Was the story true? Did Milligan really exist? If any doubt were possible on this point, did it not also throw suspicion on the story of Strangwyn, and the ten thousand pounds? Will grew serious at the reflection. He had never conceived a moment's distrust of Sherwood's honesty, nor did his misgiving now take that form; the question which troubled him throughout to-day was—whether Godfrey Sherwood might be a victim of delusions. Certainly he had a very strange look; that haggard face, those brilliant eyes—

So disquieting was the suspicion that, at dosing time, Will could no longer resist an impulse to betake himself to Morley's Hotel. Sherwood had said that Milligan was there only for a few days, until the wealthy Irishman could find a furnished house suitable to his needs whilst he remained in London. Arrived at the hotel, he inquired for his friend; Sherwood had dined and gone out. Will hesitated a moment, then asked whether Mr. Milligan was to be seen. Mr. Milligan, he learnt, had gone out with Mr. Sherwood. So Milligan did exist. Will's relief at settling this point banished his doubts on all the others. He turned westward again, and through a night of soft, warm rain walked all the way to his lodgings.

On the third day after, late in the evening, Sherwood paid him a second visit. Godfrey was in high spirits. He announced that Milligan had taken a house near the Marble Arch, where he also, as secretary, would have his quarters, and that already a meeting had been convened of the leading London vegetarians. Things were splendidly in train. Then he produced an evening newspaper, with a paragraph, which spoke of the serious illness of Mr. Strangwyn; recovery, it was said, could hardly be hoped for.

"What's more," cried Sherwood. "I've seen Ted Strangwyn himself. Nobody could behave better. The old man, he assured me, couldn't last more than a day or two, and he promised—quite spontaneously, I didn't say a word—to pay his debt in full as soon as ever his father's will was proved, which will be done as quickly as possible. —And now, have you thought over what I said the other night?"

"Thought—yes."

"With not much result, I see. Never mind; you must have time. I want you to meet Milligan. Could you come to lunch next Sunday? He invites you."

Warburton shook his head. He had never cared for the acquaintance of rich men, and was less than ever disposed to sit at their tables. All his anxieties regarding Sherwood's mental condition having been set at rest, he would go on with his grocer's life as long as need be, strengthened with the hope that shone before him.

The end of July had come. After a week of rain, the weather had turned bright, with a coolness at morning and evening very pleasant at this time of year in London streets. Warburton had business in the City which he must needs see to personally; he was on the point of leaving the shop, dressed as became a respectable citizen, silk hat and all, when in the doorway appeared Miss Bertha Cross. A certain surprise marked her smile of recognition; it meant, no doubt, that, never before having seen Mr. Jollyman save bareheaded and aproned, she was struck with the change in his aspect when thus equipped for going abroad. Immediately Mr. Jollyman doffed his hat and stepped behind the counter.

"Please don't let me keep you," said Bertha, with a glance towards Allchin, who was making parcels at the back of the shop. "I only want some—some matches, and one or two trifling things."

Never had she seemed so embarrassed in making a purchase. Her eyes fell, and she half turned away. Mr. Jollyman appeared to hesitate, he also glancing towards Allchin; but the young lady quickly recovered herself, and, taking up a packet of something exhibited on the counter, asked its price. The awkwardness was at an end; Bertha made her purchases, paid for them, and then left the shop as usual.

It was by the last post on the evening after this day that Warburton received a letter of which the exterior puzzled him. Whose could be this graceful, delicate hand? A woman's doubtless; yet he had no female correspondent, save those who wrote from St. Neots. The postmark was London. He opened, "Dear Mr. Warburton"—a glance over the leaf showed him—"Sincerely yours, Rosamund Elvan." H'm!

"Dear Mr. Warburton,—I am settled in my lodgings here, and getting seriously to work. It has occurred to me that you might be able to suggest some quaint corner of old London, unknown to me, which would make a good subject for a water-colour. London has been, I am sure, far too much neglected by artists; if I could mark out a claim here, as the colonists say, I should be lucky. For the present, I am just sketching (to get my hand in) about Chelsea. To-morrow afternoon, about six o'clock, if this exquisite mellow weather continues, I shall be on the Embankment in Battersea Park, near the Albert Bridge, where I want to catch a certain effect of sky and water."

That was all. And what exactly did it mean? Warburton's practical knowledge of women did not carry him very far, but he was wont to theorise at large on the subject, and in this instance it seemed to him that one of his favourite generalities found neat application. Miss Elvan had in a high degree the feminine characteristic of not knowing her own mind. Finding herself without substantial means, she of course meant to marry, and it was natural that she should think of marrying Norbert Franks; yet she could not feel at all sure that she wished to do so; neither was she perfectly certain that Franks would again offer her the choice. In this state of doubt she inclined to cultivate the acquaintance of Franks' intimate friend, knowing that she might thus, very probably, gather hints as to the artist's state of mind, and, if it seemed good to her, could indirectly convey to him a suggestion of her own. Warburton concluded, then, that he was simply being made use of by this typical young lady. That point settled, he willingly lent himself to her device, for he desired nothing better than to see Franks lured back to the old allegiance, and away from the house at Walham Green. So, before going to bed, he posted a reply to Miss Elvan's letter, saying that he should much like a talk with her about the artistic possibilities of obscure London, and that he would walk next day along the Battersea Embankment, with the hope of meeting her.

And thus it came to pass. Through the morning there were showers, but about noon a breeze swept the sky fair, and softly glowing summer reigned over the rest of the day. In his mood of hopefulness, Warburton had no scruple about abandoning the shop at tea-time; he did not even trouble himself to invent a decorous excuse, but told Allchin plainly that he thought he would have a walk. His henchman, who of late had always seemed rather pleased than otherwise when Warburton absented himself, loudly approved the idea.

"Don't you 'urry back, sir. There'll be no business as I can't manage. Don't you think of 'urrying. The air'll do you good."

As he walked away, Will said to himself that no doubt Allchin would only be too glad of a chance of managing the business independently, and that perhaps he hoped for the voluntary retirement of Mr. Jollyman one of these days. Indeed, things were likely to take that course. And Allchin was a good, honest fellow, whom it would be a pleasure to see flourishing.—How much longer would old Strangwyn cumber the world?

With more of elasticity than usual in his rapid stride, Will passed out of Fulham Road into King's Road, and down to the river at Cheyne Walk, whence his eye perceived a sitting figure on the opposite bank. He crossed Albert Bridge; he stepped down into the Park; he drew near to the young lady in grey trimmed with black, who was at work upon a drawing. Not until he spoke did she seem aware of his arrival; then with her brightest smile of welcome, she held out a pretty hand, and in her melodious voice thanked him for so kindly taking the trouble to come.

"Don't look at this," she added. "It's too difficult—I can't get it right—"

What his glance discovered on the block did not strengthen Will's confidence in Rosamund's claim to be a serious artist. He had always taken for granted that her work was amateurish, and that she had little chance of living by it. On the whole, he felt glad to be confirmed in this view; Rosamund as an incompetent was more interesting to him than if she had given proof of great ability.

"I mustn't be too ambitious," she was saying. "The river suggests dangerous comparisons. I want to find little corners of the town such as no one ever thought of painting—"

"Unless it was Norbert Franks," said Will genially, leaning on his stick with both hands, and looking over her head.

"Yes, I had almost forgotten," she answered with a thoughtful smile. "In those days he did some very good things."

".Some remarkably good things. Of course you know the story of how he and I first met?"

"Oh, yes. Early morning—a quiet little street—I remember. Where was that?"

"Over yonder." Will nodded southward. "I hope he'll take that up again some day."

"Oh, but let me do it first," exclaimed Rosamund, laughing. "You mustn't rob me of my chance, Mr. Warburton? Norbert Franks is successful and rich, or going to be; I am a poor struggler. Of course, in painting London, it's atmosphere one has to try for above all. Our sky gives value, now and then, to forms which in themselves are utterly uninteresting."

"Exactly what Franks used to say to me. There was a thing I wanted him to try—but then came the revolution. It was the long London street, after a hot, fine day, just when the lamps have been lit. Have you noticed how golden the lights are? I remember standing for a long time at the end of Harley Street, enjoying that effect. Franks was going to try it—but then came the revolution."

"For which—you mean, Mr. Warburton—I was to blame."

Rosamund spoke in a very low voice and a very sweet, her head bent.

"Why, yes," replied Will, in the tone of corresponding masculinity, "though I shouldn't myself have used that word. You, no doubt, were the cause of what happened, and so, in a sense, to blame for it. But I know it couldn't be helped."

"Indeed, it couldn't," declared Rosamund, raising her eyes a little, and looking across the river.

She had not in the least the air of a coquette. Impossible to associate any such trivial idea with Rosamund's habitual seriousness of bearing, and with the stamp of her features, which added some subtle charm to regularity and refinement. By temper critical, and especially disposed to mistrustful scrutiny by the present circumstances, Warburton was yet unable to resist the softening influence of this quintessential womanhood. In a certain degree, he had submitted to it during that holiday among the Alps, then, on the whole, he inclined to regard Rosamund impatiently and with slighting tolerance. Now that he desired to mark her good qualities, and so justify himself in the endeavour to renew her conquest of Norbert Franks, he exposed himself to whatever peril might lie in her singular friendliness. True, no sense of danger occurred to him, and for that very reason his state was the more precarious.

"You have seen him lately at Ashtead?" was his next remark.

"More than once. And I can't tell you how glad we were to see each other! I knew in a moment that he had really forgiven me—and I have always wanted to be assured of that. How thoroughly good and straightforward he is! I'm sure we shall be friends all our lives."

"I agree with you," he said, "that there's no better fellow living. Till now, I can't see a sign of his being spoilt by success. And spoilt in the worst sense, I don't think he ever will be, happen what may, there's a simplicity about him which makes his safeguard. But, as for his painting—well, I can't be so sure, I know little or nothing about it, but it's plain that he no longer takes his work very seriously. It pleases people—they pay large prices for it—where's the harm? Still, if he had some one to keep a higher ideal before him—"

He broke off, with a vague gesture. Rosamund looked up at him.

"We must try," she said, with quiet earnestness.

"Oh, I don't know that *I'm* any use," replied Will, with a laugh. "I speak with no authority. But you—yes. *You* might do much. More than any one else possibly could."

"That is exaggerating, Mr. Warburton," said Rosamund. "Even in the old days my influence didn't go for much. You speak of the 'revolution' caused by—by what happened; but the truth is that the revolution had begun before that. Remember I saw 'Sanctuary' while he was painting it, and, but we won't talk of that."

"To tell you the truth," returned Warburton, meeting her eyes steadily, with his pleasantest look, "I saw no harm in 'Sanctuary.' I think he was quite right to do what he could to earn money. He wanted to be married; he had waited quite long enough; if he hadn't done something of the kind, I should have doubted whether he was very much in earnest. No, no; what I call the revolution began when he had lost all hope. At the time he would have given up painting altogether, I believe; if it hadn't been that he owed me money, and knew I wanted it."

Rosamund made a quick movement of interest.

"I never heard about that."

"Franks wouldn't talk about it, be sure. He saw me in a hobble—I lost everything, all at once—and he went to work like a brick to get money for me. And that, when he felt more disposed to poison himself than to paint. Do you think I should criticise the work he did under these circumstances?"

"No, indeed! Thank you, Mr. Warburton, for telling me that story."

"How exquisite London is at this time of the year!" Rosamund murmured, as having declared it was time to be walking homewards, they walked slowly towards the bridge. "I'm glad not to be going away. Look at that lovely sky! Look at the tones of those houses.—Oh, I *must* make use of it all! Real use, I mean, as splendid material for art, not only for money-making. Do advise me, Mr. Warburton. Where shall I go to look for bits?"

Walking with bent head, Will reflected.

"Do you know Camberwell?" he asked. "There are good little corners—"

"I don't know it at all. Could you—I'm afraid to ask. You couldn't spare time—?"

"Oh yes, easily. That's to say, during certain hours."

"On Monday say? In the afternoon?"

"Yes."

"How kind of you!" murmured Rosamund. "If I were only an amateur, amusing myself, I couldn't give you the trouble; but it's serious I *must* earn money before long. You see, there's nothing else I can do. My sister—you know I have a sister?—she has taken to teaching; she's at St. Jean de Luz. But I'm no use for anything of that kind. I must be independent. Why do you smile?"

"Not at you, but at myself. I used to say the same thing. But I had no talent of any kind, and when the smash came—"

They were crossing the bridge. Will looked westward, in the direction of his shop, and it struck him how amusing it would be to startle Rosamund by a disclosure of his social status. Would she still be anxious for his company in search of the picturesque? He could not feel sure—curiosity urged him to try the experiment, but an obscure apprehension closed his lips.

"How very hard for you!" sighed Rosamund. "But don't think," she added quickly, "that I have a weak dread of poverty. Not at all! So long as one can support oneself. Nowadays, when every one strives and battles for money, there's a distinction in doing without it."

Five minutes more, and they were in Oakley Crescent. Rosamund paused before reaching the house in which she dwelt, took the campstool from her companion, and offered her hand for good-bye. Only then did Warburton become aware that he had said nothing since that remark of hers about poverty; he had walked in a dream.

## CHAPTER 32

August came, and Strangwyn, the great whisky distiller, was yet alive. For very shame, Will kept his thoughts from that direction. The gloomy mood had again crept upon him, in spite of all his reasons for hope; his sleep became mere nightmare, and his day behind the counter a bilious misery.

Since the occasion last recorded, Bertha Cross had not been to the shop. One day, the order was brought by a servant; a week later, Mrs. Cross herself appeared. The querulous lady wore a countenance so nearly cheerful that Warburton regarded her uneasily. She had come to purchase tea, and remarked that it was for use during a seaside holiday; you could never depend on the tea at seaside places. Perhaps, thought Will, the prospect of change sufficed to explain her equanimity. But for the rest of the day he was so glum and curt, that Allchin frequently looked at him with pained remonstrance.

At home, he found a telegram on his table. He clutched at it, rent the envelope. But no; it was not what he expected. Norbert Franks asked him to look in that evening. So, weary and heartsick as he was, he took the train to Notting Hill Gate.

"What is it?" he asked bluntly, on entering the studio.

"Wanted a talk, that was all," replied his friend. "Hope I haven't disturbed you. You told me, you remember, that you preferred coming here."

"All right. I thought you might have news for me."

"Well," said Franks, smiling at the smoke of his cigarette, "there's perhaps something of the sort."

The other regarded him keenly.

"You've done it."

"No—o—o; not exactly. Sit down; you're not in a hurry? I went to Walham Green a few days ago, but Bertha wasn't at home. I saw her mother. They're going away for a fortnight, to Southwold, and I have a sort of idea that I may run down there. I half promised."

Will nodded, and said nothing.

"You disapprove? Speak plainly, old man. What's your real objection? Of course I've noticed before now that you have an objection. Out with it!"

"Have you seen Miss Elvan again?"

"No. Have you?"

"Two or three times."

Franks was surprised.

"Where?"

"Oh, we've had some walks together."

"The deuce you have!" cried Franks, with a laugh.

"Don't you want to know what we talked about," pursued Warburton, looking at him with half-closed eyelids. "Principally about you."

"That's very flattering—but perhaps you abused me?"

"On the whole, no. Discussed you, yes, and in considerable detail, coming to the conclusion that you were a very decent fellow, and we both of us liked you very much."

Franks laughed gaily, joyously.

"*Que vous etes aimables, tous-les-deux*! You make me imagine I'm back in Paris. Must I round a compliment in reply?"

"That's as you like. But first I'll tell you the upshot of it all, as it shapes itself to me. Hasn't it even dimly occurred to you that, under the circumstances, it would be—well, say a graceful thing—to give that girl a chance of changing her mind again?"

"What—Rosamund?"

"It never struck you?"

"But, hang it all, Warburton!" exclaimed the artist. "How *should* I have thought of it? You know very well—and then, it's perfectly certain she would laugh at me."

"It isn't certain at all. And, do you know, it almost seems to me a point of honour."

"You're not serious? This is one of your solemn jokes—such as you haven't indulged in lately."

"No, no. Listen," said Will, with a rigid earnestness on his face as he bent forward in the chair. "She is poor, and doesn't know how she's going to live. You are flourishing, and have all sorts of brilliant things before you; wouldn't it be a generous thing—the kind of thing one might expect of a fellow with his heart in the right place—? You understand me?"

Franks rounded his eyes in amazement.

"But—am I to understand that she *expects* it?"

"Not at all. She hasn't in the remotest way betrayed such a thought—be assured of that. She isn't the sort of girl to do such a thing. It's entirely my own thought."

The artist changed his seat, and for a moment wore a look of perturbed reflection.

"How the deuce," he exclaimed, "can you come and talk to me like this when you know I've as good as committed myself—?"

"Yes, and in a wobbling, half-hearted way which means you had no right even to think of committing yourself. You care nothing about that other girl—"

"You're mistaken. I care a good deal. In fact—"

"In fact," echoed Warburton with good-natured scorn, "so much that you've all but made up your mind to go down to Southwold whilst she is there! Bosh! You cared for one girl in a way you'll never care for another."

"Well—perhaps—yes that may be true—"

"Of course it's true. If you don't marry *her*, go in for a prize beauty or for an heiress or anything else that's brilliant. Think of the scope before a man like you."

Franks smiled complacently once more.

"Why, that's true," he replied. "I was going to tell you about my social adventures. Who do you think I've been chumming with? Sir Luke Griffin—the great Sir Luke. He's asked me down to his place in Leicestershire, and I think I shall go. He's really a very nice fellow. I always imagined him loud, vulgar, the typical parvenu. Nothing of the kind—no one would guess that he began life in a grocer's shop. Why, he can talk quite decently about pictures, and really likes them."

Warburton listened with a chuckle.

"Has he daughters?"

"Three, and no son. The youngest, about seventeen, an uncommonly pretty girl. Well, as you say, why shouldn't I marry her and a quarter of a million? By Jove! I believe I could. She was here with her father yesterday. I'm going to paint the three girls together. —Do you know, Warburton, speaking without any foolish vanity, what astonishes me is to think of the enormous choice of wives there is for a man of decent appearance and breeding who succeeds in getting himself talked about. Without a joke, I am convinced I know twenty girls, and more or less nice girls, who would have me at once, if I asked them. I'm not a conceited fellow—am I now? I shouldn't say this to any one else. I'm simply convinced of its being a fact."

Warburton declared his emphatic agreement.

"Seeing that," he added, "why are you in such a hurry? Your millionaire grocer is but a steppingstone; who knows but you may soon chum with dukes? If any man living ought to be cautious about his marriage, it's you."

The artist examined his friend with a puzzled smile.

"I should like to know, Warburton, how much of this is satire, and how much serious advice. Perhaps it's all satire—and rather savage?"

"No, no, I'm speaking quite frankly."

"But, look here, there's the awkward fact that I really have gone rather far with the Crosses."

Will made a movement of all but angry impatience.

"Do you mean," he asked quickly, "that *she* has committed herself in any way?"

"No, that she certainly hasn't," was Franks, deliberate reply, in a voice as honest as the smile which accompanied it.

"My advice then is—break decently off, and either do what I suggested, or go and amuse yourself with millionaire Sir Luke, and extend your opportunities."

Franks mused.

"You are serious about Rosamund?" he asked, after a glance at Warburton's set face.

"Think it over," Will replied, in a rather hard voice. "I saw the thing like that. Of course, it's no business of mine; I don't know why I interfere; every man should settle these matters in his own way. But it was a thought I had, and I've told it you. There's no harm done."

# CHAPTER 33

When Warburton reached his lodging the next evening he found a letter on his table. Again the fine feminine hand; it was the second time that Rosamund had written to him. A vague annoyance mingled with his curiosity as he tore the envelope. She began by telling him of a drawing she had made in Camberwell Grove—not bad, it seemed to her, but she wished for his opinion. Then, in a new paragraph:

"I have seen Norbert again. I call him Norbert, because I always think of him by that name, and there's an affectation in writing 'Mr. Franks.' I felt that, when we talked of him, and I really don't know why I didn't simply call him Norbert then. I shall do so in future. You, I am sure, have little respect for silly social conventions, and you will understand me. Yes, I have seen him again, and I feel obliged to tell you about it. It was really very amusing. You know, of course, that all embarrassment was over between us. At Ashtead we met like the best of friends. So, when Norbert wrote that he wanted to see me, I thought nothing could be more natural, and felt quite glad. But, as soon as we met, I saw something strange in him, something seemed to have happened. And—how shall I tell you? It's only a guess of mine—things didn't come to foolish extremities—but I really believe that the poor fellow had somehow persuaded himself that it's his duty to—no, I can't go on, but I'm sure you will understand. I was never so amused at anything.

"Why do I write this to you? I hardly know. But I have just a suspicion that the story may not come to you quite as a surprise. If Norbert thought he had a certain duty—strange idea!—perhaps friends of his might see things in the same way. Even the most sensible people are influenced by curious ideas on one subject. I need not say that, as soon as the suspicion dawned upon me, I did my best to let him understand how far astray he was going. I think he understood. I feel sure he did. At all events he got into natural talk again, and parted in a thoroughly reasonable way.

## CHAPTER 33

"I beg that you won't reply to this letter. I shall work on, and hope to be able to see you again before long."

Warburton threw the sheet of paper on to the table, as if dismissing it from his thoughts. He began to walk about the room Then he stood motionless for ten minutes. "What's the matter with me?" this was the current of his musing. "I used to think myself a fellow of some energy; but the truth is, I know my mind about nothing, and I'm at the mercy of every one who chooses to push me this way or that."

He took up the letter again, and was about to re-read it, but suddenly altered his mind, and thrust the folded paper into his pocket.

Eight days went by. Will had a visit from Sherwood, who brought news that the whisky distiller had seemed a little better, but could not possibly live more than a week or two. As regards the vegetarian colony all went well; practical men were at work on the details of the scheme; Sherwood toiled for ten hours a day at secretarial correspondence. Next day, there came a postcard from Rosamund.

"Work ready to show you. Could you come and have a cup of tea to-morrow afternoon?"

At the conventional hour Will went to Oakley Crescent. Not, however, as he had expected, to find Miss Elvan alone; with her sat Mrs. Pomfret, in London for the afternoon. The simple and kindly lady talked as usual, but Will, nervously observant, felt sure that she was not quite at her ease. On the other hand, nothing could have been more naturally graceful than Rosamund's demeanour; whether pouring out tea, or exhibiting her water-colours, or leading the talk to subjects of common interest, she was charming in her own way, a way which borrowed nothing from the every-day graces of the drawing-room. Her voice, always subdued, had a range of melodious expression which caressed the ear, no matter how trifling the words she uttered, and at moments its slightly tremulous murmur on rich notes suggested depths of sentiment lying beneath this familiar calm. To her aunt she spoke with a touch of playful affection; when her eyes turned to Warburton, their look almost suggested the frankness of simple friendship, and her tone was that of the largest confidence.

Never had Will felt himself so lulled to oblivion of things external; he forgot the progress of time, and only when Mrs. Pomfret spoke of the train she had to catch, made an effort to break the lazy spell and take his leave.

On the morrow, and on the day after that, he shirked business during the afternoon, excusing himself with the plea that the heat of the shop was insufferable. He knew that neglect of work was growing upon him, and again he observed that Allchin seemed rather pleased than vexed by these needless absences. The third day saw him behind the counter until five o'clock, when he was summoned as usual to the back parlour to tea. Laying before him a plate of watercress and slices of brown bread and butter, Mrs. Allchin, a discreetly conversational young woman, remarked on the continued beauty of the weather, and added a hope that Mr. Jollyman would not feel obliged to remain in the shop this evening.

"No, no, it's your husband's turn," Will replied good-naturedly. "He wants a holiday more than I do."

"Allchin want a 'oliday, sir!" exclaimed the woman. "Why he never knows what to do with himself when he's away from business. He enjoys business, does Allchin. Don't you think of him, sir. I never knew a man so altered since he's been kept to regular work all the year round. I used to dread the Sundays, and still more the Bank holidays when we were here first; you never knew who he'd get quarrelling with as soon as he'd nothing to do But now, sir, why I don't believe you'll find a less quarrelsome man anywhere, and he was saying for a joke only yesterday, that he didn't think he could knock down even a coster, he's so lost the habit."

Will yielded and stole away into the mellowing sunshine. He walked westward, till he found himself on the Embankment by Albert Bridge; here, after hesitating awhile, he took the turn into Oakley Street. He had no thought of calling to see Miss Elvan; upon that he could not venture; but he thought it barely possible that he might meet with her in this neighbourhood, and such a meeting would have been pleasant. Disappointed, he crossed the river, lingered a little in Battersea Park, came back again over the bridge,—and, with a sudden leap of the heart, which all but made his whole body spring forward, saw a slim figure in grey moving by the parapet in front of Cheyne Walk.

They shook hands without speaking, very much as though they had met by appointment.

"Oh, these sunsets!" were Rosamund's first words, when they had moved a few steps together.

"They used to be my delight when I lived there," Will replied, pointing eastward.

"Show me just where it was, will you?"

They turned, and went as far as Chelsea Bridge, where Warburton pointed out the windows of his old flat.

"You were very happy there?" said Rosamund.

## CHAPTER 33

"Happy—? Not unhappy, at all events. Yes, in a way I enjoyed my life; chiefly because I didn't think much about it."

"Look at the sky, now."

The sun had gone down in the duskily golden haze that hung above the river's vague horizon. Above, on the violet sky, stood range over range of pleated clouds, their hue the deepest rose, shading to purple in the folds.

"In other countries," continued the soft, murmuring voice, "I have never seen a sky like that. I love this London!"

"As I used to," said Warburton, "and shall again."

They loitered back past Chelsea Hospital, exchanging brief, insignificant sentences. Then for many minutes neither spoke, and in this silence they came to the foot of Oakley Street, where again they stood gazing at the sky. Scarcely changed in form, the western clouds had shed their splendour, and were now so coldly pale that one would have imagined them stricken with moonlight; but no moon had risen, only in a clear space of yet blue sky glistened the evening star.

"I must go in," said Rosamund abruptly, as though starting from a dream.

# CHAPTER 34

She was gone, and Warburton stood biting his lips. Had he shaken hands with her? Had he said good-night? He could not be sure. Nothing was present to him but a sense of gawkish confusion, following on a wild impulse which both ashamed and alarmed him, he stood in a bumpkin attitude, biting his lips.

A hansom came crawling by, and the driver called his attention—"Keb, sir?" At once he stepped forward, sprang on to the footboard, and—stood there looking foolish.

"Where to, sir?"

"That's just what I can't tell you," he answered with a laugh. "I want to go to somebody's house, but don't know the address."

"Could you find it in the Directory, sir? They've got one at the corner."

"Good idea."

The cab keeping alongside with him, he walked to the public-house, and there, midway in whisky-and-soda, looked up in the great red volume the name of Strangwyn. There it was,—a house in Kensington Gore. He jumped into the hansom, and, as he was driven down Park Lane, he felt that he had enjoyed nothing so much for a long time; it was the child's delight in "having a ride"; the air blew deliciously on his cheeks, and the trotting clap of the horse's hoofs, the jingle of the bells, aided his exhilaration. And when the driver pulled up, it was with an extraordinary gaiety that Will paid him and shouted good-night.

He approached the door of Mr. Strangwyn's dwelling. Some one was at that moment turning away from it, and, as they glanced at each other, a cry of recognition broke from both.

"Coming to make inquiry?" asked Sherwood. "I've just been doing the same thing."

"Well?"

"No better, no worse. But that means, of course, nearer the end."

## CHAPTER 34

"Queer we should meet," said Warburton. "This is the first time I've been here."

"I can quite understand your impatience. It seems an extraordinary case; the poor old man, by every rule, ought to have died weeks ago. Which way are you walking?"

Will answered that he did not care, that he would accompany Sherwood.

"Let us walk as far as Hyde Park Corner, then," said Godfrey. "Delighted to have a talk with you." He slipped a friendly hand under his companion's arm. "Why don't you come, Will, and make friends with Milligan? He's a splendid fellow; you couldn't help taking to him. We are getting on gloriously with our work. For the first time in my life I feel as if I had something to do that's really worth doing. I tell you this scheme of ours has inconceivable importance; it may have results such as one dare not talk about."

"But how long will it be before you really make a start?" asked Warburton, with more interest than he had yet shown in this matter.

"I can't quite say—can't quite say. The details are of course full of difficulty—the thing wouldn't be worth much if they were not. One of Milligan's best points is, that he's a thoroughly practical man—thoroughly practical man. It's no commercial enterprise we're about, but, if it's to succeed, it must be started on sound principles. I'd give anything if I could persuade you to join us, old fellow. You and your mother and sister—you're just the kind of people we want. Think what a grand thing it will be to give a new start to civilisation! Doesn't it touch you?"

Warburton was mute, and, taking this for a sign of the impressionable moment, Sherwood talked on, ardently, lyrically, until Hyde Park Corner was reached.

"Think it over, Will. We shall have you yet; I know we shall. Come and see Milligan."

They parted with a warm hand-grip, and Warburton turned toward Fulham Road.

When Warburton entered the shop the next morning, Allchin was on the lookout for him.

"I want to speak to you, sir," he said, "about this golden syrup we've had from Rowbottom's—"

Will listened, or seemed to listen, smiling at vacancy. To whatever Allchin proposed, he gave his assent, and in the afternoon, without daring to say a word he stole into freedom.

He was once more within sight of Albert Bridge. He walked or prowled—for half an hour close about Oakley Crescent. Then, over the bridge and into the Park. Back again, and more prowling. At last, weary and worn, to the counter and apron, and Allchin's talk about golden syrup.

The next day, just before sunset, he sauntered on the Embankment. He lifted up his eyes, and there, walking towards him, came the slim figure in grey.

"Not like the other evening," said Rosamund, before he could speak, her eyes turning to the dull, featureless west.

He held her hand, until she gently drew it away, and then was frightened to find that he had held it so long. From head to foot, he quivered, deliciously, painfully. His tongue suffered a semi-paralysis, so that, trying to talk, he babbled—something about the sweetness of the air—a scent from the gardens across the river—

"I've had a letter from Bertha Cross," said his companion, as she walked slowly on. "She comes home to-morrow."

"Bertha Cross—? Ah, yes, your friend—"

The name sounded to Warburton as if from a remote past. He repeated it several times to himself.

They stood with face turned toward the lurid south. The air was very still. From away down the river sounded the bells of Lambeth Church, their volleying clang softened by distance to a monotonous refrain, drearily at one with the sadness of the falling night. Warburton heard them, yet heard them not; all external sounds blended with that within him, which was the furious beating of his heart. He moved a hand as if to touch Rosamund's, but let it fall as she spoke.

"I'm afraid I must go. It's really raining—"

Neither had an umbrella. Big drops were beginning to splash on the pavement. Warburton felt one upon his nose.

"To-morrow," he uttered thickly, his tongue hot and dry, his lips quivering.

"Yes, if it's fine," replied Rosamund.

"Early in the afternoon?"

"I can't. I must go and see Bertha."

They were walking at a quick step, and already getting wet.

"At this hour then," panted Will.

"Yes."

Lambeth bells were lost amid a hollow boom of distant thunder.

"I must run," cried Rosamund. "Good-bye."

# CHAPTER 34

He followed, keeping her in sight until she entered the house. Then he turned and walked like a madman through the hissing rain—walked he knew not whither—his being a mere erratic chaos, a symbol of Nature's prime impulse whirling amid London's multitudes.

## CHAPTER 35

Tired and sullen after the journey home from the seaside, Mrs. Cross kept her room. In the little bay-windowed parlour, Bertha Cross and Rosamund Elvan sat talking confidentially.

"Now, do confess," urged she of the liquid eyes and sentimental accent. "This is a little plot of yours—all in kindness, of course. You thought it best—you somehow brought him to it?"

Half laughing, Bertha shook her head.

"I haven't seen him for quite a long time. And do you really think this kind of plotting is in my way? It would as soon have occurred to me to try and persuade Mr. Franks to join the fire-brigade."

"Bertha! You don't mean anything by that? You don't think I am a danger to him?"

"No, no, no! To tell you the truth, I have tried to think just as little about it as possible, one way or the other. Third persons never do any good in such cases, and more often than not get into horrid scrapes."

"Fortunately," said Rosamund, after musing a moment with her chin on her hand, "I'm sure he isn't serious. It's his good-nature, his sense of honour. I think all the better of him for it. When he understands that I'm in earnest, we shall just be friends again, real friends."

"Then you are in earnest?" asked Bertha, her eyelids winking mirthfully.

Rosamund's reply was a very grave nod, after which she gazed awhile at vacancy.

"But," resumed Bertha, after reading her friend's face, "you have not succeeded in making him understand yet?"

"Perhaps not quite. Yesterday morning I had a letter from him, asking me to meet him in Kensington Gardens. I went, and we had a long talk. Then in the evening, by chance, I saw Mr. Warburton."

"Has that anything to do with the matter?"

"Oh, no!" replied Miss Elvan hastily. "I mention it, because, as I told you once before, Mr. Warburton always likes to talk of Norbert."

"I see. And you talked of him?"

## CHAPTER 35

"We only saw each other for a few minutes. The thunder-storm came on.—Bertha, I never knew any one so mysterious as Mr. Warburton. Isn't it extraordinary that Norbert, his intimate friend, doesn't know what he does? I can't help thinking he must write. One can't associate him with anything common, mean."

"Perhaps his glory will burst upon us one of these days," said Bertha.

"It really wouldn't surprise me. He has a remarkable face—the kind of face that suggests depth and force. I am sure he is very proud. He could bear any extreme of poverty rather than condescend to ignoble ways of earning money."

"Is the poor man very threadbare?" asked Bertha. "Has his coat that greenish colour which comes with old age in cheap material?"

"You incorrigible! As far as I have noticed, he is quite properly dressed."

"Oh, oh!" protested Bertha, in a shocked tone. "Properly dressed! What a blow to my romantic imagination! I thought at least his coat-cuffs would be worn out. And his boots? Oh, surely he is down at heel? Do say that he's down at heel, Rosamund!"

"What a happy girl you are, Bertha," said the other after a laugh. "I sometimes think I would give anything to be like you."

"Ah, but you don't know—you can't see into the gloomy depths, hidden from every eye but my own. For instance, while here we sit, talking as if I hadn't a care in the world I am all the time thinking that I must go to Mr. Jollyman's—the grocer's, that is—as we haven't a lump of sugar in the house."

"Then let me walk with you," said Rosamund. "I oughtn't to have come worrying you to-day, before you had time to settle down. Just let me walk with you to the grocer's, and then I'll leave you at peace."

They presently went forth, and walked for some distance westward along Fulham Road.

"Here's Mr. Jollyman's," said Bertha. "Will you wait for me, or come in?"

Rosamund followed her friend into the shop. Absorbed in thought, she scarcely raised her eyes, until a voice from behind the counter replied to Bertha's "Good-morning"; then, suddenly looking up, she saw that which held her motionless. For a moment she gazed like a startled deer; the next her eyes fell, her face turned away; she fled out into the street.

And there Bertha found her, a few yards from the shop.

"Why did you run away?"

Rosamund had a dazed look.

"Who was that behind the counter?" she asked, under her breath.

"Mr. Jollyman. Why?"

The other walked on. Bertha kept at her side.

"What's the matter?"

"Bertha—Mr. Jollyman is Mr. Warburton."

"Nonsense!"

"But he *is*! Here's the explanation—here's the mystery. A grocer—in an apron!"

Bertha was standing still. She, too, looked astonished, perplexed.

"Isn't it a case of extraordinary likeness?" she asked, with a grave smile.

"Oh, dear, no! I met his eye—he showed that he knew me—and then his voice. A grocer—in an apron?"

"This is very shocking," said Bertha, with a recovery of her natural humour. "Let us walk. Let us shake off the nightmare."

The word applied very well to Rosamund's condition; her fixed eyes were like those of a somnambulist.

"But, Bertha!" she suddenly exclaimed, in a voice of almost petulant protest. "He knew you all the time—oh, but perhaps he did not know your name?"

"Indeed he did. He's constantly sending things to the house."

"How extraordinary! Did you ever hear such an astonishing thing in your life?"

"You said more than once," remarked Bertha, "that Mr. Warburton was a man of mystery."

"Oh, but how *could* I have imagined—! grocer!"

"In an apron!" added the other, with awed voice.

"But, Bertha, does Norbert know? He declared he had never found out what Mr. Warburton did. Was that true, or not?"

"Ah, that's the question. If poor Mr. Franks has had this secret upon his soul! I can hardly believe it. And yet—they are such intimate friends."

"He must have known it," declared Rosamund.

Thereupon she became mute, and only a syllable of dismay escaped her now and then during the rest of the walk to the Crosses' house. Her companion, too, was absorbed in thought. At the door Rosamund offered her hand. No, she would not come in; she had work which must positively be finished this afternoon whilst daylight lasted.

Out of the by-street, Rosamund turned into Fulham Road, and there found a cab to convey her home. On entering the house, she gave instructions that she was at home to nobody this afternoon; then she sat down at the table, as though to work on a drawing, but at the end of an hour her brush had not yet been dipped in colour. She rose, stood in the attitude of one who knows not what to do, and at length moved to the window. Instantly she drew back. On the opposite side of the little square stood a man, looking toward her house; and that man was Warburton.

From safe retirement, she watched him. He walked this way; he walked that; again he stood still, his eyes upon the house. Would he cross over? Would he venture to knock at the door? No, he withdrew; he disappeared.

Presently it was the hour of dusk. Every few minutes Rosamund reconnoitred at the window, and at length, just perceptible to her straining eyes, there again stood Warburton. He came forward. Standing with hand pressed against her side, she waited in nervous anguish for a knock at the front door; but it did not sound. She stood motionless for a long, long time, then drew a deep, deep breath, and trembled as she let herself sink into a chair.

Earlier than usual, she went up to her bedroom. In a corner of the room stood her trunk; this she opened, and from the chest of drawers she took forth articles of apparel, which she began to pack, as though for a journey. When the trunk was half full, she ceased in weariness, rested for a little, and then went to bed.

And in the darkness there came a sound of subdued sobbing. It lasted for some minutes—ceased—for some minutes was again audible. Then silence fell upon the chamber.

Lying awake between seven and eight next morning, Rosamund heard the postman's knock. At once she sprang out of bed, slipped on her dressing-gown, and rang the bell. Two letters were brought up to her; she received them with tremulous hand. Both were addressed in writing, unmistakably masculine; the one was thick, the other was thin and this she opened first.

"Dear Miss Elvan"—it was Warburton who wrote—"I hoped to see you this evening, as we had appointed. Indeed, I *must* see you, for, as you may imagine, I have much to say. May I come to your house? In any case, let me know place and hour, and let it be as soon as possible. Reply at once, I entreat you. Ever sincerely yours—"

She laid it aside, and broke the other envelope.

"Dear, dearest Rosamund"—thus began Norbert Franks—"our talk this morning has left me in a state of mind which threatens frenzy. You know I haven't too much patience. It is out of the question for me to wait a week for your answer, though I promised. I can't wait even a couple of days. I must see you again to-morrow—must, must, *must.* Come to the same place, there's a good, dear, sweet, beautiful girl! If you don't, I shall be in Oakley Crescent, breaking doors open, behaving insanely. Come early—"

And so on, over two sheets of the very best notepaper, with Norbert's respectable address handsomely stamped in red at the top. (The other missive was on paper less fashionable, with the address, sadly plebeian, in mere handwriting.) Having read to the end, Rosamund finished her dressing and went down to the sitting-room. Breakfast was ready, but, before giving her attention to it, she penned a note. It was to Warburton. Briefly she informed him that she had decided to join her sister in the south of France, and that she was starting on the journey *this morning*. Her address, she added, would be "c/o Mrs. Alfred Coppinger, St. Jean de Luz, Basses Pyrenees." And therewith she remained Mr. Warburton's sincerely.

"Please let this be posted at once," said Rosamund when the landlady came to clear away.

And posted it was.

# CHAPTER 36

His hands upon the counter, Warburton stared at the door by which first Rosamund, then Bertha Cross, had disappeared. His nerves were a-tremble; his eyes were hot. Of a sudden he felt himself shaken with irresistible mirth; from the diaphragm it mounted to his throat, and only by a great effort did he save himself from exploding in laughter. The orgasm possessed him for several minutes. It was followed by a sense of light-heartedness, which set him walking about, rubbing his hands together, and humming tunes.

At last the burden had fallen from him; the foolish secret was blown abroad; once more he could look the world in the face, bidding it think of him what it would.

They were talking now—the two girls, discussing their strange discovery. When he saw Rosamund this evening—of course he would see her, as she had promised—her surprise would already have lost its poignancy; he had but to tell the story of his disaster, of his struggles, and then to announce the coming moment of rescue. No chance could have been happier than this which betrayed him to these two at the same time; for Bertha Cross's good sense would be the best possible corrective of any shock her more sensitive companion might have received. Bertha Cross's good sense—that was how he thought of her, without touch of emotion; whilst on Rosamund his imagination dwelt with exultant fervour. He saw himself as he would appear in her eyes when she knew all—noble, heroic. What he had done was a fine thing, beyond the reach of ordinary self-regarding mortals, and who more capable than Rosamund of appreciating such courage? After all, fate was kind. In the byways of London it had wrought for him a structure of romance, and amid mean pursuits it exalted him to an ideal of love.

And as he thus dreamt, and smiled and gloried—very much like an aproned Malvolio—the hours went quickly by. He found himself near Albert Bridge, pacing this way and that, expecting at every moment the appearance of the slim figure clad in grey. The sun set; the blind of Rosamund's sitting-room showed that there was lamplight within; and at ten o'clock Warburton still hung about the square, hoping—against his reason—that she might come forth. He went home, and wrote to her.

In a score of ways he explained to himself her holding aloof. It was vexation at his not having confided in her; it was a desire to reflect before seeing him again; it was—and so on, all through the night, which brought him never a wink of sleep. Next morning, he did not go to the shop; it would have been impossible to stand at the counter for ten minutes, he sent a note to Allchin, saying that he was detained by private affairs, then set off for a day-long walk in the country, to kill time until the coming of Rosamund's reply. On his return in the afternoon, he found it awaiting him.

An hour later he was in Oakley Crescent. He stood looking at the house for a moment, then approached, and knocked at the door. He asked if Miss Elvan was at home.

"She's gone away," was the reply of the landlady, who spoke distantly, her face a respectable blank.

"Left for good?"

"Yes, sir," answered the woman, her eyes falling.

"You don't know where she has gone to?"

"It's somewhere abroad, sir—in France, I think. She has a sister there."

This was at five o'clock or so. Of what happened during the next four hours, Will had never a very distinct recollection. Beyond doubt, he called at the shop, and spoke with Allchin; beyond doubt, also, he went to his lodgings and packed a travelling bag. Which of his movements were performed in cabs, which on foot, he could scarce have decided, had he reflected on the matter during the night that followed. That night was passed in the train, on a steamboat, then again on the railway And before sunrise he was in Paris.

At the railway refreshment-room, he had breakfast, eating with some appetite; then he drove to the terminus of another line. The streets of Paris, dim vistas under a rosy dawn, had no reality for his eyes; the figures flitting here and there, the voices speaking a foreign tongue, made part of a phantasm in which he himself moved no less fantastically. He was in Paris; yet how could that be? He would wake up, and find himself at his lodgings, and get up to go to business in Fulham Road; but the dream bore him on. Now he had taken another ticket. His bag was being registered—for St. Jean de Luz. A long journey lay before him. He yawned violently, half remembering that he had passed two nights without sleep. Then he found himself seated in a corner of the railway carriage, an unknown landscape slipping away before his eyes.

Now for the first time did he seem to be really aware of what he was doing. Rosamund had taken flight to the Pyrenees, and he was in hot pursuit. He grew exhilarated in the thought of his virile energy. If the glimpse of him aproned and behind a counter had been too great a shock for Rosamund's romantic nature, this vigorous action would more than redeem his manhood in her sight. "Yes, I am a grocer; I have lived for a couple of years by selling tea and sugar—not to speak of treacle; but none the less I am the man you drew on to love you. Grocer though I be, I come to claim you!" Thus would he speak and how could the reply be doubtful? In such a situation, all depends on the man's strength and passionate resolve. Rosamund should be his; he swore it in his heart. She should take him as he was, grocer's shop and all; not until her troth was pledged would he make known to her the prospect of better things. The emotions of the primitive lover had told upon him. She thought to escape him, by flight across Europe? But what if the flight were meant as a test of his worthiness? He seized upon the idea, and rejoiced in it. Rosamund might well have conceived this method of justifying both him and herself. "If he loves me as I would be loved, let him dare to follow!"

To-morrow morning he would stand before her, grocerdom a thousand miles away. They would walk together, as when they were among the Alps. Why, even then, had his heart prompted, had honour permitted, he could have won her. He believed now, what at the time he had refused to admit, that Franks' moment of jealous anger was not without its justification. Again they would meet among the mountains, and the shop in Fulham Road would be seen as at the wrong end of a telescope—its due proportions. They would return together to England, and at once be married. As for the grocery business—

Reason lost itself amid ardours of the natural man.

He paid little heed to the country through which he was passing. He flung himself on to the dark platform, and tottered drunkenly in search of the exit. *Billet*? Why, yes, he had a *billet* somewhere. Hotel? Yes, yes, the hotel,—no matter which. It took some minutes before his brain could grasp the idea that his luggage cheque was wanted; he had forgotten that he had any luggage at all. Ultimately, he was thrust into some sort of a vehicle, which set him down at the hotel door. Food? Good Heavens, no; but something to drink, and a bed to tumble into—quick.

He stood in a bedroom, holding in his hand a glass of he knew not what beverage. Before him was a waiter, to whom—very much to his own surprise—he discoursed fluently in French, or something meant for that tongue. That it was more than sixty hours since he had slept; that he had started from London at a moment's notice; that the Channel had been very rough for the time of the year; that he had never been in this part of France before, and hoped to see a good deal of the Pyrenees, perhaps to have a run into Spain; that first of all he wanted to find the abode of an English lady named Mrs. Cap—Cop—he couldn't think of the name, but he had written it down in his pocket-book.

The door closed; the waiter was gone; but Warburton still talked French.

"Oui, oui—en effet—tres fatigue, horriblement fatiguee! Trois nuits sans sommeil—trois nuits—trois!"

His clothes fell in a heap on the floor; his body fell in another direction. He was dead asleep.

## CHAPTER 37

Amid struggle and gloom the scene changed. He was in Kew Gardens, rushing hither and thither, in search of some one. The sun still beat upon him, and he streamed at every pore. Not only did he seek in vain, but he could not remember who it was that he sought. This way and that, along the broad and narrow walks, he hurried in torment, until of a sudden, at a great distance, he descried a figure seated on a bench. He bounded forward. In a moment he would see the face, and would know—

When he awoke a sense of strangeness hung about him, and, as he sat up in bed, he remembered. This was the hotel at St. Jean de Luz. What could be the time? He had no matches at hand, and did not know where the bell was. Looking around, he perceived at length a thread of light, of daylight undoubtedly, which must come from the window. He got out of bed, cautiously crossed the floor, found the window, and the means of opening it, then unlatched the shutters which had kept the room in darkness. At once a flood of sunshine poured in. Looking forth, he saw a quiet little street of houses and gardens, and beyond, some miles away, a mountain peak rising against the cloudless blue.

His watch had run down. He rang the bell, and learnt that the hour was nearly eleven.

"I have slept well," he said in his Anglo-French. "I am hungry. Bring me hot water. And find out, if you can, where lives Mrs. Coppinger. I couldn't remember the name last night—Mrs. Coppinger."

In half an hour he was downstairs. The English lady for whom he inquired lived, they told him, outside St. Jean de Luz, but not much more than a mile away. Good, he would go there after lunch. And until that meal was ready, he strolled out to have a look at the sea. Five minutes' walk brought him on to the shore of a rounded bay, sheltered by breakwaters against Atlantic storms above a sandy beach lay the little town, with grassy slopes falling softly to the tide on either hand.

At noon, he ate and drank heroically, then, having had his way pointed out to him, set forth on the quest. He passed through the length of the town, crossed the little river Nivelle, where he paused for a moment on the bridge, to gaze at the panorama of mountains, all but to the summit clad in soft verdure, and presently turned into an inland road, which led him between pastures and fields of maize, gently upwards. On a height before him stood a house, which he believed to be that he sought; he had written down its unrememberable Basque name, and inquiry of a peasant assured him that he was not mistaken. Having his goal in view, he stood to reflect. Could he march up to the front door, and ask boldly for Miss Elvan? But—the doubt suddenly struck him—what if Rosamund were not living here? At Mrs. Coppinger's her sister was governess; she had bidden him address letters there, but that might be merely for convenience; perhaps she was not Mrs. Coppinger's guest at all, but had an abode somewhere in the town. In that case, he must see her sister—who perhaps, nay, all but certainly, had never heard his name.

He walked on. The road became a hollow lane, with fern and heather and gorse intermingled below the thickets on the bank. Another five minutes would bring him to the top of the hill, to the avenue of trees by which the house was approached. And the nearer he came, the more awkward seemed his enterprise. It might have been better to write a note to Rosamund, announcing his arrival, and asking for an interview. On the other hand that was a timid proceeding; boldly to present himself before her would be much more effective. If he could only be sure of seeing her, and seeing her alone.

For a couple of hours did he loiter irresolutely, ever hoping that chance might help him. Perhaps, as the afternoon grew cooler, people might come forth from the house. His patience at length worn out, he again entered the avenue, half resolved to go up to the door.

All at once he heard voices—the voices of children, and toward him came two little girls, followed by a young lady. They drew near. Standing his ground, with muscles tense, Warburton glanced at the young lady's face, and could not doubt that this was Rosamund's sister; the features were much less notable than Rosamund's, but their gentle prettiness made claim of kindred with her. Forthwith he doffed his hat, and advanced respectfully.

"I think I am speaking to Miss Elvan?"

A nervous smile, a timidly surprised affirmative, put him a little more at his ease.

"My name is Warburton," he pursued, with the half humorous air of one who takes a liberty which he feels sure will be pardoned. "I have the pleasure of knowing your relatives, the Pomfrets, and—"

## CHAPTER 37

"Oh, yes, my sister has often spoken of you," said Winifred quickly. Then, as if afraid that she had committed an indiscretion, she cast down her eyes and looked embarrassed.

"Your sister is here, I think," fell from Warburton, as he threw a glance at the two little girls, who had drawn apart.

"Here? Oh, no. Not long ago she thought of coming, but—"

Will stood confounded. All manner of conjectures flashed through his mind. Rosamund must have broken her journey somewhere. That she had not left England at all seemed impossible.

"I was mistaken," he forced himself to remark carelessly. Then, with a friendly smile, "Forgive me for intruding myself. I came up here for the view—"

"Yes, isn't it beautiful!" exclaimed Winifred, evidently glad of this diversion from personal topics. And they talked of the landscape, until Warburton felt that he must take his leave. He mentioned where he was staying, said that he hoped to spend a week or so at St. Jean de Luz—and so got away, with an uneasy feeling that his behaviour had not exactly been such as to recommend him to the timid young lady.

Rosamund had broken her journey somewhere, that was evident; perhaps in Paris, where he knew she had friends. If she did not arrive this evening, or to-morrow, her sister would at all events hear that she was coming. But how was he to be informed of her arrival? How could he keep an espial on the house? His situation was wretchedly unlike that he had pictured to himself; instead of the romantic lover, carrying all before him by the energy of passion, he had to play a plotting, almost sneaking part, in constant fear of being taken for a presumptuous interloper. Lucky that Rosamund had spoken of him to her sister. Well, he must wait; though waiting was the worst torture for a man in his mood.

He idled through the day on the seashore. Next morning he bathed, and had a long walk, coming back by way of the Coppingers' house, but passing quickly, and seeing no one. When he returned to the hotel, he was told that a gentleman had called to see him, and had left his card "Mr. Alfred Coppinger." Ho, ho! Winifred Elvan had mentioned their meeting, and the people wished to be friendly. Excellent! This afternoon he would present himself. Splendid. Ml his difficulties were at an end. He saw himself once more in a gallant attitude.

The weather was very hot—unusually hot, said people at the hotel. As he climbed the hill between three and four o'clock, the sun's ardour reminded him of old times in the tropics. He passed along the shady avenue, and the house door was opened to him by a Basque maid-servant, who led him to the drawing-room. Here, in a dim light which filtered through the interstices of shutters, sat the lady of the house alone.

"Is it Mr. Warburton?" she asked, rising feebly, and speaking in a thin, fatigued, but kindly voice. "So kind of you to come. My husband will be delighted to see you. How did you get up here on such a day? Oh, the terrible heat!"

In a minute or two the door opened to admit Mr. Coppinger, and the visitor, his eyes now accustomed to the gloom, saw a ruddy, vigorous, middle-aged man, dressed in flannels, and wearing the white shoes called *espadrilles*.

"Hoped you would come," he cried, shaking hands cordially. "Why didn't you look in yesterday? Miss Elvan ought to have told you that it does me good to see an Englishman. Here for a holiday? Blazing hot, but it won't last long. South wind. My wife can't stand it. She's here because of the doctors, but it's all humbug; there are lots of places in England would suit her just as well, and perhaps better. Let's have some tea, Alice, there's a good girl. Mr. Warburton looks thirsty, and I can manage a dozen cups or so. Where's Winifred? Let her bring in the kits. They're getting shy; it'll do them good to see a stranger."

Will stayed for a couple of hours, amused with Mr. Coppinger's talk, and pleased with the gentle society of the ladies. The invitation to breakfast being seriously repeated, he rejoiced to accept it. See how Providence favours the daring. When Rosamund arrived, she would find him established as a friend of the Coppingers. He went his way exultingly.

But neither on the morrow, nor the day after, did Winifred receive any news from her sister. Will of course kept to himself the events of his last two days in London; he did not venture to hint at any knowledge of Rosamund's movements. A suspicion was growing in his mind that she might not have left England; in which case, was ever man's plight more ridiculous than his? It would mean that Rosamund had deliberately misled him; but could he think her capable of that? If it were so, and if her feelings toward him had undergone so abruptly violent a change simply because of the discovery she had made—why, then Rosamund was not Rosamund at all, and he might write himself down a most egregious ass.

Had not an inkling of some such thing whispered softly to him before now? Had there not been moments, during the last fortnight, when he stood, as it were, face to face with himself, and felt oddly abashed by a look in his own eyes?

# CHAPTER 37

Before leaving his lodgings he had written on a piece of paper "Poste Restante, St. Jean de Luz, France," and had given it to Mrs. Wick, with the charge to forward immediately any letter or telegram that might arrive for him. But his inquiries at the post-office were vain. To be sure, weeks had often gone by without bringing him a letter; there was nothing strange in this silence yet it vexed and disquieted him. On the fourth day of his waiting, the weather suddenly broke, rain fell in torrents, and continued for forty-eight hours. Had not the Coppingers' house been open to him he must have spent a wretched time. Returning to the hotel on the second evening of deluge, he looked in at the post-office, and this time a letter was put into his hand. He opened and read it at once.

"Dear old boy, why the deuce have you gone away to the end of the earth without letting me know? I called at your place this evening, and was amazed at the sight of the address which your evil-eyed woman showed me—looking as if she feared I should steal it. I wanted particularly to see you. How long are you going to stay down yonder? Rosamund and I start *for our honeymoon* on Thursday next, and we shall probably be away for a couple of months, in Tyrol. Does this astonish you? It oughtn't to, seeing that you've done your best to bring it about. Yes, Rosamund and I are going to be married, with the least possible delay. I'll tell you all the details some day—though there's very little to tell that you don't know. Congratulate me on having come to my senses. How precious near I was to making a tremendous fool of myself. It's you I have to thank, old man. Of course, as you saw, I should never have cared for any one but Rosamund, and it's pretty sure that she would never have been happy with any one but me. I wanted you to be a witness at our wedding, and now you've bolted, confound you! Write to my London address, and it will be forwarded."

Will thrust the letter into his pocket, went out into the street, and walked to the hotel through heavy rain, without thinking to open his umbrella.

Next morning, the sky was clear again, the sunny air fresh as that of spring. Will rose earlier than usual, and set out on an excursion. He took train to Hendaye, the little frontier town, at the mouth of the Bidassoa, crossed the river in a boat, stepped on to Spanish soil, and climbed the hill on which stands Fuenterabbia.

Later he passed again to the French shore, and lunched at the hotel. Then he took a carriage, and drove up the gorge of Bidassoa, enjoying the wild mountain scenery as much as he had enjoyed anything in his life. The road bridged the river; it brought him into Spain once more, and on as far as to the Spanish village of Vera, where he lingered in the mellowing afternoon. All round him were green slopes of the Pyrenees, green with pasture and with turf, with bracken, with woods of oak. There came by a yoke of white oxen, their heads covered with the wonted sheepskin, and on their foreheads the fringe of red wool tassels; he touched a warm flank with his palm, and looked into the mild, lustrous eyes of the beast that passed near him.

"Vera, Vera," he repeated to himself, with pleasure in the name. He should remember Vera when he was back again behind the counter in Fulham Road. He had never thought to see the Pyrenees, never dreamt of looking at Spain. It was a good holiday.

"Vera, Vera," he again murmured. How came the place to be so called? The word seemed to mean *true*. He mused upon it.

He dined at the village inn, then drove at dusk back to Hendaye, down the great gorge; crags and precipices, wooded ravines and barren heights glooming magnificently under a sky warm with afterglow; beside him the torrent leapt and roared, and foamed into whiteness.

And from Hendaye the train brought him back to St. Jean de Luz. Before going to bed, he penned a note to Mr. Coppinger, saying that he was Unexpectedly obliged to leave for England, at an early hour next day, and regretted that he could not come to say good-bye. He added a postscript. "Miss Elvan will, of course, know of her sister's marriage to Norbert Franks. I hear it takes place to-morrow. Very good news."

This written, he smoked a meditative pipe, and went upstairs humming a tune.

# CHAPTER 38

Touching the shore of England, Will stamped like a man who returns from exile. It was a blustering afternoon, more like November than August; livid clouds pelted him with rain, and the wind chilled his face; but this suited very well with the mood which possessed him. He had been away on a holiday—a more expensive holiday than he ought to have allowed himself, and was back full of vigour. Instead of making him qualmish, the green roarers of the Channel had braced his nerves, and put him in good heart; the boat could not roll and pitch half enough for his spirits. A holiday—a run to the Pyrenees and back; who durst say that it had been anything else? The only person who could see the matter in another light was little likely to disclose her thoughts.

At Dover he telegraphed to Godfrey Sherwood: "Come and see me to-night." True, he had been absent only a week, but the time seemed to him so long that he felt it must have teemed with events. In the railway carriage he glowed with good fellowship toward the other passengers; the rain-beaten hop-lands rejoiced his eyes, and the first houses of London were so many friendly faces greeting his return. From the station he drove to his shop. Allchin, engaged in serving a lady, forgot himself at the sight of Mr. Jollyman, and gave a shout of welcome. All was right, nothing troublesome had happened; trade better than usual at this time of year.

"He'll have to put up the shutters," said Allchin confidentially, with a nod in the direction of the rival grocer. "His wife's been making a row in the shop again—disgraceful scene—talk of the 'ole neighbourhood. She began throwing things at customers, and somebody as was badly hit on the jaw with a tin of sardines complained to the police. We shall be rid of him very soon, you'll see, sir."

This gave Warburton small satisfaction, but he kept his human thoughts to himself, and presently went home. Here his landlady met him with the announcement that only a few hours ago she had forwarded a letter delivered by the post this morning. This was vexatious;

several days must elapse before he could have the letter back again from St. Jean de Luz. Sure that Mrs. Wick must have closely scrutinised the envelope, he questioned her as to handwriting and postmark, but the woman declared that she had given not a glance to these things, which were not her business. Couldn't she even remember whether the writing looked masculine or feminine? No; she had not the slightest idea; it was not her business to "pry" and Mrs. Wick closed her bloodless lips with virtuous severity.

He had tea and walked back again to the shop, w ere as he girt himself with his apron, he chuckled contentedly.

"Has Mrs. Cross looked in?" he inquired.

"Yes, sir," answered his henchman, "she was here day before yes'day, and asked where you was. I said you was travelling for your health in foreign parts."

"And what did she say to that?"

"She said 'Oh'—that's all, sir. It was a very small order she gave. I can't make out how she manages to use so little sugar in her 'ouse. It's certain the servant doesn't have her tea too sweet—what do *you* think, sir?"

Warburton spoke of something else.

At nine o'clock he sat at home awaiting his visitor. The expected knock soon sounded and Sherwood was shown into the room. Will grasped his hand, calling out: "What news?

"News?" echoed Godfrey, in a voice of no good omen. "Haven't you heard?"

"Heard what?"

"But your telegram—? Wasn't that what it meant?"

"What do *you* mean?" cried Will. "Speak, man! I've been abroad for a week. I know nothing; I telegraphed because I wanted to see you, that was all."

"Confound it! I hoped you knew the worst. Strangwyn is dead."

"He's dead? Well, isn't that what we've been waiting for?"

"Not the old man," groaned Sherwood, "not the old man. It's Ted Strangwyn that's dead. Never was such an extraordinary case of bad luck. And his death—the most astounding you ever heard of. He was down in Yorkshire for the grouse. The dogcart came round in the morning, and as he stood beside it, stowing away a gun or something, the horse made a movement forward, and the wheel went over his toe. He thought nothing of it. The next day he was ill; it turned to tetanus; and in a few hours he died. Did you ever in your life hear anything like that?"

## CHAPTER 38

Warburton had listened gravely. Towards the end, his features began to twitch, and, a moment after Godfrey had ceased, a spasm of laughter overcame him.

"I can't help it, Sherwood," he gasped. "It's brutal, I know, but I can't help it."

"My dear boy," exclaimed the other, with a countenance of relief, "I'm delighted you can laugh. Talk about the irony of fate—eh? I couldn't believe my eyes when I saw the paragraph in the paper yesterday. But, you know," he added earnestly, "I don't absolutely give up hope. According to the latest news, it almost looks as if old Strangwyn might recover; and, if he does, I shall certainly try to get this money out of him. If he has any sense of honour—"

Will again laughed, but not so spontaneously.

"My boy," he said, "it's all up, and you know it. You'll never see a penny of your ten thousand pounds."

"Oh, but I can't help hoping—"

"Hope as much as you like. How goes the other affair?"

"Why, there, too, odd things have been happening. Milligan has just got engaged, and, to tell you the truth, to a girl I shouldn't have thought he'd ever have looked twice at. It's a Miss Parker, the daughter of a City man. Pretty enough if you like, but as far as I can see, no more brains than a teapot, and I can't for the life of me understand how a man like Milligan—. But of course, it makes no difference; our work goes on. We have an enormous correspondence."

"Does Miss Parker interest herself in it?" asked Will.

"Oh, yes, in a way, you know; as far as she can. She has turned vegetarian, of course. To tell you the truth, Warburton, it vexes me a good deal. I didn't think Milligan could do such a silly thing. I hope he'll get married quickly. Just at present, the fact is, he isn't quite himself."

Again Warburton was subdued by laughter.

"Well, I thought things might have been happening whilst I was away," he said, "and I wasn't mistaken. Luckily, I have come back with a renewed gusto for the shop. By the bye, I'm going to keep that secret no longer. I'm a grocer, and probably shall be a grocer all my life, and the sooner people know it the better. I'm sick of hiding away. Tell Milligan the story; it will amuse Miss Parker, And, talking of Miss Parker, do you know that Norbert Franks is married? His old love—Miss Elvan. Of course it was the sensible thing to do. They're off to Tyrol. As soon as I have their address, I shall write and tell him all about Jollyman's."

"Of course, if you really feel you must," said Godfrey, with reluctance. "But remember that I still hope to recover the money. Old Strangwyn has the reputation of being an honourable man—"

"Like Brutus," broke in Warburton, cheerfully. "Let us hope. Of course we will hope. Hope springs eternal—"

Days went by, and at length the desired letter came back from St. Jean de Luz. Seeing at a glance that it was from his sister, Will reproached himself for having let more than a month elapse without writing to St. Neots. Of his recent "holiday" he had no intention of saying a word. Jane wrote a longer letter than usual, and its tenor was disquieting. Their mother had not been at all well lately; Jane noticed that she was becoming very weak. "You know how she dreads to give trouble, and cannot bear to have any one worry about her. She has seen Dr. Edge twice in the last few days, but not in my presence, and I feel sure that she has forbidden him to tell me the truth about her. I dare not let her guess how anxious I am, and have to go on in my usual way, just doing what I can for her comfort. If you would come over for a day, I should feel very glad. Not having seen mother for some time, you would be better able than I to judge how she looks." After reading this Will's self-reproaches were doubled. At once he set off for St. Neots.

On arriving at The Haws, he found Jane gardening, and spoke with her before he went in to see his mother.

He had been away from home, he said, and her letter had strayed in pursuit of him.

"I wondered," said Jane, her honest eyes searching his countenance. "And it's so long since you sent a word; I should have written again this afternoon."

"I've been abominably neglectful," he replied, "and time goes so quickly."

"There's something strange in your look," said the girl. "What is it, I wonder? You've altered in some way I don't know how."

"Think so? but never mind me; tell me about mother."

They stood among the garden scents, amid the flowers, which told of parting summer, and conversed with voices softened by tender solicitude. Jane was above all anxious that her brother's visit should seem spontaneous, and Will promised not to hint at the news she had sent him. They entered the house together. Mrs. Warburton, after her usual morning occupations, had lain down on the couch in the parlour, and fallen asleep; as soon as he beheld her face, Will understood his sister's fears, White, motionless, beautiful in its absolute calm, the visage might have been that of the dead; after gazing for a moment, both, on the same impulse, put forth a hand to touch the unconscious form. The eyelids rose a look of confused trouble darkened the features then the lips relaxed in a happy smile.

"Will—and you find me asleep?—I appeal to Jane; she will tell you it's only an accident. Did you ever before see me asleep like this, Jane?"

At once she rose, and moved about, and strove to be herself; but the effort it cost her was too obvious; presently she had to sit down, with tremulous limbs, and Will noticed that her forehead was moist.

Not till evening did he find it possible to lead the conversation to the subject of her health. Jane had purposely left them alone. Her son having said that he feared she was not so well as usual, Mrs. Warburton quietly admitted that she had recently consulted her doctor.

"I am not young, Will, you know. Sixty-five next birthday."

"But you don't call that old!" exclaimed her son.

"Yes, it's old for one of my family, dear, None of us, that I know of, lived to be much more than sixty, and most died long before. Don't let us wear melancholy faces," she added, with that winning smile which had ever been the blessing of all about her. "You and I, dear, are too sensible, I hope, to complain or be frightened because life must have an end. When my time comes, I trust to my children not to make me unhappy by forgetting what I have always tried to teach them. I should like to think—and I know—that you would be sorry to lose me; but to see you miserable on my account, or to think you miserable after I have gone—I couldn't bear that."

Will was silent, deeply impressed by the calm voice, the noble thought. He had always felt no less respect than love for his mother, especially during the latter years, when experience of life better enabled him to understand her rare qualities; but a deeper reverence took possession of him whilst she was speaking. Her words not only extended his knowledge of her character; they helped him to an understanding of himself, to a clearer view of life, and its possibilities.

"I want to speak to you of Jane," continued Mrs. Warburton, with a look of pleasant reflection. "You know she went to see her friend, Miss Winter, a few weeks ago. Has she told you anything about it?"

"Nothing at all."

"Well, do you know that Miss Winter has taken up flower-growing as a business, and it looks as if she would be very successful. She is renting more land, to make gardens of, and has two girls with her, as apprentices. I think that's what Jane will turn to some day. Of course she won't be really obliged to work for her living, but, when she is alone, I'm certain she won't be content to live just as she does now—she is far too active; but for me, I daresay she would go and join Miss Winter at once."

"I don't much care for that idea of girls going out to work when they could live quietly at home," said Will.

"I used to have the same feeling," answered his mother, "but Jane and I have often talked about it, and I see there is something to be said for the other view. At all events, I wanted to prevent you from wondering what was to become of her when she was left alone. To be sure," she added, with a bright smile, "Jane may marry. I hope she will. But I know she won't easily be persuaded to give up her independence. Jane is a very independent little person."

"If she has that in mind," said Will, "why shouldn't you both go and live over there, in Suffolk? You could find a house, no doubt—"

Mrs. Warburton gently shook her head.

"I don't think I could leave The Haws. And—for the short time—"

"Short time? but you are not seriously ill, mother."

"If I get stronger," said Mrs. Warburton, without raising her eyes, "we must manage to send Jane into Suffolk. I could get along very well alone. But there—we have talked enough for this evening, Will. Can you stay over tomorrow? Do, if you could manage it. I am glad to have you near me."

When they parted for the night, Will asked his sister to meet him in the garden before breakfast, and Jane nodded assent.

# CHAPTER 39

The garden was drenched in dew, and when about seven o'clock, the first sunbeam pierced the grey mantle of the east, every leaf flashed back the yellow light. Will was walking there alone, his eyes turned now and then to the white window of his mother's room.

Jane came forth with her rosy morning face, her expression graver than of wont.

"You are uneasy about mother," were her first words. "So am I, very. I feel convinced Dr. Edge has given her some serious warning; I saw the change in her after his last visit."

"I shall go and see him," said Will.

They talked of their anxiety, then Warburton proposed that they should walk a little way along the road, for the air was cool.

"I've something I want to tell you," he began, when they had set forth. "It's a little startling—rather ludicrous, too. What should you say if some one came and told you he had seen me serving behind a grocer's counter in London?"

"What do you mean, Will?"

"Well, I want to know how it would strike you. Should you be horrified?"

"No; but astonished."

"Very well. The fact of the matter is then," said Warburton, with an uneasy smile, "that for a couple of years I *have* been doing that. It came about in this way—"

He related Godfrey Sherwood's reckless proceedings, and the circumstances which had decided him to take a shop. No exclamation escaped the listener; she walked with eyes downcast, and, when her brother ceased, looked at him very gently, affectionately.

"It was brave of you, Will," she said.

"Well, I saw no other way of making good the loss; but now I am sick of living a double life—*that* has really been the worst part of it, all along. What I want to ask you, is—would it be wise or not to tell mother? Would it worry and distress her? As for the money, you see there's nothing to worry about; the shop will yield a sufficient income, though not as much as we hoped from Applegarth's; but of course I shall have to go on behind the counter."

He broke off, laughing, and Jane smiled, though with a line of trouble on her brow.

"That won't do," she said, with quiet decision.

"Oh, I'm getting used to it."

"No, no, Will, it won't do. We must find a better way. I see no harm in shopkeeping, if one has been brought up to it; but you haven't, and it isn't suitable for you. About mother—yes, I think we'd better tell her. She won't worry on account of the money; that isn't her nature, and it's very much better that there should be confidence between us all."

"I haven't enjoyed telling lies," said Will, "I assure you."

"That I'm sure you haven't, poor boy!—but Mr. Sherwood? Hasn't he made any effort to help you. Surely he—"

"Poor old Godfrey!" broke in her brother, laughing. "It's a joke to remember that I used to think him a splendid man of business, far more practical than I. Why, there's no dreamier muddlehead living."

He told the stories of Strangwyn and of Milligan with such exuberance of humour that Jane could not but join in his merriment.

"No, no; it's no good looking in that direction. The money has gone, there's no help for it. But you can depend on Jollyman's. Of course the affair would have been much more difficult without Allchin. Oh, you must see Allchin some day!"

"And absolutely no one has discovered the secret?" asked Jane.

Will hesitated, then.

"Yes, one person. You remember the name of Miss Elvan? A fortnight ago—imagine the scene—she walked into the shop with a friend of hers, a Miss Cross, who has been one of my customers from the first. As soon as she caught sight of me she turned and ran; yes, ran out into the street in indignation and horror. Of course she must have told her friend, and whether Miss Cross will ever come to the shop again, I don't know. I never mentioned that name to you, did I? The Crosses were friends of Norbert Franks. And, by the bye, I hear that Franks was married to Miss Elvan a few days ago—just after her awful discovery. No doubt she told him, and perhaps he'll drop my acquaintance."

"You don't mean that?"

"Well, not quite; but it wouldn't surprise me if his wife told him that really one mustn't be too intimate with grocers. In future, I'm going to tell everybody; there shall be no more hiding and sneaking.

That's what debases a man; not the selling of sugar and tea. A short time ago, I had got into a vile state of mind; I felt like poisoning myself. And I'm convinced it was merely the burden of lies weighing upupon me. Yes, yes, you're quite right; of course, mother must be told. Shall I leave it to you, Jane? I think you could break it better."

After breakfast, Will walked into St. Neots, to have a private conversation with Dr. Edge, and whilst he was away Jane told her mother the story of the lost money. At the end of an hour's talk, she went out into the garden, where presently she was found by her brother, who had walked back at his utmost pace, and wore a perturbed countenance.

"You haven't told yet?" were his first words, uttered in a breathless undertone.

"Why?" asked Jane startled.

"I'm afraid of the result. Edge says that every sort of agitation must be avoided."

"I have told her," said Jane, with quiet voice, but anxious look. "She was grieved on your account, but it gave her no shock. Again and again she said how glad she was you had let us know the truth."

"So far then, good."

"But Dr. Edge—what did he tell you?"

"He said he had wanted to see me, and thought of writing. Yes, he speaks seriously."

They talked for a little, then Will went into the house alone, and found his mother as she sat in her wonted place, the usual needlework on her lap. As he crossed the room, she kept her eyes upon him in a gaze of the gentlest reproach, mingled with a smile, which told the origin of Will's wholesome humour.

"And you couldn't trust me to take my share of the trouble?"

"I knew only too well," replied her son, "that your own share wouldn't content you."

"Greedy mother!—Perhaps you were right, Will. I suppose I should have interfered, and made everything worse for you; but you needn't have waited quite so long before telling me. The one thing that I can't understand is Mr. Sherwood's behaviour. You had always given me such a different idea of him. Really, I don't think he ought to have been let off so easily."

"Oh, poor old Godfrey! What could he do? He was sorry as man could be, and he gave me all the cash he could scrape together—"

"I'm glad he wasn't a friend of mine," said Mrs. Warburton. "In all my life, I have never quarrelled with a friend, but I'm afraid I must have fallen out with Mr. Sherwood. Think of the women who entrust their all to men of that kind, and have no strong son to save them from the consequences."

After the mid-day meal all sat together for an hour or two in the garden. By an evening train, Will returned to London. Jane had promised to let him have frequent news, and during the ensuing week she wrote twice with very favourable accounts of their mother's condition. A month went by without any disquieting report, then came a letter in Mrs. Warburton's own hand.

"My dear Will," she wrote, "I can't keep secrets as long as you. This is to inform you that a week ago I let The Haws, on annual tenancy, to a friend of Mr. Turnbull's, who was looking for such a house. The day after to-morrow we begin our removal to a home which Jane has taken near to Miss Winter's in Suffolk. That she was able to find just what we wanted at a moment's notice encourages me in thinking that Providence is on our side, or, as your dear father used to say, that the oracle has spoken. In a week's time I hope to send news that we are settled. You are forbidden to come here before our departure, but will be invited to the new home as soon as possible. The address is—" etc.

The same post brought a letter from Jane.

"Don't be alarmed by the news," she wrote. "Mother has been so firm in this resolve since the day of your leaving us, that I could only obey her. Wonderful and delightful to tell, she seems better in health. I dare not make too much of this, after what Dr. Edge said, but for the present she is certainly stronger. As you suppose, I am going to work with Miss Winter. Come and see us when we are settled, and you shall hear all our plans. Everything has been done so quickly, that I live in a sort of a dream. Don't worry, and of course don't on any account come."

These letters arrived in the evening, and, after reading them, Warburton was so moved that he had to go out and walk under the starry sky, in quiet streets. Of course the motive on which his mother had acted was a desire to free him as soon as possible from the slavery of the shop; but that slavery had now grown so supportable, that he grieved over the sacrifice made for his sake. After all, would he not have done better to live on with his secret? And yet—and yet—

## CHAPTER 40

With curiosity which had in it a touch of amusement, Will was waiting to hear from Norbert Franks. He waited for nearly a month, and was beginning to feel rather hurt at his friend's neglect, perhaps a little uneasy on another score, when there arrived an Italian postcard, stamped Venice. "We have been tempted as far as this," ran the hurried scrawl. "Must be home in ten days. Shall be delighted to see you again." Warburton puckered his brows and wondered whether a previous letter or card had failed to reach him. But probably not.

At the end of September, Franks wrote from his London address, briefly but cordially, with an invitation to luncheon on the next day, which was Sunday. And Warburton went.

He was nervous as he knocked at the door; he was rather more nervous as he walked into the studio. Norbert advanced to him with a shout of welcome, and from a chair in the background rose Mrs. Franks. Perceptibly changed, both of them. The artist's look was not quite so ingenuous as formerly; his speech, resolute in friendliness, had not quite the familiar note. Rosamund, already more mature of aspect, smiled somewhat too persistently, seemed rather too bent on showing herself unembarrassed. They plunged into talk of Tyrol, of the Dolomites, of Venice, and, so talking, passed into the dining-room.

"Queer little house this, isn't it?" said Mrs. Franks as she sat down to table. "Everything is sacrificed to the studio; there's no room to turn anywhere else. We must look at once for more comfortable quarters."

"It's only meant for a man living alone," said the artist, with a laugh. Franks laughed frequently, whether what he said was amusing or not. "Yes, we must find something roomier.

"A score of sitters waiting for you, I suppose?" said Warburton.

"Oh, several. One of them such an awful phiz that I'm afraid of her. If I make her presentable, it'll be my greatest feat yet. But the labourer is worthy of his hire, you know, and this bit of beauty-making will have its price."

"You know how to interpret *that*, Mr. Warburton," said Rosamund, with a discreetly confidential smile. "Norbert asks very much less than any other portrait painter of his reputation would."

"He'll grow out of that bad habit," Will replied. His note was one of joviality, almost of bluffness.

"I'm not sure that I wish him to," said the painter's wife, her eyes straying as if in a sudden dreaminess. "It's a distinction nowadays not to care for money. Norbert jokes about making an ugly woman beautiful," she went on earnestly, "but what he will really do is to discover the very best aspect of the face, and so make something much more than an ordinary likeness."

Franks fidgeted, his head bent over his plate.

"That's the work of the great artist," exclaimed Warburton, boldly flattering.

"Humbug!" growled Franks, but at once he laughed and glanced nervously at his wife.

Though this was Rosamund's only direct utterance on the subject, Warburton discovered from the course of the conversation, that she wished to be known as her husband's fervent admirer, that she took him with the utmost seriousness, and was resolved that everybody else should do so. The "great artist" phrase gave her genuine pleasure; she rewarded Will with the kindest look of her beautiful eyes, and from that moment appeared to experience a relief, so that her talk flowed more naturally. Luncheon over, they returned to the studio, where the men lit their pipes, while Rosamund, at her husband's entreaty, exhibited the sketches she had brought home.

"Why didn't you let me hear from you?" asked Warburton. "I got nothing but that flimsy postcard from Venice."

"Why, I was always meaning to write," answered the artist. "I know it was too bad. But time goes so quickly—"

"With you, no doubt. But if you stood behind a counter all day—"

Will saw the listeners exchange a startled glance, followed by an artificial smile. There was an instant's dead silence.

"Behind a counter—?" fell from Norbert, as if he failed to understand.

"The counter; *my* counter!" shouted Will blusterously. "You know very well what I mean. Your wife has told you all about it."

Rosamund flushed, and could not raise her eyes.

"We didn't know," said Franks, with his nervous little laugh, "whether you cared—to talk about it—"

## CHAPTER 40

"I'll talk about it with any one you like. So you *do* know? That's all right. I still owe my apology to Mrs. Franks for having given her such a shock. The disclosure was really too sudden."

"It is I who should beg you to forgive me, Mr. Warburton," replied Rosamund, in her sweetest accents. "I behaved in a very silly way. But my friend Bertha Cross treated me as I deserved. She declared that she was ashamed of me. But do not, pray do not, think me worse than I was. I ran away really because I felt I had surprised a secret. I was embarrassed,—I lost my head. I'm sure you don't think me capable of really mean feelings?"

"But, old man," put in the artist, in a half pained voice, "what the deuce does it all mean? Tell us the whole story, do."

Will told it, jestingly, effectively.

"I was *quite* sure," sounded, at the close, in Rosamund's voice of tender sympathy, "that you had some noble motive. I said so at once to Bertha."

"I suppose," said Will, "Miss Cross will never dare to enter the shop again?"

"She doesn't come!"

"Never since," he answered laughingly. "Her mother has been once or twice, and seems to regard me with a very suspicious eye. Mrs. Cross was told no doubt?"

"That I really can't say," replied Rosamund, averting her eyes. "But doesn't it do one good to hear such a story, Norbert?" she added impulsively.

"Yes, that's pluck," replied her husband, with the old spontaneity, in his eyes the old honest look which hitherto had somehow been a little obscured. "I know very well that *I* couldn't have done it." Warburton had not looked at Rosamund since her explanation and apology. He was afraid of meeting her eyes; afraid as a generous man who shrinks from inflicting humiliation. For was it conceivable that Rosamund could support his gaze without feeling humiliated? Remembering what had preceded that discovery at the shop; bearing in mind what had followed upon it; he reflected with astonishment on the terms of her self-reproach. It sounded so genuine; to the ears of her husband it must have been purest, womanliest sincerity. As though she could read his thoughts, Rosamund addressed him again in the most naturally playful tone.

"And you have been in the Basque country since we saw you. I'm so glad you really took your holiday there at last; you often used to speak of doing so. And you met my sister—Winifred wrote to me all about it. The Coppingers were delighted to see you. Don't you think them nice people? Did poor Mrs. Coppinger seem any better?"

In spite of himself, Will encountered her look, met the beautiful eyes, felt their smile envelop him. Never till now had he known the passive strength of woman, that characteristic which at times makes her a force of Nature rather than an individual being. Amazed, abashed, he let his head fall—and mumbled something about Mrs. Coppinger's state of health.

He did not stay much longer. When he took his leave, it would have seemed natural if Franks had come out to walk a little way with him, but his friend bore him company only to the door.

"Let us see you as often as possible, old man. I hope you'll often come and lunch on Sunday; nothing could please us better."

Franks' handgrip was very cordial, the look and tone were affectionate, but Will said to himself that the old intimacy was at an end; it must now give place to mere acquaintanceship. He suspected that Franks was afraid to come out and walk with him, afraid that it might not please his wife. That Rosamund was to rule—very sweetly of course, but unmistakably—no one could doubt who saw the two together for five minutes. It would be, in all likelihood, a happy subjugation, for Norbert was of anything but a rebellious temper; his bonds would be of silk; the rewards of his docility would be such as many a self-assertive man might envy. But when Warburton tried to imagine himself in such a position, a choked laugh of humourous disdain heaved his chest.

He wandered homewards in a dream. He relived those moments on the Embankment at Chelsea, when his common sense, his reason, his true emotions, were defeated by an impulse now scarcely intelligible; he saw himself shot across Europe, like a parcel despatched by express; and all that fury and rush meaningless as buffoonery at a pantomime! Yet this was how the vast majority of men "fell in love"—if ever they did so at all. This was the prelude to marriages innumerable, marriages destined to be dull as ditchwater or sour as verjuice. In love, forsooth! Rosamund at all events knew the value of that, and had saved him from his own infatuation. He owed her a lifelong gratitude.

That evening he re-read a long letter from Jane which had reached him yesterday. His sister gave him a full description of the new home in Suffolk, and told of the arrangement she had made with Miss Winter, whereby, in a twelvemonth, she would be able to begin earning a little money, and, if all went well, before long would become self-supporting. Could he not run down to see them? Their mother had borne the removal remarkably well, and seemed, indeed, to have a new vigour; possibly the air might suit her better than at The Haws. Will mused over this, but had no mind to make the journey just yet. It would be a pain to him to see his mother in that new place; it would shame him to see his sister at work, and to think that all this change was on his account. So he wrote to mother and sister, with more of expressed tenderness than usual, begging them to let him put off his visit yet a few weeks. Presently they would be more settled. But of one thing let them be sure; his daily work was no burden whatever to him, and he hardly knew whether he would care to change it for what was called the greater respectability of labour in an office. His health was good; his spirits could only be disturbed by ill news from those he loved. He promised that at all events he would spend Christmas with them.

September went by. One of the Sundays was made memorable by a visit to Ashtead. Will had requested Franks to relate in that quarter the story of Mr. Jollyman, and immediately after hearing it, Ralph Pomfret wrote a warm-hearted letter which made the recipient in Fulham chuckle with contentment. At Ashtead he enjoyed himself in the old way, gladdened by the pleasure with which his friends talked of Rosamund's marriage. Mrs. Pomfret took an opportunity of speaking to him apart, a bright smile on her good face.

"Of course we know who did much, if not everything, to bring it about. Rosamund came and told me how beautifully you had pleaded Norbert's cause, and Norbert confided to my husband that, but for you, he would most likely have married a girl he really didn't care about at all. I doubt whether a *mere man* ever did such a thing so discreetly and successfully before!"

In October, Will began to waver in his resolve not to go down into Suffolk before Christmas. There came a letter from his mother which deeply moved him; she spoke of old things as well as new, and declared that in her husband and in her children no woman had ever known truer happiness. This was at the middle of the week; Will all but made up his mind to take an early train on the following Sunday. On Friday he wrote to Jane, telling her to expect him, and, as he walked home from the shop that evening he felt glad that he had overcome the feelings which threatened to make this first visit something of a trial to his self-respect.

"There's a telegram a-waiting for you, sir," said Mrs. Wick, as he entered.

The telegram contained four words:

"Mother ill. Please come."

# CHAPTER 41

Happen what might in the world beyond her doors, Mrs. Cross led the wonted life of domestic discomfort and querulousness. An interval there had been this summer, a brief, uncertain interval, when something like good-temper seemed to struggle with her familiar mood; it was the month or two during which Norbert Franks resumed his friendly visitings. Fallen out of Mrs. Cross's good graces since his failure to become her tenant a couple of years ago, the artist had but to present himself again to be forgiven, and when it grew evident that he came to the house on Bertha's account, he rose into higher favour than ever. But this promising state of things abruptly ended. One morning, Bertha, with a twinkle in her eyes, announced the fact of Franks' marriage. Her mother was stricken with indignant amaze.

"And you laugh about it?"

"It's so amusing," answered Bertha.

Mrs. Cross examined her daughter.

"I don't understand you," she exclaimed, in a tone of irritation. "I do *not* understand you, Bertha! All I can say is, behaviour more disgraceful I *never*—"

The poor lady's feelings were too much for her. She retreated to her bedroom, and there passed the greater part of the day. But in the evening curiosity overcame her sullenness. Having obtained as much information about the artist's marriage as Bertha could give her, she relieved herself in an acrimonious criticism of him and Miss Elvan.

"I never liked to say what I really thought of that girl," were her concluding words. "Now your eyes are opened. Of course you'll never see her again?"

"Why, mother?" asked Bertha. "I'm very glad she has married Mr. Franks. I always hoped she would, and felt pretty sure of it."

"And you mean to be friends with them both?"

"Why not?—But don't let us talk about that," Bertha added good-humouredly. "I should only vex you. There's something else I want to tell you, something you'll really be amused to hear."

"Your ideas of amusement, Bertha—"

"Yes, yes, but listen. It's about Mr. Jollyman. Who do you think Mr. Jollyman really is?"

Mrs. Cross heard the story with bent brows and lips severely set.

"And why didn't you tell me this before, pray?"

"I hardly know," answered the girl, thoughtfully, smiling. "Perhaps because I waited to hear more to make the revelation more complete. But—"

"And this," exclaimed Mrs. Cross, "is why you wouldn't go to the shop yesterday?"

"Yes," was the frank reply. "I don't think I shall go again."

"And, pray, why not?"

Bertha was silent.

"There's one very disagreeable thing in your character, Bertha," remarked her mother severely, "and that is your habit of hiding and concealing. To think that you found this out more than a week ago! You're very, very unlike your father. *He* never kept a thing from me, never for an hour. But you are always *full* of secrets. It isn't nice—it isn't at all nice."

Since her husband's death Mrs. Cross had never ceased discovering his virtues. When he lived, one of the reproaches with which she constantly soured his existence was that of secretiveness. And Bertha, who knew something and suspected more of the truth in this matter, never felt it so hard to bear with her mother as when Mrs. Cross bestowed such retrospective praise.

"I have thought it over," she said quietly, disregarding the reproof, "and on the whole I had rather not go again to the shop."

Thereupon Mrs. Cross grew angry, and for half an hour clamoured as to the disadvantage of leaving Jollyman's for another grocer's. In the end she did not leave him, but either went to the shop herself or sent the servant. Great was her curiosity regarding the disguised Mr. Warburton, with whom, after a significant coldness, she gradually resumed her old chatty relations. At length, one day in autumn, Bertha announced to her that she could throw more light on the Jollyman mystery; she had learnt the full explanation of Mr. Warburton's singular proceedings.

"From those people, I suppose?" said Mrs. Cross, who by this phrase signified Mr. and Mrs. Franks. "Then I don't wish to hear one word of it."

## CHAPTER 41

But as though she had not heard this remark, Bertha began her narrative. She seemed to repeat what had been told her with a quiet pleasure.

"Well, then," was her mother's comment, "after all, there's nothing disgraceful."

"I never thought there was."

"Then why have you refused to enter his shop?"

"It was awkward," replied Bertha.

"No more awkward for you than for me," said Mrs. Cross. "But I've noticed, Bertha, that you are getting rather selfish in some things—I don't of course say in *everything*—and I think it isn't difficult to guess where that comes from."

Soon after Christmas they were left, by a familiar accident, without a servant; the girl who had been with them for the last six months somehow contrived to get her box secretly out of the house and disappeared (having just been paid her wages) without warning. Long and loudly did Mrs. Cross rail against this infamous behaviour.

The next morning, a young woman came to the house and inquired for Mrs. Cross; Bertha, who had opened the door, led her into the dining room, and retired. Half an hour later, Mrs. Cross came into the parlour, beaming.

"There now! If that wasn't a good idea! Who do you think sent that girl, Bertha?—Mr. Jollyman."

Bertha kept silence.

"I had to go into the shop yesterday, and I happened to speak to Mr. Jollyman of the trouble I had in finding a good servant. It occurred to me that he *might* just possibly know of some one. He promised to make inquiries, and here at once comes the nicest girl I've seen for a long time. She had to leave her last place because it was too hard; just fancy, a shop where she had to cook for sixteen people, and see to five bedrooms; no wonder she broke down, poor thing. She's been resting for a month or two: and she lives in the same house as a person named Mrs. Hopper, who is the sister of the wife of Mr. Jollyman's assistant. And she's quite content with fifteen pounds—quite."

As she listened, Bertha wrinkled her forehead, and grew rather absent. She made no remark, until, after a long account of the virtues she had already descried in Martha—this was the girl's name—Mrs. Cross added that of course she must go at once and thank Mr. Jollyman.

"I suppose you still address him by that name?" fell from Bertha.

"That name? Why, I'd really almost forgotten that it wasn't his real name. In any case, I couldn't use the other in the shop, could I?"

"Of course not; no."

"Now you speak of it, Bertha," pursued Mrs. Cross, "I wonder whether he knows that I know who he is?"

"Certainly he does."

"When one thinks of it, wouldn't it be better, Bertha, for you to go to the shop again now and then? I'm afraid the poor man may feel hurt. He *must* have noticed that you never went again after that discovery, and one really wouldn't like him to think that you were offended."

"Offended?" echoed the girl with a laugh. "Offended at what?"

"Oh, some people, you know, might think his behaviour strange—using a name that's not his own, and—and so on."

"Some people might, no doubt. But the poor man, as you call him, is probably quite indifferent as to what we think of him."

"Don't you think it would be well if you went in and just thanked him for sending the servant?"

"Perhaps," replied Bertha, carelessly.

But she did not go to Mr. Jollyman's, and Mrs. Cross soon forgot the suggestion.

Martha entered upon her duties, and discharged them with such zeal, such docility, that her mistress never tired of lauding her. She was a young woman of rather odd appearance; slim and meagre and red-headed, with a never failing simper on her loose lips, and blue eyes that frequently watered; she had somehow an air of lurking gentility in faded youth. Undeniable as were the good qualities she put forth on this scene of innumerable domestic failures, Bertha could not altogether like her. Submissive to the point of slavishness, she had at times a look which did not harmonize at all with this demeanour, a something in her eyes disagreeably suggestive of mocking insolence. Bertha particularly noticed this on the day after Martha had received her first wages. Leave having been given her to go out in the afternoon to make some purchases, she was rather late in returning, and Bertha, meeting her as she entered, asked her to be as quick as possible in getting tea; whereupon the domestic threw up her head and regarded the speaker from under her eyelids with an extraordinary smile; then with a "Yes, miss, this minute, miss" scampered upstairs to take her things off. All that evening her behaviour was strange. As she waited at the supper table she seemed to be subduing laughter, and in clearing away she for the first time broke a plate; whereupon she burst into tears, and begged forgiveness so long and so wearisomely that she had at last to be ordered out of the room.

## CHAPTER 41

On the morrow all was well again; but Bertha could not help watching that singular countenance, and the more she observed, the less she liked it.

The more "willing" a servant the more toil did Mrs. Cross exact from her. When occasions of rebuke or of dispute were lacking, the day would have been long and wearisome for her had she not ceaselessly plied the domestic drudge with tasks, and narrowly watched their execution. The spectacle of this slave-driving was a constant trial to Bertha's nerves; now and then she ventured a mild protest, but only with the result of exciting her mother's indignation. In her mood of growing moral discontent, Bertha began to ask herself whether acquiescence in this sordid tyranny was not a culpable weakness, and one day early in the year—a wretched day of east-wind—when she saw Martha perched on an outer window-sill cleaning panes, she found the courage to utter resolute disapproval.

"I don't understand you, Bertha," replied Mrs. Cross, the muscles of her face quivering as they did when she felt her dignity outraged. "What do we engage a servant for? Are the windows to get so dirty we can't see through them?"

"They were cleaned not many days ago," said her daughter, "and I think we could manage to see till the weather's less terrible."

"My dear, if we *managed* so as to give the servant no trouble at all, the house would soon be in a pretty state. Be so good as not to interfere. It's really an extraordinary thing that as soon as I find a girl who almost suits me, you begin to try to spoil her. One would think you took a pleasure in making my life miserable—"

Overwhelmed with floods of reproach, Bertha had either to combat or to retreat. Again her nerves failed her, and she left the room.

At dinner that day there was a roast leg of mutton, and, as her habit was, Mrs. Cross carved the portion which Martha was to take away for herself. One very small and very thin slice, together with one unwholesome little potato, represented the servant's meal. As soon as the door had closed, Bertha spoke in an ominously quiet voice.

"Mother, this won't do. I am very sorry to annoy you, but if you call that a dinner for a girl who works hard ten or twelve hours a day, I don't. How she supports life, I can't understand. You have only to look into her face to see she's starving. I can bear the sight of it no longer."

This time she held firm. The conflict lasted for half an hour, during which Mrs. Cross twice threatened to faint. Neither of them ate anything, and in the end Bertha saw herself, if not defeated, at all events no better off than at the beginning, for her mother clung fiercely to authority, and would obviously live in perpetual strife rather than yield an inch. For the next two days domestic life was very unpleasant indeed; mother and daughter exchanged few words; meanwhile Martha was tasked, if possible, more vigorously than ever, and fed mysteriously, meals no longer doled out to her under Bertha's eyes. The third morning brought another crisis.

"I have a letter from Emily," said Bertha at breakfast, naming a friend of hers who lived in the far north of London. "I'm going to see her to-day."

"Very well," answered Mrs. Cross, between rigid lips.

"She says that in the house where she lives, there's a bed-sitting-room to let. I think, mother, it might be better for me to take it."

"You will do just as you please, Bertha."

"I shall have dinner to-day with Emily, and be back about tea-time."

"I have no doubt," replied Mrs. Cross, "that Martha will be so obliging as to have tea ready for you. If she doesn't feel *strong* enough, of course I will see to it myself."

# CHAPTER 42

On the evening before, Martha had received her month's wages, and had been promised the usual afternoon of liberty to-day; but, as soon as Bertha had left the house, Mrs. Cross summoned the domestic, and informed her bluntly that the holiday must be postponed.

"I'm very sorry, mum," replied Martha, with an odd, half-frightened look in her watery eyes. "I'd promised to go and see my brother as has just lost his wife; but of course, if it isn't convenient, mum—"

"It really is not, Martha. Miss Bertha will be out all day, and I don't like being left alone You shall go to-morrow instead."

Half an hour later, Mrs. Cross went out shopping, and was away till noon. On returning, she found the house full of the odour of something burnt.

"What's this smell, Martha?" she asked at the kitchen door, "what is burning?"

"Oh, it's only a dishcloth as was drying and caught fire, mum," answered the servant.

"Only! What do you mean?" cried the mistress, angrily. "Do you wish to burn the house down?"

Martha stood with her arms akimbo, on her thin, dough-pale face the most insolent of grins, her teeth gleaming, and her eyes wide.

"What do you mean?" cried Mrs. Cross. "Show me the burnt cloth at once."

"There you are, mum!"

And Martha, with a kick, pointed to something on the floor. Amazed and wrathful, Mrs. Cross saw a long roller-towel, half a yard of it burnt to tinder; nor could any satisfactory explanation of the accident be drawn from Martha, who laughed, sobbed, and sniggered by turns as if she were demented.

"Of course you will pay for it," exclaimed Mrs. Cross for the twentieth time. "Go on with your work at once, and don't let me have any more of this extraordinary behaviour. I can't think what has come to you."

But Martha seemed incapable of resuming her ordinary calm. Whilst serving the one o'clock dinner—which was very badly cooked—she wept and sighed, and when her mistress had risen from the table, she stood for a long time staring vacantly before she could bestir herself to clear away. About three o'clock, having several times vainly rung the sitting-room bell, Mrs. Cross went to the kitchen. The door was shut, and, on trying to open it, she found it locked. She called "Martha," again and again, and had no reply, until, all of a sudden, a shrill voice cried from within—"Go away! Go away!" Beside herself with wrath and amazement, the mistress demanded admission answer, there came a violent thumping on the door at the other side, and again the voice screamed—"Go away! Go away!"

"What's the matter with you, Martha?" asked Mrs. Cross, beginning to feel alarmed.

"Go away!" replied the voice fiercely.

"Either you open the door this moment, or I call a policeman."

This threat had an immediate effect, though not quite of the kind that Mrs. Cross hoped. The key turned with a snap, the door was flung open, and there stood Martha, in a Corybantic attitude, brandishing a dinner-plate in one hand, a poker in the other; her hair was dishevelled, her face red, and fury blazed in her eyes.

"You *won't* go away?" she screamed "There, then—there goes one of your plates!"

She dashed it to the floor.

"You *won't* go away?—There goes one of you dishes!—and there goes a basin!—And there goes a tea-cup!"

One after another, the things she named perished upon the floor. Mrs. Cross stood paralysed, horror-stricken.

"You think you'll make me pay for them?" cried Martha frantically. "Not me—not me! It's you as owes me money—money for all the work I've done as wasn't in my wages, and for the food as I haven't had, when I'd ought to. What do you call *that*?" She pointed to a plate of something on the kitchen table. "Is that a dinner for a human being, or is it a dinner for a beetle? D'you think I'd eat it, and me with money in my pocket to buy better? You want to make a walkin' skeleton of me, do you?—but I'll have it out of you, I will—There goes another dish! And *here* goes a sugar-basin! And here goes your teapot!"

With a shriek of dismay, Mrs. Cross sprang forward. She was too late to save the cherished object, and her aggressive movement excited Martha to yet more alarming behaviour.

## CHAPTER 42

"You'd hit me, would you? Two can play at that game—you old skinflint, you! Come another step nearer, and I'll bring this poker on your head! You thought you'd get somebody you could do as you liked with, didn't you? You thought because I was willing, and tried to do my best, as I could be put upon to any extent, did you? It's about time you learnt your mistake, you old cheese-parer! You and me has an account to settle. Let me get at you—let me get at you—"

She brandished the poker so menacingly that Mrs. Cross turned and fled. Martha pursued, yelling abuse and threats. The mistress vainly tried to shut the sitting-room door against her; in broke the furious maid, and for a moment so handled her weapon that Mrs. Cross with difficulty escaped a dangerous blow. Round and round the table they went, until, the cloth having been dragged off, Martha's feet caught in it, and she fell heavily to the floor. To escape from the room, the terrified lady must have stepped over her. For a moment there was silence. Then Martha made an attempt to rise, fell again, again struggled to her knees, and finally collapsed, lying quite still and mute.

Trembling, panting, Mrs. Cross moved cautiously nearer, until she could see the girl's face. Martha was asleep, unmistakably asleep; she had even begun to snore. Avoiding her contact with as much disgust as fear, Mrs. Cross got out of the room, and opened the front door of the house. This way and that she looked along the streets, searching for a policeman, but none was in sight. At this moment, approached a familiar figure, Mr. Jollyman's errand boy, basket on arm; he had parcels to deliver here.

"Are you going back to the shop at once?" asked Mrs. Cross, after hurriedly setting down her groceries in the passage.

"Straight back, mum."

"Then run as quickly as ever you can, and tell Mr. Jollyman that I wish to see him immediately—immediately. Run! Don't lose a moment!"

Afraid to shut herself in with the sleeping fury, Mrs. Cross remained standing near the front door, which every now and then she opened to look for a policeman. The day was cold; she shivered, she felt weak, wretched, ready to sob in her squalid distress. Some twenty minutes passed, then, just as she opened the door to look about again, a rapid step sounded on the pavement, and there appeared her grocer.

"Oh, Mr. Jollyman!" she exclaimed. "What I have just gone through! That girl has gone raving mad—she has broken almost everything in the house, and tried to kill me with the poker. Oh, I am so glad you've come! Of course there's never a policeman when they're wanted. Do please come in."

Warburton did not at once understand who was meant by "that girl," but when Mrs. Cross threw open the sitting-room door, and exhibited her domestic prostrate in disgraceful slumber, the facts of the situation broke upon him. This was the girl so strongly recommended by Mrs. Hopper.

"But I thought she had been doing very well—"

"So she had, so she had, Mr. Jollyman—except for a few little things—though there was always something rather strange about her. It's only today that she broke out. She is mad, I assure you, raving mad!"

Another explanation suggested itself to Warburton.

"Don't you notice a suspicious odour?" he asked significantly.

"You think it's *that*!" said Mrs. Cross, in a horrified whisper. "Oh, I daresay you're right. I'm too agitated to notice anything. Oh, Mr. Jollyman! Do, do help me to get the creature out of the house. How shameful that people gave her a good character. But everybody deceives me—everybody treats me cruelly, heartlessly. Don't leave me alone with that creature, Mr. Jollyman. Oh, if you knew what I have been through with servants! But never anything so bad as this—never! Oh, I feel quite ill—I must sit down—"

Fearful that his situation might become more embarrassing than it was, Warburton supported Mrs. Cross into the dining-room, and by dint of loudly cheerful talk in part composed her. She consented to sit with the door locked, whilst her rescuer hurried in search of a policeman. Before long, a constable's tread sounded in the hall; Mrs. Cross told her story, exhibited the ruins of her crockery on the kitchen floor, and demanded instant expulsion of the dangerous rebel. Between them, Warburton and the man in authority shook Martha into consciousness, made her pack her box, put her into a cab, and sent her off to the house where she had lived when out of service; she all the time weeping copiously, and protesting that there was no one in the world so dear to her as her outraged mistress. About an hour was thus consumed. When at length the policeman had withdrawn, and sudden quiet reigned in the house, Mrs. Cross seemed again on the point of fainting.

"How can I ever thank you, Mr. Jollyman!" she exclaimed, half hysterically, as she let herself sink into the armchair. "Without you, what would have become of me! Oh, I feel so weak, if I had strength to get myself a cup of tea—"

# CHAPTER 42

"Let me get it for you," cried Warburton. "Nothing easier. I noticed the kettle by the kitchen fire."

"Oh, I cannot allow, you, Mr. Jollyman—you are too kind—I feel so ashamed—"

But Will was already in the kitchen, where he bestirred himself so effectually that in a few minutes the kettle had begun to sing. Just as he went back to the parlour, to ask where tea could be found, the front door opened, and in walked Bertha.

"Your daughter is here, Mrs. Cross," said Will, in an undertone, stepping toward the limp and pallid lady.

"Bertha," she cried. "Bertha, are you there? Oh, come and thank Mr. Jollyman! If you knew what has happened whilst you were away!"

At the room door appeared the girl's astonished face. Warburton's eyes fell upon her.

"It's a wonder you find me alive, dear," pursued the mother. "If one of those blows had fallen on my head—!"

"Let me explain," interposed Warburton quietly. And in a few words he related the events of the afternoon.

"And Mr. Jollyman was just getting me a clip of tea, Bertha," added Mrs. Cross. "I do feel ashamed that he should have had such trouble."

"Mr. Jollyman has been very kind indeed," said Bertha, with look and tone of grave sincerity. "I'm sure we cannot thank him enough."

Warburton smiled as he met her glance.

"I feel rather guilty in the matter," he said, "for it was I who suggested the servant. If you will let me, I will do my best to atone by trying to find another and a better."

"Run and make the tea, my dear," said Mrs. Cross. "Perhaps Mr. Jollyman will have a cup with us—"

This invitation was declined. Warburton sought for his hat, and took leave of the ladies, Mrs. Cross overwhelming him with gratitude, and Bertha murmuring a few embarrassed words. As soon as he was gone, mother and daughter took hands affectionately, then embraced with more tenderness than for a long, long time.

"I shall never dare to live alone with a servant," sobbed Mrs. Cross. "If you leave me, I must go into lodgings, dear."

"Hush, hush, mother," replied the girl, in her gentlest voice. "Of course I shall not leave you.

"Oh, the dreadful things I have been through! It was drink, Bertha; that creature was a drunkard of the most dangerous kind. She did her best to murder me. I wonder I am not at this moment lying dead.—Oh, but the kindness of Mr. Jollyman! What a good thing I sent for him! And he speaks of finding us another servant; but, Bertha, I shall never try to manage a servant again—never. I shall always be afraid of them; I shall dread to give the simplest order. You, my dear, must be the mistress of the house; indeed you must. I give over everything into your hands. I will never interfere; I won't say a word, whatever fault I may have to find; not a word. Oh, that creature; that horrible woman will haunt my dreams. Bertha, you don't think she'll hang about the house, and lie in wait for me, to be revenged? We must tell the policeman to look out for her. I'm sure I shall never venture to go out alone, and if you leave me in the house with a new servant, even for an hour, I must be in a room with the door locked. My nerves will never recover from this shock. Oh, if you knew how ill I feel! I'll have a cup of tea, and then go straight to bed."

Whilst she was refreshing herself, she spoke again of Mr. Jollyman.

"Do you think I ought to have pressed him to stay, dear? I didn't feel sure."

"No, no, you were quite right not to do so," replied Bertha. "He of course understood that it was better for us to be alone."

"I thought he would. Really, for a grocer, he is so very gentlemanly."

"That's not surprising, mother."

"No, no; I'm always forgetting that he isn't a grocer by birth. I think, Bertha, it will only be right to ask him to come to tea some day before long."

Bertha reflected, a half-smile about her lips.

"Certainly," she said, "if you would like to."

"I really should. He was so very kind to me. And perhaps—what do you think?—ought we to invite him in his proper name?"

"No, I think not," answered Bertha, after a moment's reflection. "We are not supposed to know anything about that."

"To be sure not.—Oh, that dreadful creature. I see her eyes, glaring at me, like a tiger's. Fifty times at least did she chase me round this table. I thought I should have dropped with exhaustion; and if I had, one blow of that poker would have finished me. Never speak to me of servants, Bertha. Engage any one you like, but do, do be careful to make inquiries about her. I shall never wish even to know her name; I shall never look at her face; I shall never speak a word to her. I leave all the responsibility to you, dear. And now, help me upstairs. I'm sure 'I could never get up alone. I tremble in every limb—"

# CHAPTER 43

Warburton's mother was dead. The first effect upon him of the certainty that she could not recover from the unconsciousness in which he found her when summoned by Jane's telegram, was that of an acute remorse; it pierced him to the heart that she should have abandoned the home of her life-time, for the strangeness and discomfort of the new abode, and here have fallen, stricken by death—the cause of it, he himself, he so unworthy of the least sacrifice. He had loved her; but what assurance had he been wont to give her of his love? Through many and many a year it was much if he wrote at long intervals a hurried letter. How seldom had he cared to go down to St. Neots, and, when there, how soon had he felt impatient of the little restraints imposed upon him by his mother's ways and prejudices. Yet not a moment had she hesitated, ill and aged, when, at so great a cost to herself, it seemed possible to make life a little easier for him. This reproach was the keenest pain with which nature had yet visited him.

Something of the same was felt by his sister, partly on her own, partly on his account, but as soon as Jane became aware of his self torment, her affection and her good sense soon brought succour to them both. She spoke of the life their mother had led since coming into Suffolk, related a hundred instances to prove how full of interest and contentment it had been, bore witness to the seeming improvement of health, and the even cheerfulness of spirits which had accompanied it. Moreover, there was the medical assurance that life could not in any case have been prolonged; that change of place and habits counted for nothing in the sudden end which some months ago had been foretold. Jane confessed herself surprised at the ease with which so great and sudden a change was borne; the best proof that could have been given of their mother's nobleness of mind. Once only had Mrs. Warburton seemed to think regretfully of the old home; it was on coming out of church one morning, when, having stood for a moment to look at the graveyard, she murmured to her daughter that she would wish to be buried at St. Neots. This, of course, was done; it would have been done even had she not spoken. And when, on the day after the funeral, brother and sister parted to go their several ways, the sadness they bore with them had no embitterment of brooding regret. A little graver than usual, Will took his place behind the counter, with no word to Allchin concerning the cause of his absence. He wrote frequently to Jane, and from her received long letters, which did him good, so redolent were they of the garden life, even in mid-winter, and so expressive of a frank, sweet, strong womanhood, like that of her who was no more.

Meanwhile his business flourished. Not that he much exerted himself, or greatly rejoiced to see his till more heavily laden night after night, by natural accretion custom flowed to the shop in fuller stream; Jollyman's had established a reputation for quality and cheapness, and began seriously to affect the trade of small rivals in the district. As Allchin had foretold, the hapless grocer with the drunken wife sank defeated before the end of the year; one morning his shop did not open, and in a few days the furniture of the house was carried off by some brisk creditor. It made Warburton miserable to think of the man's doom; when Allchin, frank barbarian as he was, loudly exulted. Will turned away in shame and anger. Had the thing been practicable he would have given money out of his own pocket to the ruined struggler. He saw himself as a merciless victor; he seemed to have his heel on the other man's head, and to crush, crush—

At Christmas he was obliged to engage a second assistant. Allchin did not conceal his dislike of this step, but he ended by admitting it to be necessary. At first, the new state of things did not work quite smoothly; Allchin was inclined to an imperious manner, which the newcomer, by name Goff, now and then plainly resented. But in a day or two they were on fair terms, and ere long they became cordial.

Then befell the incident of Mrs. Cross' Martha.

Not without uneasiness had Warburton suggested a servant on the recommendation of Mrs. Hopper, but credentials seemed to be fairly good, and when, after a week or two, Mrs. Cross declared herself more than satisfied, he blessed his good luck. Long ago he had ceased to look for the reappearance at the shop of Bertha Cross; he thought of the girl now and then, generally reverting in memory to that day when he had followed her and her mother into Kew Gardens—a recollection which had lost all painfulness, and shone idyllically in summer sunlight, but it mattered nothing to him that Bertha showed herself no more. Of course she knew his story from Rosamund, and in all likelihood she felt her self-respect concerned in holding aloof from an acquaintance of his ambiguous standing. It mattered not a jot.

## CHAPTER 43

Yet when the tragi-comedy of Martha's outbreak unexpectedly introduced him to the house at Walham Green, he experienced a sudden revival of the emotions of a year ago. After his brief meeting with Bertha, he did not go straight back to the shop, but wandered a little in quiet by-ways, thinking hard and smiling. Nothing more grotesque than the picture of Mrs. Cross amid her shattered crockery, Mrs. Cross pointing to the prostrate Martha, Mrs. Cross panting forth the chronicle of her woes; but Mrs. Cross' daughter was not involved in this scene of pantomime; she walked across the stage, but independently, with a simple dignity, proof against paltry or ludicrous circumstance. If any one could see the laughable side of such domestic squalor, assuredly it was Bertha herself of that Will felt assured. Did he not remember her smile when she had to discuss prices and qualities in the shop? Not many girls smile with so much implication of humorous comment.

He had promised to look out for another servant, but hardly knew how to go to work. First of all, Mrs. Hopper was summoned to an interview in the parlour behind the shop, and Martha's case was fully discussed. With much protesting and circumlocution, Mrs. Hopper brought herself at length to own that Martha had been known to "take too much," but that was so long ago, and the girl had solemnly declared, etc., etc. However, as luck would have it, she did know of another girl, a really good general servant, who had only just been thrown out of a place by the death of her mistress, and who was living at home in Kentish Town. Thither sped Warburton; he saw the girl and her mother, and, on returning, sent a note to Mrs. Cross, in which he detailed all he had learnt concerning the new applicant. At the close he wrote: "You are aware, I think, that the name under which I do business is not my own. Permit me, in writing to you on a private matter, to use my own signature"—which accordingly followed. Moreover, he dated the letter from his lodgings, not from the shop.

The next day brought him a reply; he found it on his breakfast table, and broke the envelope with amused curiosity. Mrs. Cross wrote that "Sarah Walker" had been to see her, and if inquiries proved satisfactory, would be engaged. "We are very greatly obliged for the trouble you have taken. Many thanks for your kind inquiries as to my health. I am glad to say that the worst of the shock has passed away, though I fear that I shall long continue to feel its effects." A few remarks followed on the terrible difficulties of the servant question; then "Should you be disengaged on Sunday next, we shall be glad if you will take a cup of tea with us."

Over his coffee and egg, Will pondered this invitation. It pleased him, undeniably, but caused him no undue excitement. He would have liked to know in what degree Mrs. Cross' daughter was a consenting party to the step. Perhaps she felt that, after the services he had rendered, the least one could do was to invite him to tea. Why should he refuse? Before going to business, he wrote a brief acceptance. During the day, a doubt now and then troubled him as to whether he had behaved discreetly, but on the whole he looked forward to Sunday with pleasant expectation.

How should he equip himself? Should he go dressed as he would have gone to the Pomfrets', in his easy walking attire, jacket and soft-felt? Or did the circumstances dictate chimney-pot and frock-coat? He scoffed at himself for fidgeting over the point; yet perhaps it had a certain importance. After deciding for the informal costume, at the last moment he altered his mind, and went arrayed as society demands; with the result that, on entering the little parlour—that name suited it much better than drawing-room—he felt overdressed, pompous, generally absurd. His cylinder seemed to be about three feet high; his gloves stared their newness; the tails of his coat felt as though they wrapped several times round his legs, and still left enough to trail upon the floor as he sat on a chair too low for him. Never since the most awkward stage of boyhood had he felt so little at ease "in company." And he had a conviction that Bertha Cross was laughing at him. Her smile was too persistent; it could only be explained as a compromise with threatening merriment.

A gap in the conversation prompted Warburton to speak of a little matter which was just now interesting him. It related to Mr. Potts, the shopkeeper in Kennington Lane, whom he used to meet, but of whom for a couple of years and more, he had quite lost sight. Stirred by reproach of conscience, he had at length gone to make inquiries; but the name of Potts was no longer over the shop.

"I went in and asked whether the old man was dead; no, he had retired from business and was lodging not far away. I found the house—a rather grimy place, and the door was opened by a decidedly grimy woman. I saw at once that she didn't care to let me in. What was my business? and so on; but I held firm, and got at last into a room on the second floor, an uncomfortable sitting-room, where poor old Potts welcomed me. If only he had known my address, he said, he should have written to tell me the news. His son in America, the one I knew, was doing well, and sent money every month, enough for him to live upon. 'But was he comfortable in those lodgings? I asked. Of course I saw that he wasn't, and I saw too that my question made him nervous. He looked at the door, and spoke in a whisper. The upshot of it was that he had fallen into the hands of a landlady who victimised him; just because she was an old acquaintance, he didn't feel able to leave her. 'Shall I help you to get away?' I asked him, and his face shone with hope. Of course the woman was listening at the keyhole; we both knew that. When I went away she had run half down the stairs, and I caught her angry look before she hid it with a grin. I must find decent lodgings for the old fellow, as soon as possible. He is being bled mercilessly."

"How very disgraceful!" exclaimed Mrs. Cross. "Really, the meanness of some women of that class!"

Her daughter had her eyes cast down, on her lips the faintest suggestion of a smile.

"I wonder whether we could hear of anything suitable," pursued her mother, "by inquiring of people we know out at Holloway. I'm thinking of the Boltons, Bertha."

Mr. Potts' requirements were discussed, Bertha interesting herself in the matter, and making various suggestions. The talk grew more animated. Warburton was led to tell of his own experience in lodgings. Catching Bertha's eye, he gave his humour full scope on the subject of Mrs. Wick, and there was merriment in which even Mrs. Cross made a show of joining.

"Why," she exclaimed, "do you stay in such very uncomfortable rooms?"

"It doesn't matter," Will replied, "it's only for a time."

"Ah, you have other views?"

"Yes," he answered, smiling cheerfully, "I have other views."

# CHAPTER 44

Toward the end of the following week, Mrs. Cross came to the shop. She had a busy air, and spoke to Warburton in a confidential undertone.

"We have been making inquiries, and at last I think we have heard of something that might suit your poor friend. This is the address. My daughter went there this morning, and had a long talk with the woman, and she thinks it really might do; but perhaps you have already found something?"

"Nothing at all," answered Will. "I am much obliged to you. I will go as soon as possible."

"We shall be so glad to hear if it suits," said Mrs. Cross. "Do look in on Sunday, will you? We are always at home at five o'clock.— Oh, I have written out a little list of things," she added, laying her grocery order on the counter. "Please tell me what they come to."

Warburton gravely took the cash, and Mrs. Cross, with her thinly gracious smile, bade him good-day.

He did not fail to "look in" on Sunday, and this time he wore his ordinary comfortable clothing. The rooms recommended for Mr. Potts had seemed to him just what were needed, and on his own responsibility he had taken them. Moreover, he had been to Kennington, and had made known to the nervous old man the arrangements that were proposed for him.

"But will he be allowed to leave?" asked Bertha in her eyes the twinkle for which Will watched.

"He won't dare, he tells me, to give notice but he'll only have to pay a week's rent in lieu of it. I have promised to be with him at ten tomorrow morning, to help him to get away. I shall take my heaviest walking-stick; one must be prepared for every emergency. Glance over the police news on Tuesday, Mrs. Cross, just to see whether I have come to harm."

"We shall be very anxious indeed," replied the literal lady, with pained brow. "Couldn't you let us hear to-morrow evening? I know only too well what dreadful creatures the women of that class can be. I very strongly advise you, Mr. Warburton, to be accompanied by a policeman. I beg you will."

Late on the Monday afternoon, Jollyman's errand boy left a note for Mrs. Cross. It informed her that all had gone well, though "not without uproar. The woman shrieked insults from her doorstep after our departing cab. Poor Mr. Potts was all but paralytic with alarm, but came round famously at sight of the new lodgings. He wants to thank you both."

It was on this same evening that Warburton had a visit from Godfrey Sherwood. A fortnight ago, just after Easter, had taken place the marriage of Mr. Milligan and Miss Parker; and Sherwood, whilst his chief was absent on the honeymoon, had run down to the seaside for a change of air. Tonight, he presented himself unexpectedly, and his face was the prologue to a moving tale.

"Read that, Warburton—" he held out a letter. "Read that, and tell me what you think of human nature."

It was a letter from Milligan, who, with many explanations and apologies, wrote to inform his secretary that the Great Work could not be pursued, that the vegetarian colony in Ireland, which was to civilise the world, must—so far as he was concerned—remain a glorious dream. The fact of the matter was, Mrs. Milligan did not like it. She had tried vegetarianism; it did not suit her health; moreover, she objected to living in Ireland, on account of the dampness of the climate. Sadly, reluctantly, Mrs. Milligan's husband had to forgo his noble project. In consequence, he would have no need henceforth of a secretary, and Sherwood must consider their business relations at an end.

"He encloses a very liberal cheque," said Godfrey. "But what a downfall! I foresaw it. I hinted my fears to you as soon as Miss Parker appeared on the scene. Poor old Milligan! A lost man—sunk in the commonplace—hopelessly whelmed in vulgar matrimony. Poor old fellow!"

Warburton chuckled.

"But that isn't all," went on the other, "Old Strangwyn is dead, really dead at last. I wrote several times to him; no acknowledgment of my letters. Now it's all over. The ten thousand pounds—"

He made a despairing gesture. Then:

"Take that cheque, Warburton. It's all I have; take it, old fellow, and try to forgive me. You won't? Well, well, if I live, I'll pay you yet; but I'm a good deal run down, and these disappointments have almost floored me. To tell you the truth, the vegetarian diet won't do. I feel as weak as a cat. If you knew the heroism it has cost me, down at the seaside, to refrain from chops and steaks. Now I give it up. Another month of cabbage and lentils and I should be sunk beyond recovery. I give it up. This very night I shall go and have a supper, a real supper, in town. Will you come with me, old man? What's before me, I don't know. I have half a mind to go to Canada as farm labourer; it would be just the thing for my health; but let us go and have one more supper together, as in the old days. Where shall it be?"

So they went into town, and supped royally, with the result that Warburton had to see his friend home. Over the second bottle, Godfrey decided for an agricultural life in the Far West, and Will promised to speak for him to a friend of his, a lady who had brothers farming in British Columbia; but, before he went, he must be assured that Warburton really forgave him the loss of that money. Will protested that he had forgotten all about it; if any pardon were needed, he granted it with all his heart. And so with affectionate cordiality they bade each other good-night.

To his surprise, he received a letter from Sherwood, a day or two after, seriously returning to the British Columbia project, and reminding him of his promise. So, on Sunday, Will called for the first time without invitation at Mrs. Cross', and, being received with no less friendliness than hitherto, began asking news of Bertha's brothers; whereupon followed talk upon Canadian farming life, and the mention of Godfrey Sherwood. Bertha undertook to write on the subject by the next mail; she thought it likely enough that her brothers might be able to put Mr. Sherwood into the way of earning a living.

"What do you think we did yesterday?" said Mrs. Cross. "We took the liberty of calling upon Mr. Potts. We had to go and see Mrs. Bolton, at Holloway, and, as it was so near, we thought we might venture—using your name as our introduction. And the poor old gentleman was delighted to see us—wasn't he, Bertha? Oh, and he is so grateful for our suggestion of the lodgings."

Bertha's smile betrayed a little disquiet. Perceiving this, Warburton spoke with emphasis.

"It was kind of you. The old man feels a little lonely in that foreign region; he's hardly been out of Kennington for forty years. A very kind thought, indeed."

"I am relieved," said Bertha; "it seemed to me just possible that we had been guilty of a serious indiscretion. Good intentions are very dangerous things."

## CHAPTER 44

When next Warburton found time to go to Holloway, he heard all about the ladies' visit. He learnt, moreover, that Mr. Potts had told them the story of his kindness to the sick lad at St. Kitts, and of his first visit to Kennington Lane.

# CHAPTER 45

When Bertha, at her mother's request, undertook the control of the house, she knew very well what was before her.

During a whole fortnight, Mrs. Cross faithfully adhered to the compact. For the first time in her life, she declared, she was enjoying peace. Feeling much shaken in her nervous system, she rose late, retired early, and, when downstairs, reclined a good deal on the sofa. She professed herself unable to remember the new servant's name, and assumed an air of profound abstraction whenever "what do you call her" came into the room. Not a question did she permit herself as to the details of household management. Bertha happening (incautiously) to complain of a certain joint supplied by the butcher, Mrs. Cross turned a dreamy eye upon it, and said, in the tone of one who speaks of long ago, "In my time he could always be depended upon for a small shoulder"; then dismissed the matter as in no way concerning her.

But repose had a restorative effect, and, in the third week, Mrs. Cross felt the revival of her energies. She was but fifty-three years old, and in spite of languishing habits, in reality had very fair health. Caring little for books, and not much for society, how was she to pass her time if denied the resource of household affairs? Bertha observed the signs of coming trouble. One morning, her mother came downstairs earlier than usual, and after fidgeting about the room, where her daughter was busy at her drawing-board, suddenly exclaimed:

"I wish you would tell that girl to make my bed properly. I haven't closed my eyes for three nights, and I ache from head to foot. The way she neglects my room is really shameful—"

There followed intimate details, to which Bertha listened gravely.

"That shall be seen to at once, mother," she replied, and left the room.

The complaint, as she suspected, had very little foundation. It was only the beginning; day after day did Mrs. Cross grumble about this, that and the other thing, until Bertha saw that the anticipated moment was at hand. The great struggle arose out of that old point of debate, the servant's meals. Mrs. Cross, stealing into the kitchen, had caught a glimpse of Sarah's dinner, and so amazed was she, so stirred with indignation to the depth of her soul, that she cast off all show of respect for the new order, and overwhelmed Bertha with rebukes. Her daughter listened quietly until the torrent had spent its force, then said with a smile:

"Is this how you keep your promise, mother?"

"Promise? Did I promise to look on at wicked waste? Do you want to bring us to the workhouse, child?"

"Don't let us waste time in talking about what we settled a month ago," replied Bertha decisively. "Sarah is doing very well, and there must be no change. I am quite content to pay her wages myself. Keep your promise, mother, and let us live quietly and decently."

"If you call it living decently to pamper a servant until she bursts with insolence—"

"When was Sarah insolent to you? She has never been disrespectful to me. Quite the contrary, I think her a very good servant indeed. You know that I have a good deal of work to do just now, and—to speak quite plainly—I can't let you upset the orderly life of the house. Be quiet, there's a dear. I insist upon it."

Speaking thus, Bertha laid her hands on her mother's shoulders, and looked into the foolish, angry face so steadily, so imperturbably, with such a light of true kindness in her gentle eyes, yet at the same time such resolution about the well-drawn lips that Mrs. Cross had no choice but to submit. Grumbling she turned; sullenly she held her tongue for the rest of the day; but Bertha, at all events for a time, had conquered.

The Crosses knew little and saw less of their kith and kin. With her husband's family, Mrs. Cross had naturally been on cold terms from an early period of her married life; she held no communication with any of the name, and always gave Bertha to understand that, in one way or another, the paternal uncles and aunts had "behaved very badly." Of her own blood, she had only a brother ten years younger than herself, who was an estate agent at Worcester. Some seven years had elapsed since their last meeting, on which occasion Mrs. Cross had a little difference of opinion with her sister-in-law. James Rawlings was now a widower, with three children, and during the past year or two not unfriendly letters had been exchanged between Worcester and Walham Green. Utterly at a loss for a means of passing her time, Mrs. Cross, in these days of domestic suppression, renewed the correspondence, and was surprised by an invitation to pass a few days at her brother's house. This she made known to Bertha about a week after the decisive struggle.

"Of course, you are invited, too, but—I'm afraid you are too busy?"

Amused by her mother's obvious wish to go to Worcester unaccompanied, Bertha answered that she really didn't see how she was to spare the time just now.

"But I don't like to leave you alone here—"

Her daughter laughed at this scruple. She was just as glad of the prospect of a week's solitude as her mother in the thought of temporary escape from the proximity of pampered Sarah. The matter was soon arranged, and Mrs. Cross left home.

This was a Friday. The next day, sunshine and freedom putting her in holiday mood, Bertha escaped into the country, and had a long ramble like that, a year ago, on which she had encountered Norbert Franks. Sunday morning she spent quietly at home. For the afternoon she had invited a girl friend. About five o'clock, as they were having tea, Bertha heard a knock at the front door. She heard the servant go to open, and, a moment after, Sarah announced, "Mr. Warburton."

It was the first time that Warburton had found a stranger in the room, and Bertha had no difficulty in reading the unwonted look with which he advanced to shake hands.

"No bad news, I hope?" she asked gravely, after presenting him to the other visitor.

"Bad news?—"

"I thought you looked rather troubled—"

Her carefully composed features resisted Will's scrutiny.

"Do I? I didn't know it—but, yes," he added, abruptly, "you are right. Something has vexed me—a trifle."

"Look at these drawings of Miss Medwin's. They will make you forget all vexatious trifles."

Miss Medwin was, like Bertha, a book illustrator, and had brought work to show her friend. Warburton glanced at the drawings with a decent show of interest. Presently he inquired after Mrs. Cross, and learnt that she was out of town for a week or so; at once his countenance brightened, and so shamelessly that Bertha had to look aside, lest her disposition to laugh should be observed. Conversation of a rather artificial kind went on for half an hour, then Miss Medwin jumped up and said she must go. Bertha protested, but her friend alleged the necessity of making another call, and took leave.

Warburton stood with a hand upon his chair. Bertha, turning back from the door, passed by him, and resumed her seat.

"A very clever girl," she said, with a glance at the window.

"Very, no doubt," said Will, glancing the same way.

"Won't you sit down?"

"Gladly, if you don't think I am staying too long. I had something I wanted to talk about. That was why I felt glum when I came in and found a stranger here. It's such a long time since I had any part in ordinary society, that I'm forgetting how to behave myself."

"I must apologise for you to Miss Medwin, when I see her next," said Bertha, with drollery in her eyes.

"She will understand if you tell her I'm only a grocer," remarked Will, looking at a point above her head.

"That might complicate things."

"Do you know," resumed Warburton. "I feel sure that the Franks will never again invite me to lunch or dine there. Franks is very careful when he asks me to go and see them; he always adds that they'll be alone—quite alone."

"But that's a privilege."

"So it may be taken; but would it surprise you if they really preferred to see as little of me as possible?"

Bertha hesitated, smiling, and said at length with a certain good-humoured irony:

"I think I should understand."

"So do I, quite," exclaimed Will, laughing. "I wanted to tell you that I've been looking about me, trying to find some way of getting out of the shop. It isn't so easy. I might get a clerkship at a couple of pounds a week, but that doesn't strike me as preferable to my present position. I've been corresponding with Applegarth, the jam manufacturer, and he very strongly advises me to stick to trade. I'm not sure that he isn't right."

There was silence. Each sat with drooping eyes.

"Do you know," Warburton then asked, "why I turned grocer?"

"Yes."

"It was a fortunate idea. I don't see how else I should have made enough money, these three years, to pay the income I owed to my mother and sister, and to support myself. Since my mother's death—"

Her look arrested him.

"I am forgetting that you could not have known of that. She died last autumn; by my father's will, our old house, at St. Neots then became mine; it's let; the rent goes to my sister, and out of the shop profits I easily make up what her own part of the lost capital used to yield. Jane is going in for horticulture, making a business of what was always her chief pleasure, and before long she may be independent; but it would be shabby to get rid of my responsibilities at her expense—don't you think so?"

"Worse than shabby."

"Good. I like to hear you speak so decidedly. Now, if you please"—his own voice was not quite steady—"tell me in the same tone whether you agree with Applegarth—whether you think I should do better to stick to the shop and not worry with looking for a more respectable employment."

Bertha seemed to reflect for a moment, smiling soberly.

"It depends entirely on how you feel about it."

"Not entirely," said Warburton, his features nervously rigid; "but first let me tell you how I do feel about it. You know I began shopkeeping as if I were ashamed of myself. I kept it a dead secret; hid away from everybody; told elaborate lies to my people; and the result was what might have been expected—before long I sank into a vile hypochrondria, saw everything black or dirty grey, thought life intolerable. When common sense found out what was the matter with me, I resolved to have done with snobbery and lying; but a sanguine friend of mine, the only one in my confidence, made me believe that something was going to happen—in fact, the recovery of the lost thousands; and I foolishly held on for a time. Since the awful truth has been divulged, I have felt a different man. I can't say that I glory in grocerdom? but the plain fact is that I see nothing degrading in it, and I do my day's work as a matter of course. Is it any worse to stand behind a counter than to sit in a counting-house? Why should retail trade be vulgar, and wholesale quite repeatable? This is what I've come to, as far as my own thought and feeling go."

"Then," said Bertha, after a moment's pause, "why trouble yourself any more?"

"Because—"

His throat turned so dry that he had to stop with a gasp. His fingers were doing their best to destroy the tassels on the arm of his easy chair. With, an effort, he jerked out the next words.

"One may be content to be a grocer; but what about one's wife?"

With head bent, so that her smile was half concealed, Bertha answered softly—

"Ah, that's a question."

# CHAPTER 46

After he had put the question, the reply to which meant so much to him, Will's eyes, avoiding Bertha, turned to the window. Though there wanted still a couple of hours to sunset, a sky overcast was already dusking the little parlour. Distant bells made summons to evening service, and footfalls sounded in the otherwise silent street.

"It's a question," he resumed, "which has troubled me for a long time. Do you remember—when was it? A year ago?—going one Sunday with Mrs. Cross to Kew?"

"I remember it very well."

"I happened to be at Kew that day," Will continued, still nervously. "You passed me as I stood on the bridge. I saw you go into the Gardens, and I said to myself how pleasant it would be if I could have ventured to join you in your walk. You knew me—as your grocer. For me to have approached and spoken, would have been an outrage. That day I had villainous thoughts."

Bertha raised her eyes; just raised them till they met his, then bent her head again.

"We thought your name was really Jolly man," she said, in a half-apologetic tone.

"Of course you did. A good invention, by the bye, that name, wasn't it?"

"Very good indeed," she answered, smiling. "And you used to come to the shop." pursued Will.

"And I looked forward to it. There was something human in your way of talking to me."

"I hope so."

"Yes, but—it made me ask myself that question. I comforted myself by saying that of course the shop was only a temporary expedient; I should get out of it; I should find another way of making money; but, you see, I'm as far from that as ever; and if I decide to go on shopkeeping—don't I condemn myself to solitude?"

"It *is* a difficulty," said Bertha, in the tone of one who lightly ponders an abstract question.

"Now and then, some time ago, I half persuaded myself that, even though a difficulty, it needn't be a fatal one." He was speaking now with his eyes steadily fixed upon her; "but that was when you still came to the shop. Suddenly you ceased—"

His voice dropped. In the silence, Bertha uttered a little "Yes."

"I have been wondering what that meant—"

His speech was a mere parched gasp. Bertha looked at him, and her eyebrows contracted, as if in sympathetic trouble. Gently she asked:

"No explanation occurred to you?"

With a convulsive movement, Will changed his position, and by so doing seemed to have released his tongue.

"Several," he said, with a strange smile. "The one which most plagued me, I should very likely do better to keep to myself; but I won't; you shall know it. Perhaps you are prepared for it. Do you know that I went abroad last summer?"

"I heard of it."

"From Miss Elvan?"

"From Mrs. Franks."

"Mrs. Franks—yes. She told you, then, that I had been to St. Jean de Luz? She told you that I had seen her sister?"

"Yes," replied Bertha, and added quickly. "You had long wished to see that part of France."

"That wasn't my reason for going. I went in a fit of lunacy. I went because I thought Miss Elvan was there. They told me at her Chelsea lodgings that she had gone to St. Jean de Luz. This was on the day after she came into the shop with you. I had been seeing her. We met here and there, when she was sketching. I went crazy. Don't for a moment think the fault was hers—don't dream of anything of the kind. I, I alone, ass, idiot, was to blame. She must have seen what had happened, and, in leaving her lodgings, she purposely gave a false address, never imagining that I was capable of pursuing her across Europe. At St. Jean de Luz I heard of her marriage—"

He stopped, breathless. The short sentences had been flung out explosively. He was hot and red.

"Did you suspect anything of all that?" followed in a more restrained tone. "If so, of course I understand—"

Bertha seemed to be deep iii meditation. A faint smile was on her lips. She made no answer.

# CHAPTER 46

"Are you saying to yourself," Will went on vehemently, "that, instead of being merely a foolish man, I have shown myself to be shameless? It was foolish, no doubt, to dream that an educated girl might marry a grocer; but when he begins his suit by telling such a story as this—! Perhaps I needn't have told it at all. Perhaps you had never had a suspicion of such things? All the same, it's better so. I've had enough of lies to last me for all my life; but now that I've told you, try to believe something else; and that is—that I never loved Rosamund Elvan—never—never!"

Bertha seemed on the point of laughing; but she drew in her breath, composed her features, let her eyes wander to a picture on the wall.

"Can you believe that?" Will asked, his voice quivering with earnestness, as he bent forward to her.

"I should have to think about it," was the answer, calm, friendly.

"The fit of madness from which I suffered is very common in men. Often it has serious results. No end of marriages come about in that way. Happily I was in no danger of that. I simply made a most colossal fool of myself. And all the time—all the time, I tell you, believe it or not, as you will or can—I was in love with *you*."

Again Bertha drew in her breath, more softly than before.

"I went one day from St. Jean de Luz over the border into Spain, and came to a village among the mountains, called Vera. And there my madness left me. And I thought of you—thought of you all the way back to St. Jean de Luz, thought of you as I had been accustomed to do in England, as if nothing had happened. Do you think it pained me then that Rosamund was Mrs. Franks? No more than if I had never seen her; by that time, fresh air and exercise were doing their work, and at Vera I stood a sane man once more. I find it hard to believe now that I really behaved in that frantic way. Do you remember coming once to the shop to ask for a box to send to America? As you talked to me that morning, I knew what I know better still now, that there was no girl that I *liked* as I liked you, no girl whose face had so much meaning for me, whose voice and way of speaking so satisfied me. But you don't understand—I can't express it—it sounds stupid—"

"I understand very well," said Bertha, once more on the impartial note.

"But the other thing, my insanity?"

"I should have to think about that," she answered, with a twinkle in her eyes.

Will paused a moment, then asked in a shamefaced way:

"Did you suspect anything of the sort?"

Bertha moved her head as if to reply, but after all, kept silence. Thereupon Warburton stood up and clutched his hat.

"Will you let me see you again—soon? May I come some afternoon in this week, and take my chance of finding you at home?—Don't answer. I shall come, and you have only to refuse me at the door. It's only—an importunate tradesman."

Without shaking hands, he turned and left the room.

Dreamily he walked homewards; dreamily, often with a smile upon his face, he sat through the evening, now and then he pretended to read, but always in a few minutes forgetting the page before him. He slept well; he arose in a cheerful but still dreamy, mood; and without a thought of reluctance he went to his day's work.

Allchin met him with a long-drawn face, saying: "She's dead, sir." He spoke of his consumptive sister-in-law, whom Warburton had befriended, but whom nothing had availed to save.

"Poor girl," said Will kindly. "It's the end of much suffering."

"That's what I say, sir," assented Allchin. "And poor Mrs. Hopper, she's fair worn out with nursing her. Nobody can feel sorry."

Warburton turned to his correspondence.

The next day, at about four o'clock, he again called at the Crosses. Without hesitation the servant admitted him, and he found Bertha seated at her drawing. A little gravely perhaps, but not at all inhospitably, she rose and offered her hand.

"Forgive me," he began, "for coming again so soon."

"Tell me what you think of this idea of a book-cover," said Bertha, before he had ceased speaking.

He inspected the drawing, found it pretty, yet ventured one or two objections; and Bertha, after smiling to herself for a little, declared that he had found the weak points.

"You are really fond of this work?" asked Will. "You would be sorry to give it up?"

"Think of the world's loss," Bertha answered with raised eyebrows.

He sat down and kept a short silence, whilst the girl resumed her pencil.

"There were things I ought to have told you on Sunday." Will's voice threatened huskiness. "Things I forgot. That's why I have come again so soon. I ought to have told you much more about myself. How can you know my character—my peculiarities—faults? I've been going over all that. I don't think I'm ill-tempered, or unjust or violent, but there are things that irritate me. Unpunctuality for instance. Dinner ten minutes late makes me fume; failure to keep an appointment makes me hate a person, I'm rather a grumbler about food; can't stand a potato ill-boiled or an under-done chop. Then—ah yes! restraint is intolerable to me. I must come and go at my own will. I must do and refrain just as I think fit. One enormous advantage of my shopkeeping is that I'm my own master. I can't subordinate myself, won't be ruled. Fault-finding would exasperate me; dictation would madden me. Then yes, the money matter. I'm not extravagant, but I hate parsimony. If it pleases me to give away a sovereign I must be free to do it. Then—yes, I'm not very tidy in my habits; I have no respect for furniture; I like, when it's comfortable, to sit with my boots on the fender; and—I loathe antimacassars."

In the room were two or three of these articles, dear to Mrs. Cross. Bertha glanced at them, then bent her head and bit the end of her pencil.

"You can't think of anything else?" she asked, when Will had been silent for a few seconds.

"Those are my most serious points." He rose. "I only came to tell you of them, that you might add them to the objection of the shop."

Bertha also rose. He moved toward her to take leave.

"You will think?"

Turning half way, Bertha covered her face with her hands, like a child who is bidden "not to look." So she stood for a moment; then, facing Will again, said:

"I have thought."

"And—?"

"There is only one thing I am sorry for—that you are nothing worse than a grocer. A grocer's is such a clean, dainty, aromatic trade. Now if you kept an oil shop—there would be some credit in overlooking it. And you are so little even of a grocer, that I should constantly forget it. I should think of you simply as a very honest man—the most honest man I ever knew."

Warburton's face glowed.

"Should—should?" he murmured. "Can't it be *shall*?"

And Bertha, smiling now without a touch of roguishness, smiling in the mere joy of her heart, laid a hand in his.

## CHAPTER 47

When Mrs. Cross came home she brought with her a changed countenance. The lines graven by habitual fretfulness and sourness of temper, by long-indulged vices of the feminine will, could not of course be obliterated, but her complexion had a healthier tone, her eyes were brighter, and the smile with which she answered Bertha's welcome expressed a more spontaneous kindliness than had appeared on her face for many a year. She had recovered, indeed, during her visit to the home of her childhood, something of the grace and virtue in which she was not lacking before her marriage to a man who spoilt her by excess of good nature. Subject to a husband firm of will and occasionally rough of tongue, she might have led a fairly happy and useful life. It was the perception of this truth which had strengthened Bertha in her ultimate revolt. Perhaps, too, it had not been without influence on her own feeling and behaviour during the past week.

Mrs. Cross had much to relate. At the tea-table she told all about her brother's household, described the children, lauded the cook and housemaid—"Ah, Bertha, if one could get such servants here! But London ruins them."

James Rawlings was well-to-do; he lived in a nice, comfortable way, in a pretty house just outside the town. "Oh, and the air, Bertha. I hadn't been there a day before I felt a different creature." James had been kindness itself. Not a word about old differences. He regretted that his niece had not come, but she must come very soon. And the children—Alice, Tom, and little Hilda, so well-behaved, so intelligent. She had brought photographs of them all. She had brought presents—all sorts of things.

After tea, gossip continued. Speaking of the ages of the children, the eldest eight, the youngest four, Mrs. Cross regretted their motherless state. A lady-nurse had care of them, but with this person their father was not quite satisfied. He spoke of making a change. And here Mrs. Cross paused, with a little laugh.

"Perhaps uncle thinks of marrying again?" said Bertha.

# CHAPTER 47

"Not a bit of it, my dear," replied her mother eagerly. "He expressly told me that he should *never* do that. I shouldn't wonder if—but let bygones be bygones. No, he spoke of something quite different. Last night we were talking, when the children had gone to bed, and all at once he startled me by saying—'If only you could come and keep house for me.' The idea!"

"A wonderfully good idea it seems to me," said Bertha, reflectively.

"But how is it possible, Bertha? Are you serious?"

"Quite. I think it might be the very best thing for you. You need something to do, mother. If Uncle James really wishes it, you ought certainly to accept."

Fluttered, not knowing whether to look pleased or offended, surprised at her daughter's decisiveness, Mrs. Cross began urging objections. She doubted whether James was quite in earnest; he had admitted that Bertha could not be left alone, yet she could hardly go and live in his house as well.

"Oh, don't trouble about me, mother," said the listener. "Nothing is simpler."

"But what would you do?"

"Oh, there are all sorts of possibilities. At the worst"—Bertha paused a moment, face averted, and lips roguish—"I could get married."

And so the disclosure came about. Mrs. Cross seemed so startled as to be almost pained; one would have thought that no remotest possibility of such a thing had ever occurred to her.

"Then Mr. Warburton *has* found a position?" she asked at length.

"No, he keeps to the shop."

"But—my dear—you don't mean to tell me—?"

The question ended in a mere gasp. Mrs. Cross' eyes were darkened with incredulous horror.

"Yes," said Bertha, calmly, pleasantly, "we have decided that there's no choice. The business is a very good one; it improves from day to day; now that there are two assistants, Mr. Warburton need not work so hard as he used to."

"But, my dearest Bertha, you mean to say that you are going to be the wife of a *grocer*?"

"Yes, mother, I really have made up my mind to it. After all, is it so *very* disgraceful?"

"What will your friends say? What will—"

"Mrs. Grundy?" interposed Bertha.

"I was going to say Mrs. Franks—"

Bertha nodded, and answered laughingly:
"That's very much the same thing, I'm afraid."

# CHAPTER 48

Norbert Franks was putting the last touches to a portrait of his wife; a serious portrait, full length, likely to be regarded as one of his most important works. Now and then he glanced at the original, who sat reading; his eye was dull, his hand moved mechanically, he hummed a monotonous air.

Rosamund having come to the end of her book, closed it, and looked up.

"Will that do?" she asked, after suppressing a little yawn.

The painter merely nodded. She came to his side, and contemplated the picture, inclining her head this way and that with an air of satisfaction.

"Better than the old canvas I put my foot through, don't you think?" asked Franks.

"Of course there's no comparison. You've developed wonderfully. In those days—"

Franks waited for the rest of the remark, but his wife lost herself in contemplation of the portrait. Assuredly he had done nothing more remarkable in the way of bold flattery. Any one who had seen Mrs. Franks only once or twice, and at her best, might accept the painting as a fair "interpretation" of her undeniable beauty; those who knew her well would stand bewildered before such a counterfeit presentment.

"Old Warburton must come and see it," said the artist presently.

Rosamund uttered a careless assent. Long since she had ceased to wonder whether Norbert harboured any suspicions concerning his friend's brief holiday in the south of France. Obviously he knew nothing of the dramatic moment which had preceded, and brought about, his marriage, nor would he ever know.

"I really ought to go and look him up." Franks added. "I keep on saying I'll go to-morrow and to-morrow. Any one else would think me an ungrateful snob; but old Warburton is too good a fellow. To tell the truth, I feel a little ashamed when I think of how he's living. He ought to have a percentage on my income. What would have become of me if he hadn't put his hand into his pocket when he was well off and I was a beggar?"

"But don't you think his business must be profitable?" asked Rosamund, her thoughts only half attentive to the subject.

"The old chap isn't much of a business man, I fancy," Franks answered with a smile. "And he has his mother and sister to support. And no doubt he's always giving away money. His lodgings are miserable. It makes me uncomfortable to go there. Suppose we ask him to lunch on Sunday?"

Rosamund reflected for a moment.

"If you like—I had thought of asking the Fitzjames girls."

"You don't think we might have him at the same time?"

Rosamund pursed her lips a little, averting her eyes as she answered:

"Would he care for it? And he said—didn't he?—that he meant to tell everybody, everywhere, how he earned his living. Wouldn't it be just a little—?"

Franks laughed uneasily.

"Yes, it might be just a little—. Well, he must come and see the picture quietly. And I'll go and look up the poor old fellow to-night, I really will."

This time, the purpose was carried out. Franks returned a little after midnight, and was surprised to find Rosamund sitting in the studio. A friend had looked in late in the evening, she said, and had stayed talking.

"All about her husband's pictures, so tiresome? She thinks them monuments of genius!"

"His last thing isn't half bad," said Franks, good-naturedly.

"Perhaps not. Of course I pretended to think him the greatest painter of modern times. Nothing else will satisfy the silly little woman. You found Mr. Warburton?"

Franks nodded, smiling mysteriously.

"I have news for you."

Knitting her brows a little his wife looked interrogation.

"He's going to be married. Guess to whom."

"Not to—?"

"Well—?"

"Bertha Cross—?"

Again Franks nodded and laughed. An odd smile rose to his wife's lips; she mused for a moment, then asked:

"And what position has he got?"

## CHAPTER 48

"Position? His position behind the counter, that's all. Say's he shan't budge. By the bye, his mother died last autumn; he's in easier circumstances; the shop does well, it seems. He thought of trying for some-something else, but talked it over with Bertha Cross, and they decided to stick to groceries. They'll live in the house at Walham Green. Mrs. Cross is going away—to keep house for a brother of hers."

Rosamund heaved a sigh, murmuring:

"Poor Bertha!"

"A grocer's wife," said Franks, his eyes wandering. "Oh, confound it! Really you know—" He took an impatient turn across the floor. Again his wife sighed and murmured:

"Poor Bertha!"

"Of course," said Franks, coming to a pause, "there's a good deal to be said for sticking to a business which yields a decent income, and promises much more."

"Money!" exclaimed Rosamund scornfully. "What is money?"

"We find it useful," quietly remarked the other.

"Certainly we do; but you are an artist, Norbert, and money is only an accident of your career. Do we ever talk about it, or think about it? Poor Bertha! With her talent!"

The artist paced about, his hands in his jacket pockets. He was smiling uneasily.

"Did you know anything of this kind was going on?" he asked, without looking at his wife.

"I had heard nothing whatever. It's ages since Bertha was here."

"Yet you don't seem very much surprised."

"And you?" asked Rosamund, meeting his eyes. "Were you profoundly astonished?"

"Why, yes. It came very unexpectedly. I had no idea they saw each other—except in the shop."

"And it vexes you?" said Rosamund, her eyes upon his face.

"Vexes? Oh, I can't say that." He fidgeted, turned about, laughed. "Why should it vex me? After all, Warburton is such a thoroughly good fellow, and if he makes money—"

"Money!"

"We *do* find it useful, you know," insisted Franks, with a certain obstinacy.

Rosamund was standing before the picture, and gazing at it.

"That she should have no higher ambition! Poor Bertha!"

"We can't all achieve ambitions," cried Franks from the other end of the room. "Not every girl can marry a popular portrait-painter."

"A great artist!" exclaimed his wife, with emphasis.

As she moved slowly away, she kept her look still turned upon the face which smiled from the easel. Watching her tremulous eyebrows, her uncertain lips, one might have fancied that Rosamund sought the solution of some troublesome doubt, and hoped, only hoped, to find it in that image of herself so daringly glorified.

**Benjamin Disraeli Novels, Volume one, including Coningsby, Sybil, Tancred and Endymion**
**Benjamin Disraeli**
Benediction Classics, 2015
1182 pages
ISBN: 978-1-78139-473-1

Available from www.amazon.com, www.amazon.co.uk

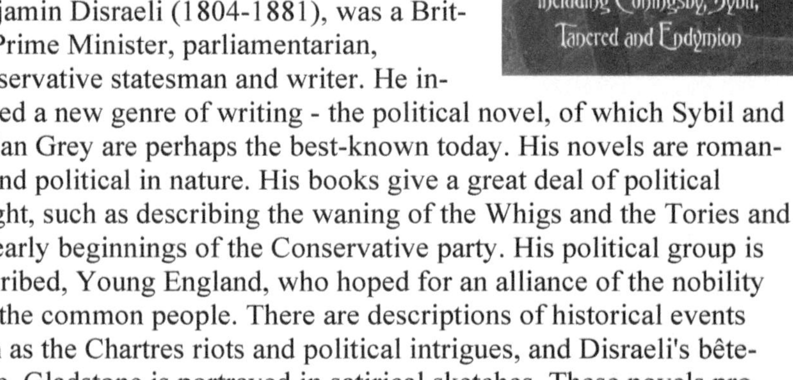


Benjamin Disraeli (1804-1881), was a British Prime Minister, parliamentarian, Conservative statesman and writer. He invented a new genre of writing - the political novel, of which Sybil and Vivian Grey are perhaps the best-known today. His novels are romantic and political in nature. His books give a great deal of political insight, such as describing the waning of the Whigs and the Tories and the early beginnings of the Conservative party. His political group is described, Young England, who hoped for an alliance of the nobility and the common people. There are descriptions of historical events such as the Chartres riots and political intrigues, and Disraeli's bête-noire, Gladstone is portrayed in satirical sketches. These novels provide a fascinating insight into Disraeli and his political landscape.

**Benjamin Disraeli Novels, Volume two, including Vivian Grey, The Young Duke and Henrietta Temple**
**Benjamin Disraeli**
Benediction Classics, 2015
1068 pages
ISBN: 978-1-78139-474-8

Available from www.amazon.com, www.amazon.co.uk

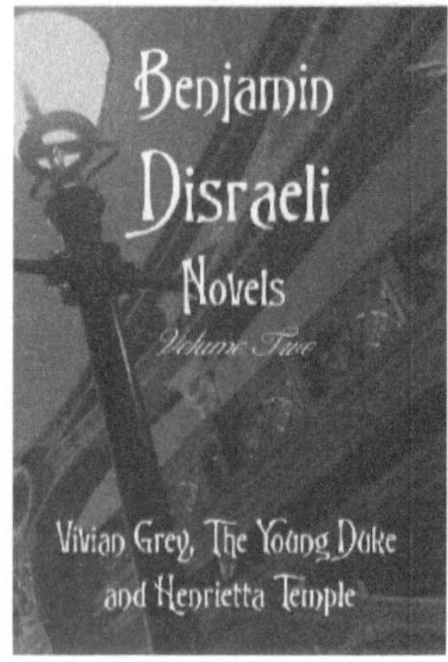

**The Novels of Elizabeth Gaskell, Volume One, Including Mary Barton, Cranford, Ruth and North and South**
**Elizabeth Cleghorn Gaskell**
Benediction Classics, 2014
1136 pages
ISBN: 978-1-78139-430-4

Available from www.amazon.com, www.amazon.co.uk

Elizabeth Gaskell (1810 - 1865), was a Victorian British writer. Her novels are fascinating to historians because they offer detailed portraits of people from every social class and she uses colloquialisms of the period. Of course, her books are also loved by a far wider audience for their moving stories, powerful relationships, social concern and the exploration of male authority.
Her six novels are contained within two volumes:
In Volume One: Mary Barton, Cranford, Ruth and North and South
In Volume Two: Sylvia's Lovers and Wives and Daughters

**The Novels of Elizabeth Gaskell, Volume Two, Including Sylvia's Lovers and Wives and Daughters**
**Elizabeth Cleghorn Gaskell**
Benediction Classics, 2014
894 pages
ISBN: 978-1-78139-431-1

Available from www.amazon.com, www.amazon.co.uk

Also from Benediction Books …
**Wandering Between Two Worlds: Essays on Faith and Art**
**Anita Mathias**
Benediction Books, 2007
152 pages
ISBN: 0955373700

Available from www.amazon.com, www.amazon.co.uk

In these wide-ranging lyrical essays, Anita Mathias writes, in lush, lovely prose, of her naughty Catholic childhood in Jamshedpur, India; her large, eccentric family in Mangalore, a sea-coast town converted by the Portuguese in the sixteenth century; her rebellion and atheism as a teenager in her Himalayan boarding school, run by German missionary nuns, St. Mary's Convent, Nainital; and her abrupt religious conversion after which she entered Mother Teresa's convent in Calcutta as a novice. Later rich, elegant essays explore the dualities of her life as a writer, mother, and Christian in the United States-- Domesticity and Art, Writing and Prayer, and the experience of being "an alien and stranger" as an immigrant in America, sensing the need for roots.

**About the Author**

Anita Mathias is the author of *Wandering Between Two Worlds: Essays on Faith and Art.* She has a B.A. and M.A. in English from Somerville College, Oxford University, and an M.A. in Creative Writing from the Ohio State University, USA. Anita won a National Endowment of the Arts fellowship in Creative Nonfiction in 1997. She lives in Oxford, England with her husband, Roy, and her daughters, Zoe and Irene.

Anita's website:
http://www.anitamathias.com, and
Anita's blog Dreaming Beneath the Spires:
http://dreamingbeneaththespires.blogspot.com

**The Church That Had Too Much**
**Anita Mathias**
Benediction Books, 2010
52 pages
ISBN: 9781849026567

Available from www.amazon.com, www.amazon.co.uk

The Church That Had Too Much was very well-intentioned. She wanted to love God, she wanted to love people, but she was both hampered by her muchness and the abundance of her possessions, and beset by ambition, power struggles and snobbery. Read about the surprising way The Church That Had Too Much began to resolve her problems in this deceptively simple and enchanting fable.

**About the Author**

Anita Mathias is the author of *Wandering Between Two Worlds: Essays on Faith and Art*. She has a B.A. and M.A. in English from Somerville College, Oxford University, and an M.A. in Creative Writing from the Ohio State University, USA. Anita won a National Endowment of the Arts fellowship in Creative Nonfiction in 1997. She lives in Oxford, England with her husband, Roy, and her daughters, Zoe and Irene.

Anita's website:
http://www.anitamathias.com, and
Anita's blog Dreaming Beneath the Spires:
http://dreamingbeneaththespires.blogspot.com

www.ingramcontent.com/pod-product-compliance
Lightning Source LLC
Chambersburg PA
CBHW020943310726
48980CB00001B/36
* 9 7 8 1 7 8 1 3 9 5 5 4 7 *